Library of America, a nonprofit organization,
champions our nation's cultural heritage
by publishing America's greatest writing in
authoritative new editions and providing resources
for readers to explore this rich, living legacy.

ELIZABETH SPENCER

Elizabeth Spencer

NOVELS & STORIES

The Voice at the Back Door
The Light in the Piazza
Knights and Dragons
Selected Stories

Michael Gorra, *editor*

THE LIBRARY OF AMERICA

Elizabeth Spencer: Novels & Stories
is published and kept in print in honor of

REBA WHITE WILLIAMS

in recognition of her dedication and support
for authors of Southern literature

with a gift from her husband
DAVE WILLIAMS

to the Guardians of American Letters Fund
established by the Library of America
to ensure that every volume in the series
will be permanently available.

Contents

THE VOICE AT THE
BACK DOOR

To David and Justine Clay

PART ONE

I *A Speeding Car*

O N A winter afternoon, unseasonably warm, a car was racing over country roads toward town. Dust, gushing from the back wheels, ran together behind in a dense whirl. On the headlands, the sun cast its thin glare above the sagebrush; it shot through the little trees, the pin oaks and the new reedy pines, and its touch pained the eye.

A large rock of gravel leaped from the wheels and whanged a mailbox. A terrapin, off on a hundred years' journey, missed death by half an inch. The car stitched a shallow curve and plunged downward, shivering: the descent was steep as a broom handle. But though the back wheels swayed, the car held the safe track, the ridges between the ruts, no broader than the edge of a nickel.

The hill emptied into a red road, quiet with sand and clay. Red clay gullies towered around, or fell away from the roadsides. No growth was on them, and some were deep enough to throw the church in. This was where the old-timers said the world was held together. Through this scarlet silence the car darted small and flat; then it ripped over a wooden bridge and was instantly swallowed in the trees of a Negro settlement.

Dogs leaped silent out of nowhere at the flying wheels and raced in pack for a way, yelping. They were mongrel hound and feist, the kind called "nigger dogs." Before the road curved, the oldest dog sat down to scratch his flea, and a young Negro woman, barefoot, stepped out on the front porch, set her hands on her hips, and stared, her eyes, like the road, growing emptier every minute.

One thing about the car: it knew the road. A country car, after a few months of driving have loosened every joint and axle and worn the shock absorbers tender and given every part a special cry of its own, pushes very fine the barrier that divides it from horses and mules. The road it knows, it navigates: dodges the washouts, straddles the ruts, nicks the bumps on the easy corner, and strikes, just at the point of balance, the loose plank in the bridge.

Five miles ahead along the road the car was traveling, an iron overhead bridge spans a brown creek with an Indian name, Pettico-cow, and a scant mile beyond that, three Negro men were quitting their work at the tie plant, shaking the sawdust out of their shoes, gathering up the lunch buckets and the work jackets. The sun had lowered into the dust line and reddened, staining the dense horizon. The three Negro men moved toward the road. The one who walked off to the side was singing to himself.

> "Quitting time done got sooner
> Most ever-ry day.
> Got to lay off two-three more niggers
> 'Fo the end of the week."

The other two Negroes exchanged a glance. Their mouths were thick and hung slightly open.

"You going to lay somebody *off*, Mister Beck?" the younger one asked.

The one who had sung moved on steadily. "Lay somebody off? I ain't said a word about laying anybody off."

"You wasn't saying it, but you sho was singing it."

"Oh, singing. That's different. You think everything a man sings he got to go and *do*?"

"I ain't studying do nor singing neither. But if somebody going to lay me off work I wants to know hit."

The third Negro was older than the first. He knew by now that another Negro is the hardest kind of boss to have. "Brer Beck ain't said nothing about firing you, boy. Brer Beck just talking to hisself. Ain't that right, Brer Beck?"

The singer ignored his question. "You niggers ain't got good sense. Did, you'd be in line for some other kind of job."

"They pays good," said the young Negro.

"They pay all right, but you ain't getting noplace. Everything you do, you do because somebody else tells you to. Me, I tell you."

"Yeah, and you got somebody else telling you."

"In a general way I have. But it's me that cuts the big orders down to the little folks. That's you. You don't do nothing but grunt and sweat. And how much money do you get? Not half as much as me."

"That's right, Brer Beck," the older Negro said, softly and with sweetness, but the younger one said, "I could quit this job tonight if I wanted to, and leave you shorthanded."

"Go on and quit then," the foreman answered. "There's plenty more just like you where you came from."

"I ain't going to quit," the young Negro said, "because it ain't but Wednesday. I thinks more of my three days pay than I does of you. Fact, I thinks more of a nickel than I does of you."

"Y'all hush," said the old Negro. "Hit's too hot to qua'l."

"Hush," said the foreman in another tone, and stopped still, listening.

From back up the road they all heard the iron bridge over Pettico-cow shake out a sound like a small foundry. From the deep points of the curves they could hear the gravel tear.

"Traveling," the older Negro said.

They had reached the edge of the road, and for the first time the three of them drew together.

When the car passed, the weeds along the road shook violently and the three Negroes were momentarily blotted out in the whirl of dust. They climbed up to the road.

"It was the sheriff," said the youngest.

"Sho was," said the oldest.

"The High Sheriff," said the foreman.

"How come him driving that fast?" asked the youngest.

"I seen his two great big old hands, laying up side by side on the steering wheel," said the oldest.

"I seen his red hair," said the youngest; "it was all slid down to his ears."

"I saw his license plates," the foreman said.

When they reached the crossroads, the young Negro turned to the foreman. "You reckon anything done happened?" he asked.

"You know as much as me, boy," the foreman said, and left them there, taking his own road for home, moving perhaps a little faster than usual.

By that time the dusty car had gained the highway, entering

it at the point near a large roadhouse painted green, bare as a barn with no trees near, set on a sweep of gravel. Inside, leaning at the window, was a man with a grizzled head cropped close and a strong wad of shoulders beneath a khaki shirt. He turned and called to another.

"You hear that car?"

"Somebody in a hurry."

"It was Travis Brevard, coming in from off the Beat Two road. Heading for town."

"Travis, huh?"

"I never saw him go that fast before. You best run into town after while, Jimmy."

"It's none of our business, Bud. Whatever it is."

"Just the same, I think you best run into town."

"Look, Bud. I'm always telling you. The best way to stay out of anything is not to get curious."

"It never hurts to know."

"It never hurts not to know. Haven't you ever heard that what you don't know don't hurt you? I thought everybody—"

"God damn it, Jimmy. Do you go into town or do I have to go myself?"

"Go yourself? Then I'd only have to go anyway, to get you safe back home. Okay, okay. I'm practically there."

He had never dreamed of not going, from the time he heard the car wheels scream onto the pavement.

But Travis Brevard, the sheriff, having reached Lacey, did nothing but slow to a tame fifteen miles an hour and circle the courthouse square. In pavement and telephone wires, bare trees, and an overcast of dust, the town, beautiful to anyone in the green seasons, now seemed shrunken and drab. But Travis Brevard took his time around the square and looked at everything closely. He was dying and he knew it; it had seemed very important to him to reach Lacey alive.

He chose to stop on the square before a small store front—one glass window and a door. Lettering on the old brick façade above read: HARPER & BRO. GRO.

He alighted from the car, a man strikingly tall, and rested one large copper-haired hand for a moment, perhaps to steady himself, against the warm hood of the car.

Then he advanced on the store.

2 *The Sheriff's Advice*

THE NEGRO delivery boy saw him first. The boy, whose name was W.B., was sitting in the far corner of the store, cross-legged on a sack of chicken feed. Duncan Harper, the proprietor, was behind the counter filling the delivery basket with items from the shelves. He first knew that something out of the ordinary was happening when he caught the white flash from the boy's eyes, and saw the rest of him grow rigid as an idol. The store-keeper turned toward the door.

The sheriff had sagged against the door frame, but neverthe-less he filled the opening. At his size and the suggestion that his weight was about to land somewhere, the store seemed to withdraw and shrink; to the grocer his property had never looked so small. Drunk, was all he thought.

"Come on in, Travis," he said. "Drag up a chair." But he noticed the reel in the sheriff's step and how riskily he lowered himself to sit down. His face was the color of a red-hot stove. Below the long thin strands of copper hair, the flesh blazed. The hair was wringing wet.

"Duncan," he said hoarsely, "I'm hot as a fox. Cut out that damn gas and give me a cold Coke."

"Sure," said the grocer, thinking that if it were whisky he would surely have smelled it by now. He pried the cap from the bottle and offered it doubtfully. "Travis, you don't look good. Let me just ring and see if Doc's in his office."

"No, you're not," said the sheriff, and poured the Coca-cola down in one tilt of the bottle. He let out a long sigh and the deep red color faded visibly. "Give me another one," he demanded.

This second bottle he sipped from. "No, Duncan, no doctor. I'll have it my way. I'm to the point, you understand, where anything I do will be wrong, so I might as well do what I want to. I knew the next one of these attacks would be the last. I only wanted to live to get home to Lacey. Would you pick a Beat Two gully for the last sight your eyes looked on? But I made it back and made my choice."

"You ought to be in bed," said the young grocer. "I'll take you home and call Doc—"

The other lifted a large hand. "I had my choice, like I said, and I said I would not go home to Miss Ada. She would spread me out on a pink bedspread and stick a thermometer in my mouth and get so scared she would forget her own name. I tell you for a fact, Duncan, I been married to Miss Ada for thirty-odd year, but I couldn't ever age her. She's nothing but a little girl and, God forgive me, but I'd rather die in a gully than on her bedspread." His breath came with difficulty, filling with a noise like a cold wind the long bellows-case of his lungs. "Then," he went on, "there was Ida Belle. Her house is a place where I could go out quiet as a match. She's been my nigger woman for fifteen years and everybody knows it, but it would likely embarrass her to have my corpse on her hands. You can't tell what they're liable to do to a nigger. She might have to leave town."

"Travis, all this talk of dying—"

"Don't butt in on me. Maybe I should have gone to the office just now, but I didn't. Maybe I've just got the big head, thinking I'm going to die, but I don't think so." He settled back, relaxing his long limbs. His breath came more easily. "Duncan, remember when you used to play football?"

"I remember."

"I used to go all the way up to the university on weekends to see you play. I went over to Baton Rouge too and down to New Orleans more than once. We would all go see you play. Then we would come home and read about it in the paper. They called you the fastest running back of the year. They named you 'Happy' Harper."

The groceryman winced. "The newspapers made that up," he said. "Nobody ever called me that. I didn't care for it, but they did it anyway."

The sheriff's gaze was concentrated on the young man's face, the serious blond features so devoid of any nerve play that a whip snapping in his face would probably not have made him shy. However, there was another dimension in his eyes. They were light brown, the color of walnut just split open. They kept a watch which missed little, and their calm did not come cheap.

"Yes, you used to bring us up, Duncan. I've seen forty thousand people stand up and yell when you began to run. I used to think I knew how you felt when the last white stripe went past."

"Not much different from winning an election maybe," said the other. "Though maybe it doesn't last as long. Not being so important."

"I don't know. Winning anything is good. I still remember how good I felt the day I won Miss Ada. You never did much in the war."

It was an accusation. The storekeeper laughed. "I did a great job in the war, Travis. I kept every juke box in Camp Shelby running with music and neon rainbows. I was so good at it they sent me out to Fort Sill, Oklahoma, to do more of the same."

"Never overseas, never an officer, let Jimmy Tallant come home from England with a hatful of medals. Now Jimmy's running that bootleg joint on the highway and paying me protection money. It's a crying shame. Once we wanted to put up a sign: 'Lacey: Home of Duncan "Happy" Harper.' Then we started to put one up: 'Lacey: Home of Jimmy Tallant.' But then you turned into a juke box engineer and now a grocery-man, and Tallant went into bootlegging. Looks like we'll never get to point with pride."

"When I was in the Army," Duncan said, "they lost my papers twice. I should have gone to OCS, but the papers stayed lost for two years."

"Then you lost your girl," said Travis.

Had this been said? The young man seemed uncertain as to whether anger was expected of him. Then he answered, "Yes, I did."

Travis lolled back in the chair. "And now you're a family man, running your daddy's little grocery store."

"If you think I couldn't have gone anywhere else and done better, you're mistaken. Even after the war, there were plenty of people over the state that remembered me. The fact is I decided to stay in Lacey because I wanted to. My wife likes it here, and I like it. There's always been a Harper on the town square. You know yourself I've got property around here and there—the grocery isn't everything. The people I grew up with are all here, and all my father's friends that are left alive. I want my children to grow up here. I don't see anything wrong with that." His face gentled suddenly. A certain anxiousness in his own defense dropped away, and he said, smiling, "For a man who claims to be dying, you've sure got a nerve."

"Dying," said the sheriff, flatly. "I forgot about it."

At these words the day sank back toward dream.

The grocer, who had taken his seat on the counter in the space where he sacked purchases, propped up a knee and turned idly to stare out the door toward the courthouse. No one on the Lacey square would have had anything but a glass door. Through it, hundreds of times in the last five years, or leaning in warm weather against the door frame, Duncan had watched the routine of the town. He had seen how day after day at midmorning and midafternoon, the girls who worked at the courthouse crossed the street to the drugstore for coffee. They came always on high heels, in the thinnest stockings, with their suits neatly pressed and their earrings shining. The narrow iron gate in the fence funneled them through and later drew them back again. All the way across the street you could hear the clatter of their heels in the high crossed hallways.

Then there were the old men, who sat on benches under the elm tree in the courthouse yard. They looked always to have been carelessly dressed and set down there by someone else. A fly was open, a shirt button missing, or a shoelace broken and retied low. Spring, summer, and fall, toiling uphill and down, they ventured out of houses where if they were loved they were no longer wanted, and came daily to this place that was theirs, a sort of no-place between the courthouse and the square because they had no business in either. Here they whittled and gossiped and spit and said Lord knows what about you. Even the politicians paid no attention to them: many a time Duncan had watched the sheriff striding by, and his heel struck past them like a hero's.

Duncan had seen funeral processions also, one so like another it was easy to forget, while the grave still yawned, just who had died. In the afternoons around four, eight yellow school buses eased past: it was about time for them now.

Look at it however you would, love it as much as you please: Lacey was dull.

Travis rose experimentally. "If I don't die today, I'm bound to sometime. What I came to say to you: I want you to take over when I'm gone."

Duncan laughed. "Preach your funeral?"

"You know what I mean. In a certain way of looking at it, I hold this county in my hand. It's better for Jimmy Tallant to be a bootlegger than for Happy Harper to peddle Wheaties. I haven't rested easy about you and I'm not the only one. Other people feel the same."

"My friends don't say so," Duncan returned.

"Your friends don't say so because it's true," the sheriff answered. He fished with a long copper-haired finger in his shirt pocket and brought out a fold of paper. "Right now I'm going home. You might as well start learning. Here's a list of country folks paid their tax today. You can go to the office and register them—somebody over there will show you how. I'll see you—"

The phone began to ring. Duncan turned aside, and as he did so he glimpsed the Negro delivery boy again. His eyes had bugged, he popped up from the feed sack like a released spring, struck the floor running, and shot out the back. Duncan wheeled.

Travis Brevard had lunged toward the counter for support, grasping as though it tried to escape him, had missed and was falling. He went to his knees. When he tried to rise, his head went down, too, and his forehead dragged the floor. He seemed to be broken in the middle. Duncan rushed to catch him, and another man, in full stride, burst through the door to help. Between them, with a slow turning motion they brought him upright. Step at a time, heavily weighted, the two of them gained the small chair, where they lowered him.

A crowd had gathered at the door; it may have been there for some time, for the man who entered had broken from it or through it. Someone was running to the drugstore for the doctor. Others were pressing into the store. As they approached, Duncan and the man who had helped him exchanged a glance. It seemed unlikely that the person with the least chance of getting there—he had had to drive in from a roadhouse two miles out on the highway—had not only made it to the scene but had also got the jump on everybody else. Whenever the story was told, his name would be mentioned. It was a name often mentioned anyway: Jimmy Tallant. It figured in most stories worth repeating and came easily off the tongue.

He spoke quickly to the grocer. "Will you be at home tonight?"

"Yes."

Then he smiled. His features were sharp and quick. In comprehension, too, he liked to stay one jump ahead. "So he wants you."

"Wanted," Duncan corrected with sudden sorrow at Travis's passing and a lash of resentment against Jimmy Tallant. Already the political picture had begun to shift and re-form in this shrewd head.

Duncan thrust the tax list into his pocket. The telephone was still ringing. Somebody asked if he wanted it answered, but he shook his head.

3 *The Sheriff's Women*

FAR INTO the early winter twilight Duncan Harper remained in the store and the store was full of people. They wanted to hear all the details of the death. For a while they talked in low tones, but gradually they spoke louder and, toward the last, one or two had cracked a joke and there had been a little scuffling, quickly dropped not so much out of propriety as because their hearts were heavy. When a silence fell, they left the store altogether, as though a program had been concluded. . . .

On a hill just at the outskirts of town, a Negro woman was sitting in a rocking chair on the front porch of her house. She was dressed in her best silk dress, the dark one she wore to church. Her hands, resting in her comfortable lap, held a handkerchief and a folded fan. She was Ida Belle, for fifteen years Travis Brevard's Negro woman. All around her front porch and the steps, other Negroes were gathered; they talked a little in low voices, or lounged silently against the porch, staring outward toward the town. Bone-white grass fringed the gullies, and in the clean winter leaflessness the white houses, the courthouse and church steeples and Confederate statue appeared to be quite close, both to one another and to the hill. Ida Belle would not go to the funeral, though she would dress for it as she had dressed today and would sit on the porch in the rocker. The other Negroes, all dressed too, would bank against the porch and fill the yard. . . .

Down in the town, in one of the larger white houses, Miss Ada, Travis's wife, lay on the bed in a darkened room. A cold compress covered her eyes and the single light bulb which burned near the dresser had been shaded with a newspaper. Two Negro girls stood one on either side, fanning her. Her cries had been silenced by hypodermic: word went out that she was "resting easier." Food had begun to arrive twenty minutes after Travis fell; there was enough of it now to last for a month. Two ladies, working hard, entered the back hallway from opposite doors. One was carrying a newspaper full of damp fern, the other a pitcher of ice.

"Hot," said the first, and pressed a sodden handkerchief to her upper lip. "It would be hot."

"And me with four to feed when I get home," said the second, pushing back a wisp of hair.

"Why don't you just go on home now, honey? *I* can manage here."

"I wouldn't dream of it! Leave poor Ada? Not for anything in the world!"

"Poor Ada!"

"Poor thing!"

Raising their eyes to heaven, they parted and swept to their imperious labor with a sigh. For women bear the brunt of everything, always. . . .

4 *The Encounter*

DUNCAN HARPER stood saying goodnight and locking the store. The lights had come on, but since his was one of the store fronts where an old-fashioned shed roof extended to the edge of the sidewalk, the larger angle of the doorway was shadowed. It was from out of the deepest plunge of the dark that the voice said, "Mister Harper?"

"Who called me?" he asked.

"I did, Mister Harper."

This time he caught the underlying negroid quality of the voice and smelled the smell. "What do you want?"

"You employ W.B. Liles?"

"No, I don't employ anybody. You've got the wrong— Oh, W.B. You mean the grocery boy? Yes, he works for me, but he—"

"Yes, he ran off. He got scared by what happened in your store. Now he's afraid you might fire him for running away. He's nothing but a child."

"No, it's all right. Tell him it's all right."

"He ran nearly all the way home, then he remembered—"

"Yes. Tell him to come in the morning as usual." Duncan turned away.

"He said there was—"

Duncan walked away. He had to get to the courthouse before the janitor left. The tax receipts were still not registered, but he could at least leave them locked in the sheriff's office. He was tired, filled with the event; perhaps for these reasons some assertive quality in the Negro had irritated him.

He crossed the street in the dark and went up the courthouse walk, past the empty benches under the elm tree. Inside the sheriff's office, he waited while the light flickered on. He looked all about him: at the dusty calendars on the walls and the rows of tax registers that reached to the ceiling, the handcuffs hung on a nail, the mounted deer head, and Travis's old suede jacket, alone on the hat tree. The wood floor was worn wavy around the stove; though they had gas now, the old building was still hard to heat, and this was where men had always stood to talk. The news of the county came here first, also the talk on a lot that went on everywhere. He looked toward the high dark windows with their carved wood moldings. It was a beautiful proud old building: it had been built before the Civil War.

The current tax register lay open on the high desk. The office force must have walked right out as soon as they heard the news. Duncan opened the register and turned a page or two, feeling the weight and smoothness of the paper.

He looked up, straight into the eyes of the same Negro man

who had stopped him on the sidewalk. He had followed ever so silently inside, and was now studying Duncan with as much interest as Duncan had shown for the tax register.

The Negro was frail, thin as though he had just come out of the jungle, but he had lost the savage's wiry drive. The force in him—and he did have it, far beyond the simple surprise of his presence—might have been mistaken for the force of a sick person who orders things to be done for him and people to do them just because he is not able to do them himself. You could not imagine his long face and high forehead undertaking to smile. He was, instead, already equipped with the kind of humor he fancied. It emerged clearly enough in the first thing he said.

"You want somebody to deliver those groceries, or don't you?"

"I forgot that order," said Duncan. "You're right."

"You certainly did. I walked three miles in to tell you. I been lecturing W.B. to do his job right ever since you hired him. He's crying now, scared you'll fire him, and scared to come back in where sheriffs can pick him out to die in front of. So I set his mind at rest. I said I'd come in."

"It's good of you," Duncan said. "I—" He pressed his hand to his brow. "Don't worry about the order. I'll take it myself. I'm late getting home as it is."

"It's W.B.'s job, Mister Harper. I intend to see that it's done."

"I'd have to go back and open the store for you."

"But if I has to go home and tell him—"

"God damn it!" Duncan burst out.

"I admits," said the Negro, after a pause, "that it was not altogether a sense of duty that got me to walk into Lacey after a hard day's work. It was in part a sense of curiosity. One sheriff dying means another sheriff coming in. I expect that means you, don't it? Mister Duncan Harper, the new sheriff?"

"It's no business of yours," said Duncan.

"It's a fact they never say a word to me. My acquaintance is not cultivated. My vote is not sought after. The truth is I got no vote to seek. If I had a vote, my acquaintance might be cultivated."

Methodically, Duncan straightened from leaning on the high counter, circled the counter, and approached the Negro.

He put his hands deep into his pockets and went back on his heels a bit. He was never in any doubt of what he could do physically, and so he could behave gently: it had been noted, in the old days, that he could bring off a tackle with a kind of politeness. His children obeyed him. He came close, and looking down on the Negro, saw in the open throat of the blue work shirt that a tendon moved stiffly at the collarbone.

"That kind of talk's no good," he seemed to be merely remarking. "On your way, boy."

The Negro withdrew from the shadow of the big white man, but he was still erect when he stopped in the door and said, "My name is Beckwith Dozer, Mister Harper. When I was a small child, my father was shot to death upstairs in this courthouse. I never been inside here before tonight."

"Oh. I see." Their eyes met and though they were alone in an empty building, and no one knew they were there, it seemed that the world listened, that a new way of speaking was about to form in an old place. They were a little helpless, too, like children waiting to be prompted. What should the words be? "There aren't many people you ought to talk this way to," Duncan said.

The Negro almost smiled. "I know that."

"It would help you to say 'Sir.'"

"I realize that."

"On your way," said Duncan.

"I wish you luck, Mister Harper," said Beckwith Dozer, and passed into the quiet dark hall. Duncan heard the words in his head for some time, and savored them there like the taste of something new, trying to decide if they mocked him, or spoke sincerely, but he could not.

5 *An Evening at Duncan's*

WHEN JIMMY TALLANT reached Duncan's house that evening, he was aware even before he stepped inside that someone had got there ahead of him. He saw the rear bumper of a car parked around the corner of the hedge, as though whoever had driven it there had considered concealing it altogether, then had decided not to. The left wing of the house where the little boy and girl slept was dark. The hall was empty, but light was coming into it from the sitting room.

He let himself in quietly, preparing to say that he had nearly beaten the door down, but no one would come. He passed into the hall at an angle that allowed him to see deep inside without being seen. He avoided the spot where the old floor moaned, and stood in the dark, watching.

The room that he spied in upon was his favorite of all in the world—the place where he cared most to be. That it was another man's living room was ironic, and of this he was all too fully aware.

It was a room whose thoroughly old-fashioned proportions had not been altered: it had a ceiling that vanished in shadow, and windows that dropped to the floor. Though scarcely pantry-size by the old standards, it was far too large for small company. Yet the woman who had touched it had understood both its own nature and what she wanted from it. She had gathered it toward the fireplace, faced every modern sort of softness and comfort into the mantelpiece. Only this part of the room was lighted, and the light did not go high. She loved to have a fire and would bring in wood for it by herself, if no one was there to help. A fire seemed to put her into some kind of timeless mood, the way it does a cat, except that she watched it, and a cat doesn't. She could not take her eyes off it, as if for fear of missing some new subtlety. She was watching it now.

She was within full view of him, curled in the armchair as usual, a small dark warm woman of unextraordinary beauty. She had no right to knowing what to do for an old house, for until she had insisted on buying this one and fixing it over nobody in her entire connection had ever had anything, and her father's family was common as pigs' tracks.

But it was not her gift for interiors that made the man in the hallway pause. He would have given her equal attention if she had been sitting on an empty Coca-cola case in a filling station.

Duncan was seated opposite her—Jimmy could see his long legs stretched out before the fire. The third person, tucked away in a deep chair, showed only a pair of bony knees crossed in oxford gray trousers. But the town of Lacey was such a size that a few inches of a person were all that was necessary to make out who it was. The only person Jimmy Tallant knew who would want, out of some quirk of youngness, to sit like an old man was Kerney Woolbright, Lacey's only gift to the Yale law school in twenty years. His voice, which had been trained to carry, carried very well indeed: Tallant realized they were discussing him.

"He's the only one who might beat you," Kerney was saying.

"But he's a bootlegger," Duncan's wife objected.

"Doesn't matter, Tinker," Kerney said. "They'll vote for him because he shot down twenty-three German fighter planes, just like they'll vote for Duncan because he set the national all-time touchdown record for a single season. Besides that, country folks like law-breakers, and besides that, he married a Grantham and is kin to half the county. The Granthams will vote their hound dogs if you get them riled."

"I wonder," Duncan said, "if it was really a shotgun wedding."

His wife nodded placidly. "Didn't you see her uptown? She's begun to show."

"I wonder how he feels about her," Kerney said.

"Ask Tinker," Duncan said. "She knows."

"You see him as often as I do," Tinker returned.

"Yes, but I didn't date him every night for five years."

"To tell the truth," said Tinker, "I'm a little bit hurt with him for marrying her."

Kerney laughed. "This sounds serious."

"It is," Duncan said.

But Tinker did not smile. "I love Jimmy," she said. "I really do. I always will."

"You see, Kerney," said Duncan, "how serious it is."

"You can make her jealous, remember," Kerney said. "Marcia Mae Hunt is home."

Canny as he was, he could not have helped knowing, even before he spoke, that he should not have said this. But perhaps he could not stop himself. He was so crazy in love with Marcia Mae Hunt's little sister, the one they called Cissy, that he schemed up ways of bringing her in.

"How *is* Cissy?" Tinker asked flatly, and gave him sweet relief.

He was going thoroughly into this subject, when Jimmy Tallant decided to walk in.

"Are you deaf? I nearly beat the door down."

Tinker brought him a drink from the kitchen.

"To the memory of Travis," Jimmy said, and raised a solemn glass.

"Will they have the election right away?" Tinker asked.

"No, regular time, August primary."

"Then who's the sheriff now?" she wanted to know.

"One of the deputies," Duncan said.

"Follansbee, of course," Jimmy said. "He's done all Travis's bookkeeping for him for years. Travis never cared for the paper work."

Kerney Woolbright laughed. "If you want to know who the sheriff really is going to be, Tinker, child, you'd better ask Woolbright."

"Then who?"

"Miss Ada. Herself."

Jimmy said, "Well I be damned."

"A courtesy appointment by the board, customary, and I heard a couple of the members say that's what they planned to do. It gives Miss Ada the fees, nothing more. She turns the job over to whomever she wants, probably Follansbee."

"That's funny," Duncan said, "Miss Ada being the county sheriff."

"Only for six months, of course," Kerney said. He grinned and added, brash as a bad little boy, "Then you two can fight it out."

"Call his mother to come for him, Duncan," said Jimmy Tallant.

"I feel like it," Duncan said.

"Junior," said Jimmy, "just because they give you a drink of whisky, it's no sign you can shoot the twelve-gauge and borrow the car."

Kerney continued to grin. "I'll let you in on a secret of my own. I'm coming out for the senate this summer."

"Senate!" Tinker stared at him. He looked so young.

"Duncan," Jimmy Tallant said, "it is my deepest conviction that the stripling has reference to the state senate, but I stand in awe before the size of his conceit. I could be wrong. Have you got your eye on Washington, boy?"

"Eventually," Kerney returned without batting an eye. "But not right away."

"You barely got into the legislature, you know."

"I know," said Kerney, "but I did get in, and I've been in for two years."

"It was a fluke. Anybody can tell you. Jenkins and Storm started fighting amongst themselves."

"And Brer Rabbit got away," said Kerney. "I know. But I also got enough votes to win, don't forget that. I'll go to the senate, too, Jimmy. They'll vote for me. If you ran for anything they'd vote for you the first go-round because you've got a war record and for Duncan because he used to tear up a football field every Saturday, but they'll vote for me for the rest of my life because I'm a politician. It's a fact."

"This makes me so unhappy," Tinker said suddenly.

Her voice fell among the three of them, sweet, unreasonable, and urgent—it was as though she had thrown something down which they all looked at for a moment before they turned to her. There were ways of associating her with unhappiness which were not pleasant to think about.

"Unhappy, darling?" Duncan smiled. He was sprawled low in the chair, elbows at equal rest, and hands clasped around his glass. A very gentle feeling for her had touched his face.

"You're so silly," she said. "All of you. Who else in Lacey has a good time besides us? You know what they do. They go to the Rotary Club and the Garden Club or church parties, or else they play bridge and gossip or else just gossip. You know the ones who stay sloppy drunk all the time, and the ones who keep nosing around after each other's husbands and wives. But all we want to do is sit around the fire and have a drink or two and talk. There aren't many things nicer to do, and you know you like it, because you come here all the time. But if you all begin running for these little two-by-four courthouse jobs in Winfield County, you're going to fight with each other and have all sorts of grudges. You aren't going to want to come here or anywhere else and talk any more. You aren't even going to want to have a drink together any more. If Duncan gets elected sheriff, I guess I'll have to go sneaking off by myself somewhere to have a decent drink. I don't like to think about it."

Her voice trailed away toward the end; in fact, her whole speech was more of a swan song than a plea, and they were not so much persuaded to deal with it as they felt how nice she was to have thought it. It was usual in her to feel that anything bad she anticipated was already accomplished and should be adjusted to rather than resisted. This bitter tinge had worn her smile a little crooked, and made it very dear.

Duncan, naturally, was the first to shake away from her. "If I do run for sheriff, Tinker, it will be for better reasons than wanting the corner office in the courthouse."

Kerney was quick. "For certain things the office can be, you mean?"

"Yes, that's it. Of course, I liked Travis same as everybody did and more, but his standards were easygoing and after twenty years in office, this county has run down till it's a grand mess."

"That's true," Kerney said.

"I'll be damned if it is," Tallant objected. "I can't agree with you. Why, Duncan, ask anybody in Mississippi what the quietest county is and they'll tell you Winfield County."

"That's on the surface. That's what Travis was good at. He could keep order at a dogfight because every dog there would be in mortal fear of him."

"All about order," Kerney said, leaning forward; "nothing about law."

"That's all right," Jimmy contended; "it's a fact that every sonofabitch black or white, east of the creek or west, thought twice before they picked up the razor because of who we had in that corner office."

"Fine," Duncan said, "but still on the surface. Under the surface, Jimmy, the sinkhole has been eating away, and you know what I mean. When Tinker and I were on the coast last spring, everywhere we went they said to us, Don't see why you folks had to come down here when you've got the neatest little Gold Coast in the USA up in Winfield County. Why, Lacey in Winfield County used to be known as the home of two senators and a governor."

"And a football star," Jimmy grumbled. "Can I help it if people like to drink? You've said yourself time and again, Duncan, you and this prodigy here, that the dry laws in this state are nothing but damn foolishness."

"Sure I have. I'll say it again, and publicly. But if prohibition is what people voted for, then I say give them what they want."

"But it isn't what they want. It's just what they voted for. Can't you get it through your head what they want? What they want is *illegal whisky*."

Kerney nodded. "I figured it all out years ago, and I think Jimmy is right. In order to get the maximum kick out of a thing, you've got to be absolutely certain it's a sin. Everybody's been led to believe in the course of a proper childhood that sex is a filthy, degrading, bestial business, and look what a lot of fun it turned out to be. Everybody has likewise been instructed that whisky is a filthy, degrading business, but half the fun of it (exactly like illicit sex) turns out to be all the maneuvering, the slipping around, the dark back doors, and the whispering: Naw I aint got none, but Joe has. So we flock to the polls to keep the old tradition alive. Really, Duncan, it keeps everybody happy:

"Preachers are happy because everybody on the church roll has signed the pledge; mothers and grandmothers and aunts are happy because not a drop of it has ever been allowed in the house; the bootleggers are happy because they are collecting from twenty to fifty per cent markups on standard brands; the state highway patrol is happy because they get up to half the markup in the shakedowns; the county sheriffs are happy because they make enough on protection money rake-offs to send their daughters to fine Eastern schools and buy Stromberg-Carlsons for their nigger mistresses—"

"Did Travis really do that?" Duncan inquired.

"Sure, he did it."

"Hush," Tinker said suddenly. "He's not in the ground yet."

"That's right," Jimmy Tallant said.

Kerney and Duncan glanced at the two who had spoken so quickly, and then their eyes met. The gesture was so involuntary, so slight, an outsider could not have discerned it. It was Duncan and Kerney's recognition of belonging to a class somewhat superior to the others, though Duncan would not have claimed any superiority even if Kerney might.

"I feel so sorry for Ida Belle," Tinker said to Jimmy.

"I do too," Jimmy said.

"She had the easiest life of any nigger woman I can think of," Kerney said. "She didn't even have to pretend to take in washing."

"That's not it, Kerney," Tinker explained. He did seem so young when he came out with things like this. "She lived with him so long, she's bound to be grieved, but she can't even go to the funeral. You know how they feel about funerals."

"It is a shame," Duncan agreed. "I thought about it at the time."

"*Couldn't* she go?" Kerney inquired. He would not stay reproved.

They looked at him.

"I'm only curious," he went on. "What would happen if she went? Would anything happen?"

"I don't know," Duncan answered thoughtfully. "Before the war, I could have said for sure, I think, that she would take a big risk to go. Since the war, I don't know."

Tallant said, "I know. There'd come a knock at her door before midnight. We would never know who knocked. But it would happen."

"What would happen?" Tinker asked.

"I don't say they'd kill her. She'd just vanish, probably."

"Well," said Kerney, "we could all go up and protect her."

Tallant laughed. "They always told me to protect Southern womanhood. I'm just now seeing what they meant."

"Whoever knocked at the door," Kerney pointed out, "he would be protecting Southern womanhood."

"Namely, Miss Ada," said Duncan.

"The sheriff moreover," said Jimmy.

"And my second cousin," Tinker said, and they all laughed, thinking not without affection of the thin, nervous, excitable little lady. In the face of the most remarkable resemblance, she refused to believe that her own cook was the daughter of a gentlemanly old doctor. "He died nursing a sick baby," she would say, "and nobody's going to tell me he would do such an awful thing." Whereupon she would open her fan and flutter it at her breast, frail weapon against a hot flash.

"I'm still not sure," Kerney said. "I'm not sure anything would happen to her."

"I tell you one thing, son," Jimmy said. "Ida Belle is not going to give you a chance to find out."

"But if she did go," Duncan said, "and something did happen to her, I bet my bottom dollar that somewhere along the line she would have dared it to happen."

He spoke with a certain anger, out of tone with the pleasantly speculative nature of their conversation. They turned to him and waited. He shifted in his chair: thinking was apt to make him uncomfortable, yet he would go off into it when he had to, like wading into cold water. This was part of a fateful simplicity in his character, something that went along with his curious absence of any purely sensual awareness—his face was a collection of matching planes. He had listened to the teacher and the scoutmaster, and later to the coach: the coach always said that was the true secret of his great career, that he could listen.

When they said in the Sunday supplement that he was unique among college athletes in that he not only made good grades but also read books, he joshed about it with the boys; but he felt secretly ill at ease until he had gone to the library and read the books the reporter said he liked. This was the first article that appeared about him, when he was only a sophomore. Later the lies and exaggerations made no difference to him. But the reporter had had good taste. It turned out that Duncan liked the books—he could listen to what they had to say, too—and when he finished these he read some more. When the word got around that this activity actually engrossed him, it was a matter of concern to responsible persons. He had, by then, a nationwide reputation. The coach called him in. "I don't know whether it's true or not," he said, "but you have to watch that sort of thing. Back when I was up at Kentucky, they had a basketball star went off on music. No harm in the thing itself, of course. But when he started meeting with some other fiddlers—well, frankly, there's always a lots of queers among people like that, and you have to watch out for them. The wrong kind of word got around. I just drop the hint to you, Harper: if you must go in for this sort of thing, keep it to yourself and mind you stick with decent people. That's all, boy."

Duncan had read far enough into the books to know this would be ridiculous to the people who wrote them;

nevertheless, he saw the coach's point. So he shook hands cheerfully and departed, being mild by nature. That was why his sharp tone now brought them up.

"Dared it to happen?" Kerney repeated.

"They try to aggravate. They try to work themselves into a position where you can't do anything but get mad, cuss them out, fire them, knock them down. I don't like to think about them that way, then every once in a while—well, one made me pretty mad today. He was little; I would have felt like an s.o.b. if I had hit him, and he would have been glad to make me feel like one."

"Who was it?" Jimmy Tallant asked.

Duncan hesitated. "I don't remember. Uncle of my delivery boy."

"Was it Dozer?" Jimmy pursued.

"Dozer. Yes. Beckwith Dozer."

"Beck Dozer," Jimmy said. "I know him well."

There was a silence. Some line had been crossed; a crack in the sidewalk had been stepped on. There was no exchange of glances.

"Why didn't you hit him?" Jimmy asked.

"Oh, now, don't start talking about hitting niggers!" Tinker cried. "I won't stand for it."

"Travis would have hit him," Jimmy said to her suddenly, and she answered at once, "But not Duncan."

"If I'd hit him he would have been glad," said Duncan.

"I don't get that," Kerney said.

"You don't deal with them every day in the week," Duncan said.

"If you had just hit him hard enough he would have forgotten to be glad about anything," Jimmy pointed out.

"I don't see it like that," said Duncan.

"Travis would have hit him," Jimmy Tallant repeated.

"Yes," said Duncan, meeting him, "and that was a bad thing about Travis."

"Bad thing? The niggers were crazy about him."

"They had to pretend they were," Kerney put in.

"What kind of talk is this?" Jimmy demanded. "Travis was the only white man I know they would ask to nigger weddings and funerals."

"That's right," Duncan agreed. "It's also true that he let a nigger man bleed to death on the floor of the jail."

"That's right too," Jimmy said.

They were silent for a moment, knowing in common with all Southerners that when the knot got too tangled it was just as well left alone.

It was just as well to tell a story.

"I was with him the night it happened," Jimmy said. "We were playing poker. The jailer's boy came over and told him. He crept up and whispered it to him and Travis said out loud, 'What nigger?' Somebody asked him what the matter was and he said, 'The boy says the nigger's dead.' Then he said 'Oh.' Flat, just 'Oh.' He had drawn out three for the discard and his hand stopped in the air. 'I never knew I hit him that hard,' he said. Everybody waited. Matt Pearson was waiting to deal. 'I had clean forgot about him,' he said. Somebody sitting outside the light said, 'You don't know your own strength, Travis,' but I don't know if he heard it. 'God have mercy on my soul,' he said. He brought down his fist with the cards and flung the cards away. 'Three, Matt. I'll take three.'"

"That wasn't all that happened," Duncan said. "Just a couple of months ago there was a wreck on the highway. A wagonload of colored people were smashed up, and five of them killed."

"I heard about it," Jimmy said. "Mighty bad."

"It was hushed up," said Duncan. "And I think I know why."

"Of course you know why," Jimmy said. "Wagon without lights—the same thing that's happened a hundred times on 82, 51, every highway in the South."

"I don't know who didn't have lights," Duncan said, "but I know where the car was coming from."

"What are you trying to say, Duncan? If you think you can lay those five niggers at my doorstep just because the fellow was drinking at Bud's. . . ."

"I didn't say I blamed you with it. I just say it's more convenient for you if the word doesn't get around that five people got killed by a man who had been drinking Grantham-Tallant wet goods."

"In other words," Kerney said, "Duncan means that protection money covers a lot of things."

"If you want to know the truth," Tallant said gloomily, "it

costs a lot and covers too damn little. The only reason I'm tempted to run for sheriff is because I'm tired of seeing $500 a month checked out to profit and loss."

"Just five hundred?" Kerney asked. "I've heard that Travis alone pulled down that much."

"He didn't," Jimmy said. "However"—he grinned suddenly —"if business expands and things ride along, there's no reason why it wouldn't be worth that and maybe more—to the right sort of person." He looked at Duncan and deliberately closed one eye.

Duncan colored swiftly. "You'd better be joking."

"Sure, I'm joking." Jimmy got up and stood with his back to the fire, empty glass in hand, warming himself. "Haven't we all been joking tonight?"

"As a matter of fact," said Duncan, "no. It's a fair warning from the start, Jimmy. If I run for sheriff and if I win, I'll shut you and Grantham down first thing."

Jimmy chose not to answer, but rather to leave him sitting there with his seriousness upon him. "It's turning a little colder." He examined the ice at the bottom of his glass. "Tinker, child, it's been a long dry day."

She uncurled and stood. "I'll fix you one, you and everybody. But if there's any more fussing, I warn you: I'll go straight to bed and read a murder mystery."

Jimmy Tallant followed her through the dark dining room and into the kitchen. "What's got into Duncan?"

She frowned, breaking out ice into the sink with annoyed rapidity. "He and Kerney. You haven't been here in a while. They sit and talk by the hour . . . niggers, politics, Truman, the South. . . ."

"Duncan's not pro-Truman?"

"No, I don't mean *that*. It's something called the 'new South.' Kerney thinks the day of the liberal is at hand. He thinks all you have to do is get a few people in a few towns to take a great big risk of being martyrs, only it will seem like a bigger risk than it actually is because people know deep down but won't admit that the old reactionary position of the South has played out to nothing but a lot of sentiment. He thinks the Dixiecrat movement was the last gasp of it."

"What big words you know, Mrs. Harper."

She laughed. "I've learned them by heart. Kerney's not interested in a solitary thing but politics. It's worse than hearing girls talk about their babies all the time."

"He's pretty interested in Cissy Hunt."

Pouring whisky, she glanced up sharply. "Sure, that's the whole thing."

He looked mystified, so she explained, though she obviously thought it was like adding two and two: "Because Duncan used to go with Marcia Mae. That's why Kerney comes here." She emphasized the last word by striking the bottle stopper in place with the palm of her small hand, a childish gesture like many of hers. It was hard to believe how shrewd she was. She gave special attention to matters of love. "Kerney *would* have to have Cissy Hunt."

"Why?"

"It's the best family in town for him to marry into. They aren't in politics, but they have influence."

So she would have her terse say about every match and marriage, driving in the slender accurate nail: she knew the reason for love was seldom love. Still, what she hardly believed in had snapped up her life—she had never loved anyone but Duncan Harper. She had known this always, from the time they were in high school.

Jimmy Tallant never had to recall that she was his first girl. He had gone with her for five years. He had taken her to dances, had parked with her on dark side roads and twisted his long intelligent limbs in every possible way around her body, which seemed so resistless. At the end of embraces incredibly extended, she would ask him to take her to the drugstore before it closed because she wanted a Coca-cola.

She had cast him into a long agony; he tread water in a lake of fire. He told her so, and she only said it wasn't her fault. Nightly, he passed from rage to tears and back again. He grew so irresistible that all the girls in the eleventh grade (to mention one group) lost their virtue to him, but nothing did him much good.

One thing: Tinker always liked to talk to him. She could even tell him about Duncan. Thus one falls in love with unhappiness, not through choosing it or wanting it, but through having to live with it. He did not know quite when she ceased to be a passion and turned into a state of mind.

She still was. He could lounge near her, against the kitchen cabinet, smoking, watching her move around and mix the drinks and hear her talk; he could remember that he had taught her to dance and smoke and kiss and drink; and he could still be moodily satisfied that she had finally got the man she always wanted. So be it ever, he thought, when suddenly she was close to him and her hand lay on his arm.

"Jimmy, don't run against Duncan."

He hesitated.

"I've never asked you for anything," she went on. "Have I?"

He saw instantly the forty ways in which this was absurd, unfair, and beside the point.

"Tink. Ole Tink." He touched her hair. "Are you happy?"

"I will be, if you won't run against Duncan."

"Whatever you say."

"You promise me?"

"I promise."

"You won't say I asked you?"

"No."

That quick, she was gone. She was telling him which drinks were whose, so he could help her take them in.

6 *Two Old Friends Meet*

THE NEXT day Marcia Mae Hunt and Duncan saw each other for the first time since she had jilted him. She had run off and married an Irishman who everyone in town insisted was a lumberjack because he was from Montana and wore a plaid shirt.

Her meeting with Duncan occurred at midmorning in front of the post office. She saw that it was going to happen before he did. He was coming alone out of the post office, tearing open some circulars, sorting out a bill or two. She had parked her convertible, gathered up her bag and gloves and had one foot out of the door when she saw him, and knew she could not turn back. The square seemed empty, but she knew from old experience that it was not. In Lacey someone was always watching, and by no means could she lack courage. She drew a breath, and her heart, which had paused, rushed to beat again. It had to happen sometime, she thought. She set both feet in their expensive well-buffed leather loafers on the pavement. She was glad that she habitually did a careful make-up, that the white collar of her blouse was clean above the beige cashmere sweater. She advanced in the mild winter sunlight, across the old brick paving before the post office.

In a moment he would look up, and see her coming toward him. It was not unlike, she recalled absurdly, the first time they had met, back when they were children.

That was the time he had happened across her back pasture with two other boys. They had been shooting jaybirds down by the branch, and carried .22 rifles with them. She was playing with the cook's little boy, making him swing her. The swing was hung from a high limb in the oak tree and the oak tree grew out of a rise, so with high swinging the flight could be perilous. She loved high swinging. That day she was going higher than ever before. "Again!" she kept screaming at the panting little black boy, knowing that when he took a notion he would quit and say "I ain't" when she wanted him to start over. But today he did not quit. He was growing and could push harder. She soared on, entranced by the dip and rise and great outward plunge.

A dreamy time elapsed between the breaking of the rope and the end of the fall. She knew what had happened. Up there, cracked aside like a whiplash, the good end of the rope snatching itself from her hand, she felt her small body take the rise anyway, without the swing to send her, and at the crest she rocked a little, sleepily. Down below she could see the creek and the place where the branch ran into it, and, over across on the bluff, the sawmill, sending up a puff of smoke. Just below there were three boys who seemed to be talking; then one of them threw his gun down and ran. She wondered where he was running.

Duncan said later it seemed to him too that she stayed up a long time. It was long enough for him to watch the broken end of the rope riding in a slack S against the sky, and to conclude when and where she would stop going up and would begin to come down. He did not know who or even what she was. The only impression he had as he threw down the gun and ran was of a positive quality of blondness—total blondness, not just a color of hair.

Then she hit him. She fell into him from above and to the left, shooting neatly into his arms. He thought at first that she had buried him so deep in the ground he would never see daylight again; the fact was that she had knocked him out and broken his collarbone. The only thing he had failed to estimate was her velocity. Otherwise, he had succeeded. She rolled safely out of his arms, and began to bellow.

Her parents came, running down the hill, and after them four or five Negro servants, and finally her brother Everett at a walk, holding his finger between the pages of a book. He did not come down the hill; being lazy as mud, he calculated he would have to climb back up it. He almost got caught in it as it was, for they kept yelling back that he was to call the doctor; but he pretended not to hear and the yard boy passed him at a run, heading back to the house to do the errand. Mr. Hunt, holding his baby close, took time to speed a look of disgust up the hill, then, turning, said something to his wife, who nodded. Everett believed they had spoken of him. Raging, he turned away. He wished that his father would die, and he called his mother a bitch. As for his sister, he wished for her simply some sort of disappearance, something that would sponge even the memory of her out of his mind. Wasn't she always into things that did not interest him, though plainly they should have done so? Last week, running to the bluff to watch the Rabbit Foot Minstrels parade into town, she had stuck a dark thorn, smooth as walnut, in her foot. Another time, greedy, she had climbed to the top of the scuppernong arbor and taken grapes right out of the sun until, reaching too far, she tipped over and fell through, flat on her stomach. Her screams were wheezy; everybody's nap was broken up. She climbed trees, had to have a pony, and went fishing with Negroes. Someday, when she got married and left—or at least when he went off to college—he was going simply to appropriate her past. He had saved the thorn and taken Kodak pictures of the pony and the fish strings.

All this he thought while he sat in the double swing in the side yard reading, and refused to look up when they passed in procession with Duncan, guiding him toward the doctor's car. "Stop twisting your hair," his mother called out, and he raged again; the page before his eyes grew actually red. The only reason he had gone even to the top of the hill was because he hoped she was dead.

He stole a glance. The Negroes were ahead, carrying a lot of useless things including blankets and a hot-water bottle. His parents and the doctor were helping Duncan. The two little boys with the rifles trailed behind, and at the very end his baby sister Cissy was hopping along on the sides of her bare feet because the sidewalk burned them—she was trailing her diaper behind her and had on nothing at all, but nobody noticed. Marcia Mae had slid in close to Duncan. She was a messy little girl, fidgety, full of reactions to everything, sometimes three or four at once, such as right now, she was happy the accident had happened, was wondering how she could work her way in to watch the doctor set the bone, she wanted to go tell the cook all about it, and she was dead to go to the bathroom. But the bone came first, being the most unusual, and she was sticking as close as she could to the boy who had saved her. He walked slow and held his arm with contemplation. He was blond too, Everett noticed, and half a head taller than Marcia Mae. Maybe they'll get married, he thought hopefully.

He was the first to think it, but in a couple of years everybody thought it. For they grew to be a fine-looking couple, fair, beautifully built, alert as a brace of hunting dogs, mettled as a young carriage span, and always going somewhere. With them on the horizon you could do two things: join their procession or go sit over with Everett in the swing, because they were It. Later, on the noble Saturdays, Duncan's football feats traveled over clicking wires to every newspaper in the world, but to Lacey this was merely a proof of something known all along: namely, that he got the best because he had the best already, that unfair way it says in the Bible that things ought to be.

What had happened to part them? Everyone gave a different answer. She had run off with a Yankee, a redheaded Irishman named O'Donnell who had got killed in the war. Nobody would ever call her by her married name. She was still Marcia Mae Hunt, the girl who was Duncan Harper's girl. An image had been violated; they were left with a sense of unease.

That morning before the post office, so many years later, the image was restored: the few who saw it would be glad to describe it to the rest, then all would have it back again, the thought of the two fair heads.

Duncan and Marcia Mae knew this, and came together with a certain stateliness in the sun—without haste. They stood talking for a while (it was, as if anyone could hear, a ritual language), parted once, turned, spoke again, walked away a second time, turned a second time, and waved goodbye. These were the gestures they had known always.

She drove through town with a steady profile. At home her mother called from the sitting room. "Is anything happening up town?" She paused, calculating. Then she said, "I ran into Duncan." "Where?" "In front of the post office." Her mother came out into the hall. "How does it seem, after all this time?"

The two women regarded each other.

Mrs. Hunt understood that her daughter had had an unhappy time of it because she had never learned anything about men. She felt that she had failed Marcia Mae by not finding some way to impart a knowledge she herself obviously possessed in quantity, as witness the darling dazzling time she had had as a girl, the foresight she had shown in selecting a man who would amount to something, to say nothing of how wisely she had weighed her assets when she had made her choice. She had judged to the dot how much her family name (Standsbury) would mean to him, and how much beauty and charm would have to be added. She had had enough, naturally.

Admirably controlled and considerate to the limits of her subtlety, the mother never mentioned her daughter's shortcomings in these matters to her face; in fact, she believed that Marcia Mae did not know what she thought of her. She was given to mentioning when she spoke of other girls who had failed to make a proper match: "She could have had so-and-so, but she didn't play her cards right."

As for Marcia Mae, she had long ago in a chill crystalline hour faced the fact that she was the daughter of a Southern belle. That meant, beyond a shadow of change, that exactly to the extent of her own attractiveness she was her mother's enemy. As she had felt the necessity of a stage presence before the post office, she felt it now, in the house she was born in.

She said, "How does it seem? We recognized each other, so I guess we haven't aged too much."

"No, I didn't mean that. I meant—"

"You mean, did my heart turn over? How could it? I never loved anybody but Red O'Donnell."

At this time it was being said on the telephone by one lady to another: "You can't tell me she ever loved anybody but Duncan Harper . . . why, she doesn't even go by her married name, nobody calls her Mrs. O'Donnell . . . and one or two people I won't name go so far as to mention she never was married to that man at all, but I don't believe that. You know, Sally Ennis's niece saw her eating a hamburger in San Diego with another man in Marine uniform who wasn't redheaded in the least. I've always understood Marcia Mae was a nice girl but, even so and notwithstanding, will you tell me why she felt compelled to elope? And if she loved that Yankee and he got the medal they said he got when she went to Washington then why wouldn't she talk about it . . . you ask her and she stares a hole . . . no, I don't believe *that* for a minute, I think she's a nice girl, but all I want to know is *why did she come back home?*"

Upstairs in her own room she closed the door. All her old things were around her—the cherry furniture, the quilt her grandmother had pieced, the radio she had got for graduation, the silver dresser set they had mailed to her when she got married. It had been dented here and there—a shame. When she looked in the mirror she wanted to surprise a child's face, lurking inside. She wanted a moment to examine that face, to ask what it had been that was so different from what everyone had assumed it was. Instead, a woman's eyes regarded her with level clarity. They had seen a great deal, had remembered it all, and told nothing, not even to herself.

Suddenly she felt like crying. The eyes were slightly surprised, they refused even to consider tears. She put her head in her hands to block out their cool regard. At this her knees shook and her wrists, as though after hard tennis.

"Why did I come back home?" she asked. "Why did I?"

And Duncan that day had questions to ask himself, too, and asked them more than once, conscious that nobody uptown mentioned her name to him. "Why did she leave me?" he wondered, and then, "Did I fail her? How?" He went to no mirror, but perhaps he was seeking after all no more than a clear look at himself.

7 *An Hour at the Hunts'*

THE FIRELIGHT was sunken as comfortably deep into the silver coffeepot as Kerney Woolbright in the armchair.

"Of course," Mr. Hunt was saying, "I don't know what the boy will do, but the last thing we need to discuss openly in this county right now is the Negro question."

"I don't know that he means to discuss it openly," said Kerney.

"You don't know," Mr. Hunt returned. "I like Duncan, always have." He laughed. "And I've seen a lot of him. But you know his family."

"Good people," said old Mrs. Standsbury, his mother-in-law. She wore a blue sack and was crocheting bootees. She had got to the age where her descendants were multiplying like rabbits.

"Good people," Mr. Hunt agreed, "but you know back during Roosevelt's first term people used to go in that store for a nickel's worth of kerosene just to hear old Phillip Harper cuss the New Deal."

"Duncan's father?" Kerney asked. He had not been brought up in Lacey.

"No, his uncle. Great-uncle, really. He was a Hoover man."

"Yes, and too hard up to buy kerosene himself to build a fire with," said Mrs. Hunt in her cool, amused voice. "But then we were all poor then. More coffee, Kerney?"

"Please, Miss Nan." He watched with pleasure the movements of her sure hands with the big veins and the rings, the practical trim of the nails, the emphatic visible contour of the bones. This was how a mature woman's hands ought to look— he had known this always. He heard the touch of silver against the thin china, and the coffee was his.

"We're poor now," said Mr. Hunt. "We just don't know it. Income tax is just around the corner."

"Everybody says that," said old Mrs. Standsbury, laying aside her work to scratch her back, "but I never notice any difference."

"Of course *you* don't," Mrs. Hunt returned, glancing at her husband.

"Well, I eat the same food you do," the old lady said without rancour and continued her work.

"Bought your new spring hat, Miss Tennie?" Kerney inquired, raising his voice a bit. Old Mrs. Standsbury's hats were beautiful, expensive, and famous. "At her age!" people said, marveling with delight, and agreed they had never seen anything like her.

"Not yet," said the old lady, "but I hope to get to Memphis next week. Nan is going to take me when she goes to the dentist."

"Dentist?" Kerney inquired. "That really sounds like hard times."

"Another inlay," Mrs. Hunt told him. "I wouldn't dream of letting Dr. Neighbors touch it."

"Old Neighbors has hammered in a many a one in his day," said Mr. Hunt. He liked to pretend it was the women folk who had torn his country loyalties.

"In his *day*, yes," returned his wife.

"Where is Marcia Mae?" Kerney inquired.

Mr. Hunt pulled himself out of a reverie. "Marcia Mae? Gone to dinner at the club. Thank God." He came out so strongly on this last that his wife glanced at him.

"Heavens, Jason."

"Well, she's worrying me to support Duncan in the sheriff's race. I seldom take a hand in local politics; too many friends here. And I certainly don't want to support the boy if he's going to make a fool of us."

"I don't think he's radical," Kerney said. "He merely wants to try out two things: enforce the liquor law and apply justice equally for black and white."

"Half the niggers will be in jail, too," said old Mrs. Standsbury.

They looked at her. They had a way of forgetting that she listened, or if she listened that she had opinions of her own.

"Oh, no, Mother," said Mrs. Hunt. She read liberal papers and always, without offending anyone, tried to see the Negro's side.

"*I* didn't say it," the old lady said. "Old Black Jonas said it a long time back. He's a nigger and ought to know."

"He was trying to please you," said Mrs. Hunt.

"He never tries to please me the way he transplants my bulbs," Mrs. Standsbury returned.

"This likker thing," Jason Hunt resumed, "you take this likker thing. Duncan's right about that. It's gotten bad in this county. There's at least one wreck on the highway every Saturday night, and there must be plenty of them we never hear about. Winfield County is notorious all over the state. This Tallant-Grantham partnership—"

"What about that, sir?" Kerney inquired.

"Well, you tell me. What about it?"

"I can't say. Jimmy's a friend—at least, I guess he is. But I have heard one or two people say it may be that he and Grantham control not just that big highway place, but pull the strings for a whole dozen others."

"And—?"

Their eyes met. Kerney grinned. "You're making me say all this, sir. You aren't running for anything; why don't you say it?"

"You're among friends," Mr. Hunt said, smiling.

"You mean there's more?" Nan Hunt was leaning forward. Men never told her anything.

"This goes no farther, Nan," her husband said. "It has been talked, however—I don't know if it's true—that some of the New Orleans syndicate that Kefauver closed down are behind the Highway 82 mess we have now in Winfield County. You take Jimmy Tallant. He's no fool. He is also no man to be shoved into a shotgun wedding. But he married Bud Grantham's daughter because Bud threatened to cut him out of the business if he didn't. Jimmy Tallant doesn't do that for a small-time bootlegger's partnership. Of course, nobody knows the straight of this. Travis Brevard didn't know it; he said all his life—"

"Toting that wad of protection money in a belt next to his skin—" Kerney put in.

"That's right. Said that Jimmy Tallant was a good Winfield County boy. Travis lived by a country code. He trusted Tallant to do the same. But Duncan now—"

"That's a different thing, isn't it, sir?"

"It is."

"I've always thought Duncan was a clean-minded boy," Nan Hunt said.

"Yes, ma'am," Kerney agreed instantly. "You are right."

"He's never amounted to much," Mr. Hunt said.

"I don't care," Nan burst out. "He's kept the store his father left him; he's stocked the things I'm used to buying; he hasn't 'renovated' and made his store front look like the inside of a bathroom; but he makes a living and lives in a quiet way, so you say he's never amounted to much."

"Yes, and where will he even get the money to make the sheriff's race, unless he asks his wife or his mother?"

"Does his mother have anything?" Nan asked.

"Plenty," said Jason Hunt, nodding. "Stashed away."

"She never spends a nickel of it on her back," said old Mrs. Standsbury. "She's worn that one dress to prayer meeting and that one old blue sweater for twenty years."

Nan smiled. "With that old long black flashlight with a head this big. Does she still have that, Mother?"

"If you'd go to prayer meeting sometime, you'd know."

Nan winked at Kerney.

"How about a drink, Nan?" Mr. Hunt inquired.

"Speaking of bootleggers—" She rose. "Soda for you, Kerney?"

"Plain water, please, Miss Nan. Can I help you?"

"Keep your seat, boy," said Jason Hunt. "Jonas is back there somewhere." He went to call the servant.

When he stood before the fireplace, glass in hand, he laughed boyishly—you saw in little flashes like this why Nan Standsbury had found him winning. "Whisky is pretty damn good at that."

"Duncan will agree with you," Kerney said. He was busy finding every chance to put a word in.

The older man became more serious. "No, and I agree with

Duncan, Kerney. He's quite right. Until we can have whisky legally, people will turn drinking into an indecent and messy business. Most people, that is."

"We certainly don't," his wife said. "Not in my house."

Kerney remembered hearing of certain parties Marcia Mae was said to have thrown back in the old days, but he said nothing.

"It's still whisky," said old Mrs. Standsbury. "Whisky is whisky. I don't care who drinks it."

"Don't mind Mother," Nan said to Kerney.

"Oh, I don't care what you do," the old lady said. She never made anyone uncomfortable, because she had told the simple truth: she did not care what they did.

The Negro man left the room, shutting the twin doors carefully.

"Kerney," Mr. Hunt asked, "who is sheriff now?"

"Why, Miss Ada, sir."

"Right. Miss Ada. And does Miss Ada know that Travis's last request was for Duncan Harper to be sheriff?"

"I don't know, sir."

"Well, don't you think it would be a good idea for somebody to tell her?"

"Me, sir?"

"Well, you, me, anybody."

"I think it would be a fine idea for you to tell her."

There was a long silence. Kerney said, "You are thinking, sir—"

"I am thinking that the likker stand is a good thing, that the Negro stand is a good thing too, but we gain nothing—we might lose a great deal—by saying so in public. I am thinking that Duncan has no experience in politics, that we do not know what he will do. I am thinking it would be much better to let him have experience for six months before he loses a race or before he wins one and gets stuck with the job and gets us stuck with him for four years."

"Oh!" Kerney scratched his head. He wondered that he had not thought of this before.

"I am saying, in other words, that I don't care to elect a man whose mistakes may have to be paid for in blood. You say Duncan wants to experiment—to try something out, I think you said. I tell you, Kerney, no one should experiment with dynamite."

"No, sir."

"Yet on such a platform he wants me to elect him."

"He didn't send me here—" Kerney began.

Nan Hunt's cool voice interposed. "I think, darling, that the voters will elect Duncan, not you." It showed at such times that she felt she had married beneath her. A tiny line of pain appeared between her eyes. Compulsively she touched her fingers there; everyone remembered her fierce headaches. But suddenly, radiantly, she relaxed. A light broke over her face. A dash of cold, stairwell air entered the room, and in the middle of it, clouding it with her perfume, a young girl was rustling, approaching. Kerney tried not to turn too fast, but he could no more keep the radiance from his face than could her mother.

"Cissy." Her father caught her hand. "You've kept this boy waiting for two hours."

"I have not, silly." She bent to touch her grandmother's forehead with a kiss. "He'd rather talk to you all than take me out in the cold anyway. Hadn't you, Kerney?"

"Well—"

"No fair, is it, Kerney?" Mrs. Hunt laughed. "Turn around, honey. Your skirt—there."

"It's six-thirty now," Mr. Hunt said. "You'll be late. Kerney. Nice to see you, boy. I'll pay that call we mentioned. But not a word of it, remember—least of all to Duncan."

"I quite understand, sir. I think it's a brilliant idea. Goodnight, sir. Coat, Cissy?"

They walked together down the long walk in the chill dark. He let her in the car, waited while she drew in her full skirts, then closed the door. She sat in the cold, settled deeply in her fur coat, waiting for the door to open, for the nice smell of cigarettes and whisky, the weight of him on the seat beside her. Kerney was so nice: he smelled nice, he talked nice, he met people well, he was going to amount to something, he was fun. Yet—

"Hurry, Kerney. We're late."

"Kiss me first."

"Oh, my lipstick, no!" But it was only a small kiss, and for just a second, his eyes looked watchfully into hers. "Hurry,

hurry!" Then, to please him, she slipped her hand through his arm. "What a silly old boy you are. Silly, silly, silly! What a funny. . . ."

She could go on like this for hours, without even thinking about it. She thought it was disgusting, but it pleased him immensely. And he was supposed to be so smart, too. She could never figure it out.

8 Miss Ada

MISS ADA was still in bed, where her husband's death had hurled her.

She was very thin and her face, devoid of make-up, had cast all its wrinkles. It was a sensitive, high-strung face, long, with well-set cheekbones and a crooked patrician nose. The eyes, luminous and somewhat exalted, fixed upon Duncan, who had come at her summons, with the misplaced fervor of a young girl reading from the Bible at a "program."

"I was so happy to learn, Duncan, that Mr. Brevard's last wish was for you to be his successor. It proves to me he was functioning right up to the last."

"Yes ma'am, he was," Duncan said. "He was as clear as ever."

"Semper fidelis!" The long thin hand swept delicately upward. "You understand me, Duncan. We cannot have the class of people Mr. Brevard *generally* appointed taking over in the Lacey courthouse, can we?"

Duncan did not answer. Class seldom entered his head; he was sure it had never entered Travis's.

"Those deputies! That office! Those spittoons! That Willard Follansbee!"

Duncan immediately recalled, by the force of Miss Ada's tone, the rich black hairs that covered Willard Follansbee, Travis's favorite deputy, down to the last finger joint.

"How could *I* be expected to deal with such people? No." Looking down, she drew circles with her forefinger around each tuft on the pink spread. "No, I think when Travis—when Mr. Brevard stopped by your store that day, he was thinking only of me."

"You do?"

"I do. Because how could *I* be expected to deal with people like Willard Follansbee? Can we have that class of people taking over in an office that is responsible to *me?*"

Duncan had a sudden wild moment of wondering if Miss Ada thought her appointment was for life. He remembered Tinker once at the store, snatched back just in time from throwing a whole wad of invoices into the stove. Her excuse, which she seemed to find adequate, was that nobody had ever told her what invoices were. More total confusions have never been rendered than by innocent women.

However, Miss Ada soon set his mind at rest.

"I realize, of course, that my position is merely titular." She colored faintly. "Just the same, they say I can appoint anybody I want to." She gave him a coy glance.

Not till then did he understand. It had taken him, he realized, uncommonly long to catch on. Because it seemed unthinkable to him that this outdated, inadequate, ridiculous old woman should have anything to say about what happened to him. Yet if she had been different, would Travis Brevard have come into a store to die?

He approached the bed and took her hand. He felt the bones slip loosely together under his hand's pressure. Could the substance under the blue twisted ridge possibly be blood?

"I'll have to think it over," he said. "I'll have to talk to—to my wife."

"Bless her heart," Miss Ada said. "That was a wonderful cake she sent over to the funeral. Not that I could eat a bite of it. But everyone said—" Suddenly her eyes fell shut. Gently, but insistently, she pulled her hand backward from his grasp. "I'm rather tired, Duncan. If you'll forgive me."

"Yes, of course."

He hesitated for an instant at the door, and it was then her eyes popped wide open and a look of distaste hastened him out.

So she had seen the weight of Travis clamped in a box and dumped in the ground; she had flicked off the hairy thought of Willard Follansbee like something nasty on her hand; now she wanted shut of Duncan too. He took his hat from the dark-stained hat tree in the hall with its mirror and side drawers, and retreated into the sun. Miss Ada's front door framed an oval of sanded glass with a flowering trellis design; it was flanked by matching rectangular sidelights. He closed the latch gently and remembered the fall of the surprisingly large eyelid, coarse as leather. Behind that door, behind that eyelid, lived the clearest conscience in town, clearer than the tiny silver bell beside the bed. He half expected to hear it ring for the colored girl, but it didn't. Miss Ada had probably gone to sleep.

9 *A Deal*

IN THE sheriff's office the next day, along about ten, Mattie Sue Bainbridge, the secretary, wrapped up good in her coat and went across the street for a cup of coffee. Willard Follansbee, mouth partly open, rared back a little more in the split-bottom chair by the stove. It had turned off freezing cold, and sound traveled far: all the way inside you could hear the iron chatter of the gate on the sidewalk when she passed through.

Willard said, "They wrap up the top part, but what do they do about the bottom?"

"Nothing," Jimmy Tallant said. He had just come in; the room was still smoking with his coldness. He spread one long raw hand quite close to the stove top. In the other he held a pair of expensive tan leather gloves.

"You know," Follansbee went on seriously, "there's a bare space that long between the top of their stockings and the bottom of their pants."

"So they tell me," Jimmy Tallant said.

"That is," said Follansbee, "if they wear pants. You think Miss Mattie Sue wears pants?"

"I never looked into it," Jimmy Tallant said. "Have you?"

"Never looked into it."

There was a long silence. Jimmy Tallant turned to warm his back, then turned again. "Well, Willard. I hear that Duncan's in the saddle now."

"'Swhat I hear too."

"You moving out?"

"No. Staying in to help him. Duncan's all right. I got nothing against him."

"I got nothing against him either. Except he thinks he's Jesus Christ."

"Does he?" Willard glanced up.

"He does."

"Travis"—Willard burst out, and Jimmy turned his back to the stove because Willard couldn't mention Travis without choking up—"Travis never meant what he said to Duncan. I bet you anything in the world you want to bet he thought he was talking to me. I bet you anything you *name* he was out of his head and thought he was talking to me."

"Only he wasn't," Jimmy said coolly. "He was talking to Duncan Harper."

"Duncan Harper. What did he ever do for Travis? Listen, whenever Travis couldn't run for sheriff by law because by law he couldn't succeed himself, I ran for sheriff for him, but it was him that was running and it was him that was always sheriff, and everybody knew it. I never grudged him."

"Yeah," said Jimmy, "and when Travis needed a nigger woman, you found a nigger woman for him."

"I went there that day," Willard recalled. He was nearly weeping again. "It was the first hot day that year, along in April, going to take the refrigerator back or make her pay for it. She was on the front porch in a purple kimono and nothing else, and it broad afternoon, drunk as a coot. 'Send me the high shurf, white man,' she said. 'Hit's the high shurf I wants to see.' I came back and told Travis, 'She's tender as cream,' I said. 'To hell with that,' he said. 'I'm going up there and get Clem Gates' refrigerator.' The next morning he paid Clem Gates for the Frigidaire, out of his own pocket."

"What's Ida Belle doing these days?" Jimmy asked.

"Nothing," said Willard. "She plays nigger blues on the Stromberg-Carlson Travis gave her. There are those that have been up there. But nothing doing. Nothing. Never will be. I'll bet money on it. It's the way Travis was. Never another one to fill his bed, or his shoes either. Duncan Harper can kiss my ass. I wish I had me a Stromberg-Carlson to play. Instead, I got to show a groceryman what to do with a poll-tax receipt."

"I wouldn't be surprised you'll be doing a few more things than that," Jimmy Tallant said. His tone had not changed, and Follansbee did not look up. Only in the way his hands and face stilled was it apparent that he knew that Jimmy Tallant had stated his business.

"I might," he said at last. When he looked up, through the silence, Jimmy Tallant was holding out his hand.

Willard did not take it. "I was just thinking the other day," he said to Tallant, "that now I'm going to be doing a good many things Travis used to do, and it don't seem right not to be getting Travis's check."

"You might have something there," said Tallant.

"Might ain't do," Willard returned.

"I'll say this," Jimmy offered, "if you really do Travis's job and yours too, you ought to be getting more. Say twenty per cent more."

Willard paused. He let out his breath slowly. "Ought ain't do either."

They stopped at the clack of heels in the high hall. Mattie Sue Bainbridge returned, hugging herself with cold. Behind her, relaxed and silent as a thought of himself, came Kerney Woolbright. He shook hands with Follansbee and Tallant in turn.

"When's Duncan coming over?" Kerney inquired.

All sorts of spiteful things occurred to Willard, but he only said, "Tomorrow, I think."

"Don't seem right in here with Travis gone," Kerney said.

The two men eyed him. They knew what he was up to, he a college man, a Yale law graduate, going to marry Cissy Hunt if it killed him, going around shaking hands and saying the commonplace thing. They didn't fall for it, but somehow they didn't challenge it either. Perhaps the reason was the uneasy feeling he gave them that he was as sharp about them as they were about him. Maybe a little sharper? They doubted that. He thrust his gloves in his overcoat pocket and warmed his hands over the stove, a little too exactly like anybody else. Tallant especially surveyed him with the eye of an old actor for a young one.

It was Mattie Sue who answered him. She said that it certainly didn't seem right, that every few minutes she caught herself thinking that was Mr. Travis just shut the outside door, and once she looked up thinking she actually saw him come in—she was all by herself with nobody else in the office, and it actually scared her. She actually thought about closing up and going home, but somebody came in.

Kerney heard this through with such sober attention that she wished there were more to say, and suddenly thanked him for the coffee he had bought her at the drugstore. She observed the two other men watching her and blushed, then began to type rapidly.

As women said of some books, there was something in Kerney for everybody.

10 *A Phone Call*

COGNIZANT OF the merits of the dial system, Kerney went home and telephoned Duncan.

"Anybody in the store?" he asked.

"Nobody but me and W.B. I'm closing for lunch."

"I'd get rid of Follansbee," said Kerney.

The wire was silent for a moment. "I can't," Duncan said.

"Sure you can."

"I can't add insult to injury, Kerney. He loved Travis like a hound dog. I told him he'd be staying on to help me."

"Yes, and what thanks do you get? He's in there this morning conniving with Tallant."

"What about?"

"You *know* what about, Duncan. You wouldn't take protection money from Tallant."

"Willard knows my policy."

"Do I have to bore a hole in your skull? Do you think Willard's going to respect your policy?"

"I don't know. I have to give him the chance."

Kerney could see Duncan as plainly as if he had gone to the store (which he hadn't wanted to do because the eye of the courthouse would follow him as certainly as God's own): Duncan warming his hand on the cat's fur, and the colored boy across the room like a maharajah's lackey, cross-legged on the sack of chicken feed, probably picking his nose. Didn't everybody know instinctively the decent thing to do? Why must Duncan Harper have the gall to insist on actually doing the decent thing?

Kerney knew within an ace what Follansbee would do: the thing that irritated him was that Duncan knew it too. Still, he was for the moment compelled to see what Duncan saw—the Follansbee so ugly, so poor, so unimportant, the aging drug-store cowboy, the third best shot at the pool hall, for whom life, like a lucky throw, had suddenly added up—its soundlessness suddenly filled with the roar of privileged cars, the rattle of handcuffs, the glamour of guns, all because Travis Brevard had looked at him one day and known what he would like. And Travis in death now stood present with Willard, bright as a saint in his simple and adoring heart. A man with his capacity for devotion must have his chance. For what? For honor?

"Okay," said Kerney. "Okay, okay, okay!"

He hung up and that was when he saw her, his mother, standing in the door with that proud little smile which said how well he looked in the gray suit.

"Good God," Kerney flared. "I thought you were shopping in the Delta."

"I changed my mind," she said.

"You heard everything I said. You could have let me know you were there."

"I don't have to let anybody know I'm in my own house," she returned, passing by him, her feelings hurt.

He caught her. "If you repeat one single damned word of what you heard just now, it'll be your own house for sure, all by yourself, because I won't be living in it any more. It was that important, do you understand? No college campus doings any more. I make you a promise: if you tell this, I leave."

"I'm not going to tell anything," she said. "I didn't hear anything you said anyway. I wasn't even listening. I was thinking how well you looked"—her voice caught—"in your gray suit."

"A likely story," Kerney said. "You didn't lose two husbands over nothing."

"*They* didn't leave me; you know very well what happened. I left—"

But he had gone upstairs and slammed the door. He gave himself a ten-year limit to be in Washington, and no eavesdropping woman who thought he was a clever child was going to keep him down.

If that was love, he hoped Cissy Hunt would never love him,

just so she married him. She would. Duncan had lost Marcia
Mae, but Cissy would marry Kerney Woolbright. Whom did
she know that was better? Nobody. And on the heels of his
confidence, fear came and touched a finger to his heart.

11 *The Raid*

TINKER DID not know a thing about politics, as she kept on
saying, but she did know that one night two weeks after Miss
Ada turned over the sheriff's office to Duncan, the National
Guard came up from Jackson to Winfield County to raid the
Grantham-Tallant roadhouse. It was misting rain, and cold.
The jonquils were in bloom and the flowering shrubs had put
out; but now everything would be nipped.

About ten-thirty Kerney knocked on the door. She heard
him stamping on the doormat and, switching on the porch
light, she marked the rime of white on his shoulders and hat
brim, and beyond him, outside, the sparse wet white dots lancing down the dark. "Snow!" she cried out with delight, and ran
past him, out into the yard, lifting her face skyward and holding
out her bare arms. Kerney watched her, smiling, and started to
follow, but she came right back in, running with a slightly man-
nered little gaiety that was nonetheless attractive.

"It won't stick," she said. "The ground's not frozen."

"It never does."

"Sometimes. Once when we were children there was a big
sleet and snow here for three days. I expect you were too young
to remember, Kerney. They turned out school and none of us
went home that I remember for a week. We made sleds and skis
and played everywhere. Everything was different. Duncan and
Jimmy and Marcia Mae Hunt and I went out rabbit hunting
together and all got lost from each other. Come on in, Kerney.
Duncan's not here, but he'll be back."

"It's as bad as being a doctor's wife for you now, I guess,"
Kerney said.

She shivered in front of the fire. She had put on, to keep
her spirits up, little gold lounging slippers and velveteen slacks.
She was practically positive that Kerney already knew where
Duncan was.

"It couldn't do any harm to tell you now," she said. "They're raiding the highway place tonight."

"Who?"

"The National Guard." She spoke with confidence, though she had no idea on earth whether there were five of them or five hundred, whether they had come in convoy trucks and dressed in olive drab with guns at their feet, the way you used to see GI's moving toward maneuvers during the war, or whether they were in policemen's uniforms, riding in long black patrol cars with the slender aerial whipping sinuous and bright from the left rear fender. She decided on the black cars and imagined their soft pneumatic shimmer through the dark, the glimmer of the snow that melted when it touched the black metal. "You don't think anybody will get hurt?"

"Hurt? I wouldn't think so. Was Follansbee along?"

"I don't know. Duncan wouldn't tell me anything at all until just before he left. Let me get you a drink."

"No thanks."

"I'll have one then."

The drink was half gone when Duncan returned. There were no long black cars with him, no men in uniform, not even Follansbee. His Chevrolet sedan skidded and gave an angry snort entering the drive.

He came in laughing.

Tinker was cross-legged on the floor before the fire. Only her eyes moved to him. He stripped off his overcoat and shook hands with Kerney.

"How did it go?" Kerney asked.

"It seems," said Duncan, "that everybody has got Tallant and Grantham wrong. You know how they make a living? They sell Coca-colas, Orange Crush, Dr. Pepper, and hamburgers, and they charge a little bit, dollar a couple, for people to come and dance to the juke boxes. Do you know how much whisky there is in all of Winfield County? One half-pint bottle belonging to old Mars Overstreet who runs that little country store. He keeps it there for a cold. He's a deacon in the Baptist Church and was right embarrassed that we caught him with it. And he really does have a cold."

Kerney's mouth tightened. "I knew this would happen. I told you."

"It was worth a try," Duncan said. "I had to give Willard a chance."

"You didn't owe him a chance. You didn't owe him anything."

"Well," Duncan said mildly, "he has more stake in the sheriff's office than anyone I know."

"He's no more than the hired help. Travis tolerated him. It's no more his business than anybody else's what you decide to do."

"I think it's probably more his business than it is yours," Duncan said.

"You don't know anything about politics," Kerney said. "You're trying to play this out like it was a football game. You want to give everybody a break and play it clean. Did anybody ever offer you anything to throw a game?"

"Hundreds of people."

"But you never took anything. Nothing. You think you can work politics that easy."

"I knew it!" Tinker said. "I just knew you'd all be fussing."

"As a matter of fact," Duncan said, "I did take something once. A wrist watch. When I found out it was meant for a bribe, I gave it back."

"I'm sure you did."

"Kerney, there's no use getting worked up over this."

"I'm sorry, Duncan. It's only that I'm for you. I'm tired tonight. I've been straining myself all day to keep out of work, and it's worn me to a nub. For God's sake, don't take me seriously. If you and I don't stick together here, we'll both stand by ourselves, because there's nobody else we can stick with and be sure of."

"I believe that," Duncan said. "I'm tired too. Let's shake on it that way and forget it for now."

Kerney met his clasp with a good grip. "I best get home," he said. "I'm Mother's baby boy and she waits up with the porch light on."

Duncan turned back from the door, saying to his wife, "He is a baby, you know. It would be too much if it didn't dawn on him every once and a while."

He came to the fire. Tinker's head came level with his knee and he pressed it close against him, moving his hand caressingly through her short dark hair. But he was not thinking of her. He was still out there on the highway where exciting things had been going on for the first time in maybe too many years, and she knew it. She tried again to see it all: black cars, men in uniform, neon reflections on the wet gravel, and the occasional glint of snow. The men in uniform were heavy and handsome and she asked him suddenly, "Was Marcia Mae out there?"

In her hair his fingers stopped still. "Yes. How did you know?"

"I just thought she probably was."

. . . He did not dare at the moment, considering Tinker's mood, to remember fully the sight of the Cadillac convertible on the outskirts of the parked cars, or the arm in the window, propped straight up with the hand against the car roof, that way she always put her arm when she was behind the wheel and the car was standing. Then the bare length of wrist between the sleeve and glove, white as the snow—the sculpture of it jumped at him and said it was she. He got a remarkable thrill of pride, not thinking she had stopped on his account especially, but thinking how game she always was, to be curious and not ashamed of curiosity, to happen along and then not pass by. She was game and she was, in her curiosity, ageless: little girl, woman, old woman, with the bright interested undemanding eyes that missed nothing. In that moment, looking toward her from where he had stopped in the lighted door of the roadhouse, he was overcome with a delight that was all innocence. He was glad that he had known her and loved her and that she had loved him, and for the first time he could take the thought of what she had done without resentment, could step right straight into it and toward her, quickly crossing the gravel, threading among the cars. As he approached, the white shadow back of the arm grew as firm as the wrist. He leaned against the window.

"Nothing here," he said.

"Nothing!"

"Nothing. It will be the same everywhere."

"Follansbee," she said.

He shrugged. "Never mind. He loved Travis so, I had to give him a chance. It's no surprise."

"I see how you felt."

"He would have been sheriff if it weren't for me."

"I see."

"Marcia Mae, I came over to tell you that it doesn't make any difference to me any more that you ran off and married somebody else."

"It was an awful thing to do to anybody," she said. "I just couldn't help it. There was nothing *personal* about it, though."

"Well," said Duncan with a wry laugh, "I don't know how personal you can get."

She laughed too. "I mean I would have done it to anyone, for"—her chin lifted—"for Red."

"I'm sure he was a great guy. And I'm sorry, Marcia Mae, about—"

"Thanks."

The short silence that followed was certainly the time when he should have gone away. But she was saying, "I'm glad you don't hate me. I couldn't stand that."

"Hate you? Listen, I don't even dwell on it any more. I think you're just a hell of a fine girl, that's all. I came to tell you—"

"You cared the other day," she said. "That day uptown. I could tell it. You resented—"

"I know."

"Then when—?"

"Just now, when I looked up and saw your arm in the window. I knew it was you. You always stop that way. It came over me that I didn't care any more. Why? I don't know why. Because I was glad to see you. That's all."

"Glad to see me?" she repeated.

"Yes, glad. Mighty glad."

"Oh."

In the second silence, he knew he should have gone away during the first one.

But a narrow face had joined them.

"I got a complaint, sheriff," Jimmy Tallant said. "One of them big soldier bastards tilted my Miami Beach Bathing Beauty Contest pinball machine and all the lights on the breasts went out. I think you ought to go have a look at it. I heard you was pretty good at fixing up radios, juke boxes, that sort of thing. You might as well accomplish one thing during the evening."

"I'll get you yet, Jimmy," Duncan said pleasantly. "You know that, don't you?"

"I'll lay money on it," Tallant said.

"I don't make big money," Duncan returned, "so I can't afford to win big money. But this is just one time I missed, Jimmy. There'll be other times."

Tallant leaned his face down to Marcia Mae. "Where do you stand on this, old buddy?"

"I side with Duncan," she said. "He'll get you, Jimmy."

"Is that gratitude? After all the whisky I've got at cost for you. Tell you what, Marcia Mae. Soon as these folks hit the road, let's you and me have a drink up close to the stove. If Duncan won't bet with me, maybe you will."

"I might have a drink with you at that," she said.

"It's snowing," Duncan remarked.

Marcia Mae held out her hand. "Snowing." She smiled with sudden charm. "Do you remember the time, Duncan, when you and I got lost out in the woods that big snow we had when we were in high school?"

"What do you mean, you and Duncan?" Jimmy demanded. "I was there and so was Tinker. We all got lost, from town and from each other."

"That's so," said Marcia Mae, "but who found us? I forget."

"We found each other," said Jimmy. "I found a nigger house I knew, and Marcia Mae hollered her way toward me with Duncan not far behind."

"And I went back and found Tinker," Duncan said. "She was crying, down by an old stump."

"I remember now," said Marcia Mae.

"Yes," said Jimmy, "we found each other. . . ."

So it now seemed to Duncan that every time in life he came on Tinker she had contrived to get herself below knee level. Maybe she looked cute and felt right on the floor, but it made him feel like a fool. "Get up," he demanded.

She came up quickly, like the good dancer she was, rising further than her feet, all the way to the tips of her toes, with that startling quality of lightness she had, as though she had shot up through water. Her eyes were dutiful.

"Tinker," he said, "we are not going to start quarreling about Marcia Mae. I've seen her exactly twice in the last ten years. The first time was the other day in front of the post office. She happened to be uptown. The second time was to-night. Why she was there I don't know, but I ought to know her pretty well and I can guess. She saw something was going on and she was curious and—"

"And brave." She said it instantly, and it made him mad.

His jaw tightened, but after a moment he forged ahead. "As for what she did to me, it was terrible at first. It would be for anybody. Later it all boiled away and cooled. There was noth-ing left but a scar in my mind somewhere. But tonight when I saw her—this is important, Tinker—I knew that I didn't care any more one way or the other. I knew that as the person I used to know, she just didn't exist any more, not for me."

"Not an attractive woman any more?"

"Attractive woman? Oh, now, that's different, Tinker. And not fair. Lots of women are attractive; I can't help knowing that. The other way around too. Tallant, for instance. You aren't ever in any doubt—"

"Tallant! He's got nothing to do with this."

"Well you started it, honey. You brought up Marcia Mae. I only thought I'd get it said once and for all, so things wouldn't pile up before we knew it."

"I didn't start anything at all, Duncan. All I asked was if Marcia Mae was out there tonight. You could have answered yes or no."

"All right then. I thought you started it. I thought you had more in mind than that. I was mistaken."

She sat curled in the chair now, the big soft one: she could get as much out of its comfort as a kitten. She was fiddling with a little steel puzzle that had come in a box of Crackerjack: she liked to eat Crackerjack. She was also observing his rather monumental efforts at complete honesty.

Tinker's father and stepmother lived in south Mississippi in what Tinker called "the most expensive pigsty in the world." They had a swimming pool and several long cars and a station wagon with the name of the estate written on the door. They gave drinking parties and so did all their friends. When they were all together, they told dirty stories, and when they sepa-rated the men talked oil production and cursed the Fair Deal and the income tax, while the women gossiped.

Tinker's own mother had left her father back in the days when people thought all the oil was in Oklahoma and Texas, and when instead of being filthy rich he was filthy poor. Not that she wanted him back. She had returned to her girlhood home, which stood empty, one wintry fall afternoon, leading Tinker by the hand. There was a red glow among the trees, which stood black and wet against the horizon. Every pane in the bay window was drenched in red. Tinker's mother hoisted her in through a window and she unlatched the front door.

Indomitable, she called a Negro in off the road to build a fire, and after that sent him, protesting and laboring as though against a physical force, into town for some groceries from Harper's store. She cooked cheese crackers and toast in a Dutch oven and made hot chocolate on the hearth. There was molasses too, so thick and cold a knife could slice it. Nothing had ever tasted so good. Later they sat on the floor before the fire and played crokinole.

The house was not really hers but nobody could stand to move her out, and she was still in it when her ex-husband's oil money bought it for her. She was in it now. She was a tall thin woman with no figure at all, and heavy hair as dark as the day she married, wound in a rope around her head. Her eyes were gentle, clear, and somewhat vacant: people said she was "off."

If there was anything Tinker did not want to do, it was to go live with either of her parents. At the same time she knew, while she sat in the chair and solved the Crackerjack puzzle, that she was closer to it than she had ever been before.

12 *Jimmy Tallant's Wife*

"WHISKY AND SEX," said Jimmy Tallant to his wife. "That's all there is. Whisky and sex. Not even money. Nobody cares about money, only the best way to throw it away. The best kind of whisky. The right kind of sex. You don't believe it? All right, take away whisky and sex and tell me the history of Lacey, Mississippi, since 'seventy-five. *Eight*een seventy-five, that is. The year we ran the damn money-grabbing Yankees out so we could swig our likker and f— our women in peace. But hell, you don't even know what happened in *seven*teen seventy-five, much less anything that's happened in Lacey in the last seventy-five years. You been living here all your life in Winfield County, but I bet you don't know one thing about it. Do you?"

"Did they find anything down at the Idle Hour?" she asked. "Did they make you pay anything?"

"You are the dumbest woman I ever saw," said Jimmy. "Here I make you a speech that Kerney Woolbright could ride to the senate like coasting in on a pair of angel's wings, and all you have to ask is whether the governor's boys rated any cash. Well, I'm not going to tell you. You don't get out that easy. You got to tell me that one thing. One historical fact." He raised a finger. "Historical."

She tried not to laugh. She ground her swollen body down under the pile of blankets and, lips quivering, put the magazine she had been reading when he came in (a detective magazine full of pictures of beauties like herself who had been murdered) in front of her face, up close. She thought he was the cutest, funniest thing she had ever seen in her life.

Then, before she knew he had moved from across the room, his long steely fingers closed painfully on her hand. "You know what your daddy said about you? He said, 'Bella ain't really a bad girl and Bella ain't really all that dumb. I reckon the fact is Bella is just silly.'"

Bud Grantham, her father, had really said that. As if to prove him right, she went off into giggles. Jimmy hitched up his pants legs and sat down on the edge of the bed as impersonally as a doctor. Then he bent her hand backward into her wrist. Her laughter ended in a gasp. "One fact I asked for. One fact I get."

"The Monroe Doctrine," she said, wild-eyed. This hurt. Didn't husbands sometimes murder the beautiful women?

"About Lacey, I said. Who the hell you think wrote the Monroe Doctrine? Old Judge Standsbury? Come on. One thing." He increased the pressure.

"You're killing me!"

"I may."

"I remember one time Daddy said—*oh!*—said that there were twelve niggers shot one time in the courthouse upstairs. In the courtroom, he said. Twelve."

He dropped her hand. "Right." He returned across the room. "But it's a hell of a thing to remember. Why did he tell you that?"

"I was little. It was cold and in the wintertime, back during the depression. We didn't have much. We went to school in the buggy."

"I remember all that."

"So he said if anybody at school ever laughed at us, or asked me why I didn't have but one dress to wear, not to say anything back, but just to leave. Then he said that about the niggers being shot in the courtroom, and said to remember when they laughed that it was their daddies or granddaddies that did it, and that they weren't all that hot themselves."

"If anybody had thought to invite him to that party," Jimmy grumbled, "he would have been up there pumping bullets in every belly he could aim at. He was mad because he got left out."

"Daddy's a good man," said Bella. "I think Daddy's just a real fine man."

"Ummm," said Jimmy Tallant.

. . . A real fine man. He remembered the old cropped bur head hunched down low and the leathery face, which was exactly the same color as his khaki shirt, bent frowning toward the floor, for it always embarrassed him to talk seriously about any woman to another man, much less about his daughter who was already an embarrassment to him. "Bella ain't really a bad girl, and Bella ain't really all that dumb. I reckon the fact is Bella is just silly. I know you never wanted her kind, but I tell you as a matter of personal experience: these high-class women can give you a lot of trouble." What Bud Grantham had in mind when he said "high-class women" was his second wife, a high-heeled, swivel-hipped woman from New Orleans who claimed to be a Creole and draped herself in a fake French accent and, on occasions, not much else. She had disappeared one night —come closing time they couldn't find her—though she had waited on some plush customers from California headed for Florida, and there was not much doubt what had happened. It seemed a funny way to go to Florida, up 82, and Jimmy kept an ear cocked for quite a while, but he never heard any more. He idly recalled that he had slept with the woman, and reflecting on the ways of sex which always lay like a senseless tangle of roots below the surface of the ground, he thought wryly that if he had known Grantham's first wife he might have to be wondering not only whose child Bella was carrying, but whose child Bella was. It was a hot day and he was getting drowsy: his head felt thick. He asked suddenly, "Bud, is Bella your own daughter?"

"What!" Grantham bellowed and jumped up.

"No, now wait a minute," Jimmy said, telling the truth. "I was thinking you might have adopted her from your brother, the one"—he paused delicately—"the one that's in Atlanta."

"Oh." Grantham sank back. He was sitting on top of the desk in the office, right back of the roadhouse. "That there was a grudge fight they fetched Herman up for. They had no call to meddle in it."

"They will do that," said Jimmy.

"Yeah." Grantham was getting sleepy too: he yawned, rubbed his eyes, then righted himself decisively. "I ain't going to shoot you."

"That's good," said Jimmy.

"She's my daughter, but that ain't to say I don't know how she is. All I got to go on is what she says, and all she says is that it's yours. If you won't marry her, how do I look? I won't turn her out, no matter what. If you won't marry her, then you're leaving me, selling out to me for good. Take till in the morning if you want to think it over."

"How much will you give me?" Tallant inquired.

"Ten thousand."

"What! I can get five times that out of you in court, Bud, and you know it."

"Go to court then," said Grantham. "We'll both be down in Atlanta with Herman."

"You wouldn't—"

"Wouldn't I? My friend, I was better off than this when I made my living grubbing for cotton and hunting coon. The penitentiary can seem like a right quiet place to be compared to what I've had to listen to at home for the last month. Oh, I could go out to California and fetch her back one of them movie stars; they'll do anything for enough jack. But I know ain't nothing going to settle her but you. She's my little girl, Jimmy, and I'm your best friend, boy. Where're all the fine ones you growed up with in Lacey? What did they do when they got through admiring the chest full of decorations you brought back with you from across the water? Did anybody offer to take you in as partner? Nobody but ole Bud—"

"Oh, cut it out," Jimmy said. They were both well aware that it was Jimmy's father who thirty years before had led the gang who shot the Negroes down in the courthouse.

Jimmy never knew when people were thinking about this and when they weren't. All his life it lay in the back of his mind except during the war when he flew the planes and did the heroic things. He had a scorn for the good families in Lacey because he figured his father had done their dirty work for them once, and then they had turned on him. The Tallants had had a most uncertain status since—or was it all settled and nobody had thought to tell them? Jimmy didn't know. He knew that he and his brother and sister had run with the nicest people who sooner or later had told them what had happened. He was aware of vital statistics: his parents had died; his brother had been killed early in the war; his sister had married out of the state and moved away. He had rented the old house, ignored his aunts and cousins, drunk too much, and never cared for any girl but a nice little nobody—Louise Taylor, the one they called "Tinker," old Gains Taylor's daughter. He had cut a path for the bombers over Germany, and thousands died. He had returned a hero, but his girl was already married. She had gone to Duncan Harper with the soft tan hair and the smile and everybody's love. When Marcia Mae Hunt had deserted him, Duncan had only to turn his head and call Tinker's name.

So what better was there to do, he asked himself, than to go into business with a man he had always liked, a man whose family had been for generations bootleggers, hunters, trappers, owners of small country stores and tiny crazy-shaped farms. He judged wryly that this was where he belonged; he would say to anybody that the Granthams were the cream of Winfield County. So the match with Bella was a natural. Was it, and everything else in his life, an outgrowth of what his father had done? He didn't know. He saw it in any case as a joke on Jimmy Tallant, and as such he could accept it.

"Cut it out," he repeated. "I'll give you the business before I'll start crying. I'll marry her, sure. Why not? . . ."

"Listen, Bella," he said to his wife, "don't you ever mention those niggers to me again. It was my daddy that led the gang that did it." Her eyes got big. "You didn't know that?" he asked her.

"Seems like, now you mention it, I did hear something about it, long years ago."

"You mean folks don't talk about it now?"

"I don't know." She was honest as an animal. "I don't know any folks that would."

"I reckon not."

"I always say," she said, "let bygones be bygones."

He did not hear her.

"In the army, overseas," he told her, "I been known to drink with niggers. Some would be together with us at the same party, or maybe enlisted men too, shut up in a pub together during an air raid. That would be a kind of party. We'd get to talking and shoot the bull. We'd take a razzing sometimes, the niggers and me, from the Yankee boys that would always be bringing up the Civil War. 'Don't fool with me,' I'd say; 'my daddy shot twelve niggers dead in one afternoon between two and two-fifteen.' Then they'd all laugh, black and white together, thinking I'd strung the long bow again, because if you talk to Yankees they never hear you; all they hear is the accent, so they figure nothing you say could be important, or even true. If it was Yankees he'd shot instead of niggers, they'd have a statue to him in the courthouse yard and I could put on my string tie and lay a wreath on it, every Memorial Day. But let it pass.

"One night in a pub during the buzz-bomb raid, I said those words, 'Don't fool with me,' I said, and the rest of it, and from way out in the corner there after they stopped laughing, just when the next close one began to sing, a voice a whole lot flatter than mine said, 'It's the truth. His daddy shot them dead.' I said, 'Where you from and what's your name?' He said, 'I'm from Winfield County, out on the old Wiltshire Road near the covered bridge. My name is Sergeant Beckwith Dozer.' Then everybody hit for cover because it was going to be a near one, and just when the silence came I walked to the door and outside. They yelled after me, but I was tight, and the way it had all turned up that way, sudden and sharp, I wanted to be right under the damn thing when it fell. If he hadn't said that about the old Wiltshire Road and the covered bridge. But he knew it, too, see? Knew what would get me where I lived. A nigger always does know how to work you. He knew how to get me through that door; though the rest of them shouted after me, Yankee voices in with the Limeys', his voice I never heard. The earth rattled and shook me down flat, so I thought I was dead. But I woke up in the night, not even scratched, and walked on back home. The next time I saw him was on the Lacey square and the war was over. But he remembered and I did too, and the bastard grinned, remembering the time he nearly killed me. Do you think if it had worked *he* would have lost any sleep? Not Sergeant Dozer."

"Beck Dozer, is that who you mean? The one who's all time hanging around?"

"He's a good man to have. Don't ever get the man who claims to like you to do your work; get the man who hates your guts, because he'll see you in hell before he'll show himself to you as anything less than the best. Sure, he hangs around; he does whatever I might happen to need him for."

He hung his shirt and tie on a hook in the closet. "Pull down the shade," he said. When she leaned to do so, she screamed and jumped out of bed. "That nigger!" she cried.

He was across the room at once, taking his revolver from the desk drawer. She caught hold of him and clung to him, pointing back toward the window. Her knees were literally knocking together.

"Turn me loose, Bella. What nigger was it?"

"That Dozer nigger. The one you were just talking about. Quick. He's going, don't you see?"

"What was he up to?"

"Walking close by the window. Looking back over his shoulder."

"Did he stop?"

"Yes. No. I don't know. Quick and you can catch him."

"Not if you don't let go of me." He steered her to the bed and set her gently down. "Take it easy. You want to lose the baby?" He went to the window and cupped his hand to his eye, peering out. He called Beck's name twice, then lowered the shade, returned to his desk, and replaced the gun. She was quaking under the cover, making noises like a puppy. He began to laugh.

"You wanted me to shoot him, Bella? You actually did, didn't you? You wanted me to shoot a nigger. All for you."

"It was scary. It was so. It scared me half to death. I don't like niggers. I'm here alone so much of the day, way out here in this house by myself, way out from town, way out on the highway. There's niggers everywhere. Anything can happen. Look at me shake."

"I'll see him tomorrow," he said. "Get over. Tonight I'll sleep by the window." He covered her with another blanket and tucked it round, all she needed to make her happy. . . .

The next day when he saw Beck Dozer, he asked him about the incident. "I crossed through your back yard, Mister Tallant," Beck said. "It happened to be the shortest way home."

"Don't do it again," Jimmy said. "We don't like strangers in our yard at night."

For some reason he had not said niggers. But then his mother had brought him up never to say nigger to a nigger's face.

PART TWO

13 *Jimmy Tallant Drives South*

A WEEK LATER Jimmy Tallant was driving southwest toward Vicksburg and the River. The snow and freeze had staunched the spring: he drove through misting rain, swamps, and advertisements. The heater smelled. The windshield wipers kicked like a weary dance team. He played the radio until he couldn't tell a cowboy song from the lady interview with the dress designer. He wished that Tinker was right there next to him, riding in front of the cigarette lighter.

At Yazoo City, after many miles in the flatland, the road veered due south, rising nobly into the hills. Along the highway now, nearing Jackson, there were many new houses. Some were regular government, FHA styles with the carport, the empty picture window open on the highway, and nothing inside the whole house, it would seem, but the "Gone-with-the-Wind" lamp right in the center of the window. Bella had bought a lamp like this and put it in the middle of her picture window. "It's a real imitation colonial antique," she had told him. Other houses were larger and swankier: imitation Southern colonial, imitation Georgian, "ranch type." They had probably cost a filthy lot of money. For this was oil country now, and what wasn't oil was cattle. All the front yards of the new houses were mushy and sparsely covered with grass. The trees in the yards stood hardly tall as a man and had been planted in pairs.

He passed some places he liked to see, houses low-set and deep in porches, screens, and tacked-on rooms that country people always add because they live from the inside of a house outward and hardly ever think about how a thing will look to themselves, much less to strangers going by in a car. Theirs was the opposite impulse from the picture window. Heavy trees belonged to them, bare pecan whose intricate branches collected a blue, wet intensity out of the cold, and disheveled old cedars. Chairs on the big front porches were propped face to the wall to get them out of the damp.

He was glad for places like these.

Yet actually he had no desire to know the people who owned them, any more than to know the people who lived in the new imitation houses. Less, in fact, because in the new ones he was liable to find somebody he had been in school with or known in the war, he was liable to be offered a drink. But nothing on earth lured him toward the old places. In Tinker he could have made peace with them. She got on well with country people and she liked country places. She was interested in what went into the soup mixture, how long it took to hook a rug, and where an antique highboy came from. The talk would mute and fade and come again—old talk you didn't have to listen to any more because you know it by heart already. But Tinker was gone, his link was broken. He sometimes wished now that he had not relied on her so much, or left behind him the road that would take him to the front yard, the shaggy tree, the screened porch, and the big Sunday dinner. Yet left it he had, and he could not go back. The very thought of it bored him to death. He would rather be riding the leaky gray monotony of highway, listening to the windshield wiper and the cowboy song, pursuing his own illegal business.

Beyond Jackson, before Vicksburg, he began to look for the station and café. He found it right where they said, an ordinary white frame building, trimmed in red, pitched out on a swath of gravel. He was the first to arrive. But the others were prompt. He had not entered the café before a black Cadillac rose over the hill from Vicksburg and slid into place beside his Ford. Its plushy wheels pressed the gravel tenderly, and its motor purred like a kitten.

Three men got out and went with Jimmy into the café. They sat down at a table covered with a red checkered cloth which matched the curtains in the windows. The windows were sweated over from the gas radiance which had overheated the upper air of the room, though the cement floor, sweating also, was chill. The proprietor came in from the station and said he thought it was too hot in there. He turned the gas down and blew his nose. He had a bad cold.

One of the men put a pint bottle of whisky on the table and asked for four glasses. He was chewing on a broomstraw. It seemed unlikely he had been near a broom on that or any other morning.

"Hear you got rid of your sheriff," he said, and shifted the straw with his tongue. The skin of his face was extremely thick and of a yellowish-brown color, the consistency and depth of discoloration often seen in sideshow barkers or men from the Southwest—it seems to come not so much from the sun as from exposure, and exposure not so much to weather as to every kind of strange affair and person and injury. He wore a dark wool shirt, a brilliant tie and a light gray hat of extraordinarily fine felt. When the glasses came he poured out a scant inch of whisky for himself and took it quickly, then drank a little water. He shoved the bottle toward the second man, who did the same. This one was dressed like the first, and looked a good bit like him, except that he had a squat face that seemed thoughtful but may only have been stupid. His hair was jet-black and very coarse, and grew in spikes out from the crown, each hair making its separate break for the open. He might have been sitting under a little plate. He looked Indian, just as the burnt-faced man looked Mexican: but then you usually thought men like them were part something else.

"Excuse me," the second man said, and pushed the bottle on to Jimmy. "Hair of the dog, you know."

Jimmy shook his head and passed the whisky on to the third, who was young, just a boy, and who wore his coat very roomy. "I'll jest wait till I get me a Coca-cola," said the boy, and grinned. There was no doubt whatever where he was from. Jimmy Tallant was probably kin to him. So this was who they got to carry the gun for them. How important were they, then, or how important did they think they were, or hope they were?

"Yeah, the sheriff," said Jimmy. "He took a notion to die."

"Just took a notion, huh?"

"Natural causes," Jimmy said. "It's still being done every once in a while."

"Yeah, so what about this new fellow?"

"That's a different thing," said Jimmy.

"What is he? A Baptist? A Jesus boy?"

"He's a sheep dog," Jimmy said. "He's going to cross the Delaware if he has to swim through the light brigade."

The second man, the thoughtful one, woke up and looked suspicious.

"I don't get you," he said.

"He's a football star," Jimmy said. "He's trying to make a touchdown."

The second man turned to the first. "If I don't get it, how is Sam going to?"

The first man took the straw out of his mouth and winked at Jimmy. "That's right. He was a football star. Won five hundred cold cash for me one time in the last thirty seconds of play. Against LSU in '39. You remember the day?"

"I remember them all," said Jimmy. "But the word I came to bring you is, he might be better in football than he is in politics."

"I understand you've been shut down for two weeks. He must be doing all right. Ain't that what they want up there, the Sunday-school class and the Epworth League? Ain't that what they vote for up in them hills? Wallace here, he's from up in them hills. Ain't that the way they are, Wally?"

The boy in the loose coat grinned. "I ain't from Winfield County. Winfield County, tha's a crazy county. I wouldn't be from Winfield County for nothing."

The thoughtful man leaned forward. "How'd he do it? We heard you had a inside man—a deputy."

"I have," Jimmy said. "He's all right and he's working. He tipped me off when they brought the National Guard up. They scoured the county and they found one half-pint. But what Harper did two weeks later he did by himself. Nobody knew it. He just drove out in a strange car with his hat pulled down to his nose and ordered a fifth from the carhop. When the boy brought it out, he had us cold. Slapped on the biggest fine in the books, confiscated ten cases of bonded whisky, and fixed it so we can't even sell beer for six weeks."

"One man walked in and did you that much damage? What did he have with him, the atom bomb?"

"I can't hurt him," Jimmy said. "It's still my place, goddam it, you haven't moved your wheels and tables up there yet. I got my reasons and I stick to them."

"The thing we came to say is, we may not move the wheels and tables up there at all. So Sam says."

"Tell Sam," Jimmy said, "that by September this man will not be in the way any longer. We have an election in August. When there's an election Harper goes."

"How do you know he will?"

"I'm going to see to it, that's how I know."

"You running yourself?"

"We're running Travis's deputy. And I'm fixing it before-hand so he can't help but win."

"How? How are you fixing it?"

"It's my county and my neck of the woods. I know better how to handle it than anybody else. If you want to get some-body else up there—"

"That's not it. Just tell us a little something."

"Something we can tell Sam."

"That's right. Just a little something we can tell Sam."

"All right," said Jimmy Tallant. "This joker, this Harper, not only wants to purify Highway 82 from one county line to the other; he's got principles drawn up about treating the niggers right. He's had the gumption not to mention this out amongst the constituency. He thinks he can do a quiet job along those lines without anybody much noticing how liberal he is. I in-tend to smoke him out."

"So then?"

"So then it takes care of itself. Ask the kid here. Nobody with one solitary idea on the Negro question has got a chance in the world of getting elected to public office in Winfield County."

"Tha's right," said the boy cheerfully. "They ain't got a chance. Nor in Tippah County either."

"So everything's under control, Mitchell," said Jimmy. "You can tell Sam."

Mitchell sneezed. He went and stood by the gas radiance, and stared at the sweat-covered windows. "God, what a joint. You couldn't pay me to live in Miss'ippi."

"There are plenty more just like it," Jimmy said gloomily, "in Alabama, Georgia, Louisiana and Texas, Montana, Utah, Idaho and Kansas. To name a few."

"It's the truth," said Pilston, the Indian-looking one. "I wonder why Mitchell picked this one."

"I remembered it," Mitchell said, "because they got a alli-gator out back."

"A alligator!" the boy repeated.

"That's right. There used to be a sign up: ten cents to see the alligator. The sign's gone, so I don't reckon he's still got the thing."

"Did you ever see it?"

"See it? No. I never seen it."

"Maybe he never did have it," said Pilston.

"Why would he put a sign up about a alligator if he didn't even have one?" the boy asked.

The proprietor came in. "Hey," said the boy, "have you got a alligator back in the back?"

"Sure," said the proprietor; "back in the back yard. Go on out and look at him if you want to. I don't charge nothing in the winter."

The boy got up. "Sure enough? Can I?"

"Sure. I'll show you."

The other three men for a moment seemed about to follow the boy and the proprietor. There seemed to be something awful about not having in the room with them a person curious to see an alligator free of charge.

Mitchell said, "They have them all out West, you know, these roadside zoos and things. They put up signs all along the way about what big Gila monsters and rattlesnakes they've got. I remember one time I was driving out to Tia Juana with a young fellow something like the boy here and we stopped to get some gas and a hamburger at one of those zoo places. Wasn't a soul around. Just a lot of yellow and red signs about what a hell of a fine place it was—I can see them yet. The kid went back to the zoo, but he couldn't find a soul. He came back and said the animals were all starving and some of them were dead. They didn't have any water. It smelled to high heaven back there, he said. A Mexican came along and said the man that owned the place had died and the woman had hitch-hiked off and never did come back. So the kid couldn't stand it. He went in and shot the snakes and the wild cats, and opened the other cages for the things to get out. That's how come I remembered this place. Everytime I see anything like a zoo place, I think of that other time. This kid here, he had to see the alligator too. They're all alike, kids like that."

"Wonder why they don't charge to see him in the winter," said the Indian-looking man.

"Alligators get cold in the winter. They ain't up to much," said Mitchell after a time.

The Indian-looking man thought it over, then said, "How the hell do you know what a alligator's up to in the winter?"

"I don't know. I'm just guessing. It stands to reason, don't it? Don't it, Tallant?"

"Sounds all right to me," Jimmy said.

"I bet he's 'sleep right now," said Mitchell. "Cold and sluggish and 'sleep. Lay you four bits on it."

"If this keeps up we'll have to go back and look at the damned thing," said the Indian-looking man.

"No we won't," said Mitchell. "We'll just ask the kid. He'll tell us."

"Okay then. We'll ask the kid."

When the boy came back, Mitchell asked him, "How was the alligator? Wasn't he cold and sluggish?"

"Mighty sluggish," the boy said, "and he looked cold."

"Was he asleep?" the Indian-looking man asked.

"He was when we came out, but then he opened his eyes. I couldn't tell if he was looking at us or not."

"See, so I don't owe you nothing. He wasn't asleep."

"He was asleep till they woke him up."

"No, we didn't wake him up. He woke himself up. Maybe he wasn't asleep."

"See, you can't tell. I don't owe you nothing. Not a dime."

They were still arguing when they got into the Cadillac.

14 *Errand by Night*

BECK DOZER would not tell his wife where he was going.

"It's best you don't know. If something happens and they ast you, it's best you can just say, He never said."

"Next time I going to marry me a field nigger," said Lucy. "Somebody too tired at night to go out and get theyselves in trouble."

"Whar you goin', Unker Beck?" asked W.B.

"Blow your nose," Beck Dozer told him. "You been running like a sugar tree all this blessed day."

He put on his town-cut coat, and English-type tweed jacket, ordered by measure from Sears Roebuck. In overalls he was apt to give the impression of being not exactly skinny but skimpy, as if there had been just enough material to make him. But in this coat, and especially when he shined his glasses on the sleeve and put them on, he brought to mind a college class-room and himself with a notebook, ready to walk in and lecture. He took a swallow of whisky from a pint bottle on the mantelpiece, then he went to a large mirror in a gilt frame and examined the knot in his tie, firming it.

Just across the room in a matching gilt frame, hung an enormous daguerreotype of Beck's father, Robinson Dozer. He had a thin face, large eyes, and wore a string tie. If Beck Dozer looked professorial, his father's face brought gentlemen to mind, and a gentleman's household, and how gentlemen liked their own kind about them, never mind who brought the whisky in and who drank it. Robinson Dozer had been one of the twelve Negroes shot down in the Lacey courthouse in 1919. He had been the emissary to the blacks, the one who had said, You all come on in; they wants to talk this thing over. Beck Dozer had been four years old when it happened: his father's murder was his earliest recollection of childhood.

"You ain't going to wear your good coat out in this rain?" his wife asked.

"Lucy," said Beck, "I gots to wear my good coat tonight."

Back in the kitchen where W.B. had gone there was a sudden lot of racket involving a tin bucket top, a pan that had been set under the leak, and a scuttle of kindling. Lucy went back and yelled at W.B. "What you thank you doing? Jest tell me that!" She returned with the baby on her arm, cleaning its face on her dress and hushing it. Beck was putting on his GI slicker.

"Don't go out in this, Beck," Lucy said. "Hit's way too bad a night."

Beck Dozer took the baby from her and set it on a pallet down before the fire. He caught her arm and pulled her after him through the door to the hall, then through the hall and front door to the porch.

Lucy was thin as a railroad track, a real nigger gal in a straight-cut cotton dress, with big bare feet, black greased hair, and a world of softness on the bone. In the big room, through the open doorways, the raining sounds talked loudly. W.B. forgot about his troubles in the kitchen. He ran into the hall and back, then leaned over the arm of the rocking chair by the fire where a pile of petticoats and skirts and an apron lay like an old soft quilt.

"Granny," he said. "Unker Beck hugging Aunt Lucy. Out on the poach. I seen hit and I knows hit."

The pile of clothes shook. A hand like a daddy longleg's foot came out and groped for him.

"He's Granny's Jesus chile," said the old woman. "He's Granny's man."

"I'se a little bitty ole black nigger," said W.B., and got the silly giggles.

Beck Dozer heard this as he left, and had the impulse to go back and tell W.B. that he was in reality half British. Nobody could have told him except Beck Dozer, nor that Beck was not his uncle but his father. As he double-buttoned his slicker high at the throat and went down the steps into the rain, he wondered now if anybody would ever know. It made him sad to think about W.B., never knowing whose he was, and sad to think of the plain little English girl who wouldn't leave a Negro Yank alone, and sad to think of himself who no matter what he argued or said had always wanted a white woman. He thought of his father too, the gilt frame being all he could do to please that gentle face, and he thought that dying should not be a public thing. He saw that everything most clear to him was sorrowful, full of Negro sorrow. He included himself in his sorrows, for he always suspected that, like his father, he was going out to deal with white people someday and never come home again.

Some hours later, both his hands were bleeding and he was standing on the hill outside a white man's house. The hill was narrow at the flank, scarcely large enough, it appeared, for the house to rest on it, so that where Beck Dozer stood at an angle back from the lighted windows he had to watch out that he didn't fall off in the gully, down amongst all the vines and varmints.

The room he could see into was a bedroom, a children's room, with an iron white-painted single bed and a crib. A young white woman with dark hair was moving about, putting two children to bed. The older one, a boy, with hair so blond it was white as his skin, turned over the wastebasket meddling in it and got blessed out for it.

Beck Dozer circled the house and gained the back door.

15 *Beck's Legal Right*

TINKER KEPT insisting she heard something until she went to the back door to see for herself, and there stood a Negro out by the steps in the rain.

"Duncan," she called. "Duncan! There's somebody here to see you."

Her husband was beside her quickly, leaning out. The Negro had not knocked, but had stood saying, "Mister Harper? Mister Harper?" over and over, and now that they saw him it seemed they had heard him for certain all the time, for no telling how long, for it is part of the consciousness of a Southern household that a Negro is calling at the back door in the night.

"It's Dozer, isn't it?" Duncan asked, shielding his brow and squinting against the rain.

"Yes, Beckwith Dozer."

"Come on in out of the wet." Duncan held the door for him. He raked the mud from his shoes on a steel mat.

"Watch out for the floor," said Tinker.

"A little mud," said Duncan.

"Not mud; he's bleeding. Don't you see his hands?"

"Good Lord, what have you got yourself into?"

"I got in a fight. That's how come I'm here."

"You wait right there while I get a towel," Tinker said. "Don't they need to be bandaged, Duncan?"

"Looks like it," he called after her. "Do you need a doctor, Beck? Are you hurt anywhere else?"

"Just my hands," said Beck Dozer.

In the kitchen, Tinker made him wash in a basin she kept put aside for the children when they hurt themselves, then dabble on some medicine while she cut strips of gauze and adhesive.

"Looks like to me," said Duncan, looking at the curiously jagged cuts and scratches, "you got mixed up with some woman owned a crosscut saw. Who've you been scrapping with?"

"Bud Grantham was who it was," said Beck Dozer. "I went out there to buy some whisky."

"He can't sell you any. I shut him down."

"That's what you think. It's going out the back door to

anybody comes along. He sold some to a white man just before me—I seen him leaving with it in a newspaper—then he said he didn't have none for me. I said, I gots the cash money, and it's just as good money as that one just now bought a fifth from you, Mr. Grantham. He spit and says, It's nigger money; don't fool yourself, nigger, it ain't never good as white money and it ain't never going to be. He threw in a word or two I wouldn't repeat before Mrs. Harper here, then I said a GI word or two back and he hit at me, but I ducked him and hit back."

"You hit Bud Grantham!" Tinker exclaimed. The idea of this Negro hitting anybody was more than you could have expected of him, as if a soggy, thin little firecracker, long after the explosion of the pack, had taken a notion to go off. But she saw his face and did not laugh. Beck Dozer blinked behind his glasses. "I had a razor," he announced.

Duncan whistled.

"He picked up a butcher knife he had there with him opening a crate of whisky and came at me with it. He started yelling for Jimmy Tallant. That's when he hacked into my hands—they was up like this to save my face from him. So I outs with my razor and gave him the quickest cut I could"—he made a nasty motion with his bandaged right hand—"and ran."

"Where'd you hit him?"

"I aimed about here." The hand moved to the side of his neck, below the ear. "But you know you can't tell when a razor goes in and when it don't. It's so fine and sharp and slices so smooth—"

"That'll do," said Duncan sharply, as Tinker shuddered.

"As I say, I aimed there."

"Yes."

"But I missed."

"That's good," said Duncan dryly.

"I got him on the shoulder instead, right between the arm and the collar bone. I heard his shirt when the cloth split, but about the flesh, like I was saying—"

"Then you might have hurt him pretty bad?"

"I might have grazed him, sure enough," said Beck Dozer, studious behind the milky shield of his glasses. "On the other hand, I might have missed him completely."

"Umm," said Duncan. "Bad. Either way. Where's the razor?"

"I threw it away in the woods."

Tinker stepped back. Beck Dozer looked down at the snowy bandages and nodded to her. "I thank you, Mrs. Harper. But whatever I done"—he turned back to Duncan—"is done. And whatever it was, a Grantham won't forget it."

He moved to sit by the stove, the way Negroes coming into the white kitchens always did in the old days when the stove burnt wood and dried them while they smoked like bread, and warmed them, too, clean through to the bone.

"If I no more than nicked Bud Grantham, if I no more than fanned the air in front of him, it's enough for him and all them other Granthams to want my black hide. I'm scared, Mister Harper. I came to ask you for custody."

"It might have been better, seeing that it's Granthams we're dealing with, if you had left town instead of coming to me."

"That's the old-timey way," said Beck Dozer. "Getting out of town never solved anything. If a Negro never takes advantage of what legal rights are open to him, he can't hope to enjoy those that ought to be open and ain't. You are the law, Mister Harper. I have come to you."

"That's all very good reasoning," said Duncan, "until a Negro picks the toughest white man in Winfield County for fancy razor work. If you're so damned philosophic about this, you should have done about two seconds of thinking beforehand."

"But I didn't," said Beck Dozer.

"It looks that way," said Duncan. He went to telephone the Idle Hour, Grantham's house, and Jimmy Tallant's, but received no answer to any, whereupon he called the Woolbrights' and discovered that Kerney had taken Cissy Hunt to the picture show in Stark. He reentered the kitchen carrying his hat, his GI slicker slung over his arm, one pocket heavy with his gun.

"You don't agree with me," inquired Beck Dozer, "that a Negro must use the law in good faith wheresoever and whensoever the opportunity arises?"

"Except for all the soevers, you might be quoting me," said Duncan. "Okay then. We'll go to jail."

"Jail?" said Tinker at once.

"I may be late," Duncan told her. "I'll try to call you. Lock the house up good. If Kerney calls in, tell him to come up to the jail."

She had been scalding the basin at the sink. Now she went anxiously to him. "Jail?"

Duncan smiled. "He asked for custody, darling. That's what custody means. I have to put him in jail to keep him safe from the Granthams."

"It's my legal right," Beck Dozer explained to her kindly.

"I'm sorry you're mixed up in any of this," she said, helping him with the slicker.

From the back door, she leaned out, calling after them, "Duncan, look for Jimmy."

He turned at the car door. "For Tallant?"

"Yes, he—he'll *know*."

The rain rustled between them. "You're right. He will." The car door closed.

16 *The Jailer*

UPSTAIRS, the jail was so black you could not even see the iron bars. From below, Mr. Trewolla, the jailer, at last found the switch; a bulb that hung from a dusty cord shed a thin light about them. All the cells stood empty with the cold, sweaty black iron doors slightly ajar, and when the big door that closed the stair ceased to send forty kinds of echoes walking amongst the shadows, you could hear the coal dust near the stove smashing unpleasantly beneath their damp shoes. But this was an ordinary sound, better than the big door. At the touch of the key, at the pull of the hinges, almost at the brushing of a sleeve, the door's voice stirred; a little more and it might have formed a word—the very one you never wanted to hear.

The only person in jail was a Negro woman named Lu, sitting over in the corner on a broken chair.

"Oh, Jesus, Brer Beck," she said, "I never thoughts to see you here."

"What you doing in here?" he asked her.

"I had to eat," she said. "Anybody ought to eat. How you do, Mister Harper!"

Duncan remembered her well. She was a slump-shouldered Negress who wrapped her head in a rag and carried her chin low and to one side, angling a sour eye at the world. Tinker had hired her, being unable to get anyone else, right after their second child was born. She did not steal or tote, but was of a complaining nature. She had nothing, she said; her children had nothing; they had to go to school barefoot over frozen roads; her mama and papa lived with her and should have furnished her a little from the old age, but they couldn't get the old age because they had the law title to that old pieced-together house that all of them lived in; and her husband should have helped her at least to raise the lawyer's fee to transfer the title of the house so her mama and papa could be legally penniless and get the old age, but her husband took up with a yellow. About this point of hearing the story for the fifth time, Tinker raised up suddenly in bed and told her, "There's a ten-dollar bill on the mantelpiece. Take it and buy those children some shoes and don't you ever come in this house again."

"The cawn bread ain't done," said Lu.

"Then it'll just have to burn up," said Tinker.

Lu thought. "You firing me?"

"I certainly am," said Tinker.

"Oooo!" said Lu, and woke up the baby.

"If I goes on relief next," Lu told her, "I has to say how come."

"You can say you talk too much," said Tinker, and fell back, exhausted.

Lu thought again. "Does I?" she asked.

"Your sister has got food," said Beck Dozer to Lu. "To my personal knowledge."

"You needn't think she's going to give me none," said Lu. "What you done done to your han's?"

"Why won't she give you none?"

"She too stingy. Me and her's twins and she was bawn sucking on both tits."

"You're not going to want to stay up here long," Duncan told him, "unless you can find some way to hush her."

He went downstairs.

Mr. Trewolla was an old man with liver spots on his hands and a hernia which he thought about tenderly, all the time. He had been the jailer for twenty years, for longer than Travis Brevard had been sheriff. He took a dim view of all sheriffs and town marshals. A deacon in the Baptist Church, he had considered Travis a loose character, and had felt comfortably backed up by God when Travis died. He thought of Duncan as a boy who had a lot to learn, but since he understood around town that Duncan would "take a drink," and that his wife "took a drink" with him, he felt the chances of his learning anything were small indeed. Mr. Trewolla honestly believed that anybody who would "take a drink" would do "most anything." Nobody could tell him: every Saturday night he saw plenty of the kind of thing whisky could do. He held complicated opinions on every arrest, but these opinions, like tortuous country roads that all led to the same dreary hamlet, invariably ended: "Whisky, you know. Whisky."

Mrs. Trewolla, his big fat wife, cooked turnip greens and sowbelly for the prisoners every day on the wood stove downstairs. Then after she took a bath and powdered, she would go uptown in the afternoons, walking around visiting, telling everybody exactly the things Mr. Trewolla had already said. "Daddy says," she would begin, then she would quote, all the way through, "Whisky, you know. Whisky. Just like Daddy says." She did not have the imagination to alter anything.

Duncan stood in the hall of the jail and looked through into the living room where a hooded metal lamp was burning beside the armchair. Mr. Trewolla, in his green eyeshade, had gone back to reading the newspaper. Behind him the high old-fashioned windows rattled in their frames when the wind sluiced the rain against them. Duncan had recently read about a man at the university who had made a study of jails and had come up with the information that only five jails in the state of Mississippi took an unskilled person of average intelligence more than twenty minutes to break into or out of. He did not think that the Lacey jail was one of the five. It was among Mr. Trewolla's duties to make a yearly report on the condition of the jail. Mr. Trewolla had done this faithfully every year, but every year had always said the same thing—that the jail was sound as ever.

Duncan entered the living room and laid Mr. Trewolla's keys on the table.

"Have a seat, have a seat," said Mr. Trewolla. He laid aside his newspaper.

Duncan felt too rushed to sit down, but he did it anyway.

"Looks bad in Korea," said Mr. Trewolla.

"Yes, sir, it does. I'd hate to be fighting in all that mud and ice."

"They ought to have done what MacArthur told them. It's enough to make you sick. That fool Truman. Trying to tell the finest general of our time how to fight a war. Trying to tell us down here in Miss'ippi what we got to do for niggers."

"He's got his faults," said Duncan.

"Faults! Name me one virtue he's got. You can ask Mrs. Trewolla what I've said about him from the beginning. Ha!"

"Mr. Henry, about this boy upstairs—"

"Drunk?"

"No, sir, I want to tell you. There may just possibly be trouble. He says he's been in a scrap with Bud Grantham. He came to me for custody. Grantham and Tallant would bend heaven and earth to give me trouble. They may come for him—you can't tell."

"What was he doing at Grantham's?"

"Trying to buy some whisky."

"Then it's dog eat dog," said Mr. Trewolla. "The best thing you could do was let Grantham handle him. They've got their ways, those fellows. They deal with rough cases all the time."

"He asked us for nothing but his right. That is, if he's telling the truth. We're going to give it to him, even if they try to take the jail apart. You see, if I can prove they're still selling whisky, I can throw the book at them."

"You can what?"

"I can ruin them. Confiscate everything."

"Nothing is going to stop them, in my opinion," said Mr. Trewolla. "Don't think you've cramped their style. There's just as much going out the back door as ever went out the front. I been knowing that. Said it at the time."

"Mr. Henry, the only thing I want you to do is keep that nigger safe."

Mr. Trewolla's nervous old man's hand with the yellowed

nails fumbled with his eyeshade. He scratched his forehead where the mark of the shade showed red across his indoor skin.

"You'll never get a conviction. You going to carry a nigger's evidence in front of a grand jury?"

Duncan rose. "I'm trying to carry out one step at a time what the law says is the right thing, Mr. Henry." He smiled. "I never heard of a law against the law, did you?"

Mr. Trewolla followed him to the front door. "And what's that nigger trying to do? Commit suicide?"

"I don't claim to understand it all so far, Mr. Henry, but I hope to before the night's over. Let's just keep him safe and don't let anybody in unless they've come from me. Don't you think that might be best?"

"If that's your orders, why then—"

"I'd think it might be better for Miss Annie to go over somewhere else."

"I'm staying right here with Daddy," said Mrs. Trewolla at once from the other side of the kitchen door.

"Whatever you think. Goodnight then, Mr. Henry, and thank you. Goodnight, Miss Annie."

"Goodnight, boy."

"You heard it all," said Mr. Trewolla to his wife the minute the door closed; "what do you make of it?"

"What do you make of it, Daddy?"

"There's something funny about it."

"That's exactly what I said, Daddy. There's something funny about it."

"You remember Duncan's uncle, old Phillip Harper. He was a Hoover man. The only vote cast for Hoover in Lacey and Winfield County in 1932 was Phillip Harper's."

"But Duncan is sweet," said Mrs. Trewolla suddenly, with fat conviction. "He sat down and talked to you. He thought about me staying here. You know that was sweet, Daddy."

"I'm telling you right now," said Mr. Trewolla, who was far more alarmed by an opinion from his wife than by anything Duncan had done, "there's funny politics mixed up in this. You'll see. I never thought I'd wish for Travis Brevard back in office. I *know* what whisky is, but funny politics—!" He shook his head, readjusted his eyeshade, and shuffled back to the rocking chair, the lamp, and the newspaper.

17 *A Call to Kerney*

DUNCAN FELT the need of Kerney so much that he telephoned the movie house in Stark from the pay station in the drugstore and had him paged.

"There's a nigger in the woodpile," Duncan concluded, "in addition to the one in the jail. I think Tallant is back of it."

"Then there's a hook in it somewhere," said Kerney, "at the very least."

"I can't get anybody I can depend on," said Duncan. "Trewolla is set in his ways and thinks I'm still in knee britches, and Follansbee is off God knows where, though I certainly don't want him."

"You can deputize, you know."

"But it makes me look a fool to deputize over nothing."

"Then what are you planning to do?"

"Go look for Tallant and Grantham first, and try to get the straight of it."

"Suppose you don't find them?"

Duncan paused. "Then I'll go sit in the jail with the nigger, I guess. What's the matter, Kerney?"

"Nothing; I was laughing. Can't you lock him in the jail and leave him there?"

"The jail is nothing," said Duncan. "You could break into it with a can opener."

"Look," said Kerney, "I'll take Cissy home now and come up and check with you. Maybe we can figure something out. Duncan?"

"What?"

"It's raining too hard to lynch a nigger. It's too cold."

"It's what?"

"It's the wrong time of year, too. These things are supposed to happen in the middle of September after it hasn't rained for forty weeks, after all the cattle have died of thirst and their stench rolls in from the country and there's so much dust the sun looks bloody all day long. Isn't that right?"

"I don't know," said Duncan. "I never saw a lynching."

"I never did either," said Kerney. "All I know is what I read in William Faulkner. Duncan?"

"Yeah?"

"I just thought. I never heard of a Negro that would make a farce out of a lynching, let alone his own."

"You never met Beck Dozer," said Duncan.

"No, I never did. See you later, Duncan."

"See you later."

18 *The Squaring Off*

IN JIMMY TALLANT'S house on the highway a little light burned through the rain; it seemed a friendly sight in an otherwise doleful, chill, muddy, self-centered world.

Inside, in the bedroom, Jimmy Tallant's wife Bella was sitting on the arm of the easy chair with a magnifying mirror in her hand, pulling out her eyebrows. Jimmy stood in the door watching her for a while, wondering why she was doing it, until he remembered that if he asked her she would probably tell him.

"What are you trying to do, get rid of all of them?"

"It said in this magazine article," Bella explained, in her care not looking up, "that I'm the age to do it this way."

"What age is that, and what way do they mean?"

"Well, they said that back in the 1930's Marleen Deetritch and Jean Harlow used to know how to make their faces look more sophisticated by refining the line of their eyebrows, but that women finally revolted from that fashion and went in for the natural look. They said that was still all right for young girls up to when they got around twenty-five, but after that that a woman owed it to her maturity and poise to use every device to give herself more sophistication—"

"Yes, but Bella, are you absolutely sure that when you get through there you are going to have a sophisticated look?"

She put down the glass and thought it over. "If you don't ever try anything, you don't ever change at all."

"You best stop that kind of changing before you start it. Turn around and look at me. Lord, Bella, you're going to scare the doctors when you go to the hospital."

"I ain't done yet," she said, and picked up the mirror sadly. "I read another article. It was written by a doctor, an M.D., only he's a famous psychiatrist too; I forget his name. Anyway, it said that at this particular point when you're pregnant, husbands ought to be especially considerate and thoughtful. This doctor said that in his personal opinion husbands were personally responsible for one-third of all miscarriages, and that all that the husbands caused were pure and simple psychological cases. That's what it's called: The Psychological Miscarriage. I saved it out for you to read. It's over there on the dresser."

"God," said Jimmy, "if everything's so damned psychological, suppose I have a psychological miscarriage? Had you thought about that?"

"There is such a thing," she said earnestly, "as a psychological pregnancy. I know because Elsie Mae Henderson had one, remember?"

"Just so you didn't read it in another article," he said.

"I haven't got anything to do but read articles," she said; "that and *True Detective*. Just waiting for my time to come."

"You might try washing the dishes. I bet you haven't touched them."

"You never did send me the nigger," she said.

"I tell you every goddamned time it comes up. I can't get the nigger since the joint shut down."

"You could go and get the nigger!" she shouted at him, and began to cry.

"You've got so damned important since you're really going to have that baby there's not any staying in the same house with you. I never heard of a baby taking so long to get here. Seems like you've been pregnant for at least a year. You better not give me one of those psychological run-arounds, miscarriage or otherwise. I'll have this marriage declared so null and void I'll not only swear you're a virgin, I'll even believe it. The kitchen is full of coffee grounds and rotten orange peels. There's bacon grease all over the sink and a whole raw egg busted in one stove eye. The living room is full of dirty glasses from three nights ago, and there's a washtubful of cigarette ashes turned upside down in the middle of the rug."

"My back hurts me all the time," she said. "It hurts me so bad sometime I think I'll just die. And I'm all time wanting to wee and then I can't."

He advanced on her. "I'm not going to live in filth. I hate it. There are women who keep their houses straight with pains in the back, pains in the head, no help, a husband and two or three children to cook for three times a day, seven days a week. You don't have much to do. So for God's sake, do it!" He took a swat at her, but whether he intended it to land was not clear to either of them, because she began to giggle as though it were a romp and caught his hand, dropping the mirror which broke on the floor. It was a ten-cents-store mirror, the kind that magnifies on one side. She spent many hours a day with it, doing minute things to her face.

"Stop, stop. Stop, silly. There's somebody at the door! Don't you hear them? Somebody at the front door."

He did hear. He let go her arm, which she began to nurse. He stared at the broken pieces of mirror for an instant. "Seven more years' bad luck. Well, clean it up."

He shut the bedroom door behind him and crossed the living room. Out on the doorstep stood Duncan Harper, his slicker gleaming with rain.

"I've been trying to call you," he said. "Your phone out of order?"

"Not that I know of. Come in."

"I'm looking for Bud Grantham," Duncan said. "You haven't seen him?"

"As a matter of fact, I have," said Jimmy Tallant. "He can't see anybody, now or later. He had an accident tonight."

"It might have been a fight he had," Duncan said.

"It might have been."

There sounded a wail from the next room. "My daddy's hurt and you never told me!" The door clattered open—the damp had swelled the wood, so that it stuck on the jamb.

"Get on back to bed, honey," said Jimmy. "You know you oughtn't to be up. It's nothing serious or I would've told you." She hung in the door, mouth open, wrapper drooping about her shoulders, eyebrows mismatched, and in all her pregnancy so honestly uncomfortable that Duncan felt sorry for her. "Good evening, Bella," he said.

She looked just like one of her cousins who used to sit in front of him in one grade and comb her hair over and over with a pink comb. She had the bobby pins all piled up before her open book and a little mirror propped in the pencil rack, and when the teacher asked her a question all she heard was her name and all she said was, "I don't know."

"Hello, Duncan." She looked around the living room. In truth, an oversized ash tray lay upside down in the middle of the carpet, and ash had tracked away from it on either side. "Isn't everything a mess?" she said.

"I know how it is," Duncan reassured her. But even as he spoke he could hear in his head Tinker's slow laden steps around the house, up to the minute of going to the hospital, putting clean things into orderly dresser drawers.

"Sure," said Jimmy. "He knows how it is."

"No, he doesn't," she said quietly, and closed the door between them.

"Come on back here where she won't hear us," Jimmy said, and led him into what Bella called the "dinette," where he lighted a large gas radiance. They stood near it, warming. The rain beat a steady drum. They found it awkward to be alone together. "Well, sheriff?"

"I want to see Bud Grantham."

"All right. I'll tell you what you do. You follow the old Wiltshire road for ten miles till you get right this side of Black Hawk, then you take off up a hill without any gravel. There's a bob-wire gap about a half a mile on, that's how you'll know you got the right road. About another half mile you have to ford a branch. After that it's only two more miles to where Bud's gone to."

"He couldn't have got back there in this rain. Nobody could."

"His brother came for him. You see, Granthams are like that, Duncan. Every time one of them gets sick, they figure they're going to die, and they got to die on the old homestead or they won't go to heaven. So Bud heads home if he has to swim the branch with galloping double pneumonia."

The gas heated quickly. In the living room Jimmy drew out chairs for them both and offered Duncan a cigarette. "How about a drink?"

"No thanks."

"If you want to go back there, Duncan, you'll have to go without me. I tried to get him to stay here—"

"He must have had a doctor; that is, if he's so bad off he went home to die."

"That's another funny thing," said Jimmy. "Bud don't hold with doctors. Bud's a herb man. He's got an aunt who stirs all this stuff up in pots on a stove out in a little outhouse about the size of a pantry. She doctors every Grantham in the county —no, Duncan, it's true. You haven't been out in those woods, I bet, since all of us used to rabbit-hunt. You haven't kept up your connections. How should you know?"

"You aren't convincing me of much," said Duncan. "I've got my doubts that Grantham is so much as scratched. Still, there's a nigger come to me for custody. I've put him in jail and now I'm answerable for him."

"There's no answerable to it. A nigger that jumps a Grantham is answerable to the other Granthams. That means me."

"Then you'll have to deal with me first. There are two types of mess I'm not going to stand for in this county. The likker traffic is one, and nigger trouble is the other."

"It's widely known," said Jimmy Tallant, "how you feel."

At the scorn in his tone, Duncan rose impulsively. "You've got no right to play with important things like these. They reach out to be bigger than us or Winfield County. Bootlegging isn't like having a still out in the back pasture any more. It pulls a lot of wires all over the country. I've heard that you're going to put gambling in, that a New Orleans syndicate is backing you. What are you trying to make out of Winfield County? You're big-talking now about lynching a Negro. Maybe you don't mean any real harm to him, but suppose the thing gets out of hand? There's a national press that stands ready to jump on all such as this, and they never get the straight of things. They make us all sound like a bunch of barefoot morons who love to smell black meat burning."

"I'm not what you'd call a public-spirited citizen, for a fact," said Jimmy. "I care about as much about the national press and the nigger organizations as they care about me and the niggers. And that, as you know, is exactly nothing."

"At least you could care about your own people."

Jimmy narrowed the lids of his foxy eyes. "I've appreciated your hospitality from time to time. I've taken right much pleasure from your drinking-whisky."

"We've always been glad to have you. Tinker's devoted to you, Jimmy."

"In your place I wouldn't have stood for it," Jimmy said.

"Now you're after saying I don't care much about her. If that's what you mean—"

"I even named her," Jimmy went on. "Her name was Louise. Louise Taylor. I started calling her Tinker because she was counting off some buttons on her dress one day at school. She said tinker tailor, and I wouldn't let her get any farther. Every time I would say, Who? Who's Tinker Taylor? till she got mad at me and cried. She was a true old compass, Tinker was, and every time I took her out and looked at her, the needle pointed north. Every time I said, Who do you love? she said Duncan." He rose and went to the window.

"It's true things never worked out for us the way we thought they would," Duncan said earnestly. "But what's done is done. I don't think our private lives should have anything to do with the nigger in the jail, or the bootlegging business, or the sheriff's race. I think you've got to face public things in another frame of mind."

"My father did a public thing," said Jimmy Tallant. "He shot Robinson Dozer, among others, and that's Dozer's son that's sitting in the jailhouse. You'd be surprised how private it makes me feel."

He had been looking out the window while he spoke—Bella's picture window she'd had to have, to be like everybody else; the imitation colonial antique Gone-with-the-Wind lamp was not lighted. So when he said what he did about his father and turned away from the rainy dark toward Duncan, who stood near the mantelpiece, he looked out of certain long shadows and seemed a greater distance away than he actually was. His face, so sharp when the mind sped, held now a touch of the hound's sadness, but above all it was a lonely face, pulled in like the rain off the wild stretches. He made you think of telephone poles leaning infinitely on along a highway that went forever toward the mountains. You could no more talk to him than you could talk to a song.

"I hate to say this," said Duncan, going toward the door, "but until this election is over and I've won, or you've found some way to lick me, I don't think you'd best be dropping by the house again."

Jimmy Tallant did not answer him or protest. He did not bat an eye. It seemed that his face darkened slightly, as though dark had come strongly between them through the front door when Duncan opened it.

"I might drop by the jail and get that nigger," he said.

"I'll be ready for you," said Duncan.

19 *The Vigil*

"You GOTS a long time to wait," said Beck Dozer. "It's not but ten o'clock."

"If it's much later maybe they'll be too sleepy or too drunk," Duncan said.

"But in the earlier hours, or so I have read, they still have got their daylight minds. It takes the midnight mind to do the black deed to the black man."

"Oh, Jesus," said Lu. "Don't make it sound so *true*, Brer Beck."

Duncan laughed. "All you niggers ought to be preachers with a carload of nigger women saying Oh Jesus don't make it sound so true, every time you paused to mop your brow. You could preach them in and out of hell all day long, stop long enough to go outdoors and eat fried chicken, and take a different one home every night."

"And you think that would be the end," said Beck Dozer, "of the so-called Negro question."

"They call it bread and circuses," said Duncan.

"Why, so they do," said Beck.

"This is the first time I done ever darkened a jail door," said Lu. "And now look."

The two men were seated in cane-bottom chairs on either side of the cold stove. The Negro woman had retreated into the corner of the nearest cell and had begged Duncan until he had locked her in. She wanted to make sure that an iron door stood between her and whoever might arrive. Duncan had tried to make her go home as soon as he had returned from Jimmy Tallant's.

"S'pose I meets 'm on the stairs?" she had asked.

"But you can't now," said Duncan.

"Why can't I?"

"Because they aren't there."

"S'pose I meets 'm at the do'?"

"But nobody's outside. Look out there; it's empty."

"S'pose I meets 'm on the road?"

"You can see the road, too, in the streetlight. You can see nearly all the way around the courthouse. Nobody's there."

"But when I gets to the *turning* of the road, what if I meets 'm there?"

Duncan had not answered. It would be just Lu's luck to meet a pack of drunk Granthams, sure enough, and get hurt by mistake.

"With they bob-wire whups," Lu went on, "and they fat pine kindling wood. With they coal oil and they blow torches—"

"Hush up, woman," said Beck Dozer. "It ain't you, it's me, and anyway I understand that kind of thing is out of date. I hope somebody has told them so."

He sat angled a bit forward in the stiff little chair, keeping his weight off the corner where the cane had worn through. He had placed his hands one on either knee and the white bandages showed annoyingly clear in the dim light.

He said to Duncan, "Why don't you go downstairs with Mister Trewolla?"

"Mister Trewolla's bedtime is nine o'clock. I let on I was just coming up to check on you, then going along home myself."

"You don't want Mister Trewolla to think you're casting aspersions on him, in other words."

"No more than I can help," said Duncan.

Lu had found an empty cigarette package in the corner, had spread it out carefully and was dismembering it, piece at a time, with her long picky fingers. You could hear the cellophane come apart at the seams, then she moved on to the printed paper, then the tinfoil.

"I wonder where is Mister Kerney Woolbright," Beck Dozer asked.

Duncan did not answer. He got up, took a restless turn back

past the cell doors, looked up the narrow circular stair that led up to the death cell, the cupola of the jail.

"There ain't a soul up here to help you," said Beck. "In past time, or so I hear, white folks could raise a number just like each other to stick together on these things, but you can't even find one honest deputy. Either you is the only man around with principles, or everybody else is stitching their principles together out of a different bolt of goods."

"It so happens I'm the only man that's sheriff," said Duncan, "and that I haven't tried to deputize. Now shut up. If there's anything worse than Lu talking every minute, it's you talking every minute."

He looked down through the narrow barred window into the jailyard, the streetlight glow of the hollow square, his own grocery an obscure ridge in the store line along the farther side.

He was wondering himself what had happened to Kerney Woolbright.

20 *The Attack*

IT WAS twelve midnight, as Beck Dozer had predicted, before they came.

From the windows Beck and Duncan watched them get out of the car, which had arrived stodgily, slushing through the puddles. They piled out endlessly, like the old clown act at the circus, and milled about, turning their big shoulders to the rain's slant and swapping a word or two until a familiar figure came up wirily from behind the ignition and led them through the gate. By count there were only seven.

Lu began to wail, like something way off in the woods before dawn on a clear spring night. The sound, mounting, became less mysterious and more like Lu.

"Shut that up," Duncan said. "I can't hear anything that's going on."

But all she did was change pitch. Beck crossed quickly to Lu's cell and stuck his face halfway through the bars. He spoke roughly.

"It's that kind of noise they wants out of a nigger. It's what they're waiting for you to do. It makes them feel good when you sound like that. It tells them they got you where they want you for another fifty, hundred, two hundred years. I says to shut up because I personally can't stand to listen to it, Lu Johnson. Nobody studying you. You think Jesus done forgot you?"

"Jesus," said Lu, and hushed suddenly. "He ain't never forgot me yet, Brer Beck."

"Then set there and think about Him till I tells you you can quit."

In the quiet, voices rose to them from the hall below, brushing now and again a tender spot in the iron. Mr. Trewolla was at the door in his bathrobe, trying to explain things without his teeth.

"Orders ith orders," said Mr. Trewolla. "He'th told me not to let you in."

"I just want to talk to him," said Jimmy Tallant.

"Don't you let him through that door," Duncan called out from above. "I've talked to him once tonight already. If he wants to talk again, I'll come downstairs."

"You thee?" said Mr. Trewolla.

"Some things have come to light since I saw Duncan. Grantham's willing to settle the whole thing with no harm done to anybody. I have to see the nigger too. Five minutes will settle it. Okay?"

Mr. Trewolla sneezed.

"Okay," said Jimmy Tallant.

A large young Grantham boy beside him laid a shoulder to the door which Mr. Trewolla had cracked open to talk. The screws that held the chain-bolt locks fixed in the old wood wrenched free, splintering.

"You better go put some socks on, Mr. Henry," Jimmy Tallant advised, as he stepped inside. "You can catch cold mighty quick like that, especially this kind of weather."

"Duncan!" Mr. Trewolla called toward the ceiling. "In thpite of everything I could do—!"

"That's okay, Mr. Henry," Duncan answered, this time from behind the iron door at the head of the stair. "Just get on back in the back."

"You come back here to me, Daddy," Mrs. Trewolla called. "You leave those awful people alone."

"It's dog eat dog," said Mr. Trewolla, going to obey Mrs. Trewolla. "Nothing in the world but likker-heads. If I'd had my gun, now, but whisky'th, whisky, just like I always say."

"It's a mighty brave man," said Jimmy, "would come to meet six Granthams without even a beebee gun. Not to mention a Tallant."

The Granthams stood politely about in the hall like Granthams invited to a party in a stiff house. One said, "You wouldn't of thought he would of come to the front door without no gun. But he sho' did do it. He didn't have no gun at all. None I seen anyway."

"Turn that light out," Duncan said rapidly to Beck. "Here's the key. That little winding stair there leads up to the death cell. They can't shoot at you there. Lock yourself in good."

He checked his automatic, and took his stand behind the door. The bottom two-thirds of the door was solid iron, plated and bolted like the sides of a battleship, but the upper third was barred. Through the bars, looking down the stairs, which from the first landing upward narrowed to the width of a ladder, he saw Jimmy's face surface toward him, pale against the dull iron gloss around about, and with that same distance in it he had noticed before, so that, rising steadily toward him, its distance increased—just as a star falling seems to be palpably near the earth the instant before it vanishes in space, or as a car hurtling out of a highway gains a point in the glittering light where it seems to still and then reverse, or as a dying face still retreats the closer down you bend to hear the words and stay the breath, or as a man turns from a rainy window to say, "My father did a public thing." Then Beck switched out the light.

Granthams came up the stairs, banging and clattering, and by the time the noise died Duncan could make out Jimmy's features again, now nearer than ever in the dark. Down near the bottom two Granthams were talking to each other. They used to be just that way, Duncan recalled, when he went to school with them. They were always five grades behind and had never been known to finish out a school year, because they came to school only when cotton picking was done and before spring plowing started, always provided the hunting season was poor. So when the teacher lined the classes up after recess to march them inside through the halls, she did not even try to quiet the Granthams. They were at the end of the line shoving each other, marveling at the size of their own great big fists, bigger already than most men's on the town square ever got to be, and the misery and terror of anything not Grantham or Grantham kin that crossed their path was the misery and terror of the Pygmy who got in the giant village by mistake and walked down the street apologizing all the way. A Grantham by himself could be docile, and sometimes discovered sweetness and grew so good it would seem his own goodness was the only thing that amused him. So Granthams who got separated from other Granthams during the war came back from the Army sometimes leading fine girls who looked proud to be their wives, and so they moved into town or into other towns, and so the tribe had thinned. But Granthams together were another matter. Somebody had wronged them once—perhaps a British king had gone too far. Whatever it was, it wouldn't happen again. Granthams were good as a king; they were better than a nigger. Nobody ought to forget it. The proud "highwhite" servant made them spit. Granthams left living back in the woods now had few friends except each other; yet a man like Jimmy Tallant, who had shown those foreigners over there how to fight a war, had known who he wanted to be home with when they got through pinning the ribbons on him.

Duncan recalled, too, that the day he had entered Camp Shelby, in the same bunch with himself was a boy who happened to fall in beside him after the sergeant had dismissed them. "I think I'll go back to town," said the boy. "Town!" Duncan said. "Didn't you hear what he just said? We can't go outside camp for two days." "Yeah, well I just thought I'd go in for a little while. I thought you might want to come." Duncan stared, then laughed. "But you can't! Don't you know this is the Army? You have to take orders." The boy was mild, but there was flint in him. He regarded Duncan and a mild spark fell. "You don't want to go, I'll go ahead on by m'self," he said, and walked away. They had considerable trouble with him before he would make up his bed the way they had in mind, or keep his effects the way the diagram wanted. It wasn't that he didn't understand them.

Jimmy Tallant said, "Y'all boys shut up down there."

"Y'all hush," the Granthams said to one another.

"I should have picked up the keys from Trewolla," said Jimmy.

"He hasn't got them," said Duncan. "They're all on my side of the fence."

"I was prepared for that," said Jimmy. "Hey, Lewis! Are you ready with that blowtorch?"

"I'm ready, Cud'n Jimmy."

"I've got a gun," Duncan said, "and I aim to use it on the first person tries to burn that lock."

"Whereabouts is your gun?" Jimmy Tallant inquired.

"Right here in my hand."

"Everybody knows that Duncan Harper tells the truth. It's why he made so many touchdowns. Are you ready there, Lewis?"

"Ready, Jimmy!"

"Okay, then, shoot!"

A single brilliant flare illumined the whole interior, and Lu shrieked once from the cell.

21 *Council of War*

THE NIGHT that Duncan Harper felt duty-bound to go sit in the jail and protect that nigger that had been in England during the war, naturally nobody wanted to get mixed up in it. Still, along about eleven-thirty with the town as quiet as snow, a good many people got restless and drove up to the jail. They stopped in the street where they could watch from a distance, and sat in their cars; and some rode by time and again, asking what had happened. Probably nobody thought that there would be any trouble, else they would not have brought their children with them.

When Kerney Woolbright got to town, he took Cissy Hunt straight home. Marcia Mae was out on the porch swing in the cold, and insisted on riding up to the jail with him. Cissy was prevailed upon to come inside the house, but it was accepted in the family that nobody could do anything with Marcia Mae. She wore loafers and a slouchy raincoat with a hood and sat in the corner of the back seat. She had been walking in the rain, she said, and was wet. She assailed Kerney with certain remarks.

"Wonder what his wife is doing all this time?"

"Whose wife?"

"Duncan's."

"Oh, Tinker, you mean. She's home with the children, I'd think."

"Has she changed much?"

"You haven't seen her?"

"No."

"I expect she's just as she always was."

"A real cute girl," said Marcia Mae.

He drove around the corner without replying.

"You see her often, I guess," Marcia Mae went on. "What's she like?"

"She's like herself," said Kerney. "There's nobody quite the same."

Marcia Mae would have thought that out of all the average American-looking girls she had ever seen, Tinker Taylor was the most average American-looking of them all, but she recognized the rebuff and took it. Maybe Cissy ought to marry Kerney, after all, she thought idly. He had spoken up like a man.

They drew up across from the jail, on the side of the street next to the courthouse, at a little distance from the other cars. Watching across the rainy yard toward the jail, they saw when the windows blazed blue-white, heard the woman scream, and saw the windows light a second time. . . .

As a matter of fact, the light was a flash bulb. Duncan recognized it instantly for what it was, because they had once gone off in his face all the time.

Duncan Harper's life had taken an unusual course mainly because his nerve centers enjoyed a remarkable balance. Under extreme pressures toward action, he could reason through any number of possibilities and choose one with as much leisure as he might choose lunch from a menu, and all in the five seconds it was said to take a good tackle to rush the backfield. They said that from the stands he seemed not to be moving at all, that he looked dazed or maybe just lazy, as if he might yawn. Then the pass would be aloft and landing, or you would glimpse his heels rounding right end.

So when he was standing back of the door with the gun in his hand and Jimmy Tallant said "Shoot!" and the flash bulb went off, he realized he had the best opportunity anybody could ask for killing Jimmy Tallant. He could have said for the rest of his life that he had thought the flash was gunfire. He knew now too that Jimmy wanted himself shot; he understood now the strange distances he had noted before in the face which as the light glared pressed upward closer to the bars with a look like a high diver's plunging toward twelve inches of water in a dishpan. But Duncan did not fire. He would hardly have killed anybody, even someone he despised, and he did not despise Jimmy. A second bulb went off. When Lu's cry died in the iron, there came the splintering of the tiny bulbs, dropped on the hall floor below.

After that, they all went away. They filed out the jail door in the dark, tramped through the cinders, and loaded into the muddy car. When they entered the square from the jail drive and saw cars massed silently in the rain, one of the Granthams leaned from the window and fired a pistol. He may have thought he was shooting straight up, and the car lurched, or he may have had his wrist deflected by the narrow opening of the window; however it happened, the bullet went low and broke the ventilation window in one of the parked cars. In passage it sang a tune in several ears and, dying, it angled a scar into a brand-new Pontiac fender. The Grantham, when he fired, had sounded the high-pitched exulting yell that some people say is the old Rebel yell. If anybody had asked him why he fired the shot, he would have said that something came over him.

Anyway, before whatever it was came over him and he leaned out and yelled and fired, the people in Lacey who were watching were as ready as Mr. Trewolla to speculate unfavorably on the subject of Duncan Harper. But then the bullet made its little music, and they remembered what dangerous people Granthams really were. The man who got his ventilator window broken had his wife and grandbaby with him. Granthams were lawless and bad.

Nobody left. They all sat waiting after the load of Granthams had screamed away through the rain: you could hear the gears mesh a half mile away on the long drag running outward toward the highway. Still they waited. When Duncan's car at last drew out of the jailyard, some of the townsmen alighted to stop him. He stepped out and stood hatless, talking in the rain. Lights in the nearer cars flashed on, and he was plain there in the crossbeams, his fair hair feathery under a bright crust of rain.

He had won again.

It was easy to idealize Duncan Harper. He was never proud; you could not spoil him. He was fine yet familiar-looking. He seemed to present no complicated problem. It seemed he always felt just what a person ought to feel.

That night when he stepped out into the eyes of Lacey, ranked behind the black car-hoods and rain-glazed windows, he stepped for a second time in heroism.

Then Kerney Woolbright had crossed the street and was drawing him aside.

"It's time you came," Duncan complained. "What in hell happened to you?"

"I had to get hold of the Humphreys County sheriff and talk him into coming over. I figured if nobody in Lacey would take sides, we ought to have help from somewhere."

"When I was up there waiting for God knows what, I doubted you were coming at all. I'm sorry, Kerney." He put out his hand impulsively, and Kerney grasped it.

"What did Tallant want?" Kerney asked. "What was that light?"

"They took two pictures," Duncan said. "That's all."

"Pictures? Of you, of the Negro, of what?"

"When I heard them coming inside, I told the Negro to get himself upstairs to the death cell and lock the door; then there was so much racket I didn't hear him go. When the flash went off, I noticed him standing there by me, just a little to the back."

"Then you think it's one of Tallant's concoctions."

"Yes, and I half suspect the Negro of being in on it. He was nervous, but not scared enough. He kept talking too much."

"But what will they do with the pictures?" Kerney asked.

"We'll have to wait and see."

A car roared round the square and drew up short beside them, splashing mud. It was McCutcheon, the Humphreys

County sheriff, enormous in his custom-built trousers. He heaved himself out of the front seat and struggled erect to meet Duncan. Standing, he propped himself up on a stout short walking stick. Two deputies were with him. They remarked that in time past Travis would have asked them in the office and offered them a drink, but they understood everything was changed. They said people in Winfield County had to pick a nigger fight every once in a while these days in place of getting drunk.

The Lacey crowd had thinned by the time they drove away. Duncan followed Kerney to his car and sat inside for a moment, out of the rain.

"So what about the Negro?" Kerney asked.

"It's custody he asked for, and he's going to get it."

"No excitement after all," said Marcia Mae.

Duncan had not noticed her before and he started, turning, and saw her emerging from the dark bundle on the back seat which he had not even taken for a person. She was shaking back the clumsy raincoat hood from her bright hair.

"Since nobody else will lynch him, let's go lynch him ourselves."

The men were silent. Her confident Hunt voice, with the smoky tint it had always held, framed now and again a Yankee crispness on a word, reminding them of her life's distance since ten years ago—no, nothing that happened here could seem important to her.

Duncan pointed toward the courthouse whose upper story rose whitely into the rain, while out beyond, whiter still, the inevitable Confederate soldier's statue held a stern guard toward the North. "Upstairs there," he scolded her, "twelve Negroes were shot down in cold blood."

"When was that?" she asked.

"Nineteen-nineteen," said Kerney, "or was it twenty? Somewhere along in there."

"Oh," she laughed. "I thought you meant last year."

"You've heard about it," said Duncan, "all your life."

"Yes, now that you mention it. I've heard it and forgotten it because I don't care. If I don't care nobody cares. I'm no different from anybody else. Nobody our age in town could say offhand who was there or why."

"Jimmy Tallant's father was there," said Kerney, "for one."

"Yes," said Duncan, "and Beck Dozer's father, for another."
Kerney whistled.

"They both knew it," Duncan went on. "Tallant would do a
toe dance around a volcano. I could have shot him by mistake
tonight when the flash went off in my face. It looks to me he's
been trying to die for years."

"I wish," said Marcia Mae, "that I was anybody's secretary in
some big city. And that every morning I got up and put on a
gray suit and a clean white blouse and went to work in a beautiful soundproof air-conditioned office one hundred and one
floors up, with streamlined filing cabinets and a noiseless electric typewriter. I wish I had a little apartment with a view from
the window of nothing but skyscraper tops. Then I would be
happy."

"No, you wouldn't," Duncan said.

Now all the cars had gone away but theirs. They were left
with the old square. The two streetlights bleared in the wet.
The last car, disappearing, jolted in a rut by the filling station.
Its taillight described the corner. Then it was nothing.

"Why wouldn't I be happy?" she demanded.

"You'd have to get up early every morning, for one thing.
For another, you'd get bored."

Kerney felt that the two of them were alone in the car, that
he was not there at all.

"So many things are boring nowadays," she said. "Why is
that?"

"It's part of getting old," said Duncan.

"I take it hard. Harder than most people do."

"I don't know whether you do or not," he answered.

22   *A Path Leads Backward*

IF ANY one household was most afflicted by the new law en-
forcement principles in Winfield County, it was Duncan Harper's. On Saturday nights, as Tinker had predicted, people no
longer wanted to stop and talk. Wednesday-night trips to the
next county for bingo had to go as well. And Jimmy Tallant
never came.

After the heavy rains, the sun had come out and discovered a jungle. To human beings it seemed that their bodies had got involved in the rich growth; thinking went laboriously—the mind seemed to work like a motor under too great a dredge of oil. Vines drew the fences down to earth, and the leaves on every kind of growing thing looked too large, like an elephant ear. It had also become suddenly hot.

Down on the terrace just back of the house, Tinker found that grass had forced up overnight between the bricks. She went down on Sunday afternoons with her trowel and scissors, working on her knees until the sun lowered. Her little girl Patsy, freshly out of her winter overalls, ran miniature errands for her, talking a blue streak. The work seemed an excuse for getting out of doors and for meeting Sunday by doing a thing that was not everyday.

For Sunday, whether you have a hangover or not, is a restless time. There is the thing that Saturday night held out to you and never quite gave, but there is no use complaining to Sunday. It is stone deaf, and does not even know your name.

Earlier, Duncan had taken his son for a walk in the woods.

The boy, who was around ten, had hair so blond as to be white, and for this reason they all called him Cotton. He was sailing comfortably into the future under his father's banners; it had been impressed upon him early that he was not to talk about football outside the family. Usually nobody in the family wanted to talk about it either, but at the moment he was enjoying a day of grace and had felt encouraged to reveal, while crossing a barbed-wire fence, that he had changed his life's ambition to being a big-league baseball pitcher, instead of a football star.

"Why? Do you like baseball better than football?"

"No, I still like football best. But there's already a Harper that's an All-Time Great in football. I want to be an All-Time Great in something else. I thought baseball would be the next best thing. Then when Patsy grows up, she could be a girls' tennis champion. If Mother has another little boy, he could —let's see, what could he do?"

"Track, maybe?"

"I don't like track. It's not a game."

"Swimming?"

"That's no game either. Maybe basketball. Lightweight people are good in basketball."

"Why is he going to be so lightweight?"

"Because he'll be so little."

"What makes you think Mother wants another little boy?"

"I don't know. I thought maybe she might."

Duncan sat down. They had gained the middle of a roll of pasture underneath a bluff. The cows had cropped the grass short there. He leaned back on the hillside in the sun.

"Mother wouldn't let you do that," said the boy. "You'd catch cold."

"But Mother isn't here. Won't I still catch cold?"

The boy caught on and laughed. "I don't know."

"We used to find Indian arrowheads on this hill."

"Who did?"

"Oh, your mother and I."

"Was she your girl friend, Daddy?"

"Of course she was."

"Your girl friend all the time?"

"Most of the time."

"You had another girl friend besides Mother!" But these matters did not really interest him. He had begun to tumble about on the hillside like a puppy, making foolish noises.

"Don't act silly," said his father. "Let's go down to the branch."

"Can I carry the shotgun?"

"You know I've told you a hundred times. You can not carry the shotgun."

"Maybe Mother could have *two* more children," said Cotton.

"Oh? What's the fourth one for?"

"Well, ice sports are real important some places. Not around here because there isn't any ice, but up North they are. This would make a good ski jump, if there was ever any ice on it. It would make a good place for a swing."

"A swing! Who told you that?"

"Nobody. I just thought of it."

"That's funny. There used to be a swing here. Right from that big tree limb."

"Let's build one here again sometime."

"We can't. It isn't our land."

"Whose land is it?"

"Let's go down this path," said his father.

A bank of plum bushes and willows screened the branch from the pasture. The path down to the watering ford was cleft two feet deep or more into the bank, chopped in slowly by the hooves of cattle. A muscle of current curved into the shaggy bank. Duncan and Cotton jumped to an island of sand, then across the stream. They sat down on the sandy farther bank. The small sound of the current filled the open space between the stream and a thicket of willows.

"We used to build dams here," Duncan said.

"Dam is an ugly word. You said an ugly word."

"Would you like to build a dam?"

"You said another—"

"Cotton, I told you to stop acting silly."

Stricken by his father's sudden change of tone, the child tried hard not to cry, and finally succeeded. They often said to him on such occasions: "Be a man, don't cry." He now said this to himself, and found it worked.

"I'll tell you something that's true," said Duncan. "When you want to stop acting silly, start doing something. Now think of something you can do."

"All right, I've thought of something."

"What is it?"

"Go wading."

"Good, we'll both go wading."

They both removed their shoes and socks, and laid them up on the grass, away from the sand. Duncan unloaded the gun and put it down on his coat. The water was chilly and only the top crust of sand was warm. The boy's feet were still tender from having gone shod through the long wet spring. His toes curled at the touch of the water. Duncan rolled up his pants legs and splashed across and slightly upstream to where an old fence post lay on the higher bank. He loosened it from one end, lifting it as though from its grave, for an outer strip of it had rotted into the earth. Black bugs shot away into the brush and a few maggots made a sluggish, agonized gesture at the sudden sunlight. Duncan observed this for a moment, then he laid the post in the water, across the narrowest neck of the branch.

"What's that for?" asked the boy.

"Go on and wade," said Duncan. "I'm going to build a dam."

He scooped out a ditch in the stream's bed, laid the post there and leveed it in place with dripping handfuls of sand. Then he began to bring heavy damp sand from the bank.

Presently the water downstream ceased splashing. Cotton was standing near him to watch. Drops of bright water fell from his fingertips. Little drying rims of sand had formed on his legs.

"Can I help you, Daddy?"

"No, thank you."

"Please, Daddy."

His father straightened and they grinned at each other, understanding the game. "I thought you didn't want to build a dam. I thought you'd rather wade."

"I changed my mind."

"All right then. You can help me."

They both began to carry sand in double handfuls, holding it out before them like bowls too full of something. The water backed up gradually behind the dam. It hunted patiently, found the weakest place, and struck through.

"It won't hold," said Cotton, staunching it desperately.

"I saw some rocks over yonder a little way. And some chunks of log from an old pigpen." Duncan pointed.

"Oh boy! We could build a big dam with those."

"Sure we could."

"Let's go." Cotton began to run.

"Wait a minute. Listen. This will be good. You get the rocks and the wood and build one up here and I'll go down the branch a little piece just around the corner there and build another one. When it all backs up good and strong, you can break this one and make a real flood. Then you can run down to where I am and watch the water break the other one. Won't that be fine? That is, if you don't mind working hard."

"I don't mind working. I like it. I can beat you finished."

"Don't forget to leave your spillway running right up to the last. You saw what happened before."

"I won't!" He ran again. "When I'm almost through I'll holler."

"Holler loud. And wait till I answer you. You hear?"

"Okay. I'll holler real loud."

He was hard at work already, trustworthy, concentrated, and happy. Under the sun that fell on the ruined pigpen, his white hair grew hot as glass. A tuft would not lie down at the crown. He did not hesitate to tackle heavy loads of rock and logs. The big thing was that he and his father were working together. This knowledge, like the sound of the branch, filled the open space he moved in, and more than the sunlight, shadow, or greenness, made its quality. He did not feel it when his legs and arms got tired. He enjoyed majestic securities.

He laid the last stone, sealing the spillway. The dam was an austere production, tough with stone and thatchings of wood, packed in with wet sand and firmed across the top. He had worked for an hour.

He stood straight and called his father. After he had called several times, he realized the truth. His father was playing a joke on him. The water mounted imperceptibly behind the dam, which was holding well. He ran downstream. When he burst through the plum thicket, a new reach of the branch curved before him. There was another ford, muddy and pocked with hoofprints, and far over to the left a fence corner and a wet brown field beyond, empty and taking Sunday. Besides these, there was only a confusion of new leaves up the bank to his right, and a silence full of birds. There had never been the start of a dam.

"It's ready, Daddy; come out! It's ready; stop hiding!"

He did not know how many times he raced back and forth, people being always foolish as children when they are betrayed, and children being very foolish indeed. He was suddenly frightened, and returning at a walk through the thicket, he began to cry.

Then he stopped dead still. His father was sitting on the higher bank beside the path that they had followed down from the pasture above. He was staring at the boy. The dam still held, but the water had backed up behind it in a pool and begun to swirl. Duncan sat with his head lowered. There was green stain on his cheek and pressed into his hair, and his clothes were twisted strangely.

"Were you there all the time, Daddy?" There was no answer, and Cotton wondered for a terrible minute if this man was his father at all. He pulled a weed and began miserably to peel it.

The water struck free, first a trickle, then a loud gush, which faded.

"I built it real good," said Cotton.

When the water made the noise it made, the man seemed to come to himself. With an athlete's decision of movement, he jumped from the bank and cleared the stream and, bending, swung the child affectionately against him.

"It was a wonderful dam," he said. "It was the best I ever saw."

"But where was yours, Daddy?"

"You know when I went down around the corner? Well, there was a man came by who wanted me to help him head his cow back to the pasture. We had to climb all up through the woods. I'm sorry I had to leave you by yourself. Let's go home now."

They put on their shoes and walked back. Duncan shot the gun twice to amuse him. On the way they stopped by Duncan's mother's, the house that was low in front but tall in the back, with a long wooden flight of steps dropping down into the back yard. They all three sat together on the steps and ate teacakes out of a crock. When they reached home, Tinker was not long in discovering that Cotton had fever and had to be put to bed.

"You shouldn't have let him go wading," said Tinker.

"It's May," Duncan said.

"I know, but you know what a late spring we've had, and the water was still cold, I bet. I bet you let him sit on the wet ground too and probably let him get too hot dragging all that stuff around in the sun. You ought to think about things like that when I'm not there."

The little girl began to sneeze.

"I guess that's my fault too," said Duncan.

"No, it's my fault. I took her down with me to weed the terrace, and the brick is still damp." She turned away from the sink. There was a cup towel, as usual, tied around her small waist and she dried her hands on it, found a piece of Kleenex and blew the child's nose.

Later, after she had put them both to bed in the twilight, Duncan's mother telephoned and told her how Duncan had come by with Cotton and they had sat on the back steps eating teacakes, what Duncan had said, what she had said, what Cotton had said. She lived alone and appreciated every little attention, and she was always wanting to remind Tinker of this.

Tinker hung up the phone. The twilight in the house, wide open to the outdoors, had just passed gold. The free Sunday quiet of the light called up the love of innocence in her heart, and with it the ritualist's faith in the innocent trappings of the day: a walk in the woods, playing at the branch, a visit to Grandmother's, children. I'm foolish and wrong, she confessed to herself, not to trust what I know I can trust. Duncan, she thought, and at his name tears sprang at once to her eyes.

She looked in on the children. Tired from the day outside, Cotton slept already, an arm flung wildly out, and Patsy whispered something, as she was apt to do, and shut her eyes again. Tinker closed the door softly. She moved through the filmy light in the hallway and saw how every pretty thing she had cast its long graceful shadow. From the threshold of the living room she saw Duncan on the couch. His sleeping hand hung toward the floor.

She knelt and unbuckled her sandals and, stepping free of them, went and sat on the bit of couch beside him. She unbuttoned his shirt and was about to lay her head down when she saw the red mark in the skin itself, and beside it the lipstick stain.

From long habit, out of even so deep a sleep, he threw his arm up around her, and she dropped down to the floor with a little moan.

23 *Picture in the Paper*

"It's happened," said Kerney Woolbright.

He stood in the door of the sheriff's office. Duncan was alone, Mattie Sue Bainbridge having gone across the street for her morning Coke.

He looked up from the desk at Kerney once, then taking greater care, he looked again. "What's happened?"

"It's come out," said Kerney. "After two months. I kept wondering. I guess you have too."

"I don't know what you mean. What are you talking about?"

Kerney tossed a newspaper open before him on the desk. It was a Chicago paper for Negroes; the outer pages were pink. Negroes were always sending the white people's laundry back wrapped in pages of this paper, or others like it, as if they hadn't thought what they were doing or there wasn't any other paper around the house.

"There's a picture of you inside," said Kerney, "in quite a prominent position—the one they took in the jail. You've got a gun in your hand and Beck Dozer is behind you. You look real good. Handsome."

"That's nice to hear," said Duncan.

"Also," Kerney went on, "there is an article here about you. It tells how proud everybody ought to be of you, born and raised in Mississippi and yet defending a Nee-grow. Nobody can understand it, but they all think it is wonderful. You are a champion of civil rights, you are a defender of the black race. In Chicago, friend, you are solid. In Winfield County you'll probably be everybody's least favorite grocer till the day you die."

"'Lone hero,'" Duncan read, "'in a gallant defense of a hapless Negro—'"

"'Nee-grow.'"

"'. . . falsely suspected of a minor offense against a local café owner, Sheriff Duncan Harper of Winfield County, Mississippi, successfully turned away from the cell door an angry lynch mob. . . .'"

"I always said," Kerney remarked, "that you were everybody's hero."

"Oh, shut up, and try to figure out who might have sent them this article."

"They have reporters all over the South," said Kerney. "Tallant may have written it himself."

"It's signed. 'Cuthbert Owsley.' What a name! It sounds like a Tallant-type invention. How else would they get the names, the dates, all the details? But we can't go on guesswork. We have to know."

"The trouble with that is, it takes time, and we haven't got the time to waste. The first thing to do is to hit back good and strong. Buy space in the paper, or print a handbill and show Tallant up for what he is."

"I can't accuse him without knowing."

"You don't have to accuse. You can insinuate. I'll write it, or rather we can do it together. You can suggest that Tallant bribed the nigger to pose for the picture, then sent the story in. You know that's the size of it. But you've got to say it quick."

Duncan shook his head. "I've got to know first. When I walk back across to the grocery store, I want to go with my shoes clean."

"You got in trouble before by not listening to me," said Kerney.

"You weren't born and raised in Winfield County, Kerney. You wouldn't know a lot of people around here as well as you do if it hadn't been for me. The Hunts, for instance. I gave you a good name with Mr. Jason."

Kerney stood undecided. "You're saying we ought to stick together."

"I've always thought we had the same feeling about things. If I'm wrong, why then—"

"You aren't wrong; we do."

"I'm willing to risk losing a race to—"

"But that's just it!" Kerney cried with a sudden lost wild boyishness. "It doesn't matter to you!" His picture, labeled Candidate for the Senate, Third District, had just appeared on the telephone poles. He recovered quickly and, stepping toward the desk, laid his hand palm down between them. It was a long-fingered, thin hand, the kind that held the pen that was mightier than the sword. "I've got to have this county's record, Duncan."

"I want to see you win," said Duncan. "I'll do everything possible to see that you do, that we both do."

"If Tallant and Grantham get back in the saddle—"

"Are you sure you've counted all my cards? Tallant is the brains there, and I wonder if he really wants to lick me."

They looked at one another, and both of them thought of Tinker.

"Meanwhile," Duncan continued, pointing to the paper, "I'll have to work this out in my own way, Kerney."

Mattie Sue Bainbridge came back. "Miss Winfield County Courthouse," said Kerney, "of 1950." He laid his hat across his heart.

Mattie Sue wrinkled up her mouth and blushed. "You're the craziest thing!" she said.

"Give me a piece of tablet paper, Mattie Sue," Duncan said, when Kerney had disappeared.

He bent over the paper at the small desk by the window, writing laboriously with his left hand.

"dear Mr. Editor: I am a negroe in Wingfeeld county, Mississippi, who wish to get in tuch with the man who sent in the peice which tell about mister Duncan Harper our sherriff. You say the man is name mister Cuthbert Owsley, but there is not a man of this name in Wingfeeld. It is important to some of us negroes because we have made up a club (secret) for our civil rites and wishes to find all who will help us. Yours truely, A. P. Abbott."

He sent Mattie Sue to the post office with the letter along with a note to the postmistress to put any mail for A. P. Abbott in the sheriff's box.

Three days later an answer came. "Cuthbert Owsley is the nom de plume of one of our valued correspondents in your area. His name is Mr. Beckwith Dozer. We wish you great success with your civil rights organization."

Duncan read it over twice and a pair of eyes seemed to be regarding him out of gold-rimmed glasses.

"This doesn't make any sense at all," he thought and, catching up his straw hat, went out to find Beck Dozer.

24 *Beck Thinks It Over*

DUNCAN DROVE to the tie plant, but it was shut down for the day, so he followed first one side road, then another, until he reached the mailbox with "Dozer" written on it. The ink had bleared under the "Z." He left his car on the road, close in beside the bank, and climbed the narrow dusty path where a child had been playing with spoons and snuff bottles. The house was a plain two-wing country house with a hall down the middle and a gable to the right. Once at the top of the bluff above the road the ground was flat as a pan and went flatly back into the wood behind. The fence around the front yard was fancy calf wire that had seen better days; the front gate was weighted with a plowshare. No one was in sight, yet the sense of human presence lay strong everywhere, as in the old story of the ship that is found empty at sea. Duncan minded his country manners and stood by the gate, calling.

"Anybody home?"

"'Home?'" said the wood behind the house.

A tiny black boy scampered across the open hall. Someone moved inside the gabled window. In the back yard a dog barked and would presently trot around the corner of the house, stand in the front path, and bark again. Duncan waited.

After so long Beck Dozer emerged into the hall and came directly down the steps. "Git away," he said to the dog. He wore new overalls and an old work shirt that clung to his small shoulders.

"I've come to ask who Cuthbert Owsley is," said Duncan. He held the Chicago paper in his hand.

"You already know," returned Beck. "Don't you?"

"Then I have another question too."

"Go ahead."

They talked across the gate, standing equal distance back from it, not lounging against it as two white men might when they talk together, but looking straight into each other's eyes, and Duncan commenced to see the advantage of Beck's glasses.

"What crazy streak makes you do business with a man like Jimmy Tallant who doesn't give a damn if all the niggers in Winfield County get wiped out one way or another as long as he has a free hand on Highway 82?"

"Mister Tallant and I are tied together on account of what his daddy did to mine. He wouldn't lose me, nor let me come to harm for anything in this world. He's my main protection in this life. That and he pays me for what he gets me to do. He's paid me high as $200 for some jobs. You take that night I was up at the jail with you. That's what he gave me for it."

"So how did you really get your hands cut?"

"That was the only hard part. I did it myself on somebody's new bob wire."

"These Chicago articles—what are you trying to do with them?"

"They pay pretty good too. I gave you a good enough name, didn't I?"

"You gave me such a good name you as good as lifted me out of the sheriff's race, and you damn well know it. If you're trying to help your people—"

"I don't run in pack, Mister Harper. I'm not trying to help anybody but me. I said that when I came on back down here to live after the war was over. Any Negro with little enough sense to choose to come back to Mississippi to live, had better hew his own road and not look to right nor left."

"Is that what you call yourself doing?"

"It's what I does."

"I don't believe a word of it," said Duncan with such force the Negro fell silent.

"You've seen a light these days," Duncan went on. "All of you have. You keep casting around for the best way. You want to deal equally with white men but you don't know who to trust. You'd rather have Mr. Willard Follansbee in office instead of me?"

"To be honest with you, Mister Harper, I prefer the status quo. You can climb the status quo like a step ladder with two feet on the floor, but trying to trail along behind a white man of good will is like following along behind somebody on a tightrope. As he gets along towards the middle his problems are likely to increase, and soon he gots to turn loose of me to help himself."

"I stayed with you at the jail," Duncan reminded him. "I didn't like it, but I did it. You were the one cheating that night, not me."

"I remember." He stood blinking for a moment, then he opened the gate. "If you'd care to step inside the yard a minute, Mister Harper, there's something I'd like to show you."

To their right, tall althea bushes framed a path that led down to a house scarcely larger than a privy. Beck unlocked the door and pushed it wide. Duncan looked in on a square room where two long hand-hewn benches and two tables faced a raised platform with a desk and chair. Behind, a blackboard was set neatly into the wall. The three remaining walls were lined with bookshelves, these giving way only to the windows. From an iron stove in the far corner came the scent of coal dust.

"I lights a fire in here every so often during the winter. They tell me damp is not good for books."

Duncan glanced over the shelves. They held mainly leather-bound sets, perfectly arranged. Many titles were in Latin with authors he had heard of somewhere; memories stirred in him of vague desires he had once felt to know what these very books said. His own reading had been largely in the English and American books his professors had talked about most, and later in modern books that Kerney was apt to like mentioning. And he remembered, too, one night in summer sitting in the porch swing with Marcia Mae, how Nan Hunt had come out to bring them coconut cake and fresh peach ice cream she had taken for them ahead of time out of the freezer, salt-packed for Sunday. They begged her to stay and talk to them, and some-how the talk turned to reminiscence—somehow she had come to say, her voice very sweet, "I wonder what happened to the old library Senator Upinshaw gave to Robinson Dozer when he died? I suppose they must have destroyed it when they killed Robinson. A thing like that knows no bounds."

"They left the library, then," Duncan said to Beck. "And the school too."

"I used to say that to myself," said Beck. "At least they left his books the Senator gave him. At least they couldn't touch the books. But you know, Mister Harper, it finally came to me why they hadn't done it. You know why? They didn't do it because they didn't care."

"Can you read these books?" Duncan asked.

"No. Can you?"

"No."

"You are the first white man I ever showed the inside to."

"You're the first Negro I ever invited to my house to talk business with. I need your help."

"Help for what?"

"I want to expose how Tallant got that picture. I want you to be in on it."

Halfway to the gate they stopped. The Negro grew cold right in the sun and shook. He could not answer the white man with any poise, so he stood noticing the sights of the season. The chickens shuffled for worms on the spring ground; wood smoke came from the washpot out back along with the slap of a sheet being pounded on the board; jaybirds screamed in an oak tree down near the road. The dog slept, sprawled in the sun. A little naked Negro boy came out the door and halfway down the front steps, where he squatted like a savage.

"Git back in the house," Beck told him. "What you mean outdoors without your clothes?"

He turned finally to Duncan. "I tell you, Mister Harper, you are the only white man to see inside my papa's school, but Mister Jimmy Tallant knows it's there because he asked me once what it was. I think maybe he's thought too, So they left the books, and then I think maybe he's gone on to think, They left them because they didn't care. Mister Tallant and I, we're yoked up together, you might say. There isn't anything one of us thinks that the other one hasn't thought too. They say a nigger's got to belong to some white man."

"You believe that?"

"No," said Beck, and sighed.

"I won't force you to come," said Duncan, "or pay you anything for doing it."

"Lord knows, the Granthams will have my hide on the door before night come, if I do this."

"I count on Mr. Tallant," said Duncan. "I don't think he'll let them hurt you."

"You don't *think*! It's not you, it's me!"

"It might be me! It could be me! Don't you know it might come to that?"

"All right then. I'll come."

When the gate stood between them again, Beck asked him, "Why you wants to act like this, Mister Harper?" and one of his dark cheeks gleamed wet, smeared down from the gold rim of his glasses lens.

"No reason," Duncan returned. "I want to do what's right, I guess. That's all."

The slight Negro stood watching the big genial figure of the white man descending the steep path with paced, confident control of motion, and he felt his unease deepen. In a country where the motives for doing things are given names like honor, pride, love, family, greed, passion, revenge, and hatred, "right" had an odd inadequate sound. Beck shivered again in the smooth sunlight and thought that he had warmed the books so carefully and now needed warmth himself. He entered the house and there sat his wife's grandmother, Granny (Aunt Mattie, the white folks called her), drawn up to a little low fire.

"Granny, are the Harpers Yankees?"

He had struck a moment when her mind was clear.

"No, son, dey's here all along. Dey's cu'us, dat dey is, but dey ain't Yankees."

"Cu'us how?"

"Jes' cu'us. Jes' like I say."

25 *Talk on the Lawn*

"LOOKS LIKE Duncan's done him a do," said Jason Hunt.

They had sat out on the lawn since supper and now it was dark, and their shapes in the wicker chairs scarcely impressed another shadow. But they saw each other clearly, through long knowledge. Kerney was there, his long legs stretched out in the grass, elbows propped on the chair arms, fingers laced. From time to time, with the toe of his shoe he scratched his leg where a mosquito bit him, or a gnat. The gnats were getting worse. Nan Hunt kept a Flit gun beside her and sprayed every few minutes. It was the only time of year, she said, when she approved of her daughters' smoking. "But you smoke yourself," said Marcia Mae finally. Everybody had waited so long for somebody to say this, there didn't have to be any answer.

Old Mrs. Standsbury, sitting erect with her thick short legs crossed, said, "Yes, she certainly does." She was wearing her sack against the night air and kept her hands thrust in the folds. She wore a diamond pin low at her throat, which was soft as a girl's.

"You tell them about it, Grand," said Jason, using the children's name for her. He had had in him a love for her growing many years. There would never be any need to mention it. He sometimes thought of it as the most satisfying force in his life.

"I never wanted any of my children to smoke," the old lady said, "but they all did it anyway."

"Just like Cissy," said Kerney, wanting her name in it.

"Huh?" said Cissy, who had not been listening. She knew she was sitting just beyond where Kerney would have liked her. He wanted to hear her breath, or graze her arm as though by accident when he raised his hand. A little out from the rest, in a loose peasant skirt, one knee hugged against her, Marcia Mae sat low in a canvas beach chair, a huddle, darker than the others.

"You approve of how he's handled it, sir?" Kerney asked.

"Duncan? Yes, I approve in general. I think he might have done it quicker. I think he might have talked to me, to somebody older."

"*I* talked to you, you remember," Kerney said.

"I remember. But Duncan—he never comes to me."

"Must he?" Nan Hunt inquired. The edge was in her voice.

"Apparently not," said Jason, dryly.

"What did he do?" Cissy asked.

"I've told you three times," said Kerney. "You don't listen."

"I'll listen now," she said. "What did Duncan do?"

"Oh, Lord," said Marcia Mae.

"You don't ever read the papers?" her mother asked her.

"I read the funny papers," she said. They laughed. "Tell me," she insisted. "Grand doesn't know either."

"Do you know, Mother?" Nan asked, raising her voice.

"Know what?" She was a little deaf.

"About what Duncan did."

"The piece in the paper, you mean?"

"That's right."

"What did she say?"

"I said *yes. The piece in the paper.*"

"Certainly I know. I read the paper every day."

"She keeps up," said Jason.

"Well, you children won't let me cook or work in the yard with Jonas. I have to do something. I can't crochet all day long."

"There, Mother. You're exactly right."

"Of course, she's right," said Jason.

"For crying out loud," said Cissy. "Will *some*body tell me—"

"Yes, somebody will tell you," said Jason, "but where do we have to start?"

"You'll have to go back to when Duncan was born," said Marcia Mae.

"Then you'd better tell her," said Nan. "You'd know more about that than anyone else."

But Marcia Mae fell silent, and Kerney at once commenced relating:

"It was just after Duncan closed up the highway place—now you must remember hearing about *that*, Cissy—there was a Negro named Beck Dozer came to him and asked for custody, claiming he'd got in a fight with Bud Grantham and Bud was sure to get him. It was raining like hell and Duncan couldn't locate anybody but Jimmy Tallant, who claimed they'd taken Bud back up in the hills, maybe to die. Duncan shut the Negro up in jail, but old Trewolla's not the most forceful character in the world, and Duncan wasn't easy in his mind. He didn't want either to sound the alarm over nothing, so he just stayed up in the jail with the Negro. Sure enough, the Granthams came and Tallant with them, walked right by Trewolla and were heading upstairs for the Negro when Duncan stopped them. At that point, they shot two pictures with a flash bulb and went away."

"That was the night," said Jason, "that one of the Granthams fired a gun out of pure devilment and almost hit old Morris's grandbaby."

"That's right. And the night I brought Cissy home early from the picture show in Stark."

"I remember that. It was raining."

"Yes. Then finally, the picture of Duncan and the Negro in the jailhouse comes out in a Chicago Negro paper, the kind they're sending out all over the South now, with an article saying Duncan is a defender of the colored. Come to find out the whole show was a put-up job—there never was a fight with Grantham, and Dozer was paid a fat fee for his part in it. This lays the carpet for Follansbee to walk into office. It was a stunty way to do it, but Tallant is that kind."

"He likes to play games," said Jason. "It amuses him."

"Why couldn't Duncan just tell everybody how it all happened?" Cissy asked.

"Because in politics," said Marcia Mae, "everybody agrees to confuse a perfectly simple issue that everybody understands."

"No," said Jason, "that is eventually what Duncan did do, Cissy, but he had to tell it in some forceful way, in print. He came out with a paid political statement in last Sunday's paper, containing along with his own statement a sworn statement by Beckwith Dozer. Is that nigger still alive, Kerney?"

"So far as I know, sir."

"He won't be living here much longer, then," said Jason.

"Duncan also stated," Kerney continued, "that he was not the willing subject of comment from any outside group, that as long as he was sheriff he was managing things for the constituency and nobody else."

"So that's the size of it," said Jason. "I suppose he'll run it again when the campaign heats up and they start circulating that picture and the Chicago article as handbills."

"There's going to be money poured in against Duncan," Kerney said.

"From who?" Cissy asked.

"Who indeed!" Nan said. "People who want to sell whisky in Winfield County."

"Then Duncan will have to circulate handbills," said Jason, "reprints of *his* article, and the whisky people will go in with the Chicago Negro people to circulate more handbills denying Duncan's handbills, and the beer people will go in with the Baptist Church, only the Baptists won't know it's the beer people, and circulate handbills saying Keep Whisky out of Winfield County, and Tallant will still make money because somehow or other on election day with everything shut up tighter than Dick's hatband, everybody is going to contrive to get"—he slapped a mosquito—"Goddam it—dead drunk.

"I have my objections to Duncan," he went on, "and always have had; still he's a decent sort of fellow, and I hate to see him get lost in this sort of mess."

"Isn't there a chance he won't get so lost as you think?" Nan inquired.

"He seems some way," Jason reflected, "always to go in over his head. I've noticed that about him."

Marcia Mae stirred restlessly. For a few minutes past, heat lightning had been flashing in the west.

Kerney said respectfully but firmly, "I'm not sure that's true of Duncan, Mr. Jason. I see a lot of him. He thinks the time has come to progress a little, but he wants to do it in the right way. Doesn't that always make people seem slow?"

"Jason means to say you can't be right unless you talk to the right people," Nan Hunt said.

"God knows, Nan—!" It sometimes seemed to Jason that his wife had turned into evil.

The front screen door slammed, and brought them all to notice that Marcia Mae had left them.

"So now, Cissy," Kerney asked, "do you understand?"

"About what?" asked Cissy.

Later she followed him out to the car where it sat under the cedars in the drive. They sat in the car and had a cigarette and she let him kiss her a few times. Then she drew away and laid her cheek down in the window, against the metal of the door. Honeysuckle smelled so strong you could not even smell the car.

"I know about Duncan and Marcia Mae, Kerney."

After a long silence, he said, "How did you know?"

"She goes back in the woods to walk sometimes, and one day I was out near where the path goes down to the tennis court when I saw her coming up through the trees. She looked pretty and happy and she was singing something, then she saw me. She got mad, and mean—goodness! She said I had followed her. It made me so mad I could spit. I went and told Mother on her and Mother said we all had to be patient, that Marcia Mae acted peculiar because her husband had got blown up and she went off by herself to be unhappy. Then I thought, She sure wasn't unhappy when I saw her before she saw me. But I didn't say anything to Mother and then I knew about Duncan. Goodness!" She laughed. "A scandal in the family. You guess everybody knows it?"

"People have been waiting to know it ever since she hit town," Kerney said.

"How did you know?"

"I went by the office to find Duncan a couple of weeks back. He wasn't in, so I went to his house. Tinker was sitting out in the back yard with the lawn mower, trying to make up her mind to get up and use it. Then she looked up and saw me and I knew I'd better not say, Where's Duncan? God bless her."

"You feel all that sorry for her?"

"There's nobody like Tinker."

"It's funny. Men always feel that about Tinker, but she doesn't have any girl friends at all, does she?"

"You women are such snobs, that's the only thing. You think, Oh, Tinker *Taylor*. The one that chased Duncan Harper till he finally married her. She's nobody but old Gains Taylor's daughter."

"I don't think anything of the kind. I just think she's hard to talk to. I tried to talk to her at the garden party last summer, but she wouldn't say anything."

"She probably felt uncomfortable in stockings and heels," said Kerney. "She's the original woman. All the rest of you are playing paper dolls."

"Well I like that!"

He held her back from opening the car door and they scuffled a moment. "Want to go for a ride?" "No." "Want to go get a Coke?" "No." "Want a drink?" "No." "Want a kiss?" "No. No, no." "Cigarette?" "Umm. One more."

"What do you think about it?" he asked her. "If it's true?"

"About Duncan and Marcia Mae? It's their business, I guess. It's her own life. That's the way she's always acted."

"But what do *you* think?"

"I think she's crazy," said Cissy. "Where's the future in it?"

Kerney shrugged. "Maybe they still love each other. Maybe he'll leave Tinker, and they'll get married."

"She wouldn't have him. She wouldn't before and wouldn't again." She said this in her chill proud little voice.

He put his hand under her chin and turned her face to his. "But if he wasn't married and if you were she, what would you do then?"

"You wouldn't catch me on a deal like that. I used to have this awful crush on Duncan. I still just think he's wonderful. But you know what I'd tell him? I'd tell him to go jump in the lake."

"But suppose—suppose it was me instead of Duncan? What would you do then?"

She stared at him a moment and then burst out laughing. "Why, Kerney Woolbright! If you aren't the craziest thing! Do you think for one minute—Kerney!"

"Hush," he said. "Stop laughing."

She stopped finally and put her cigarette out, snuffing it carefully in the ash tray. "I've got to go in." She turned to him. Her face, serious, lovely, melting, came lifting toward him, and to herself she knew exactly how she looked in her young softness. She saw herself better than she saw him, how her eyes were velvet, her mouth tender, and her dark hair all intricate with the swelling night.

So he kissed her and as they drew apart his hand, in midimpulse of caress, fell short and touched her cheek instead. He saw how slight such moments were, and wondered at love's terrible deflections. That night he lost more than his usual quota of sleep over her, twisting on the crumpled sheets, eluded continually by a mosquito.

Cissy, meanwhile, quarreled with her mother about having to go back down and latch the screen, played the radio awhile, filed her pretty nails, and went to sleep.

26 *The Rejected Ones*

THE BLUE glitter of Tinker's little Chevrolet, coming out of the east, was marked by Jimmy Tallant long before he saw her inside or knew she was going to stop there. He stood with his hands in his pockets out in front of the roadhouse, which was now no more or less than a filling station with a couple of gas pumps, a Coca-cola cooler, and a snack stand. He or Bud opened the place just enough to keep up their license with the gas company. As a matter of fact, Jimmy liked to be up there by himself. He had his morose side, and alone he watched endlessly the trucks come snorting to the crest of the hill to the west, admired the triumphant boom in their descent, or from the long shimmering eastern approach the razzle-dazzle of the new cars in the sun, making such a little sound when they passed, exactly like an ounce of air pressure being released from a tire, and there went a ton of sweet metal, lancing at eighty toward the Mississippi and beyond. It was not the cars themselves that intrigued him, though questioned at any moment he could have said instantly what make, what year, and what model, but the sense of the linked immensities of America, the feeling that he and his two gas pumps and roadhouse were all another flicker in the eye of the traveler who found nothing there out of place. So the long hot hours passed, one after the other: Charleston, Atlanta, Birmingham, Meridian, Shreveport, Dallas, Houston, El Paso, Tucson, San Diego: the sun blazed on them all, and everywhere a man stood before a roadhouse, near two gas pumps, arms folded, and watched the highway.

Then he saw the car that looked like Tinker's and he forgot the U.S.A., for she was slowing down, a quieter dazzle tossed about the blue hood, and the gravel crackled beneath the tires.

"Well!" He leaned into the window. "If it isn't herself. The rich man's beauty and the poor man's dream. Get out, lamb child. I wanted to see you most in the world."

Beneath her dark glasses her mouth smiled. She wore, as always, a true lipstick color. For coolness her dark hair was caught up from the nape by a black grosgrain band.

"Where've you been, honey?" he asked.

The red mouth talked to him. "Over to the picture show in Stark."

"The picture show? Right after lunch on a day like this?"

"Well, I got somebody to keep Cotton and Patsy for a change. I walked right out the door when she walked into it."

"What was on at the show?"

The mouth hesitated. "Isn't that silly? I can't even think— Jimmy, I wanted to ask you if you knew a Negro to do my wash. Duncan is wearing about a dozen shirts a day. I don't know why shaking hands with people should get so many shirts dirty."

"Everybody asks me about niggers since Duncan shut me down. But hell, I can't even find anybody to wash dishes in my own kitchen. You might try Beck Dozer's wife, though. She'll take in a little sometimes if she needs the cash."

"I'll drive by there now."

"You know how to go. It's the old Wiltshire road, the first cutoff past the covered bridge."

"I remember. Yes." She did not move to turn the ignition.

"But you couldn't remember the name of the show." He still could not see her eyes. He did not need to.

She put both small hands on the wheel and laid her forehead down on them. "Oh, Jimmy. What am I going to do?"

"I don't know, baby. You've just got to ride out the storm, I guess."

"They'll never come apart. Only she—if she'd been any kind of woman she never could have left him before. How can he forgive her now?"

"How can you forgive him?"

"I don't forgive him. I can't stop loving him, that's all."

"Then there you are."

"You remember how she used to play tennis when we were all in high school? All afternoon; I can see her yet. In white shorts and a black leather belt and a white boy's shirt. She could hit a ball as hard as a boy. She'd throw everything behind the racquet, leave the ground. Grit her teeth. I bet when she's in a rut she gets like that. I bet when she—"

"You'll make yourself sick," said Jimmy. "Come inside out of this sun. There's a room in the back where it's cool."

She opened the car door. "We'd better drive it around to the back," he said. "Lacey is another name for the Gestapo."

"You think I give a happy damn? Let them see the car. Let's make it all more interesting for them."

But he shoved her gently over and took the car around to the back himself. Just off the office was a bedroom where he and Bud used to take turns about sleeping the morning through when the business was on the boom, and they didn't shut down till dawn came and bled the neon. It was neat, this room, with a linoleum rug, a brass bed, a cane rocking chair with a cretonne-covered cushion, and a pair of straight curtains in the window which the Negro cook had made himself out of a pair of flour sacks. There was an old-timey Victorian bowl and pitcher, soap-dish and chamber-pot set stacked up on the dresser. A Negro had once offered it to Jimmy in exchange for a fifth of whisky. Jimmy had no use for it, but he pitied an honest thirst. Later it came in handy, for Bud had been known to rent the room to couples when the little houses out at the side were all filled.

Jimmy raised the window and propped it in place, then turned on the electric fan.

"It's shady back here now. Lie down, honey. It'll be cool in here in a minute."

He brought back two Cokes from the cooler and packages of Nabs. She took a few thirsty swallows and then sat holding the bottle, forgetting it.

"Jimmy, what am I going to do?"

"My theory is that you work this kind of thing out so that you live it one day at the time. You don't see things in big blocks of months and years, or what awful thing is finally going to happen. You just say, Now let's see. What am I going to have for supper?"

"I've said that already. I already know."

He saw her neat kitchen where there were no gadgets: the smooth marble slab she rolled the biscuits on, the grease-blackened pans she cooked her muffins in, and the big butcher knives, not bought out of a store, but the kind the Negroes made out of scrap steel, the hickory handles steel-hammered in place, and she had a whetstone too. One time during one of her summer parties when they had all gathered down on the terrace she had been slicing some ham in the kitchen and had cut herself. Duncan, who had been drinking more than usual, had picked up the knife. "Look at the size of this thing," he kept saying. "Her hand is about the size of a baby's. You wouldn't think she could pick it up, you wouldn't think—." He held it out before him. "You're letting her bleed to death," Jimmy remarked, so that Duncan's hand went tight on the hickory handle. They all knew each other too well. She, meanwhile, had stopped the blood herself, having recalled something she learned in Red Cross class about a big vein—she forgot its name.

Jimmy turned her wrist and there lay a small white line.

"The thing is," she was saying, "no awful thing is going to happen. They can go on like this forever. She doesn't want a husband, she just wants a man. You think she wants to cook and keep a house? You think she'd love a child if she had one?"

"I think it's possible that she might."

"She doesn't love anything, she wouldn't know how. She doesn't know what love is."

"Let's get off this one, Tinker. Everybody knows about love. Men, women, children, and coon dogs. They all know. It's the big old wide-open secret of the world, honey. I've loved you all my life, for instance. You think I ever have to tell you or anybody else?"

"Oh, Jimmy." She began to cry a little and he sat down by her to comfort her, holding her against his shoulder. "It should be after a high-school dance," she said, even smiling a little.

"Except I never got you on a bed before. I suppose I neglected to mention it."

They remembered his long agonized speeches, the times he used to break out laughing at himself.

"Yes, you did once before. The night Marcia Mae's and Duncan's engagement came out in the paper. I went to Memphis with you and went up to the hotel room with you."

"And then got drunk and then got sick and then passed out. You never gave me a chance."

"I'm such a common girl. I do such awful things. You didn't think less of me?"

"I never thought more of you."

"How do you manage, Jimmy? Duncan always says you like to be unhappy. That if you were happy you wouldn't know what to do."

"Duncan pursues happiness and I don't. That's the whole difference. He needn't talk smug. Right this minute I may be a sight happier than he is."

She sighed and dropped her head. "Men like to talk."

"You think it's all her fault, don't you?"

"Of course it's her fault. She left him, ran off with that lumberjack."

"Honey, he wasn't a lumberjack."

"All right, what difference does that make? The minute she came back she started after Duncan again."

He was silent.

"Well, whose fault do you think it was? His?"

"I don't think she would have left him if he hadn't failed her someway."

She stiffened to make some wifely defense, but thought better of it. "We can sit here for hours and say nasty things about them."

He smiled. "Well, let's do."

"Let's be mean."

"I hate blondes, don't you?"

"Despise them. They tell you lies."

"And they're dumb."

"And stuck up."

"And mean and—"

"*Jimmy!*"

The shout from outside the empty roadhouse struck them both silent.

Jimmy said rapidly, "It's Bud. I'll put him off. The door there goes into the rest room and it opens out the side. You can watch your chance and get out that way."

The next instant he was through the door to the office, and she could hear Bud Grantham calling again, and Jimmy answering.

27 *A Hasty Conference*

THEY MET in the office door.

"Have they come yet?" Bud asked.

"Has who come yet?"

"Who's back there then?"

"Nobody. I was taking a nap, for Chris'sake."

"Don't give me that. There's a car out back."

"Oh yeah, I know. Hanley sent his nigger in the Chevvy demonstrator. Somebody told him his new hog-wire fence was broken down back in the bottom. The nigger left the car up here in the shade."

"I thought they might have come."

"Who might have come?"

"Sam called this morning. I left word at the house with Bella."

"I haven't been home."

"You didn't eat at home?"

"I ate uptown, at the café."

Bud said, "You ain't doing right by my little girl, Jimmy. And her with a chap to care for."

"Listen," said Jimmy, "there ain't a woman living in this

world don't say Praise God when her husband can't make it home to dinner. I was only being thoughtful. You think any man likes to eat in a café when he could put his feet under his own table? Now come on. What about Sam?"

"He called from New Orleans, or rather got Mitchell to call for him. He—"

"*Jim—meee!*"

The door far up toward the front of the roadhouse slammed and they heard the drag of loose heels on the concrete floor. It was Bella. They both lowered their eyes, like boys caught in something. Neither one of them ever really wanted to see Bella. As a matter of fact, Jimmy liked her better than Bud did. She frequently amused him; he sometimes pitied her; and when he felt both of these things at once he became quite fond of her and could make her happy for weeks at a time by letting her know it once. But the only thing she ever did to Bud was make him nervous.

She stood in the door where Bud had moved out of it. She was wearing the flowered wrapper, the one they had told her when she bought it looked enough like a dress to wear it uptown and she had believed them, and a pair of high-heel slingback white shoes, grass-stained, with the heels broken inward and the strap that was supposed to hold them up lying under her instep. She wore the baby at her waist as if it were a big bow tie.

She said to Jimmy, "Are you back here?"

"Looks like I am. Doesn't it?"

She giggled. "Silly! Daddy come by the house this morning. He said to tell you there was a man from New Orleans called —Daddy! Are you back here too?"

"Wipe his mouth," said Jimmy.

"I didn't bring nothing for it." She caught up the hem of her skirt.

"I should have worn a tie," said Jimmy. "We could use that." He looked at the child. "God damn, what a face. Come here, Buster." He took the baby and held it folded together under one arm in a manner unorthodox but firm. The baby grew extremely happy and began to sputter.

"Miss Annie Miller uptown," said Bella; "she told me yesterday he looked exactly like you."

"She must have lost her eyesight," said Jimmy. "He looks more like an Apache Indian chief than he does me or you or Bud or half-dozen Granthams all put together." He thrust the baby suddenly in Bud's face. "You notice a resemblance?" he inquired. "See anything you want to claim?"

The baby was indeed uncommonly dark. He had a thick crop of spiky black hair that stuck out around his brow, saucer fashion. "Koochee koochee," went Bud, wiggling one tough old brown finger. "Koochee koochee koo. Don't give him to me, Jimmy. Fannie had seven but I was ever a-scairt to hold one. Koo, baby. Koo, baby. Koo."

"Whose car is that one I saw out back?"

"Huh? Oh, car. Is it still back there?" Jimmy craned out the window. "Hanley's nigger he sent up to check the fence down in the pasture. Left it up here in the shade."

"Hey, *Tallant*!" The door of the roadhouse banged again and a man's voice rang.

"Old home week," said Jimmy. "I think it's the Candidate."

"I called him," said Bud. "Sam will want to see him. That was all right, wasn't it? They aim to put the skids under this Harper thing. We might as well put all we got behind it."

Jimmy sighed. "Sure, I know. It's just that Follansbee is my personal nomination for the man least calculated to put me in a mood for weaving daisy chains." Willard appeared in the door. "Well," said Jimmy, "if it isn't the white hope of Winfield County. Only you look more like the black hope than the white one. Christ a'mighty, man, don't you know if you're running for office you've either got to look like a one-gallus tramp and slobber tobacco juice, or make a halfhearted pass at looking like a gentleman? When did you shave last?"

Follansbee touched his chin. It was not really a chin, only a gable on his neck. "This morning," he said. "I shave every morning. It just grows so fast, that's all. Means I'm virile, Jimmy. Full of sap and spark."

"That ain't the way I heard it," said Jimmy.

"How'd you hear it?"

"It means you're going to grass. For a fact it does. Didn't you know that dead people's hair keeps growing, growing, growing. That's all *they're* busy doing. Going to grass."

"Oooooo!" said Bella. "It's the truth. I read it in a magazine."

"Bella, my heart," said Jimmy. "Why don't you get the hell on out of here? There must be a whole pile of things the mother of one has to do around the house."

"Travis's hair," said Willard dolefully, settling back on his head the hat he had lifted as Bella left (he lifted it now about a million times a day). "I reckon if that's so what you said, his old red hair must be a yard long by now, with five months to grow in."

"It's laying all around him in the coffin," Jimmy said. "All around his shoulders."

"Hush up!" Bud Grantham said. "You're tempting the devil, Jimmy, you and Willard, talking about the dead. It ain't fittin'."

"Well, we've all got to join him someday," said Willard.

"It's a fact," said Jimmy.

"I don't dispute it," said Bud.

"Jimmy, about those folks that are coming up here—"

"Talk to Bud. He caught the phone."

"You both know what they want. They want to put money back of Willard."

"Money, yes," said Jimmy. "But why come up here?"

"Well," said Bud, "to see where the money's going to go to, I reckon, just like anybody else. They've had experience in these things."

"That's just the trouble," said Jimmy. "They've had too much experience. I don't know if I like it much."

"We've got to have their money to fight this Harper thing."

"That's what they want us to think," Jimmy said. "That we've *got* to have it."

"Well, don't we have to?" Willard asked nervously. He was at that point in a race—about six weeks before the election—that comes to every political candidate whether he is running for the Presidency or justice of the peace in the smallest crossroads in west Texas: he had to win. It had become a total necessity.

"I don't like the way the wind's blowing," said Jimmy. "Look. They come up here, they offer to pour money in. How much do you think they'll offer?"

"We mentioned five thousand," said Bud, "the first go-round."

"But they're making a special trip. Suppose they mention ten thousand, fifteen? What then? Do we take it?"

"We'd look silly not to," said Willard.

Jimmy turned on him. "Will you keep out of this? What do you mean *we*? You don't own a stick of this place. It's Bud's and it's mine, and what we say you abide by."

"I never meant to meddle," said Willard.

"What do you think we ought to do then?" said Bud. "You got to hurry up, Jimmy. They're on the road and traveling."

"I'm thinking maybe we shouldn't take anything."

"Nothing!" Willard squeaked.

"Look," said Jimmy, "I planned the right way to throw this thing our way and there's no reason on earth why it won't work. All you got to do is keep it up and keep it up and keep it up that Duncan Harper is a nigger lover. The keystone is the picture we took: we embroider from there, we quote him, we tell stories about him, and maybe none of it is quite the truth, but we've always got to lead back to that picture which is down in black and white and nobody can dispute it.

"On the other hand, if we get scared and take this money, what then? We win the race, but we've sold ourselves. We've sold our right to say how much gambling equipment we want to put in, who we aim to hire and why; pretty soon we won't even be allowed in the room when they count up the cash. They can sweet-talk all they want to about there aren't any strings on this money, but you know and I know, Bud, that there are always strings. It's exactly like taking federal funds to build your houses, to plant your land, to buy your cotton nobody else wants. No strings on that either except pretty soon the government owns your soul and you sit and cuss it till you're blue in the face, but if somebody mentions taking that precious parity away from you, you squall like the last of a noble line threatened with imminent castration. I'm sorry but I'm too much of a states-righter to see this any other way. If you're subsidized you're sunk. I've got a natural love for the business Bud and I had built up here together, and I'm enough of a Winfield County citizen to want to tell those sons o' bitches to go back where they came from."

"It's your business and mine," said Bud, "for a fact."

"I don't know," said Willard gloomily. "All that talking is all right, Jimmy, but when the time comes you haven't been coming down the line."

"What do you mean?"

"You pulled that one off after I tipped you the National Guard was coming up: they didn't find a drop. Okay. But two weeks later Harper comes out singlehanded and shuts you down. There were those standing by to cart him off neat and quick that night, but you stalled. Then up at the jail, okay, you wrapped that one up, picture and all. But two weeks later Harper gets the nigger to come out and say it was a put-up job and what then? You don't lay a finger on the nigger. You don't let anybody else tend to him either. It ain't like you, Jimmy. There are those that keeps on saying you're just projecking around, that you don't want to win this race at all. They say that Harper's wife's got the Indian sign—now, I never said it, Jimmy. I never even thought it. But if people are saying it, then you ought to know about it, is the way I feel. I honestly do."

"He sho' don't lay a finger on that nigger," said Bud. "And won't let nobody else."

"Seems like it's you that's the nigger lover," said Willard. "If a nigger double-talked me that way I'd have me a showdown before nightfall."

"All right then, run it without me," said Jimmy. "I'll get out right now. Walk out of here and never come back. Bud, you can write Willard's speeches. Willard, you can bargain with Sam and his crew. Both of you can decide how much money you want, how much share you're willing to give for it. I'm tired anyway. It's time I took a vacation. Every morning I say to myself, Here I am thirty-five years old and I've never seen Niagara Falls or Mammoth Cave. Or maybe I'll go West. There's things to see—"

"Jimmy, for God's sake," Willard said, "I think I hear the car. Whatever I said, I take it back."

Bud Grantham hauled his shoulders together. "It's nothing to prank about, boy. Old Bud wouldn't know his own name without you to tell it to him."

The screen door far out front slammed and numbers of foot-steps sounded and stopped. There came a murmuring, but this time no one called.

Jimmy went out to greet them. He hoped to hell that Tinker had seen her chance and taken it, but he had not heard the car.

28 *The Gang Visits Lacey*

THIS TIME there were four of them. There were Mitchell again and the Indian-looking man, Pilston, and the boy who carried the gun for them. And there was Sam himself. Sam was a gentlemanly-looking man who did not weigh very much, and though all the men were taller than he, he did not seem short either. He wore a light blue Palm Beach suit, crisply pressed, a white shirt, and a navy tie with a maroon figure. He was bald with a benevolent rime of white hair, and his eyes were a clear blue. He gave a sort of definition to the two older men who were with him: Jimmy had not thought of them as thugs before. But he failed somehow to define the boy who carried the gun. He only made him seem younger than ever, and chewing gum that way made it seem a toy pistol that he wore beneath his arm, probably one that had come full of candy.

Jimmy shook hands with the boy heartily. "Hello, Wally. Still like your work?"

"There ain't any work to it," said Walter. "All I do is ride around in the car and look out the window."

"You mean you ain't used that thing yet? There ain't been anybody mean enough to shoot?"

"It looks like it," said Walter. "Only it ain't shooting anybody they got in mind. No more than a policeman shoots people. I'm kind of like a policeman, see?"

"That's a new one," Jimmy said. "What about that, Mitchell? The kid here says he's like a policeman."

"We explained it all to him," said Mitchell. "We talked it all over with him and we all came to that conclusion. That's right, ain't it, Wally?"

The boy grinned, shifting the gum to the other jaw. "'At's right."

"This boy here," said Sam to Bud Grantham with pride, "can shoot a gun better than anyone I have been privileged to observe. I've had some idle time in recent months and I've spent pleasant hours watching the kind of mark he can strike. He doesn't miss, that's all. He simply does not miss."

"Is he really that good?" Jimmy asked Mitchell.

"He can shoot all right," said Mitchell.

"How good are you, Wally?" Jimmy asked. He liked Wallace. He felt he knew him by heart.

Wallace grinned. "Well, up in Tippah County where I'us bawn, that's where I learned to shoot, from my Unker Chollie Klappert—up there they usta say I could take the middle claw off a killdee's foot on the far side. It always come easy to me, shooting."

"Chollie Klappert your blood uncle?" Jimmy asked.

"Sure is."

"I'm kin to them myself. That makes us cousins."

"Well I swan," said the boy. He was pleased.

Sam said, "I dislike to change the subject, but I think we'd best get down to business. This office is all right, but it's rather small, don't you agree? Now if we could have some light out in your main room and pull two of the tables together . . . ?"

He gestured toward where Jimmy sat in the window, blocking the larger part of the view with his shoulders. "Sure," said Jimmy. "We can do all that and we can serve you a drink of whisky for real hospitality. But we better tell you first off that Bud and Willard here and me been talking this deal over and we've decided that we're against it. We've got this election sewed up anyway; there's no need for outside help. As for the business we do with you after the election, we've discussed that months ago, before Travis Brevard died, though I never got to sound him on it. Willard here has been sounded and is agreeable provided certain interests of his own are protected. Bud and I, we deal with Willard, and we deal with you and we deal with Duncan Harper. We do the dealing. Now if that's clear we'll have a drink on former contracts and call it a day. I've got—"

"*Jim-mee!*"

The screen had banged again and the heels were sounding on the concrete. Bella was back. She would have the baby with her, Jimmy knew. He took advantage of the moment to look out the window, and he could stop sweating, for Tinker had got away.

Bella stood in the door. She always wanted to look at people up close. She used to meet everybody that stopped even long enough to use the rest room back when the roadhouse was open, and now she was lonesome, and to add to it she needed a certain number of people every day to tell her how cute the baby was.

She had on make-up this time and a proper dress. Jimmy spieled out the introductions without even uncrossing his knee. Sam was smooth as butter—it was enough to make you cry; and Mitchell got clumsily to his feet. The boy from Tippah County took Bella's appearance as the most natural thing in the world—it would seem that women carrying babies had showed up in most situations of his life. So the turn passed round to the fourth, the Indian-looking man, and Jimmy still could not remember his name. It was the name that stopped him, and while he was still staring trying to think of the name, he found instead that the face he was looking into, framed with spiky black hair, was more familiar than it had any right to be and still be on a man whose name he couldn't call. He saw that the face was muting like the coils in a juke box from scarlet to purple, the way a baby's face colors when it screams its head off at night for nothing but pure unadulterated meanness.

The room had grown deathly silent, until at last Bella, who had apparently been hard put also to remember the man's name, burst into a smile of innocent delight.

"If it ain't George! George Pittman!"

"Pilston," said the Indian-looking man, and swallowed.

"Pilston. Sure. What on earth made me say Pittman? I declare, I said to Jimmy the other day that I'm alltime getting—"

She trailed off, seeing that they were all silent and downcast, and at last her face burned (for memory walked as slowly into Bella's brain as a solitary hen in midafternoon deciding for some reason to climb the crosswalk and hop into the henhouse). She looked wildly from Pilston to the baby, who were staring at each other in primitive horror, the baby's face unfortunately reflecting not only Pilston's every feature but his emotions as well. Then she said, "Oh." It was a little sound uttered in a little girl's honest voice, and on it she turned and fled.

After a time Jimmy Tallant gave a short laugh and walked out of the room.

Every so often things happen to a person which are like others that have happened, and in these things, even if they are bad or foolish or disgraceful, the person finds his identity is reaffirmed, and so he is at peace. He had grown up in the shadow of what his father had done—all his growing indeed had been raising his head closer to that knowledge. Tinker had not chosen him. Even in the blind senseless dark of poor Bella another man's seed had contrived to run home and lock the door against his own.

But not being really a bitter person, it was not that he thought so much about it as that he felt cast back again into his old lonely freedom. So as he went down through the field to the woods back of the roadhouse, having recalled an appointment to meet Beck Dozer, he went whistling absently, and once picked up a stone to see how far he could throw it.

Back up the hill in the roadhouse office, Bud Grantham at last straightened from where he had been leaning against the desk with his shoulders hunched to let his old tough brown head sink low between them. When he stood up he looked gravely around him.

"You folks make yourselves at home. I best go and see about my girl. Her mother died when she was scarce the size of that one with her and I was never the one to raise a pack of little chaps, as time over and again it's proved to me I was never the one for it."

Leaving, he drew out a great handkerchief, and from outside they heard him honk his nose.

Sam, all the while, had sat cleaning and paring his nails with a nickel-plated gadget. His hands were white, clean and firm, like a surgeon's and he cut the hangnails cleanly free on all ten pure white fingers, without a trace of blood. He at last folded the gadget back upon itself and dropped it into his coat pocket. He dusted his knees. Then he looked at Mitchell.

"Ignoring various family complications which have arisen, I conclude that Mr. Grantham and Mr. Tallant do not wish to do business with us today."

"It looks like it," said Mitchell.

"Well," said Sam, "we have a long hot drive ahead, and before someone or other of them decides to come back and shoot Mr. Pilston here, I suppose we had best be on our way." He made a gesture of rising, when Willard Follansbee, who had been thinking in the corner for some time, said, "Wait" in a tone of despair.

"Yes?" said Sam.

"He don't want to win the race," said Willard. "He ain't going to lift a hand to win it. Everybody knows it."

"Not want to win? Why on earth not want to win?"

"I'll tell you, but don't you say I told you. He's crazy about Duncan Harper's wife. She can turn him any way."

Sam sat thinking. "That clears it. I thought myself, he does not want to win." He straightened. "Go get him, Mitchell."

"Where from?" Mitchell asked, rising.

"His house, I would think."

"He didn't go home," said Wallace, the boy, who had been sitting where he had a glimpse out the window. "I seen him head down that field and towards the woods."

"You go with Mitchell then, Wally. And quickly, please."

29 *The Point of Panic*

As DUNCAN had once before, Tinker came to Beck Dozer's house, saw where the "Z" had run on the mailbox and drew her car into the shallow curve out of the main road. She ascended the path to the gate and stood outside it.

"Anybody home?"

"'Home?'" said the wood.

A young Negro woman, thin and straight as a broomstick, dressed in a straight-cut gingham dress, came down the steps and out to open the gate for her. Her head was wound in a white rag and she wore straws in her ears.

"Come on in," she said to Tinker. "The mosquitoes gits bad out cheer this time of day."

Tinker accompanied her to the house. The Negroid effluvium touched her round, mingled with a drift of wood smoke from the back, and the scent of spring water which draws itself clean out of the earth and brings with it of all earth only its black odor.

"Does Aunt Mattie still live with you?" she asked.

She had suddenly, by the smell of the house, remembered the old woman, though she had not thought of her for years. She had been very sick once when she was a child, and Aunt Mattie had invited herself in and stayed with them and nursed her. When the fever left her, she was weak as a baby and had to learn to walk again. Aunt Mattie would take her up in her lap and sit near the window with her. It was April and the spring was just turning to a deeper warmth—this was a new time and Tinker felt herself new again. With fever's sensitivities she had heard them talking it that she would die and seen them looking it too, but Aunt Mattie had not wavered and had had no time for them: the spoon with the food in it had come at her in the black hand with the nails blue-gray like the silver spoon, had come at her, and come again. Her mother cried in the kitchen, "You put bacon grease in it again!" and wept she was so vexed. In bed Tinker heard it and her tongue came out and licked. That was why it had tasted so good and strong and black, not because it came off the blackness of the hand with the spoon. When she sat weak in the window and Aunt Mattie held her feet together under an old piece of cotton blanket, she thought she had been born out of Aunt Mattie's lap. Aunt Mattie was not a bit modest. "Mattie done save this precious," she told her. "Hadn't been for Mattie you'd be gone from here. Yo' mamma don' know nothing about dis chile like Mattie knows her."

Lucy said, "Yes'm, Granny's here. You wants to come and speak with her?"

Tinker followed her inside, through a dim hallway where a door led off into a large room with a bed in the corner and chairs grouped around a cold fireplace. In the far rocker, the largest, Aunt Mattie was waiting out the time under an old pile of quilts. Her thin hands kept together on her lap, and her head leaned to one side as if trying to catch a little light from the window. The hair was white, kinky and very short: it hugged the old skull and made a neat fitting of itself, all the way around. The wrinkles ran downward and were cleft deep; Aunt Mattie had not played around with age. She was so nearly blind she was aware only of strong sunlight. Yet she could hear well enough.

"Here's somebody come to see you, Granny," said Lucy.

Tinker put her hand on Mattie's. "I haven't seen you in a long time, Aunt Mattie."

The old hands moved caressingly, exploring the fingers and wrist with a fine tremulous dry touch.

"I doan' know you, chile, but doan' tell me. Talk twel I hears your family voice."

"When I was sick one time you came and nursed me."

"They ain't a chile in this town can't say I didn't. White folks doan' know nothing about they churen."

"I'm married now myself, Aunt Mattie. I've got two children of my own."

"I hears your voice now. You's Emmie Taylor's chile."

"That's right."

"I mind the mawning they tole me you's sick. I was down by the branch at the ole place, boiling sheets. They come down the heel and say to me, You know Miss Emmie Taylor's little girl? They had to keh her home from school today she took so sick. So I says right then, Take this clothes-punching stick. Miss Emmie Taylor cain' keh for no sick baby. So that's when Mattie come, honey."

"You saved my life, Aunt Mattie," said Tinker, kneeling down so that her hand rested comfortably between the fingers that held so lightly, pressing now and again to emphasize a word. She had not meant it so, but when she knelt tears came easily, rushing, and fell warm on Mattie's hands and her own. Mattie did not question her. "There, baby. There. Hit's going to be all right."

Her head sank then and she cried all over. Mattie groped across her head, her shoulders, caressing her. "There, baby. There, baby. She Mattie's chile."

She rose when she was done and found her bag for a handkerchief. Lucy had retired, who knew when, or would ever know? She was a Negro, and her tact was of this quality.

The room rested deep in twilight. Tinker walked into the open hallway. She glanced back fondly toward Aunt Mattie, but did not return. She knew that Mattie now perhaps thought she had come yesterday or last year, and would not know her if she spoke again.

The tears had left her exalted and hushed. She thought with a gratitude as immense as a clear sky that today there had been Mattie and Jimmy to ease her. She sat down gravely on the porch steps.

A man ran into the house from the back steps. It seemed that Lucy had entered the hall from some side door the instant that he was calling, "Lucy! Lucy!"

Tinker sprang up and saw him say, "I gots to run, Lucy. It's Mister Jimmy Tallant. Somebody shot him—"

"Lawd, Beck, was it you?"

"No, but they'll think so. They thinks so now."

"Who thinks? How come they thinks?"

"I was coming along the path, hoping to see did Mister Tallant have any little job for me, when I heard some talking and a shot, right close, but I never thought nothing except it was somebody out hunting, till I looked over in the edge of the pasture and there was a man laying and nobody else near. I come up close to see who and there was blood running out and I says, 'Oh God, it's Mister Tallant!'"

"Was he dead?"

"I don't know. There wasn't time to see. Then's when I saw two white men walking away up at the rise of the hill toward the highway, and I thought I better get away from here, but one was coming back already, pointing at me and hollering, 'You can say what you want to, but we know you did it, nigger. We saw you and we know and you sure better run! You better get lost, nigger!'"

"Oh Jesus, Beck!"

"What chance I got, Lucy, if they say it was me? What can I do? I gots to run, Lucy, as fast and far as I can. . . ."

Tinker was running herself by then, back along the path to the woods that Beck had fled from. She was the first after Beck Dozer to find him.

Bud Grantham, some little time after the New Orleans car had driven away, had begun to look for him here and there, and so came upon them both in the dewy corner of the pasture just at dusk, she on her knees in blood beside him, tearing cloth from his shirt.

"Call an ambulance!" she cried across the field.

He ran at once to obey, not completely understanding. He felt that day that his tough old heart had been grieved once, and now again, beyond anything it had been fitting to expect. To Bud nothing seemed to be happening decently, and it was at this, as much as for fear that Jimmy was seriously injured, that he almost wept as he made for the telephone.

PART THREE

30 *The Sisters*

NAN HUNT had a caller. The girls, Cissy and Marcia Mae, sitting out on the side porch where they had hurried and quickly shut the curtained French doors because they weren't dressed and had no wish to talk to anybody, could hear from within the murmuring rise and fall of ladies' voices. They did not make out the words.

Cissy was doing her nails. A manicure case waited on the floor beside her chair and she held a large open bottle of polish remover clamped between her bare knees. She wet bits of cotton with the remover and cleaned the old polish away in gaudy smears. The reek of the chemical was all out of proportion to the importance of the affair, but so, for that matter, was Cissy's degree of concentration upon it. Gunshot would scarcely have disturbed her. Her nails grew in firm ovals out of the moist pads of her fingertips; she enticed them to a shapely length with her emery boards. Marcia Mae, who glanced now and again over her plain hands, could not resist watching her sister's strategies.

Cissy was nineteen, and poised that summer at a moment of femininity so intense that her virginity seemed scandalously out of order in the universe. The flesh of her arm was soft as freshly molded butter; even the redolence of the bathroom when she left it held something all lazily like a sigh. She was not at all beautiful; perhaps she was not even pretty: she made everybody so nervous that nobody knew any better how she looked than Kerney Woolbright did, with her eyes like chocolate fudge still warm from the pan and her hair as glossy as a blooded chestnut's coat. If the fact of her innocence was disturbing, the question of her self-knowledge was worse: every touch of the file lured the little hands into a greater sensual alertness—was Cissy so unaware of this?

"If you paint them now," said Marcia Mae, "I'll scream."

Called up, Cissy questioned that she had been addressed. Her little uncertainties were charming. She touched her tongue to her bottom lip before she spoke.

"Didn't you ever like to paint your fingernails? When you were my age, I mean."

She had almost said "when you were young," and Marcia Mae knew it.

"Some women, even at thirty, can still manage that sort of thing."

"Mother says you ought to quit it, though, after you're mature."

"You mean to say you admit you're immature?"

Cissy, like a plot of lush foliage reluctant to stir in the breeze, only yawned. Her voice, like her mother's, was seldom raised. But she was apparently not without kindness.

"I wish I had grown up when you did," she said. "You all had a lot more fun. I used to be jealous of you, always going somewhere with Duncan and Jimmy and Tinker Taylor. I used to wish I would hurry up and grow too. But it isn't all that much fun."

"We did have fun. But there were lots more of us than just four."

"You were the main ones. Things didn't happen without you."

"Yes, we were the main ones."

"You and Duncan always went in Jimmy Tallant's car."

"That's because Duncan never had a car of his own."

"No! I didn't know that!" In Cissy's time, for a man not to own a car seemed as bad as if he never brushed his teeth or shined his shoes. "But he was a big football player!" Her sense of shock increased.

Marcia Mae laughed. "Duncan Harper was the only All-American in captivity, I reckon, who never so much as owned a Ford, let alone a Cadillac."

"Is he still that way?" Cissy asked.

She did not look up, but in the ensuing silence she steadily painted a fingernail with a tiny brush.

"You'll have to ask his wife," said Marcia Mae.

Cissy painted another nail. "You know, Kerney is just crazy about her. He likes her more than he does me."

"There's something pathetic about her," said Marcia Mae. "She makes men think she has to be protected. God knows from what."

"She's common," said Cissy and dipped her little brush.

"Men don't care if women are common," said Marcia Mae.

"Look what she did," Cissy pursued, "when Jimmy Tallant got shot. She went all out, stopping the blood, getting an ambulance, crying right in front of everybody, sitting all night in the hospital. I'd just die before I'd do anything like that. It's like crying out loud at a funeral, or saying you're constipated."

"What a prissy little thing you are!" said Marcia Mae.

"It isn't just me. Everybody said that, said she ought to be ashamed taking things over like that when it was another woman's husband. Even Grandmother said so, and she never talks about anybody."

"Oh nuts. I don't like her either, but that's not the reason. I think you've got a right to get worked up over anybody's shot husband you want to."

"Then why don't you like her?"

Marcia Mae hesitated. "I didn't really mean I don't like her. I mean I didn't like her when I knew her best. That was nearly ten years ago."

"Well, why didn't you like her then?"

Marcia Mae set both hands into her waistline and, sitting up straight as though weary from long traveling, flexed her slender back. "Well, she was always so little and cute. Her fanny bobbled when she crossed the room. She would listen to shady stories, but she wouldn't tell them. She went with Tallant for years and never gave an inch."

"Never did what?"

"Never slept with him, I mean."

"Should you?" inquired Cissy, who had taken root in her mother's virtuous advice that if you gave a man what he wanted he wouldn't want it any more.

"Should you, shouldn't you? I don't know. I think it's wrong to parade it like a bowl of cream before a cat. I think it's disgusting."

Cissy capped her little filthy-smelling bottle and spread her fingers out on her bare knees to dry.

"But maybe she's changed now," said Marcia Mae.

She lighted a cigarette and drew her knees up in the swing and circled them with her arms. She had really fine legs, better than her sister's, whose ankles were too round and thighs shapeless where the little-girl fat had not cleared away. But Cissy, if she lived to be a hundred, would never have an inch of flesh that would hold a candle to Marcia Mae. Marcia Mae's ankle shot down as straight and trim as a blade, and it was fleet: even in repose it ran and halted to make the stroke and ran again. A certain clean physical intonation of superiority —carriage, people say—she would have perhaps had anyway, being well-born, but the limbs' decisive justness, the back's subleties, the neck's pride—all these she had earned without knowing it, climbing high into the grape arbor, racing with Negro children to see the minstrel parade, swinging whole mornings through out in the pasture swing. When the yard and the woods and the Negro children fell away into a dream world (though they were all still there, the sense of them had vanished), she had gone on to tennis and in college spent more time in the swimming pool, they said, than in class. On her idle wrist now a round gold watch no bigger than a dime was bound by a gold snake chain. She glanced at it now and again.

Before the two girls the level side lawn spread away like a gracious open fan. Its grass was soft gray-green, rich this year by reason of the wet spring. The black shadows which embossed it fell where they would: feathery, but in grand possession, toward dawn, lightly sustaining the big dew, they shrank up tight and black toward noon, and swelled darkly on till five or thereabouts when the sun shot a glare through, this being the only hour you could not enjoy sitting out in the yard. Flowering shrubs flourished in their accustomed places, deep-rooted and assured as trees. There were a few flower beds near the porch steps and one or two far out, very far, there where the bluff dropped suddenly and Jason Hunt had strung a white-painted chain for fear someone might fall in the dark —he could even be sued. Not much was blooming now at this high point of summer with all its layered green and shadow. Roses were in bloom, and certain stiff common flowers like zinnias and marigolds, but none of these were on the lawn. It seemed to have had its own way about things, and if it had rejected roses, that was that.

The fact was, however, that the lawn took a terrible amount of labor. Nan Hunt talked about it so much nobody heard her any more. She was out every morning in a large straw hat, with shears and work gloves. She directed a Negro boy, who drove her to distraction. She wouldn't "get rid of him" because he had a "growing hand," but you had to "keep in behind him" because he was "not worth killing." He cost her a great deal of anguish, and after dinner every day ran the power mower, a wonderfully sleepy sound for napping. His name was George, and right now he was sitting on the far side of the cedar tree out back of the kitchen, dozing. He was the same who used to play with Marcia Mae and had pushed her in the swing so many times, including the day the rope broke on the rise and slung her up so high and she looked down out of mid-air and saw a boy throw down his gun and run and wondered why he did it. A bumblebee warred twice against the porch screen; a green lizard ran across a flagstone.

With effort like rising out of deep waters, Marcia Mae re-heard her own last voice, and added, "Maybe I would like her all right now. Maybe I would like her just fine. I don't know."

"You could go call on her," Cissy suggested.

"Damn it, Marjorie Angeline," for this was Cissy's true outlandish name, "I'll go to see who I please."

Cissy yawned again. "I wish I had a Coke. I'm sleepy."

"So do I. Go get us one."

"My nails aren't dry. Besides, I can't go through the living room without speaking to whoever is in there with Mother."

"You could go around the house," suggested Marcia Mae.

"Umm," said Cissy, meaning that she didn't want to.

Marcia Mae stood up and, tucking her shirt into her shorts, caught up a wrap-around skirt from the back of her chair.

"Going for a walk?" Cissy ventured.

But her sister did not seem to have heard her.

"Now Mother will make me come speak to the company," Cissy complained.

"You'll survive," said Marcia Mae, and went off arrow-straight across the lawn. The path lowered her, gently at first, then quickly; her high bright head vanished downward among the trees.

31 *A Rendezvous*

LITTLE BY LITTLE, only as much each time they met as her pride would allow, Marcia Mae had told Duncan about her life away from Lacey. Slowly, she had brought herself to admit that this was why she had come home, to tell him everything. He was the only one to hear that behind the high proud look she had whenever Red O'Donnell was mentioned, lived the memory of a marriage that had not been a raging success.

The big handsome Irishman had loved to drink and party; he had loved the figure he cut in Marine officer's uniform. He thought his Southern bride was the prettiest girl he'd ever seen, and because he had always lived in California, he was pleased to be ordered to the San Diego Marine base. For the first few months he was charming, generous, and gay.

Then routine began to weigh on him. He was assigned to paper work at the base, which bored him; his opinion of his superior took hours to describe and he described it every night when he got home. On weekends he felt it necessary for them to go to parties with other young married couples of the service. He could whip a party together in no time, inviting along as his best friends in creation people whom he had met a few hours before in a bar. These people, Marcia Mae said, invariably seemed all right; they were attractive, well-dressed, well-paid, often amusing. She learned that after a certain point in the evening's drinking it was best not to enter any bedroom. Once after midnight she discovered that when looking for an ash tray it was more tactful not to walk back of the sofa. One night Red vanished for several hours with a movie bit actress somebody had brought along; he claimed afterwards not to have remembered anything after ten o'clock. They had a terrible fight—it seemed he expected women to fight, and moreover expected her to be angry with him, but not for very long.

A day or two later, his ex-wife appeared. He had never mentioned that he had one. They still owned some property together in Los Angeles and what she had in mind was that he make over the property to her in lieu of back alimony. "I don't really owe her any alimony," Red explained to Marcia Mae. "I was just supposed to pay it till she married again and she married inside two months. But now she's got another divorce, so she claims I have to start paying her again. If anybody ought to have alimony it was me." And he would plunge into the long list of her faults. When she telephoned, however, which was often, he became as docile as you please and made appointments with her to discuss business or see lawyers. Marcia Mae put her foot down. "You either stay with me or go back to her," she told him. "Do you want to go back to her?" "Oh, no," he said dolefully. "She spends too much money." He was sitting on the couch in the living room of the duplex they lived in, and was heartily worrying about himself. Marcia Mae burst right out laughing. From that moment she stopped believing that she loved him or ever had. "You get rid of her," he begged. "You start answering the phone and say I'm out of town." She seemed not to be able to stop laughing. He was finally offended. "I don't see what's so funny," he said. "The joke is on me," she told him. "I left the best man in the state of Mississippi for you—for this."

She began to think of leaving him, but she was too hardheaded to do it right away; she hated the thought of the news going back home, of the people who would say "Uh-*huh*, I told you so." While she was still debating, she learned to be fond of him in a way, the way one feels for a child after taking care of it for a time. "Which only proves," she told Duncan, "that I never loved him. I was never hurt enough."

His orders came, and he was gone. On shipboard he wrote her two passionate letters in a style not quite illiterate, begging her pardon for everything and saying how sweet she was. She had to admit that she cried over them.

One day she came back walking from the grocery store to their duplex on a sunny California winter day and saw the telegram on the table where the cleaning woman had left it. She knew already what it said. She put some coffee on the stove first, thinking that if the coffee was going before she read it, then afterward she would have to do something about the coffee. Later she went to the beach in the car Red had left with her and walked by the sea for a long while.

Later communications filled in some details: the telegram had merely stated a fact. Finally a picture formed quite clearly in her head. There had been ten men gathered in a fringe of palms just off the beachhead at Tarawa. A grenade had come bouncing out of the jungle and rolled at their feet; it was seconds from detonation. Nine of the men had plunged to earth, face downward, clutching into the ground, but the tenth had leaped deliberately upon it and had been blown to smithereens. She could imagine the island: palm trees rising in a proud disheveled way, strong sun, the sea and white curling foam, the square-nosed landing craft rolling in and every so often a bright flash of fire. And there at center stood ten men just before a moment of impetuous decision. She was linked back to the time she had first laid eyes on Red O'Donnell, a carelessly handsome man walking straight toward her the moment he set eyes on her at a soldier's dance, saying in his confident Yankee way, "You're not to dance with anybody but me," and thirty minutes later, "You don't know it yet, but you're going to marry me." It was his sense of freedom that had drawn her. Of course, he would jump on a grenade if he wanted to. Now he was a war hero.

The nine men he had saved appeared one at a time or in pairs, always in dress uniform, presented themselves with great formality and told her their stories, turning the Marine dress cap in their big hands and sitting forward on the edge of the sofa. Then, very likely, the man next door in the duplex would knock and say, "The Missus thought you might like this," and it would be an upside-down cake or a pot of Brunswick stew or half a lamb roast. Then the Marine would be persuaded to stay. Life for Marcia Mae at that point entered a kind of beautiful vacuum. The woman next door cooked herself crazy, the sun shone, the flowers bloomed, the men Red had saved all fell in love with her, the car Red had left ran like a dream.

She was out on the beach for a picnic one night with the ninth and last one. The sun had set far out over the ocean, and she said, "Now it will go on to Tarawa, and shine on the beach there and the sea and the little bit of jungle with the palm trees, just exactly the way it was shining when Red blew himself up." So the ninth man said, "Who told you the sun was shining?" She couldn't remember. "It was rainy," said the Marine, "with a heavy wind, the tail of a typhoon, we kept saying. Things were confused. I kept thinking I had forgotten something. It was hard to do the simplest thing. Salt water blew down my back. I was sitting by O'Donnell in the LCI coming in, and I said, 'There's salt water down my back, for Christ's sake,' and he said, 'Mine, too.'" After a time he said to Marcia Mae, "I don't see what difference it makes whether he got blown up in the sun or in the rain." She said, "I don't see why either, but it does." She asked him, "When are you going home?" "It's like I told you," he said, "I don't want to leave you ever at all." "Yes," she said, "but think of what you've got back home," because she had heard all this from eight before him, and knew exactly how to impress it on him. "There *is* the wife and kids," he said. "I guess responsibility is what you might call it." "I think you might," she agreed.

With the illusion of the sunlit explosion, her last hold on a dream vanished too. Her husband's valor was extensively publicized and she found that the woman next door was not the only one eager to do things for her. She accepted a free business course, got good jobs one after another, keeping them only so long as they interested her. She was twice engaged, but her enthusiasm waned decidedly each time.

One day she came back to Lacey.

Now that she was very near the end of telling Duncan Harper everything she could remember of her years away, she wondered what would happen next. Walking, she came from the woods into open pasture, took off the skirt that had shielded her legs from scratches and some idea about snakes, and threw it over her head for protection against the July afternoon sun. As she came down to cross the branch by one of the many small fords the cattle made, she heard footsteps approaching from a path hidden in trees. She withdrew along the sandy stream, concealing herself in a thicket that came down into the water.

A Negro boy came into view, carrying a molasses bucket full of blackberries in either hand. She watched the innocent gliding white of his eyeball. The tin bucket touched sunlight. He stepped straight into the stream; water sucked and sloshed into the diamond-shaped cut-out places in his rubber boots. The rich black fruit lay piled above the buckets' mouths, but the boy's easy stride held every berry safe. She knew the way of a wood enough to know he could not possibly see her. How was it he made her feel that he knew she was there?

She waited till his footsteps died quite away on the roll of pasture behind her. Then for motion there was only a buzzard, high up, asleep on the air, and for sound a cricket that woke, wound once, then drowsed again. Every leaf, grass blade, and twigged arm of brush seemed hushed in contemplation of the heat, and motion went so against this prevalence that it took a penalty: she was wet with sweat and trembling when she gained the top of the bluff and saw the car waiting for her where the old road forked. Black spots danced before her eyes. When she saw no one inside, she gasped.

Then Duncan called to her. To escape so much hot metal he had gone a short distance away to the edge of the bluff and was sitting in the shade of an old beech tree. He had taken off his coat and rolled up his sleeves. Sun through the narrow leaves speckled his arms and turned the hairs golden. She came to him and he drew her down and close to him with one arm.

"You're shaking. What's the matter?"

"I thought I would have a sunstroke." Their voices had fallen at once to whispers.

They clung together; kissing, their heads sank against the tree trunk. At last she pulled apart from him and straightened, saying, "How awful in this weather. It makes me feel like a bitch."

"You looked worried when you came up the path. I was watching you."

"Cissy has been baiting me again, the disgusting child! You can't tell me she doesn't know I see you. Coming through the pasture I heard a colored boy and hid from him. Then when I saw the car without you in it, I thought at first it must be someone else's car and we'd be trapped."

"You're having a hard day."

She broke a twig between her fingers. "I don't actually feel guilty myself. I feel that other people are trying to make me say I'm wrong whether I think so or not. I've always hated that about Lacey. They all know how right they are. Anybody who disagrees is wrong. Why shouldn't I see you? Who else is there in the world I'd want to talk to? If we want to meet for dinner right uptown in the café and sit there till closing time, whose business is it to have any opinion about it?"

He did not mention whose business it could be said to be, but only observed, "It might be a little hard to convince anybody, sure enough, that the only thing between us was conversation."

She almost flared up at him; but the rueful humor in his tone was too familiar and dear, and what he said was true. She laughed in spite of herself.

"Oh, Duncan, I do love you. I know you love me, even if you won't tell me so."

A cricket wound a dry spiral of sound into the heat. She was forever coming at him in a new way with this question. She raised her eyes to his and caught him watching her with the worried, removed look people have for sick children.

"I knew you had to see me, Marcia Mae. I knew that all along."

"You're going to make it out you were only doing your duty!" She hurled down a handful of broken twigs. "You're the most dishonest person I've ever known."

"All right, just suppose I said, Yes, I love you, I'll never leave you! What next? What would you want me to do about it?"

"Well—" She hesitated. "I never thought we could be happy staying here. Beyond that—" She made a little gesture. "I don't want to try to run your life for you."

He laughed. "You just want me to leave my family and home and business. Beyond that I'm perfectly free."

"Nobody made you find me that Sunday in the woods! Nobody made you show up today, no, nor any other day!"

They fell unhappily silent.

She spread out her wrap-around skirt and lay on it face downward, propped on her elbows. She pulled up grass, clearing a little bare space to draw in with a stick.

"How is Jimmy Tallant?" she inquired.

"About the same. It's touch and go. I stopped by the hospital this morning and they let me in to talk to him for a minute. He still says some strange white man shot him."

"Everybody thinks it was that Negro. Even the Negroes think so. Jonas told me."

"Well, I don't think so," said Duncan.

"You think it was some white man Jimmy Tallant never saw before and nobody has ever seen since?"

"I think Tallant and Grantham were up to their necks in crooked business. It could have been any number of people."

"The first person there was Tinker, wasn't it? What does she say?"

"Just what she always said. That she was at Dozer's when he ran in and said Jimmy had been shot. Nobody was with Jimmy when Tinker got to him. Bud Grantham contends that Dozer did it, though he didn't see it happen."

Marcia Mae wrote "Tinker" on the bare space of ground, then erased it with her fist.

Duncan ground out a cigarette under his heel. "She'd tell me anything she knew."

"Listen!" said Marcia Mae and looked up from writing "Duncan" on the ground. "I thought I heard someone."

"There's nothing. You're nervous today."

"I always expect people to jump out of trees on us. I always feel better inside."

He stood up presently, knocking the dust from his trousers, and put down his hand to her. "We'll go inside then."

They walked together up a disused, shady path which gave on an open space with a deserted Negro house. The gate was broken in, the yard weed-grown; gigantic purplish-crimson Negro plants, the kind called "prince feathers," plumed above the steps and the floor of the sagging porch. Marcia Mae had found the house and had first brought them there. If they were happier going down the familiar path together than they had been so far that day, it was perhaps because they had come to equal terms in a common attraction.

Marcia Mae realized this, and wondered if he came with her only to give her, generously, this sense of an equality they had lost. The thought depressed her; she forgot it, but it returned again when she lay with a hand under her head on the little pile of cotton left over from last year's picking—they had found it in the only room of the house not full of wasps. The shadows had lengthened, streaking the bare dusty floor. They had not spoken for a long time; then Duncan turned abruptly to her from the window, demanding, "Why did you leave me? *Why?*"

There was finality in his voice; this time he would have to know. Looking toward him in surprise, she understood that his need to see her had been as great as hers for him. She saw his searching baffled eyes and knew that impossible as it seemed, she would have to try to answer him.

32 *What She Remembered*

AT THE TIME, ten years before, her reasons had all seemed very clear, but now there was no one answer she could give him. She could see what she had done only in terms of what she remembered, and she did all she could, which was to start remembering again.

"That summer," she said. "That awful summer."

"It was terrible, yes."

"My brother died."

"Everett. Early in June."

"We had to put off the wedding."

"I remember."

"There is one thing I have to say that nobody has ever said." She sat up. "It's better Everett died. Nobody would come out and say so, but everybody thought it. You wouldn't say so either."

He winced, turning away. "If everybody does know things like that, what's the good of saying them? It seems kinder not to."

"Kind! Duncan, I saw with my own eyes how glad Daddy was when Everett died. Mother felt it, and all the love she'd had for Everett, the weak one, her only son, turned into hate for Jason. She was left living with the man who'd killed him—"

"Killed him?"

"Wanted him dead. People hear wishes as loud as guns."

"You think it was all your father's fault, the way Everett was?"

"No, it was Mother's too. They pulled him two ways. He was sensitive and lazy and clever and he never found himself. Daddy bought him a gun. He made him go deer hunting. They stood on a stand together in the freezing cold and mist from before daylight on till ten and when the deer came by, Daddy shot and said 'Shoot' to Everett. Everett was funny when he told me about it. He said he knew the gun had to go off, so somehow or other he jerked the trigger. He said the miracle was that he didn't hit Daddy. He said he couldn't have come within a mile of the deer. But when it fell, Daddy, to cheer him up, said, 'You got him, Son, you got him!' Then he dragged

him out to where the deer had fallen and was heaving to rise
and run again with one leg shattered and the heart torn but
still pumping out the hot blood. Daddy kept a death grip on
Everett to keep him from running away, then he slit the deer's
throat with his knife and shoved Everett down to bathe his
face in the blood. The old hunter's ritual, you know. Everett
saw the big soft eyes veiling over, and the shattered bone in
the leg poking up and Daddy's hand coming at him with big
globs of blood smoking on it. He began to vomit and say, 'I
didn't do it, you did it, you did it!' He broke away and ran. He
met some of the other hunters coming in to see the kill. They
laughed about it. Daddy was humiliated. He told everybody
that Everett was sick and he took him home that night. Everett
did get sick, as it turned out. Mother stowed him away under
hot-water bottles. He was sick all during Christmas. His fever
nearly broke the thermometer. Daddy wouldn't come in the
room. When Everett lay in bed recuperating, he cut out little
bits of velvet and silks and taffetas from Grandmother's rag bag
and made Cissy a wonderful doll. It was the prettiest doll I ever
saw, a Turkish doll with long balloon pants bound in silver at
the ankles and a wicked black mustache. And a fez. Daddy saw
Cissy with it and said, 'Where'd you get that, Baby?' She said,
'Everett made it for me.' He reached out his hand to take it.
'Don't you touch it,' Mother said. I was there. I saw it all. I
felt sorry for all of them, but I didn't understand. Now that I
understand it, I don't feel anything any more. Once you know
whodunit, you don't care about the book any longer. They
killed him. I understand it. He was miserable. I think it's better
he's dead."

"I had the impression," said Duncan, "that Everett died of
bronchial pneumonia."

"Yes, but they had set up the pattern long ago. When anybody rejected him, he got sick. Mother would nurse him. The
last time was your fault, actually."

"Me! What on earth do you mean?"

"He had finished college. He was supposed to go to work,
find a job, *do* something. Life was closing in on him, tightening
over him like a fist. He wandered out of one room and into
another and read in stuffy corners. The summer got hotter and

hotter. Daddy wouldn't look at him. I was too kind to him. Grandmother was knitting him some Argyle socks. Mother planned the meals just for him.

"He used to ride around in the car with us at night. I thought he enjoyed that. We'd make him quote us poetry. He never seemed to want to go home.

"He didn't want to leave us alone because he didn't want us to make love. He was in love with you, Duncan. Now don't deny you knew it."

He did not answer.

"He was out in the garden alone," she continued, "or out near the sundial beyond the cedars or in first one room and then the other where the sun had left for the day—there are lots of rooms in our house—I can't tell you just how many there are right off, because when I'm away I remember some at times and others at other times—but it does seem to me when Everett died he took with him some rooms I can't find any more. He had an imagination and it was always going—imagining, imagining. That's different from thinking. It pulls everybody off base, makes them nervous. When it's going on in one room, the room you're in looks dead and plain because that other one is so alive. So he drank too much, standing on the back porch sipping whisky through the long sweet awful dusks, and read every book not only in our house but in the library and all he could borrow from other people in town. I think it must have been the day he put down the last one that we had all gone away. I was in Stark for fittings on my trousseau, and Mother and your mother were up at the church to talk about decorations. The house was empty and you were in your empty house. He got up and went to you."

"I never told that to a soul, Marcia Mae, not even you."

"He told me himself when his fever got high. He kept saying, 'Duncan hates me now, I know Duncan hates me,' and I would say, 'Why, Everett?' and he would say, 'I saw him in his house and now he hates me.' When he died and I knew Daddy was glad, that was when I tried to get you to run away with me. Do you remember?"

"We were sitting in the yard," he recalled, "in that double swing where Everett used to read books all afternoon. My

mother came up the walk and went inside. You said that was
the fourth time she'd been to call since the funeral, then you
said you weren't going to be nice about it, that the reason she
came was that she loved being in with the Standsbury family.
You said you were sick of everybody agreeing to cover up the
plain truth by being nice to one another. Then you said we had
to leave home."

"It was a day a lot like this one: hot, shady, beautiful, still.
The lawn was lovely and the house was quiet. You could even
think that death was something like poetry. When the swing
went back I thought, With all this horror in people how can
things look so beautiful? and when the swing went forward I
thought, It is so beautiful maybe the horror isn't real, and then
I put my foot on the ground and stopped the swing, because I
saw them both, both together, the beauty and the horror, like
one gorgeous rotten fruit. That was when I knew we'd have to
leave. I had an absolute conviction of it."

"The only thing you didn't consider was that your having an
absolute conviction of something did not mean that I would
have it too. You threw it all at me at once."

"Just as it came to me, right in the swing."

"You wanted me to sell the grocery store and my property,
and we would take the money and go West, take one of the
coaching jobs I kept getting letters about, wait till my draft
number was called. Then you would follow me around to army
camps or, if I went overseas, you would get a defense job and
wait for me to come back and then—and then what? I forget."

"Oh, just that we'd start from nothing but ourselves, clean,
out West somewhere. We couldn't stay in the South and be
free. In the South it's nothing but family, family. We couldn't
breathe even, until we left. I explained it all. When I finished
you said, 'Do you guess it's too soon after the funeral for us to
go to a nice cool movie?'"

"At that point you jumped up, slapped me in the face, and
walked into the house. From then on I never had any peace.
You said we had to leave, that I didn't know a bad thing when
I saw it."

"You were very patient. You said you were all your mother
had, that your property was all here, that Jason had already
turned over some of his business to you, that he would make

over more in time, that we would have a house of our own
—way across town all by ourselves—imagine! You said I was
just upset over Everett." She paused until he looked at her. "If
there's anything these ten years prove, Duncan, I hope at least
you know now that *I was not just upset over Everett*."

He did not reply to her vigor, her assertiveness. He came to
her and held her close to him. "I failed to understand you. Is
that what you're saying?"

"It wasn't only me you failed to understand. It was everything."

But she had softened. She studied the lines around his eyes,
running back into the boyish fuzz of hair that his blondness
kept, shading out a more definite hairline. She pressed up the
skin of his brow and watched the long horizontal lines disap-
pear, and then as her hand relaxed saw their inevitable return.

"Before he died," she went on finally, "Everett thought there
were soldiers out by the summerhouse. They were in ragged
clothes, he said, all gathered around somebody or something
on the ground, and talking, until one left and ran toward the
house. This was a hot afternoon. It had threatened a storm at
dinner, but it blew over, then things seemed drier and stiller
than before. Flies had come into the house. The soldier went
past the corner of the porch. Everett kept asking where he'd
gone. Grandmother said that her mother told how during the
Civil War some soldiers had stopped on the lawn. One of them
was sick and they were afraid he had cholera. They wouldn't
bring him in the house, but one of them finally came to ask for
water and food. She couldn't recall the rest of the story."

She said: "The day I really left you, I didn't have any idea
I was doing it. I walked out of the house just before the afternoon broke. Those were long days after Everett died. It
seemed that the heat would never climb high enough, satisfy
itself enough, to start down again. Mother had to start taking
shots for her headaches. Daddy kept right on calling you in
to talk business. We had let them put the wedding off three
months. There was a war in Europe. You said we couldn't hurt
the family now, we ought to help them. Mother was asleep in
a pitch-black room. I thought I was so nervous because maybe
I was getting the curse. I walked down through the cedars and
out into the sun. I had not walked to town since I was a child.

People looked at me on the street without speaking, it seemed so odd to see Marcia Mae Hunt walking. I had forgotten how broken the old sidewalks were, with cow hooves printed in them. I thought I would buy a Coke at the drugstore and walk back home, then I saw at the drugstore that the Greyhound bus was in. It was going East. So I got on it and rode over to Stark.

"As I was drinking another Coke at the Stark drugstore, I saw a sign up that said there was a dance at Willett Hill for the members of the armed forces. It said the bus would stop at the schoolhouse at seven to pick up the girls from Stark. I drank the Coke and went to the movies and ate popcorn. Then I ate a hamburger in the café. And a piece of coconut pie. I was just on time for the bus to the dance. The other girls were all dressed up in low-cut peasant blouses. They had artificial flowers pinned in their hair and too much black lipstick on. They also wore fancy strapped sandals and had their toenails painted. But they were mainly country girls, you know, and hadn't done any of this in too wise a way. They seemed to feel sorry for me, because I had on a tailored cotton skirt and shirt and scarcely any make-up. Finally one of them pulled a spare artificial flower out of her bag and offered it to me. It was a red poppy and smelled of dime-store powder. I thought at first I would put it in my hair if it killed me, but then I knew I couldn't. Whatever I meant by going off like that, it wasn't for a pack of country girls to call me 'Hun' and offer me Dentyne.

"At the dance they all left me and herded in little bunches on one side of the room and giggled, waiting for the soldiers to come ask them to dance. All the soldiers, instead, began to ask me to dance. For one thing, I was alone; for another, I was a blonde. It never hurt anything, being a blonde. The little soldiers were sweet, touching somehow, like Confederate soldiers are, and I remembered the soldiers Everett saw on the lawn, though you didn't believe he saw them. We argued and argued, you remember? It was Jimmy Tallant who said, 'For Christ's sake, Duncan, let her believe it if she wants to.' And you said, 'I don't care if *she* believes it; she wants *me* to believe it too.'"

Duncan recalled, "And Tallant yelled, 'Well, believe it too then, for Christ's sake!' We were all over at Stark at the café, and all a little tight on beer."

"Tinker said, 'I believe it, Marcia Mae.'" After a silence, Marcia Mae added, "She has a soft voice."

"Yes, she has."

"Will Tallant live or die?"

"They still can't say."

"I looked for you that summer, Duncan. I looked and looked. I trailed every scent like a bloodhound and bayed all night at empty trees. I wanted, passionately, for you to understand. If I could have showed you once why we had to get away, that they were turning our love into a complicated family thing, that they had killed Everett and oh, you kept going to talk business with Daddy and saying that Everett was out of his head with high fever, and you didn't, couldn't, wouldn't understand!"

"I suppose Red O'Donnell understood perfectly," said Duncan.

"That's funny," she said, "I never once expected him to. He was a Yankee."

She said: "He wasn't even supposed to be at the dance. He was a Marine on a three-day pass from the Pensacola base, determined to hitch-hike as far through the South as time would allow, any direction he got a ride. He had waited an hour in Willett Hill for a ride and when nobody stopped he kept reading the sign for the soldiers' dance. Finally he thought, If nobody comes along for another fifteen minutes, I'll go to the dance. He went and there I was. We called it destiny.

"We left the dance. We went to an all-night café and tourist court out at the highway junction. We kept drinking whisky in a booth. I kept getting him to talk to me. He might have been a creature from Mars. He had no consciousness of families, small towns, roots, ties, or any sort of custom. I expected lightning to strike him. I had always taken so much for granted. I had never gone with anyone but you. I thought I knew everything, but here was someone unconcerned with everything I knew. I won't deny remembering anything about it, though some of it was always awfully vague, but I woke in a cabin of the tourist court at three A.M., cold sober, saying, 'Marcia Mae Hunt, what are you doing here?' I did exactly what I told myself to do and came straight home. On the bus. The driver let me off at the corner.

"It was a warm night with a moon, very sweet. I remember it so well. I was tired and the house had never looked so good. I thought, Well, what a crazy thing I did. White houses in the South in the summer at night, with all the big trees so dark and deep, they float, you know, and the sweet air that comes through the window and over your bed—

"Well, unfortunately, there was a light on upstairs. Mother was worried; she had thought I was out with you, but you had called around eight, then some lady in town called and asked Mother why I went to Stark on the bus and an old friend of Mother's from Stark called and asked what I was doing over there in the picture show by myself eating popcorn. Then Mother called you back and promised to make me call you the minute I came in. All this that night. The next morning a cousin from Willett Hill telephoned to say she had heard but could not believe that I had come to the soldier's dance *alone*, and by afternoon you and Daddy had had a conference about just how upset was I really over Everett's death, and afterwards I saw you and said, 'Let's get out of here, let's go now.' You said, 'Marcia Mae, I'm pretty damn sick of your carrying on this way.' You said, 'You might as well realize that I'm not going one step anywhere, and you aren't either.' Mother was calling out of the bedroom to remind me for the fourth time that I hadn't been uptown to get the mail—she still didn't think it proper for her to go about. She had a great greed for sympathy notes and kept getting them from old boy friends. Daddy called at me from the library, 'Are you going to run uptown for your mother, or do I have to do it?' And I looked at you and knew you thought there was nothing on the face of the earth that ought to stand in the way of my going uptown for the mail. I despised you, Duncan, for the first and last time. It was an awful feeling.

"So I went uptown to get the mail.

"Red O'Donnell was standing out in front of the drugstore where the bus had dropped him. He had sweated out his only two shirts and had bought a plaid cotton sports shirt. Westerners are like that; they'll wear whatever they feel like wearing. They think it's nobody's business what they have on. I was never so glad to see anyone. He could have been in overalls.

I thought the best thing I'd ever done was get drunk and go to a tourist court with a strange Marine. I thought, At least he's free. I said to myself, I wish I were free like that. Then I thought, I love him."

It was not clear at what point twilight had commenced its serious summer ritual. Already the shadowy, dusty room seemed a reflected place and silence a spell impossible to break by any means close at hand. Then they heard the bump against the door.

They had already decided what they would do if anybody came along. They had discovered a small windowless room, a storeroom perhaps, or closet, set between the two larger rooms. Marcia Mae was to close herself inside there while Duncan got rid of whoever it was.

When he heard the sound he was instantly on his feet, bringing her up with him, and as she showed alarmingly no inclination to stir, he pushed her toward the little low door. The sound came again, but louder and with more intention, a thud and shove against the door's lower half, as if someone struck a knee there. Duncan walked directly forward then, removed the wooden peg from the latch, and opened the door.

It was a dog, a mongrel hound the color of the Mississippi River, whose hide was nothing but a coat of paint over the skeleton, and whose eyes were totally prepared for human life, understanding at one time both the giant succulent unplucked hambone and the dishpan full of scalding water. The hindquarters were set low at a bias, alert to dodge and flee; while one forepaw rested bravely, even handsomely, and the other was lifted in all the gentility of prayer. His nose had pushed the door.

"It's just a dog," he turned to call to her, but saw she had not moved to hide. He flushed with annoyance at her, but before he could speak they both grew suddenly ashamed; so he stepped outside and, sitting on the door sill, began to coax the dog back to him.

The animal came in low to the ground, the tail wagging between his legs. Speaking quietly, Duncan was at last allowed to stroke the low head. Marcia Mae sat down on the sill beside him, tucking her clothes together. "He's shaking all over, poor thing," she said compassionately, but when her hand moved the dog leaped away, and would not return, though he longed to.

"You frightened him," said Duncan. "You put out your hand too fast. Here, boy. Here." He whistled softly. "He probably lived here," he went on, "else why would he be trying to come into a house where there isn't any smell of food? Probably when the family left here to go to Detroit and work in the dee-fense plant, they had to leave him."

"Yes," she said, "only that would be so long ago."

"They say they don't forget," said Duncan. "It's the hound blood."

"We sit here mourning over a damn nigger dog," she said, "as though we had nothing better to bother us."

The dog crept halfway in and lay down, observing everything about them. A little more and he would have belonged to them. When it grew as dark outside as it had been inside the cabin, they walked back to the car. The dog hovered, following at greater and greater distances, until their departure left him alone with his hour's bewilderment of heart.

33 *The Way Back Home*

WHEN HE drove back to Lacey, Duncan did not go immediately home. He noticed with relief that his mother's house looked empty, so he stopped there and went inside, walking into the unlocked hallway and back to his old room, the one she kept just as he had always had it. Duncan was an only child.

The room was almost dark, but he did not switch on the lamp. He sat down in the straight chair at his old high-school desk, his head lowered. There was always with Marcia Mae the problem of her vividness: whether she fell out of the sky at him or climbed up a hill to meet him, it took a while for him to right himself.

From the empty Negro house she had returned to the car with him and had sat for a time on the front seat beside him. At last she said, "Duncan, I cannot bear this sneaking and hiding and deceiving."

"You don't see how it is."

"No, I don't," she said. "One other thing I can't bear is to say goodbye."

She jumped out and ran away down the hill before he could say a word. His first impulse had been to follow her, but he did not quite obey it; then it was too late. He had watched her hair, combed simply back behind her ears, toss from side to side as she ran. He could see it still. She had not looked back once.

He faced it now, admitting that what they had had was over; that they had reached the end of what they had to tell. He wondered if he was any nearer answering what he had asked himself so often: "Why did she leave me?" She had told him, certainly, everything she knew.

He tried to bring all of it into one statement. She had left him because he would not run away with her and be free from the evil she saw in her family and in the whole South. It wouldn't do to think, Marcia Mae is just that way: emotional and sudden and proud. She did see something different from what he saw, and had tried in vain to show it to him; like pointing out something on the edge of a distant wood, the effort had come to nothing. He did not believe that the Hunts were worse than anybody else, or that you escaped from anything when you left Lacey and the South. Still it was what she saw and what he did not see that had torn them apart.

He remembered his father, a patient, soft-spoken man, trying to read the paper after supper while his great-uncle Phillip walked up and down the room saying that the New Deal was unconstitutional. "I tell you, Henry, I tell you," he had cried to Duncan's father, "I can endure poverty, I can endure starvation. Let ten thousand depressions sweep down upon us! I take my stand upon the Constitution! That man is promising bread, jobs, and easy money in return for our freedom! Do you realize it, Henry? Do you realize what this means?"

"How can you stand it every night?" Duncan heard his mother ask once while his father stood in his nightshirt, about to switch the light off. "If you try to stop it, he only gets worse," he said. "If you really cross him, he'll move out again." Uncle Phillip had done them that way once because Duncan's mother had twice forgotten to send his linen to the washerwoman. "Woman!" he had risen from the table announcing, "the same roof shall shelter us no longer!" He had moved down to the hotel. Duncan's father let him go, refused to discuss him even in the family, and three weeks later in the store asked him home for supper. He came meekly, this terror of children uptown on the square, possibly driven on by the strings the hotel cook left in the beans. Mrs. Harper, standing at the front window with her little boy, said, "Oh, mercy, your father's got him back. Look how well your father walks," she said with pride. "He's a gentleman." They watched while Henry opened the gate for Uncle Phillip, who leaned back on his walking stick and huffed a moment from the climb. "I do believe that Uncle Phillip's getting old," said Mrs. Harper wistfully. "Run put another plate on the table."

There was never any doubt that it was in Duncan's father's mild grasp that the stability of the family lay. He had died when Duncan was in high school, surviving Uncle Phillip by two years. Though he had married late, a much younger lady, he was still not an old man. It was judged that he had never been very strong. Their last two years as a family had been unquestionably happy. Released from the burden of Uncle Phillip, Henry Harper spread himself amiably among old friends. He was proud of his fine-looking boy who was attracting notice everywhere the way he played football. It amused him that Jason Hunt sometimes stopped in the store to talk. Though he never said so, he was conscious that back in the old days Hunts used to come to town on Saturday in a wagon, wearing shoes for the first time that week. But Jason had been a smart one: he had set out to marry a Standsbury, and he had done it. His daughter was pretty enough; everybody said how nice she looked with Duncan.

One day in the early fall Duncan had come home from football practice and been surprised to see his father's hat and cane on the hall tree. He found his father lying down. He lay in his shirtsleeves and suspenders, his button collar open at the throat. "I felt a little tired at the store, son. I wanted to rest a little before supper." "Do you need anything? Are you sick?" "No, just tired. Where's your mother?" "It must be Auxiliary day." "It always is," said Henry Harper, and smiled. This was a joke they shared. Duncan went back to the kitchen for a drink of water. From the back porch he looked out on a familiar calm stretch of yard, dropping down to a barn, a chicken yard, and a small orchard. He smelled the dusty stir of autumn in the twilight—it always said football to him and school opening —and there was that other quality beneath the eagerness and color that tried to speak and could not, so he had never known what it was, except that it was sad. He heard his mother come in, and presently she called him from the bedroom. His father had just died. So ever after he knew that the name of the other quality in autumn was death, and that it was sad, but only sad —there was nothing terrible about it. He did not believe that he and his father would ever have quarreled.

In what small light was left he looked about him, noting without further interest his cabinet of football trophies, the big handsomely bound book of newspaper clippings resting on a special shelf. In the closet he found another book he had suddenly remembered; it was really a large folder, and inside were crumbling samples of insect life, butterflies, moths, and such like, mounted on stiff sheets and labeled. This had been his Boy Scout project one summer and some of the lettering, he recognized, had been put there by Tinker Taylor, who had been helping him. "I declare," his mother said one day after Tinker had gone home, "that girl is just crazy about you. That child!"

Maybe football hadn't been such a good thing after all, he thought, taking comfort from the careful, loving uprightness of the lettering that she had done for him. He put up the book in its right place, switched out the lamp, and left, passing in the hall the door to the room where his father had died. His mother still had not come home. Maybe this too was Auxiliary day.

He considered that he knew himself by certain things, by their certain manner of being themselves that identified them with his deepest self. He wanted, positively now, to go home to his wife and children.

Duncan Harper was a citizen of Lacey, that was it. Just answering a question about love could not alter this fact. Just saying "Come away" could not change it. It was his strongest and final quality.

34 *What Tinker Knew*

HE FOUND his family all together in the kitchen. Tinker was getting supper and talking to both children at once—they were forever carrying on conversations with her on two completely different subjects, each unaware that the other was speaking at all. Cotton, who was standing near the door, was interrupted in a long story by the sense of someone near him. He looked up and said, "Hello, Daddy."

"You're getting tall as I am," Duncan said. "How tall are you?"

"No, precious," said Tinker to Patsy, who was sticking her finger in the biscuit dough. "It isn't good to eat."

"Tinker, I—"

She glanced up. The wooden spoon continued to move rapidly. She was the instant before turning the dough out to knead.

"People have been calling you all afternoon. If you look on the phone table."

He lied automatically. "I was up at Mama's."

She stopped dead. "Why don't you move up there? Why don't you eat up there too? Isn't her cooking better than mine?"

"Hush, Tinker—the children. I want us to talk—I want to tell you—"

"Yes, the children," she said, louder than before. "See how they've grown. Can you think of their names?"

He crossed toward her, and at his approach she flinched and ran backward from him. It was when she released her hold on the spoon and pan that she seemed to turn wild.

"Tinker! Darling, listen—!"

"'Darling'! You've got me mixed up!"

The next step forward he took, she snatched an empty preserves jar from the shelf and hurled it at him, and after that a potato, which struck him painfully, just below the eye. Her hand seemed about to pick up a large knife, but just then she gasped, whirled, and dashed down the back steps into the dark. Patsy shrieked and ran after her, but the screen door whammed to in her face. She started wailing. Cotton only blenched and clung to the wall exactly where he stood, as though the house itself had tilted. Something boiled over on the stove. "Turn it off," his father told him, pointing him relentlessly into the cloud of steam, then he too ran out into the dark.

Tinker reached the barn ahead of Duncan and fled up into the loft. He tried to follow but two steps broke under his weight and the whole structure quivered flimsily. She crouched in the dark above him like a small animal run to its den. He could hear her breathing and see what looked to be the glint of her eyes. He was forced to remember how people said her mother one day had picked up and left old Gains because he wouldn't stop driving the Model T around and blowing the horn. She had taken Tinker and simply repossessed the house she had lived in as a child, was still in it. The town had therefore judged Mrs. Taylor crazy; they said she was "off."

And Tinker herself had run away home from the playground at recess because they'd laughed at the suit her mother had made for her from an old "costume." It was navy wool with big pearl buttons the size of moons. They had worked on it together, her mother teaching her to turn a hem, baste, and square a corner. All for nothing: it would not "do." She had run from their terrible laughter, and on the sidewalks heard for a long time, before she would stop or turn, a boy's steps running and a boy's voice: "Louise. Louise Taylor. Don't run so fast. Wait for me." He had taken her to the drugstore and they had had a Coca-cola, and people told them they ought to be in school. She had looked along the straw, down into the glass where the ice was fading color. "I think your dress is real pretty, Louise." Still sipping, she raised her eyes full to his, and before the straw could suck in the glass she was in love.

"I'm not going anywhere, Tinker. I'm never going to leave you. Whatever there's been is over now—over for good."

He could hear her breathing going on from the run, but couldn't know what she felt or but what she might launch a rusty piece of pitchfork in his face—no telling what was up there handy.

"You ran away another time, remember? I ran after you. I bought you a Coca-cola, remember? And Tinker, you remember the summer you helped me make the butterfly book? It's still up at Mama's. I found it today. I could still tell your handwriting. You were a lot of help."

He had made her cry. He could hear her snuffling like a puppy; she never cried out loud. When she stopped he said, "Louise?"

After a while she crawled to the edge of the loft and looked down into his face. "Duncan, there's something I never told you. You know the day Jimmy got shot? I had stopped to see him and four men from New Orleans came there. They wanted to put money in the race against you. There was somebody named Sam in charge and Pittman, Pilston, something like that, and another name I can't remember, and a boy named Wallace who had a gun."

She told him all she could think of.

"But where were you? How did you hear this?"

"There's a bedroom off the office where they were talking. Jimmy hid me in there." She shook some trash out of her hair. "I would have told you, but I thought it might help you. The last thing I've wanted to do lately was help you. I'm coming down now." She accomplished this without his help, straining every rotten step to the cracking point, though none broke.

"But Tinker, all this time, and you never told me. Don't you realize—"

"Duncan Harper, if you say another word about it, I'll go right straight up that ladder again, and I'll *never* come down."

When they returned to the house they found it tranquil. Kerney Woolbright, election-weary, thin as a string, was sitting in the living room.

"It sure gets my goat," he said as Duncan walked in, "that Jimmy Tallant, lying up in the hospital still having blood transfusions after two weeks and twice reported dying, has got more power in this damned election than you and me put together. He may be hiding Beck Dozer himself. I've shaken this county like a persimmon tree, and I can't find a single lead to who shot him if it wasn't Dozer, and you with everything you can do through the sheriff's office can't find out where Dozer must be hiding. That damn nigger-paper photo stares at me off every goddamn telephone pole. I tell you, Duncan, if we can't lay it on the line at the speaking Saturday, we're licked."

"It so happens something new has come to light," said Duncan. "I think I know who shot Tallant, and I think I can prove it before the Saturday speaking."

"You what? But who—?"

"I can tell you what it is, but not where I got it from. Relax while I call New Orleans, Kerney. I really think we've got this made."

Tinker discovered the children in the bedroom, being entertained by Bimbo, the colored boy who brought the buttermilk by in the evenings. He had found them sobbing in the kitchen, steam gushing up on the hot stove, and had not only saved the supper but had engrossed both them and himself in a long story:

"Man, he got the eyes like this here, and man, he got the long ole swored bill coming out like this, and all pebbled out with little bitty old fine sharp teefies—yo' daddy's razor *blade* ain't no sharper than what them teefies is. And he go zooming in the water when the big old fantail move—that's his motor —and every once in a while out of purey dee devilment he come up for air and he jump Ker-*flop*! and sound so loud that niggers picking cotton a mile off in the field looks up and says, 'You hear that? There jump that old mean garfish what's bigger than a mule.'"

Cotton, who was sitting on the floor listening with his mouth open, was relieved to see his mother appear in the door; but Patsy, whose eyes had grown enormous, whispered solemnly, "It's a great big garfish." She was seated on Bimbo's knee, and was staring into his face like a devotee before an idol, and indeed she was to worship him, all her childhood long.

35 *Jason Takes a Hand*

THE NEXT day was Friday, the day before the big political speaking, and Jason Hunt felt he had put things off as long as he could be expected to. From his office in the wing of his home, he put in a call for Kerney Woolbright and waited there for him, savoring the summer morning breeze and the smell of dew, which had bent the rich grass. He had a love for the country and could spend time with pleasure by watching simple details of it. This part of his property reminded him time and again of the country place where he was brought up. A gully was always a gully, but here and there vines mantled it: jackson vine, virginia creeper, ivy, honeysuckle, and at the rough points farther down the fall, trumpet vine and elderberry. Wisteria clothed his dying cedar; the mistletoe did not kill his oak, and storms, for all people told him of shallow roots, had yet to bring it down across his house. So when he closed his uptown office (he called it "retiring"), he had built an office here, adding one more wing to an already overgrown, haphazard house, setting himself above the wilder and least tended part of the grounds—the lawn his wife fretted over, where garden parties were held and guests strolled, was not visible to him here.

It was strange how his family, all within the same walls, had had a tendency to withdraw. Marcia Mae, her high room brooding abovestairs (he thought she woke at night and smoked), his dead son's room that nobody entered but guests, Cissy (he smiled) tucked away back of the side porch with her tester bed she had begged to have and a jungle of scented jars and jugs nobody dared to touch. And Nan, all silken, touching a glass stopper to her ears—she kept her room too hot in winter and must darken it when her headaches struck and took her off with them into suffering none of them would ever know. Only his mother-in-law's room stood free of all uncomfortable privacies. Her bed was covered with the patchwork quilt, the old-timey gaudy kind that he liked; her room was closed only for her afternoon nap. Otherwise, her doors were open all day long, and even at night, as long as the light burned and she lay propped on pillows in a lacy jacket to read first the Bible and then *The Ladies' Home Journal*, nobody stopped to knock.

Jason contrived to spend part of every day alone with her, and sometimes they did not speak. In his younger days he had considered her a burden. Now he felt simply that he had won through to her, and not only to her but to his office with everything just as he liked it, and to his yard and trees that seemed blessed in an Old Testament way, they flourished so. He could think now of his son without bitterness and of his wife without anger. He had learned you could not rule. Neither, however, could you withdraw entirely so long as God left you about. From experience judgment grew, and must emerge to give the touch where it seemed needed most. This he believed.

From his vantage point at the window, he observed the young man hastening up the walk. His face was earnest and his step firm. Jason recalled that he had also watched Duncan Harper approach to his summons, and had always discovered a slight irritation in his big indolent bearing—as on the football field, Duncan never seemed to hurry. Facing Duncan's steady eyes wherein responsibility sat large, Jason had explained the intricate Hunt affairs and felt in the boy an even deeper lack. It was not that Duncan did not understand when Jason expounded business, only that he would have given Jason exactly the same attention if a country store or a sawmill had been at stake. He had no more sense of greed than a child had lust; not that Jason approved of greed, but to have at least the sense of it seemed a proof of manly thinking and developed a firmer hand on the reins.

But this second boy was a different matter. Cissy had played the family role where Marcia Mae had not deigned: she "kept him guessing" as every Southern family advises, and politics dazzled before him in the same maddening sort of game. The boy was thin and walked with a stoop and someday soon now the knife-blade wrinkle between the eyes would not go away, even when he smiled. The first hurdles were always the hardest. Jason felt, in short, a likeness to himself in Kerney Woolbright that he had never felt in Duncan Harper. Yet he wished to proceed with caution, for the two were friends and were known as running mates. What had drawn this up? Young political ideals, brave things to say about Negroes? Or love of his two daughters?

Jason stripped a cigar and pared it in the wastebasket. He had short attractive hands, browned by the outdoors, and he met Kerney's practiced political shake with as true a clasp as Winfield County could offer.

"Sit down, boy, and talk to me a little. An old man gets to feel all out of it nowadays."

"Sorry I'm late. I came from town as soon as they told me."

"It's a bad day to bother you, I'm afraid. Four days before the primary."

"The funny thing is, sir, I was coming by to talk to you today. I was about to call you up."

"Well, then! Great minds, and all that."

"Yes, sir, but I've been wanting to come for some time and talk things over. The trouble has been that Duncan has been busy and I've been busy, so we've had no time to talk to one another. I finally saw him last night. We're pretty well committed to taking a similar stand on things. I felt I had to talk with him before I could see you and know I had the right answers."

"And now do you know?"

Kerney smiled. "I think so. Yes, sir."

"It has seemed a little odd to me," said Jason, toying with a useless sea-shell inkstand from Coral Gables, Florida, which somebody in the family had seen fit to surprise him with, "that you and Duncan have insisted on this partnership, no matter how friendly you may be personally. You're running for the state senate, he for county sheriff. The territories are not the same, and the two offices are bound to involve different kinds of issues."

"That's perfectly true, sir. I've been aware of that all along. But Duncan and I agree there are certain large issues abroad in the state and that every politician had better face them. Duncan and I are the same kind of folks, you might say. We're young; we're college graduates; we think we represent a type that ought to get into Mississippi politics on every level. It would be natural for people to associate us anyway. We think we're only taking a fair advantage to join forces on every forward-looking policy."

"Umm. And the certain large issues you mentioned, Kerney. We're back where we were last winter, aren't we? Right after Travis died, I suggested we work Duncan in as the sheriff appointment. You said then it was Negroes and the prohibition laws that concerned you two most. You said that Duncan wanted a fair deal for Negroes, and that he wanted to shut down Grantham and Tallant. Is that right?"

"Yes, sir, it—"

"Well, Kerney. Tallant is shut down. There's no doubt about it."

They were silent. Kerney sat looking at his hands and his brow flushed slowly.

"Tallant is shot to pieces, sir. Is that what you mean to say?"

"I couldn't help thinking it," said Jason.

"Mr. Jason, if you're implying that Duncan's policies are

responsible for Jimmy Tallant getting shot, I think you're being unfair. I—"

"I never meant to imply anything, Kerney. I merely remarked
that one can not help thinking about Tallant now when prohibition is mentioned, just as when you mention Negroes now,
one can hardly help thinking about the Dozer Negro who may
have tried to murder him."

"Sir, there's one thing you may not know yet. This is in
strictest confidence. Duncan and I have learned that some men
from a New Orleans gambling syndicate were up here to see
Tallant the afternoon of the shooting. We know there was a
quarrel."

"How do you know that?"

"Duncan says he is not at liberty to say."

"Well, what is being done?"

"They will be located in New Orleans if possible, questioned
and arraigned if possible for attempted manslaughter."

"A slippery question," said Jason. "Ferreting gangsters out
of New Orleans to answer for a small-time fracas in the back-
woods. Even if they were up here that day, what makes you so
sure they did it?"

"The Negro—"

"The nigger ran. As far as I can see, Kerney, somebody has
yet to run after him."

"But Tallant insists the Negro is innocent."

"He would naturally do that. It's always galled Jimmy that
his daddy was the one that shot Dozer's father."

"Yes, and Duncan feels for that very reason that Beck Dozer
would never have fired on Tallant. There's been a tie between
them for years. Duncan says they've kept each other company
about the past."

"Interesting," said Jason. "But now what?"

"Duncan believes that Beck will come in and give himself
up for custody until he can be proved innocent. He believes
that Beck will take the risk and have the trust. He thinks if
Beck won't do this, no Negro in the world will. I'm tempted to
defend him myself if the case should go to court." He stopped
for breath; his eyes were eager. "If the New Orleans lead yields
anything, then Tallant and Grantham will be ruined for good."

Jason said, "You're clear in your head, of course, what is going to happen to Duncan at the polls?"

"You mean he's going to lose?"

"People want to vote for Duncan, Kerney, but the fact is that this sort of thing is not going down. You know that, don't you, when you associate yourself with him?"

"You mean then, that I'm going to lose, too?"

"People want to vote for you, too, Kerney. They remember how you came out ahead two years ago in the legislature's race. You were clever to split the vote that way and win. They like clever bright boys. They'd like to vote for you again. There's nobody against you but old Mavis over in Wyatt County, and people are sick and tired of seeing his face on the posters. I don't know. Maybe you and Duncan have the right line on this business, gangsters and all. Maybe Dozer is worth the kind of sacrifice you're making for him. But I certainly think you'll have to give up entirely any idea of getting the office you're supposed to be seeking." He smiled, his tough-skinned face spilling instantly and graciously all its store of charm. "You'll forgive me speaking plainly, boy. I've seen enough of you around the house for quite a while to get to feel like you're one of the family. With a little urging I might have called myself talking to a son of my own."

Whatever Kerney felt about this did not reveal itself in his face. "Thank you, sir," he said, adding, "I have faced the idea of losing the race, sir."

"Faced it, yes. But have you thoroughly made up your mind to it?"

"I felt it might be worth—" He stopped. He did not look at Jason or avoid him either, and his face became even more deeply his own possession. Kerney Woolbright was neither ugly nor handsome, and though he had the features neither of aristocracy nor of common folk, he might have been placed in either. But above every other quality his face was his own: the large pointed nose, narrow chin cleft in the center, and eyes sheltered deeply in brows and lashes belonged to no one but Kerney Woolbright, a fact that grew more positive every day.

"How old are you, Kerney?" Jason Hunt asked gently.

"Twenty-five, sir."

"As young as that! I thought as much, but it always seems impossible. A college degree, Yale law degree, two years in the legislature, and now—well, who knows? You carry it all well. I never thought before that you got ahead of yourself in any way. Some young men do. And some, of course, only sons with a mother alone who has enough money, would say they had responsibility enough and just sit down, if you follow me. Some stick one toe out in the water and see how cold it is and they've had enough for the rest of their natural-lives." He laughed. "I was one of a big family. It was never left to me to decide. They snatched me up and threw me in over my head and it was sink or swim from then on. If anybody looked back to see which one I did, I was too occupied to notice. I've got a sneaking suspicion, though, that nobody looked. I hope I've never been the kind of fellow to say everybody has to do it my way or it isn't done right. You've had a big opportunity for going ahead, and you've kept the trace chains tight and the singletree riding level. If I had had the money to go to college, I'd have gone into the law, I always thought, that or medicine. The law is the right thing for stepping off into politics. I thought the other day, You must have seen politics ahead of you all along, Kerney."

"You're right, sir. I have."

"The same time I wondered that, I was sitting out here in the office by myself watching the cat out there watching a jaybird and the jaybird watching God alone knows what, and I thought, What is Duncan Harper doing in politics? Isn't this sort of a sudden idea?"

"He's been interested in politics for a long time, sir."

"Yes, so have I. But I'm not about to start running for something."

"Travis Brevard asked him—"

"So they say. Do you think if Travis had had even a sneaking suspicion that Duncan took liberal views, he would have asked him to run for dogcatcher, let alone sheriff? Travis was asking a football star, nothing else."

"Duncan knows that, sir."

"What is Duncan living on these days? The store can't be bringing in much with somebody else hired to run it."

"I don't know about his finances. He still finds time to write a little insurance. I think he has some property in town and maybe a place or two in the country. You know how it is."

"I ought to," said Jason, and they exchanged a smile. Nobody could name a business in Winfield County that Jason Hunt had not at some time been in it. "He has a nice house," Jason continued. "Of course, his wife's father has that oil money."

Kerney was about to speak again, though what he would say seemed uncertain to him, when Jason Hunt rose and spoke with swift strength.

"In my opinion Duncan Harper has no business in politics. He is not only inept, he may even be dangerous. You instead have every business to be in politics. He has no right to ruin your career, as it will be ruined, Kerney, in this race, for good."

Kerney had risen also. His face flamed completely red; that was all he showed.

"Duncan is my friend, sir," he said firmly.

"I have every respect for friendship," said Jason Hunt, and put out his hand. "Good day, my boy. Miss Nan and I are always pleased to see you. Come back whenever you can."

36   *Beset on Every Side*

WHEN HE came from the steps that dropped from Jason's office to the yard, Nan Hunt called to him from somewhere within the house. It was a testament to the absolute charm of her voice that she could win his attention at that moment.

"I know you're busy, but can you come here just a minute?"

He skirted the corner of the house with its rich slumberous shrubbery, and hastened up the low steps to the front gallery. She stood near the turn of the porch, back of the green glider.

"We want you for dinner tomorrow night after the speaking," she told him. "Perhaps Cissy mentioned it."

"No—oh, yes, yes she did, I think. Excuse me, Miss Nan. The heat and politics together are too much for me." He came toward her, threading amongst the rocking chairs, but she stepped back from him saying, "Kerney," and he had to turn the farthest corner of the porch, puzzling, to find her again. She stood near the wall. The walnut just outside shadowed them; the sun had not yet struck through: they were as sheltered and private as if they had suddenly entered a little grove. Her hand held his wrist, and her face so swiftly near him had transformed itself on the moment. He had never seen her like this before. She was touched back into youth as startlingly as though she had just died; she seemed never to have had a headache in her life; she was more beautiful than both her daughters; and she said, "Whatever he advised you, don't do it. I don't know what it could be. He does not discuss his business with me; I have no notion. But if there is a murmur of your heart against him, then follow your heart. Oh, believe me, believe me, Kerney! You will never be sorry!"

Kerney's intellect was catlike; thrown into a tailspin, it had a tendency to reappear on its feet. He thought at once: Was Jason Hunt *this* bad? The hand on his sleeve, not small, more strong than weak, was still of an indescribable fragility, and the whole woman like a flower nurtured to that perfect bloom which, inexchangeable for any other, is flawed only by its sur-roundings: it is a trifle too heavy for its stem, and what climate yields its proper airs? Certainly Mississippi seasons were all too coarse for her. What man could ever pass the long trials of her indisputable discriminations? Jason Hunt had failed, and Kerney knew that he would fail too. There remained to her the exquisite intimacies of pain, and what subtle memories one could not even guess at. Thus he rapidly reasoned himself apart from her, and though he replied with gallantry and affection that would have seemed genuine to almost anybody, he left her lonelier than before, for if she seldom risked a gesture of the heart, she had not forgotten how to recognize one. Her dia-monds blinked but she did not; she parted from him graciously.

The irony of his reaction to her was that he had already made up his mind to reject Jason's ideas before she suggested it. The scales had already tipped decisively; his step had been certain as a saint's. But her appearance in the matter had thrown Jason into unexpected light, and not so much Kerney's decision, but the whole apparatus of it was shaken. For if Jason was wrong about Duncan, and Nan unjustified about Jason, then Duncan might conceivably be miscalculating about Beck Dozer, which put Kerney Woolbright on shaky ground, and was not good.

To add to his confusion, Cissy appeared on the path before him.

"Silly," she said. "You almost ran into me without looking. All time thinking about politics. Silly."

"Cissy," he said, and put an arm around her. "Walk with me down the walk and listen to me a minute."

"Well, I'm listening. What's the matter?"

He could not begin. He had no way to explain. "Don't say I told you, but I may not win the race. I may lose."

"Is somebody else running besides old Mr. Mavis?"

"No, honey, that's not it."

"But who on earth would vote for old Mr. Mavis instead of you? You're just worrying over nothing."

He went a little way down the flight of wooden steps that led to the street, and sat down, drawing her down beside him. He had foreseen her among young Washington matrons, photographed on the White House lawn.

"You haven't even noticed my new dress." She spread wide around her knees a chambray skirt of yellow, paneled in white cotton eyelet. "You don't notice anything any more. We never get to go anywhere. You never tell me anything."

"Cissy, please don't tell this to anybody, but I—"

"You always say that! You know I won't tell anything!" But, alas, she told everything she knew to everybody she knew, and they both knew it. But he never challenged her when she insisted this way, and he did not now.

"What were you going to tell me, Kerney?"

He shook his head. "I just don't have time now, honey. I have to go uptown."

"I don't like the way you're doing me, Kerney. I meant to wait and tell you after the election. I just don't like it. I don't want anybody who's going to be all the time leaving me about important things they won't talk about. You never do explain anything to me. All I'm supposed to do is talk baby talk to you. I do it when I don't feel like it one bit. I think it's the silliest thing I ever heard of. I get sick myself sometimes. I'm not going to do it any more, either. I tell you that right now."

He got up and went slowly down the steps toward his car, which in his haste he had left in the road instead of ascending the drive. He entered the scalding sun and paused, turning back. There were tears in his eyes, but he judged she could not see them. She rose from the ankles, sturdily, without touching anything.

"You're treating me the way Daddy treats Mother. He never tells her anything. If your business is all that important, and you're all that important, then I've got to be important too. Either that, or I'm going to quit liking you. You needn't think I can't, Kerney, not for a minute."

He went away without saying anything. He felt like a small boy, unjustly injured, and wanted to go home and be called soft names.

It happened to Duncan, he thought. Now it's happening to me.

PART FOUR

WILLARD FOLLANSBEE, child of scorn, sat in one of Bud Grantham's hide-bottom chairs with his straw hat in his lap. He looked about as delighted with the world as the world was with him, but his abiding consolation was that both he and the world knew it.

"They don't want me. I don't kid myself none. They don't even like me. When they voted for me before they's voting for Travis, just on account of he couldn't succeed himself. When they vote for me this go-round they'll be voting against Harper. The thing I aim to make certain sure of tomorrow is that they get an earful of plenty to vote against Duncan Harper *for*. You know, Bud, I can't stand the sight of that fellow."

"I never thought he was such a bad type," said Bud Grantham. "I never felt nothing unkindly towardjuh him." He ran one tough old finger across three warts in the palm of his hand. He had been to the conjure woman a week ago, but so far they hadn't shed.

"Listen," said Willard, "I get to where I can't stand the sight of the hat on his head or the shirt on his back. I can't decide when I don't like him the most, when he comes in the door or when he goes out the door. I tried to decide it yesterday, but s'help me, I couldn't."

"Folks like him in general," said Bud, "or so I'm told."

"Listen," said Willard, "I been treading lightly over him when I speak. But did you realize before, Bud, that country folks don't care nothing atall about football?"

"I knew," said Bud, "that Bud Grantham don't care nothing for it. I couldn't care less. I don't even care at the time, much less ten years later. I don't even put a two-dollar bet in on the pool."

"You tell me honestly, Bud. How do we stand?"

"We stand to win, is my feeling. But you know my heart ain't in it so much, Willard, what with Jimmy laid up and the place shut down. I got nothing to do all day but swat flies."

"Yeah, it's bad, I know. How you figger we stand to win?"

"Because Harper ain't caught the nigger yet. Everybody thinks the nigger shot Jimmy. I don't think he's going to catch that nigger. If you want to trample on him when you speak, that's the ground you ought to trample over. There's a might of folks in this county just crazy about Jimmy, and it don't set well that a nigger can shoot him down and go scot-free. Tell the truth, it don't set well with me. I'd like to get my hands on the nigger my own self."

"God help him to stay lost, is the way I look at it. If I laid hands on him first, he'd never get to Duncan Harper alive. I think he knows too much. I think that's why he run."

"I think he done it," said Bud.

"If he done it, how come Jimmy won't say so?"

"On account of what his daddy done. Jimmy don't find the way of resting easy over that. Don't ask me how come. We all got our peculiarities."

"On the other hand," said Willard, "looks like he could have made up something better than what he did. Jimmy's been laying up in that hospital for two weeks with all them nurses singlefooting up and down for him, talking way down weak: 'It was a strange white man. Somebody out hunting. Never laid eyes on him.' I've knowed him to make up better than that to pass the time during a slow hand of poker."

"If you think the nigger didn't do it, who do you think did? You said Sam sent them boys back there to talk to Jimmy. He didn't say nothing atall about trying to kill him."

"It's true," said Willard. "But how come them to give up the idea of talking to him that quick."

"Well, you were there, and heard what they said. I'd gone on up to the house. Run through it one more time for me, Willard."

"It was after you followed Bella back over to the house. Pilston and Sam and me set there in the office and didn't say much except I think Pilston did remark once on the temperature, that it was unusually high, and I said he was right. Then I heard a shot, but I didn't think nothing about it. I knew the kid they had with them carried a gun, but if I thought anything, I thought somebody was just pranking with it."

"I'm all time hearing shots off in the woods," said Bud. "It don't signify no more to me than a axe ringing. You take just this morning. I heard two right close together off down towardjuh the creek."

"That day," said Willard, "you never heard but one. But, like I say, I didn't think nothing. Wasn't a minute later that Mitchell come to the door and called Sam out into the main part of the Idle Hour to tell him something. Sam came straight back, polite and cool as a preacher in the cool of Sunday morning before the singing and the sermon and the fried chicken, and says that they've decided not to talk to Jimmy right now after all. Mitchell says he's back in the woods arguing with some nigger. He says he and Wally were headed on back when they heard a shot from down there. 'Naturally,' he says, 'we don't care to be involved in any local matter. We prefer to drive along now, attend to some business over in the Delta,' he says, 'and strike back here long about nine or ten o'clock.' Mitchell had already gone and got in the back seat with the boy, and Sam and Pilston took the front, with Pilston driving. They said 'So long till later,' and drove off West, toward the Delta. They never came back."

"They might have heard about Jimmy in time not to come back," said Bud. "News being what it is when it comes to traveling."

"All I said to myself at the time was, 'Well, Jimmy's finally decided to handle that Dozer nigger for double-crossing him.' I didn't want to meddle in his business, so I drove on back to town. It wasn't till I heard Jimmy was in the hospital that I seen the light. So that's how come they left so quick, I says. They done it themselves."

"I think they caught the nigger at it," Bud said. "I think, like they said, they never wanted to be mixed up in nothing of that type. If Pilston had gone into the woods, now— But what call for quarrel was there, Willard, between Jimmy and Mitchell?"

"The one toting the gun was that boy."

"If I remember right, him and Jimmy had just struck up a kinship right after they come."

"That wouldn't make no difference to folks like them."

"I think it was the nigger," said Bud.

They sat silently for a time in Bud's room with the old iron bed, the washstand, and the desk pushed over against the wall. The ledgers were there, for Bud, like a conscientious accountant, brought them home from the office at the Idle Hour and sometimes tried to figure out where he ought to enter his expenses.

"I think it was the nigger, too," said Bella, walking in.

"He don't talk to you, either?" Willard asked.

"No more than to anybody else since he's been up yonder in the hospital, but one time he told me a story about when he was overseas. He run into the Dozer nigger and the Dozer nigger tried to kill him. Did you know that, Daddy?"

"I don't know nothing about overseas," said Bud.

"Jimmy's funny about that nigger," said Willard, "for a fact. You'd think he'd bought him and paid cash for him. He's that attached."

"Where you going, honey baby?" asked Bud. "All diked out."

She had got herself up in a cool sleeveless summer cotton with big Hawaiian flowers on it, and her hair was brushed smooth, her make-up careful. She was not such a bad-looking girl.

"I'm going to the meeting, Daddy," she said. "I was hoping you could come go with me."

"I best stay with the chap," said Bud. "Is he sleep?"

"Lucy's coming to stay with him. You come on now, Daddy. I promised I'd bring somebody. They had it all divided off last night. You could get in the Tomorrow I'll Take Jesus As My Savior group, or you could choose the Tomorrow I'll Speak to Someone about Jesus group, or you could be in the Tomorrow I'll Bring Somebody Else to the Meeting group. So I picked that one."

"Can't you just speak to him about Jesus and go on?" Willard asked.

"No, because I promised this other one. It wouldn't be doing right, would it?"

"It's a fact I ought to go," said Bud. "Bella's mama never missed a night; we had our own bench saved for us, me and her and all the chaps. They couldn't open a meeting without us. My own mother went morning *and* night. I've seen the time she'd get up sick to go. I never seen a better woman. Not in all my borned days. You tell 'em up there, baby, that your old daddy's a sinner, but his heart's with 'em, and he aims to get there yet."

A voice called from out in the dark.

"Miss Bella? Oh, Miss Bella?"

"It's Lucy," said Bella. "Come on in, Lucy."

"That's Beck's wife, ain't it?" Willard asked, as the quiet, thin Negro girl entered from the back porch and halted just inside the screen door. She wore a dark, straight-cut cotton dress and low-quarter tennis shoes. She had wrapped the hem of an old pillow slip around her head, for she had straightened her hair that day, using the hair grease and the hot-iron comb, just as if something special might be about to happen. She was at once aware from Mister Willard Follansbee's glance that the white cone on her head looked attractive, but she did not remove it.

"Come here, girl," said Follansbee.

Shy, tall, soft, she moved to the edge of the lamplight.

"Come here!" he repeated, pointing to a straight chair, and when she hesitated he seized her by the wrist and flung her into it. "Where's Beck at?"

"I don't know, sir."

"Look at me." He jerked up her face.

"I said I don't know, sir. I ain't seen him."

"You ain't seen him," Willard mimicked. "It's going on three weeks. What's he doing—or is he doing without?"

Lucy turned her head aside. She was conscious of the white man's slack jaw where the stiff black hair roots were visible like punctures and the breath moved in and out. She went dull all over, animal, African, obedient to the forcing whip. "I ain't seen him," she repeated.

"'I ain't seen him,'" Willard mocked. "Listen, nigger, you know the worse thing a white man can do to a black man, don't you?"

"I don't know, sir."

"You don't? You never heard what happens to a black man if he tries anything with a white woman?"

"Beck ain't done nothing. There wasn't no white lady."

"You tell Beck to stay gone from here. 'Cause if I see him it ain't going to make no difference if there was a white lady or there wasn't a white lady. It's going to be the same for Willard Follansbee. Willard Follansbee. That's me. You understand?"

"Yes, sir."

"What you going to do?"

"If I see him, I tell him."

"Tell him what?"

"To stay way from here."

"Stay way how come?"

"'Count of what you'd do."

"What would I do? You tell me." He bent suddenly close to her. "You tell me."

"Willard," said Bud Grantham and put a stubby old hand between them, shoving the man back from her, "you done said enough, considering there's a lady present."

"Oh," said Willard, recovering, "damn if I didn't forget." He glanced to where Bella stood just out of the light, leaning forward in close scrutiny of Lucy's face. Willard ran his fingers through his long thin straight black hair, pulling it away from his wet brow. He turned his back on Bella and walked uncertainly toward the dark back screen door.

"Oo," said Bella, straightening up with something like a shudder, or maybe a rabbit running across her grave, "y'all ought'n to do Lucy that away," and she added, though whether to make her feelings plausible to the men or to herself was not clear, "If you bother her, she won't look after the baby good, and it's time I was at church."

"Run on along, baby," said Bud Grantham. "It's all agoing to be all right."

"Can I tell 'em you'll come next time, Daddy?"

"You tell 'em that."

Lucy rose and moved toward the door of the room where Bella was staying.

"His bottle's in the icebox, Lucy," Bella called back. "Don't forget to heat it."

38 *The Helpless One*

BECK NEVER let Lucy work in white folks' houses. He made good enough money when he was foreman at the tie plant, before all these things started happening. Now when they sent for her she was scared to go and scared not to go. She hardly knew day from night any more, and moved from one thing to the next without being able to say what she was doing.

After she had fed the little baby and joggled him and changed him, she knew beyond a doubt what the white man was waiting there for. He was walking around in Mister Bud's room by himself, drinking Mister Bud's whisky. Mister Bud himself was out on the back porch in the dark, rocking and singing along with the white-folks tent meeting down the road.

> "There is a fountain filled with blood
>   Drawn from Immanuel's veins,
>   And sinners plunged beneath that flood . . ."

She accepted what would happen. A Negro, lowered past a certain line of misfortune, no longer counts on cleverness: she did not think how she could divert him, contrive to upset the baby, win the other man's attention. Some savage instinct made her scrounge down low in the corner between the window and the bed. She took off her white headwrap and laid it on the counterpane.

> "The dying thief rejoiced to see
>   That fountain in his day;
>   And there may I, though vile as he . . ."

Out on the back porch, Mister Bud was belling like a hound. The room was dark. When the door opened, and light entered, she turned her head low. If he didn't quit breathing so loud, he would wake up the baby.

She recalled the time she used to go down to the Sanders' house, the white-folks kitchen where Aunt Mattie used to cook. On the sidewalk one day by the hill up Mister Sanders' pasture, that old white man stopped her. It was spring and the iris blades felt cold on her legs. Aunt Mattie had raised her nice: she didn't know what he meant. She couldn't have been more than nine or ten. When she came crying into the kitchen, Aunt Mattie looked her over good, then gave her some coffee. The white lady, Miss Jessie Sanders, took on worse than Mattie. "That awful old man. He ought to be ashamed! I'd like to let him know exactly what I think of him." "Yes'm," said Mattie, "nex' time she know to run '*fo*' he see her, stid of after." But Miss Jessie still took on. She took on and took on. She told her husband at the dinner table. "That awful old thing," she said. "To hear him pray out loud in church! You think he'd died and gone to heaven." "Did he hurt her, Mattie?" Mister David called back to the kitchen. "Naw suh," said Mattie, taking her own sweet time. "I reckon he too old." "Nasty thing," said Miss Jessie. . . .

When Lucy walked back through the woods, tears lay along her cheeks like scars. The days for running to Aunt Mattie were gone long ago. She couldn't even tell Beck what the white man had done. He would feel it worse than she did. He might even do something crazy. Right after she first married Beck, the yellow boy she had been married to before kept shining around. He wanted to come sit on the porch on Sunday and talk. Beck wouldn't have it. Little as Beck was, he said he would kill that nigger if he kept on coming by. That was how she knew about Beck.

"He sound asleep, Mister Bud," she had said. "My own chillen ain't had they supper."

"You can go," said Bud Grantham. "Bella'll be home now in a minute. I hear they're singing the invitation hymn."

They sure enough were.

> "Just as I am, without one plea,
> But that thy blood was shed for me
> And that thou bid'st me come to thee
> O Lamb of God, I come! I come!"

Brother Simmons at the Bear Ma'sh M.E. Church used that one too, but Lucy felt too ill-used to take satisfaction from it. She followed a twisting, wooded path that led her beyond the field where Mister Jimmy Tallant had got shot, climbed through two barbed-wire fences and went over a stile. She passed a spring, set back deep in a hollow where the water winked and shifted like an eye, and there gushed out into the night air the deep earth smell of black loam. The night was thick with life: it sang or buzzed or chanted or chirped or jumped off into the bog or ran through the leaves, and a lot of it probably had no business out on this side of the grave. Lucy had never bothered much about h'ants.

Not that she doubted them. Black people are night people, and you do not drive a Southern road at any unearthly hour without seeing them along the roadsides, going somewhere, or marking at a distance across the field the oil lamp burning full wick within the cabin. Sometimes, passing near a cabin that is totally dark as though for sleep, one hears break out again the low mingling of many voices; no crisis has brought them there, but the instinctive motion of their strange society has behaved like a current deep down in the river, and here they are. Savage, they came to a savage land, and it took them in. White people, already appalled by floods and rattlesnakes, malaria, swamps, tornadoes, mud, ice, sunstroke, and typhoid fever, felt compelled to levee out the black with the same ruthless patience with which they leveed the Mississippi River. They were driven to do what they did, not by any conviction of right or wrong, but by the simple will to survive. Meanwhile, Negroes married the land. Its image is never complete without them; if they are out of the picture, they are only just around the corner, coming or going, or both. They are not really as afraid in the night as most white people are. Whiteness is a kind of nakedness to the dark world, and Lucy, who had all the fear she could do with, went to no trouble to imagine more. She moved on in her blackness, and her heart, sick and numb, burned tender as the eye of a night creature, alive in the dark.

"Who?" she asked plain out when the figure appeared ahead of her, silhouetted down a little free length of path.

"It's me, Aunt Lucy." It was W.B.

"You ain't heard nothing?" she asked when they came together.

"Nothing from Unker Beck. Mister Duncan is at the house, though."

"Doing what?"

"He in setting by Granny. Claim she nussed his papa when his papa died, and laid him straight and all. Claim she cared for his mama after his mama birthed him. He done tole me all about it once befo'."

"What he coming for now? It ain't no interest of mine who nussed his daddy and eased his mammy. If Granny done it, look at Granny. Who's caring for her now?"

"We is, Aunt Lucy."

"We sho' is. Don't you tell that white man nothing, W.B. Ain't nobody to help Beck but Beck."

"I ain't tole him nothing."

"Ack like you dumb, ack like you crazy, but don't say nothing to a white man. Wall yo' eyes like you ain't got good sense. You hear me, W.B.?"

"Yes'm, Aunt Lucy. I hears you."

"Beck call hisself being so smart. Going to make first this deal with the white, then the next one better still. There ain't no dealing with white folks, this one *or* the next one. I reckon Beck know hit now. Turn aloose of me and hush, W.B. I ain't got time for you to be no baby. You gots to be a man."

"Aunt Lucy, Unker Beck never done it. Unker Beck never shot Mister Jimmy Tallant."

"No, he never, W.B. But when the white folks think you done something, you just well's to run."

"I run the day Mister Travis Brevard died."

"Then you knows about your Unker Beck. He done the same."

39 *The Distances Between*

"HE MUST have his own chance to decide," said Duncan, speaking very slowly. "He must have his own choice. If Mister Willard Follansbee wins the election, he and Mister Bud Grantham will kill Beck if they can find him. You'll have to leave here, leave your house and home to go to him. The reason people say they don't want to vote for me is because I let Beck get away. If Beck will come back, I will protect him. You know I'll protect him because I did it once before, up at the jail."

"I don't know where he at," said Lucy.

"Me neither," said W.B.

"Yo' daddy had the prettiest ca'edge hoss I most ever seen," said Aunt Mattie. "The day you's born it come up a little whipping storm and Mister Henry Harper hitched his buggy up at the top of the heel and come walking for me. 'How come us walking, Mister Henry, and you with yo' spohty ca'edge?' 'I gots to spoht my equipage uptown tomorrow, Mattie, and you ain't gwy catch me splashing it up on no nigger road.' But Lawd, in dem days the roads in town was apt to slush up bad as any."

"We know now that Beck did not shoot Mister Tallant. We have a good start on finding the people who did. We may find them any minute now. The last I heard, the police had located them, down in New Orleans; it's just a matter of getting them to confess. If Beck will trust me and come give himself up, then everybody will know he wasn't mixed up in anything. Nobody can say he was."

"Mister Jimmy Tallant ain't going to let them do nothing to Beck."

"Mister Jimmy Tallant has had two weeks to call the name of the man that shot him, and he hasn't called it yet. It would bust his business if folks knew that New Orleans gamblers were putting money in this sheriff's race. You haven't got to do anything that will cause you trouble, anything to put you in danger. You just have got to get word to Beck exactly what I say and let him decide."

"I don't know where he at," said Lucy.

"Me neither," said W.B., who was watching the white man he used to work for. In spite of everything he was pleased to death that Mister Duncan had come to their house.

"W.B. could go," said Duncan. "I know W.B. well because he's worked for me. Folks said, That boy is too little to know where to take groceries, but I didn't think so. I said, He's a good boy and a smart boy. He'll learn. I was right. Wasn't I, W.B.?"

Lucy saw the child grin from ear to ear, and his absence of fear scared her. "Git yonder in the kitchen and see what is the baby got in to."

"Yes'm."

He skipped past Granny to obey.

All evening, with the sound of children in the house, Aunt Mattie felt she was in heaven. She had just gone in and looked at Miss Edna Harper's new baby; he was grown and in the room here now—she did not mistake who was there, though all her eyes could see was the kerosene lamp flame they lighted for her every time it got dark. Mister Henry Harper had just brought her to the door, he had let her in the front, the way she always came in to her white folks, and she'd gone straight on back to where Miss Edna was moaning. In heaven you talked to whoever came to mind or into the room, it was the same, and did anybody know for sure this wasn't it right now?

"Hit was the prettiest baby," said Aunt Mattie, "the whitest white chile I done ever seen."

Lucy flashed Duncan a look of scorn. Her walls were dark walls and the old woman with her perfectly round, addled eyes and her cap of hair short and kinky as a man's (for all her hundred and who knew how many years, it was gray, not white, and never would lose its tenacity to color)—the old woman sat under a dark old quilt and even her fingernails were the rich deep amber color of old tree bark, and the andirons in the swept fireplace were black as old muffin pans. What was white?

"Beck got to do what he do in he own time," she said.

"That's exactly right," said Duncan. "But he can't do anything unless you tell him how things stand."

"In dem days," said Aunt Mattie, "ever'thing Miss Edna Harper say do Mister Henry Harper done. But she couldn't do nothing atall with old Mister Phillip, po' lady. If he wasn't a caution! I'se hanging out that chile's diapers out on the back porch when I heard them scufflings under the steps. Dere dey was, Mister Phillip and dat black gal that toted the milk. 'Ain't you shame?' I says. 'It not but ten o'clock in the morning, and a baby just bawn yestiddy in this house. I gwy have you churched, nigger.' 'Go on away from here, Mattie,' Mister Phillip says. 'You tend to your'n and I'll tend to mine.' Hee! Hee! He never seed me afterwards he didn't mention it. 'Did you get her churched, Mattie?' Hee! Hee!"

"How I know where Beck at?" said Lucy. "Maybe he in New Orleans, maybe he in Memphis. I don't know. What I got to do with where he at?"

"You know," said Duncan.

W.B. came back. This time he stopped by Granny's chair. Her hand touched his arm, groping up and down his sleeve. "He's Granny's man he is. Ain't nothing gwy harm him. Nare a ha'nt come nigh, nare a cross-eyed nigger. He Jesus' lamb."

Duncan picked up the kerosene lamp from the table and crossed to where the large daguerreotype of Beck Dozer's father hung on the wall.

40 *Robinson Dozer*

THE FACE in the daguerreotype was thin and severe and the hair the true woolly African neatness of fit, the texture of a good rug. The head was held rigidly high, but neither, it would appear, through consciousness at having a picture made, nor from the restraint of the high boiled collar. The eyes seemed concerned.

This man, or so the story went, had given up his job as butler in the fashionable Standsbury house and had moved with his family to the country outside Lacey where he owned a little legacy of land. There was a good-sized Negro-tenant and free-farmer population in that area: Robinson Dozer founded a little school in his own front yard.

His parents had been slaves of a senator, John Lucian Upinshaw, "Senator John." The old man, living poorly after the war in a splendid house, had wished to spend his last years educating the children of his former slaves. Robinson Dozer had sat on a bench with the other Negro children out in the guesthouse in the front yard—the one the Senator had converted into a library. Robinson's eyes were big as a raccoon's; his mouth hung open long enough for a jenny wren to nest in it; and he remembered every word that Senator John said.

Senator John thought that Southerners should have started this sort of thing years ago; he felt compassion for these black innocents so violently kicked into freedom; he thought that only the educated mind was fit for American citizenship. His mind burned clearly. He thanked God for this calling here in his old age, his poverty, the ruin of his country. One frosty morning an hour before his class, he fell on the back steps and broke his hip.

He sent his niece to tell the Negro children, but what with all the excitement of the fetching and carrying, she forgot to go. The black children sat on the benches in the law office for forty-five minutes in hypnotized silence; then, as though someone had signaled, they bolted. They ran in terror across the lawn, dropping the tablets and pencils along the garden path. Propped high in a mahogany four-poster, his stout old leg intricately distended toward the ceiling by a homemade pully, the Senator announced he would continue his classes in his bedroom.

Next morning, he sent his grandson down to the guesthouse to bring the students in. When at last the boy came shivering back across the frozen yard and said that nobody had come, he became nervous and extremely irritated. He guessed the truth, that nobody had got to them the day before; he commanded that everyone in the house be marshaled to go out and search for them all over the plantation, to bring in every one of them if it took till sundown. After a while, his daughter came into his room.

She had a paper full of cornfield peas and she shelled them with jerking motions while she talked, casting hulls by the handful into a bucket, funneling the peas into a boiler. She was running the house now. Her husband had been killed at Shiloh. She used to cry at night and play songs on the piano at twilight, but now she did not have time for either one. Her bare arms were broken out in red spots where she had been out in the garden gathering the peas and turnip greens—that was all they had to eat now: first peas, then turnip greens and turnips, cooked with a bit of salt pork. She did not notice any longer that it was cold: a fire in a room was apt to make her say she was burning up, whereupon she would stamp out, as though mad at somebody. A Union officer and ten strange Negroes had raided the smokehouse three days before and left them with no meat at all. She had penned two shoats right at the back door, and said she would raise them if she had to move them into her bedroom.

"Papa," she said, jerking the hulls away from the part that was food, "Papa, I can't have the children going out of sight of the house. It's dangerous on the roads now. I have to take Holcomb and the shotgun with me when I go to town in the buggy. If those little niggers appreciated what you're do-ing they'd come back. The answer is they don't appreciate it. You're not teaching them anything," she went on pitilessly; "you're wasting your time and your strength, out there in that cold office. I don't know that I want them in here anyway, smelling up my house. Every child on this place is working; why can't they?"

"Working! Why, Liza, child, what do you call work? I've raised a sweat on the little rascals out there in the cold; you wouldn't believe how much they've learned. They know the alphabet, and how to cipher, the names of some few states, and can print a sentence or two on paper. They're learning the story of Thomas Jefferson and how he set his slaves free. Think of it, Liza! In a scant fifty years from savagery!"

"Savagery! They're animals, if you ask me. They aren't as good as savages. There's Nanny and old Luke and who else? Nobody. They come to the back door wanting something to eat. 'Go to the Yankees': that's what I ought to say. But I don't. 'All right,' I say, 'I planted that garden with these two hands, and I sweated down to nothing hoeing it, and when nobody else is around, who goes out and gets the vegetables? Me. But all right. Go cut me some kindling wood, go straighten up the back fence where that crazy cow got her yoke caught, go in the woods and get me a new hoe handle. Then you can come and eat same as we do, turnip greens and side meat, corn bread and potlikker, and if that ain't good enough for you, go to the Yankees and see what you get.' That's what I say."

"You poor child. Having to do all this work. I'm sorry, Liza."

"It isn't only work, Papa. It's danger, night and day. You never know what's going to happen next. They can start burning houses again; they can turn *us* into slaves; they're crazy, I tell you; they can do anything."

"Liza, don't get upset."

"Upset!" This was too much. She told him everything, tearing the hulls viciously apart, things that were happening in town, along the roads, at the capital, all over the South.

"Why wasn't I told?" he asked sternly.

"I didn't want to worry you. You couldn't do anything about it."

He knew then that he was old. Easing the leather-bound volume aside, taking off his spectacles, he agreed, "No, I couldn't do anything."

"You seemed happy enough, teaching little niggers."

Not only old, childish. He had to be humored. He sighed. What had gone with his daughter's gentle tongue? He was not used to being wounded by women. "Poor Liza. Poor little girl."

They heard Aunt Nanny scolding in the hall. "You say you wants to see him, well, go ahead on in and see him. I ain't got time to waste on trash like you is."

In the high white doorway, there appeared the Negro boy with the raccoon eyes in the small face.

"Why," said Senator John, "it's Robinson Dozer. He's come for his lesson. Get on out into the kitchen with your pea-shelling, Liza. I'm lying here worthless, but I can teach this boy."

The old man never walked again. He went about in a wheel chair for years till he died, and it was Robinson Dozer who pushed him everywhere, reciting Presidents. The family mocked him, sometimes to his face, walking to the chant of "Washington, Adams, Jefferson, John *Quincy* Adams, Madison, Monroe. . . ." They did this when they got him by himself. They didn't dare mock him in front of Senator John. He eventually moved into the house with the old man, slept in the trundle bed, and padded in and out with slop jars, water for shaving, trays of food, and books, books, books. The family said that all he could learn was the Presidents' names, just as they said that this was all the old Senator had memory enough left to teach him.

But one day at the dinner table one of the cousins said he had heard them wheeling around in the back yard together speaking French. "French!" There was a silence. "Or maybe it was Latin," said the cousin. "Well, I hope so," said Eliza. "Teaching that black thing French. The idea!" "Granddaddy don't know any French to teach him," said another cousin, Davy, a great sarcastic boy. "Naw, he don't know French." "*I* didn't think he remembered Latin either," said Eliza. "Maybe he don't," said Davy. "I don't see how Vernon would know. Maybe Robinson was teaching African to Granddaddy." "It wasn't English," said Vernon. "Holler see's there any more bread."

When Senator John realized he was perhaps engaged in a dangerous thing, it was too late to stop. An intellectual thirst is impossible to sate. Waking in the first dawn, the old man would lie regarding with the tenderness of a parent, the frail boyish form outlined under the covers of the flat bed near the hearth. "What will happen to him?" he thought. "What have I done to him?" In his will he left a little farm to Robinson

Dozer, from his holdings in the county. Also that part of his library which had no pertinence to the state.

By rights Robinson Dozer should have gone North.

Eliza told him as much, the day after the funeral. "I'll always be as good to you as I can because of Papa. But there's not going to be anybody else like him, not down here. As I said when Xavier got killed in the war, This is another life I've got to start, another person I've got to be. You can stay here as long as you want to—"

"I've packed already, Miss Eliza. With your permission, I'll be leaving this afternoon."

"Oh." She gave him a hard look but she did not inquire into his business. "If I were you, I'd sell the land Papa left you and find some place up North. I'll write a note to Judge Standsbury. Maybe for Papa's sake he'll write letters to that college in the East. Do you want me to do that?"

He had been laughed at in her house, and he would not, could not, ask for anything. "Whatever you would like to do, Miss Eliza."

She turned abruptly to her desk, pulling paper forward from the pigeonholes, drawing out blotter, inkstand, and pen. "If it weren't for Papa—" The letters came out blackly aslant, but the words, as always in letters or conversations "outside the family," were courteous and warm.

Judge Standsbury, seated in his law office near the fire, said "Ummm" three times to the letter. He had no idea what to do with Robinson Dozer. His air of benevolent learning imparted the impression that he knew everything practical as a matter of course. When he took off his glasses and pressed his brows between two fingers he seemed to be weighing a number of diverse possibilities. Actually he was provoked at this whim of old John's, educating a colored boy, and the way John had reached out and snagged him from the other side of the grave.

"What do you plan to do once you get up North, Robinson?"

"I should first like to acquire a college degree, sir, then possibly secure a position as a teacher. I might even look into the law."

"Ummm," said Judge Standsbury.

In the grate a lump of soft coal burst from within and two parts of it tumbled out on the floor. Judge Standsbury watched

Robinson's appreciative handling of the fire tongs and shovel, as if the feel of the wrought iron pleased him. As indeed it did. Along with a taste for Latin prose, Robinson had acquired a tendency to feel at home under hand-carved moldings.

"These affairs will take a little time, Robinson, a little time."

"I recognize that, Judge Standsbury."

"You mean to go back out to Miss Eliza's?"

"Miss Eliza and I do not have too successful an understanding."

"Then I think you'd better come down to stay at our place, Robinson, while we're waiting for these—er, matters to go through."

In the ten years that Robinson was the Standsbury butler, the matter of his going North was never mentioned again. Judge Standsbury sometimes woke in the night and thought with a twinge in the direction of the old Senator's grave that he had never written letters for Robinson. But Robinson had never mentioned the matter again. Well, he was a whole lot better off down here and probably knew it. Hadn't they taken him in? Easy, easy now, Judge Standsbury slid back into sleep.

The truth was, Robinson could never bring himself to ask for anything. In summer he wore a white coat; in winter a black one with a white boiled shirt, starched collar, and black string tie. If he was superior to all the Negroes, he was no less superior to all the whites, for the Standsbury household was a sociable one—not much given to books. Robinson lived gravely among silver, polished woods, and heavy glass decanters. In his room off the kitchen he read the books the Senator had left him. None of the Standsbury children dared enter his quarters. He was the terror of their youth.

The first anybody knew that Robinson had a wife and two children was the day he left the Standsburys for good. He led his family into the parlor where everyone was assembled just following Sunday dinner, and introduced them all around. He was already packed, he said, and would be leaving within the hour. Then he led the way from the room.

"So that's how Robinson spent his Sundays," said Judge Standsbury after the entire family had passed ten minutes in silence, something of a record. He had not dared say this in front of Robinson.

Ever after the Standsburys remembered him and talked about him, for living with Robinson in the house was a memorable thing. A glance from him was worse than a beating from their parents. The parents, too, had felt supervised, and had been known to leave the house to quarrel so that Robinson would not overhear them. His opinions were never expressed; hence everyone worried all the time about what he thought. When guests came, Robinson gave the Standsburys great prestige. In fact, his service with them solidified them in the opinion that they were aristocrats; before, they had often suspected that they were not. Yet they were never really comfortable with him, and his departure liberated their spirits so much that things looked rather perilous for a week or so. Judge Standsbury came to the table once in his shirtsleeves, and the children were discovered romping barefoot in the best parlor. But nobody said they wanted him back because neither they nor anybody else ever really liked Robinson. The old Senator had loved him, and this love had emancipated him, had made him independent, learned, scornful, superior, and unkind.

When he left he went back to the piece of land the Senator had willed him, which had been what Judge Standsbury was asked to sell for him to finance his way up North. Here he took possession from the former tenant and began to farm. For the first time in his life he wore a pair of overalls, blue-black at first and heavy as sailcloth, bending harshly to his thin limbs' motion, but finally a blue as delicate as spring sky reflected in an old window, and as gently textured as silk.

Word drifted back to town that Robinson had started a school for Negroes. Soon now, he was seen in town on Saturdays, not in overalls, but in the old black suit and string tie. He had long been a story, now he was a "character." Negroes, who had never liked the "high-white" Standsbury butler, accepted him, and even white people treated him with respect, called him 'Fessor without joking, and sometimes gave him a small donation. It was believed that you could not really teach Negroes anything; it was reported that Robinson could not get them to attend classes any more than the town schoolmaster could, but even when Vardaman stumped the state with the message that "every nigger you educate is another nigger you have to kill," it was not said anywhere in Lacey that the school was a bad thing until the First World War was over and the boys came home.

Three of the boys were big black bucks from Robinson's part of the county. They had learned a thing or two in France, they felt, and they called on Robinson to tell him about it. Later, they started taking lessons from Robinson at night. One of them had contrived to lose an arm in France: he got a disability check from the government, and the other two borrowed from him unmercifully, so they did not have to go to work. They were often remarked uptown on the square and not only on Saturday. There was something sinister about them: their togetherness, their size, their not working, their swagger, their watchfulness. It was hoped that Robinson was not putting any ideas in their heads. "Or vice versa," a man like Acey Tallant might say, flipping his cigarette into the open grate in the chancery clerk's office. He "traveled" during the week, gave the impression of statewide political connections, and was wont to check by the courthouse on weekends to see what was going on.

The three Negro veterans wore their uniforms, woolen shirts and khaki peg-top pants with wrap leggings that tapered to their wide army shoes. There was talk that Negroes would try to push for the vote since the war ended, that veterans would organize to this end; some said that Negroes had volunteered in order to get to France and sleep with white women; now that they were back, people said, they were crazy for more of the same. An automobile dealer ordered them out of his showroom because they had got in the habit of coming in and loitering all afternoon around the stove. Henry Harper said they always came into his grocery store after dark along about closing time and would not say what they wanted for an unaccountable long time. His uncle, old Phillip Harper, chased them out one night with his walking stick. They seemed determined to make people nervous. White people had been glad to listen at first to their experiences in France, but now they were tired of it; the same story four times over would not work any more; Negroes, if worthless, were at least supposed to be charming or funny. Robinson Dozer, as a matter of fact, had got tired of them too. He was still trying to make them stop talking about France so they could learn something, when the troubles started.

In quick succession a white farmer's cotton house was burned down, another had his pigs let out, a third was driving to town when the wheels of his buggy came off. White householders began to feel uncomfortably far from town, indeed from one another, and count themselves greatly outnumbered by the Negro farmers and renters. Unfortunately, at this time a white farmer's daughter drowned in Pettico-cow.

It had been a season of dry weather and she was found in the shallows of the deep hole where she had died. Or perhaps she had not died in the water, but had been thrown in afterward. She was heavily bruised about the head and face, and there were said to have been signs of violence on her elsewhere, but since the family would on no account allow her to be examined, all descriptions of them conflicted. The path that led from Robinson Dozer's house to the country road ran along the creek bank for a time—it ran, in fact, quite near the deep hole.

The father of the girl at first, in his grief, got out his gun to go and kill the three Negro veterans. His neighbors restrained him. Negroes outnumbered them three to one, but relations had always been peaceful, even pleasant. The families of the boys were "good Negroes." There were surely better ways to handle this.

After the funeral, the white men met and talked far into the night; the next day a sober wagonload drove into town, calm in the sense of having reached just decisions without resort to violence. They had two demands to make: first that the three veterans be arrested immediately on suspicion of murder and, even if they appeared innocent beyond doubt, that they be made to leave the county for good; second, that Robinson Dozer's school be closed. "You see what happens," they said, "when you try to educate a nigger."

The three Negro veterans said that the first they heard of the girl's death was when they were arrested on the town square. Following the arrival of the latest disability check they had spent several days pleasuring themselves over in the Delta at a Negro settlement known as Coontown. Several hundred Negroes there must have seen them and remembered them, but though they sent urgent messages not one appeared to say so. The sheriff locked them up in the jail, the farming delegation turned homeward in the creaking wagon, the town passed uneasy nights.

Robinson Dozer was exercised; he made several patient trips between town and his home. He called on the sheriff, talked with the veterans, was closeted with Judge Standsbury for an hour. Secretly he did not so much care what happened to the boys; he did not want his school to be closed. He gained permission, at last, to assemble a black delegation: the parents of the boys (it then emerged that two of them were brothers), two leading Negro freeholders, and himself. The white delegation promised to return, and Judge Standsbury himself agreed to preside. Though tired, Robinson supped in the evening with dignity, spoke little with his family, and composed himself early for bed. The time had been set for two-thirty; the place was the courthouse.

Robinson Dozer with his delegation arrived at the courthouse an hour before the appointed time. He arranged this purposely. He did not want anybody saying that the niggers didn't care. The white delegation had been in town since morning. They scarcely ever saw town except on Saturdays, so they made a picnic of it, ate a box lunch, bought one thing and another, and jawed a good bit in the stores. In the drugstore they saw Acey Tallant—he had just come back to Lacey from a trip out of the state. He asked a lot of questions but his only comment was that "things had certainly gotten out of hand." He was seen later in the newspaper office, and again in the café, whence he crossed decisively to the pool hall.

Up at the courthouse, the sheriff sent the Negro deputation upstairs to the large courtroom to wait. He sent a man with a shotgun to stand at the door. He had the windows open for the first time that spring, and the flies were about to run him crazy. Around two o'clock he sent two armed deputies to the jail for the three veterans. A tubby, jolly, rather simple-minded man, his theory was that Negroes should be kept intimidated by a big show of handcuffing and guns. "You can do anything with 'em," he said, "as long as you keep the hell scared out of 'em." Playing solitaire at his desk, he heard the step of the three prisoners and the two white men resound in the big halls and pass up the staircase.

Judge Standsbury spent a calm morning, ate a good dinner, and settled for a little nap before going up to the courthouse. Several times the phrase, "Friend of black and white alike," occurred to him, for he had gained the age where what they could not escape saying in the newspapers when he died wandered pleasantly through his mind. He felt gratified that Robinson had had at last to call on him about something. Robinson had made all of the Standsburys feel uncomfortably that things would someday be the other way around. The judge napped with the Memphis paper on his chest and his feet covered by an afghan. At two-fifteen he rose, put on his coat, buttoned his vest, adjusted the heavy gold chain which caught the sun so skillfully, selected his handsomest silver-mounted walking cane and, wishing to be not more than a few minutes late, started briskly toward town.

The chubby sheriff, hearing the trample of a dozen men in the hall, came out of his office to see what was going on. The men were all from town or nearby; none of them had any personal connection with the matter in hand. They looked pleasant enough, however; the only noticeably sinister thing about them was that they were all of about the same appearance—tall, active, with weathered faces, neither young nor old—you might have thought that somebody had chosen them. The sheriff knew them all, and that they were part of his constituency.

"Where you boys going?" he asked.

"Just upstairs. Just to see what's going on."

The man who had answered was Acey Tallant. Everyone had expected him to be the spokesman. He looked like the others, only more so—he was always in some slight way different from any group he was discovered among. And he was discovered among them all. He hunted with men richer than himself who liked him well enough but said he would never amount to very much. He was not originally from Winfield County, but had married into a good family there. He talked about property in neighboring counties and in the Delta, sold a bit of insurance, managed some real estate for his wife, and was known to hold some sort of intermittent job with a state office in Jackson. If you asked what it was he would tell you, but five minutes later it would seem you were no clearer on it than before. He was attractive to women. Always, when he talked to anyone he managed to make it seem that he was wasting valuable time, and for this subtlety to make its perfect stamp required a man like the chubby sheriff, holding an uncertain grip on a small job, hoping he was popular with everybody.

"Y'all not toting guns or anything?"

"Of course we ain't."

"I don't want any trouble, you know."

"Trouble? Who said anything about trouble? We're just curious."

"Okay then. If you promise."

"Sure we promise."

The chancery clerk around the corner blew his nose on a large white handkerchief, went back into his office and shut the door. "I think you'd better go home," he said to his secretary. "In fact, I think we both better go home."

Upstairs, in the courtroom, the windows were open on the warm February day. Somebody had had the forethought to build a fire in the stove that morning, but now in the steady early afternoon warmth, the heat was superfluous and formed a visible sleepy glaze on the air.

Robinson Dozer had selected, with a teacher's instinct, a chair at the end of the table where the court clerk sat when court was in session. He now wore round gold-rimmed glasses before his round 'coon-dark eyes; he kept his hands folded on the table before him and his face showed nothing. The three Negro veterans, from the habit of standing around stoves to talk about what they had seen in France, were standing by the stove now, albeit they were running sweat down the collars of their khaki woolens. They had got sluggish in the heat and their mouths hung slightly open. Their three pairs of eyes saw three directions of nothing. The four older Negroes, their parents, had taken a bench together and were sitting now facing the empty judge's stand as though they had come early for church. The two freeholders sat on the front row near the table. The men wore their best suits, with ties. The women wore silk dresses and hats; one took snuff and another fanned herself. Over in the far corner of the large room, another Negro couple were sitting. They had come to see Judge Standsbury about getting a divorce, had been mistaken for part of Robinson's group, and had been sent upstairs by the sheriff. Now they wished to leave, but when they went to the door to explain, one of the deputies ordered them back. Awkward, obedient, ignorant, hoping only to please, they did not attempt to say more, but repeated, "Yes suh, yes suh," and drew away. They would not say anything now until somebody asked them something. Frightened, sitting close together, they began to think they did not want to get a divorce after all.

When the crowd of strange white men appeared in the center aisle of the courtroom, Robinson Dozer did not at first turn his head. "It looks like the niggers done taken over," said Acey Tallant. Robinson seemed to be looking them over, but the light glazed on his lenses and no one could tell but what he was contemptuous.

"We are expecting Judge Standsbury," he said.

"When you talk to me, nigger, you better say 'Mister.'"

"I don't know your name, sir."

"Then I'll tell you something funny. You ain't ever going to know my name. My name don't matter. I'm white and you're black, that's all that you and me need to know."

The delegation of farmers, seeing that Judge Standsbury was approaching the courthouse doors from the opposite side, gathered away from where the wagon was hitched by the iron fence and started together across the lawn. They were halfway to the door when the firing started and had to break apart and scatter when one of the Negro veterans, jumping from the upstairs window, nearly fell on top of them. It was the one-armed one who, ever since he had had his narrow escape in France, was apt to panic at the approach of danger. He had simply run out of the open window as though he would run on the air, and was still running with his legs and the one arm pumping perfectly together, when the white men saw him and scattered. It was thought the fall killed him, but the men were warned to stand aside while someone fired into his body from above.

Judge Standsbury was just entering the courthouse door when the shots began echoing and resounding. Plaster fell around him as he ran upstairs, but they would not let him in. He wept openly and called for Robinson and at last was carried home, completely broken up. The family reassured him until he died that nothing that had happened was his fault, and he tried to go on with his law practice. Yet it seemed to him that to the extent he would not let what had happened in the court-house stop him in his work, the work was vitiated, and to the extent that he would let it stop him, not only the work but he himself ceased to exist. "He'll never be any good any more," the family said to one another. "Nothing named Tallant is ever coming in this house again." Yet one of his granddaughter's best friends was Acey Tallant's son. "Wouldn't he just die?" they said to one another, but by then he was dead already.

Beckwith, Robinson's youngest son, could still remember that they waited past sundown that night for his father to come home, that nobody ate anything all day, that when he giggled once his mother slapped his face, and that no lamp was lighted.

Then the car came jouncing, rattling down the dry-rutted country road, and in its yellow approach the shadows walked like giants, paused, heard the silence, then the sound, and walked on. Then it was dark again. His sister clutched him by the shoulders and he held on to her knee. Finally his mother, who seemed to have it all in her head exactly when to do things, went out into the yard with his brother and together they carried in his father's body.

They washed him and dressed him in his other black suit, the old one, put on a clean boiled shirt and starched collar with the black string tie, and laid him out in bed. He lay straight and frail under the covers, and his head on the pillows was small as a child's. You would have thought he had died right there, decently. That was what everything they were doing seemed to be trying to pretend. But his mother said, in front of them all, though talking to Beck, who was the littlest:

"It's this they taken him up for, so's they could cast him down. Say Yes suh and No ma'am and You sho' is right, and don't ever say nothing else. What face you got, keep for the black. Yo' daddy never learned it. You see what done happened to him."

41 *An Impulse Restrained*

DUNCAN HARPER lowered the lamp from Robinson Dozer's picture, and turned to Lucy. They each in their own way knew the whole story, but whether they had been told it or not or by whom would never be clear. Southerners hear parts of stories with their ears, and the rest they know with their hearts.

"If Beck will come to me," said Duncan, "I swear to do everything for his own good."

Aunt Mattie's rocker creaked. "I says to Mister Henry Harper many's the time, 'Mister Henry, how come you is such a gemman and yo' uncle so triflin' a man?' Said it right in front of Mister Phillip. But Mister Phillip he jes' giggle. 'I'll have you churched, Mattie, don' watch out. Sho' gwy have you churched.'"

"I don't know where he's at," said Lucy.

For an instant Duncan's eyes met W.B.'s. Then he set the lamp on the table and took his hat.

"Dey always tell it on Mattie, When Mattie got any sass to say, Mattie sass you to the face. But Mattie loves her white folks. What dey gwy do 'thout Mattie? Who gwy love 'em like Mattie do?"

The white man's step was in the hall, on the porch and path. They heard the plowshare scrape against the gate, heard him stumble once going down the hill; then the car door slammed and the starter touched the motor.

Lucy looked down for where W.B. was standing, but W.B. had vanished. She moved instantly to the far corner of the room and was back in the kitchen with W.B. by the collar and the buggy whip raised over his head before he could lower the foot that he was putting the shoe on.

"Where you think you going? Answer me that! You think you going to be the smart one, doing what the white man say. You think somebody going to buy you a ice cream on Saddy. You well's to learn right now, boy. You's a nigger, and you ain't never going to be nothing else. You don't learn it now you ain't going to live to learn it tomorrow. If I don't learn you, who is?"

The whip was keen, and her thin arm drove it terribly upon

him. He danced at first, then threw up his hands and fought the blows like wasps, cried for her to stop, squirmed free and ran. He might have got away from a man, but she brought him down before he had gone two steps, and never missed a stroke. She tore his shirt to shreds and brought blood out of him, and kept right on till the whip broke, teaching him, the only way she knew how, the thing she thought he had to learn.

"Nigger! Nigger! Nigger!" she cried, beating him, and her throat shone wet with her tears.

42 *Jimmy Comes Home*

A FEW MINUTES after Willard Follansbee had left Bud Grantham's house, another car pulled up before the front, and Jimmy Tallant himself alighted gingerly. He saluted the young doctor who had driven him there from the hospital.

"And take it easy," said the doctor through the window. "You got everybody's blood in Winfield County in you now. You've about drained us dry, to tell the truth."

"They lost blood and you lost sleep. I know I put you over the jumps. Thanks for everything, Doc."

"Goodnight. If you need anything, holler."

"'Night."

Wobbly, he felt as tall as a telephone pole, and assailed the steps to the front gallery like an old man. From the room he peered out to the back porch where Bud still rocked and sang away, though in a calmer style than when the meeting fired him:

> "Shall we gather at the river
>   Where bright angel feet have trod,
>   With its mighty waters ever
>   Flowing by the throne of God?
>
> "*Yes*, we'll gather at the river . . ."

"Well, I'll be damned," said Jimmy to himself.

He entered the room where he knew Bella would be staying. He propped a pillow against the headboard of the bed, and let himself down with a sigh. He switched on the bedside light to see the time. In the crib, the baby opened its eyes and regarded him in Indian silence from under the spiky jut of hair. "Hi, Buster," said Jimmy. The baby knotted its fists to yawn, squirmed, and went back to sleep. Jimmy turned out the light.

"Is that you, honey baby?" Bud asked from the porch.

The more Jimmy thought about answering, the less he seemed to find the strength to do it.

"Your old daddy's been setting here thinking tonight, sugar foot," said Bud, through the window. "I'm going with you to the meeting tomorrow night. I'm tired to death studying about this election, and I don't want dealing with them New Orleans fellows, no more than Jimmy did. I'm weary of this wicked earth, and if that preacher don't watch out I'll rise and tell it right out in front of everybody. Bud Grantham was raised to know left from right good as any. My mother was as fine a woman as ever walked the earth. I'm going on to bed now, baby."

"Well, I'll be damned," Jimmy said to himself again, hearing Bud's steps pass down the back gallery toward the bathroom.

The bed where Jimmy lay stood near the front windows of the house, and when the shade was raised one could watch the highway down the distance of the gravel drive. Bud's house had stood there long before they had straightened the roads and paved them. It had once been a country place, hard to get to as any other, but known to be worth the trouble for what you could get wrapped in a newspaper by driving around to the back and blinking the lights three times.

In those days there was every size of child around the house to play with, and every kind of dog to hunt with. As a boy, Jimmy used to go home with Granthams from school, spend the night or the weekend, hunt for coon and 'possum. There had been a well in the back yard—you let a tin pipe down for the water; at night in winter you could hear the dogs under the house when they scuffled for comfort, bumping the beams, or dreamed about a rabbit, or yawned with the high *Iiii* sound. In summer there were peaches like gold to eat, all off three or four old trees that grew on the slope where you went down to the still. And the still itself, all bowered thick in green brush, vine and secret path, was the place of rite and the hushed tone: with solemnity—pride and humility unlikely to occur again—Jimmy had learned its mysteries.

Now there was the highway instead of the old crooked road (which the supervisors had at least graveled better than any other road in the county), and water came in pipes; the still was gone in favor of the Idle Hour, and whisky, though wrapped in a newspaper the same as ever, bore a bonded government stamp and a different flavor.

No wonder Bud Grantham was weary of this wicked earth. Jimmy Tallant got pretty sick of it himself.

A car eased off the highway, and approached the house so slowly that when it stopped at the front steps the wheels scarcely turned at all.

Bella's voice came distinctly, the instant the motor died. "How in the world did you know where I was at is what I can't figure out."

Another voice, a man's, was not so clear.

"Oh," said Bella. "They told you because they'd seen me go past to the meeting."

The man talked so long then that Jimmy had given up hearing any more, though Bella kept saying over and over, "Well, I think you're just the sweetest thing." Then she said, "But you just don't know how crazy I am about Jimmy. He's the sweetest thing in the world." Then she said, "I feel right bad about the baby myself, that is, if favor means anything. I'm not for sure. Some say it does, some say not." And finally she said, getting out of the car, "But I think you're just the sweetest thing in the world, Mr. Pilston."

"Well, I'll be goddamned," said Jimmy to himself.

When she tipped in and closed the bedroom door, she switched on the light and nearly shrieked.

"Hush," said Jimmy. "Bud's asleep and so's the baby."

"Were you wake? Were you there all the time?"

"No, I been asleep too. I just now woke up. Why?"

"Well, I been down to the tent meeting. There was a man drove me home."

"Who was it?"

"One of them Moreheads from over in Leflore. He was at the meeting."

"Which one? Angus?"

"Not him. It was one I never have seen before. Funny, I can't call his name. He asked about you."

"That right?"

"I thought maybe you heard the car and all. I just didn't want you to think nothing."

"I see."

Suddenly, she beamed. She came to him and gave him a great big kiss. "How you feel, darling?"

"Mighty puny," said Jimmy.

"Can I get you anything? How about a glass of sweet milk?"

"I was aiming to tell you soon as you got back, Bella. I think I best go down to sleep in the Idle Hour. The house is probably in a mess, and there's not but one bed up there anyway."

"You can't sleep with me!"

"I'm too stove up, honey. You know that. We couldn't have any fun anyway."

"Oh. Well, how long's it going to be, Jimmy? Before we can?"

"I don't know." He loosened a hangnail with his thumb. "Doc says a year or two."

"A year!" Her mouth seemed to have fallen permanently open.

"How's the preacher?" Jimmy asked. "Any good?"

"I just can't stand it, Jimmy. What on earth am I going to do? I never heard of such a thing as that. The doctor told me the bullet went through the lower part of your right lung and the upper part of your stomach, and that the most delicate operation he ever performed was getting it out of you and sewing you back up again, but I don't see why your lung and your stomach's got anything to do with what you want to do with the rest of you."

"My injuries," he said, fending her off, "are my own business. Don't mess with me, Bella. You know I had three hemorrhages in the hospital, doing no more than lying flat on my back."

"Yeah, I know, Jimmy, but a year—!"

"At the least. Maybe two."

She sat with her hands knotted in her lap.

"You remember that Mr. Pilston?" she said suddenly.

"Sure, I remember him."

"Well, if there ever was anything between him and me, which everybody thought there was on account of the baby took a notion to look like him—I ain't saying there was, understand? —but *if* there was, then it was mainly your fault."

"*My* fault! I don't know how in the hell you figure that."

"Well, it was because I was so crazy about you, and first you'd pay attention to me and then you wouldn't. If you got drunk you'd dance with me, tell me how pretty I was and all, but sober you wouldn't look at me twice except to poke fun at me. It was then I got frustrated."

"You got what?"

"Frustrated."

"You're still reading those blooming magazines."

"Well, if it's true, does it matter whereabouts I found it?"

"I reckon not, honey."

"I got to feeling like if you wouldn't pay me any mind, I wished somebody would come along who would pay me some mind. The word they use for that is frustration."

"I think you're a nice girl, honey," said Jimmy, and kissed her on the forehead. "I don't blame you for anything you've done. Now you find me a blanket or two because I'm so weak I'm liable to get cold even in this weather, and fetch me the flashlight. It's time I got to bed."

Nothing would do but that she went down to the Idle Hour with him and made the bed for him.

"I meant to ask Bud," he said. "Has Follansbee been around?"

"He was out here tonight before I went to the meeting."

"What'd he say? Anything?"

"Lucy came to look after the baby for me. He was trying to get out of her where Beck was. Said if he found Beck he was going to treat him the same as if Beck had raped a white woman."

"God," said Jimmy. "What a scummy joker that Follansbee is."

"Jimmy, darling, just let me stay down here with you a little old while."

"I'm tired out, honey. I'm so weak I'm folding up."

"Well." She plumped the pillow and laid it straight, but he propped it against the headboard and lay down as he had in the room at Bud's. She kissed him goodnight, and picked up the flashlight. At the door she turned. "You don't love me," she told him quietly. "That's the whole thing."

She went away behind the flashlight beam, through the dark.

43 *Stain of the Past*

HE STAYED for some time without moving to undress, twirling a penny box of matches between his thumb and forefinger. He tossed it aside, pulled himself up, and went through to the office, where he found first the light switch, then the telephone, and dialed a number.

"Hi, Tink," he said happily.

"Jimmy! Where are you?"

"Back home."

"But you weren't supposed to be out till next week."

"There was some woman having twins across the hall. They decided I'd be better off at home."

"Do you feel all right?"

"Sure, I'm fine. Oh, Tinker, thanks for the transfusion."

"Don't mention it. Duncan tried to give some, but he wasn't the right type."

"I'm having cards engraved to mail out. You'll both get one."

She giggled.

"How are things, Tink?"

"Okay. Everything's okay."

"Then I guess Harper must be home."

"Yes, he is. You want to talk to him?"

"Please."

A moment later Duncan's clear voice was saying hello. What don't I like about him, Jimmy wondered, all aside from hating his guts for marrying Tinker. There's something else. . . .

"I appreciated you offering me some of your blood, Harper."

"I tried," said Duncan, "but it wasn't the same type."

"They tell me," said Jimmy, "that I've got the commonest damn blood there is."

"What class does that put me in?"

"The blue class, probably. Say, Harper, you know you kept deviling me up at the hospital to tell you who it was shot me?

Well, I've thought it over. Follansbee's out to get Dozer. I was afraid of that all along. I don't like to do this on account of Bud. But all things being considered I'm ready to turn everything I know over to you."

Duncan said, after a moment, "What kind of a deal is this?"

"No deal at all. I'm on the level. I can't locate Dozer for you, but I can fix it so everybody will know he had nothing to do with it. If you want to drive out here, we can fix up a statement."

"A statement on what?"

"You may not know. There were some gambling gentlemen from New Orleans by to see me that day—"

"I had a very good source of information about that. In fact, she was just the other side of the door."

"Let's keep her out of this."

"You listen to me, Tallant. You been lying up there in that hospital keeping shut-mouthed for two and a half weeks while this thing of Dozer got good and hot from one end of the county to the other. What happened could happen; you were sitting back to let this election fall right in your lap. As long as Woolbright and me were on the spot you were willing to watch us fry. Now you've got word the tide has turned. As a matter of fact, I'm at home waiting for New Orleans to call any minute. You needn't think you can jump on the band wagon and good as say to everybody, Look what I did! Kerney and I broke this thing and we're about to break you and you know it. You've had your chance. You've got less sense of public good than any man I ever saw, and if you ask me—" He stopped.

"Finish it," said Jimmy. "You were going to say I came by it naturally."

"I didn't say that," Duncan returned, his voice cooling. "If you'd come around sooner it would be different. But here at the eleventh hour— We don't want your help, Tallant. That's all."

Jimmy replaced the telephone, switched out the light, and closed the dusty office. When he gained the bed and sank down again, he was shaking.

He remembered what Bud Grantham had said through the window: Weary of this wicked earth. But Bud could do what Jimmy couldn't. Bud would rise in a meeting someday, if not this summer, then the next one, and tell his sins and let Jesus save him. When all the doors were shut, a lot of folks knocked at that one. They claimed it always opened. Well, I'll never know, Jimmy thought.

I even tried to get that boy to kill me, he thought, hardly believing it all himself. Even that didn't work, though it might have if Tinker hadn't come . . . Tinker Taylor . . . cowboy sailor. . . .

He raised up the matchbox to read what it said on the cover, when his hand grew tired as death; he let it fall, and presently he slept.

PART FIVE

44 *The Public Enemy*

I N NEW ORLEANS, in the summer, the early morning is apt to have a false freshness, as if somebody had sprayed a big black stevedore with cologne. About ten the city begins to sweat: the sun is like a red-hot stove lid, only nobody looks at the sun, the heat being a condition in which one exists, and is not to be seen any more than air or the grace of God. All the subtle diplomacies of civilization enter into circumventing the heat: it obviously cannot be met on open field. There is air conditioning now for everything from movie palaces to dim little bars, but there are patios too, and latticed porches, shut-tered windows, and polished hallways deep down the stairwell with old glass shielded from the glare. In Audubon Park the swans drift to the shade as it blackens, and down on Tchoupa-toulos Street women go about all day in their slip and house-shoes, and an electric fan looks at them with one big eye from head to toe, toe to head, while they nap in the afternoon. With a car, you can take the shore drive along Lake Pontchartrain, though there is no shade and sometimes even the breeze off the water is hot. Down in the French Quarter you can buy tall frosted glasses with minty mixtures, cold as snow, though al-cohol is always heating and will give you an awful wallop when you go out again. Then there are the oyster bars.

The oysters come in every day out of the beds in the river and the lake, and it is supposed to be dangerous to eat them in the summer, but they are kept directly on ice and are so good, especially when you have a hangover, that to many people it is worth the chance. A man takes them off the ice and breaks them open with an oyster knife and serves them by the dozen on a plate of ice. You can mix yourself a sauce out of catsup with a little Worcestershire sauce, lemon juice, and a dash of horseradish, though for an uneasy stomach lemon juice alone is enough. These, along with a tall cold glass of beer, will go a long way toward fortifying the soul to endure the heat of the day.

There is not much crime in New Orleans in the summer. At night, on weekends, Negroes carve each other to fancy bits with a razor, but if you put all the Negro crimes in the paper there would be no room for international affairs. Down on Bourbon Street, which burns at night like a pool of oil, homosexuals sometimes make nasty petulant scenes in the bars. But a people so earnestly concerned with keeping cool do not find the materials of crime ready to hand, and nothing about the young man who was eating oysters and drinking beer and the older man who had joined him would have told the waiter that one was from the intricate society of the underworld and the other a plainclothes man from the city detectives. Their conversation looked casual, not even businesslike. It might have been about the weather, how hot it was.

"You seen Sam?" the older man asked the young one. He picked his teeth with a match stub and watched the other lift an oyster till it severed from the shell.

"Not since last night. I won't see him either. He fired me."

"What you plan to do now?"

"I'm fixing to go back home, I reckon." The oyster glided down his throat. He took a swallow of beer. "It ain't nothing like New Orleans, but maybe that's a good thing."

"What is home at?"

"Up in Mississippi. Up in Tippah County."

"Well, there's one thing certain."

"What's that?"

"You might go back to Tippah County, but you sure got to detour by Winfield."

An oyster actually paused in the boy's throat. "Sam," he said, and swallowed. "That's how come he fired me. The sonofabitch. He told on me. If they was to tell on each other, they'd start shooting. It just goes to show you, I ain't one of them. They knew it and I knew it. I never was."

"There aren't any charges I know of. You're just wanted to give evidence." The detective ordered himself a beer, then, on second thought, a half-dozen oysters.

"There couldn't be any charges, because I never tried to do nothing. It was completely accidental. It was the first shot I missed since four years ago when Unker Chollie Klappert said, 'If you'll go real easy you can shoot the marker off that hen's foot.' But she lifted her foot up somehow or 'nother and the bullet nicked her on the leg, so Unker Chollie said we was obliged to have her for dinner."

"Yes, and what about this other little accident? Just how did it happen?"

"I never hated anything so bad in my life," the boy said. "I always did like Mr. Tallant, though I never had met him but one time before, but the time we drove up in Miss'ippi to see him, we found ourselves to be kinfolks. Sure did. He was one of Unker Chollie's cousins, the one I was just now talking about with the hen. I don't know which side of the family, so maybe we was only connected. Anyway I sure did like him. If I was just ranking the folks I know I'd rather shoot by accident, I'd put him closer to the bottom than anybody outside of Unker Chollie Klappert and Aunt Darr. And Mama, naturally. Never seen him but twice. But that's how I feel about it."

"Yeah, so how did this get to happen?"

"Sam and Pilston and Mitchell went up there to Franklin to see about farming out some gambling equipment. They were going to put some money into the sheriff's race so it would be safe to operate. But Mr. Tallant didn't much want to trade with them about the election. About that time Mr. Tallant's wife come in toting a baby which Sam said later was Pilston to the life, though I couldn't notice much resemblance. Don't never seem to me a little baby looks like any*thing*, let alone any*body*. Yet there's them that claim to see it. I don't reckon that's got the world and all to do with anything, except then was when Mr. Tallant got up and left the room. Sam sent me and Mitchell after him to bring him back and settle up about the election."

"So then?"

"So then we followed him on back of the roadhouse across a pasture and down a hill, back to the edge of a field where some woods started. We hollered to him to come on back, and Mitchell said, 'You better do like we tell you; this boy here's got a gun.' He turned around and started laughing. Real friendly and easy, like he was every other time. He said, 'You better take the gun yourself, Mitchell. You'll never get that boy to shoot me. I wish you could. Me and Wally's kinfolks, and what you asking for ain't done. But then I tell you, Wally,' he said, 'I hone to see how good you can shoot. You take this four-bit piece and when I thumb it in the air like that' —he thumbed it—'you see can you bring it down for me.' He thumbed it up again and when he stopped talking he looked at me and stopped laughing. He had the saddest face I ever saw. It was mournful. It called to mind a song Unker Chollie said he used to get on the old earphone radio set out of Shreseport, went 'Look down, look down that lonesome road before you travel on.' I always liked that song and thought it many's the time traveling round in the car with Sam and Mitchell and them. Then he was holding the fifty-cent piece on his thumb and saying, 'How good can you shoot now, sure enough? It must be a sight to behold.' So I said, 'It is a sight.' Then he said, real soft, 'Then shoot for me, Wally,' and he thumbed the coin, but where it had been sailing up free towards the trees it missed that time and only went about a foot high; I guess it never cleared him. Then was when I shot, having made up my mind to it. I don't know if you know anything about shooting or not, but once your mind tells your finger to pull that trigger it don't make no difference if a elephant gets in the way, you're going to shoot.

"It must be laying somewhere around there still, that four-bit piece, plugged. For I hit it, and him too. The minute I saw what had happened, I started to run towards him, but Mitchell grabbed me and got the gun out of my hand. 'You get on back up that hill,' he said. 'Don't, you'll stay down here and keep him company.' Mitchell taken charge of everything. He seen a nigger down the hill, down in the bottom, and went on back to scare him away so he couldn't tell he seen us there.

"It was later we heard from up there that Mister Tallant wasn't dead. I was mighty glad to hear it. Glad! I was downright thankful."

"It squares with what Mitchell says," said the detective, "almost word for word." He dusted the cracker crumbs from his mouth and polished off his beer. "I got to go send a wire up to Winfield County. Seems they had all decided that nigger you say Mitchell scared off had done the shooting, and some boy up there is having a hell of a time getting elected sheriff when he couldn't find the nigger or you either."

"I can't say how it happened, except by the way he was looking, so solemn and sad, his eyes pulling at me. You believe in himotism? Maybe he himotized me."

"Where you going to be?"

"Right here."

"Not going to hunt up Sam?"

"That bastard better stay away from me. Him and his talk about the 'code.'"

"He never told you to hit Tallant. What accident you had was your accident. I think Sam's played it straight. If you'd done it *for* him, he'd have backed you."

"He could have told me. Talked to him an hour last night. All he said was he couldn't afford me any more. Never mentioned Mr. Tallant, Winfield County, Miss'ippi, or Highway 82."

"I reckon he was scared anybody that could have one accident like that could have two."

"Two. I already had two. You remember I told you about that old hen. I never ought have got mixed up in this kind of business, but I always thought you ought to put your talents to use."

"I'm counting on you to wait here for me, Wally."

"Glad to," said the boy, and smiled at him gently.

45 *The Fugitive*

EARLIER THAT morning, up in Franklin County, Beck Dozer walked in the back door of his own house.

"Lawd, Beck," said Lucy, "is it sho' nuff you?"

"It's me," said Beck. "You going to give your baby a kiss?"

"I sho' is."

He swung her around and set her down again. "What time is it, Lucy?"

"I don't know, but it's early. Granny ain't off the slop jar yet. Lord to God, Beck, you scared me half to death."

"Got any coffee?"

"There's some on the stove. Us had a scontious time in this house last night. I most had to beat the stuffing out'n W.B."

"How come?"

"Mister Duncan Harper come out here again makes the third time since you been gone. He got on W.B. to make him go find you."

"What for?"

"Tell you how-all he going to pertect you, how-all he got

the chance to win the 'lection if you shows up, what-all he aim
to want to do. W.B. ain't got a grain. Time Mister Duncan left
he out in the kitchen wif one shoe on reaching for the other
one."

"How come you not to let him go? You think I can't do my
own thinking?"

She went on mixing corn batter in an enamel pan, now and
again dipping water in from the bucket on the shelf, beating it
with a flopping sound that seemed to be part of what she said.

"I think you don't git yo'se'f right straight on back over to
Humphreys County, you going to land in a peck of trouble.
Mister Duncan ain't the onliest one got the word for you. I
seen that other'n running for shurf, Mister Willard Follansbee
—*he* claim do he see you first he going to do you like what they
does when a nigger get with a white woman."

"Unker Beck," said W.B., coming in in his shirttail, "Aunt
Lucy done frail the life outer me."

"You think you telling sump'n," Lucy said. "Well, you ain't."

"Come here, boy," said Beck. "Lord, Lucy. You'd think he
was mixed up with a wildcat. Time going to come, W.B., when
you going to go wheresoever you feels called on to go, no
matter who tries to stop you. Is that right?"

"Sho' right, Unker Beck."

"Don't call me uncle any more, W.B. I'm your blood daddy,
son. You are my own natural child."

Lucy stopped still with everything. She did not understand
all she knew about Beck, but every time he brought out something fresh, he gentled her more. "I been knowing it all the
time, Beck. But he ain't. W.B. ain't."

"I sho' ain't," W.B. said, in soft self-contemplation.

"Where his mama at?" Lucy asked.

"She in England, where she always was. In London. You
don't have to know all about it, Lucy. She wrote me a letter
saying she couldn't work and keep him too and that her husband was working too and wanted shut of him, since he was
black. She said if I'd send her the money there was an American
woman getting a divorce and coming back to the U.S., and she
could get him in by her. Either that or she'd put him in a home
over there. She would have done it too. All them folks over
there in England, they take their children when they ain't no

bigger than W.B. and send them to school, then they're shut of them, they don't have to see them much more. So I wrote her to send this child to me. That was the time I went up North. It all worked out. The woman brought him to a hamburger and beer place in Harlem, and left him by himself, sitting in the booth. We had it all planned on the telephone. She didn't want me to see her, or be seen with me. She was scared about the law, somehow or other."

"His mammy just give him away, never thought no more of it?"

"They're not like us. Don't seem they care for chillen like we do."

"Sho' don't," said Lucy. She took down a black iron griddle with a handle like a loop of string, lifted an eye from the stove, and set the griddle over the flame.

"You glad I'm your daddy?" Beck asked W.B. "Want to, you can say Daddy. Go on. Say Daddy."

"I can't, Unker Beck," said W.B., overcome with the shyness of names. He put his face in Beck's shoulder.

Holding the spoon firm in the cup with his finger, Beck drained off his coffee and set it aside. He pulled the boy closer to him.

"You liable to have a little white baby one of these days, black boy. Don't giggle. What you laughing for? Turn your face around here, and listen what your daddy tells you.

"If a child of yours want to go North, you let him go along; that is, if you're not already North yourself. If you marry light enough, your children might cross the color line, but if they do, you tell them to make sure when they marry a white girl that she's really one hundred per cent pure white, because if she's not she's apt to wind up with a black baby and that might not go down so well with her folks. That is, if anybody still cares much by that time. In another thirty years or so, Lucy, they might just think it's cute to have a dark child. Look how they all gots to have a sun tan. You ever thought about that? The day of the white skin might be near about over.

"I read up on all such as this, son. Your Aunt Lucy don't know, and most white folks don't either, but if you're going to mess around on the color line you just as well to understand it.

I never exactly meant to mess with the white, but the British women came running to the black skin."

Lucy spread bacon grease on the griddle with a rag swab wrapped on the end of a little cedar stick. The grease spit like sleet. "Was she a real white lady?" Lucy asked. She portioned out the batter in cakes on the hot griddle.

"W.B.'s mama? She wasn't any prize. She looked like she was about half-starved, just like you."

"That accounts for that big old boat W.B. been talking about ever since he got here."

"I remembers hit jest as plain," said W.B.

"Don't say hit. Say I remember it."

"I remember it."

"That's right." He rose and reached down three plates from the safe, then the molasses bucket, and went to the back porch to bring the butter in from the icebox.

"Don't you use up all that butter," Lucy said. "There ain't no more."

She set the first of the batter cakes on the table. Beck helped himself, thrusting his fork in to the hilt. He smiled.

"You know I told you my sister brought W.B. in a boat across Lake Michigan. How come you so dumb? Granny knows better than you. I bet she knows folks don't cross Lake Michigan in a boat."

"Granny don't know nothing. She don't know no more than me."

"Anybody knows that."

"I can't help it if I'm dumb," said Lucy. "You want some more coffee?"

"Just a tap. Mind how you pours that sorghum, W.B.!" He spooned sugar into his cup.

"The city of London," he resumed, "is what I would call the white man's city. It is cold and dark and dirty. Sometimes they have the fog and sometimes they have the rain or maybe a little wet dirty snow, or then again it might just be cloudy. But there is always *some*thing, summer and winter, all mushy and run together. They sit in little steamy café-looking places and drink tea. The tea is the color of dishwater, but it tastes good, or maybe everything else tastes so bad you just think it tastes good. They all sit and read the paper or look straight ahead of themselves. They don't talk to one another much, except when they're drinking in the pubs. They don't notice the girls that wait on the tables. You take and let the door fly open and a big black good-looking GI walk in with a great big smile and an eye for the ladies, and every girl in that place is going to want to follow him down the street when he goes out again. It's only natural. Our white boys, they had an easy time in London. There's girl after girl there that nobody has ever yet told they were pretty. Maybe they *ain't* pretty, understand, but we all come to feel that this was partly the reason. We had to step careful and gather with the Yankee boys for company in the pubs, but when it came to women—man! we were all over that town.

"Such as it was. It is, as I was saying, the white man's city. You don't hear the jazz along the street like in New York, or the blues like in New Orleans. New York is getting to be a nigger town, and New Orleans always was. I knew a fellow in the Army that came from San Francisco. He said his town wouldn't be nothing atall without the Chinaman. I'm inclined to believe all this because if ever a city was in need of color it was London. You leave the white man to himself, I said, and this is what the white man does.

"The Negro city, on the other hand, rests on the Equator by the Ocean between the Mountains and the Sand. It is a pure-white city with little shade trees all along the streets and an artesian well on every corner. The men dress all in clothes white as sheets, which looks good because they are so black. The women are black too, but they dress in different-colored clothes, yellow and red and bright blue, with all different kinds of skirts, some long and tight and switchy, some long and full, some short and tight, some short and pleated. There's no such thing as this year's style or last year's style. They can choose how they like it. Then they wear gold earrings in their ears."

"And in they nose," said Lucy, and refilled his plate. "I done heard about it."

"That's one style that's gone out," said Beck. "They changed all that."

"Whereabouts is this place?" asked W.B. "Is it close as Memphis?"

"It's in Africa," said Beck, "on the west coast."

"Where is Africa?" asked W.B.

"It's too far to walk. Don't you know about Africa? Don't you learn anything in school?"

"'Cose he know," said Lucy. "He just showing out." She scratched between her plaits with a hairpin. "Watch these here hot cakes for me, W.B. I gots to go get Granny up. She be done gone to sleep again on the pot."

When she had installed the old woman in her chair for the day, had smoked and aired the room and let the light in, and put the baby on his pallet in the kitchen, giving him a cold biscuit to gnaw on, she ordered W.B. without any fooling to go and get his clothes on, and began to get out of Beck what she wanted to know.

"You ain't going into town?"

"Whatever I does, Lucy, you ain't stirring a step out of this house. You stay here with Granny. They all time claiming up in town how they love Aunt Mattie, done saved their lives, birthed their children, laid out their dead, mingled with the smallpox for them. Well. Maybe they love her and maybe they don't. Maybe they'd shame to come in the house where she is. You stay indoors. It's a speaking day, and our race must not be conspicuous. You don't know what that word means. I got nobody to talk to. My daddy had a senator. All his life he could stay right quiet, after twenty years of talking about Cicero and Plato."

If he was blaming her, she didn't know it clearly. She could not hear him well, but whether because her ears had dulled or his voice had weakened, she could not say. He stopped speaking and looked at her, and the way the light fell she could see right through his glasses to his eyes. She knew why he had been talking such a blue streak, and why he couldn't think of any more to say. She saw his fear begin. She saw it climbing toward hers like two people about to meet, and from that moment she believed he would die that day. She thrust her hand out before her, as though she fended something away. She felt her hand grow cold in the outward strain of the muscles, and saw below the gold rim of Beck's glasses the scorch of tears, and around the edge of his hair, the gray rime of sweat.

"You still can catch the train. Go on up North. Go to Chicago. Ain't nobody coming to look for you. You can send me word. When Granny dies—"

"Granny dies! You couldn't kill Granny with a machine gun."

"Beck, please go on up there. Take W.B. if you want to. You can send me the money to come. I'll bring Granny with me."

"I came home to change to my good clothes," said Beck.

"Beck, go on back to Humphreys County! The white ain't for us. They ain't for nobody but theyselves. It ain't for us to mingle."

"They gots to learn," said Beck, rising. In the catch of light his glasses were opaque again, and luminous. "They can't learn off nobody but us. All these years we been backing up, and you see they never have learned anything."

"It don't have to be you that learns them!"

"It's got to be somebody," he said. "Might be some nigger with half my brains, somebody who'd make a mess of things. Papa never made a mess of anything. That's how come they don't rest easy about him till this good day."

He went to find his Sunday clothes. When he came out, W.B. was all dressed up too and stood alongside of him, both of them in their coats and ties, like wanting her to send them off somewhere, and it as hot as it was going to get.

"Where you think *you* going?" Lucy demanded.

"*He* taking me," said W.B.

It struck Lucy that they were doing her wrong.

"I ain't about to walk into Lacey all by myself. W.B. knows how to do. I told him. We going through and across the creek, over in back of Mister Mars Overstreet's store, out there where all the gullies are. I plan to wait there while W.B. circles into town, to the back of Mister Harper's house. Mister Harper can come out and get me, if that is what he wants so bad."

"You just as crazy as you can live," said Lucy, getting mad. "All them white folks in town today, all drinking. If you had to get hold of Mister Harper whyn't you stay over in Humphreys County and talk to the shurf over there? Whyn't you call him on the telephone from somewheres way off?"

"Because it's not just Mister Harper to think about. It's that town I think of. It's where my papa died."

"You just determined!" Lucy cried. She was really mad now. "Any day but this one you could have picked. Oh, no. W.B., don't you go a step of the way. Yo' Unker Beck think he smart, but he acting downright crazy now. You needn't think you going to get any big fun'al outer me. I don't care what your policy cover."

"We gots to go on now," said Beck, "before it gets too late."

Tremulous, half in tears, she stood for some time sulking near the stove. She felt ill-used, and thought of her first husband, that limber, yellow, shiny boy, all the time joking and joshing. If he ever went off it was for something like a woman; he never got determined where white folks were concerned. Then he left her mind like steam out the window. "Beck!" she cried, and ran after him. "Beck, Beck, Beck!" She was headlong on the path, crying outright.

She saw them down at the bottom of the hill, where the path crossed a footbridge over the spring-branch. They were walking hand in hand. "Beck!" He turned and W.B. turned. Beck lifted his hand. She halted on the slope.

"You go on back to the house, Lucy," he told her. "Look after Granny and the baby. Don't go outdoors."

Down near them, the branch made its clear small running sound.

She turned without saying any more and walked away home, just as he told her. She felt suddenly at peace, doing exactly as he said.

46 *The All-Day Speaking*

HOT WEATHER clouds, voluminous, processional, pearly, rode high over Lacey. Out in the county the crops were laid by; nobody traveled in the fields. The country stores were all locked up, and so was farm machinery in the sheds, with the tanks and crankcases drained and spare parts locked in the houses. Bad dogs were chained to run on a wire. Good dogs pursued the cars a little way, gave up, and turned back home. In the old days they could have gone too, trotting just behind the wagon, or underneath it, for shade. In lots of ways it seemed like a Sunday; in others not so much.

Tinker dressed in her navy that she had not had on since June. She smoothed the white piqué collar before the mirror, wondering if a bit more starch would have brought another vote to Duncan. Whatever her collar, the children were shining triumphs of her hand. Sometimes it happened that soap and water, fresh clothes, damp-brushed hair, and shoes produced two marvelous creatures, docile to tears, too good for the human race, apt to glow in the dark, their eyes full of the secret that would set the world free. "Look how pretty Mama looks," Patsy whispered to Cotton, who gazed up at her in guileless adoration. "You all go get in the car," said Tinker. She was too well acquainted with their hellish moments to be unduly swayed.

Duncan, too restless to wait for everyone to dress, had gone ahead to the school grounds where the speaking would be. Driving through town, Tinker saw Kerney in conversation with a group on the drugstore corner. She stopped almost in the middle of the street, the way people always would do in Lacey, and honked to him. He glanced her way twice before he crossed to her.

"One look at these two," said Kerney, admiring the children, "and Willard Follansbee himself will vote for Duncan."

"I scrubbed them within an inch of their lives this morning and now they're in a coma. They haven't been this clean since last Easter."

"What I need in this race is a pair of those."

"It isn't hard. Happens every day."

"So they tell me."

"Kerney, has Duncan found you?"

"I haven't seen him, no."

"He wants to tell you that he talked to New Orleans again this morning. The police were expecting to get the straight dope on who shot Jimmy within the next hour or so, and were going to wire the minute they knew. The boy at the telegraph office will run the wire over to the speaking, and if he finds you first he'll give it to you. Is that straight?"

"Letter perfect," said Kerney, and smiled at her, leaning in the window. "Tinker, you're the prettiest girl in Lacey."

"Watch out. I'll tell Cissy."

"I don't care if you do. I've told her myself. You're the prettiest, and the sweetest. I've never known anybody as sweet as you."

"It's meant a lot to me, the way you've stuck by Duncan. It's made all the difference to him."

He did not stir. "You have such pretty eyes," he said.

She reached over to pat his hand. "We're blocking traffic. Good luck!"

She drove on. She had seen in the rear-view mirror the handsome nose of the Hunts' convertible, and the two girls, Marcia Mae and Cissy, riding with the careless poise of people going to the beach. Marcia Mae was wearing a straw field hat to keep off the powerful sun, and she and Cissy both were half-masked in dark glasses. Tinker's smoothly groomed dark head was bound in a strip of white piqué—her summer hat—and she had even put on hose and carried short white gloves.

The convertible in turn pulled up beside Kerney Woolbright.

"I've come to hear you make a speech," said Cissy, immensely pleased with herself. "Tell me what it's going to be about, so I can look intelligent."

"Little girls shouldn't bother their pretty heads with nasty old politics," said Kerney.

"He's going to lose," said Marcia Mae. "I've been telling her all morning, but she won't listen. Duncan's going to lose, and Kerney is too."

At the school grounds, Duncan located Tinker and came to sit with her in the car. Patsy sat in his lap, put his straw hat on over her ribbons and curls, picked up his large hand as though it were a puppy and gave it a passionate kiss.

"She's discovered kissing," said Tinker.

"I thought politicians kissed babies. Seems it's the other way around. Did you tell Kerney about the wire from New Orleans?"

"Yes, haven't you seen him?"

"He should be here by now."

"He was up on the drugstore corner."

"They're all telling me I've got to explain about the Dozer case. Follansbee is distributing handbills of that damn picture Tallant had taken at the jail. He's written a lot of crap to go with it. You can tell he did it, instead of Tallant. There's not a correct sentence in the whole thing."

"What does it say?"

"Same old thing. I'm a nigger lover, protecting Dozer at any cost because he works for the nigger papers. Thank God, Kerney speaks in the morning. He's going to lay it on the line for me."

"He seemed upset this morning. I thought he was going to cry. He kept telling me how pretty he thought I was."

"He can say that again."

She laid her two small hands with the expertly lacquered nails side by side on the Chevrolet emblem in the center of the steering wheel.

"I think everything's all right between us now. I think it always will be."

He flipped the soft end curl of her hair with his finger. "I know it will be. I'm sorry anything had to happen. Do you know how sorry I am?"

"I think it had to happen. I always thought it had to, in the back of my mind."

"I thought so too, I guess."

And quickly as though he had told her a joke, she had turned and smiled at him.

"What had to happen, Daddy?" Cotton asked. He was standing on the floor of the back seat, leaning reflectively between them in that satisfying way children can make use of a car as though it were a house.

"Daddy had to run for sheriff, darling," said Tinker.

"You mean you're sorry you had to run for sheriff?"

"No, not exactly, but Daddy doesn't like to make speeches."

"*I* think Daddy means he's sorry he made you hit him in the face with a potato."

"*I* made *her*—well, see who's side he's on."

"There's not any side to be on, precious," said Tinker, and smoothed his hair.

"I want some ice cream," said Patsy.

Parked off at an angle down in the shade near where the bunting trailed down from the outdoor speakers' platform, Marcia Mae did not turn her head but saw just the same from her mask's corner the family group in Duncan's car.

"Isn't Duncan too bucolic for any use?"

"What does that mean?" Cissy asked, who thought maybe it was an illness like dropsy.

"Oh, so damn family-group. Little curly-haired cherubs, little home-grown wife. Thank God I'm not tied down that way."

But just the same her heart ached.

"Why would Kerney nearly cry?" Tinker asked.

"He hates the thought of losing. But you can't tell. He may

make them see the truth. How can you ever know how deep a fake nigger-issue goes? We don't even know for sure how deep a real one goes any more. And Kerney's a good speaker, which I'm not. I had a lot of good friends around these parts, and I sold them on Kerney. His name has got around."

"How did you sell them, Daddy?" Cotton asked.

"Well, talking to them. I knew them all from the old football days."

"From when you were an All-time Great," said Cotton.

"I want some ice cream," said Patsy.

"If Kerney speaks in the morning, when do you speak?" Tinker asked.

"Not till afternoon. Kerney's running for district office— that puts him before lunch, a good spot, right after the gubernatorial candidates. I'm with the locals, later on. By then we're sure to have heard from New Orleans."

"Ice *cream!*"

"They've been so good," Tinker explained, opening the door. "All right. You all come on."

Over at the long table under the sycamore trees, the Garden Club ladies in their flowered voile dresses fanned flies away from the chicken salad, potato salad, fried chicken, ham, deviled eggs, rolls, pies, cakes, and relishes. Tinker spoke to all the ladies in turn and bought ice cream sandwiches for the children. She told them each separately to lean over when they bit it and to hurry and finish it before it melted. She straightened from explaining this to Patsy, and there was Marcia Mae. Seen by so many they could not do other than greet each other, and stand talking for a while.

Soon now the white collar of Tinker's dress would wilt, what with children and the heat, just as her white cotton gloves would acquire a streak of grease somehow, and grass stain would mark her spectator pumps. Marcia Mae presented a more unfenced appearance, as it were, in her ribbed cotton skirt and tailored linen shirt, her loafers soft as gloves on her narrow naked feet: a political speaking was no more worth dressing for than a soldier's dance.

Both these women, by turning their heads, might have seen across the level school grounds to the spot beside the see-saws where Marcia Mae Hunt had looked at Louise Taylor's made-over coat-suit with pearl buttons the size of moons, and said, "That's the funniest-looking dress *I* ever saw," in her voice that was always a little rough, like raw silk—she had never been known to lower it. Looking aside together, they would have seen the past as one turns to see a person who already stands at the elbow. For in a small town, in a society whose supreme interest is people, the past exists physically—empty chairs expect the dead and not in vain. So, turning thus to admit they both remembered, to look again on what they remembered, they might have discovered forgiveness, or at least a moment of companionship. But they had been again too recently in contest, and felt compelled to meet each other's eyes with all the steady honesty of guilt and ask the most hypocritical questions.

Marcia Mae reflected, escaping on the excuse that she had to take a Coca-cola to Cissy, that practically everybody in Lacey felt constrained around her for one reason or another; she wouldn't accept invitations, tell her life story, or remember to speak to people. She scuffed the heels of her loafers at the pleasure of release from this latest encounter. She retained a satisfying impression of Tinker too carefully matched in navy and white, even to navy and white pumps. You would wonder perhaps if in her navy bag there was not a white handkerchief with a navy figure. She regained the leather seat of the convertible and surprised Cissy with the Coca-cola.

"It's not cold enough," said Cissy, feeling.

"I can't help that," said Marcia Mae.

Cissy drank. "I saw you talking to Mrs. Duncan Harper." She smiled her little fat smile.

"Don't be such a brat," said Marcia Mae.

"I want to see Kerney," Cissy complained.

"No doubt you will."

He was near them now, detaching himself from a group of men in straw hats and white shirts. Marcia Mae felt suddenly that she wanted to see him, too. She slid from the convertible seat and went to him. His eyes at least presented her with no discomfort—a born politician on speaking day, trim without elegance in his seersucker suit, what could he be saying to her except, "You and I are the smart ones; we know how things really are." He looked at her so much that way that she actually believed it.

"Cissy awaits," she told him. "She forgot to give you the summons for dinner tonight."

"I haven't got time to talk to her now," said Kerney. "Besides, I already know about it. Miss Nan told me." He waved at Cissy, who had contrived to look impassive behind her blinders and gave no sign.

The platform was empty except for a man tinkering with the microphone. He kept saying, "Testing. Is that all right, Mac?" The words were small in the three big mouths on top of the soundtruck.

"I've never seen such a crowd," said Marcia Mae. "There must be two thousand people here. I always forget how many country people there are."

"It's a common failing," said Kerney.

Still in black for her husband's death, Miss Ada Brevard appeared between them, fanning mightily. Thin and nervous, conscious of a better world where political speakings were not allowed, Miss Ada had but one matter to take up with Kerney and she saw no reason to make a secret of it.

"I have just this minute been told, Kerney, that Duncan is opposed to segregation in the schools! I'm more distressed than I can tell you. Can this possibly be true?"

"Why, Miss Ada," said Kerney, "not that I know of."

"Edna Colquit just heard it with her own ears. She told me. Mr. Colquit asked him right out what he would favor if the Supreme Court ruled out segregation in the schools, and he said in that case we should have to work out some way to comply with the ruling."

"Why, Miss Ada—"

"If you nice young people in politics begin this kind of talk, to whom, oh, to whom shall we turn?"

"Miss Ada, I—"

"You realize what this means to me, Kerney. I, *I* appointed Duncan to office. I was sheriff myself when Mr. Brevard died. Why, I said to Edna, 'It's the basis of our Southern way of life that the black should not mingle with the white. Our forefathers fought and died, Kerney—'" Her voice quite broke. The thought of the culture that had bred her seemed to blow against her like a wind too strong; she was shaken in it, like a high frail bough.

"There, there." Kerney grasped her little arm.

She raised her head high. "If Mr. Brevard had known that any such thing could be in Duncan Harper's mind, he could never, could never, never—"

"He didn't know," Kerney said hastily. "I think you can rest assured of that."

"I said to Edna, 'If he's going to have ideas like that, I shall just have to take the rostrum myself and say I never knew it when I appointed him. I see no recourse.' Is it true that he is hiding that Dozer Negro?"

"Why, goodness, Miss Ada, I'm sure that Duncan—"

"He has always seemed such a sweet boy, such a handsome boy, such a gentleman!" She was as dewy and fresh with tears as a girl, as grieved as an old piano tune.

"Here he comes now," said Kerney. "Why don't you just talk to him?"

"Why, I shall! I will!" She furled her fan for the encounter.

Duncan, who was obviously headed for Kerney, tangled immediately in her nets. He floundered amongst them, shifting from one hip to the other, standing here, circling there, but could he be rude to Miss Ada? He could not.

Marcia Mae said to Kerney, "You came a long way from convincing her of anything good about Duncan."

"You don't convince people like Miss Ada of anything," said Kerney.

"Somebody convinced her of a few things somewhere along the line. She's the most convinced person I've seen in a long time."

"That's just the trouble," Kerney said, "with this whole part of the country. Do you know," he chose suddenly to confide, "a college friend of mine, practicing in New York now, passed through yesterday and called me. I said I didn't have time to see him. What could I say to him? What can we ever say?"

"Look at Duncan," said Marcia Mae dreamily. "In college he was all lean meat and bone. Leanness is a good thing, a good fast thing: people with their foot in the road are lean and fast, like you, Kerney, with your mind churning and burning away. If you stay in Lacey you'll get fat. First the thickening waistline, then the bald spot in the back. You won't be able to get away either, when old ladies stop you on the street. Only you won't be too nice to leave, like Duncan. You'll be too bored to try."

Kerney hardly heard her. Waiting for a word with Duncan, he was more sharply aware of what Duncan was saying. He heard things like: "I don't think we can possibly secede again, Miss Ada. We tried that once, you remember . . . No, I don't say I believe in integration right away, but I do think that whatever the Supreme Court decides to rule, the country sooner or later has to go along with . . . you see, the Constitution. . . ."

My God, thought Kerney Woolbright, he's going to explain the Constitution to Miss Ada. "Tell Duncan I couldn't wait," he said to Marcia Mae. He turned on his heel; and his anger seemed to him at the outset like the loss of temper occasioned by hitting an elbow or at the end of a long day typing a document with the carbon reversed; but it did not fade as it should have: it continued to seethe and fume on his way to the rostrum, to threaten to possess him if he did not find a way to halt it. The Constitution, he thought, the *Constitution*. He felt that he would strangle in a sense of impotence that warred against every instinct of his soul. . . .

From the car under the sycamore shade, Tinker saw Duncan and Marcia Mae come close to collision, exchange a taut greeting, and part.

"Who's that yellow-headed lady with Daddy?" Cotton asked.

"Her name is Mrs. O'Donnell," said Tinker.

Cotton threw a gun to his shoulder. "Pow, Mrs. O'Donnell. Pow, pow!" He was apt to start firing on anybody.

"Hush," said Tinker. "She'll hear you. That isn't nice."

"Pow, Mith O'Donnell," said Patsy without firing anything.

"Testing," said the three big horns from the soundtruck. "I think it's all right now, Mac."

Kerney Woolbright and the electrician passed each other on the rostrum steps.

Duncan came to the car window. "I'm going to sit in the audience, down near the front. Kerney is bound to mention things that concern us both, and I want to be in evidence to back him up."

"Who was that yellow-headed lady, Daddy?" Cotton asked.

"A lady named Miss Hunt," said Duncan.

"I'm named Mith O'Donnell," said Patsy and grinned at him blissfully.

"They asked who she was," Tinker explained, "and I said Mrs. O'Donnell."

"You were right, of course," said Duncan. He pressed his hand into his brow as though his head hurt. "Miss Ada should have brought a Confederate flag to wave. I'll be glad when all this is over." Then he was gone.

47 *The Messenger*

SKIRTING THE town cagily on his way to Duncan Harper's house, W.B. passed in back of a Negro cabin where a little boy was playing keeps by himself in the back yard. He was crawling around the ring on his hands and knees and shooting hard with a big glass taw. W.B. himself had an agate, and Unker Beck kept a big ball-bearing out of a tractor to shoot with.

The little Negro playing marbles was talking to himself: "Oh, you shoots it and you spins it and you breaks it down the middle, oh you takes it sump'n like this and you goes sump'n like this and— You kin play wif me, black boy, if you got a taw."

"I ain't so black," said W.B. "I half white. I just learned it."

"I half white too," said the boy. "My daddy's a white man, only he died in Mist' Duncan Harper's grocery sto."

"I seen him do it," said W.B.

"My name is Robert," said the boy, "but they calls me James."

"They calls me W.B."

"Is that your name?"

"Uh-huh."

"You can have some breakfast, want to."

"Thank you, but I can't. I got to find Mister Duncan."

"Mist' Duncan Harper the shurf now in place of my daddy."

"I know hit."

"Who want the shurf?"

The woman who asked this stood at the back door. She was large and blowsy. She wore a soft cotton robe with flowers on it, and she was the pleasing rich color of coffee with a lot of real cream stirred in it.

"I does, Miss Ida Belle," said W.B. "My daddy's sont me to find him."

"Yo daddy? Who yo daddy?"

"My Unker Beck Dozer. He really my daddy. I half from England."

"Sho'nuff?"

"Yes'm. Is."

"Looks like Beck done better than me. How come he ain't ever tole it?"

"He never wanted to hurt Aunt Lucy's feelings."

"Is her feelings hoit now?"

"She don't act like it."

"Well, then?"

"I'o'no'm."

"I does. Beck giving hisself airs. 'Hoit Lucy's feelings.' I got no time for Beck. He give me the pain."

"Where he give you the pain, Mama?" asked the little boy playing marbles.

"Hush up, James. Come here, W.B."

Beyond the back gallery the door stood open on a big room. There was a tall mirror in it on a stand with a heavy gold frame running all the way around. When he used to deliver groceries, he got good at looking in back doors. There was also a record playing softly. The windows had drawn curtains. The glass in the mirror looked like water. The room looked cool.

"You going to Mister Duncan Harper's house?" asked Ida Belle.

"Yes'm."

"Then you go to Mister Duncan's house, but don't you go a step farther. Mister Duncan ain't there, you tell Miss Tinker, or you set there till he come home. Don't you go in town. Don't you go down to that speaking. You know Mister Willard Follansbee?"

"Yes'm, I knows him."

"He come to see me yestiddy trying to get me to say where Beck was at. If he catches you, he'll chop you up and fry you like a chicken, boy. You go to Mister Duncan's and don't you stir a step."

"I ain't right sure," said W.B., "that I wants to go to Mister Duncan's."

"No, now you best do that," said Ida Belle, kindly, like a schoolteacher. "Beck counting on you to do that. Just don't take no chances."

"Yes'm."

When he came into town he walked down the white-folks streets with his head ducked. A white lady inside a house, put up a window and said, "Hey, boy!" He stopped and looked at her. "Do you deliver groceries?" she asked.

"No'm," he said. "My name Willie."

"Willie what?"

"Willie Beckwith."

"Well, I reckon you aren't the one." She put down the window.

When he reached Mister Duncan Harper's house there wasn't anybody at home. He went to the back steps and sat down, two steps from the top. He wanted to go home to Granny and Aunt Lucy. He felt that he had to wait and say what Unker Beck told him to, seeing that it was the day he learned Unker Beck was his daddy. He believed that when Mister Duncan Harper came everything would be all right.

48 *Kerney Woolbright Makes a Speech*

THE TOWN master of ceremonies, the mayor, was announcing that Kerney Woolbright, candidate for the state senate from the Third Senatorial District, would be the first of the legislative candidates to speak. The benches were filling, and knots of talking people loosed to rearrange themselves, turn toward the rostrum and fold their arms, for careful listening.

Kerney Woolbright, no matter what they thought of him personally, was known to be an orator, and people will turn out to hear an orator, and give him attention. Voting is another thing. Voting has nothing to do with speaking, or the size and silence of the crowd. What it does have to do with has yet to be finally discovered.

Duncan Harper gained the front row. There was a country shyness about the way it was vacant, except for a few old men, one deaf, one crippled, one obese, and one habitually drunk. He nodded to them all, and they smiled with what looked like

derision, as was their habit. One shook his hand, and he felt
the craggy forefinger knuckle that all the fingers had bent and
fled from.

Here and there, as he had passed through the crowd that was
retracting itself inward toward the rostrum and pulling its scattered elements together, certain phrases were repeated: "Went
to school up North somewhere . . . this nigger business . . .
talker, but I . . . him and Harper . . . in the legislature did
he . . . school up North but him and Harper. . . ."

Kerney rose, came easily to the microphone, and began to
speak without preliminaries. He thanked the proper people,
firmly reviewed his career as a Winfield County boy who had
gone to school first at the state university, later to Yale in the
North from whence he had returned—the instant he got his
diploma, it would seem—to the joys of Winfield County. Here
he had hoped to settle down to a quiet life as a lawyer, but
service to the people of the state of Mississippi seemed to attract him more every day in an age when young men seemed
regrettably inclined to place private ambition first, and public
duty last in their thoughts, if indeed they thought of it at all.
People sometimes told him he ought to enjoy life, make lots of
money, and wait for advanced years to serve the public, but he
personally thought that when men got to the age of President
Truman they owed it to the country to retire. This pulled a
laugh, for Kerney's opponent was considerably older than he,
and everybody was against Truman.

"A fine wife you're going to make," said Marcia Mae, glancing at Cissy. "You've got to learn to laugh at his jokes."

"He makes me sick," said Cissy. "I wish I hadn't come."

A young man appeared at the flank of the convertible near
Cissy's elbow. He was a reporter from a town in another county.

"You're Cissy Hunt, aren't you? I met you over at Moon
Lake last summer. I don't guess you'd remember me."

"Oh, sure, I remember. Sure I do."

"I hear this is the fair-haired boy over here that's speaking
now. I hear you're engaged to him, Cissy."

"Oh, goodnight. It gets to where you can't be friends with a
boy people don't say you're engaged. We're good friends. But,
goodnight—"

"It was his speech my boss sent me over here to cover. Seems there might be some angle on the race question in it."

"I don't know," said Cissy. "Politics just confuses me. I just don't know a thing about it."

"Neither one of you is ever going to know," said Marcia Mae, "if you don't listen to what he's saying."

"Oh, he's just on what he thinks about taxes now; that's not much of an issue. Then he'll review his voting record in the legislature and pledge support to the free textbook program. That gets him over to schools, and through the door to the nasty mean hateful old federal government in Washington that wants to exploit our fair Southland and thinks they can tell us what to do and what not to do. Then he gets to segregation and white supremacy, which is what I'm waiting for."

"This is my sister, Mrs. O'Donnell, Bob—"

"Preston. How do you do, ma'am. Cissy, your boy friend's got a good voice."

"I haven't even got a boy friend, I keep telling you. Goodnight."

"A girl like you is bound to have ten boy friends. What's the matter with these hillbillies? Why don't you come over to the Delta?"

"I'd love to. When can I?"

"I want to hear the speech," said Marcia Mae.

"See you later," said the reporter. He unslung his camera and moved across the grass, picking his way around the crowd toward the rows of seats and the red-white-and-blue-draped platform. Up there before a plain wooden rostrum with a pitcher of water, a water glass, and a microphone, a man was speaking. His hands held lightly to either side; his easy forward-leaning stance had been calculated long ago, and the sway of his shoulders, the lift of his chin, the gestures now of his hands, now of the whole arm were like the riding of an expert horseman, who no longer thinks of the rein or the spur, but only of calling the horse to its zenith, and Kerney's horse was the crowd, which had grown as silent as the sky.

". . . And now, my friends," said the three big horns, "I come with reluctance to an issue which lies closer to all our hearts than everything else I have said put together. I say that

I speak with reluctance, for there are friends among you to whom my words may give pain. I would ask them to remember that a public servant cannot speak, cannot act, cannot even wish in a private way. Where the public good is at stake, he cannot wish for personal joys. Where he must fulfill a public duty, he cannot hope always to please his friends.

"Good men and women of Winfield County, I know your feeling about the institution of racial segregation in our Southern way of life. I have walked among you these past few weeks and talked with you, and I know your spirit. What you have believed once, you still believe; what you have fought for once, you will fight again to defend, for you are strong, proud people and you do not change. I state to you solemnly, friends, my belief that no man has a right to ask for your vote who cannot serve you from his heart. I pledge you here, from this platform, that no matter what stand the federal government of the United States—the President, the U.S. Senate, or the Supreme Court—may take on this issue, I, Kerney Woolbright, will defend our Southern viewpoint, our Southern traditions, and the will of our Southern people, as long as God gives me breath.

"I come now to a more immediate issue. Exactly two weeks ago this very day, a Winfield County citizen whom you all know was shot and seriously wounded. A Negro man, widely suspected of this shooting and known to have been at the scene of the crime, disappeared immediately afterwards and has not been seen since. I am not the sheriff of this county and it is not my business to say to you what should or should not be done. But it is being said that nothing has been done to bring this Negro to justice, and it is further being said that I, Kerney Woolbright, am party to protecting this Negro as a fugitive from arrest and from whatever due process of the law may follow therefrom. I wish to state to you that nothing could be further from the truth.

"Duncan Harper stands on Tuesday for election to sheriff of Winfield County. Far be it from me to tell you how you should vote. The vote is your sacred instrument of power: let no man dictate to you in whose service you shall enlist it.

"Duncan Harper is said by many to be a friend of mine, and they are right. He is my friend and a friend to all of you. He has brought me cheering to my feet with thousands in the days when he was a national football hero, and all the sports honors this nation can offer were heaped upon his head. But friendship, my fellow citizens, as I have said, cannot and indeed should not make a demand higher than the demands of the public good. I do not attempt to defend or condemn Duncan Harper or any of his actions. I prefer to say simply that he will speak for himself.

"But I, Kerney Woolbright, hereby publicly disassociate my candidacy from the candidacy of Duncan Harper. Inasmuch as we are friends, I love him still. Inasmuch as misunderstanding may malign him, I deplore it. Inasmuch as his will conflicts with yours, I condemn him.

"As a simple citizen of Winfield County, like yourselves, I have a vote to cast for sheriff.

"Duncan Harper will not receive my vote.

"Men and women of Winfield County, I thank you."

49 *Duncan Retreats*

As KERNEY finished his speech, there was at first a stunned murmur from the crowd, a shout or two of "Pour it on, boy," and "You tell 'em, Woolbright," and from somewhere a shrill whistle.

Duncan rose and walked up the trampled grass between the rows of seats. People craned to see his face, but it showed nothing. He walked easily and steadily, for he had once learned well how to pass through a cheering gauntlet as though nothing had happened.

He gained the car and slid under the wheel, reaching for the ignition.

"I'd better take you and the children home," he said. "There's liable to be some ugly doings down here."

"Duncan, no. I'll take them home. You stay here. They may give you a chance to speak."

"Tinker, you know I'm no speaker. That's the last thing I'm good at. I'll wait my turn, give them a chance to cool down. Right now I don't want to see anybody."

"All right." She slid over, releasing the wheel to him. "But I don't think it matters, Duncan, who shot Jimmy or what you ever hear from New Orleans. I don't think anybody cares. I think all they care about is to make sure that everybody they vote for favors segregation."

"Well, maybe so. At one time I thought things might have been different. I know this much: I just have to go along with it the way it's always looked to me. I have to follow it through the way I started it. I can't care too much any more what they want."

"Kerney cares. He cared too much."

"Kerney said he wasn't going to vote for you, Daddy," Cotton said.

"Don't talk to me about Kerney, either one of you."

The family rode silently with him, past the empty courthouse square, the drugstore corner, the stores, with the sign of HARPER & BRO. GRO.

"I always hated football," said Duncan. "I never wanted to play. The coach in high school was nothing but a math teacher who hadn't thought about football in ten years until he saw me and Essie Sanders playing kick and catch after school one day. He watched for five minutes, and the next day talked the principal into organizing a team—the first we ever had in Lacey. But I wasn't trying, I wasn't trying anything at all. I never got to finish the work for my Scout badge because of him and his football team. I used to think I'd do it the next summer, but it was always the next summer."

They had pulled up into their own front yard.

"Go play in the sand pile," said Tinker to her children. "Run on!" she had to order, for Cotton stood needing her. "Look after Patsy for me," she told him. She followed Duncan into the house. Here she fished out a bottle of whisky she had stashed away, and gave him a stiff drink. Twice she sent Cotton back into the yard.

"I only wanted to be a groceryman like Daddy," Duncan told her. "I wanted to walk in the woods on Sunday with my family. I never imagined my name in all the papers, I never dreamed Travis Brevard would walk in my store and die. Tinker, don't you leave me! Promise me."

"Leave you, Duncan? *Leave* you?" She thought he might as well have been imploring her not to start speaking Chinese. In all her life the thought of leaving him had never crossed her mind once.

He turned away from her, and stood facing the cold fireplace, resting his foot on the brass andiron.

"We sat in here, do you remember, the evening after Travis died. We were full of something about to happen. You said we mustn't start running for things." He gave a short laugh, then turned back to her, saying calmly, "They're all too intense for me, you see. Kerney, Marcia Mae, even Willard Follansbee. They are taken and swept by things inside them—here." He laid his hand across his breast. "It must be that I hardly know at all how they feel. Things seem pretty obvious to me, by and large. This Negro thing. Segregation, civil rights— What else is there to say any more but that they should have an equal chance? How can there be anything else to say? But Kerney had to win. If I had felt strongly enough that I had to win, you see, I might have—Tinker, do you understand?"

"No," she said at once. "I think he did an awful thing."

"Yes, so do I. But if I could see how he must have felt!"

"There's never been a time when I didn't adore you," she said.

"They say there's something funny about my family," he went on. "I know people say the Harpers are peculiar. I never knew why, except maybe Uncle Phillip voting for Hoover."

They both laughed.

"If they say it about your family, what on earth do you think they say about mine?"

"Daddy? Daddy."

"Cotton," said Tinker, "if I have to tell you one more time—"

"But I keep trying to tell Daddy. W.B. is out in the back. He says he knows where Beck Dozer is."

"Oh." Duncan left quickly for the back of the house, and Tinker was alone with the boy.

"Come here, darling. Come talk to Mother."

"Mother, Daddy said he never did want to play *football*."

"Well, now. Well, now. I guess Daddy said something he didn't mean, don't you?"

"But Daddy wouldn't do that, would he?"

"Everybody does that, sometimes."

"Even Daddy?"

"Daddy less than anybody. But sometimes even Daddy."

Duncan returned hastily. "Beck is waiting for me down back of Mars Overstreet's store. If I hurry and get him I can put him in custody over in Humphreys County and still be back in time to speak at two o'clock."

"Are you going now?"

"Right now. Yes."

She dusted off her stocking feet and slipped into her shoes. Like the children, she always took them off the minute she got in the door. "I'm going with you."

"You stay with the children."

"The children are all right. Wherever you go today, I'm going too."

When they passed the town square, she was the first to see what had happened. The window of Harper's grocery was broken. There was a jagged hole like a star in the lower half; one point reached several feet upward into the painted letters. If she had known any way to shield him from the sight she would have taken it. Instead she laid a hand on his arm, hoping he would not see.

But he always looked at the store. She felt the shock go through him to the bone.

50 *The Public Man*

WHEN KERNEY WOOLBRIGHT came down the steps of the rostrum, the forethrust of the crowd was already upon him. People greeted him with relief—in the tangle of everything that had been talked about Duncan and Kerney and Jimmy Tallant and Beck, they were glad to get back to something they could understand without question, the way they understood a sermon on God so loved the world.

Some felt that Kerney should not have said right out that he wouldn't vote for Duncan, but others, arguing the point back into line, said, "Why not?—it's the way I feel myself. I like Harper, but he's said too many doubtful things."

If we had stood together, Kerney thought. If we had stood together.

His thinking went on lonely, like going down an empty valley in a strange country, while Kerney, with his hat in hand and his Lincoln-like stoop for catching every word, remained talking, nodding, listening gravely, shaking hand after hand.

When he turned to move away from the crowd, three coun-
trymen with aging boy-faces made him the center of a walking
huddle.

"We decided we done fooled around too long," said one.

"We going nigger-hunting tonight," said another. "We hear
he's over in Humphreys County."

The third said, "Want to come?"

"I'm due to make a banquet speech in Wayne tonight," said
Kerney. "You boys take it easy. Go talk to Tallant."

A leading gubernatorial candidate drew him aside, laid an
arm around his shoulder, and talked for a moment, creating
a favorable impression. Willard Follansbee stood in his path,
wearing his white linen campaigning suit and red tie that
stirred memories of Bilbo. The hairs on his hands and those
barely subdued to the skin surface of his throat and face appeared richly purple in so white a territory, established with the
tropical weight of fuel oil in a bucket. When he removed his
straw hat, it was as if one of a species had thrust its head out at
the appointed hour. Another effect the white had was to make
his teeth look yellow. He put out his hand and Kerney took it,
not without nausea.

"Hell of a fine speech," he said. "Just a hell of a fine speech."

Kerney gained the Hunt convertible.

"Can I bum a ride?"

"You certainly cannot," said Marcia Mae. Determined not to
so much as look at him, she kept craning her head nervously
back, waiting for a rift in the crowd.

"Can I, Cissy?"

"Sure. Hop in."

Marcia Mae turned on her at once. "Don't you know what
he's done? Didn't you hear what he said up there?"

"You mean you're not going to let him ride home because
of something he said in a speech? That's the silliest thing I ever
heard of."

"You mean to say you are? Don't you know he just stabbed
his best friend in the back? Publicly?"

"I don't understand anything about it and neither do you.
You always want to make a big fuss."

"If you let him in this car, I'm getting out of it."

"Well, get out then," said Cissy.

"Wait," said Kerney. "I'll walk—"

But she had flashed past him, flinging the door shut almost on his finger. He could no more have stopped her than a buzz saw.

"Let her go," said Cissy. "She just gets like that."

He took over the wheel and backed gingerly to make the turn. People waved to him, and some came up to shake his hand. When he maneuvered the car free on the road to the square, he reached into his back pocket for a handkerchief and felt that something which had been secure there two hours before was now not there at all. He searched again, frantically, prodding into his pockets, halting the car. Then he saw that Cissy was reading from a yellow paper.

"This is the longest telegram I ever saw," she said.

"Give me that." He snatched it. "Where did you get it?"

"It was out on the seat there. It's to Duncan Harper. It's not even yours."

"They brought it to me. I thought it was mine."

"I bet you didn't," she said. "You kept it because it says they've found the man mixed up in that shooting."

"Don't be silly. Why would I do that?"

"Well," she said, "because you didn't want anybody to know it wasn't the Negro after all. How could you talk against the Negro if everybody knew for sure he hadn't done anything?"

Kerney stared at her. "Who told you that?"

"Told me?"

"Will you take off those damn glasses and look at me?"

He reached to unmask her eyes, but a car honked behind him. He drove on, but at the square he took an abrupt swing to the right and picked up speed. He drove away from the direction of the highway, past Duncan Harper's house, past outlying houses, far out, going faster.

"Where on earth are you going?" Cissy asked.

"Who was that you were talking to while I was speaking? Some man with a camera on his back?"

"Oh that was Bob Preston. He works for the Rosedale *Eagle*."

"What did he want?"

"He said I ought to come over in the Delta more and go to

parties. It sounded like fun. I bet they have a good time over there."

He swung off into a hard-packed country road, deeply shaded—the cemetery road.

"You must be crazy," said Cissy, "driving way out here."

He swung the wheel again, sharply, entering a lane even more secluded, quiet, abandoned. Through the low oak limbs and sassafras growth, the iron palings of the cemetery fence were visible. The ground lay thick with the droppings of the oaks. When he cut the ignition, something went right on chirping in the brush. There was no feel of houses near.

He reached over himself and stripped the dark glasses from her face.

"Cissy, if anyone ever asks you about that telegram, you are going to say you don't know anything about it. You will do that for me, won't you, Cissy?"

She inspected a chip in her nail polish. She was somewhat out of humor with him, and was getting hungry. She would not look at him. "Okay. I won't say anything."

He was silent for a time—dissatisfaction in his long young face, his thick young springy hair, his lowered lashes, his full, resting mouth. He turned to her, one arm staying upon the wheel just where it had deflected the car into the lane, while the other extended along the back of the seat. He reached out his hand gently.

"Cissy—?"

She drew back from his touching her at all. "I don't know if I want to help you about that telegram or not. I'll have to ask Papa."

"You'll not do any such thing!"

She thought at first that someone else had seized her from behind, actually by the hair, but seeing it was nobody but Kerney she had some notion he must be going really crazy and tried her little contemptuous manner of flinging free, putting her chin in the air, and saying what she expected to be done for her. But the one who got flung was she, straight down—could Kerney be this strong?—her head struck the doorframe painfully. She struggled up, about to be really scared. "Oh," she said, for her elbow honestly slipped on the leather seat and she fell back, again hitting by accident on a posture, an angle, and a sensation it had been for some time now so pleasing to dream about in bed. "Oh," she kept saying in various ways until his mouth stopped her. She discovered she had been absolutely right in thinking how boring most things were.

When she began to listen again, there was still that bit of chirping in the brush. Her dress was all unbuttoned and her pretty cotton eyelet underthings dragged awry. She did not mind; this was why they were so pretty. She saw the chrome door handle, the sleek gadgets on the dashboard, and above her the rich oak limbs.

"Will you tell?" His head had fallen to rest above her heart.

"Tell? Oh, they'd never let us back together if I told."

"I mean about the telegram."

The telegram was like a stray piece of paper washing up and down in the ocean.

"I don't care about it," she said.

He raised his head. "But I do."

His hand moved through her hair again, caressing and firm.

"Then I won't. I won't tell. Never, never."

51 *Under One Roof*

THE BIG Hunt house stood wide open to gather breezes out of the hot day. Though the people in it were all over it and at considerable distances from one another, their consciousnesses were nonetheless linked and conversant, like music.

Nan stood alone in the dining room, putting out silver for her dinner in the evening. She heard her daughter run in the front door and scamper to her room.

"Cissy? Where on earth have you been? Nellie saved you some dinner in the oven. Is Kerney there? There's enough for him, too, isn't there, Nellie?"

"Yas'm." Nellie answered from way out at the servant's table, shoveling turnip greens, cornbread, potlikker, and sidemeat all together on her fork.

"You gwy set there and eat all day, Miss Nellie?" the yard boy asked her from the steps.

"Ef'n I wants to," said Nellie. Conversation did not distract her.

"I want to talk to Kerney for a minute," Jason called, from far off in his office wing, lying on a coarse dark quilt brier-stitched from large pieces of men's suit scraps. He was about to nap, had removed his shoes and coat. The morning paper lay by the narrow bed.

"Have you got anything over your feet, Jason?" Nan asked.

"On a day like this? Lord, Nan."

"All right, you know how you are."

"I know it's hot."

"Don't turn the fan on without putting something on your feet."

From her own room, open on the hall, old Mrs. Standsbury said, "Is Kerney there? Tell him I certainly am glad he broke with Duncan Harper."

Jason laughed. "You're supposed to be deaf, Miss Tennie."

"She hears everything she wants to," said Nan.

"I just think somebody ought to say what they think about Duncan never chasing that Negro. It's going to get so Negroes can come right in the same house with you. It's high time somebody spoke up for law and order. The Negroes will take us all over, don't watch out."

"You hear dat?" said the yard boy from the steps.

"Hears 'em," said Nellie, and drew near her plate an enormous leftover slice of mince pie.

"Kerney!" It was Marcia Mae from the far end of the porch, beyond the corner, knocking a ping-pong ball. She would shove the table against the wall, and play that way alone by the hour. "Kerney, come here!"

He appeared, having threaded through the porch furniture to join her. She kept up the spaced knocking of the little ball: wall, table, table, strike; table, wall, table, table, strike. Her backhand wrist with the little paddle was her silky tennis drive in miniature. She had shed her skirt in favor of a pair of tailored shorts.

"I don't take back anything I said," she told him, sniping the ball. "You betrayed Duncan Harper. You stabbed him in the back."

"I don't recall ever hearing that you stuck by him," Kerney said.

"If I had stuck by Duncan," she said, leaning far forward to catch a small bounce at the net, "I would be a Lacey housewife, putting muffins in a hot stove this minute. And you, after Tuesday, if you had stuck with Duncan, would be a has-been politician, a small-town drinking lawyer. I know how it is. You were afraid of being bored. Nevertheless, I am going to do everything in my power to keep Cissy from marrying you, Kerney."

"It won't do any good," said Cissy, from behind. "I'm going to marry him anyway."

Marcia Mae lifted her palm and let the celluloid ball sail into it. She laid down the paddle and turned. They were standing together, dew-fresh and far too bright. Marcia Mae was not reminded by their moist, parted lips and shining eyes of a small house somewhere, scorched food, and the journey home with news from the doctor's office; instead she could peer through their happiness as through a keyhole into a world where all these sweet young matters were never to be overly valued, like attractive knickknacks on the gleaming top of a strong desk.

"You understand him?" Marcia Mae asked, levelly.

"What's it to you?" Cissy countered, and lifted her little chin.

Marcia Mae walked through to the dining room where her mother ranked out the silver.

"There's a big one on the way," she warned. "Brace yourself."

"What?" Nan had lifted the coffeepot, and her fingers tightened on its handle. It was as though someone had set off a buzzer system in her nerves, but the pot remained perfectly level.

"She's decided to marry him."

In her mother's face, swift as the tripping of a Kodak shutter or the glint of a narrow blade held into the vision so that for an instant it disappears altogether, Marcia Mae saw unmistakable horror and sickness of heart, and she thought of small, fine bones put to strain beneath the flesh. "I thought she would." She healed instantly—they were in the doorway. "Children!"

"Marcia Mae told you! Oh, she shouldn't!"

"So that's where you were! We couldn't imagine."

Jason came pounding in in his sock feet. "Well, baby girl!" He was kissing her over and over, and wringing Kerney's hand. "As if you didn't have enough handshaking to do."

"I'm going to tell Grand," said Cissy, and vanished.

"You hear that?" Nellie said and stopped eating pie.

"Hear what?" asked the yard boy.

"Miss Cissy, Mister Kerney getting ma'd." She went into the kitchen and came back with a dish of cut lemons. "They needn't think they going have no wedding in this house till cotton picking done. I can't he'p it who they is. All them things is done in the kitchen."

"Who getting ma'd?"

"Miss Cissy. Mister Kerney Woolbright."

The Negro boy was lounging his length against the steps. "I thought they's ma'd already."

"You a crazy nigger," said Nellie. "You know who yo' daddy was? That cross-eyed nigger used to drive Miss Hope Mullens's cows to paster, that's who."

"I ain't never heard that," said the boy.

"Then it's time you did."

"About the speech this morning, sir," Kerney was saying to Jason.

"You couldn't do anything else, Kerney. I wanted to talk to you about it. You probably feel pretty bad over it. But everybody I talked to felt the same way I did, that Duncan's a fine boy and they hate to go against him, but he's lost his head on this Dozer thing. He undertook to say to somebody he thought the niggers would be voting in a few more years. Maybe they will be, but nobody who talks that way can expect to win an office. You couldn't let him ruin your chances. I think, in fact, boy, that you behaved with good sense and courage, and I said to myself at the time, If I ever had a son, I'd want him to be like that. Able to take a thing in hand, and drive it—"

He stopped, and as his voice faded in the shadowy room and his active brown hand unclasped, he remembered a bit behind the two women that he had indeed had a son who had hated him and who had died.

Nan stepped in and put her cool lips to Kerney's cheek. "So welcome to the family, dear."

Marcia Mae went out to the glider on the front porch and hugged her knees. Inside, Cissy had wakened old Mrs. Standsbury out of her nap. She had been dreaming about her girlhood and kept saying, "Marry who? Kerney? Kerney who?"

Jason followed Kerney into the hallway. "I never try to interfere or make suggestions in anything you young people have in mind. Just let me know whenever I can help. It's the main pleasure I get out of life nowadays, helping my children, and you mustn't begrudge it to me. You'll excuse me if I don't come out in my sock feet. I guess you ought to know by now where the door is."

When Kerney passed Marcia Mae he gave no sign of noticing her, and she could not tell if he had pretended this or not. His face revealed nothing of him except his identity: it was as if he had carried his own portrait by.

She rose and reentered the house. Cissy and Nan were still in the dining room, though Cissy had already fetched magazines and they were leaning together near the corner of the sideboard where light came in strongest through the bay window. The approach of a wedding brings out a nineteen-year-old side in every woman, and you would have thought them two girls together, each satisfied at the snail-slow turning of the thick, slick, beautifully photographed pages. "I saved all the June magazines this year," Nan said in her amused voice. "I can't imagine why."

Marcia Mae remembered the spring before she was to have married Duncan, how it had warmed so wickedly, so fulgently toward June, the quarrel over white satin, the heavy paper in the announcements, the search for white camellias in quantity so late in the year, the proud high-arching storms.

"Duncan speaks at two o'clock," she said. "Are you going?"

They both turned quickly—she might have snapped a whip on their backs.

"I'm not," said Cissy. "The only reason I went this morning was to hear Kerney."

"I never try to go out to these things any more," said Nan. "I explained that to Kerney this morning."

Fine, between her eyes, one could see across the room the little wire that would presently begin to throb and tauten, would drag her at last, helpless, stumbling, in agony, into a blackened room, and on a canopied bed, behind a fast shut door, take all its pleasure of her.

Marcia Mae left them together and looked in on her grandmother. The old lady lay propped on two pillows, in her summer dressing gown, an afghan throw drawn up to her waist. She stayed quieter, with folded hands, than the pretty familiar objects that winked on her dresser.

"I hope I don't die before they have the wedding."

"Die!" Marcia Mae laughed. "You're never even sick."

"I'm still going to die," said the old lady. "You don't think I'm silly enough to think I'll live forever, do you?"

"I didn't know it ever worried you," said Marcia Mae. "You read the Bible all the time."

"I didn't say it worried me. Worry's a sin."

"Grand, you remember when all those Negroes were shot in the courthouse back right after the First World War?"

"Remember it? Yes, I remember it well."

"What did Grandfather Standsbury think of it?"

"Think of it? He thought it was terrible, like everybody else."

"I mean didn't he always feel guilty about it, as if he might have stopped it from happening if he had got up there in time?"

"I was mighty glad he didn't get up there till it was over. Those men were murderers, that Acey Tallant especially. Your grandfather couldn't have done a thing with them. He always thought he could, but he couldn't."

"Yet he always felt guilty, didn't he? It haunted him till the day he died, didn't it?"

"I don't know if it did or not. If he thought about it all the time, he never told me. He would never have been one to unburden his worries on his dear ones. He was a mighty fine family man, always loving and considerate. From the day we married till the day he died, there was never anything of what you'd call real trouble between us. My wish was what he wanted—he loved a happy home. I took it all for granted in those days, but God's let me live to see what a precious thing it was. Nowadays, with people flaunting marriage around like a new dress, that is, if they bother to get married at all—why, they carry on worse than Negroes. They don't want to call anything right or wrong. Your grandfather was a far cry—" She stopped speaking, noticing that her granddaughter was gone, but kept on thinking without interruption, smiling faintly, out of great pleasure of spirit, though she felt no undue excitement and had scarcely ever been moved to tears.

Retreating to her high room, Marcia Mae changed her shorts for the corded cotton skirt, ran the silver-mounted comb through her hair, and holding the silver hand mirror to catch the best light, painted her mouth. Blotting Kleenex between her lips, she glanced far down to where three sparrows preened themselves around the leak the garden hose made at the hydrant. Movable sprays ran all day now on the lawn; the yard boy trundled them about to different spots, and still the earth hardened and grass faded from the top half-downward. There where the little birds shook drops from their wings, the ground would not at first absorb the moisture, as perfectly dry cloth takes its time about wetting. Out far, by the edge of the lawn, the leaves on a low maple branch hung dusty, dry, distinct and still. The heat would linger till November yet, but summer was over now, had left the first thing it leaves, the heart, and Marcia Mae knew she would soon be going away. She would take off the house and the town and the people there, like taking off her clothes, one thing at a time, before dressing new from the skin out—new place to live, new job, and somewhere, a new man.

But this I do, she thought, and turned resolutely, dropping the tissue with its red print into the wastebasket, resealing the lipstick, laying down the mirror. This one thing I do.

She caught up her bag, the worn soft leather that pleased her. She ran downstairs.

"Marcia Mae!"

It was her father.

She kept on out the front door, but in the yard she veered, circled the wing of the house and halted under his office windows. "Daddy?"

He appeared back of the screen. "Where are you off to, Marcia Mae?"

"To hear Duncan speak. Do you want to come?"

"I told you from the first, Marcia Mae, that I don't approve of Duncan's ideas in this race. I don't want to be put in a position of having to show publicly what I think of him."

"But I do want to show what I think of him. I want the chance to say I'm for him."

"You cannot play with this nigger business, Marcia Mae. That Dozer Negro has been bound for trouble exactly the same way his father was. If Duncan had handled things right—"

"You mean if Duncan had come to you for orders. If he had taken lessons in how to be a hypocrite."

"You're being very hard. I foresaw trouble for Dozer years ago. I tried to get him to go North. None of this counts with you. I've made money out of this county for forty years, given jobs to everybody worth a plugged nickel, kept this house up and you children fed, clothed, and flying around in automobiles. I reckon this makes me a crook. I wouldn't go down there to that speaking, Marcia Mae. Duncan is talking for something that's going to come, but I tell you it cannot be spoken out for. I reckon that makes me a hypocrite. But I don't want you around where there's any trouble."

"I have to go," she told him. "I have to stand with Duncan's friends. Don't you understand why I have to?"

"I guess so." His face disappeared from the window, then showed again. "You're grown." He vanished, this time for good.

52   *An Army Gathers*

SHE DROVE OUT, swinging the convertible expertly out of the thick-layered shade into the heat and dust, and skirting the hot square, moved rapidly away toward the schoolhouse and the speaking grounds.

The cars had already gathered, filling the grounds. The benches were tight-packed and people were standing close in and sitting on the fenders of the nearest cars. The loudspeaker gaped open its three monstrous throats. But the spot they all faced, the rostrum, was empty.

Marcia Mae was forced to park on the right side of the campus and walk a good distance through the car-crowded space.

A game, she thought. You would have thought it was a game. On football weekends at the university, the campus was one big parking lot, and people from every part of the state, from all over the South, too, sat eating their lunches with the car doors open in the dry fall heat. Along the sidewalks from the town, the children sold programs and chrysanthemums with satin ribbons, and shouted their wares from the cold-drink stands. The steady beat of walking filled the air: the flattering, feminine high heels that Southern girls wore to the big games along with their new fall suits, their little hats; the paced, lazy, well-shod, decisive walking of Southern men. Everywhere you heard them say Harper. Close your eyes and it fell out of the air at you, here loud, there soft, here with a Rebel yell before it, there with a furtive handshake on a bet.

In one way or another they were all there to see him, and she, Marcia Mae, for two straight years (the only time in the history of the university) marched as Homecoming Queen between the chancellor of the university and the captain of the team, and received from the Governor of the state an enormous bouquet of white chrysanthemums with satin ribbons eight inches wide, and stood smiling while the three-hundred-piece band arranged on the field to spell "UM" played "Let Me Call You Sweetheart," and a crowd of 30,000 stood solemnly and the men removed their hats, just as if it had been "The Star-Spangled Banner" or news of the President's death or the outbreak of a war. . . . "Jason Hunt's daughter." "Yeah." "From up in Lacey, too." "Yeah." "High-school sweethearts." "So they say." "Never went with anybody else." "Well, he's got plenty, Jason has." "Yeah." "Shows where football will take you, man." "Over the fifty-yard line." "What you talking about? Goal to go."

They're all here again, she thought, on account of him.

People looked at her silently. She saw a tall, angular country fellow she had known as a child but whose name she could not remember. He had a neck like a turkey gobbler's, grizzled, scaly, and fumed, from the sun or some complaint; his eyes were amused and kind. He did not mind being ugly. To him she would never be anything but a funny little girl.

"Why is everybody so quiet?" she asked, half-whispering lest her voice rise over the crowd.

"They don't aim to agree with him," he told her. "On anything." He smiled at her, ever so gently.

"None of them? None?"

"I don't undertake to say none, Miss Marcia. Let's leave it at ninety-nine and some odd per cent."

She thought, I don't believe that, and moved on toward the benches. Just at the end of one toward the back, a man of the town, a friend of her father's, got up and gestured with his hat that she take his seat. She shook her head.

"I'm going further down. Where is he?"

"It's ahead of time yet. I guess he'll come."

"He'll come. It's not like him to back out."

"I don't think it is either."

"He'll come unless something has happened."

"I think so too."

With the touch of his hat, he detained her from entering the heart of the crowd.

"I wouldn't go any further in, Marcia Mae."

"Why? What—"

"Well, I wouldn't, that's all. Listen."

She heard then the hum of the crowd. No sound rose distinctly above any other, but the quality was resolute and passionate. It was like men marching somewhere, nearer all the time. It was like the rustle of hymnbooks in the big tent meeting just after the first number is called. It was as certain as storm and morning, and unreasonable as blood.

The crowd was one.

The instant she realized it, it went through her like lightning. She was terrified.

Jason Hunt, who had followed his daughter secretly, watched her from the shadow of a countryman's pick-up. He saw the halt and start and straightening of her fine carriage, as when in the dark seeded pasture all its own, the thoroughbred smells the wild thing that everybody said left these parts long ago, and the narrow head flings high and the tender ears leap forward. The hoof, trimmed and blackened, has never lifted except to be admired. Through the whitewashed palings the sheathed claw thrusts and touches earth and bears weight. They had said to her all her life: "Don't go too far from town . . . It's Saturday; don't go down on the tennis court by yourself, not in the afternoon . . . Be careful . . . Be sure there's a man along." So this was why.

A young man touched her arm. "Your daddy says he changed his mind about coming. He says for you to come on back there with him."

"No." Even on the one word, her voice shook. She said again, firmly, "No."

She whirled and hurried off the other way, going back to her own car. Somebody obviously had to get to Duncan. Somebody had to warn him what he was about to come strolling into. I can do this for him, she thought. This. At least this. There was some kind of forever in it—the way she thought about it.

The young man went back to Jason Hunt. "She wouldn't come," he said.

Jason watched her drive away, and scratched behind his ear. It wasn't like her to run off. "Okay," he said. "Thanks anyhow."

53   *Three Children Play*

PATSY, COTTON, and W.B., left alone, first ate Puffed Wheat with cream and sugar, then some ice cream and little cakes. They then went to the back door and looked out into the yard toward the sand pile, but the yard looked too big and bright today to play out in. On the way back through the kitchen, Patsy remembered a tin of candy everybody else had forgotten about, and climbed on a chair to drag it down. The candy had grown old and Cotton did not want anything else sweet, but W.B. put one in each jaw and so did Patsy.

In the living room they sat on the floor and started teaching W.B. how to play I Doubt It, but Patsy got the cards sticky and Cotton said they were his cards and put them back into the box. When he felt the sticky surfaces of the cards, Cotton felt he would cry, though not about the cards. There was a feeling he had often now, as if he had swallowed a little light bulb whole. He would try to draw his breath, or yawn it away, but it stayed, cold and hollow, down in his stomach. If he got near his mother when he cried about something, only then would it grow warm and go away.

Patsy said she didn't want to play cards any more anyway.

"W.B. is my horse," she said. "I can ride him."

She climbed on his back and put her arms around his neck. W.B. began to trample around the couch on his hands and knees, riding Patsy on his back.

"Giddyap," she said, kicking him with her bare heel.

W.B. made a galloping motion. Patsy squealed.

"Y'all stop," said Cotton. "Don't do that."

But they paid no attention to him. He bent, coming close with the blocking technique Duncan had taught him, and spilled them both on the rug. Patsy tumbled on her fat behind; W.B. sprawled out on his back.

"Y'all play something else," said Cotton.

He was still worried because his daddy had said he didn't like football.

"You're the meannest thing," said Patsy. "I like W.B. a whole lot better than you, and he's colored."

"I just half colored," said W.B. promptly, sitting up. "I also half white."

The children studied him silently.

"If you are half white," Patsy asked, "where *are* you half white?"

"I don't know," said W.B., puzzling. "I hadn't thought to look."

"Then ride me like a horse again," said Patsy. "Let's gallop."

"No," said Cotton, coming between them. "Don't play that."

"You're the meannest thing," said Patsy and hit at him. "Help me beat up Cotton, W.B." It was a grand idea. Her eyes got big. "Together we really could."

But W.B. backed off. "Naw now, Patsy, naw. Let go, Patsy. Les us leave Cotton be."

"Play something else," said Cotton.

"I don't want to play anything else. I don't want to!"

She had started to cry when they heard the knocking at the front door.

"It's Mister Willard Follansbee, I bet," said W.B. "He want to fry me like a chicken. He after me."

"You go hide," said Cotton. "I'll say you aren't here."

But it was only a blond lady, the one they had seen down at the schoolhouse that morning. She wanted to know where

Duncan was and he told her just what he'd heard them say: out at Mars Overstreet's store beyond the Pettico-cow Creek bridge. She seemed an outside lady and spoke in a foreign way.

"Where on earth is that?" she asked. "How do you get there?"

"I don't know," he said.

He stood connecting her with stories instead of anything here, so when she stared, bent, and suddenly kissed him, he wasn't surprised. He wished she had not gone away.

54 *The Stampede*

ANOTHER BESIDES Jason Hunt had wondered at Marcia Mae's departure from the speaking grounds. Unused to making his own decisions, Willard Follansbee was worrying that day with the nervous intensity of a cotton gin. Where was Harper? If Harper didn't come, he, Willard, could speak first. Good. But what if Harper showed up with some last-minute stuff from New Orleans? Bad. What if the nigger got in safe to Harper and told what he knew? Where was Marcia Mae going? The sweat gathered in salty pearls about his brow and trickled down the back of his neck into his collar. What with dust, sweat, and hair oil, his head itched like fire. Was Marcia Mae going to find Harper?

Across the street from the school grounds, a boy came out the screen door of a small sandwich and cold-drink shop, and crossed toward the crowd. Follansbee stood far on the outskirts in his white suit and flaming tie; the boy located him after a moment's search.

"Somebody just called in from out in the country," said the boy. "They say Harper's done got the nigger."

He stood in the offhand way that many Southern boys have, telling the most remarkable news without expression or elaboration.

"When did they call?" Willard demanded.

"Just now. Just this minute."

"Where from in the country?"

"You know Mars Overstreet's store? They were just leaving it."

As the boy left, one of a group of men near Willard had moved to stand at his shoulder. Now the others closed in; among them were the three who had stopped Kerney Woolbright earlier and asked him to go with them to hunt Beck Dozer down.

"I wouldn't be surprised," said Willard, "if Harper just might need our help to bring that nigger in."

"What y'all fixing to do?" a man called to them.

Willard drew his little pack away toward his car, obviously in conference. "You boys take it easy," another voice advised.

Several of the men piled into the car with him. One turned back, changing his mind, and watched them drive away. A friend joined him. "Might as well go see what they're up to." They got in a mud-splashed pickup, two others crowding into the cab with them at the last minute, and drove away after Willard.

Nobody seemed to know quite what had happened. In watching them go, everybody close by had let the boy get away, back to the sandwich shop. Several people, like bees straying from the central swarm, ran across to question him, but learned nothing; his father had forbidden him to do more than deliver the message. They found him obedient and stubborn as a mule.

Questions flew around. Where was Duncan Harper? Marcia Mae Hunt? Willard Follansbee? Here and there a man turned away from where he was standing and found either his own car or that of a friend who might want to drive uptown in case anything was going on. First, one car went; then, two minutes later, another, this one, like Willard's, with several passengers. For five minutes longer the crowd endured the strain. For five minutes every head was turned toward the empty road which told nothing. The murmur grew into a hubbub. Speculation was instantly repeated as fact: they were bringing the nigger into Lacey; Duncan Harper had found who shot Jimmy; a wire had come from New Orleans for Duncan Harper; the nigger was dead all along; Follansbee and Duncan were in a fight on the square. Through every statement the same thread ran: something was happening somewhere. It seems strange that curiosity can multiply into as strong a desire as wanting to get out of a burning building.

A man said quietly to his wife: "They're fixing to cut loose here in a minute. Let's get out while we can." He caught her by the hand and made for his car, and the stampede was on.

Jason Hunt found himself hopelessly trapped in the rush. Several people had jumped into his car to ride with him, without saying by your leave. Baby, baby, he kept thinking. What had she gone rushing off into this time? He did not see how such a dusty riot of machines would ever untangle. But one by one they shook loose; with a roar of the motor, some old Ford with a rattling fender won a path into the schoolhouse drive and gained the town street. After it came a sleek two-toned Oldsmobile.

Soon they were all free and coursing one behind the other with increasing certainty, for the first to reach the town square were not long in learning that Marcia Mae had stopped at the drugstore to ask the way to Mars Overstreet's store in the country.

55 *At the Store*

MARS OVERSTREET'S store was a grocery–filling station, sitting high on a crazy bluff to the left of the road five miles out beyond the tie plant and the Pettico-cow Creek bridge. In the winter when the smaller roads washed out or got too muddy for travel, the store was a sort of branch post office for the neighborhood. There was a dusty radio inside where people came to listen to the World's Series or the war news or the football game, though mainly they came to talk to one another and get the local events thrashed over. Anybody who for one reason or another had decided not to go to town on Saturday afternoon was apt to show up and stand around without saying much. Even today, with the county drained into Lacey for the political speaking, there were two young men in the store along with old Mrs. Overstreet, who being deaf and of no political turn of mind—she did not think women should have had the vote—had been left in charge of the store. She was back of the counter reading the paper, her glasses low on her nose and a yellow pencil stuck in her knot of hair.

The two men were alike—not in appearance, for one was short and dark, the other tall and brown; nor in the events of their lives, for one had just returned home after two years' fighting in Korea and the other was said to be taking refuge in the hills from the husband of a woman over near the River —and were spending all their time together because each felt himself enhanced for other people by an adventurous atmosphere which failed to do him any personal good at all, and each felt that perhaps if he were the other, life might have yielded up the secret. They were, in short, bored to death.

They were never observed talking to one another, only standing together, each in an attitude. The tall one, the one who had just come from Korea, liked to lean against something without exactly sitting on it, and fold his arms low across his chest the way John Wayne did in the movies. The short one, who was slightly bowlegged, kept his head ducked low with one hand on his hip and the other holding a cigarette the way one picks a berry, so that the smoke had stained between all his fingers and part of the palm. The question Mrs. Overstreet had asked five minutes before—or was it ten?—was still to be heard from time to time in the store. It had been:

"Whyn't y'all at the speaking?"

In order to get rid of it, like swatting a fly, the short one dropped his cigarette on the concrete floor, ground it out with his shoe, and answered through a mouthful of smoke.

"Just didn't go, I reckon."

Mrs. Overstreet finished the funny paper and turned to the editorial page. Her head rose and fell, drawing her eye up and down the columns; she was winnowing out what she meant to read. She released another question into the room:

"Wonder why there wasn't never a write-up in the Memphis paper when Travis Brevard died?"

Then she began to read in earnest.

Her words came and went, came and went. The tall brown one gave a yawn that staggered him.

"Was. Was a nice little squib, about that long." He opened two fingers, but did not trouble to unfold his arms. "Mama sent it to me."

"Funny I never saw it," said Mrs. Overstreet. "I thought I saw everything in the paper. Hardly ever miss a thing."

"Maybe she got it out of another paper."

Mrs. Overstreet took off her glasses and lowered the newspaper. "The *Tribune*!" She could not accept this. "You don't mean Wessie Stevens reads the *Tribune*!"

"No'm," said the tall man. "She takes the *Commercial*, same as everybody."

"Well then." Restored to orthodoxy, Mrs. Overstreet replaced her glasses and put the paper up again before her face. "I hardly ever miss anything. Funny I never saw it." Clearly, she did not believe it had ever been printed.

The shorter man turned a cigarette out of a torn pack, struck a cheap, large-flame lighter to it, and walked to the window. He said something in a voice which never carried beyond the person nearest him, though whether this was its quality or his intention could not be known, and Mrs. Overstreet, behind her newspaper, took a notion that when people spoke they ought to make themselves heard. She absolutely demanded to know what he had said.

Surprised, he turned about, regarding her with beautiful, bucolic, unintelligent eyes, which the woman whose husband was supposed to be chasing him had probably found irresistibly romantic.

"I just said I wisht it would rain."

"Everybody does," said Mrs. Overstreet, impatiently.

"That's all I said."

"What?"

"I said that's all I said."

"Maybe if we'd all quit talking about rain, it would go on and do something."

The two looked at each other, shrugged, and went to the window. They stood there so long, Mrs. Overstreet noticed them. "What is it?" she asked.

"It's somebody driving up in the side yard."

"Getting out?"

"No'm, just stopping. Why, it's Duncan Harper, him and his wife."

"Duncan Harper coming in here?" Mrs. Overstreet laid down the paper on the counter, and put her glasses, which were a great trial to her, on top of it, and came to the window. "He's walking out down the bluff," she said. They all observed that this was true.

The tall man stepped through the side door and stood watching.

"He's coming back towards the bluff with a nigger. I bet you anything it's that Dozer nigger."

"What nigger?" the dark one asked.

"You know that nigger. Took a shot at Jimmy Tallant here last month."

"Sure I know. I used to know him personally. You reckon he's been back there all this time?"

"I reckon he was."

"He's got a nerve," said Mrs. Overstreet. "He's had everybody dancing to his own sweet tune. Using the back of my land to hide in. Look at him, talking along with Duncan Harper. He thinks he's good as I am, now, don't he?"

But she was only marveling. She would have sounded the same if she had been watching an acrobatic troupe.

The dark young man went out of the store to join the other, and the two sauntered across the yard toward Duncan and Beck.

56 The Challenge

WHEN DUNCAN called from the path down to the cotton house, Beck's woolly head poked out immediately from the door.

"I wants to go into Lacey," Beck told him.

"I can't risk that," said Duncan. "You'll go into the next county for custody."

"How come you think I waited for speaking day if not for all the white folks to be gathered in town? I wants to go into Lacey like my daddy did."

"I guess you must want to go out of Lacey like your daddy did. Do you long to get dumped in your own front yard like a sack of meal?"

"Times have changed," said Beck.

"I thought times had changed too," said Duncan, "but this morning I found out they haven't. You're looking at the man who's going to get the smallest vote for sheriff in the history of Franklin County."

"On account of me?" said Beck and stopped walking.

"Partly you. Partly Mister Kerney Woolbright turning against me. And mainly people not wanting to vote for anybody with one single liberal thought toward the black race."

"If I had a vote it would be yours, Mister Harper."

"If I could get you one, I would."

"And still," said Beck, "I would like to ride into Lacey."

"I don't give a damn what you'd like," said Duncan.

He was conscious of the biases and willfulness that Beck put himself together with, until his character was as whorled as the grain of a tree that had grown up through the middle of a harrow. There was no way not to think of Uncle Phillip, who was also always pulling against the tide, and just then he recalled for the first time in his life something his mother had told him once when Uncle Phillip had provoked him to the point of murder. "His wife ran off with his best friend," she said. "You have to take that into account. Now don't you ever mention it, especially not to him." I guess it was enough to make a Hoover man of him, Duncan thought, and as quickly as that the gap of sympathy that had stood all these years between his uncle and himself was closed. For he knew now that he too would be seen in Lacey as an eccentric; possibly it would be the only way he could be tolerated. "He went off on the race question," they would say, as though he had taken up some Oriental religion; "It was the strangest thing." Strange enough to take the place of his football record as the story people told about him. Curiously, these reflections did not oppress him. The people around Lacey who were said to be peculiar took up the major part of the town; but perhaps their peculiarity, whether acquired deliberately or incidentally, gave them what they wanted—it freed them from what people expected of them. He felt freer already. I can read more now, he thought, and have a drink in the evenings after work, and just then Kerney Woolbright leaned across the grocery counter, looked up at him with trustful boyish eyes and said, "Do you guess Cissy Hunt would give me a date?" and Marcia Mae, poised to serve beside the fresh chalk line, shook a damp strand from her forehead and flashed him a smile. He heard glass splinter—*who* could have done it? He never wanted to know—and he was back with Uncle Phillip, closer than ever. Cresting the path he saw the two young men approaching them from the store. The day was not over yet.

"Do you mean to say that nigger was back there all the time?"

"We'll help you take him in."

"No need for that. Beck and I are old friends. He came to give himself up."

"You can't ever tell what a nigger will do," said the dark man.

"Sure can't," said the tall one, and hooked a thumb in his belt. "He tried to kill Jimmy Tallant, didn't he?"

"He wasn't the one," said Duncan. "It was a white man did it. Ask Tallant."

"That Jimmy Tallant," said Mrs. Overstreet from the side door behind them and died laughing.

"How do you do, Mrs. Overstreet," said Duncan and tipped his hat.

"Pretty well, thank you, Duncan, considering the heat."

"You can't go by what Tallant says," said the tall man. "He'd just as soon lie to you as look at you. Ask him what time it is, he'll look at his watch and tell you thirty minutes off, just to see what you'll do. Ain't that right, Ed?"

"That's right," said the other.

"That nigger there," said the first, jerking his chin at Beck, "what he needs is for somebody to scare the hell out of him a couple of times. He thinks he's good as I am. You going to have trouble like this till somebody does it to him. I know what I'm talking about."

"I reckon we'll just get on along," said Duncan. "If I thought there was any harm in him, I don't guess I'd have brought my wife along when I came for him."

The two men did not want to give ground.

"I hear you're against segregation, want to let the niggers vote," said the tall one. "Is that right?"

Duncan flushed. "Why don't you go to the speaking and hear what I've got to say?"

"Why should I if you can tell me yes or no right now? Do you or don't you?"

"I haven't got time to waste on you," Duncan said.

"*Waste* on us? You don't talk much like a politician to me. You ask for our vote and you're talking like that?"

"You can vote for whoever you want to," said Duncan. "The way you're talking, I wouldn't want to claim you on my side."

He walked between them, clearing a sort of wake that Beck could follow in. Beck was so carefully expressing neither one thing nor the other that he fell neatly when the tall man tripped him.

"His side," said the dark one and sniffed a couple of times as though his nose bothered him. "Must think he's still playing football."

Mrs. Overstreet, who had retreated into the store, stuck her head out the door, and called to the two as if they had been her own little children.

"Edward! Perrin! Youall come straight inside right this minute!"

"Duncan!" Tinker cautioned from the car window.

"Don't, Mister Harper," Beck said, from the ground.

They were right. Duncan halted, unclenching his fist, turning away. He helped Beck get up.

"They're just trying to pick a fight," said Tinker. She was leaning across the wheel, speaking from the driver's window. That placed her in the center of the front seat with a space on either side.

"They're never out of one thing they don't get into another!" Mrs. Overstreet called to Duncan.

Duncan slid in under the wheel. Beck had crossed before the radiator and now opened the opposite door of the car. He was about to break the front seat forward and let himself in the back, when Duncan glanced toward him, and his hand paused. In that particular slant of light, Beck's glasses failed for once to shield his eyes.

So it comes down to this, Duncan thought. *To the tiniest decision you can make. To the slightest action. In front of people daring you to do what you believe in and they don't.*

"There's plenty of room in the front," he said.

Beck looked down at Tinker, in recollection of the lady who had bandaged up his hands. For an instant she wavered, then shifted aside toward Duncan. "Of course there's room," she said.

"Well I'll be goddamned," said the tall man to the other. "Do you see that?"

Before Duncan could start the motor, they stood beside

him, their faces thrusting in the window. "Somebody's got to stop a thing like this," the tall one said flatly.

"We're in a hurry," Tinker said, feeling just the way Mrs. Overstreet had felt, the way badly brought-up children always make a woman feel. "Youall get out of the way."

The hand of the tall one snaked deftly in toward the ignition key, but before Duncan could strike it aside, Tinker had set her live cigarette on it. The man recoiled with a shriek, carrying away with him on the flesh a good quarter of an inch of burning ash, and fell backward, sprawling over his companion, who had bent downward from the window. Duncan took the chance to back away. As he swirled into the drive, coasting down to the road, "They've thrown us later than ever," he said. "I'll be an hour late to the speaking grounds."

"I wants to ride into Lacey," said Beck Dozer.

"I'm taking no chances with you," said Duncan. "I'll just have to be late."

"I think you'd better stop and see about that front tire," said Tinker.

"The tire?"

"Yes. That boy, that awful little black-headed one. He was up to something with it when he bent down."

"To the tire? What would he do?"

"I don't know. I wouldn't put anything past them."

"It seems to ride all right," said Duncan. "I don't have time to stop," he added.

She relighted what was left of her cigarette. Her brown eyes watched him from the mirror.

"I thought I'd be dead before this time of day," said Beck, riding philosophically, his hand holding to the bar that braced the ventilation window, his legs crossed in his best trousers, his shoes shining under the coat of dust.

The car swayed with the curves. Tinker thrust her heel harder to the floorboard. "Do you have to go so fast, Duncan?"

"I should have told them," he said. "When they asked if I wanted Negroes to vote, I should have said right out, Yes I do. There's no middle ground on this. Kerney's seen to that. I have to come right out with what I mean."

"You were afraid for Beck," she said.

"That's it."

They passed the Negro settlement where the women took in washing, and were gone before the dogs, lazy in the heat and drought, had time to more than lift their tongues out of the dust. They ripped over the Pettico-cow Creek bridge and the dry boards jumped up and clattered. They passed the tie plant. Nearing the highway and the juncture where the road ran out at the Idle Hour, the gravel thickened, the road widened, the curves spun them in wider arcs.

"There's something coming," Tinker said. "Look at all that dust."

Duncan pressed the horn for a couple of blasts and leaned closer to the wheel. He saw no need to slacken speed; he was a quick, accurate driver and he knew the road. But he was not prepared for Marcia Mae.

She came flashing out of a curve ahead, her yellow hair wild in the wind; when she saw him coming, she half-turned back to point behind her. She was calling something. She had always been a terrible driver.

There behind her, bursting from the curve, came another car, jammed with men, and Follansbee at the wheel. She was trying to warn him.

Duncan decided at once to take advantage of the curve to get past both cars, though he was well enough acquainted with Marcia Mae to know she might have some wonderful idea. And she did. With Follansbee coming close upon her, she slammed on her brakes, squinting her eyes and bracing herself for the shock.

Duncan felt a moment of extraordinary pride in her. It wasn't such a bad idea. It had taken nerve. It was even working. There went Willard, skidding on a wild bias through the gravel to his right, unable to swing toward Duncan's half of the road and sure to blam the convertible. Marcia Mae herself had very nearly blocked the road; her radiator had deflected toward him in the sudden stop.

Duncan swerved to skim past her, making it by a thread. Weeds rattled against his fenders. He would have to bring the wheel down sharply left to regain his track, then reverse into the road's tilt—it could be done.

He saw the nose of a pick-up appear in the curve. He cut the wheel down, braking momentarily, and before he could switch back for the quick reversal, he felt and heard it at once—the feeling as though his left knee had given suddenly beneath him at full stride in a tricky run, the sound like gunshot in his ear: a blowout. The wheel leaped violently in his grasp.

57 A Rush to the Scene

JIMMY TALLANT had spent the day in his empty roadhouse; he had decided for reasons of health to stay away from the speaking. He heard the first car leave the highway, making for the country, but was too late to see who was in it. When the second passed he was at the window. Marcia Mae's shank of hair signed the sky for him, and zip from over the highway rise came Follansbee, hell for leather, car loaded to the gills, and a country pick-up riding close to his taillight.

It took Jimmy about one revolution of the tires to realize that the only person Marcia Mae Hunt and Willard Follansbee had in common was Duncan Harper. Had the first car been his? And if so, was Tinker with him?

Jimmy's car stood near the entrance; he had fudged a day or two on his doctor's orders not to drive, and had gone into town earlier for a pack of cigarettes. He was bending to the ignition switch when he heard, from a little distance within the rolling country where the road ran, the bang of a blowout followed by a shriek of brakes and crashing of metal. Tinker! His thought came louder than the sounds had. At once he was speeding through the gravel, through shoals of yellow dust that in the still hot day showed no volition either to settle again or ebb into the air currents. Now it thickened to the absolute density of mud; now it cleared on a space of road so innocent that Jimmy wondered if he had already passed whatever had occurred.

He had not. Here at the crest of a curve, with puffs of dust still rising from it, the pick-up lay in a ditch to the right of the road, half-overturned. Two wheels stuck up in the air; he saw the fore one stop turning. Men were crawling out of the cab and sitting along the edge of the ditch. One saw Jimmy pass and ran after him, waving an arm. There ahead was Marcia Mae's convertible stopped in the middle of the road. Not a scratch was on it and it was empty.

Jimmy pulled up behind and stopped.

Marcia Mae shouted to him from the drop at the right of the road.

"Oh God, Jimmy! It's awful! Duncan's tire blew out and he turned over twice, right into Follansbee. Follansbee and all those men are crawling out of a gully, but I can't find Duncan's car at all! Come help me find him, Jimmy—"

"Was Tinker with him? Was she?" He was already over the edge of the slight embankment that sloped, then more sharply dropped, to a ravine split into two rambling wooded sections. "*Was she?*" He shook her.

"Somebody was. There were three, I think."

He pulled away from her. He was listing from his long stay in the hospital, as uncertain of his direction as a feather in the air. "Come on," he said, and plunged down at a run.

"It must be that way," she said, pointing right.

"Here!" He stopped his descent, slipping on the loose Mississippi earth. A large gash in the weeds at his feet showed where a car's weight had struck and glanced off. He thought he heard a cry. He took the short steep way down, half-sliding. Behind him, Marcia Mae stumbled and fell, so that he came to the wrecked car ahead of her, saw who was inside and what had happened and hurried on, searching.

Down a cowpath something alive crawled up out of a shallow ditch and caught him by the knees. It took him a minute to recognize Beck Dozer. The glasses were gone, for one thing, so that his face looked like any colored boy's who had gone and got into trouble on Saturday, but young, very young. Blood was streaming back around his temples as if somebody had beat him over the head.

"Get up, for God's sake," said Jimmy, "and tell me if his wife was in the car too."

"She was," said Beck, shaking like a puppy. "Oh, Jesus, yes. Don't leave me, Mister Jimmy, please."

But he ran again. Where? He circled, thrusting back bushes, weeds, and vines. He called. At last he found her.

She was a little way down the hill from where he had seen the gash in the earth. She had not sailed far, but she had certainly gone high, had succeeded in clearing a clump of small locust trees and landing in a little shady space. By an old stump that had turned white and was sprouting vines and mushrooms he found her lying on her side. She had an arm under her head and looked relaxed and assured there, as if she had chosen the place to take a nap in.

At the sight of her he was suddenly no longer terrified, even though he believed at first that she was dead.

By that time the country road above them was filling with cars; in minutes more the highway itself was blocked and all the traffic on U.S. 82 was baking in the sun. Through traffic could curse all it pleased: a town had turned out to see its own history. Slick with sweat, caked with dust, burned at the touch of metal, fanning, roasting in their own cars, the people of Lacey drove every inch as near as they could to the scene, and some got out to walk nearer while others sat waiting for the news.

Slowly it came back to them, an item at a time, some of it wrong. The highway patrol arrived, clearing a way for the ambulance that had got no farther than the hilltop beyond the Idle Hour where it stood blinking yellow and red, red and yellow, the colors blurring in the sun as fire will do. At last it maneuvered into the country road with its siren purring, and here it crept more slowly than ever, the parked cars shifting and backing to make room, and fresh dust spewing. After a time a doctor, impatient, alighted; he thought he could do better on foot.

Those who had first reached the scene of the wreck were rewarded. Already they had heard all the firsthand stories—stories that would be good for generations. Now they were privileged to see authority arrive and stretchers carried up the hill. Last of all, they witnessed Jimmy Tallant emerge, and walking with him with a cloth to the blood on his head, the Negro man, Beck Dozer.

Seeing the clumps of people gathered on the road and roadsides and in the fields beyond, Jimmy stopped and said, raising his voice so everybody could hear him: "Beck Dozer has got to go into town to the doctor to get his head sewed up. If anybody tries to stop him they've got to stop me first. I'd like to get it straight right now that whoever shot me it certainly wasn't Beck, and it's time everybody stopped making out that it was. I answer for Beck, and if he ever tried to shoot me, I'd take damn careful aim the next time I saw him and shoot him back. But nobody else is going to do it. All this mess—all this —happened on account of Duncan Harper being determined to keep Beck Dozer safe. Well, here he is and he's still alive and he's going to stay alive. I answer for him. I hope that's clear."

A path opened to let him through to his car. The white man and the Negro drove away through silence; not a hand was lifted and not a word was said.

The ambulance had gone ahead of them already, and Tinker had been taken to her mother's house. She had just been knocked out, the doctor said, so he had given her a shot to keep her that way.

When Jimmy turned from the highway into the town road, Beck spoke. "I rides into Lacey," he said. "I rides into town like my daddy did." He held the cloth to his head, sitting by the white man, and watched every street go past.

At the doctor's office they sewed him up, giving him a needle to deaden the pain and afterward a paper box of pills to take in the night in case he waked up hurting. He was wrapped in bandages again, as snow-white as Mister Duncan Harper's wife had got out for him. He paid in cash, and Jimmy Tallant took him home.

Lucy came out to meet him after the car had gone. W.B. stood behind her on the steps, and inside through the window, he could make out the shadow of Granny in the chair by the fireplace.

"Jesus!" said Lucy. "Is you bad hurt?"

"Not too bad."

"What they done to you, Beck?"

"Nothing. Nothing except take care of me. I feel like it's been a year since this morning. My glasses got broken." He reached his son and put a hand on his shoulder, looking down into his eyes.

"I got bad news for you, son. Mister Duncan Harper is dead."

58   Jimmy Gets Busy

LATE SUNDAY afternoon, a couple of Lacey citizens actually rode out to the Idle Hour and asked Jimmy Tallant if he would allow his name on the ballot for sheriff.

"We hear that Bud Grantham has taken up religion," said one, with an uneasy laugh. "We thought maybe you'd like to take up politics."

Jimmy was sitting on the counter inside the main room of the bare roadhouse, hugging his knee. He wore a clean white shirt with the cuffs turned back, a tie loose at the throat, and a gold tie pin on a chain. His hair was slicked down with water, and he was chewing gum. He looked, in fact, like a country fellow about to go out on a summer date. It was reported later that he didn't even get up.

"You better go easy," he said. "You don't know how I feel about the race question."

They both laughed outright. "We know there's no need to ask you."

"Then you won't be interested to know I favor equal rights."

"We're serious about this, Jimmy. We've checked the law: in case of a candidate's death before election, a write-in vote is legal. We're willing to get out the quiet word all over the county starting this minute, if you'll give us the green light."

"Seriously, then, what have you got against Willard Follansbee? He's still on the ticket."

"Nothing, except nobody wants him. They just don't want to vote for him. If Harper was still in it, Follansbee would win because Harper favored nigger rights."

"I just got through telling you: I also favor nigger rights."

The two stood silent. "We considered you might at least think of it as a compliment."

"I think you haven't counted your blessings," said Jimmy. "If you ask me, you've got the perfect candidate and don't know it. He's not going to get religion like Bud Grantham and feel like the likker business is not godly. He's not going to wonder if a nigger has a right to an equal hearing or a fair deal. On every issue that arises, you gentlemen will not have to ask,

'Where does our sheriff stand?' You will know. I cannot really imagine why you've taken a notion you don't care for Willard Follansbee. Maybe he's not as good-looking as I am. He hasn't got very much chin. But you have to recall that Duncan Harper was even better-looking than I am, and you certainly didn't want him. You think it over and try to be tolerant and remember that not everybody is born with the best looks in the world. As for Follansbee's character, I can personally vouch for him. He is the true mirror of your deepest convictions. Hand-picked by Travis Brevard. Trained in office. Knows his job. Why, if he had been the sheriff appointee instead of Duncan Harper, Duncan Harper would still be alive this minute."

"I said that myself," said one, nodding.

"Of course, the nigger might be dead," said Jimmy.

"Well, I don't think dead necessarily. There's some still think that nigger ought to be run away from here."

"Well, then, there you are. Follansbee would probably see eye to eye with you. Of course, the way *I* feel, anybody tries anything with Dozer has to answer to me. Personally."

The two looked uncomfortable. "Well," said the spokesman, "if you took up a notion like that about Dozer, everybody would understand. You'd have a right to it."

"I am not to be trusted," said Jimmy. "I am basically unsound." As they left, he said, "Take it easy."

Along about second dark, with the revival singing flooding up from down the highway, another car stopped and presently there came a scratching at the back door. Jimmy went through the dark to open it.

"Evening," he said to Pilston, who came near to fainting in his arms. "I had to say it was Bella wanted to see you," he explained, switching on the light. "Otherwise you wouldn't have come, would you?"

"I reckon not," said Pilston, shrinking down in a straight chair by the lamp as though bracing himself for the third degree or worse.

"You can relax," said Jimmy. "I'll get us a drink. We might as well be sociable. The truth is, I wouldn't harm a hair of your head, Pilston. I would defend you to the grave."

Bella stopped by the roadhouse on her way home from church. "It was just the best sermon yet," she said, just before she saw Pilston. "Mercy!" She thought they might be going to fight over her.

Her innocence came out so truly then that Jimmy lowered his eyes and for once words failed him. She gathered the nature of things all by herself.

"You want me to go on and go with him, don't you?"

"I married you because of what you said about the baby," Jimmy told her. "You knew that at the time."

"I thought I was telling the truth," she said. "It was you I remembered best."

"That's not the way they run these things."

"It might be true still. It looked like you to the life when it was tiny. Maybe it'll look two or three ways more before it's grown. It might get to look like you again."

Pilston shook his head. "You can always tell Indian blood. My mother was a pure-breed Sioux."

Jimmy cleared his throat. "Pilston here has been telling me he's resigned from the gambling business."

"There's not too much future in it," said Pilston, "not in this part of the country anyway. Time you get going good they elect somebody wants to clean you out. There ought to be laws to protect you. Have it one way or the other, but have it permanent. Instead you can't tell. There's no stability." He shot a sly look at Bella. "I told her all this. I had a little talk with Bella night before last. It was while you were still in the hospital."

"That so?" said Jimmy.

"I've put aside a little pile. She knows about it."

"Well now," said Jimmy, "I just as well take my hat and go for a little stroll. Give you two a chance to talk some more."

Bella sat with her feet side by side on the concrete floor. "But it's you I love, Jimmy." That stopped him.

"The thing is," Pilston told her, right out, "he don't care nothing at all about you. He never has, I bet you, and he ain't going to. If a woman loves a man and he don't love her, she can love him more and more, but it don't change him. At least, that's been my experience. Ain't that right?"

"I know it," said Bella. "It's how come I been going to the meeting all the time. I was counting on the Lord to help me."

"Well," said Pilston, "maybe the Lord has. They tell me He moves in mysterious ways."

"He's a sensible-talking man, Bella," Jimmy said, in advisory tones, and left them.

Outside, he found Beck Dozer waiting, and paid him. "He got here before you could get back," said Jimmy.

"Oh, I rode with him," Beck said. "He was over in that Delta bingo place, just like you guessed."

"Do you know if there's anything in the Bible about the father of your children being your legal husband?"

"I don't recall any such," said Beck. "Wouldn't it give some people a number of different wives?"

"They say you can find anything in the Bible," said Jimmy. "When you go home, see can you locate me a text."

"If I finds such a scripture, I might have to abide by it."

"Um," said Jimmy. He was apt to trail off into thinking now, and his thinking always went this way: Why me?

It did not seem possible. If life was blind, how could it suddenly wish him well? Why had not he died in a field in the wood, shot by accident, with Tinker bending over him to help him, instead of Duncan, smashed out of life in a car wrecked by accident, with Marcia Mae covering the sight of him until they pulled her away, and bright blood clung in her hair? And Duncan, the poor bastard, at least was trying to do good; while he, Jimmy Tallant, had never been known to try to do anything good.

He and Beck walked to the front of the roadhouse and, picking up gravel, took turns throwing at a telephone post across the highway. Jimmy struck it first—it rang to the heartwood —and Beck paid him a nickel. They played twice more, and retired in a sweat to a bench by the roadhouse steps.

"I go around in every waking hour thinking on that wreck," Beck confessed. "I think and think, and what I always ask is, 'Why him?' If somebody had to die, why wasn't it me?"

"It wasn't that somebody had to die," Jimmy said restlessly. "He did get killed. It just happened that way. There's nothing to wonder about. You just take it the way it is."

"Mister Harper was a gentleman," said Beck, from the end of the bench. "One is obliged to say it, for it's true."

"You're right," said Jimmy, sitting back with his knee hugged, adding at last with finality—it was perhaps the first time in his life he had ever thought or spoken of Duncan without a lurking scorn—"He was a gentleman."

On the highway coming from Lacey, a car was approaching. Slowing as it neared, it seemed to drift silent on the black strip, the lights widening. The gravel by the roadhouse rustled. The car stopped just beyond the two gas pumps. In the dark it was impossible to make out who the two inside were. Neither Jimmy nor Beck stirred. The figure nearer the wheel spoke without turning his head. His voice identified him as the one who had questioned Jimmy earlier about running for sheriff.

"Did you mean that, Jimmy, what you said about favoring equal rights?"

"I meant it," Jimmy said. He did not move.

In the long pause the insects choired, louder, it would seem, than the revival singing had been.

"You haven't thought it over? Don't want to change your mind?"

"No."

The pause this time was longer yet. Then the one at the wheel started the motor. The car pulled to the edge of the highway, waited while a heavy truck boomed past, then moved away in the direction of Lacey.

"They wanted you to run for sheriff?" Beck inquired.

"Yeah."

"Just for a minute in there, when they got right still, I thought maybe they were going to say, 'Well, equal rights or not, run anyway.' Did you think that?"

"It crossed my mind," said Jimmy.

"They say these matters are very delicate," Beck remarked. "If they had said, 'Run anyway,' I might have shouted 'Hallelujah!' and spoiled everything for another fifty years. You can't tell."

"No, you can't tell."

EPILOGUE

When the Bough Breaks

"I DIDN'T SEE SO much of it," said Mrs. Overstreet. "I never did like nigger trouble, though I understand—ought to by now, goodness knows—that it's necessary sometimes. I just didn't want to watch it, you know. There was Duncan Harper to get him, and them two boys in the store, Perrin Stevens and Edward Price, they run out there. So I started to go in the back room of the store and shut the door. I thought to myself, I reckon I ought to watch, there'll be so many people asking me about it, but I just hope he gets him away from here without nothing happening to him.

"Then I recollected all of a sudden I had seen Duncan's *wife* in the car! I said to myself, It couldn't be right: nobody would go to arrest a nigger with his wife in the car, so the next thing I was fixing to do besides telling Perrin and Edward to behave (always into something, them two) was call her into the store with me if it looked like anything. But by then, bless Pat! Perrin Stevens was sprawled out on the ground hugging his hand where Tinker Harper had burnt him with her cigarette, and Edward Price was sprawled out by him where Perrin had tripped over him. *And* the nigger was up in the front seat.

"I said to myself, I never yet saw a fugitive from justice treated in such style, though they claim there're prisons out in California where they don't want to hurt the crooks' feelings, so everybody acts like nobody never done nothing at all, and they're all just there for fun. A nigger at that! I know he never done it, but didn't anybody know it for sure at that time, least of all Duncan Harper. Well, the boys was upset and I was upset, though I'm sorry as anybody, you understand, that Duncan had that wreck. I don't say, Served him right. Nobody ought to say that. It ain't Christian.

"Perrin Stevens wore his hand wrapped up for a week, but him and Edward never talked so much about it, except to say that if any nigger had to be riding in the front seat along with a white man and a white man's wife when there was a whole back seat empty, and it August, they didn't want to hear nothing about it that time either. But if Edward did anything to

293

the tire I never saw it. I think he more than aptly got knocked over when Perrin drawed his hand back where she burnt him and then Duncan stepped on the gas. You can ask him though.

"Looks cloudy today, though the paper just said: Fair. Continued Warm. I'm so tired of reading Continued Warm. I'm almost tempted to write a letter. Listen, you can call it warm if you want to, but to me it's *hot*. H-O-T, hot. It ain't a hard word. Look it up."

Having listened with his usual good care throughout this declaration, Kerney Woolbright paid his respects and drove back to town. There was a little whipping wind abroad, though it was not yet noon. Dust ran across the road in furrow widths. The iron bridge over Pettico-cow Creek sounded dangerously like thunder.

He parked the car on the square, and began to walk around without seeming to, talking to this one and that one: though apparently in casual progress toward some minor business, he was really not going anywhere at all. People congratulated him on winning the race, and joshed him about the announcement of his engagement to Cissy Hunt, which had appeared in the Sunday paper.

"She had to wait till after the election before she'd say the word," they said. "Cissy's not so dumb."

"No," said the postmistress, who had just locked up for dinner, "they mailed all the stuff in to the paper on the Monday before the voting. I'll have to take up for Cissy on that. Looks like we're going to get that rain."

Kerney ran into Perrin Stevens, the Korean War veteran, as he was coming out of the pool hall. Perrin stuck his thumbs in his belt and slouched back against the wall with one foot to prop himself.

"Naw, I never said much to him that day, Kerney. Me and Edward come running out of the store to help him, the way anybody would. Then he said the nigger was his friend, that was the first thing that threw us off. It sort of riled me. He never knew at the time, it turned out, but what that very nigger had fired on Jimmy Tallant in cold blood. In cold blood, man. Then he never thanked us neither. And on top of that —put the nigger in the front seat! I'm like you, Kerney. I never heard your speech that day, but I know how you felt. You liked

Duncan, he was your friend, but who in the South can go along on stuff like that? I tell you, I been in the war over yonder fighting them damn little varmints, and it's the same story in the Army. I don't care what the nigger-loving reporters write back to the nigger-loving newspapers. I'm telling you because I seen it. It's the same story.

"You can't give them responsibility because they don't know what it is. If you get too many of them in one regiment you might as well call off the war and shoot craps. If you don't segregate them there's always trouble. When one gets out of line, they all get out of line. We had a lot of them in our outfit—smokes, the Yankee boys call them. We had it understood. The PRO—public relations officer, you know—kept writing back how brave they were, and every time one came up for a medal, the CO signed it. He said he didn't want Mrs. Roosevelt flying over to Korea to talk to him. I don't care how much fruit salad they wear. When the situation comes, the whites know how to handle it. Duncan Harper was due a piece of my mind that day—I didn't know at the time he had just heard a piece of yours. His wife burnt my hand, I guess Ma Overstreet told you if you saw her. Look-a there. You can still see the scar. All right. I don't hold nothing against her. Women don't have to figure out too much what their men are up to. She better not ever *talk* to me about it—I'll tell her that right now. And that nigger better watch his step, that's all I got to say.

"Somebody said the other day that Ed Price and me must have had something to do with that tire blowing out, but I'm glad to say I never touched it. It seemed more like a act of God to me, though I'm the last person to say I'd want to see Duncan Harper even with a sprained ankle, let alone dead. I used to be proud to say I was from Winfield County just because Duncan Harper lived here. It don't seem right to think he's dead.

"But, hell, you touch this race thing, Kerney, and it kicks like a mule. A mule. Hell! A elephant."

Kerney had to run for his car, not so much to escape rain which had begun to fall in disks, as to make sure of getting home (three blocks away) in livid lightning and dark at noon like judgment day. The storm was so intense that when he ran into the house from the porte-cochere, the current was already off and his mother, whose occupation was gone the minute she could not cook for him, was sitting in front of the fireplace in the living room, as though ready to receive guests.

"I think it's a tornado," she said to him conversationally when he appeared in the door. "I was in one in the Delta once, and if I'm right the eye should arrive within the next few minutes."

He looked past her. Small branches, broken, went skidding past on a flood of air, and wet green leaves plastered to the panes. She was usually very nervous about things, so he concluded she must be coping with what she considered real danger instead of the imaginary kind. He broke into a cold sweat and trembled on the stair.

"I wouldn't go upstairs if I were you," she called out. "You're safer on the ground floor."

But he had, obviously, to get to his room; the same as she had to sit with her back straight and legs crossed, as though chatting with people at tea.

The wind was like a large hand laid deliberately to the side of the house. He expected to see the door of his room crush to flinders before he could open it. But he let himself in and, closing the door, lay down in the middle of the bed and lighted a cigarette.

The familiar top of the pecan tree had disappeared from the window; now it came flailing back, fighting like a cat somebody was trying to drown. Lightning exploded in his ear. He sweated at every pore and shivered from cold. His mother had sent him to Sunday school for a few years as a child, but the main thing he knew about religion was looking at some Gustave Doré illustrations either for the Bible or for *Paradise Lost* —he could not remember which. He always thought of those pictures during thunderstorms and how the glory seemed all mixed in with horror: angels like a bee swarm going on forever, and heaven like having opened the door to the jumping-off place. He was always afraid of lightning.

Yet when the phone rang he knew he would answer it, because Beck Dozer was supposed to call him, so with tongue dry in his mouth he hurried through to the extension in the hall abovestairs.

"Hello," said Beck, "I reckon it's dangerous to be using the phone, but I promised to call you soon as I knew." He sounded cheerful.

"Do you know?"

"Yes, I know."

"Then tell me."

"He's staying over in Stark and eats at a little highway café called the Feed Bag. You know where it is?"

"Yes, I know."

"He's staying there because there's a man in the Delta after him for running around with his wife. But he gets there to eat every evening around six."

"Okay, but I'd better hang up. It's storming. . . . What?" The phone crackled.

"I said when do you pay me?" Beck asked.

"Any time. I don't care. I got to hang up. . . . Tonight at seven by the old Idle Hour. Okay. Sure."

He dropped the phone in its cradle as if it were red-hot.

After another hour his mother called from the top of the stair.

"We still can't cook; the current's still off."

"I'm not hungry," he replied.

She came to the door. "I thought we were gone that time. I really did."

He lay in his sock feet, his knees drawn up, smoking.

"Come on," she said, "we'll fix some sandwiches and tea. There's ham anyway."

"I'm not hungry, Mother. I'll be down when I get hungry. Now I'm not hungry at all."

"All right. But you haven't been eating enough. You have to keep your strength up. Senator." She smiled fondly, almost tearfully. "Senator Woolbright."

He did not answer and she went away. The thunder kept breaking and mending, breaking and mending, farther and farther away, while the rain made a low loving sound on the roof. When the room grew like a hotbox he opened the window. In late afternoon the sun came through a streak, like dawn at four o'clock. What was green was burning green, and light on the drought-dulled ground seemed about to make rainbows. You could smell all the sweet small limbs and leaves where the storm had broken them open.

Around five-thirty he drove to pick up Marcia Mae and they went to Stark to find Edward Price. Beck had worked well.

Kerney entered the little highway place called the Feed Bag at ten past six, and Edward Price was there, eating hamburger steak and french fried potatoes in the far corner, in a booth, alone.

Kerney sat down.

"He better not fool with me," said Edward Price, by way of conclusion to the story of the last time he had seen Duncan Harper. Substantially, his account was the same as Perrin Stevens' and Mrs. Overstreet's.

"But he's dead," said Kerney, rubbing his brow with his handkerchief. There, across the indentation his hatband made, sweat liked to collect. It was cool outside, but inside there, a big electric fan on a pole, hatrack tall, did nothing but make the air closer than ever.

"I know he's dead," said Edward Price, and drank some iced tea. When he put the glass down, crumbs of ground beef and corn bread floated to the bottom along with the stirred sugar. His mouth left an arc of grease at the rim. "He's dead, and that goes to show you. We know what's what about things. We know how we like them."

His nails were broken off, and grease was black under them as evenly as though a woman had done it on purpose as a manicure. His hair had grown too long. But doubtless during the romantic episode in the Delta he had slicked up and looked better, maybe with a white shirt on, the tie knotted low and the top button open, the cuffs turned back once on his wrists, smelling of a good hair tonic, with his large dark heavily lashed eyes and his air of knowing what he meant about things. He might have seemed then what the woman thought she might as well have.

"I voted for you," he said, irrelevantly. "After I heard what you said, and had seen what I saw, I checked to see if my poll tax was paid up and sure enough it was. So I voted for you."

"A good thing to do," said Kerney, falling into his automatic politician's street banter. He found himself staring at the thick-cut, white, fried potatoes on which Edward Price was now engaged in pouring tomato catsup. Kerney's stomach gave a lurch. He did not know if he was hungry or sick, and could not at the moment remember having eaten anything for weeks, though if this were true his mother would certainly be having a fit. He stretched out his arm full length and gripped the side of the table, bringing himself near across toward Edward Price, who stopped with a loaded fork and his mouth wide open.

"Did you do it?" Kerney demanded, in agony.

"Do what?" He put down his fork with the food on it.

"That tire that blew out for Duncan Harper was cut, slit. You could see it. I saw it when I went and looked at the wreck. If it was cut, somebody cut it. Nobody will do anything to you, least of all me. I don't want any trouble. I don't want to tell anybody. I just want to *know*. I've *got* to know."

He had played it all wrong, he realized. In fact, he had not played it at all. He of all people, Kerney Woolbright, who was cagy and smart, a shrewd poker-hand, a born politician. He had not even waited to be called. He had thrown his cards face up on the table, and himself on the mercy of a stranger. He was like the young girl in her first crush, unable to wait to say I love you; he was like the pretty new schoolteacher turning from the blackboard to ask: Who threw that? Who threw it? Who? Tell me! Who?

"Go talk to Perrin Stevens," said Edward Price. "I never had nothing to do with it." He returned to his food; his thick lashes lowered like little curtains over his dark sullen unreliable eyes.

". . . So," said Kerney to Marcia Mae, when he returned to the car, "I lost my head. I didn't play it right. He wouldn't say."

She lighted a cigarette from the dashboard. "It's just as well."

"What do you mean?"

"Kerney, we're both of us sweating blood over this because we want to find an out. We want to say that if Edward What's-his-name cut the tire, then that caused the wreck, then it was his fault what happened to Duncan. But even if we found that out, we'd still be just as much involved as ever. I've thought this over every way in the world, and more often than not I get right mad at Duncan for dying. It's the only unfair thing he ever did." Then she said suddenly, "I went to see Tinker."

"You *what*?"

"Yes, I did. I took myself down, and went by after supper one night so nobody would see me. The little boy came to the door—he's so like Duncan around the eyes. I told him to tell her who I was, and she came right out. We sat on the front porch alone together and I told her why I came running about

Duncan that day, because he never realized how vicious people could be and that the crowd was in a terrible mood waiting for him and that I couldn't see him walk in in such an innocent way. She didn't say anything, so I kept on talking. I told her that I had tried to make Duncan leave her, but he wouldn't, just as long years ago I tried to make him leave Lacey and my family and his family, but he wouldn't. So I just gave it over to her like that, you see, Kerney—my whole long love for Duncan. When you tell something you give it away.

"She followed me down the walk to the gate, and I said it had meant a lot to me to talk to her and I hoped it hadn't worried her too much. She said no and said too there was one more thing that I might not remember. She said that in school I once had laughed at a dress her mother had made her. I said, Well, I didn't remember, but I was sorry about it. That seemed to be all between us, so I left. I feel better now. I feel if I hadn't done it, I'd always be like a raw seam, something left to ravel out into time—some vague sort of death. Do you see?"

He did not answer. Having retraced the highway from the Feed Bag to the Winfield County line, he was now approaching the old Idle Hour, which was more a shell every day, since the gas pumps had been taken away and then the windows boarded up. They said that Bud Grantham had gone back to farming and that Jimmy Tallant was buying land and would put cattle in.

He turned into the drive. The gravel was heavy from the rain. He circled toward the back, braked, and cut the motor. It was nearly night, a relieved night; the earth had learned it could rain again.

Down in the wet pasture you could dimly make out from the hill the shaggy lines of green woods beyond, the elbow of a path. Down there a man had walked, flung rocks at a tree, then flipped a half a dollar in the air for a boy to shoot at.

A step crushed the stones, and Beck Dozer appeared.

"I was taking in the sunset," he explained, "along the highway west. Did you find him, Mister Woolbright?"

"I found him, yes."

"Did he say he cut the tire?"

"No."

"Did he say he didn't cut the tire?"

"No."

"Well. So you don't know, do you?"

"No."

"And I don't know either," said Beck leaning against the car. "I don't know if a single hand was raised against me or not. They do a lot of talking, they'll still go mark the X on the ballot in favor of the man like yourself who says he wants to keep me from marking X on another ballot, but the curious thing to me is that I, Beckwith Dozer, am still alive. I haven't even been run out of town. You use the Negro question to fetch votes with, Mister Woolbright, but to me it's a matter of whether my hide is on my back or ornamenting the barn door. For this I would like to know whether or not he actually damaged the tire. You owe me ten dollars, by the way."

Kerney opened his wallet and drew out the bill. After he had handed the money to Beck he held the billfold open still. "There is someone who knows."

"Who?"

"You were sitting on the far side of the car and didn't see. Duncan is dead. It was Mrs. Harper who kept asking that somebody stop and look at the tire. What did she see that made her think something might be wrong with it? Have you asked her?"

"No," said Beck, after a time. "This I won't do for you, Mister Woolbright. What she knows she knows. Her knowledge is not for sale."

"Well then," said Kerney, "let's put it this way. You see Jimmy Tallant all the time and sooner or later, maybe right now, maybe not, Jimmy is going to see Mrs. Harper. Lucy goes down to help her. W.B. is always underfoot. Sometime or other, one of you might hear her say and tell the others. Isn't that possible?"

"It's possible," said Beck. "But if it happened, I don't think I would tell you, Mister Woolbright. The only thing I know to tell you to do is to go ask her yourself."

"Yes. Yes, of course," said Kerney. "I could do that."

Late, they drove into the Hunt driveway under the slow-dripping trees. The family was all out in the yard beyond, strolling; it was too wet to sit in the yard chairs, but who could stay out of the cleansed air? They turned and waved. They walked apart from one another, in various directions; here was a flower, there a broken shrub, here a lost tennis ball, yonder a view of the west. Jason leaned in the car window.

"Well, did you find him?"

"Yes, sir."

"Did he say anything?"

"No, sir. I couldn't get a thing out of him."

"Well then. We've done all we can." He looked westward for a minute, then he said, "By the way, Kerney. I've heard a thing or two in town about a matter I probably ought to take up with you. I'm sure there's nothing to it; just if you hear anything, you won't be surprised. The boy at the telegraph office says he delivered to you the message that the man who shot Tallant had been arrested in New Orleans. He said he brought it to you right before the speaking."

A long lavender cloud reclined in the west. It lay easily in a broad cleared stretch of sky, and seemed, what with the thicker lingering clouds above, like an island in a peaceful sea, and Kerney remembered things from English poetry about sailing to the isles of the blest. Few people ever got the chance that Kerney Woolbright had now.

"I remember," said Cissy, and poked her gleaming chestnut head affectionately under her father's arm from where she smiled and crinkled her eyes just slightly at the corners, in the soft way of Southern girls, saying to Kerney without words, "At last, my darling, you are here." She said to her father, "I was in the car when they brought it."

"I see," said Jason, in some alarm, still speaking to Kerney. "But did you know what was in it? Did you read it?"

So, all unheralded, blessed as rain, salvation had broken over him. He paused, setting the words in their proper rank, the way a good lawyer is trained to do. He took another look at the lavender cloud which seemed to tarry for him. He always believed he would have spoken.

"He gave it to Duncan," said Cissy. "They were right near the car. I saw him do it."

"Did you read it beforehand?" Jason asked.

"No, he gave it to him just like it was," Cissy said. "I was right there in the car."

"Cissy, will you please hush. I'm asking Kerney."

"I didn't open it, sir," said Kerney. "I thought that since I had been forced to go against Duncan's platform I no longer had the right to deal in his business. He left orders with the telegraph office to deliver anything to either one of us, but that was when he thought we were still together on the Beck Dozer question."

"So you just turned it over to him?"

"Yes, sir, I did."

"Strange. You would have expected him to get up and make some kind of public announcement. Everybody was curious. Well, he's dead now and we can't inquire, perhaps we shouldn't speculate. Let him rest."

"I feel the same, sir. It's why I never mentioned it."

"Yes. Well, come on in to supper, Kerney. We'll be eating shortly. I smell chicken and hot biscuits. You don't have so much of an appetite in hot weather, but since the rain has cooled things off—well, we'll keep her in there cooking them as long as we can sit there and eat them. I once ate twenty-five, or so Nan vows."

"I *counted* that many," said Nan, joining them, a bough of wisteria in one hand, held outward so as not to drip on her dress. "Look, isn't this lovely? The storm broke it off. Come on in, Kerney, and mix us a drink before supper. We'd love to have you stay."

Dark upon the sidewalk—for preoccupation, no matter how blond you are, is a darkening force—Marcia Mae went from Kerney's car to the house. He was afraid of her, but more afraid of her away than there with her, so he accepted the invitation. While he mixed drinks in the kitchen, the special Collins he could do so well for hot weather, she came through; again at the table as the silver fork tines sank into the tender meat that parted so easily from the bone while the polished knife blade cut the brown grilled crust, he felt her eyes cross and recross him, her face beautiful and pale, for she had been forgetting her make-up, even lipstick, lately, and had to be reminded of it.

As he took leave after supper he met her head-on on the steps with nobody near, and this time he could not avoid her: her eyes were a warrant and cornered him legally.

"I classed myself with you," she told him. "I take it back. I was mistaken. But don't worry. I won't make a big scene.

Why should I tell what everybody already knows except Grand, and she doesn't care? They know, but you are one of them now and they will protect you. They will organize themselves for evasions and excuses, they will indulge in endless beautiful subtleties, they will get the door of heaven open for you if they have to unscrew the golden hinges, for your sake and their own. You're safe. Nothing can touch you. Don't worry about anybody, least of all me."

She ran fleetly up the steps past him and indoors. He had no chance to speak. He went down the walk to the car.

A tumult raged in him. He could still go back and say the words to change it all: to make himself an outcast, an exile, a hero. But who would understand? He at least had *understood* what Duncan did. Who would understand him? God, maybe? God by Himself was not enough. Besides, didn't every big politician, statesman, national figure have something of this nature in his past, something he'd had to endure once, to compromise on? It had hurt him to the quick maybe—he would never think of it without pain, never the whole remainder of his life—but this was after all the burden he must bear with him along the way he had to go. The way was service, his country's service: he had to heed the people's will.

He braked suddenly. Without being conscious of it, he had driven wanderingly, around and around the town, and here he was before Duncan's house, Tinker's house. A light burned inside, rounding outward on the hill, cloud-soft upon the darkness. His own headlights stated something strict before him. Between the road there where he was and the hill and house which folded her in, her and hers, darkness was the gulf, darkness the wall, and darkness the only answer; for he could not go in. This final dishonesty he could not commit.

I loved her, he thought, or whispered. I loved her so much.

And fortunately for whatever people might think of him, nobody passed him while he was stopped there, his head laid forward on his arms which were folded across the steering wheel, crying aloud with great innocent sobs, like a little boy.

THE LIGHT IN THE PIAZZA

To John

I

ON A JUNE AFTERNOON at sunset, an American woman and her daughter fended their way along a crowded street in Florence and entered with relief the spacious Piazza della Signoria. They were tired from a day of tramping about with a guidebook, often in the sun. The cafe that faced the Palazzo Vecchio was a favorite spot for them; without discussion they sank down at an empty table. The Florentines seemed to favor other gathering places at this hour. No cars were allowed here, though an occasional bicycle skimmed through; and a few people, passing, met in little knots of conversation, then dispersed. A couple of tired German tourists, all but harnessed in fine camera equipment, sat at the foot of Cellini's triumphant Perseus, slumped and staring at nothing.

Margaret Johnson, lighting a cigarette, relaxed over her apéritif and regarded the scene which she preferred before any other, anywhere. She never got enough of it, and now in the clear evening light that all the shadows had gone from —the sun being blocked away by the tight bulk of the city— she looked at the splendid old palace and forgot that her feet hurt. More than that: here she could almost lose the sorrow that for so many years had been a constant of her life. About the crenellated tower where the bells hung, a few swallows darted.

Margaret Johnson's daughter Clara looked up from the straw of her orangeade. She too seemed quieted from the fretful mood to which the long day had reduced her. "What happened here, Mother?"

"Well, the statue over there, the tall white boy, is by Michelangelo. You remember him. Then—though it isn't a very happy thought—there was a man burned to death right over there, a monk."

Any story attracted her. "Why was he burned?"

"Well, he was a preacher who told them they were wicked and they didn't like him for it. People were apt to be very cruel in those days. It all happened a long while ago. They must feel sorry about it because they put down a marker to his memory."

Clara jumped up. "I want to see!" She was off before her mother could restrain her. For once Margaret Johnson thought, Why bother? In truth the space before them, so satisfyingly wide, like a pasture, might tempt any child to run across it. To Margaret Johnson, through long habit, it came naturally now to think like a child. Clara, she now saw, running with her head down to look for the marker, had bumped squarely into a young Italian. There went the straw hat she had bought in Fiesole. It sailed off prettily, its broad red ribbon a quick mark in the air. The young man was after it; he contrived to knock it still further away, once and again, though the day was windless; his final success was heroic. Now he was returning, smiling, too graceful to be true; they were all too graceful to be true. Clara was talking to him. She pointed back toward her mother. Oh Lord! He was coming back with Clara.

Margaret Johnson, confronted at close range by two such radiant young faces, was careful not to produce a very cordial smile.

"We met him before, Mother. Don't you remember?"

She didn't. They all looked like carbon copies of each other.

He gave a suggestion of a bow. "My—store—" English was coming out. "It—is—near—Piazza della Repubblica—how do you say? The beeg square. Oh yes, and on Sunday, si fanno la musica. Museek, bom, bom." He was a whole orchestra, though his gestures were small. "And the lady—" Now a busty Neapolitan soprano sprang to view, in pink lace, one hand clenched to her heart. Margaret Johnson could not help laughing. Clara was delighted.

Ah, he had pleased. He dropped the role at once. "My store —is there." A chair was vacant. "Please?" He sat. Here came the inevitable card. They were shoppers, after all, or would be. Well, it was better than compliments, offers to guide them, thought Mrs. Johnson. She took the card. It was in English except for the unpronounceable name. "Via Strozzi 8," she read. "Ties. Borsalino Hats. Gloves. Handkerchiefs. Everything for the Gentlemens."

"Not for you. But for your husband," he said to Mrs. Johnson. In these phrases he was perfectly at home.

"He isn't here, unfortunately."

"Ah, but you must take him presents. Excuse me." Now Clara was given a card. "And for your husband also."

She giggled. "I don't have a husband!"

"Signorina! Ah! Forgive me." He touched his breast. Again the quick suggestion of a bow. "Fabrizio Naccarelli."

It sounded like a whole aria.

"I'm Clara Johnson," the girl said at once. Mrs. Johnson closed her eyes.

"Jean—Jean—" He strained for it.

"No, *John*son."

"Ah! Van Johnson!"

"That's right!"

"He is—cugino—parente—famiglia—?"

"No," said Mrs. Johnson irritably. She prided herself on her tolerance and interest among foreigners, but she was tired and Italians are so inquisitive. Given ten words of English, they will invent a hundred questions from them. This one at least was sensitive. He withdrew at once. "Clara," he said, as if to himself. No trouble there. The girl gave him her innocent smile.

Indeed, she could be remarkably lovely when pleased. The somewhat long lines of her cheek and jaw drooped when she was downhearted, but happiness drew her up perfectly. Her dark blue eyes grew serene and clear; her chestnut hair in its long girlish cut shadowed her smooth skin.

Due to an accident years ago, she had the mental age of a child of ten. But anyone on earth, meeting her for the first time, would have found this incredible. Mrs. Johnson had managed in many tactful ways to explain her daughter to young men without wounding them. She could even keep them from feeling too sorry for herself. "Every mother in some way wants a little girl who never grows up. Taken in that light, I do often feel fortunate. She is remarkably sweet, you see, and I find her a great satisfaction." She did not foresee any such necessity with an Italian out principally to sell everything for the gentlemens. No, he could not offer them anything else. No, he certainly could not pay the check. He had been very kind . . . very kind . . . yes, yes, very, very kind. . . .

II

B UT FABRIZIO NACCARELLI, whether Margaret Johnson had cared to master his name or not, was not one to be underestimated. He was very much at home in Florence where he had been born and his father before him and so on straight back to the misty days before the Medici, and he had given, besides, some little attention to the ways of the stranieri who were always coming to his home town. It seemed in the next few days that he showed up on every street corner. Surely he could not have counted so much on the tie they might decide to buy for Signor Johnson.

Clara invariably lighted up when they saw him, and he in turn communicated over and over his innocent pleasure in this happiest of coincidences. Mrs. Johnson noted that at each encounter he managed to extract from them some new piece of information, foremost among them, How long would they remain? Caught between two necessities, that of lying to him and not lying to her daughter, she revealed that the date was uncertain and saw the flicker of triumph in his eyes. And the next time they met—well, it was too much. By then they were friends. Could he offer them dinner that evening? He knew a place only for Florentines—good, good, very good. "Oh, yes!" said Clara. Mrs. Johnson demurred. He was very kind, but in the evenings they were always too tired. She was drawing Clara away in a pretense of hurry. The museum might close at noon. At the mention of noon the city bells began clanging all around them. It was difficult to hear. "In the Piazza," he cried in farewell, with a gesture toward the Piazza della Signoria, smiling at Clara, who waved her hand, though Mrs. Johnson went on saying, "No, we can't," and shaking her head.

Late that afternoon, they were taking a cup of tea in the big casino near Piazzale Michelangelo when Clara looked at her watch and said they must go.

"Oh, let's stay a little while longer and watch the sun set," her mother suggested.

"But we have to meet Fabrizio." The odd name came naturally to her tongue.

"Darling, Fabrizio will probably be busy until very late."

It was always hard for Mrs. Johnson to face the troubling-over of her daughter's wide, imploring eyes. Perhaps she should make some pretense, though pretense was the very thing she had constantly to guard against. The doctors had been very firm with her here. As hard as it was to be the source of disappointment, such decisions had to be made. They must be communicated, tactfully, patiently, reasonably. Clara must never feel that she had been deceived. Her whole personality might become confused. Mrs. Johnson sighed, remembering all this, and began her task.

"Fabrizio will understand if we do not come, Clara, because I told him this morning we could not. You remember that I did? I told him that because I don't think we should make friends with him."

"Why?"

"Because he has his own life here and he will stay here always. But we must go away. We have to go back home and see Daddy and Brother and Ronnie—" Ronnie was Clara's collie dog—"and Auntie and all the others. You know how hard it was to leave Ronnie even though you were coming back? Well, it would be very hard to like Fabrizio, wouldn't it, and leave him and never come back at all?"

"But I already like him," said Clara. "I could write him letters," she added wistfully.

"Things are often hard," said Mrs. Johnson, in her most cheery and encouraging tone.

It seemed a crucial evening. She did not trust Fabrizio not to call for them at their hotel, or doubt for a moment that he had informed himself exactly where they were staying. So she was careful before dinner to steer Clara to that other piazza—not the Signoria—once the closing hour for the shops had passed. Secure in the pushing crowds of Florentines, she chose one of the less fashionable cafes, settling at a corner table behind a green hedge which grew out of boxes and over the top of which there presently appeared the face of Fabrizio.

She saw him first in Clara's eyes. Next he was beaming upon them. There had been a mistake, of course. He had said only piazza piazza. How could they know? Difficile. He was so sorry. Pardon, pardon.

There was simply nothing to be gained by trying to stare him down. His great eyes showed concern, relief, gaiety as clearly as if the words had been written on them, but self-betrayal was unknown to him. Trying to surprise him at his game, one grew distracted and became aware how beautiful his eyes were. His dress gave him away if anything did. Nothing could be neater, cleaner, more carefully or sleekly tailored. His shirt was starched and white; his black hair still gleamed faintly damp at the edges; his close-cut, cuffless gray trousers ended in new black shoes of a pebbly leather with pointed toes. A faint whiff of cologne seemed to come from him. There was something too much here, and a little touching. Well, they would be leaving soon, thought Mrs. Johnson. She decided to relax and enjoy the evening.

But more than this was in it.

When she finally sat back from her excellent meal, lighting a cigarette and setting down her little cup of coffee, she glanced from the distance of her age toward the two young people. It was an advantage that Clara knew no Italian. She smiled sweetly and laughed innocently, so how was Fabrizio to know her dreary secret? Now Clara had taken out all her store of coins, the aluminum five- and ten-lire pieces that amused her, and was setting them on the table in little groups, pyramids and squares and triangles. Fabrizio, his handsome cheek leaning against his palm, was helping her with the tip of one finger, setting now this one, now that one, in place. They looked like two children, thought Mrs. Johnson.

It was as if a curtain had lifted before her eyes. The life she had thought forever closed to her daughter spread out its great pastoral vista.

After all, she thought, why not?

III

B UT, OF COURSE, the whole idea was absurd. She remembered it at once when she woke the next morning, and
flinched. I must have had too much wine, she thought.

"I think we must leave for Rome in a day or two," said Mrs.
Johnson.

"Oh, Mother!" Clara's face fell.

It was a mistake to set her brooding on a bad day. The
rain which had started with a rumble of thunder in the early
morning hours was splashing down on the stone city. From
their window a curtain of gray hung over the river, dimming
the outlines of buildings on the opposite bank. The carrozza
drivers huddled in chilly bird shapes under their great black
umbrellas; the horses stood in crook-legged misery; and water
streamed down all the statues. Mrs. Johnson and Clara put on
sweaters and went downstairs to the lobby, where Clara was
persuaded to write postcards. Once started, the task absorbed
her. The selection of which picture for whom, the careful printing of the short sentences. Even Ronnie must have the card
picked especially for him, a statue of a Roman dog. Toward
lunch time the sun broke out beautifully. Clara knew the instant it did and startled her mother, who was looking through
a magazine.

"It's quit raining!"

Mrs. Johnson was quick. "Yes, and I think if it gets hot again
in the afternoon we should go up to the big park and take
a swim. You know how you love to swim and I miss it too.
Wouldn't that be fun?"

She had her difficulties, but when they had walked a short
way along streets that were misty from the drying rain, had
eaten in a small restaurant, but seen no sign of anyone they
knew, Clara was persuaded.

Mrs. Johnson enjoyed the afternoon. The park had been re-
freshed by the rain, and the sun sparkled hot and bright on
the pool. They swam and bought ice cream on sticks from the
vender, and everyone smiled at them, obviously acknowledging a good sight. Mrs. Johnson, though blonde, had the kind

of skin that never quite lost the good tan she had once given it, and her figure retained its trim firmness. She showed what she was: the busy American housewife, mother, hostess, cook, and civic leader, who paid attention to her looks. She sat on a bench near the pool, drying in the sun, smoking, her smart beach bag open beside her, watching her daughter, who swam like a fish, flashing here and there in the pool. She plucked idly at the wet ends of her hair and wondered if she needed another rinse. She observed without the slightest surprise the head and shoulders of Fabrizio surfacing below the diving board, as though he had been swimming under water the entire time since they had arrived.

Like most Italians he was proud of his body and, having made his appearance, lost no time in getting out of the water. He was in truth slightly bowlegged, but he concealed the flaw by standing in partial profile with one knee bent.

Well, thought Mrs. Johnson, it was just too much for her. She watched them splash water in each other's faces, watched Clara push Fabrizio into the pool, Fabrizio pretend to push Clara into the pool, Clara chase Fabrizio out among the shrubs and down the fall of ground nearby. Endlessly energetic, they flitted like butterflies through the sunlight. Except that butterflies, thought Mrs. Johnson, do not really think very much about sex. The final thing that had happened at home, that had really decided them on another trip abroad, was that Clara had run out one day and flung her arms around the grocery boy.

These problems had been faced, they had been reasoned about, patiently explained; it was understood what one did and didn't do to be good. But impulse is innocent about what is good or bad. A scar on the right side of her daughter's head, hidden by hair, lingered, shaped like the new moon. It was where her Shetland pony, cropping grass, had kicked in a temper at whatever was annoying him. Mrs. Johnson had been looking through the window, and she still remembered the silence that had followed her daughter's sidelong fall, more heart-numbing than any possible cry.

Things would certainly take care of themselves sooner or later, Mrs. Johnson assured herself. She had seen the puzzled look commence on many a face and had begun the weary maneuvering to see yet another person alone before the next meeting with Clara. Right now, for instance—Clara could never play for long without growing hysterical, screaming even. There, she had almost tripped Fabrizio; he had done an exaggerated flip in the air. She collapsed into laughter, gasping, her two hands thrust to her face in a spasm. Poor child, thought her mother. But then Fabrizio came to her and took her hands down. In one quick motion he stood her straight and she grew quiet. Something turned over in Mrs. Johnson's breast.

They stood before her, panting, their sun-dried skin like so much velvet. "Look," cried Clara, and parted the hair above her ear. "I have a scar over my ear!" She pointed. "A scar. See!"

Fabrizio struck down her hand and put her hair straight. "No. Ma sono belli. Your hair—is beautiful."

We must certainly leave for Rome tomorrow, Mrs. Johnson thought. She heard herself thinking it, at some distance, as though in a dream.

She entered thus from that day a conscious duality of existence, knowing what she should and must do and making no motion toward doing it. The Latin temperament may thrive on such subtleties and never find it necessary to conclude them, but to Mrs. Johnson the experience was strange and new. It confused her. She believed, as most Anglo-Saxons do, that she always acted logically and to the best of her ability on whatever she knew to be true. And now she found this quality immobilized and all her actions taken over by the simple drift of the days.

She had, in fact, come face to face with Italy.

IV

SOMETHING SURELY would arise to help her.
One had only to sit still while Fabrizio—he of the endless resource—outgeneraled himself and so caught on, or until he tired of them and dreamed of something else. One had only to make sure that Clara went nowhere alone with him. The girl had not a rebellious bone in her, and under her mother's eye she could be kept in tune.

But if Mrs. Johnson had been consciously striving to make a match, she could not have discovered a better line to take. Fabrizio's father was Florentine, but his mother was a Neapolitan, who went regularly to mass and was suspicious of foreigners. She received with approval the news that the piccola signorina americana was not allowed to so much as mail a postcard without her mother along. "Ma sono italiane? Are they Italian?" she wanted to know. "No, Mamma, non credo." And though Fabrizio declaimed his grand impatience with the signora americana, in his heart he was pleased.

A few days later, to the immense surprise of Fabrizio, who was taking coffee with the ladies in the big piazza, they happened to be noticed by an Italian gentleman, rather broad in girth, with a high-bridged Florentine nose and a pair of close-set, keen, cold eyes. "Ah, Papà!" cried Fabrizio. "Fortuna! Signora, signorina, permette. My father."

Signor Naccarelli spoke English very well indeed. Yes, it was a bit rusty perhaps, he must apologize. He had known many Americans during the war, had done certain small things for them in liaison during the occupation. He had found them very simpatici, quite unlike the Germans, whom he detested.

This was a set speech. It gave him time. His face was not at all regular; the jaw went sideways from his high forehead, and his mouth, like Fabrizio's, was somewhat thin. But his eye was pale, and he and Mrs. Johnson did not waste time in taking each other's measure. She sensed his intelligence at once. Now at last, she thought ruefully, between disappointment and relief, the game would be up.

Sitting sideways at the little table, his legs neatly crossed, Signor Naccarelli received his coffee, black as pitch. He downed it in one swallow. The general pleasantries about Florence were duly exchanged. And they were staying? At the Grand. Ah.

"Domani festa," he noted. "I say tomorrow is a holiday, a big one for us here. It is our saint's day, San Giovanni. You have perhaps seen in the Signoria, they are putting up the seats. Do you go?"

Well, she supposed they should really; it was a thing to watch. And the spectacle beforehand? She thought perhaps she could get tickets at the hotel. Signor Naccarelli was struck by an idea. He by chance had extra tickets and the seats were good. She must excuse it if his signora did not come; she was in mourning.

"Oh, I'm very sorry," said Mrs. Johnson.

He waved his hand. No matter. Her family in Naples was a large one; somebody was always dying. He sometimes wore the black band, but then someone might ask him who was dead and if he could not really remember? Che figura! His humor and laugh came and were over as fast as something being broken. "And now—you will come?"

"Well—"

"Good! Then my son will arrange where we are to meet and the hour." He was so quickly on his feet. "Signora." He kissed her hand. "Signorina." Clara had learned to put out her hand quite prettily in the European fashion and she liked to do it. With a nod to Fabrizio, he was gone.

So the next afternoon they were guided expertly through the packed, noisy streets of the festa by Fabrizio, who found them a choice point for watching the parade of the nobles. It seemed that twice a year, and that by coincidence during the tourist season, Florentine custom demanded that titled gentlemen should wedge themselves into the family suit of armor, mount a horse, and ride in procession, preceded by lesser men in striped knee breeches beating drums. Pennants were twirled as crowds cheered, and while it was doubtless not as thrilling a spectacle as the Palio in Siena, everyone agreed that it was in much better taste. Who in Florence would dream of bringing a horse into church? Afterwards in the piazza, two teams in red and green jerseys would sweat their way through a free-for-all of kicking and running and knocking each other down. This was medieval calcio; the program explained that it was the ancestor of American footballs. Fabrizio, whose English was improving, managed to convey that his brother might have been entitled to ride with the nobles, although it was true he was not in direct line for a title. Instead, his cousin, the Marchese della Valle—there he went now, drooping along on that stupid black horse which was not distinguished. "My brother Giuseppe wish so much to ride today," said Fabrizio. "Also he offer to my cousin the marchese much money." He laughed.

Fabrizio wished his English were equal to relating what a figure Giuseppe had made of himself. The marchese, who was fat, slow-witted and greedy, certainly preferred twenty thousand lire to being pinched black and blue by forty pounds of steel embossed with unicorns. He giggled and said, "Va bene. All right." He sat frankly admiring the tall, swaying lines of Giuseppe's figure and planning what he would do with the money. Giuseppe was carried away by a glorious prevision of himself prancing about the streets amid fluttering pennants, the beat of drums, the gasp of ladies. He swaggered about the room describing his noble bearing astride a horse of such mettle and spirit as would land his cousin the marchese in the street in five minutes, clanging like the gates of hell. He knew where to find it—just such an animal! Nothing like that dull beast that the marchese kept stalled out in the country all year round and that by this time believed himself to be a cow. . . . Unfortunately, the mother of the marchese had been listening all the time behind the door, and took that moment to break in upon them. The whole plan was cancelled in no time at all, and Giuseppe was shown to the door. There was not a drop of nobility in his blood, he was reminded, and no such substitution would be tolerated by the council. As Giuseppe passed down the street, the marchese had flung open the window and called down to him, "Mamma says you only want to impress the American ladies." Everyone in the street had laughed at him and he was furious.

Perhaps it was as well, Fabrizio reflected, not to be able to relate all this to the Signora and Clara. What would they think of his family? It was better not to tell too much. Fabrizio's brother Giuseppe had enjoyed many successes with women and had developed elaborate theories of love which he would discuss in detail, relating examples from his own experience, always with the same serious savor, as if for the first time. No, it was very much wiser not to speak too much of Giuseppe to nice American ladies.

"My father wait for us in the piazza at this moment," Fabrizio said.

Sitting beside Mrs. Johnson in the grandstand during the game, Signor Naccarelli dropped a significant remark or two. Her daughter was charming; his son could think of nothing else. It would be a sad day for Fabrizio when they went away. How nice to think that they would not go away at all, but would spend many months in Florence, perhaps take a small villa. Many outsiders did so. They wished never to leave.

Mrs. Johnson explained her responsibilities at home—her house, her husband and family. And what did Signor Johnson do? A businessman. He owned part interest in a cigarette company and devoted his whole time to the firm. Cigarettes—ah. Signor Naccarelli rattled off all the name brands until he found the right one. Ah.

And her daughter—perhaps the signorina did not wish to leave Florence?

"It is clear that she doesn't," said Mrs. Johnson. And then, she thought, I must tell him now. It was the only sensible thing, and would end this ridiculous dragging on into deeper and deeper complications. She believed that he would understand, even help her to handle things in the right way. "You see—" she began, but just then the small medieval cannon which had fired a blank charge to announce the opening of the contest took a notion to fire again. Nobody ever seemed able to explain why. It was hard to believe that it had ever happened, for in the strong sun the flash of powder, which must have been considerable by another light, had been all but negated. All the players stopped and turned to look, and a man who had been standing between the cannon and the steps of the Palazzo Vecchio fell to the ground. People rushed in around him.

"Excuse me," said Signor Naccarelli. "I think I know him."

There followed a long series of discussions. Signor Naccarelli could be seen waving his hands as he talked. The game went on and everyone seemed to forget the man who every now and then, as the movement around him shifted, could be seen trying to get up. At last, two of the drummers from the parade, still dressed in their knee breeches, edged through the crowd with a stretcher and took him away.

Signor Naccarelli returned as the crowds were dispersing. He had apparently been visiting all the time among his various friends and relatives and appeared to have forgotten the accident. He took off his hat to Mrs. Johnson. "My wife and I invite you to tea with us. On Sunday at four. I have a little car and I will come to your hotel. You will come, no?"

V

T EA AT THE NACCARELLI HOUSEHOLD revealed that the family lived in a spacious apartment with marble floors and had more bad pictures than good furniture. They seemed comfortable, nonetheless, and a little maid in white gloves came and went seriously among them.

The Signora Naccarelli, constructed along ample Neapolitan lines, sat staring first at Clara and then at Mrs. Johnson and smiling at the conversation without understanding a word. Fabrizio sat near her on a little stool, let her pat him occasionally on the shoulder, and gazed tenderly at Clara. Clara sat with her hands folded and smiled at everyone. She had more and more nowadays a rapt air of not listening to anything.

Giuseppe came in, accompanied by his wife. Sealed dungeons doubtless could not have contained them. He said at once in an accent so Middle Western as to be absurd: "How do you do? And how arrre you?" It was all he knew, except Goodbye; he had learned it the day before. Yet he gave the impression that he did not speak out of deference to his father, whose every word he followed attentively, making sure to laugh whenever Mrs. Johnson smiled.

Giuseppe's wife was a slender girl with black hair cut short in the new fashion called simply "Italian." She had French blood, though not as much as she led one to believe. She smoked from a short ivory holder clamped at the side of her mouth, and pretended to regard Giuseppe's amours—of which he had been known to boast in front of her, to the distress of his mama —with a knowing sidelong glance. Sometimes she would remind him of one of his failures. Now she took a place near Fabrizio and chatted with him in a low voice, casting down on him past the cigarette holder the eye of someone old in the ways of love, amused by the eagerness of the young. She looked occasionally at Clara, who beamed at her.

Signor Naccarelli kept the conversation going nicely and seemed to include everybody in the general small talk. There was family anecdote to draw upon; a word or two in Italian sufficed to give the key to which one he was telling now.

Some little mention was made of the family villa in a nearby paese, blown up unfortunately by the Allies during the war— the Americans, in fact—but it was indeed a necessary military objective and these things happen in all wars. Pazienza. Mrs. Johnson remarked politely on the paintings, but he was quick to admit with a chuckle that they were no good whatsoever. Only one, perhaps; that one over there had been painted by Ghirlandaio—not the famous one in the guide books—on the occasion of some ancestor's wedding, he could not quite remember whose.

"In Florence we have too much history. In America you are so free, free—oh, it is wonderful! Here if we move a stone in the street, who comes? The commission on antiquities, the scholars of the middle ages, priests, professors, committees of everything, saying, 'Do not move it. No, you cannot move it.' And even if you say, 'But it has just this minute fallen on my foot,' they show you no pity. In Rome they are even worse. It reminds me, do you remember the man who fell down when the cannon decide to shoot? Well, he is not well. They say the blood has been poisoned by the infection. If someone had given him penicillin. But nobody did. I hear from my friend who is a doctor at the hospital." He turned to his wife. "No, Mamma? Ti ricordi come ti ho detto. . . ."

When they spoke of the painting, Clara admired it. It was of course a Madonna and Child, all light blue and pink flesh tones. Clara had developed a great all-absorbing interest in these recurring ladies with little baby Jesus on their laps. She had a large collection of dolls at home and had often expressed her wish for a real live little baby brother. She did not see why her mother did not have one. The dolls cried only when she turned them over, they wet their pants only when you pushed something rubber, and so on through eye-closing and walking and saying "Mama." But a real one would do all these things whenever it wanted to. It certainly would, Mrs. Johnson agreed. She was glad those days, at any rate, were over.

Now Clara stared on with parted lips at the painting on which the soft evening light was falling. She had gotten it into her little head recently that Fabrizio and babies were somehow connected. The Signora Naccarelli did not fail to notice the nature of her gaze. On impulse she got up and crossed to sit beside Mrs. Johnson on the couch. She sat facing her and smiling with tears filling her eyes. She was all in black—black stockings, black crepe dress cut in a V at the neck, a small black crucifix on a chain. "Mio figlio," she pronounced slowly, "è buono. Capisce?"

Mrs. Johnson nodded encouragingly. "Si. Capisco."

"Non lui," said the signora, pointing at Giuseppe, who glanced up with a wicked grin—he was delighted to be bad. The signora shook her finger at him. Then she indicated Fabrizio. "Ma lui. Si, è buono. Va in chiesa, capisce?" She put her hands together as if in prayer.

"No, ma Mamma. Che roba!" Fabrizio protested.

"Si, è vero," the signora persisted solemnly; her voice fairly quivered. "È buono. Capisce, signora?"

"Capisco," said Mrs. Johnson.

Everyone complimented her on how well she spoke Italian.

VI

"GALILEO, Dante Alighieri, Boccaccio, Machiavelli, Michelangelo Buonarroti, Donatello, Amerigo Vespucci. . ." Clara chanted, reading the names off the row of statues of illustrious Tuscans that flanked the street. Her Italian was sounding more clearly every day.

"Hush!" said Mrs. Johnson.

"Leonardo da Vinci, Benvenuto Cellini, Petrarco. . . ." Clara went right on, like a little girl trailing a stick against the palings of a picket fence.

Relations between mother and daughter had deteriorated in recent days. In the full flush of pride at the subjugation of Fabrizio to her every whim, Clara, it is distressing to report, calculated that she could afford to stick out her tongue at her mother, and she did—at times, literally. She refused to pick up her clothes or be on time for any occasion that did not include Fabrizio. She was quarrelsome and she whined about what she didn't want to do, lying with her elbows on the crumpled satin bedspread, staring out of the window. Or she took her parchesi board out of the suitcase and sat cross-legged on the floor with her back to the rugged beauties of the sky line across the Arno, shaking the dice in the wooden cup, throwing for two sets of "men," and tapping out the moves. When called, she did not hear or would not answer; and Mrs. Johnson, smoking nervously in the adjoining room, thought the little sounds would drive her mad. She had never known Clara to show a mean or stubborn side. Yet the minute the girl fell beneath the eye of Fabrizio, her rapt, transported, Madonna look came over her, and she sat still and gentle, docile as a saint, beautiful as an angel. Mrs. Johnson had never beheld such hypocrisy. She had let things go too far, she realized, and whereas before she had been worried, now she was becoming afraid.

Whether she sought advice or whether her need was for somebody to talk things over with, she had gone one day directly after lunch to the American consulate, where she found, on the second floor of a palazzo whose marble halls echoed the click and clack of typing, one of those perpetually young American faces topped by a crew cut. The owner of it was sitting in a seersucker coat behind a standard American office desk in a richly panelled room cut to the noble proportions of the Florentine Renaissance. Memos, documents, and correspondence were arranged in stacks before him, and he looked toward the window while twisting a rubber band repeatedly around his wrist. Mrs. Johnson had no sooner got her first statement out —she was concerned about a courtship between her daughter and a young Italian—than he had cut her off. The consulate could give no advice in personal matters. A priest, perhaps, or a minister or doctor. There was a list of such as spoke English. "Gabriella!" An untidy Italian girl wearing glasses and a green crepe blouse came in from her typewriter in the outer office. "There's a services list in the top of that file cabinet. If you'll just find us a copy." All the while he continued looking out of the window and twisting and snapping the rubber band around his wrist. Mrs. Johnson got the distinct impression that but for this activity he would have dozed right off to sleep. By the time she had descended to the courtyard, her disappointment had turned into resentment. We pay for people like him to come and live in a palace, she thought. It would have helped me just to talk, if he had only listened.

The sun's heat pierced the coarsely woven straw of her little hat and prickled sharply at her tears. The hot street was deserted. Feeling foreign, lonely and exposed, she walked past the barred shops.

The shadowy interior of an espresso bar attracted her. Long aluminum chains in bright colors hung in the door and made a pleasant muted jingling behind her. She sat down at a small table and asked for a coffee. Presently, she opened the mimeographed sheets which the secretary had produced for her. There she found, as she had been told, along with a list of tourist services catering to Americans, rates for exchanging money, and advice on what to do if your passport was lost, the names and addresses of several doctors and members of the clergy. Perhaps it was worth a try. She found a representative of her ancestral faith and noted the obscure address. With her American instinct for getting on with it, no matter what it was, she found her tears and hurt evaporating, drank her coffee and began fumbling through books and maps for the location of the street. She had never dared to use a telephone in Italy.

She went out into the sun. She had left Clara asleep in the hotel during the siesta hour. A lady professor, whose card boasted of a number of university degrees, would come and give Clara an Italian lesson at three. Before this was over, Mrs. Johnson planned to have returned. She motioned to a carrozza and showed the address to the driver, who leaned far back from his seat, almost into her face, to read it. He needed a shave and reeked of garlic and wine. His whip was loud above the thin rump of the horse, and he plunged with a shout into the narrow, echoing streets so gathered-in at this hour as to make any noise seem rude.

After two minutes of this Mrs. Johnson was jerked into a headache. He was going too fast—she had not said she was in a hurry—and taking corners like a madman. "Attenzione!" she called out twice. How did she say *Slow down*? He looked back and laughed at her, not paying the slightest attention to the road ahead. The whip cracked like a pistol shot. The horse slid and, to keep his footing, changed from a trot to a desperate two-part gallop that seemed to be wrenching the shafts from the carriage. Mrs. Johnson closed her eyes and held on. It was probably the driver's idea of a good time. Thank God, the streets were empty. Now the wheels rumbled; they were crossing the river. They entered the quarter of Oltr'arno, the opposite bank, through a small piazza from which a half-dozen little streets branched out. The paving here was of small, rough-edged stones. Speeding toward one tiny slit of a street, the driver, either through mistake or a desire to show off, suddenly wheeled the horse toward another, almost at right angles to them. The beast plunged against the bit that had flung its head and shoulders practically into reverse; and with a great gasp in which its whole lungs seemed involved as in a bellows, it managed to bring its forelegs in line with the new direction. Mrs. Johnson felt her head and neck jerked as cruelly as the horse's had been.

"Stop! STOP!"

At last she had communicated. Crying an order to the horse, hauling in great lengths of rein, the driver obeyed. The carriage stood swaying in the wake of its lost momentum, and

Mrs. Johnson alighted shakily in the narrow street. Heads had appeared at various windows above them. A woman came out of a doorway curtained in knotted cords and leaned in the entrance with folded arms. A group of young men, one of them rolling a motorscooter, emerged from a courtyard and stopped to watch.

Mrs. Johnson's impulse was to walk away without a backward glance. She was mindful always, however, of a certain American responsibility. The driver was an idiot, but his family was probably as poor as his horse. She was drawing a five-hundred-lire note from her purse, when, having wrapped the reins to their post in the carrozza, the object of her charity bounded suddenly down before her face. She staggered back, clutching her purse to her. Her wallet had been half out; now his left hand was on it while his right held up two fingers. "Due! Due mila!" he demanded, forcing her back another step. The young men around the motorscooter were noticing everything. The woman in the doorway called a casual word to them and they answered.

"Due mila, signora!" repeated the driver, and thrusting his devil's face into hers, he all but danced.

The shocking thing—the thing that was paralyzing her, making her hand close on the wallet as though it contained something infinitely more precious than twenty or thirty dollars in lire—was the overturn of all her values. He was not ashamed to be seen extorting an unjust sum from a lone woman, a stranger, obviously a lady; he was priding himself rather on showing off how ugly about it he could get. And the others, the onlookers, those average people so depended on by an American to adhere to what is good? She did not deceive herself. Nobody was coming to her aid. Nobody was even going to think, It isn't fair.

She thrust two thousand-lire notes into his hand and, folding her purse closely beneath her arm in ridiculous parody of everything Europeans said about Americans, she hastened away. The driver reared back before his audience. He shook in the air the two notes she had given him. "Mancia! Mancia!" No tip! Turning aside to mount his carriage, he thrust the money into his inner breast pocket, slanting after her a word that makes Anglo-Saxon curses sound like nursery rhymes. She did not understand what it meant, but she felt the meaning; the foul, cold, rat's foot of it ran after her down the street. As soon as she turned a corner, she stopped and stood shuddering against a wall.

Imagine her then, not ten minutes later, sitting on a sofa covered with comfortably faded chintz, steadying her nerves over a cup of tea and talking to a lively old gentleman with a trace of the Scottish highlands in his voice. It had not occurred to her that a Presbyterian minister would be anything but American, but now that she thought of it she supposed that the faith of her fathers was not only Scottish but also French. A memory returned to her, something she had not thought of in years. One Christmas or Thanksgiving as a little girl she had been taken to her grandfather's house in Tennessee. She could reconstruct only a glimpse of something that had happened. She saw herself in the corner of a room with a fire burning and a bay window overlooking an uneven shoulder of side yard partially covered with a light fall of snow. She was meddling with a black book on a little table and an old man with wisps of white hair about his brow was leaning over her: "It's a Bible in Gaelic. Look, I'll show you." And putting on a pair of gold-rimmed glasses he translated strange broken-looking print, moving his horny finger across a tattered page. In this unattractive roughness of things, it was impossible to escape the suggestion of character.

It came to her now in every detail about the man before her. Even the hairs of his grey brows, thick as wire, had each its own almost contrary notion about where to be, and underneath lived his sharp blue eyes, at once humorous and wry. Far from being disinterested in his unexpected visitor who so obviously had something on her mind, he managed to make Mrs. Johnson feel even more uncomfortable than the specimen of American diplomacy had done. He was, in fact, too interested, alert as a new flame. She had a feeling that compromise was unknown to him, and really, come right down to it, wasn't compromise the thing she kept looking for?

Touching her tea-moistened lip with a small Florentine embroidered handkerchief, she told him her dilemma on quite other terms than the ones that troubled her. She put it to him that her daughter was being wooed by a young Italian of the nicest sort, but naturally a Roman Catholic. This led them along the well-worn paths of theology. The venerable minister, surprisingly, showed little zeal for the workout. An old war horse, he wearied to hurl himself into so trifling a skirmish. He wished to be tolerant . . . his appointment here after retirement had been a joy to him . . . he had come to love Italy, *but*—one could not help observing. . . . For a moment the sparks flew. Well.

Mrs. Johnson took her leave at the door that opened into a narrow dark stair dropping down to the street.

"Ye'll have written to her faither?"

"Why, no," she admitted. His eyelids drooped ever so slightly. Americans . . . divorce; she could see the suspected pattern. "It's a wonderful idea! I'll do it tonight."

Her enthusiasm did not flatter him. "If your daughter's religion means anything to her," he said, "I urge ye both to make very careful use of your brains."

Well, thought Mrs. Johnson, walking away down the street, what did Clara's religion mean to her? She had liked to cut out and color things in Sunday school, but she had got too big for that department and no pretense about churchgoing was kept up any longer. She wanted every year, however, to be an angel in the Christmas pageant. She had been, over the course of the years, every imaginable size of angel. Once, long ago, in a breathless burst of adoration, she had reached into the Winston-Salem First Presbyterian Church Ladies Auxiliary's idea of a manger, a flimsy trough-shaped affair, knocked together out of a Sunkist orange crate, painted gray and stuffed with excelsior. She was looking for the little Lord Jesus, but all she found was a flashlight. Her teacher explained to her, as she stood cheated and tearful, holding this unromantic object in her hands, that it would be sacrilegious to represent the Son of God with a doll. Mrs. Johnson rather sided with Clara; a doll seemed more appropriate than a flashlight.

Now what am I doing? Mrs. Johnson asked herself. Wasn't she employing the old gentleman's warning to reason herself into thinking that Clara's romance was quite all right? More than all right—the very thing? As for writing to Clara's father, why Noel Johnson would be on the trans-Atlantic phone within five minutes after any such suggestion reached him. No, she was alone, really alone.

She sank down on a stone bench in a poor plain piazza with a rough stone paving, a single fountain, a single tree, a bare church façade, a glare of sun, the sound of some dirty little black-headed waifs playing with a ball. "Careful use of your brains." She pressed her hand to her head. Outside the interest of conversation, her headache was returning and the shock of that terrible carriage ride. She did not any longer seem to possess her brains, but to stand apart from them as from everything else in Italy. She had got past the guide books and still she was standing and looking, and her own mind was only one more thing among the things she was looking at, and what was going on in it was like the ringing of so many different bells. Five to four. Oh, my God! She began to hasten away through the labyrinth, the chill stench of the narrow streets.

She must have taken the wrong turning somewhere, because she emerged too far up the river—in fact, just short of the Ponte Vecchio, which she hastened to cross to reach at any rate the more familiar bank. A swirl of tourists hampered her; they were inching along from one show window to the next, of the tiny shops that lined the bridge on both sides, staring at the myriads of baubles, bracelets, watches, and gems displayed there. As she emerged into the street, a handsome policeman, who, dressed in a snow-white uniform, was directing traffic as though it were a symphony orchestra, smiled into the crowd that was approaching along the Lungarno, and brought everything to a dramatic halt.

There, with a nod to him, came Clara! He bowed; she smiled. Why, she looked like an Italian!

Item at a time, mother and daughter had seen things in the shops they could not resist. Mrs. Johnson with her positive, clipped American figure found it difficult to wear the clothes, and had purchased mainly bags, scarves and other accessories. But Clara could wear almost everything she admired. Stepping along now in her hand-woven Italian skirt and sleeveless cotton blouse, with leather sandals, smart straw bag, dark glasses and the glint of earrings against her cheek, she would fool any tourist into thinking her a native; and Mrs. Johnson, who felt she was being fooled by Clara in a far graver way, found in her daughter's very attractiveness an added sense of displeasure, almost of disgust.

"Where do you think you're going?" she demanded.

Clara, who was still absorbed in being adored by the policeman, could not credit her misfortune at having run into her mother. Mrs. Johnson took her arm and marched her straight back across the street. Crowds were thronging against them from every direction. A vender shook a fistful of cheap leather bags before them; there seemed no escaping him. Mrs. Johnson veered to the right, entering a quiet street where there were no shops and where Fabrizio would not be likely to pass, returning to work after siesta.

"Where were you going, Clara?"

"To get some ice cream," Clara pouted.

"There's ice cream all around the hotel. Now you know we never tell each other stories, Clara."

"I was looking for you," said Clara.

"But how did you know where I was?" asked Mrs. Johnson.

They had entered the street of the illustrious Tuscans. "Galileo, Dante Alighieri, Boccaccio, Machiavelli, Michelangelo . . ." chanted Clara.

This is not my day, sighed Mrs. Johnson to herself.

She was right about this; alighting from her taxi with Clara before the Grand Hotel, she heard a cry behind her:

"Why, Mar-gar-et John-son!"

Two ladies from Winston-Salem stood laughing before her. They were sisters—Meg Kirby and Henrietta Mulverhill— a chatty, plumpish pair whose husbands had presented them both with a summer abroad.

Now they were terribly excited. They had no idea she would be here still. They had heard she was in Rome by now. What a coincidence! They simply couldn't get over it! Wasn't it wonderful what you could buy here? Linens! Leather-lined bags! So cheap! If only she could see what just this morning—! And how was Clara?

Constrained to go over to the Excelsior—their hotel, just across the street—for tea, Margaret Johnson sat like a creature in a net and felt her strength ebb from her. The handsome salon echoed with Winston-Salem news, gossip, exact quotations, laughter; and during it all, Clara became again her old familiar little lost self, oblivious, searching through her purse, leafing for pictures in the guide books on the tea table, only looking up to say "Yes, ma'am," and "No, ma'am."

"Well, it's just so difficult to pick out a hat for Noel without him here to try it on," said Mrs. Johnson. "I tried it once in Washington, and—" I've been blinded, she thought, the image of her daughter constant in the corner of her vision. Blinded —by what? By beauty, art, strangeness, freedom. By romance, by sun—yes, by hope itself.

By the time she had shaken the ladies, making excuses about dinner but with a promise to call by for them tomorrow, and had reached at long last her hotel room, her headache had grown steadily worse. She yearned to shed her street clothes, take aspirin, and soak in a long bath. Clara passed sulking ahead of her through the anteroom, through the larger bedroom, the bath, and into her own small room. Mrs. Johnson tossed her bag and hat on the bed and, slipping out of her shoes, stepped into a pair of scuffs. A rap at the outer door revealed a servant with a long florist's box. Carrying the box, Mrs. Johnson crossed the bath to her daughter's room.

Through the weeks that they had dallied here, Clara's room had gradually filled with gifts from Fabrizio. A baby elephant of green china, its howdah enlarged to contain brightly wrapped sweets, grinned from a table top. A stuffed dog, Fabrizio's idea of Ronnie, sat near Clara's pillow. On her wrist a charm bracelet was slowly filling with golden miniature animals and tiny musical instruments. She did not have to be told that another gift had arrived, but observed from a glance at the label, as her mother had not, that the flowers were for both of them. Then she filled a tall vase with water. Chores of this sort fell to her at home.

Mrs. Johnson sat down on the bed.

Clara happily read the small card. "It says 'Naccarelli,'" she announced.

Then she began to arrange the flowers in the vase. They were rather remarkable flowers, Mrs. Johnson thought—a species of lily apparently highly regarded here, though with their enormous naked stamens, based in a back-curling, waxen petal, they had always struck her as being rather blatantly phallic.

Observing some in a shop window soon after they had arrived in Florence, it had come to her to wonder then if Italians took sex so much for granted that they hardly thought about it at all, as separate, that is, from anything else in life. Time had passed, and the question, more personal now, still stood unanswered.

The Latin mind—how did it work? What did it think? She did not know, but as Clara stood arranging the flowers one at the time in the vase (there seemed to be a great number of them—far more than a dozen—in the box, and all very large), the bad taste of the choice seemed, in any language, inescapable. The cold eye of Signor Naccarelli had selected this gift, she felt certain, not Fabrizio; and that thought, no less than the flowers themselves, was remarkably effective in short-circuiting romance. Could she be wrong in perceiving a kind of Latin logic at work—its basic quality factual, hard, direct? Even if nobody ever *put* it that way, it was there; and no matter what *she* might think, it was, like the carrozza driver, not in the least ashamed. A demand was closer to being made than she liked to suppose: Exactly where, it seemed to say, did she think all this was leading? She looked at the stuffed dog, at the baby elephant who carried sweets so coyly, at the charm bracelet dancing on Clara's wrist as her hand moved, setting in place one after another the stalks with their sensual bloom.

It's simply that they are facing what I am hiding from, she thought.

"Come here, darling."

She held out her hands to Clara and drew her down on the edge of the bed beside her. Unable to think of anything else to do, she lied wildly.

"Clara, I have just been to the doctor. That is where I went. I didn't tell you—you've been having such a good time—but I'm not feeling well at all. The doctor says the air is very bad for me here and that I must leave. We will come back, of course. As soon as I feel better. I'm going to call for reservations and start packing at once. We will leave for Rome tonight."

Later she nervously penned a note to the ladies at the Excelsior. Clara was not feeling well, she explained, and the doctor had advised their leaving. They would leave their address at American Express in Rome, though there was a chance they might have to go to the Lakes for cooler weather.

VII

To the traveller coming down from Florence to Rome in the summertime, the larger, more ancient city is bound to be a disappointment. It is bunglesome; nothing is orderly or planned; there is a tangle of electric wires and tram lines, a ceaseless clamor of traffic. The distances are long, the sun is hot. And if, in addition, the heart has been left behind as positively as a piece of baggage, the tourist is apt to suffer more than tourists generally do. Mrs. Johnson saw this clearly in her daughter's face. To make things worse, Clara never mentioned Florence or Fabrizio. Mrs. Johnson had only to think of those flowers to keep herself from mentioning either. They had come to see Rome, hadn't they? Very well, Rome would be seen.

At night, after dinner, Mrs. Johnson assembled her guide books and mapped out strenuous tours. Cool cloisters opened before them, and the gleaming halls of the Vatican galleries. They were photographed in the spray of fountains and trailed by pairs of male prostitutes in the park. At Tivoli, Clara had a sunstroke in the ruin of a Roman villa. A goatherd came and helped her to the shade, fanned her with his hat and brought her some water. Mrs. Johnson was afraid for her to drink it. At dusk they walked out the hotel door and saw the whole city in the sunset from the top of the Spanish Steps. Couples stood linked and murmuring together, leaning against the parapets.

"When are we going back, Mother?" Clara asked in the dark.

"Back where?" said Mrs. Johnson, vaguely.

"Back to Florence."

"You want to go back?" said Mrs. Johnson, more vaguely still.

Clara did not reply. To a child, a promise is a promise, a sacred thing, the measure of love. "We will come back," her mother had said. She had told Fabrizio so when he came to the station, called unexpectedly out of his shop with this thunderbolt tearing across his heart, clutching a demure mass of wild chrysanthemums and a tin of caramelle. While the train stood open-doored in the station, he had drawn Clara behind a post and kissed her. "We are coming back," said Clara, and threw her arms around him. When he forced down her arms, he was crying, and there stood her mother.

Day by day, Clara followed after Mrs. Johnson's decisive heels, always at the same silent distance, like a good little dog. In the Roman Forum, urged on by the guide book, Mrs. Johnson sought out the ruins of "an ancient basilica containing the earliest known Christian frescoes." They may have been the earliest but to Mrs. Johnson they looked no better than the smeary pictures of Clara's Sunday-school days. She studied them one at a time, consulting her book. When she looked up, Clara was gone. She called once or twice and hastened out into the sun. The ruins before her offered many a convenient hiding place. She ran about in a maze of paths and ancient pavings, until finally, there before her, not really very far away, she saw her daughter sitting on a fallen block of marble with her back turned. She was bent forward and weeping. The angle of her head and shoulders, her gathered limbs, though pained was not pitiful; and arrested by this Mrs. Johnson did not call again, but stood observing how something of a warm, classic dignity had come to this girl, and no matter whether she could do long division or not, she was a woman.

To Mrs. Johnson's credit she waited quietly while Clara straightened herself and dried her eyes. Then the two walked together through the ruin of an open court with a quiet rectangular pool. They went out of the Forum and crossed a busy street to a sidewalk cafe where they both had coffee. In all the crash and clang of the tram lines and the hurry of the crowds there was no chance to speak.

A boy came by, a beggar, scrawny, in clothing deliberately oversized and poor, the trousers held up by a cord, rolled at the cuffs, the bare feet splayed and filthy. A jut of black hair set his swart face in a frame, and the eyes, large, abject, imploring, did not meet now, perhaps had never met, another's. He mumbled some ritualistic phrases and put out a hand that seemed permanently shrivelled into the wrist; the tension, the smear and fear that money was, was in it. In Italy, especially in Rome, Mrs. Johnson had gone through many states of mind about beggars, all the way from Poor things, why doesn't the church do something? to How revolting, why don't they ever let us alone? So she had been known to give them as much as a thousand lire or spurn them like dogs. But something inside her had tired. Clara hardly noticed the child at all; exactly like an Italian, she took a ten-lire piece out of the change on the table and dropped it in his palm. And Mrs. Johnson, in the same way that people crossed themselves with a dabble of holy water in the churches, found herself doing the same thing. He passed on, table by table, and then entered the ceaseless weaving of the crowd, hidden, reappearing, vanishing, lost.

She closed her eyes and, with a sigh that was both qualm and relief, she surrendered.

A lull fell in the traffic. "Clara," she said, "we will go back to Florence tomorrow."

VIII

IT WASN'T THAT SIMPLE, of course. Nobody with a dream should come to Italy. No matter how dead and buried the dream is thought to be, in Italy it will rise and walk again. Margaret Johnson had a dream, though she thought reality had long ago destroyed it. The dream was that Clara would one day be perfectly well. It was here that Italy had attacked her, and it was this that her surrender involved.

Then surrender is the wrong word too. Women like Margaret Johnson do not surrender; they simply take up another line of campaign. She would go poised into combat, for she knew already that the person who undertakes to believe in a dream pursues a course that is dangerous and lonely. She knew because she had done it before.

The truth was that when Clara was fourteen and had been removed from school two years previously, Mrs. Johnson had decided to believe that there was not anything the matter with her. It was September, and Noel Johnson was away on a business trip and conference which would last a month. Their son was already away at college. The opportunity was too good to be missed. She chose a school in an entirely new section of town; she told a charming pack of lies and got Clara enrolled there under the most favorable conditions. The next two weeks were probably the happiest of her life. With other mothers, she sat waiting in her car at the curb until the bright crowd came breasting across the campus: Clara's new red tam was the sign to watch for. At night the two of them got supper in the kitchen while Clara told all her stories. Later they did homework, sitting on the sofa under the lamp.

Three teachers came to call at different times. They were puzzled, but were persuaded to be patient. Two days before Noel Johnson was due to come home, Mrs. Johnson was invited to see the principal. Some inquiries, he said, had been felt necessary. He had wished to be understanding, and rather than take the evidence from other reports had done some careful testing of his own under the most favorable circumstances: the child had suspected nothing.

He paused. "I understand that your husband is away." She nodded. "So you have undertaken this—ah—experiment entirely on your own." She nodded again, dumbly. Her throat had tightened. The word "experiment" was damning; she had thought of it herself. No one, of course, should experiment with any human being, much less one's own daughter. But wasn't the alternative, to accept things as they were, even worse? It was all too large, too difficult to explain.

The principal stared down at his desk in an embarrassed way. "These realities are often hard for us to face," he said. "Yet, from all I have been able to learn, you did know. It had all been explained to you, along with the best techniques, the limits of her capabilities—"

"Yes," she faltered, "I did know. But I know so much else besides. I know that in so many ways she is as well as you and I. I know that the doctors have said that no final answers have been arrived at in these things." She was more confident now. Impressive names could be quoted; statements, if need be, could be found in writing. "Our mental life is not wholly understood as yet. Since no one knows the extent to which a child may be retarded, so no one can say positively that Clara's case is a hopeless one. We know that she is not one bit affected physically. She will continue to grow up just like any other girl. Even if marriage were ever possible to her, the doctors say that her children would be perfectly all right. Everyone sees that she behaves normally most of the time. Do I have to let the few ways she is slow stand in the way of all the others to keep her from being a whole person, from having a whole life—?" She could not go on.

"But those 'few ways,'" he said, consenting, it was obvious, to use her term, "are the main ones we are concerned with here. Don't you see that?"

She agreed. She did see. And yet—

At that same moment, in another part of the building, trivial, painful things were happening to Clara—no one could possibly want to hear about them.

The serene fall afternoon, as she left the school, was as disjointed as if hurricane and earthquake had been at it. Toward nightfall, Mrs. Johnson telephoned to Noel to come home. At the airport, with Clara waiting crumpled like a bundle of clothes on the back seat of the car, she confessed everything to him. When he said little, she realized he thought she had gone out of her mind. Clara was sent to the country to visit an aunt and uncle, and Mrs. Johnson spent a month in Bermuda. Strolling around the picture-postcard landscape of the resort, she said to herself, I was out of my mind, insane. As impersonal as advertising slogans, or skywriting, the words seemed to move out from her, into the golden air.

Courage, she thought now, in a still more foreign landscape, riding the train back to Florence. Corraggio. The Italian word came easily to mind. Mrs. Johnson belonged to various clubs, and campaigns to clean up this or raise the standards of that were frequently turned over to committees headed by her. She believed that women in their way could accomplish a great deal. What was the best way to handle Noel? How much did the Naccarellis know? As the train drew into the station, she felt her blood race, her whole being straighten and poise, to the fine alertness of a drawn bow. Whether Florence knew it or not, she invaded it.

As for how much the Naccarelli family knew or didn't know or cared or didn't care, no one not Italian had better undertake to say. It was never clear. Fabrizio threatened suicide when Clara left. The mother of Clara had scorned him because he was Italian. No other reason. Everyone had something to say. The household reeled until nightfall when Fabrizio plunged toward the central open window of the salotto. The serious little maid, who had been in love with him for years, leaped in front of him with a shriek, her arms thrown wide. Deflected, he rushed out of the house and went tearing away through the streets. The Signora Naccarelli collapsed in tears and refused to eat. She retired to her room, where she kept a holy image that she placed a great store by. Signor Naccarelli alone enjoyed his meal. He said that Fabrizio would not commit suicide and that the ladies would probably be back. He had seen Americans take fright before; no one could ever explain why. But in the end, like everyone else, they would serve their own best interests. If he did not have some quiet, he would certainly go out and seek it elsewhere.

He spent the pleasantest sort of afternoon locked in conversation with Mrs. Johnson a few days after her return. It was all an affair for juggling, circling, balancing, very much to his liking. He could not really say she had made a conquest of him: American women were too confident and brisk; but he could not deny that encounters with her had a certain flavor.

The lady had consented to go with him on a drive up to San Miniato, stopping at the casino for a cup of tea and a pastry. Signor Naccarelli managed to get in a drive to Bello Sguardo as well, and many a remark about young love and many a glance at his companion's attractive legs and figure. Margaret Johnson achieved a cool but not unfriendly position while folding herself into and out of a car no bigger than an enclosed motorcycle. The management of her skirt alone was enough to occupy her entire attention.

"They are in the time of life," Signor Naccarelli said, darting the car through a narrow space between two motorscooters, "when each touch, each look, each sigh arises from the heart, the heart alone." He removed his hands from the wheel to do his idea homage, flung back his head and closed his eyes. Then he snapped to and shifted gears. "For them love is without thought, as to draw breath, to sleep, to walk. You and I—we have come to another stage. We have known all this before— we think of the hour, of some business—so we lose our purity, who knows how? It is sad, but there is nothing to do. But we can see our children. I do not say for Fabrizio, of course—it would be hard to find a young Florentine who has had no experience. I myself at a younger age, at a much younger age —do you know my first love was a peasant girl? It was at the villa where I had gone out with my father. A contadina. The spring was far along. My father stayed too long with the animals. I became, how shall I say?—bored, yes, but something more also. She was very beautiful. I still can dream of her, only her—I never succeed to dream of others. I do not know if your daughter will be for Fabrizio the first, or will not be. I would say not, but still—he is figlio di mamma, a good boy—I do not know." He frowned. They turned suddenly and shot up a hill. When they gained the crest, he came to a dead stop and turned to Mrs. Johnson. "But for her he has the feeling of the first woman! I am Italian and I tell you this. It is unmistakable! That, cara signora, is what I mean to say." Starting forward again, the car wound narrowly between tawny walls richly draped with vines. They emerged on a view, and stopped again. Cypress, river, hill, and city like a natural growth among them—they looked down on Tuscany. The air was fresher here but undoubtedly very hot below. There was a slight haze, just enough to tone away the glare; but even on the distant blue hills outlines of a tree or a tower were distinct to the last degree —one had the sense of being able to see everything exactly as it was.

"There is no question with Clara," Mrs. Johnson murmured. "She has been very carefully brought up."

"Not like other American girls, eh? In Italy we hear strange things. Not only hear. Cara signora, we *see* strange things also. You can imagine. Never mind. The signorina is another thing entirely. My wife has noticed it at once. Her innocence." His eye kept returning to Mrs. Johnson's knee which in the narrow silk skirt of her dress it was difficult not to expose. Her legs were crossed and her stocking whitened the flesh.

"She is very innocent," said Mrs. Johnson.

"And her father? How does he feel? An Italian for his daughter? Well, perhaps in America you, too, hear some strange words about us. We are no different from others, except we are more—well, you see me here—we are here together—it is not unpleasant—I look to you like any other man. And yet perhaps I feel a greater—how shall I say? You will think I play the Italian when I say there is a greater—"

She did think just that. She had been seriously informed on several occasions recently that Anglo-Saxons knew very little about passion, and now Signor Naccarelli, for whom she had a real liking, was about to work up to the same idea. She pulled down her skirt with a jerk. "There are plenty of American men who appreciate women just as much as you do," she told him.

He burst out laughing. "Of course! We make such a lot of foolishness, signora. But on such an afternoon—" His gesture took in the landscape. "I spoke of your husband. I think to myself, He is in cigarettes, after all. A very American thing. When you get off the boat, what do you say? 'Where is Clara?' says Signor Johnson. 'Where is my leetle girl?' 'Clara, ah!' you say. 'She is back in Italy. She has married with an Italian. I forgot to write you—I was so busy.'"

"But I write to him constantly!" cried Mrs. Johnson. "He knows everything. I have told him about you, about Fabrizio, the signora, Florence, all these things."

"But first of all you have considered your daughter's heart. For yourself, you could have left us, gone, gone. Forever. Not even a postcard." He chuckled. Suddenly he took a notion to start the car. It backed at once, as if a child had it on a string, then leaping forward fairly toppled over the crest of a steep run of hill down into the city, speeding as fast as a roller skate. Mrs. Johnson clutched her hat. "When my son was married," she cried, "my husband wrote out a check for five thousand dollars. I have reason to think he will do the same for Clara."

"Ma che generoso!" cried Signor Naccarelli, and it seemed he had hardly said it before he was jerking the hand brake to prevent their entering the hotel lobby.

She asked him in for an apéritif. He leaned flirtatiously at her over a small round marble-topped table. The plush decor of the Grand Hotel, with its gilt and scroll-edged mirrors that gave back wavy reflections, reminded Mrs. Johnson of middle-aged adultery, one party only being titled. But neither she nor Signor Naccarelli was titled. It was a relief to know that sin was not expected of them. If she were thinking along such lines, heaven only knew what was running in Signor Naccarelli's head. Almost giggling, he drank down a red, bitter potion from a fluted glass.

"So you ran away," he said, "upset; you could not bear the thought. You think and you think. You see the signorina's unhappy face. You could not bear her tears. You return. It is wise. There should be a time for thought. This I have said to my wife, to my son. But when you come back, they say to me, 'But if she leaves again—?' But I say, 'The signora is a woman who is without caprice. She will not leave again.'"

"I do not intend to leave again," said Mrs. Johnson, "until Clara and Fabrizio are married."

As if on signal, at the mention of his name, Fabrizio himself stepped before her eyes, but at some distance away, outside the archway of the salon, which he had evidently had the intention of entering if something had not distracted him. His moment of distraction itself was pure grace, as if a creature in nature, gentle to one word only, had heard that word. There was no need to see that Clara was somewhere within his gaze.

Signor Naccarelli and Mrs. Johnson rose and approached the door. They were soon able to see Clara above stairs—she had promised to go no farther—leaning over, her hair falling softly past her happy face. "Ciao," she said finally, "come stai?"

"Bene. E tu?"

"Bene."

Fabrizio stood looking up at her for so long a moment that Mrs. Johnson's heart had time almost to break. Gilt, wavy mirrors, and plush decor seemed washed clean, and all the wrong, hurt years of her daughter's affliction were not proof against the miracle she saw now.

Fabrizio was made aware of the two in the doorway. He had seen his father's car and stopped by. A cousin kept his shop for him almost constantly nowadays. It was such a little shop, while he—he wished to be everywhere at once. Signor Naccarelli turned back to Mrs. Johnson before he followed his son from the lobby. There were tears in her eyes; she thought perhaps she observed something of the same in his own. At any rate, he was moved. He grasped her hand tightly, and his kiss upon it as he left her said to her more plainly than words, she believed, that they had shared together a beautiful and touching moment.

IX

LETTERS, INDEED, had been flying; the air above the Atlantic was thick with them. Margaret Johnson sat up nights over them. A shawl drawn round her, she worked at her desk near the window overlooking the Arno, her low night light glowing on the tablet of thin airmail stationery. High diplomacy in the olden days perhaps proceeded thus, through long cramped hours of weighing one word against another, striving for just the measure of language that would sway, persuade, convince.

She did not underestimate her task. In a forest of question marks, the largest one was her husband. With painstaking care, she tried to consider everything in choosing her tone: Noel's humor, the season, their distance apart, how busy he was, how loudly she would have to speak to be heard.

Frankly, she recalled the time she had forced Clara into school; she admitted her grave error. Point at a time, she contrasted that disastrous sequence with Clara's present happiness. One had been a plan, deliberately contrived, she made clear; whereas, here in Florence, events had happened of their own accord.

"The thing that impresses me most, Noel (she wrote), is that nothing beyond Clara ever seems to be required of her here. I do wonder if anything beyond her would ever be required of her. Young married girls her age, with one or two children, always seem to have a nurse for them; a maid does all the cooking. There are mothers and mothers-in-law competing to keep the little ones at odd hours. I doubt if these young wives ever plan a single meal.

"Clara is able to pass every day here, as she does at home, doing simple things which please her. But the difference is that here, instead of being always alone or with the family, she has all of Florence for company and seems no different from the rest. Every afternoon she dresses in her pretty clothes and we walk to an outdoor cafe to meet with some young friends of the Naccarellis. You would be amazed how like them she has become. She looks more Italian every day. They prattle. About what? Well, as far as I can follow—Clara's Italian is so much better than mine—about movie stars, pet dogs, some kind of car called Alfa-Romeo, and what man is handsomer than what other man.

"I understand that usually in the summer all these people go to the sea, where they spend every day for a month or two swimming and lying in the sun. They would all be there now if Fabrizio's courtship had not so greatly engaged their interest. Courtship is the only word for it. If you could see how he adores Clara and how often he mentions the very same things that we love in her: her gentleness, her sweetness and goodness. I had expected things to come to some conclusion long before now, but nothing of the sort seems to occur, and now the thought of separating the two of them begins to seem more and more wrong to me, every day. . . ."

This letter provoked a trans-Atlantic phone call. Mrs. Johnson went to the lobby to talk, so Clara wouldn't hear her. She knew what the first words would be. To Noel Johnson, the world was made of brass tacks, and coming down to them was his specialty.

"Margaret, are you thinking that Clara should marry this boy?"

"I'm only trying to let things take their natural course."

"*Natural* course!" Even at such a distance, he could make her jump.

"I'm with her constantly, Noel. I don't mean they're left to themselves. I only mean to say I can't wrench her away from him now. I tried it. Honestly I did. It was too much for her. I saw that."

"But surely you've talked to these people, Margaret. You must have told them all about her. Don't any of them speak English?" It would seem unbelievable to Noel Johnson that she or anyone related to him in any way would have learned to communicate in any language but English. He would be sure they had got everything wrong.

"I've tried to explain everything fully," she assured him. Well, hadn't she? Was it her fault a cannon had gone off just when she meant to explain?

Across the thousands of miles she heard his breath and read its quality: he had hesitated. Her heart gave a leap.

"Would I encourage anything that would put an ocean be-tween Clara and me?"

She had scored again. Mrs. Johnson's deepest rebellion against her husband had occurred when he had wanted to put Clara in a sort of "school" for "people like her." The rift between them on that occasion had been a serious one, and though it was smoothed over in time and never mentioned subsequently, Noel Johnson might still not be averse to put-ting distances between himself and his daughter.

"They're just after her money, Margaret."

"No, Noel—I wrote you about that. They *have* money." She shut her eyes tightly. "And nobody wants to come to America, either."

When she put down the phone a few minutes later, Mrs. Johnson had won a concession. Things should proceed along their natural course, very well. But she was to make no per-manent decision until Noel himself could be with her. His coming, at the moment, was next to impossible. Business was pressing. One of the entertainers employed to advertise the world's finest smoke on a national network had been called up by the Un-American Activities Committee. The finest brains in the company were being exercised far into the night. It would not do for the American public to conclude they were inhal-ing Communism with every puff on a well-known brand. This could happen; it could ruin them. Noel would go to Washing-ton in the coming week. It would be three weeks at least until he could be with her. Then—well, she could leave the decision up to him. If it involved bringing Clara home with them, he would take the responsibility of it on himself.

Noel and Margaret Johnson gravely wished each other good luck over the trans-Atlantic wire, and each resumed the burden of his separate enterprise.

"Where'd you go, Mother?" Clara wanted to know, as soon as Mrs. Johnson returned.

"You'll never guess. I've been talking with Daddy on the long-distance phone!"

"Oh!" Clara looked up. She had been sitting on a footstool shoved back against the wall of her mother's room, writing in her diary. "Why didn't you tell me?"

"I didn't know that's who it was," she lied.

"But I wanted to talk to him, too!"

"What would you have said?"

"I would have said—" She hesitated, thinking hard, staring past her mother into the opposite wall, her young brow contracting faintly. "I would have said: 'Ciao. Come stai?'"

"Would Daddy have understood?"

"I would have told him," Clara said faithfully.

After that she said nothing more but leaned her head against the wall, and forgetful of father, mother, and diary, she stared before her with parted lips, dreaming.

Oh, my God, Margaret Johnson thought. How glad I am that Noel is coming to get me out of this!

X

AFTER HER HUSBAND'S telephone call, Margaret Johnson went to bed in as dutiful and obedient a frame of mind as any husband of whatever nationality could wish for. She awoke flaming with new anxiety, confronted by the simplest truth in the world.

If Noel Johnson came to Florence, he would spoil everything. She must have known that all along.

He might not mean to—she gave him the benefit of the doubt. But he would do it. Given a good three days, her dream would all lie in little bright bits on the floor, like the remains of the biggest and most beautiful Christmas tree ornament in the world.

For one thing, there was nothing in the entire Florentine day that would not seem especially designed to irritate Noel Johnson. From the coffee he would be asked to drink in the morning, right through the siesta, when every shop, including his prospective son-in-law's, shut up at the very hour when they could be making the most money; up through midnight when mothers were still abroad with their babies in the garrulous streets—he would have no time whatsoever for this inefficient way of life. Was there any possible formation of stone and paint hereabout that would not remind him uncomfortably of the Catholic Church? In what frame of mind would he be cast by Fabrizio's cuffless trousers, little pointed shoes, and carefully dressed hair? No, three days was a generous estimate; he would send everything sky-high long before that. And though he might regret it, he would never be able to see what he had done that was wrong.

His wife understood him. She sat over her caffè latte at her by-now-beloved window above the Arno, and while she thought of him a peculiarly tender and generous smile played about her face. "Clara," she called gently, "have you written to Daddy recently?" Clara was splashing happily in the bathtub and did not hear her.

Soon Mrs. Johnson rose to get her cigarettes from the dresser, but stopped in the center of the room, where she stood with her hand to her brow for a long time, so enclosed in thought she could not have told where she was.

If she went back on her promise to Noel to do nothing until he came, the whole responsibility of action would be her own, and in the very moment of taking it, she would have to begin to lie. To lie in Winston-Salem was one thing, but to start lying to everybody in Italy—why, Italians were past masters at this sort of thing. Wouldn't they see through her at once? Perhaps they already had.

She could never quite get it out of her mind that perhaps, indeed, they already had. Her heart had occasionally quite melted to the idea—especially after a glass of wine—that the Italian nature was so warm, so immediate, so intensely personal, that they had all perceived at once that Clara was a child and had loved her anyway, for what she was. They had not, after all, gone the dreary round from doctor to doctor, expert to expert, in the dwindling hope of finding some way to make the girl "normal." They did not *think*, after all, in terms of IQ, "retarded mentality" and "adult capabilities." And why, oh, why, Mrs. Johnson had often thought, since she too loved Clara for herself, should anyone think of another human being in the light of a set of terms?

But though she might warm to the thought—and since she never learned the answer she never wholly discarded it—she always came to the conclusion that she could not act upon it, and had to put it aside as being, for all practical purposes, useless. "Ridiculous," she could almost hear Noel Johnson say. Mrs. Johnson came as near as she ever had in her life to wringing her hands. Oh, my God, she thought, if he comes here!

But she did not, that morning, seek out advice from any crew-cut diplomat or frosty-eyed Scot. At times she came flatly to the conclusion that she would stick to her promise to Noel because it was right to do so (she believed in doing right), and that since it was right, no harm could come of it. At other times, she wished she could believe this.

In the afternoon, she accompanied Clara to keep an appointment at a cafe with Giuseppe's wife Franca and another girl. She left the three of them enjoying pretty pastries and chattering happily of movie stars, dogs, and the merits of the Alfa-Romeo.

Clara had learned so much Italian that Mrs. Johnson could no longer understand her.

Walking distractedly, back of the hotel, away from the river, she soon left the tourist-ridden areas behind her. She went thinking, unmindful of the people who looked up with curiosity as she passed. Her thought all had one center: her husband.

Never before had it seemed so crucial that she see him clearly. What was the truth about him? It had to be noted first of all, she believed, that Noel Johnson was in his own and everybody else's opinion a good man. Meaning exactly what? Well, that he believed in his own goodness and the goodness of other people, and would have said, if asked, that there must be good people in Italy, Germany, Tasmania, even Russia. On these grounds he would reason correctly that the Naccarelli family might possibly be as nice as his wife said they were.

Still, he did not think—fundamentally, he doubted, and Margaret had often heard him express something of the sort —that Europeans really had as much sense as Americans. Intellect, education, art, and all that sort of thing—well, maybe. But ordinary sense? Certainly, he was in grave doubts here when it came to the Latin races. And come right down to it (in her thoughts she slipped easily into Noel's familiar phrasing), didn't his poor afflicted child have about as much sense already as any Italian? His first reaction would have been to answer right away: Probably she does.

Other resentments sprang easily to his mind when touched on this sensitive point. Americans had had to fight two awful wars to get Europeans out of their infernal messes. He had a right to some sensitivity, anyone must admit. In the first war he had risked his life; his son had been wounded in the second; and if that were not enough he could always remember his income tax. But there was no use getting really worked up. Some humor would prevail here, and he was not really going to lose sleep over something he couldn't help.

But Clara, now (she could almost hear him saying), this thing of Clara. There Margaret Johnson could grieve for Noel, almost more than for herself. Something had happened here which he was powerless to do anything about; a chance accident had turned into a persisting and delicate matter, affecting his own pretty little daughter in this final way. An ugly finality, and no decent way of disposing of it. A fact he had to live with, day after day. An abnormality; hence, to a man like himself, a source of horror. For wasn't he dedicated, in his very nature, to "doing something about" whatever was not right?

How, she wondered, had Noel spent yesterday afternoon, after he had replaced the telephone in his study at home? She could tell almost to a T, no crystal-ball gazing required. He would have wandered, thinking, about the rooms for a time, unable to put his mind on the next morning's committee meeting. As important as it was that no Communist crooner should leave a pink smear on so American an outfit as their tobacco company, he would not have been able to concentrate. He likely would have entered the living room only to find Clara's dog Ronnie lying under the piano, a spot he favored during the hot months. They would have looked at one another, the two of them, disputing something. Then he would presently have found himself before the icebox, making a ham sandwich perhaps, snapping the cap from a cold bottle of beer. Tilting beer into his mouth with one hand, eating with the other, he might later appear strolling about the yard. It might occur to him (she hoped it had) that he needed to speak to the yard man about watering the grass twice a week so it wouldn't look like the Sahara desert when they returned. When *they* returned! With Clara, or without her? Qualms swept her. Her heart went down like an elevator.

"Signora! Attenzione!"

The voice was from above. A window had been pushed wide and a woman was leaning out to shake a carpet into the street. Margaret Johnson stopped, stepping back a few paces. Dust flew down, then settled. An arm came out and closed the shutters. She went on.

And quite possibly Noel, then, as dusk fell, his mind being still unsettled, would have walked over three blocks and across the park to his sister Isabel's apartment. Didn't he, in personal matters, always turn to women? Isabel, yes, would be the first to hear the news from abroad. She would not be as satisfactory a listener as Margaret, for being both a divorcee and something of a businesswoman (she ran the hat department in Winston-Salem's largest department store) she was inclined to be entirely too casual about everybody's affairs except her own. She would be beautifully dressed in one of her elaborate lounging outfits, for nobody appreciates a Sunday evening at home quite so much as a working woman. She would turn off the television to accommodate Noel, and bring him a drink of the very best Scotch. When she had heard the entire story of the goings-on in Florence, she would as likely as not say, "Well, after all, why not?" Hadn't she always advanced the theory that Clara had as much sense as most of the women she sold hats to? "They're going to want a dowry," she might add.

Now, mentioning a dowry that way would be all to the good. Noel would feel a great relief. He disliked being taken advantage of, and he was obviously uneasy that the Naccarellis were only after Clara's money. Wouldn't Margaret be staying in the best hotel, eating at the best restaurants, shopping in the best shops? The Italians had "caught on," of course, from the first, that she was well off. But now, through Isabel, he would have a name for all this. Dowry. It was customary. "Of course, they're all Catholics," he would go on to complain. Isabel would not be of any use at all there. Religion was of no interest to her whatever. She could not see why it was of interest to anybody.

Later, as they talked, Isabel would ask Noel about the communist scare. She would be in doubt that the crooner was actually such a threat to the nation or the tobacco company that a song or two would ruin them all; and was all this trouble and upset necessary—trips to Washington, committee meetings, announcements of policy and what not? Noel would not be above reminding her that she liked her dividend checks well enough not to want them put in any jeopardy. He might not come right out and say this, but it would cross his mind. More and more in recent years, Noel's every experience found immediate reference in his business. Or had he always been this way, if, in his younger years, less obviously so? Yet Mrs. Johnson remembered once on a summer vacation they had taken at Myrtle Beach during the depression, Noel playing ball on the sand with the two children when a wind had driven them inside their cottage and for a short time they had been afraid a hurricane was starting. How they had saved to make that trip!—that was all Noel could recall about it in later years. But at the time he had remarked as the raw wind streamed sand against the thin tremulous walls—he was holding Clara in his lap—"Well, at least we're all together." The wind had soon dropped, and the sea had enjoyed a quiet green dusk; their fear had gone, too, but she could not forget the steadying effect of his words. When, at what subtle point, had money come to seem to him the very walls that kept out the storm? Or was the trouble simply that with Clara and her problem always before him at home, he had found business to be a thing he could, at least, handle successfully, as he could not, in common with all mankind (poor Noel!), ultimately "handle" life? And business was, after all, so "normal."

Whatever the answer to how it had happened—and perhaps the nature of the times had had a lot to do with it: depression, the New Deal, the war—the fact was that it had happened, and Margaret knew now that nothing on earth short of the news of the imminent death of herself or Clara, or both, could induce Noel Johnson to Florence until the business in hand was concluded to the entire satisfaction of the tobacco company, whose future must, at all personal cost, be secure. On the other hand, since she had already foreseen that if he came here he would spoil everything, wasn't this an advantage?

She had wandered, in this remote corner of the city, into a small, poor bar. She lighted a cigarette and asked for a coffee. Since there was no place to sit, she stood at the counter. Two young men were working back of the bar, and seeing that she only stared at her coffee without drinking it, they became extremely anxious to make her happy. They wondered whether the coffee was hot enough, if she wanted more sugar or some other thing perhaps. She shook her head, smiling her thanks, seeing as though from a distance their great dim eyes, their white teeth, and their kindness. "Simpatica," one said, more about her than to her. "Si, simpatica," the other agreed. They exchanged a nod. One had an inspiration. "Americana?" he asked.

"Si," said Mrs. Johnson.

They stood back, continuing to smile like adults who watch a child, while she drank her coffee down. At this moment, she had the feeling that if she had requested their giant espresso machine, which seemed, besides a few cheap cups and saucers and a pastry stand, to be their only possession, they would have ripped it up bodily and given it to her. And perhaps, for a moment, this was true.

What is it, to reach a decision? It is like walking down a long Florentine street where, at the very end, a dim shape is waiting until you get there. When Mrs. Johnson finally reached this street and saw what was ahead, she moved steadily forward to see it at long last up close. What was it? Well, nothing monstrous, it seemed; but human, with a face much like her own, that of a woman who loved her daughter and longed for her happiness.

"I'm going to do it," she thought. "Without Noel."

XI

SIGNOR NACCARELLI was late coming home for lunch the next day; the water in the pasta pot had boiled away once and had to be replenished. He was not as late, however, as he had been many times before, or as late as he would have preferred to be that day; and though his news was good, his temper was short. Signora Johnson had talked with her husband on the telephone from America. Signor Johnson could not come to Italy from America. He could not leave his business. They were to proceed with the wedding without Signor Johnson. He neatly baled mouthfuls of spaghetti on his fork, mixed mineral water with a little wine, and found ways of cutting off the effusive rejoicing his family was given to. The real fact was that he was displeased with the American signora. Why, after dressing herself in the new Italian costume of printed white silk which must have cost at least 60,000 lire in the Via Tournabuoni—and with the chic little hat, too—should she give him her news and then leave him in the cafe after thirty minutes, saying "lunch" and "time to go" and "Clara"? American women were at the mercy of their children. It was shocking and disgusting. She had made the appointment with him, well and good. In the most fashionable cafe in Florence, they had been observed talking deeply together over an apéritif in the shadow of a great green umbrella. It would not be the first time he had been observed with this lady about the city. And then, after thirty minutes—! An Italian man would see to manners of this sort. This bread was stale. Were they all eating it, or was it saved from last week, especially for him?

Signora Naccarelli, meanwhile, from the mention of the word "wedding," had quietly taken over everything. She had been more or less waiting up to this time, neither impatient nor anxious, but, like a natural force, quite aware of how inevitable she was, while the others debated and decided superficial affairs. The heart of the matter in Signora Naccarelli's view was so overwhelmingly enormous that she did not have to decide to heed it, because there was nothing outside of it to make this decision. She simply *was* the heart—that great pulsing organ which could bleed with sorrow, or make little fish-like leaps of joy, and which always knew just what it knew. What it knew in Signora Naccarelli's case was very little and quite sufficient. Her son, Fabrizio, was handsome and good, and Clara, the little American flower, so sweet and gentle, would bear children for him. The signora's arms had yearned for some time for Clara and were already beginning to yearn for her children, and this to the signora was exactly the same thing as saying that the arms of the Blessed Virgin yearned for Clara and for Clara's children, and this in turn was the same as saying that the Holy Mother Church yearned likewise. It was all very simple and true.

Informed with such certainties, Signora Naccarelli had not been inactive. A brother of a friend of her nephew was a priest who had studied in England. She had fixed on him already, since he spoke English, as the very one for Clara's instruction. That same afternoon she set about arranging a time for them to meet. Within a few days, the priest was reporting to her that Clara had a real devotion to the Virgin. The signora had known all along that this was true. A distant cousin of Signor Naccarelli's was secretary to a Monsignore at the Vatican, and through him special permission was obtained for Clara to be married in a full church ceremony. At this the signora's joy could not be contained, and she went so far as to telephone Mrs. Johnson and explain these developments to her, a word at the time, in Italian, at the top of her voice, with tears.

"Capisce, signora? In chiesa! Capisce?"

Mrs. Johnson did not capisce. She thought from the tears that something must have gone wrong.

But nothing had, or did, until the morning in the office of the parroco, where they gathered a little more than two weeks before the wedding to fill out the appropriate forms.

XII

W HAT HAD HAPPENED was not at all clear for some time; it was not even clear that anything had.

The four of them—Clara and Fabrizio, with Margaret Johnson and Signor Naccarelli for witnesses—were assembled in the office of the parroco, a small dusty room with a desk, a few chairs and several locked cabinets that reached to the ceiling, and one window looking down on a cloister. In the center of the cloister was a hexagonal medieval well. It was nearing noon. Whatever noise there was seemed to gather itself together and drowse in the sun on the stone pavings below, so that Mrs. Johnson experienced the reassuring tranquility of silence. Signor Naccarelli, hat in hand, took a nervous turn or two around the office, looked at a painting that was propped in the back corner, and with a sour down-turning of his mouth said something uncomplimentary about priests which Mrs. Johnson did not quite catch. Fabrizio sat by Clara and twirled a clever straw ornament attached to her bag. So much stone was all that kept them cool. The chanting in the church below had stopped, but the priest did not come.

The hours ahead were planned: they would go to lunch to join Giuseppe and Franca his wife and two or three other friends. Of course, Mrs. Johnson was explaining to herself, this smell of candle smoke, stone dust, and oil painting is to them just what blackboards, chalk and old Sunday-school literature are to us; there's probably no difference at all if you stay open-minded. To be ready for the questions that they were there to answer, she made sure that she had brought her passport and Clara's. She drew them out of their appropriate pocket in the enormous bag Winston-Salem's best department store had advised for European travel, and held them ready.

Signor Naccarelli decided to amuse her. He sat down beside her. Documents, he explained in a jaunty tone, were the curse of Italy. You could not become a corpse in Italy without having filled in the proper document. There were people in offices in Rome still sorting documents filed there before the war. What war? they would say if you told them. But, Mrs. Johnson assured him, all this kind of thing went on in America too. The files were more expensive perhaps. She got him to laugh. His quick hands picked up the passports. Clara and Fabrizio were whispering to one another. Their voices too seemed to go out into the sun, like a neighborhood sound. Signor Naccarelli glanced at Mrs. Johnson's passport picture—how terrible! She was much more beautiful than this. Clara's next—this of the signorina was better, somewhat. A page turned beneath his thumb.

A moment later, Signor Naccarelli had leaped up as though stung by a bee. He hastened to Fabrizio, to whom he spoke rapidly in Italian; then he shot from the room. Fabrizio leaped up also. "Ma Papà! Non possiamo fare nulla—!" The priest came, but it was too late. He and Fabrizio entered into a long conversation. Clara retreated to her mother's side. When Fabrizio turned to them at last, he seemed to have forgotten all his English. "My father—forget—remember—the appointments," he blundered. Struck by an idea, he whirled back to the priest and embarked on a second conversation which he finally summarized to Clara and her mother: "Tomorrow."

At that, precisely as though he were a casual friend who hoped to see them again sometime, he bowed over Mrs. Johnson's hand, made an appropriate motion to Clara, and turned away. They were left alone with the priest.

"Tomorrow" . . . "domani" Mrs. Johnson knew by now to be the word in Italy most likely to signal the finish of everything. She felt, indeed, without the ghost of an idea how or why it had happened, that everything was trembling, tottering about her, had perhaps, without her knowledge, already collapsed. She looked out on the priest like someone seen across a gulf. As if to underscore the impression, he spread his hands with a little helpless shrug and said, "No Eeenglish."

Mrs. Johnson zipped the passports back into place and went out into the corridor, down the steps and into the sun. "Domani," the priest said after them.

Holding Clara by the hand, she made her way back to the hotel.

The instant she was alone she had the passports out, searching through them. Would nothing give her a clue to what had struck Signor Naccarelli? She remembered stories: the purloined letter; the perfect crime, marred only by the murderer's driver's license left carelessly on the hotel dresser. What had she missed? She thought her nerves would fly apart in all directions.

Slowly, with poise and majesty, the beautiful afternoon went by. A black cloud crossed the city, flashed two or three fierce bolts, rumbled half-heartedly and passed on. The river glinted under the sun, and the boys and fishermen who had not been frightened inside shouted and laughed at the ones who had. Everything stood strongly exposed in sunlight and cast its appropriate shadow: in Italy there is the sense that everything is clear and visible, that nothing is withheld. Fabrizio, when Margaret Johnson had touched his arm to detain him in the office of the parroco, had drawn back like recoiling steel. When Clara had started forward with a cry, he had set her quickly back, and silent. If they were to be rejected, had they not at least the right to common courtesy? What were they being given to understand? In Florence, at four o'clock, everything seemed to take a step nearer, more distinctly, more totally to be seen.

When the cloud came up, Mrs. Johnson and Clara clung together pretending that was what they were afraid of. Later they got out one of Clara's favorite books: Nancy Drew, the lady detective, turned airline hostess to solve the murder of a famous explorer. Nancy Drew had so far been neglected. Clara was good and did as she was told about everything, but could not eat. Late in the evening, around ten, the telephone rang in their suite. A gentleman was waiting below for the signora.

Coming down alone, Mrs. Johnson found Signor Naccarelli awaiting her, but how changed! If pleasant things had passed between them, he was not thinking of them now; one doubted that they had actually occurred. Grave, gestureless, as though wrapped in a black cape, he inclined to her deeply. Margaret Johnson had trouble keeping herself from giggling. Wasn't it all a comedy? If somebody would only laugh out loud with enough conviction, wouldn't it all crumble? But she recalled Clara, her eye feasting on Fabrizio's shoulder, her finger exploring the inspired juncture of his neck and spine; and so she composed herself and allowed herself to be escorted from the hotel.

She saw at once that his object was to talk and that he had no destination—they walked along the river. The heat had been terrible for a week, but a breeze was blowing off the water now and she wished she had brought her shawl.

"I saw today," Signor Naccarelli began in measured tones, but when Mrs. Johnson suddenly sneezed, "Why did not you tell me?" he burst out, turning on her. "What can you be thinking of?"

Stricken silent, she walked on beside him. Somehow, then, he had found out. Certain dreary, familiar feelings returned to her. Meeting Noel at the airport, Clara behind in the car, wronged again, poor little victim of her own or her mother's impulses. Well, if Signor Naccarelli was to be substituted for Noel, she thought with relief that anyway she should at last confess. Instead of Bermuda, they could go to the first boat sailing from Naples.

"It is too much," went on Signor Naccarelli. "Two, three years, where there is love, where there is agreement, I say it is all right. But no, it is too much. It is to make the fantastic."

"Years?" she repeated.

"Can it be possible! But you must have understood! My son Fabrizio is twenty years old, no more. Whereas, your daughter, I see with my two eyes, written in the passport today in the office of the parroco: twenty-six! Six years difference! It cannot be. In that moment I ask myself, What must I say, what can I do? Soon it will be too late. What to do? I make the excuse, an appointment. I see often in the cinema this same excuse. It was not true. I have lied. I tell you frankly."

"I had not thought of her being older," said Mrs. Johnson. Weak with relief, she stopped walking. When she leaned her elbow against the parapet, she felt it trembling. "Believe me, Signor Naccarelli, they seemed so much the same age to me, it had not entered my mind that there was any difference."

"It cannot be," said Signor Naccarelli positively, scowling out toward the noble skyline of his native city. "I pass an afternoon of torment, an inferno. As I am a man, as I am a Florentine, as I am a father, as I long for my son's happiness, as—" Words failed him.

"But surely the difference between them is not as great as that," Mrs. Johnson reasoned. "In America we have seen many,

many happy marriages with an even greater difference. Clara —she has been very carefully brought up; she had a long illness some years ago. To me she seemed even younger than Fabrizio."

"A long illness." He whirled on her scornfully. "How am I to know that she is cured of it?"

"You see her," countered Mrs. Johnson. "She is as healthy as she seems."

"It cannot be." He turned away.

"Don't you realize," Mrs. Johnson pleaded, "that they are in love? Whatever their ages are, they are both young. This is a deep thing, a true thing. To try to stop what is between them now—"

"*Try* to stop? My dear lady, I will stop whatever I wish to stop."

"Fabrizio—" she began.

"Yes, yes. He will try to kill himself. It is only to grow up. I also have sworn to take my life—can you believe? With passion I shake like this—and here I am today. No, no. To talk is one thing, to do another. Do not make illusions. He will not."

"But Clara—" she began. Her voice faltered. She thought she would cry in spite of herself.

Signor Naccarelli scowled out toward the dark river. "It cannot be," he repeated.

Mrs. Johnson looked at him and composure returned to her. Because whether this was comedy or tragedy, he had told her the truth. He could and would stop everything if he chose, and Fabrizio would not kill himself. If Mrs. Johnson had thought it practical, she would have murdered Signor Naccarelli. Instead, she suggested that they cross over to a small bar. She was feeling that perhaps a brandy. . . .

The bar was a tourist trap, placed near to American Express and crowded during the day. At night few people wandered in. Only one table was occupied at present. In the far corner what looked to Mrs. Johnson exactly like a girl from Winston-Salem was conversing with an American boy who was growing a beard. Mrs. Johnson chose a table at equidistance between the pair and the waiter. She gave her order and waited, saying nothing till the small glass on the saucer was set before her. It was her last chance and she knew it. It helped her timing considerably to know how much she detested Signor Naccarelli.

"This is all too bad," said Mrs. Johnson softly. "I received a letter from my husband today. Instead of five thousand dollars, he wants to make Clara and Fabrizio a present of fifteen thousand dollars."

"That is nine million three hundred and seventy-five thousand lire," said Signor Naccarelli. "So now you will write and explain everything, and that this wedding cannot be."

"Yes," said Mrs. Johnson and sipped her brandy.

Presently Signor Naccarelli ordered a cup of coffee.

Later on they might have been observed in various places, strolling about quiet, less frequented streets. Their talk ran on many things. Signor Naccarelli recalled her sneeze, and wondered if she were cold. Mrs. Johnson was busily working out in the back of her mind how she was going to get fifteen thousand dollars without her husband, for the moment, knowing anything about it. It would take most of a family legacy, invested in her own name; and the solemn confidence of a lawyer, an old family friend; a long-distance request for him to trust her and cooperate; a promise that Noel would know everything anyway, within the month. Later, explaining to Noel: "In the U.S., you would undoubtedly have wanted to build a new house for your daughter and her husband. . . ." A good point.

"You must forgive me," said Signor Naccarelli, "if I ask a most personal thing of you. The Signorina Clara, she would like to have children, would she not? My wife can think of nothing else."

"Oh, Clara longs for children!" said Mrs. Johnson.

Toward midnight, they stopped in a bar for a final brandy. Signor Naccarelli insisted on paying, as always.

When she returned to her room, Margaret Johnson sat on her bed for a while, then she stood at the window for a while and looked down on the river. With one finger, she touched her mouth where there lingered an Italian kiss.

How had she maneuvered herself out of further, more prolonged, and more intimately staged embraces without giving the least impression that she hadn't enjoyed the one he had surprised her with? In the shadow of a handsome façade, before the stout, lion-mouth crested arch where he had beckoned her to stop—"Something here will interest you, perhaps"—how, oh how, had she managed to manage it well? Out of practice in having to for, she shuddered to think, how many years. Nor could anything erase, remove from her the estimable flash of his eye, so near her own, so near.

"Mother!"

Why, I had forgotten *her*, thought Mrs. Johnson.

"Yes, darling, I'm coming!" In Clara's room she switched on a dim Italian lamp. "There, now, it's all going to be all right. We're going to meet them tomorrow, just as we did today. But tomorrow it will be all right. Go to sleep now. You'll see."

It's true, she thought, smoothing Clara's covers, switching out the light. No doubt of it now. And to keep down the taste of success, she bit hard on her lip (so lately kissed). If he let me out so easily, it means he doesn't want to risk anything. It means he wants this wedding. He wants it too.

XIII

IN THAT AFTERNOON'S gentle decline, Fabrizio had found himself restless and irritable. Earlier, he had deliberately ignored his promise to meet Giuseppe, who was doubtless burning to find out why the luncheon had not come off. That day he travelled unfamiliar paths, did not return home for lunch, and spent the siesta hours sulking about the Boboli Gardens, where an unattractive American lady with a guidebook flattered herself that he was pursuing her. Every emotion seemed stronger than usual. If anyone he knew should see him here! He all but dashed out at the thought, entered narrow streets, and in a poor quarter gnawed a workingman's sandwich—a hard loaf with a paper-thin slice of salami. When the black cloud blew up he waited in the door of a church he had never seen before.

About six he entered his own little shop, where he had been seldom seen of late and then always full of jokes and laughter. Now he asked for the books and, finding that some handkerchief boxes had got among the gloves, imagined that everything was in disorder and that the cousin was busy ruining his business and robbing him. The cousin, who had been robbing him, but only mildly (they both understood almost to the lire exactly how much), insisted that Fabrizio should pay him his wages at once and he would leave and never return voluntarily as long as he lived. They both became bored with the argument.

Fabrizio thought of Clara. When he thought of her thighs and breasts he sighed; weakness swept him; he grew almost ill. So he thought of her face instead: gentle, beautiful, it rose before him. He saw it everywhere, that face. No lonely villa on a country hillside, yellow in the sun, oleanders on the terrace, but might have inside a chapel, closed off, unused for years, but on the wall a fresco, work of some ancient name known in all the world, a lost work—Clara. He loved her. She looked up at him now out of the glass-enclosed counter for merchandise, but the face was only his own, framed in socks.

At evening, at dark, he went the opposite way from home, down the Arno, walking sometimes along the streets, descending wherever he could to walk along the bank itself. He saw the sun set along the flow, and stopping in the dark at last he said aloud, "I could walk to Pisa." At another direction into the dark, he said, "Or Vallombrosa." Then he turned, ascended the bank to the road and walked back home. Possessed by an even deeper mood, the strangest he had ever known, he wandered about the city, listening to the echo of his own steps in familiar streets and looking at towering shapes of stone. The night seemed to be moving along secretly, but fast; the earth, bearing all burdens lightly, spinning and racing ahead—just as a Florentine had said, so it did. The silent towers tilted toward the dawn.

He saw his father the next morning. "It is all right," said Signor Naccarelli. "I have talked a long time with the signora. We will go today as yesterday to the office of the parroco."

"But Papà!" Fabrizio spread all ten fingers wide and shook his hands violently before him. "You had me sick with worry. My heart almost stopped. Yesterday I was like a crazy person. I have never spent such a day."

"Yes, well. I am sorry. The signorina is a bit older than I thought. Not much, but— Did you know?"

"Of course I knew. I told you so. Long ago. Did you forget it?"

"Perhaps I did. Never mind. And you, my son. You are twenty-one years, vero?"

"Papà!" Here Fabrizio all but left the earth itself. "I am twenty-three! The sun has cooked your brain. I should be the one to act like this."

"All right, all right. I was mistaken. But my instinct was right." He tapped his brow. "It is always better to discuss everything in great detail. I felt that we were going too quickly. You cannot be too careful in these things. But my son—" He caught the boy's shoulder. "Remember to say nothing to the Americans. Do you want them to think we are crazy?"

"You are innamorato of the signora. I understand it all."

XIV

A<small>T THE WEDDING</small> Margaret Johnson sat quietly while a dream unfolded before her. She watched closely and missed nothing.

She saw Clara emerge like a fresh flower out of the antique smell of candle smoke, incense and damp stone, and advance in white Venetian lace with so deep a look shadowing out the hollow of her cheek, she might have stood double for a Botticelli. As for Fabrizio, he who had such a gift for appearing did not fail them. His beauty was outshone only by his outrageous pride in himself; he saw to it that everybody saw him well. Like an angel appearing in a painting, he seemed to face outward to say, This is what I look like, see? But his innocence protected him like magic.

Clara lifted her veil like a good girl exactly when she had been told to. Fabrizio looked at her and love sprang up in his face. The priest went on intoning, and since it was twelve o'clock all the bells from over the river and nearby began to ring at slightly different intervals—the deep-throated ones and the sweet ones, muffled and clear—one could hear them all.

The Signora Naccarelli had come into her own that day. She obviously believed that she had had difficulties to overcome in bringing about this union, but having got the proper heavenly parties well-informed, she had brought everything into line. Her bosom had sometimes been known to heave and her eye to dim, but that day she was serene. She wore flowers and an enormous medallion of her dead mother outlined in pearls. That unlikely specimen, a middle-class Neapolitan, she now seemed both peasant and goddess. Her hair had never been more smoothly bound, and natural color touched her large cheeks. Before the wedding, the wicked Giuseppe had seen her and run into her arms. Smiling perpetually at no one, it was as though she had created them all.

Signor Naccarelli had escorted Margaret Johnson to her place and sat beside her. He kept his arms tightly folded across his chest, and his face wore an odd, unreadable expression, mouth somewhat pursed, his high, cold, Florentine nose drawn toughly across the bridge. Perhaps his collar was too tight.

Yes, Margaret Johnson saw everything, even the only person to cry, Giuseppe's wife, who had chosen to put her sophisticated self into a girlish, English-type summer frock of pale blue with a broad white collar.

I will not be needed any more, thought Margaret Johnson with something like a sigh, for before her eyes the strongest maternal forces in the world were taking her daughter to themselves. I have stepped out of the picture forever, she thought, and as if to bear her out, as the ceremony ended and everyone started moving toward the church door, no one noticed Margaret Johnson at all. They were waiting to form the wedding cortege which would wind over the river and up the hill to the restaurant and the long luncheon.

She did not mind not being noticed. She had done her job, and she knew it. She had played single-handed and unadvised a tricky game in a foreign country, and she had managed to realize from it the dearest wish of her heart. Signora Naccarelli was passing—one had to pause until the suction of that lady in motion had faded. Then Mrs. Johnson moved through the atrium and out to the colonnaded porch where, standing aside from the others, she could observe Clara stepping into a car, her white skirts dazzling in the sun. Clara saw her mother: they waved to one another. Fabrizio was made to wave as well. Over everybody's head a bronze fountain in the piazza jetted water into the sunlight, and nearby a group of tourists had stopped to look.

Clara and Fabrizio were driving off. So it had really happened! It was done. Mrs. Johnson found her vision blotted out. The reason was simply that Signor Naccarelli, that old devil, had come between her and whatever she was looking at; now he was smiling at her. The money again. There it was, forever returning, the dull moment of exchange.

Who was fooling whom? she longed to say, but did not. Or rather, since we both had our little game to play, which of us came off better? Let's tell the truth at last, you and I.

It was a great pity, Signor Naccarelli was saying, that Signor Johnson could not have been here to see so beautiful a wedding. Mrs. Johnson agreed.

Though no one knew it but herself, Signor Johnson at that very moment was winging his way to Rome. She had cut things rather fine; it made her shudder to realize how close a schedule she had had to work with. Tomorrow she would rise early to catch the train to Rome, to wait at the airport for Noel to land, but wait alone this time, and, no matter what he might think or say, triumphant.

He was going to think and say a lot, Noel Johnson was, and she knew she had to brace herself. He was going to go on believing for the rest of his life, for instance, that she had bought this marriage, the way American heiresses used to engage obliging titled gentlemen as husbands. No use telling him that sort of thing was out of date. Was money ever out of date, he would want to know?

But Margaret Johnson was going to weather the storm with Noel, or so at any rate she had the audacity to believe. Hadn't he in some mysterious way already, at what point she did not know, separated his own life from that of his daughter's? A defective thing must go: she had seen him act upon this principle too many times not to feel that in some fundamental, unconscious way he would, long ago, have broken this link. Why had he done so? Why, indeed? Why are we all and what are we really doing? Who was to say when *he*, in turn, had irritated the selfish, greedy nature of things and been kicked on the head in all the joyousness of his playful ways? No, it would be pride alone that was going to make him angry: she had gone behind his back. At least so she believed.

Though weary of complexities and more than ready to take a long rest from them all, Mrs. Johnson was prepared on the strength of her belief to make one more gamble yet, namely, that however Noel might rage, no honeymoon was going to be interrupted, that Signor Naccarelli was not going to be searched out and told the truth, and that the officials of the great Roman Church could sleep peacefully in rich apartments or poor damp cells, undisturbed by Noel Johnson. He would grow quiet at last, and in the quiet, even Margaret Johnson had not yet dared to imagine what sort of life, what degree of delight in it, they might not be able to discover (rediscover?) together. This was uncertain. What was certain was that in that same quiet she would begin to miss her daughter. She would go on missing her forever.

She was swept by a strange weakness. Signor Naccarelli was offering her his arm, but she could not move to take it. Her head was spinning and she leaned instead against the cool stone column. She did not feel able to move. Beyond them, the group of tourists were trying to take a picture, but were unable to shield their cameras from the light's terrible strength. A scarf was tried, a coat; would some person cast a shadow?

"Do you remember," it came to Mrs. Johnson to ask Signor Naccarelli, "the man who fell down when the cannon fired that day? What happened to him?"

"He died," said Signor Naccarelli.

She saw again, as if straight into her vision, painfully contracting it, the flash that the sun had all but blurred away to nothing. She heard again the momentary hush under heaven, followed by the usual noise's careless resumption. In desperate motion through the flickering rhythms of the "event," he went on and on in glimpses, trying to get up, while near him, silent in bronze, Cellini's Perseus, in the calm repose of triumph, held aloft the Medusa's head.

"I did the right thing," she said. "I know I did."

Signor Naccarelli made no reply. "The right thing": what was it?

Whatever it was, it was a comfort to Mrs. Johnson, who presently felt strong enough to take his arm and go with him, out to the waiting car.

KNIGHTS AND DRAGONS

PART ONE

I

Martha Ingram had come to Rome to escape something: George Hartwell had been certain of it from the first. He was not at all surprised to learn that the something was her divorced husband. Martha seldom spoke of him, or of the ten years she had spent with him. It was as though she feared if she touched any part of it, he would rise up out of the ground and snap at her. As it was he could sometimes be heard clear across the ocean, rumbling and growling, breathing out complaining letters and worried messengers, though what had stirred him up was not clear. Perhaps he was bored, thought Hartwell, who never wanted to meet the bastard, having grown fond of Martha, in his fussy, fatherly way. He was her superior at the U.S. cultural office, and saw her almost every day, to his pleasure.

The bastard himself Hartwell had also seen in a photograph that Martha had showed him, drawing it from her purse while lunching with him in a restaurant. But why carry his picture around? Hartwell wondered. Well, they had been talking of dogs the other day, she explained, with a little apologetic shrug and smile, and there was the dachshund she had been so fond of, there on the floor. But Hartwell, staring, was arrested by the man—that huge figure, sitting in the heavy chair with some sort of tapestry behind, the gross hands placed on the armrests, the shaggy head, and big, awkwardly tilted feet. Martha's husband! It made no sense to think about, for Martha was bright and cordial, neither slow nor light-headed, and she had a sheer look that Hartwell almost couldn't stand; he guessed it was what went with being vulnerable. "He looks German," protested Hartwell. She thought he meant the dog. "Dear old Jonesie," she said. Hartwell chuckled uneasily. "No, I meant him," he said. "Oh. Oh, yes. Well, no, Gordon is American, but it's funny your saying that. He studied in Germany and his first wife was German." "What happened to her?" Martha tucked the photograph away. "She died. . . . I was Gordon's student," she added, as though this explained something.

Why did the man keep worrying her? Why did she let him do it? Hartwell did not know, but the fact was, it did go on.

But sometimes the large figure with the shaggy head left her alone and she would be fine, and then she would get a letter from a lawyer she'd never heard of, speaking of some small lacerating matter, or an envelope addressed in a black scrawl with nothing but a clipping inside on a political issue, every word like a needle stab, considering that he knew (and never agreed with) how she felt about things. And if one thought of all the papers he had gone shuffling through to find just the right degree of what he wanted! And sometimes some admirer of his would come to Rome and say he wasn't eating at all well and would she please consider. "He never ate well," she would answer. "Only large quantities of poor food." She thought of all the hours spent carefully stirring canned cream of mushroom soup. And yet—thinker, teacher, scholar, writer, financial expert, and heaven knew what else—he had been considered great and good, and these people were, she understood, his friends. She tried to be equable and kind, and give them the right things to drink—tea, or Cinzano, or scotch—and show them around the city. "But *he* never says he would be better off if I were there," she would make them admit. "He never says it to you, or me, or anyone." Then she would be unsteady for a week or two.

Nobody can change this, she decided; it will always be this way.

But she grasped George Hartwell's sympathy, and knew that when he gave her some commission outside Rome, it was really done as a favor and made her, at least, unreachable for a time.

"Do you want to go to Genoa?" he asked her. It was June.

He was sitting at his large friendly disorderly desk, in the corner office of the consulate, and he was round and cherublike, except for a tough scraggle of thin red hair. There was always a cigar stuck in the corner of his mouth. He scrambled around among manila folders. "Arriving in Genoa," he explained, "cultural exchange people, heading eventually for Rome. But in the meantime they've excuses for wanting to see Milano, Padova, Lago di Como, perhaps going on to Venice. Italian very weak, but learning. Guide with car would be great help."

"But who are they?" She always had a feeling of hope about moving toward total strangers, as if they would tell her something good and new, and she would go away with them forever. She took the files as he found them for her. "Coggins . . . what an odd name. Richard Coggins and wife Dorothy and daughter Jean."

"That's the ones. Some friend of the family's wrote Grace about them. We've got to do something a little extra for them, but it just so happens I have to go to Florence."

Martha smiled. George's wife Grace, out of an excess of niceness, was always getting them into things. She wanted everyone to be happy, she wanted things to "work out." And so it followed, since she herself was away in Sicily, that one wound up having to be helpful for a week or two to a family named Coggins. "Mr. Coggins is an expert on opera, George, no kidding. Did you know that? Look, it says so here."

"That we should be floating somebody here to lecture the Italians on opera," George Hartwell complained. "Any six waiters in any one of a hundred trattorie in Rome can go right into the sextet from *Lucia* for fifty lire each. Italian women scream arias during childbirth. What can we tell any Italian about opera?"

"I wonder," said Martha, "if they listen to us about anything."

"Martha! That's the remark we don't ever make!" But he laughed anyway, shuffling papers. "Here we are. The others make a little more sense. . . . James E. Wilbourne and wife Rita. No children. Economist . . . thesis brought out as book: *New Economic Patterns in* . . . et cetera. He won't stick with the group much, as is more interested in factories than art galleries."

"Maybe the worst of the Coggins' is their name."

"You'll go then?"

"Yes, I'll go."

"Atta girl."

But, certainly, she thought, moving through the sharp June shadows under the trees around the consulate, something will happen to change these plans—there will be a cable in the hall or someone will have come here. She entered her summer-still apartment through all the devious stairways, corridors, and cortili that led to it. "Sequestered," George Hartwell called her, as though knowing it was not the big terrace and the view alone she had considered in taking a place one needed maps and even a compass to reach. The sun and the traffic noises were all outside, beyond the windows. There was no cable, no telephone message, but—she almost laughed—a letter. She recognized the heavy black slant of the writing and slowly, the laugh fading, slit it open. To her surprise the envelope was empty. There was nothing in it at all. He had probably meant to put a clipping in; it was a natural mistake, she thought, but some sort of menace was what she felt, being permanently lodged in the mind of a person whose love had turned to rejection. "Forget it," Hartwell had advised her. "Everybody has something to forget." But, alas, she was intellectually as well as emotionally tenacious and she had, furthermore, her question to address to the sky: how can love, in the first place, turn into hate, and how can I, so trapped in hatred, not suffer for it?

In his apartment, the expensive, oak-panelled, high-ceilinged place in New York's upper Seventies, crusted with books and littered with ash trays, she had lived out a life of corners, and tiny chores had lengthened before her like shadows drawn out into a sunslant; she had worn sweaters that shrank in the back and coloured blouses that faded or white ones that turned grey, had entertained noble feelings toward all his friends, and tried to get in step with the ponderous designs he put life to, like training hippopotami to jump through hoops. There had been the long rainy afternoons, the kindness of the porter, the illness of the dog, the thin slashing of the brass elevator doors, the walks in the park. She still felt small in doorways. Not wanting to spend a lot, he had had her watched by a cut-rate detective agency, whose agent she had not only discovered at it, but made friends with.

She crumpled the empty envelope and dropped it in the wastebasket, bringing herself up with a determined shake rather like a shudder.

2

MARTHA INGRAM would always remember the first sight she had of her new Americans at the dock in Genoa. She got a chance to look them over before they saw her. She had to smile—it was so obviously "them." They stood together in clothes that had seen too much of the insides of suitcases and small metal closets in ship cabins; they were pale from getting up early after an almost sleepless night at sea, and the early breakfast after the boat had gone still, the worry over the luggage, would have made them almost sick. The voyage was already a memory; they waved halfheartedly, in a puzzled way, to a couple who, for ten days, must have seemed their most intimate friends. They formed their little huddle, their baggage piling slowly up around them, while the elder of the two men —Mr. Coggins, beyond a doubt—dealt out hundred-lire notes to the porters, all of whom said that wasn't enough. The Coggins girl's slip was too long; she was holding a tennis racket in a wooden press. She looked as if she had just got off the train for summer camp. Her mother had put on one white glove. The young man, Wilbourne, gloomy in a tropical-weight tan suit, seemed hung over. Was this Mrs. Wilbourne sprinting up from behind, her hand to her brow as if she had forgotten something? But it was somebody else, a dark girl who ran off crying "Oh, Eleanor!" Mr. Coggins had greying hair that stood up in a two-weeks-old bristle. His lips were struggling with a language he believed he knew well. He understood opera, didn't he? "Scusatemi, per favore. . . ."

Martha hated to break this moment, for once they saw her, they would never be quite like this again. "Are you, by any chance, the Coggins'?" They were. How thrilled they were, how instantly relieved. They had been expecting her, but had not known where to look. It was all open and friendly beyond measure. Martha became exhilarated, and felt how really nice Americans were. So the group formed instantly and began to move forward together. "Taxi! Taxi!" It was a word everyone knew. . . .

Two weeks later George Hartwell rang them up. They had crossed Italy by then and had reached—he had guessed it— Venice. How was it going?

"Well, fine," Martha said. "It's mainly the Coggins'. Mrs. Wilbourne couldn't afford to come and stayed behind. She's flying out to Rome in a week or so. George, did you ever know an economist who didn't have money problems?"

He chuckled.

"Mr. Wilbourne doesn't stay with us much. He goes off to visit industries, though God knows what he can learn with sign language. It's churches and museums for the Coggins'— they're taking culture straight."

"Should I come up and join you with the other car?" His conference was over in Florence; he was feeling responsible and wondering what to do.

"We managed okay with the baggage rack. They've shipped nearly everything ahead." She felt obscurely annoyed at being found. "How did you know where we were?"

"I remembered that pensione, that little palace you like. . . ."

It was indeed, the pensione in Venice, a building like a private palace. It had once been some foreign embassy, and still kept its own walled campo, paved in smooth flagstones, ornamented with pots of flowers, boxed shrubs and bougainvillea. The tall formal windows opened on a small outdoor restaurant. "You mean we get all this and two meals a day?" Mr. Coggins was incredulous. "And all for six thousand lire each," chanted Mrs. Coggins, who was by now a sort of chorus. That was the first day. Jim Wilbourne, angrily complaining about some overcharge on the launch from the station, joined them from Padova just in time for a drink before dinner, and they felt reunited, eating out in the open with the sound of water, by candlelight. They decided to stay on for a day or two.

One afternoon they went out to the Lido—all, that is, except Martha, who had decided she would spend the time by herself, revisiting one or two of the galleries. When she came out of Tintoretto's Scuola into the quiet campo where the broad shadow of a church fell coolly (had everyone in Venice gone to the Lido?), there in a sunlit angle, a man, with a leather briefcase but no apparent business, stood watching. The campo, the entire area, all of Venice, indeed, seemed entirely deserted. There had been no one else in the gallery but the ticket seller— no guide or guard—and even he seemed to have disappeared. The man with the briefcase held a lighted cigarette in his free hand, a loosely packed nazionale, no doubt, for the smoke came gushing out into the still air. When he saw Martha pause and look at him, he suddenly flung both arms wide and shouted, "Signora, signora! Che vuol fa', che vuol fa'?" "I don't know," Martha answered. "Non so." "Something has gone wrong!" he shouted across the campo, waving the briefcase and the ciga- rette. "Somewhere in this world there has been a terrible mis- take! In questo mondo c'è stato un terrible errore!"

Martha walked away to the nearest canal and took a gon- dola. Mad people show up all over Italy in the summer; they walk the streets saying exactly what they think, but this was not like that: it was only sciròcco. The air was heavy. She remem- bered Tintoretto's contorted figures with some desire to relax and straighten them out, and the cry from the man with the briefcase, comic and rather awful at once, swept through and shook her.

Already the sky was beginning to haze over. On a clothesline hung behind an apartment building, a faded red cloth like a curtain or a small sail, stirred languorously, as though breath- ing in the heat itself. The boat's upcurving metal prow speared free, swinging into the Grand Canal. Even here the traffic was light; the swell from a passing vaporetto broke darkly, rocking the gondola in a leaden way.

At dinner everyone was silent. Jim Wilbourne ate very lit- tle and that with his elbow propped beside his plate, Martha judged that the Coggins' bored him; they seemed another or- der of creature from himself. Some days before he had wanted to know what Italian kitchen appliances were like. The kind of apartment he wanted in Rome absorbed him.

Jean Coggins, who had sunburned the arches of both feet at the Lido, looked about to cry when her mother said sharply: "If you insist on having wine, you could at least try not to spill it." Mr. Coggins, whose brow was blistered, sent back his soup which was cold, and got a second bowl, also cold.

To Martha the silence was welcome, for always before when gathered together, they had done nothing but ask her about

the country—politics, religion, economics, no end of things.
She was glad they had at last run down, like clocks, and that
they could find themselves after dinner and coffee out in the
back courtyard because some fiddlers had happened to pass.
The guests began to dance, first with one another, then with
strangers, then back to known faces again. When the music
turned to a frantic little waltz, Jim Wilbourne stumbled twice,
laughed and apologized, and led Martha to a bench near the
wall, where they were flanked on either side by stone jars of
verbena.

"I'm so in love with that girl," he said.

Martha was startled. What girl? The waitress, one of the
guests, who? There wasn't any girl but the Coggins girl, and
this she couldn't believe. Yet she felt as the guide on a tour
must feel on first noticing that no one is any longer paying
attention to cathedrals, châteaux, battlefields, stained glass or
the monuments in the square.

Jim Wilbourne offered her a cigarette, which she took. He
lighted it, and one for himself.

"Out at the Lido this afternoon," he went pleasantly on,
"she got up to go in the surf. Her mother said, 'You're getting
too fat, dear. Your suit is getting too small.' For once I could
agree wholeheartedly with Mrs. Coggins."

So then it was Jean Coggins. "But she's only a kid," Martha
protested.

"That's what I thought. I was ten days on that damn boat
and that's what I thought too. Then I caught on that she only
looks like a kid because her parents are along. She's nineteen,
actually. And rather advanced," he drily added.

"But when—?" Martha exclaimed. "I've never seen you near
each other."

"That's strange," said Jim Wilbourne.

She almost laughed aloud to think how they had so quickly
learned to walk through walls; she felt herself to be reasonably
observant, quite alert, in fact. But she was also put out—she
and George Hartwell were not really delighted to have Americans who leaped into la dolce vita the moment the boat docked
—if not, in fact, the moment they embarked. She got up and
walked to the wall where she stood looking over the edge into
the narrow canal beneath. From under the white bridge a boat

went slowly past, a couple curled inside; its motor was cut down to the last notch, and it barely purred through the water. Before Jim Wilbourne came to stand beside her, the boat had slipped into the shadows.

"Italy always has this romantic impact," Martha began. "You have to take into account that the scene, the atmosphere—"

"Generalizations," Jim Wilbourne teased her, quoting something she was fond of saying, "are to be avoided."

"No, it's true," she protested. "After a year or so here, one starts dreaming of hamburgers and milkshakes."

"Indeed?" He flicked his cigarette into the water and turned, his vision drawn back to where Jean Coggins was dancing with the proprietor's son Alfredo, the boy who kept the desk. Her skirts were shorter, her heels higher, her hair, a shambles on her return from the beach, had been brushed and drawn back. She had put on weight, as her mother said, and she did, to Martha's surprise, look lovely.

Martha, who disliked feeling responsible for people, toyed with the idea of seeking the elder Coggins and hinting at what she knew, but there in the faraway shadows, around and around a big oleander pot, the Coggins' were dancing cheek to cheek. Richard Coggins accomplished a daring twirl; Mrs. Coggins smiled. The two grubby musicians, with accordion and fiddle, who had brought an empty fiasco and offered to play for wine and tips, had not even paused for breath for an hour. They could go on like this all evening.

Sciròcco, Martha thought, deciding to blame everything on the weather.

She slipped away, walking inside the broad dimly lit hall of the pensione. It looked shadowy and lovely there, its wide doors at either end thrown open to the heavy night. On the beamed ceiling reflections from water were always flickering, breathing, changing. Behind the desk a low light burned, and the proprietor, a tubby shrewd-faced man, was bending over one of his folio-sized account books. He had told Martha that the pensione was owned by a Viennese lady, who came there unannounced twice a year. She might descend on him, like the angel Gabriel, he had said, at any moment. So he kept his nose to his figures, but now, as Martha went by on her thoughtful way upstairs, he looked up.

"Ah, signora," he said, "there's nothing to do about it. Non c'è niente da fare." But what he meant, if anything, was not clear.

She heard the lapping of tiny waves from everywhere, and through a window saw the flowers against the wall, hanging half closed and dark as wine.

3

IN PIAZZA SAN MARCO where she went the morning after with some idea of keeping her skirts clear of any complications, Jim Wilbourne nevertheless appeared and spotted her. Through hundreds of tables and chairs, he wove as straight a line toward her as possible, sat down and ordered, of all things, gelato. He was wearing dark glasses as large as a pair of windshields, and he dropped off at once into a well of conversation —he must have enjoyed college, Martha thought. The scarcely concealed fascism of Italy troubled him; how were they ever to bring themselves out into democracy?

"Quite a number have jumped completely over democracy," Martha said.

"I simply cannot believe," he pursued, trying to light a cigarette with any number of little wax matches, until Martha gave him her lighter, "that these people are abstract enough to be good Communists. Or Democrats either, for that matter. I think when the Marshall Plan came along they just wanted to eat, and here they are on our side."

"Oh, I really doubt they're so unaware as you think," Martha said. "The idea of the simple-hearted Italian—not even English tourists think that any more."

"I don't so much mean simple, as practical, shrewd, mainly a surface life. What would happen, say, if this city turned Communist right now? Would one Venetian think of hauling the bones of St. Mark out of the cathedral and dumping them in the lagoon? I just can't see it."

"The Coggins' seem to like everything just the way it is," Martha laughed.

"Do you see that character as I do? As long as Richard Coggins can hear some ragazzo go by whistling 'O soave fanciulla,' he's gone to paradise for the afternoon. The more ragged the ragazzo is, the better he likes it. I have two blind spots; want to know them? Opera and religious art. A million churches in this country and quite likely I'm not going to like a single one of them."

"So no wonder you keep escaping us."

"Oh, it's been pleasant enough; you've done your best to keep us happy. And then, there's daughter Jean—" He paused, adding, "Don't get me wrong," though she had no idea what that meant. By now he was eating through a mountain of ice cream, striped with caramel and chocolate, piled with whipped cream and speared with wafers.

"The Coggins' are going down to Rome tomorrow," he went on. "As you know they've got this meeting with Coggins' opposite number, somebody who's going to the States to tell us all about jazz."

"I ought to know about it," Martha said. "I went to enough trouble to set it up. Anyway, it's chamber music, not jazz."

"Okay, Mrs. Ingram. So you'll get me straightened out some day; keep at it. Anyway, I wondered if maybe you wouldn't stay on a day or so, with Jean and me. She thought it would be a good idea; we could all go to the Lido."

"That might be fun," said Martha.

"If you're worried about the Coggins'—well, don't. Him and his bloody opera plots. Ketchup all over the stage, women's heads bellowing out of sacks. Is he serious? Those people were born to be deceived."

"The real hitch for me is that I have a schedule back in Rome. I only made this trip to please my boss."

"It can't be all that important," he pursued, though it was obvious to her that by actually mentioning deception he had spoiled it all.

"Anyway," she pointed out gently, "in this weather the water will be no good at all for swimming. There's sure to be a lot of rain."

"How nice to know so much."

She maneuvered easily, but the fact was he puzzled her. Are they all turning out like this, she wondered, all of them back there? Yet he consistently gained her attention, if that was what he wanted; she had found him attractive from the start, though she had assumed he was accustomed to creating this sort of reaction, and would not have thought it remarkable if he noticed at all. As for herself, she wanted only to place a face value on him. Tanned, solid, tall, dressed even to his watchband with a sort of classical American sense of selection, he was like something hand-picked for export; if you looked behind his ear you might find something to that effect stamped there. He was very much the sort who showed up in ten years leading a group of congressmen by the nose and telling them what to look for and where, though when on home leave she might encounter him even before that, being interviewed on some TV show. It would be like him to leap out at me, right in a friend's living room, she thought. And when he had appeared in Venice a few evenings back, she had been looking toward the bridge he crossed to reach them and had seen him mount up angrily, suddenly, against the horizonless air. He gave her then, and fleetingly at other times as well, the impression of being seen in double, as people always do who carry their own image in their heads.

"How can you smoke and eat ice cream at once?" she asked him.

He stopped, both hands, with spoon and cigarette, in air. He looked from one to the other. "Funny. I didn't know I was." He dropped the cigarette at once, smashing it out carefully.

"I've been wondering how to tell you this," he said, still looking down, but straightening as he finished. "It just happens that I seem to know your former husband rather well."

The bright level surface between them on which she had, in her own way, been enjoying the odd sort of quarrel they had been having, tilted and she slid definitively, her heart plunging downward. So another one had arrived.

"Why didn't you say so before?" she asked him.

"It isn't so easy to say, especially if—"

"If you have a message," she filled in.

She sat looking out at the square. It had filled with tourists, mainly Germans moving in a slow, solemn, counterclockwise procession, ponderous, disorderly, unattractive, as though under tribal orders to see everything. There were the pigeons, more mechanical still, with their wound-up motions, purple feet and jewel-set eyes. And then there was a person, all but visible, right at home in Venice, moving diagonally across the great colonnaded ellipse of the piazza, head down, noticing no one, big shoulders hunched forward under his old tasteless tweed jacket, grey-black hair grizzled at the nape. He was going to the corner drugstore, somewhere near East 71st and Madison. The smell of a late New York summer—just a morning hint of fall—was moving with him, strong enough to dispel the scent of European cigarettes, the summer-creeping reek of the back canals. He would spread books on the counter, stir coffee without looking at it, clumsily allow the bit of lettuce to drop from his sandwich.

"Not so much a message," Jim Wilbourne said.

"You see, people are always turning up when I least expect them!" She longed now simply not to sound helpless.

"Oh, then," he said, in a relieved voice, "you must already know about the accident."

"Accident!" She started like a quiet, lovely insect into which someone has suddenly stabbed a pin; her wings quivered; her eyes were fixed.

"Oh my God, now I've done it!" She tried twice to speak but failed and the voice below the green mask soon continued: "I think he's all right now."

"Oh. . . . Then nothing serious happened—" She drew a shaky breath.

Jim Wilbourne glanced out across the square. "There was some doubt about his being able to walk, but I think—" He broke off again, tentative, mysteriously cold.

Martha stirred compulsively, as though to shake herself free of whatever net had fallen over her. In doing so, her knee struck the little table, rattling the cups and spoons. She remembered the letter on the table in Rome, and the emptiness of the envelope was now her own. "He was always a completely awful driver," she was presently able to continue. "Go on, now you've started. Tell me the rest."

Were they reading lines to each other? Nothing, even turning the table completely over, bringing three waiters rushing down upon them with long arguments about paying for the glassware, would have quite restored her bearings, or loosed her from this cold current into which he seemed deliberately to have plunged them both. "Tell me," she insisted.

His vision seemed, behind the glasses, to pass her own. "Oh, it wasn't a driving accident. But who should tell you this?—it's not my business to. He was out hunting with one of his patients, up in the Berkshires. I never thought that aspect of it made too much sense—well—to take a mental patient hunting, that is. Almost like an experiment, just to see if he'd do it to you on purpose. I never meant to get into all this. But since he is okay now, you naturally will be relieved to know—"

The entire piazza, thickening steadily in the closing weather, had become a total wet-grey illusion. "This isn't Gordon Ingram," Martha said. "It can't be."

"Gordon? No, Donald Ingram. The psychologist, you know. My wife studied with him at Barnard. Well, he does have an ex-wife in Italy. It was just that we were sure—"

Martha was really angry now. "I think you invented the whole thing!" She had not quite lost control. Sparing herself nothing, she had hoped, as though striking off a mask, to find something unequivocal and human facing her, to lose the sensation of conversing with a paper advertisement for shirts and whiskey.

"No, honestly. Quite sincerely, I promise you. It was just a natural mistake."

If there was a person back of the glasses, she had missed him completely. She was not going to succeed in confronting him with anything, for his voice, with as much sameness as a record, went on, "—a natural mistake."

Well, she supposed it was true. She sat looking down into the treacly dregs of espresso in her cup, into which a drop or two of the oppressive mist occasionally distilled and twinkled. She gathered up her bag, lighter, a couple of packages including a glass trinket and a book she had bought for a friend, and got up to leave.

Jim Wilbourne leaped to his feet. He was halted by the waiter, who had arisen from nowhere to demand payment. Now he was running after her. "Wait!"

She turned. "If I don't see you . . . I may take the train down, to stop off in. . . ."

Just as he reached her a whole family of German tourists walked straight into him, knocking off his green glasses. Martha had the startling impression that an entirely new face had leaped into place before her, in quick substitution for the one she had been across from at the table. It was even saying different things: his tone now openly challenged her: "So you won't?" "No." "Not for even a day?" "Exactly."

Their faces, contesting, seemed for an instant larger than life; yet she could remember, recalling the exchange, no further words than that, and the moment must have faded quickly, for in retrospect it seemed telescoped and distant in the vast sweep of San Marco. Jim Wilbourne was backing away as though in retreat, and Martha stood holding her packages while two pigeons at her feet plucked at the smashed bits of his glasses. There was no weakest blot of sun and she wandered out of the square into the narrow labyrinth of Venice where the lions had mildew on their whiskers and St. George slew the dragon on every passing well.

She had looked back once, in leaving the arcades, thinking she had left a camera on a chair, and had seen Jim Wilbourne with Jean Coggins, who must have been nearby all along. They were standing near the corner of the arcade, talking. The girl had a white scarf wrapped around her hair. The vision flickered, and was gone.

He would have been angry with me anyway, she told herself. The story was only an excuse, a pretext. But why should I have angered him?

She walked, moving sometimes with clumps and clots of people, at other times quite alone, beginning to settle and stabilize, to grow gentle once more after the turmoil, the anguish, which his outlandish mental leap at her had, like a depth charge, brought boiling up inside her. She took a certain view of herself: someone, not unusual, who had, with the total and deep sincerity of youth, made a mistake; now, the mistake paid for, agonizingly paid for, the only question was of finding a workable compromise with life. But now at this point did she have to learn that there was something in life which did not want her to have even that? The threat seemed distinctly to be hanging in the air, as thick as the threat of heavy weather.

I should have talked more with the man with the briefcase, she thought, for, far from being mad, he had got things exactly right. Perchè in questo mondo è stato veramente un errore terribile. Don't I really believe that Jim Wilbourne's errore terribile was deliberate? She had accused him of it, certainly, and she did believe it.

She had believed more than that, looking back. She had thought that he was simply stirring up the Jean Coggins romance to question her authority—but that was before she had actually seen the girl standing there.

Martha stopped and almost laughed aloud. She had been about to walk straight into a wall, an architectonic device painted upon it to suggest continuing depth where none existed. The laugh would have bounced back at her, perhaps from the false corridors, the steps and porticos and statuary of that very wall. Laughter was a healthy thought, nonetheless, which said that not so many things pertained to herself as she sometimes seemed determined to believe. And as she stood there a woman much older than herself, grey, but active and erect, walking with the easy long stride of Venetians, who are good at walking because they are always doing it, went past and entered a doorway, bearing a net of groceries—la spesa —in one hand. Just before she entered, she glanced up, and a cat uncurled itself from the column base near the entrance where it had been waiting, bounded past the woman's feet and entered the door in one soft flowing motion. The door closed.

Martha recalled her apartment in Rome; how easily and comfortably it closed about her once she had got past the place where the messages waited and, beyond, found the salotto empty and free. How quietly then she took out her work and spread it on the table, opened the shutters out to the terrace in summer, or bent in winter to light the fresh fire the maid always left.

A new season lay ahead. Perhaps the messages would begin to dwindle now, and not so many couriers would show up; time perhaps had no other result but the dissolution of things that existed, and after this something new came on. Martha, if she never had anything worth calling a new life, would have settled simply for a new silence. It would happen, she believed, when Gordon Ingram finally went back totally to his friends, who would convince him that if his young failure of a second wife ever existed, she had had no right to. (And let it even be true, she thought; if it makes him content, why, I'll believe it too.) She thought then of Jim Wilbourne and Jean Coggins, off somewhere together in the city's rich labyrinth.

Asking the direction of the Grand Canal from a young woman who was eating chocolate, she went off in the way she was told.

4

SOMETIME after four it began to rain—the city, more than ever like a grey-ghost ship, a hynoptic evocation, nodded into the thicker element. The rush and whisper of rain came from every distance. Inside, the air clung like cloth. The maids at the pensione hastened about closing the shutters; they set the restaurant up indoors and brought candles out to decorate the tables—Martha felt she was viewing a new stage-set, a change of scene. Like an opera almost, she thought, and at that moment, sure enough, here came the Coggins', skimming in together hand in hand through the rain. Now they were laughing together at the door and soon, from the desk, were appealing to her. "Have you seen Jean?"

She said she hadn't, but Jean herself came along not much later, walking alone through the rain. She had been sightseeing in a palace, she said, and had got lost when she left it. "You go right upstairs and take a hot bath," Mrs. Coggins said.

Jean went by, making wet tracks, and looking curiously at Martha, of whom she was somewhat in awe. Her foreign clothes, her long fair smoothly put-up hair, her intelligence, and near absence of make-up made her seem to Jean like a medieval lady in a painting. "I can't tell what she's thinking," she had complained to Jim Wilbourne. And he had said nothing at all.

The Coggins' called Martha aside and confided to her with shining eyes that they had experienced a most curious phenomenon since coming to Venice. They had been able to relive in great detail, vividly, their entire past lives. Martha, who could not think of anything worse, nodded, smiling. "How wonderful," she said. "Marvellous," they assured her.

In the heavy air Martha had all but dissolved, and went upstairs to take a nap. She left the two Coggins' murmuring below. Tomorrow they would all be in Rome; there would be the sun.

She slept and dreamed.

In the dream Gordon Ingram was standing along some country road, in New England, among heavy summer trees, and saying, "You see, I have been severely injured in a hunting accident. I cannot come there; please understand that otherwise I would." He looked very young, like the young man in photographs she had seen of him, taken long before they met, standing in the sort of hiking clothes he must have worn in walking over Europe in days, vacations, the like of which would never come again. She was reaching out her hand and saying, as in a formal note to someone, "I sincerely regret . . . I deeply regret. . . ." It seemed the first thing they had had to talk about in many years; the first time in many years that he had spoken to her in his natural voice. The rain-coloured shadows collected and washed over the image and she half woke, then slept again, but could not summon up the dream. She remembered saying to herself, perhaps aloud, "What a strange city this is." For it lay like a great sleeping ear upon the water, resonant and intricate. All the while the rain poured vastly down and could be heard even while sleeping and dreaming, speaking one continuous voice.

In a half-daze she woke and dressed and went downstairs, and at the desk found a note for herself. Jim Wilbourne had just left; he had probably let in the ragged splash of water near the door. He had written a scribble to say that he would see them all in Rome. She crumpled the paper and dropped it in a wastebasket back of the desk. She tried to ring George Hartwell, but could not reach him; the line seemed muffled and gave her only a vague wavering sound. The operator, after a time, must have shut her off for the day. But she remembered that George had said once, one evening when he had drunk too much, that Americans never lose their experience abroad, they simply magnify it. "It's the old trick of grandfathers," he had said. "Before the fire they make little motions and big shadows dance on the wall. Europe is the wall the shadows dance on." His voice went with her for a step or two.

There was nothing to do till dinner and she went upstairs again. The smell of cigarettes hung stagnant in the upper hall and from somewhere a shutter banged in the shifting wind. She pursued stairways and long halls, passed alcoves and sudden windows. Everything was as dark as her dream had been when it faded. A lance had whistled past her ear, and the impression persisted that she moved in a house of death.

PART TWO

5

I~N ROME~ that fall she stopped herself just before telling a friend that her husband had been wounded in an accident. This was very odd, for the fall was bright and sane, and she was at the time nearly eclipsed in cleaning up a lot of George Hartwell's extra chores. The cultural effort had taken on new life that year; the lectures were well received, the social events congenial; pools, lakes, marshes of American good will were filling up everywhere, and all Italians, you would think at times, were eventually going to splash and mingle in them, and the world would never be the same again.

A letter from a lawyer came to Martha, suggesting a price for some property she had owned jointly with Gordon Ingram. It should have been settled long before; it was only since they had gone so happily into it—this small wooded crook of land beside a stream in New York State—that she could never bear to discuss it. But why wouldn't he write me about it? she wondered. Why get somebody else? She sat with the letter and realized something: that if he had had an accident it would have been about here that it happened, right on this bit of land. There were some rocks and a stream below a slope, screened by maple trees.

At last she wrote: "Dear Gordon: Do take the property outright. I do not want any money for it. Will sign whatever transfer is necessary. Martha."

But he could not stand brief notes, simple transactions, direct generosities. Her motives now would suspend him for days. When people dealt with him too quickly, he always suspected either that he had made them too good an offer, or that they were trying to shake away from him; and so, suspicious, obscurely grieved, he would begin to do what he called considering their own good; he would feel it his duty to make a massive reevaluation; he would call all his friends. He would certainly call them all about Martha.

They had all discussed her to death anyway; for years she had interested them more, it seemed, than they interested themselves. They had split her up and eaten her, some an arm and some a neck and some the joints of her fingers.

Sitting at her desk on a Sunday morning, in sunlight, Martha pressed her palm to her brow. Should she mail the letter at all, or write to the lawyer instead, agreeing to everything, or write to her own lawyer to take it over? And must all life, finally defeated, turn itself over with a long expiring grateful sigh into the hands of lawyers? No, she thought with sudden force; I will keep it a personal matter if both of us have to be accidentally wounded. It is, after all, my life.

So in the end she wrote two letters, one to the lawyer and one to Gordon Ingram. Once, before she left the States for Italy, a year after her divorce, she had run squarely into him in New York, getting out of a taxi she had hailed, and before she could stop herself she had almost screamed, and that must have been terrible for him—poor Gordon. But she well knew that if she deceived herself by thinking she knew how he felt, she might act upon it, with sympathy, and trap herself, falling a victim of his pride.

It seemed to her in retrospect that while she debated her letter that Sunday morning, the sun went away; sensually, in recollection, she could almost feel it slipping from her hair, her cheek, her shoulder, and now Rome was deep in winter, with early dusks, blurred neon on the rush of shining streets. Tramontana, the wind from the mountains, struck bitterly, or heavy weather moved in from the sea; the great campagna around Rome became a dreary battlefield of contentious air, and one had to be sorry for the eager Americans, there for one year only, who now had to learn that a sunny, amiable, amusing, golden land had passed in one night into a dreary, damp, cold dungeon of a world where everybody was out to cheat them and none of them could get warm. Martha was used to it. She had been there several years and she liked it. Far stranger to her had been that sudden shift of weather in Venice, back in the summer. It had plunged her, like a trapdoor opening under her feet, into a well of thought she could not yet get out of. She must have been deeply in it the very day when, going home in an early dark after tea with friends, she had run into Jim Wilbourne.

She had seen the Wilbournes fairly often during the fall. Rita Wilbourne, though somewhat more flamboyant than Martha cared to think about—she wore chunky jewelry, bright green and corals, colored shoes—was energetic in getting to know people. She studied Italian, learned it quickly, and took up a hobby—she would make ceramics. It had been a Grand Idea and now it was beginning to be a Great Success. All one room of the Wilbourne apartment had become a studio. It exuded the smell of solvents and plasters.

There had been intermittent invitations. George and Grace Hartwell, the Wilbournes, and Martha Ingram often found that they had gravitated into the same corner at a party, or were ringing each other up to come over for supper on rainy Sundays. What did they talk about so much as the Coggins'?

Jean Coggins had a job in a glove shop on the Piazza di Spagna. About once a week, every young Italian in Rome made a point of coming in and buying gloves. Some did nothing but walk back and forth before the window for hours. The owner was having to expand.

Richard Coggins was the success of the entire cultural program. His Italian, once it quit rhyming like opera, was twice as fluent as anyone else's; he learned, he learned! He was invited —a great coup for the American image—to address the opera company in Milan. His lectures were packed and ended with cheers and cries. (Bravo! Bis, bis!) Oh, no one had ever furnished more party talk than the Coggins'. Yet there was something enviable about their success.

One night at the Wilbournes' apartment after dinner, Jim Wilbourne remarked: "Jean Coggins' effect on Italian men began to happen the minute the boat docked. It was spontaneous combustion. Do you remember Venice, Martha?"

Martha looked puzzled. She shook her head. The trouble was she remembered nothing but Venice; it was a puzzle which had never worked out for her; what exactly did he mean?

"There was some boy who kept the desk—Alfredo, his name was."

"Oh, yes, the proprietor's son."

"What happened?" someone—Hartwell's wife—wanted to know.

"Well, they were hitting it off so well that she wanted me to persuade Martha—you must remember this, Martha—to stay on a day or so, so that her parents would let her stay too. The only catch was she didn't want me to mention Alfredo: it seems the Coggins' believe that Italian men are incorrigibly passionate or something. She nagged me until I promised to do it, but the only excuse I could think of was to say I was interested in her myself."

Everyone laughed. "So what happened?" they wanted to know.

"Well, I got nowhere with Martha. She got out of it very well."

"What did you say?" Hartwell asked her.

"I forget"—she let Jim Wilbourne finish his story.

"She said she'd like to stay on but she had some appointments or other—very grand she was."

Hartwell, after a hard week, had had a drink or two more than usual. He gave Martha a hug. "I love this girl."

"But I was in the dark myself," Martha protested. She soon followed Rita into the next room to look at her workshop.

"So she tried to be philosophic, which for a Coggins is something of a strain, to put it mildly. She went off in the rain with Alfredo, off in Venice somewhere, and called it a day."

"I wouldn't have thought these two colors would go at all," Martha said to Rita, who had joined her. "But you've made them work."

"Yes, but Italians are so bold with their colors. I think it must be something in the sunlight here—when there's any sun, of course." She picked up two sections, handle and basin, from an unfinished hors d'oeuvres dish. "You see, you wouldn't think that would do well, but I find the more I experiment—" Her bracelets jingled together as her hands moved. They were thin, quick, nervous hands with tinted nails. Grace Hartwell had told Martha that the Wilbournes were expecting a child. Why is George such a puritan? Martha wondered. You'd think I'd struck a blow for freedom by keeping lovers apart.

"Did you, by any chance," Martha asked Rita, "know a Professor Ingram at Barnard?"

"Oh, yes, but not at Barnard. I went to Columbia. He teaches there occasionally, one semester every so often. Yes, I not only knew him, but we were sure for a time that you must be the former Mrs. Ingram. She's somewhere in Italy. It's odd your asking that."

"I'd just recalled when we were talking of Venice that Jim mentioned him to me there. And several other times," she lied, "people have assumed that he—I never met this person, of course."

"But beginning to feel you know him rather too well?"

"I also heard he had been in some sort of accident last summer. Did you know anything about that?"

"Oh, that must be another Ingram still. No, unless something happened just recently—"

The ceramics were laid out in a bare, chilly servant's room on a large makeshift table, strips of wallboard held up by a smaller table underneath and supported on either end by chairs. The effect was of a transferred American look, makeshift and practical, at no pains not to negate the parquet floor, a scrolled mirror now layered with cement dust. A small French écritoire had been pushed into a corner, and beside it, a gilded baroque angel holding a torch stood face to the wall. The room had probably been intended as a smoking or drawing room off the salotto. They had dined on frozen shrimp from the PX, and only in here with the ceramics was the odor escapable. Why would anyone buy frozen American shrimp in Italy? Martha had wanted to ask, but had not. It had been answered anyway, at dinner; Rita was afraid of the filth in the markets. But the markets were not filthy, Martha thought, murmuring how delicious it was.

"Hey, Martha!" Hartwell again.

"We're busy," Rita called.

"Information required," Grace Hartwell said.

"They always want you to tell them things, don't they?" said Rita, with a moment of woman's sympathy. "If I were you, I wouldn't."

Martha came to the doorway, her shawl tugged around her. Her hands felt cold. Hartwell was lighting his third cigar. Would he not, singlehanded, eventually drive out both shrimp and ceramics smell? "Martha, I thought siròcco was a wind.

Jim here says it's not. He says in Venice it's nothing but heavy weather. Now you settle it."

"I believe it's an African wind," she said, "and causes storms all along the coasts, but sometimes the wind doesn't get as far as Venice, especially in the summer, so then you have heavy weather and rain."

Jim Wilbourne laughed. "You mean it is and it isn't."

"I guess that makes you both right," she agreed, and smiled.

All their faces were momentarily turned to her. There was some way, she realized, in which, in that moment, she drew them, the two men primarily, and because of the men, inevitably, the women as well. She would have as soon dropped at once whatever force this was, dropped it off like her shawl on the threshold and walked away. But to where? she wondered, To where? No one can abdicate the earth.

Yet she kept on wondering this in some corner of her mind until the night she ran into Jim Wilbourne, down in the low Renaissance quarter of the city, in the windy, misty, December cold. In brushing past they recognized each other, and for some reason, startled, she slipped on an uneven paving stone so that he caught her back from falling. Then he asked her into a café and they had a drink together. She felt she was seeing him after a long absence.

He had changed somewhat; she noticed it at once. He was paler than in Venice, no longer seemed so well turned-out; needed a better haircut, had a cold. He was complaining about Italian medicine; it was his wife's having a miscarriage only a week or so after their dinner party that had got them so sensitive to these matters. Martha thought how soon the bright young Americans began to look tarnished here. The Wilbournes had had some squabble with the landlord about their apartment. He had believed that Rita, who had begun to sell her ceramics, was obviously using the place for business purposes, so he drew up papers demanding either eviction or a larger rent. Martha had heard this through the grapevine, in the same way she had learned that there had been some disagreement with American friends about a car. All these were the familiar complications of Roman life, which only the Coggins' seemed to escape. *Their* landlord had dreamed of an opera career when young, and as a result brought them fresh cheeses from the country, goat's milk, ropes of sausages. The Wilbournes, stubbornly American, were running against the Italian grain, so of course everything was going wrong. Yet Jim Wilbourne did work hard; it was this that Hartwell always said, as though making up for something.

Jim Wilbourne asked her the name of the pensione where they had all stayed in Venice. A friend of his was going up. "But do you think they'd enjoy it this time of year?" she asked. "What's the matter, the weather?" The weather, obviously; she hardly needed, she thought, to nod. "I must be thinking of Verona." He frowned. "There was a big fireplace—?" She shook her head. "I don't think so."

The door of the café stuck on the way out; getting it to work, he gave her an odd smile. He walked along with her for about a block, then, saying something about somewhere he had to be, he turned abruptly and went back the other way.

She turned around in the cold misty street, looking after him. The street was long and narrow and completely deserted, the shop windows covered over with iron facings which had been bolted to the pavement. Almost involuntarily, she lifted her hand. "Wait!" She did not speak very loudly and it was a wonder he heard her at all. He did stop, however, and looked back.

She began to walk toward him, and presently he even came a step or two to meet her. She stood huddled in her dark coat. The damp got in everywhere. She shifted her feet on the cold wet stones. "It's a silly thing to ask—I keep meaning to mention it whenever I see you, then I always forget. Do you remember a conversation we had in Venice when you said that someone you knew named Ingram—you mistook him for my husband—had been shot in a hunting accident?"

"I had hoped you'd forgotten that. It was a hell of a conversation. The whole place was depressing: some start for a year in Europe." He did not exactly look at her, but past her in a manner so basically unsatisfactory to her she would have liked to complain about it. Then when he did look at her, her face, she realized, slanting up to him, must have become unconsciously strained. She laughed.

"I'm shivering in this cold. This is ridiculous, of course. I wouldn't have remembered it at all, but Rita mentioned it to me, not long ago—this same man, I mean. But what she said was that he never had any accident at all. Neither he nor anyone else she knew."

"Well?"

"Well, I simply wondered what the connection was. Why did you say it at all?"

"I must have got him confused with someone else."

"Oh, I see. Someone you know and she doesn't?"

He did not reply.

"Was that it?" she insisted.

"Lots of questions," he remarked, amusing himself, though he was not what she could call light about it. "I guess I just don't remember it so well as you."

"It was in San Marco, in Venice. You ran after me and broke your dark glasses and just after that Jean Coggins came there —to meet you."

Watching him was like looking up into a dark mirror, or trying to catch some definite figure embedded in glass. Yet his features were singularly without any motion at all. She had, as she had had before, the impression of a photographed face.

"Oh, yes, Jean Coggins. . . ." She thought for a moment he would not continue. "She wanted you to stay on, she got me to ask you. I told you that," he added, impatiently. "In fact, I went to some trouble to tell you. As for her coming there, I don't remember that—I don't think it happened."

A Lambretta sputtered behind her, turning with a cough into the narrow, resounding street. The echoes clapped, climbing up to the high tile eaves above them. Pools of rain, surfaced in the uneven paving, seamed and splashed. Jim Wilbourne and Martha Ingram stepped back into a shallow alcove against an iron door, where large white letters were painted, advertising the name of the shop. The roar mounted with an innocent force and turmoil which seemed close to drowning them, then it passed, faded, turned a corner. They both stepped back into the street.

"All this seems to have got on your mind in some sort of way," Jim Wilbourne said. "Here, come on, I'll walk you home."

The damp chill had crept up to her ankles, but she did not stir, though he caught her elbow to urge her forward. Her private idea of him was beginning to form; namely, that he was a sort of habitual liar. He might, if this was correct, be incapable of telling the truth even when it would do him no shred of harm to do so, even when it might be better that way. Any exact nature of things he was called upon to reconstruct might seem always to escape him. Hartwell had called her in once about a mix-up which had involved Jim Wilbourne and she had said then that she thought he was absentminded, but Hartwell protested, "That simply won't hold a thing like this." Then she said, "I don't think he would do anything to damage his work." They were, between them, she and Hartwell, aware of new Americans, newer than themselves, perhaps different, perhaps more nearly right, than they who had been "out here," "away from things" for longer. The feeling was that people, like models of humanity, might quickly become obsolete in some overruling set of American terms even now, beyond their knowledge or power, being drawn up; so their confidence grew weak before the solid advantage of the Wilbourne image. He was so definitely American-looking, while Hartwell had recently given in to shoes with pointed Italian toes which looked extremely odd on him, and Martha went habitually to Roman dressmakers and looked extremely well, though hardly Fifth Avenue. So with this thinking interchanged between them, Hartwell agreed not to make an issue of the Wilbourne default, and let the matter slide.

Martha said to Jim Wilbourne, "Naturally it got on my mind. It concerned me, didn't it?"

"Not at all. It concerned me, Jean Coggins and a man you used to be married to."

She gave a laugh that did not sound altogether pleasant, even to herself. "A rather close relationship," she said. Rambling about in those half-dreams which Gordon Ingram's giant mahogany bed, like being lost on a limitless plateau with the same day's journey always in prospect, seemed both to encourage and deny, she had often thought the relationship could be a lot closer, yet now she regretted most the times that it had been. She would have liked to extinguish those times not only out of memory but out of time itself.

They began to walk off together in her direction. She protested against being any trouble to him, but he did not seem to hear her, and soon he was walking ahead at a rapid, nervous pace she found hard to keep up with in her thin shoes. His long legs and narrow heels kept striking accurately down before her. The streets were narrow and dark and his raincoat went steadily on, as though its light colour cut a path for them.

"Jean Coggins," he told her with his short hoarse laugh, "has a lot of boy friends but never gets to bed with any of them. We found this out from the maid whose sister works for the family of one of the boys. She's a grand girl in topolinos, picnics, out among the tombs. She could probably make love in a sarcophagus. Her morals are well-defined, but what if she never gets over it?"

"How do her parents get along with all this?" Martha asked.

"Her parents," said Jim Wilbourne, "are still in Venice, dancing around a flower pot."

This was not only funny, but true; Martha often saw them there herself.

He slowed his step, letting her catch up even with him, and for a moment caught her hand. "Why do I always talk to you about Jean Coggins?"

"It does get monotonous," she admitted.

"I can't think why I do it. She's comical. All the Coggins' are comical."

"You told me you loved her. You're probably still trying to get out of that."

"I don't know. It was the Italian boy—"

"Yes, I know. Alfredo."

"I remember now I told her to ask you yourself, about staying on in Venice, but she didn't have the nerve. She found you awe-inspiring, your intelligence, authority, something—I don't know. As for me, I had some sort of strong feeling for you, right from the first. I imagined you felt the same, but then—" He broke off, but added, rather drily, "Your attention was elsewhere. You seemed—enclosed."

She said nothing, walking, hearing their footfalls on the stones, and how sometimes the sound of them interlocked and sometimes not.

"I try not to think of myself at all," she ventured. And this was true; she would have put herself quite outside her own harsh, insistent desire for him, if this had been possible. As it was not, she meant simply to hold it aside.

"Well, you don't succeed," he said pleasantly. "Nobody does."

"You took that way of getting my attention by telling me that Gordon—that my husband—" Only to get that question out of the way! She felt she could get herself intellectually right, at least, and as for the rest— But striving with him to get it answered only drew her deeper in and her feeling mounted that it was no more possible to make him speak openly to her than to make an intelligent animal consent to converse.

"I kept trying to get out of it, once I started it," he reminded her. "But nothing seemed to work. I had some notion you were slipping away from me; you did it repeatedly—it was a question of whether anything on earth could reach you at all. On that peculiar day, the question seemed what you might call urgent."

"But even on a peculiar day," she argued, "to make up death like a parlor game—"

He stopped walking. "I didn't invent any death. You did—or seem to have."

It was true. Her heart filled up with dread. Not even her dream had mentioned death. The wildest leap of all had been her own.

"Oh, God!" she murmured. "Oh my God!" She stood before him, her head turned severely aside. They had reached the top of her street, and from the far end there came, in the narrow silence, the trickle of a commonplace little fountain. The mist, shifting, prickled sharply against her cheek. Some minutes back, from high up among the roofs and terraces, a cat had mewed, trapped on a high ledge.

He drew her in, quickly, easily, against him. The motion for them both was accurate beyond measure, and the high tension between them broke up almost at once. At its sudden departure, she gasped sharply. His arm still tightly around her, he brought her to her doorway and leaned against it with her. A small boy went past without a glance, and then a girl in a swinging coat, who looked twice and then away. The street came back to them, constricted, grey-black, high and dim.

"You've made too much of a mystery of this," he said. "I wanted to see you before, but—well, obviously, it was difficult. And then how could I be certain what went on with you?"

"I don't know," she said, but rousing somewhat out of the muffled clamour of her senses, she thought to ask: "How did you know that anything went on?" to which he did not reply.

She thought of his various hesitances and evasions in terms of his life being elsewhere: how could he manage to get into hers without disturbing his own? The problem could have any degree of intensity for him. She fully intended to say this, when he said:

"There's nothing very unusual about all this that I can see. You've wanted him out of the way all along. You wanted me to get rid of him. You see that, don't you?"

And he had cast her, with one casual blow, straight into madness.

She was back in her terrible private wood where the wind howled among the thorn trees; she was hearing the roar of the gun down by the stream, the crash of the autumn-garish leaves. She was racing to get there in time and the thorns tore her gown and her flesh. "Out of the way," "get rid of him"— these phrases were plainly and diabolically murderous, and she could not hear either one or echo it without a shudder. How could Jim Wilbourne speak with such an absence of horror? An accomplice speaks this way, she thought, brought too late into the action to have any but the most general notion of it, but once there, what way can be taken back to the time before him? With a staggering mental effort, nothing short of heroic, she closed down the lid on her chestful of bedlam, and said to him calmly:

"You must understand: hatred is too much for me. I can't face it; you have to believe that." He stirred, shifting her weight entirely against his arm and shoulder, but as he said nothing, she presently hurried on: "We would be here anyway, whether you had told me that miserable story in Venice or not. We'd still be here—I know that's true!"

This declaration was so swift and plain, it caught them in like all of truth, in one warm grasp, so that she felt it might never have ended, until he drew back to point out: "My darling, of all places in the world to make love! Do I break the door down? Haven't you got a key?"

She drew herself back, collecting the shreds and rags of what she had been thinking. Something was being ignored; she found it about the same time as she located the key. "But you do see what I meant to say." Her hand lay urgently on his arm. "It's important to me to know you understand."

"I understand it isn't true. You'd never have called me back tonight if it hadn't been for what you call my miserable story in Venice. And you know that, Martha, don't you?" He gave her a demanding shake. "Denying it—that's no good."

"I know, I know, but I—" The words rushed out at last like a confession. She felt a deep pang of relief and was unable to finish what she had begun by way of protest. She felt shaken and outdone. All her life she had longed for some world of clear and open truth, reasonable and calm, a warm, untroubled radiance (the sort of thing that Gordon Ingram wrote about so well), but though she thirsted like the dying for it, it never appeared to her and she wondered if every human being was not surrounded by some dark and passionate presence, opaque and confusing, its face not ever to be discerned without enormous cost. The rush of her emotion had thrown her fully against him, and she disengaged herself slowly. He let her go.

"I never meant to injure you," he said at last. "It's only that —well, I suppose in this case it matters, keeping straight on things."

Straight! She almost burst out laughing. Well, she thought somewhat wearily, all her rush toward him brought to a complete stop, she supposed he *had* gone to some high degree of concentrated effort to keep her straight. As for the straight of *him*, it was such another question, it made her dizzy to think about it. The truth about even so slight an episode as the Coggins girl alone would have quite likely baffled a detective force. And where, for that matter, had he been going tonight? In a return to her native aristocratic detachment, she could not bring herself to ask him things like this; perhaps it was because she did not really want to know.

She turned, finding her key in her bag, and tucking her hair up with one hand, unlatched the door. It was a small winter- and night-time door cut within the larger portone, and sprang easily back so that she stepped inside the dimly lit interior at once. She looked back reluctantly to observe him. He had not pressed in behind her but stood as she had left him. It was only that one arm was thrown out against the door. The crumpled sleeve of his coat, the white inch of cuff, the set of his hand, pressed into her senses like the bite of a relief. His gaze, meeting hers, did not implore her for anything. His face was simply present, and would be, she recognized, as it had been for a long time now, present and closely with her whether she shut it out or not. From somewhere she had gained the strength to take it now, deliberately, whenever the moment came, between her two hands.

She nodded, and bending sideways to avoid the low frame, he stepped inside. The closing door made a soft definitive thud, echoing strongly within, but only once, dully, in the narrow street outside. She mounted the long stairs, proceeded through corridors and turnings, archways and landings. She did not look back or speak, but moved quietly on ahead of him.

She had lived a year at least, she thought, since running into him in the Via de' Portoghesi.

PART THREE

6

GEORGE HARTWELL got the news in Milano. By then it was summer, summer even in Rome which he had left only two days ago to help maneuver the Milan office through a shake-up; and the weather finally pleased everyone. The old damp, closed medieval shrunken city, which had all but destroyed them all, had evaporated in one hour of this glorious new season. And what could have happened in it that was not gone with it? he wondered, and read the letter once more.

On Sunday morning he was driving there. It's the least I can do for her, he thought, just in case. In case of what? The road flickered up, the sea appeared and melted away and crashed in again. In case, in case, he thought, and soon might even make a song of it, and go bellowing as operatically as Richard Coggins all along the sea road south, past Santa Margherita, Porto Fino, with Tarquinia ahead and Santa Marinella . . . the plains, the mountains and the sea.

In some ways he wondered if it was a serious matter at all. Is any personal matter, he asked himself, a serious matter any longer? Isn't a personal matter simply a bug in the machine? Get rid of it as quickly as possible, or one of the rockets in your space capsule might jam. Push button C with all due reverence, for any other one will be your doom. The sea grew pink, then crimson, then a blue so deep and devastating he thought he would give up all considerations and sit out several days on a rock. Then life would change, if we would do that. If every other person, every other week. . . .

A Lambretta roared up out of a curve, all but shaving the paint from his left front fender. He did not slacken speed, but drove on. He was not going to go and sit on any rock, ever, not even if they dropped the bomb next week.

Martha Ingram, all this time, was serenely alone upon her terrace, drying her long hair in the sun. Observant as a cat in the morning still, she had just seen far down in the little square below, where the fountain twinkled, the last courier come and go, a rich little white-haired lady from Connecticut, some cousin or friend (was it?) of Gordon Ingram's—Martha could not remember her name. The sun stood at ten and a large daytime moon floated in the sky, pale, full-blown as a flower, it seemed a contrivance of the imaginary sort, fragilely mounted for effect. Was it because she could not remember the name that she had not gone to the door? The name, actually, had been called to her attention no earlier than yesterday, when a note had come, written from the lady's hotel—the Grand, of course, nothing less. (Martha had often thought that Gordon Ingram was in Rome and staying at the Grand, which would have suited him so; they had large fronded palms in the lobby, and the steps which broke the interior floor between the reception area and the lounge were so long you could never find the end of them.) Martha wondered what she had done with that note—she didn't know.

Just now, through the beautiful weather, an hour earlier in the summer morning the Italian messenger from the embassy had come with a dispatch case for her: she was to add a stack of reports for Hartwell and take them in the next morning. Well aware of the season, the Italian, whose name was Roberto, was amiable and conversant and invited her for an afternoon at the beach. He had his sister's car, he said, by way of recommendation, and had recently visited the States. Martha agreed the beach would be nice; she had got together with him on several minor problems recently and had found him astute. He was, in a pleasant way, a sort of social spy; he could tell an arrivato a mile off, and he knew ways of isolating, or deflecting, people. If Hartwell had found some way of listening to someone like Roberto during the winter past, the Coggins' would not have leaped to such prominence in the cultural program that people now had the Americans all taped as opera lovers. So what Roberto was in turn going to want . . . questions like that flowed along easily with Roman life; they were what it was about. She thought of that gently sparkling sea and what a slow progress she had made toward it through heavy weather a year ago, back when it all began.

Going out, Roberto passed by the porter and the little lady in blue. Martha could hear by leaning over the terrace that the porter (whom she had bribed) was saying over and over: "La Signora Ingram non c'è . . . la Signora Ingram è fuori

Roma." Roberto stopped by the fountain; turning swiftly, he seemed to stamp himself with a kind of ease on his native air. "Si, si, c'è . . . la signora c'è . . . l'ho appena vista." Then, catching some glance from the porter, he retreated. "O, scusi . . . uno sbaglio. . . ." He turned, a little grey Fiat, the sister's car, no doubt, his goal, but the little lady shot after him, quick as a rabbit. She caught his sleeve. "I am looking for Mrs. Ingram. She lives here. Now would you be so kind." "Non parlo inglese, signora. Mi dispiace. . . ." How quickly, Martha thought, they did solidify. She had always, from the first, had some knack of getting them on her side. But was it fair that poor little lady friends of the family should get the runaround? Le prendono in giro, Martha thought. They are leading her in a circle. A little more and she would go down and open the door, come what might.

She never saw any friends, messengers, from the States any more. She never read her mail. And when the little lady looked up, she ducked cleverly behind the parapet of the terrace, bringing her hair, which she had just shaken damp from the wet scarf to dry, down with her. She loved the warmth on the back of her neck, the sun's heat reaching to the roots of her hair, through the fabric of her dress. Who would leave it for a minute to descend three stone flights that still smelled like winter?

So the rich lady cousin went away in her fitted blue summer coat with the funny squat legs V-ing down from the broad behind into the tiny feet in their specially ordered shoes. What a world of shopping, the kind these ladies did, came back to Martha as she watched her go. And there was her loud English to the porter (the louder we speak the more chance we have), and then for the sweeter part, her brave attempt at Italian: "Voglio parlare con la Signora Ingram, per cortesia." It was as if someone had said that if the lady's duty lay in climbing a mountain at once, she would not even have stopped to change clothes.

The porter was not touched in the least. "No, signora. La Signora Ingram non c'è. L'appartamento è vuoto." They went on and on, their voices in counterpoint, echoing in the wide-open hallways below, now touching the fountain, now climbing to the terrace. If I could think of her name, Martha thought, I might weaken and let her in. Surely she has nothing to do with, knows nothing about, the property in New York State which they must have got me to sign something in regard to or they would not now be so determined to get me to sign something releasing it. You would think they had found a deposit of gold and diamonds six inches beneath the soil, though it is quite possible that I am holding up a real estate development. Who can tell what goes on back in that green dream across the Atlantic?

The porter kindly called a cab. Now he would earn two ways —the tip from the lady, and Martha's bribe. All he had to do was be as adamant as a barred door, which was his true nature anyway. The lady rode off in her hat of blue-dyed feathers with the tight veil, fitting sleekly as it had been carefully planned to do, over her white hair, her two million wrinkles. She held her neck up straight, giving orders to the driver, an indomitable little white duck.

If I could have thought of her name, I would have let her in, thought Martha, as the cab disappeared from the square. She wasn't as bad as the rest of them, I do remember that. Martha knew too, by the slight degree of feeling by which even mad people recognize character, as though fingers upon a fine string in the dark had discovered a knot in it, that the lady in blue was not indulging in ugly suspicions as to if and why lies had been told her. She was saying that she simply did not know. That was all.

Oh, mythical bird, vanishing American lady! She had been, Martha felt certain, the last courier.

Martha picked up her hairbrush and, drawing her chair close to the edge of the terrace, she began to brush her hair. The bells had begun to ring, and she had put her hair up when George Hartwell drew up in the square below, hot and rumpled and jaded, hitching up the handbrake sharply. So I was right to have the papers ready for him, Martha thought, but it wasn't especially the papers he had come there for. He tossed his hat aside and sat down in the sun.

He held out a letter to her, though it had come to him. "Your sister says you don't answer your mail," he told her, stirring the coffee she brought him. "She also wants you to know that Gordon Ingram is very sick. He is in New York Hospital."

"I haven't answered much mail recently," Martha admitted. "I've scarcely read my mail at all."

A long silence grew up between them. Hartwell's wife was in the States attending their son's graduation from prep school in Massachusetts. Everyone had begun to be displaced. The Wilbournes were gone, Jim to take a job on some new economic council for advising private industry, and Rita to open a ceramics shop, having shipped loads of material, not quite legally, through embassy channels. They had left their flat in a mess, having sneaked out unexpectedly three days early: Hartwell still had calls from the landlord. The parquet was ruined, the mirrors. . . .

How was it that the sun seemed literally to warm one's heart? Hartwell now thought kindly of Martha Ingram's husband for the first time in his life. The poor old bastard, was what he thought. A man that age. Quite likely he's dying.

"So will you consider going there?" he asked her. "It can be arranged."

In the sun her hair shimmered like a fine web. Hartwell had once said about Martha Ingram when he was drunk, "Being from Springfield, Missouri, I am moved by women with grave grey eyes," which, as everyone told him, made no sense at all. It was a flight that failed. He had had some reference to his mother, aunt, some old magazine picture, or advertisement, maybe, showing a lady who wore her long hair up, face partly turned aside, serious and quiet. It was his way of worrying out loud. For his wife had speculated that there was undoubtedly a man in her life, but who? Hartwell used to think it over in the office alone and then wad paper up and hurl it at the wastebasket.

A slight movement just now of a curtain through one of the terrace windows made him think of Jim Wilbourne's even, somewhat longish, smoothly observant face, his nervous gesture of banging the heel of a resoled American shoe against a desk or chair leg when he talked, his cough and cigarettes and short hoarse laugh. Anybody, thought Hartwell, but Jim Wilbourne. Yet there she was, shining and fair, surfaced out of a long hard winter.

"Going there?" she repeated, as if he had mentioned a space ride. "It's nothing he's suggested. Don't tell me she said that."

"No," Hartwell admitted, "but look at it anyway. . . . You haven't even read it." She had taken it, but it was lying on her lap. When she moved, it slid to the terrace and she did not pick it up.

"But I know anyway," she said. "The last time I saw him was in Venice. He did not even look my way."

"Venice! Your husband was not in Venice," Hartwell corrected her, with a slightly chilly feeling.

She tucked one foot meditatively beneath her. "You see how crazy I am," she pointed out.

After some time, Hartwell said, "Intentionally crazy, I take it?"

"It's necessary," she finally replied.

At this Hartwell stopped drinking coffee, perhaps forever.

"What are you thinking?" she asked him.

"I think the weather is better," he said.

"That isn't what you think," she said gently, and gently too she went so far as to pick up the letter and place it—most untrustworthily—upon the table.

A small bell in a small church rang close by. It had a lovely clear sound and one actually looked about, expecting to see it, as though for a bird which had burst out singing.

"If only you could have got by without Wilbourne!" Hartwell cried, astonishing himself.

Martha built a pyramid out of burnt matches beside the milk pitcher. "He's gone. And anyway, what was it to you?"

"I didn't like him," said Hartwell arbitrarily. "This has happened before. It's nothing new. Those tall young men. . . ." It had happened all his life, in fact; he never having been one of them. At Harvard he had seen them, in the clothes of that day, older, of course, than himself, their strong easy step moving down corridors; and at Oxford, English tall with heavier bone structure, their big knees ruddy and tough in the blear cold. Now they were younger and would be younger still, but the story was still the same. "One expects such brilliance, and what happens? A moderately adequate work program, someone dear to me damaged"—she gave him a glance but did not stop him —"and now this headache of an apartment going on and on into the summer."

They had wrecked their apartment when they left, Jim and

Rita Wilbourne. The parquet, the mirrors, the plumbing, the furniture. It was a vengeance on the landlord whose nature was infernal, and who had made their life a grating misery for the whole year. Now Hartwell had to listen to the landlord; he came once or twice a week to Hartwell's office; he would come tomorrow. "Signor console, deve capire che sono un uomo giusto e gentile. . . . You must understand I am a just and honorable man." The world was smeared and damaged, and Martha's craziness obsessed him, the more because she having completed herself he was in some ways crazier than she, else why would he let the landlord in for these interminable visits complaining of something which he could be said to be responsible for only in the vague sense of directing an American program in which Jim Wilbourne had, for a short time, taken part?

"You are linking me, George," she half-teased him, "to what the Wilbournes did to the landlord. Is that reasonable?"

"No, it isn't. It isn't reasonable at all. It just happens to be the truth, that's all. And anyway, you didn't see it—you didn't get the guided tour after they carried out the crime and ran away to Naples in the night. Carelessness is one thing, disorder left by people who aren't so tidy, something not at all nice about it, smelly maybe, but still human. But Rita and Jim Wilbourne had taken hammers, crowbars, scissors . . . !" He had begun, somewhat ludicrously, to shout.

Martha thought it was time somebody repaid a Roman landlord in kind, though anything short of crucifixion seemed genteel, but even to think of a Roman landlord seemed out of place in the timeless, non-bitterness of a Sunday morning full of sun.

"If he found that was the only way to get even," she said, "there may even have been some logic in it. I'm sure he got no more than even, and maybe no less. You forget he was an economist, so that might have something to do with the way he felt; I really don't pretend to know."

"I'm sure you would know more than I would," Hartwell said, somewhat recovering himself.

"I know he was the only one who could deal with Gordon Ingram—I do know that. But I never thought of him as smashing apartments up, though now that you mention it—"

The little church bell stopped ringing about then, and she wondered at Hartwell, this stupor of moral horror in his face, and predicted, the instant before he did it, that he would ask for a drink. She went and got it, drifting free and anchorless through her apartment, then going off to rearrange some flower pots, having no more ties than a mobile, invisibly suspended in the sun. Yet she was kind enough to reassure him. "If my judgment of him is worth anything, he seemed more quiet than not."

"Quietly murderous?" Hartwell murmured and fell into the scotch with a sigh.

She had to recognize, for by turning her head she could even see what made a space for itself rather constantly in her mind—how the room just beyond the tall windows onto the terrace looked now. They would have both known a long chain of rooms like that from childhood on, known their quiet, with shadowy corners and silent chairs and pictures that look only at one another, ornaments of no earthly connection to anything one knows about or can remember, and known too the reason for their precise quality, even down to the slow wind of dust motes in the thin slant of winter sun, the cool rest the marble has in summer, and the small light of the lamps: the reason being that somebody has been got rid of in them. In spite of her, their thoughts, like profiles in a modern painting, merged and coalesced: she appeared as one of a long line of women who have rooms like this: invariably handsome, well-dressed, detached, goalless, they have struck at life where it lived, unnaturally, because it grew unbearable.

He recalled from his long lost Missouri days, various women, their features indistinct, but their spirits clear to transparency, who lived in shady white houses with green latticework under the porch where the land sloped away. In varying degrees of poverty and wealth, they gave up their lives day by day, like sand running through a visible hourglass, to some trembling cross old father or invalid brother or failure of a husband or marvellously distorted and deeply loved child. But out and away from this monotony, they ranged far and wide among friends of the town, accepted, beloved, understood, praised. He saw them shift through that lost world with the sureness of angels, and though he said to himself it was lost, the thought occurred to him that it was perhaps only himself that was lost to it; for certainly it was there still: what made him think it wasn't? It was still there and going on, and repeating moreover its one relentlessly beautiful message, that you had to stand what you couldn't stand, or else you couldn't live at all. And for the first time it came to him that Martha Ingram did not, any longer, exist. He felt a pang of missing her, as though sometime back somebody had come in the office and told him the bad news and he had done all the decent things.

Whereupon she looked at him, reflectively, through the sun, and all the fabric of his fantasy crumbled. At least in the warm intelligent effigy of the flesh she was still there and still able to get through to him. She was all but pointing out to him that he didn't really know, how could he know just how it was? It was inhuman; it was monstrous—that was the first thing to know. Therefore, who was to say what she had or hadn't had the right to do about it?

7

As to whether or not she was really there any more, she could have said that she had simply become the winter past. Its positive motion against her, which seemed at times as blindly relentless as a natural force breaking up her own life, would always be with her. But it could not, unlike a natural force, ever be forgotten, for human faces had appeared in it and voices had cried to her, human motion had struck her down, and by these things, grasped at, sometimes only half understood, she had been changed for good, and could never escape them. It had been a definitive season.

But why George Hartwell now had to rush back into its devastating glooms and vapours, the flicker of its firelights, and quick gasps of its passions, so grotesquely lighted up in shadow play against the walls of his good and gentle heart—that she could not say. She did not really want to say. He seemed distant to her. She was fond of him. She could not have been any more or less than that if he had wanted her to, and he would never say so if he did, even, she supposed, to himself. She could, however, indulge him. He had his curiosity, so much a part of his affection—she could honor both by letting him in on things. She doubted if she would ever go so far as to say very much about the evening she had run into Jim Wilbourne on the Via de' Portoghesi, but in a way by just recalling it, it could be in some way shared by George Hartwell's openness in her direction, which she might have been leaning over to pat on the head, like a house pet. But then, of course, he would want to get past all that as hastily as possible, and on to the next thing, the next stone in her private torrent, and she guessed, looking back that that would have been the Boston lawyer. In January, wasn't it?

Yes, she could share that with George. She could even tell him about it, for she would not forget a single detail of it, even down to the grey suit the lawyer was wearing. He was all grey, in fact, all over, even to his cuff links, hair, and tie, and his name was grey as well—Bartram Herbert. He was a close friend of Gordon Ingram's. She had known him for years.

He flew in in the afternoon, to Ciampino, just as his tele-gram had said he would. She did not meet the plane, and had even decided that she would leave the city for Naples, but unable to make herself do so, showed up exactly where he had asked her to, the Flora lobby near the Porta Pinciana. She even arrived on the exact hour, clasped his hand with a pale smile and turned her chilly cheek for a token kiss. He took her down to have a drink with him in the bar. Next he ordered a cab to Ranieri's (had he reserved by cable, she wondered?), which is an old-fashioned Roman restaurant where the carpets sink deeply in and the soft chandeliers swing low and the waiters murmur in French, bending at Monsieur's elbow, and he said (this being the kind of place his voice was best adapted to), "Gordon feels some income should be set up from the land for you. It is on his conscience because you may remember that some of your parents' legacy went into the original pur-chase; it was not noted in the deed of sale and indeed could not be; this is only a matter of personal conscience, as I'm sure you must appreciate correctly."

She was wearing a stern black suit and noticed, in a discreet but enormous mirror in a heavy frame, how pale she looked, though perhaps it was only the lighting, how subdued she sat, almost clipped out with scissors. She watched the neat insertion of his pointed spoon in the melon he had discov-ered on the menu and was now enjoying, and longed to say, "But you and Gordon were directors in that trust company that failed in the crash—I heard all about it—and somehow you never got precisely ruined, though of course ruined was the word you used for yourself but it was never visible." But she did not. She wondered if it was not too easy to suspect dishonesty where people are really only loyally seconding one another's ideas, echoing one another's politics and views of humanity which sound despicable, only to prove their com-mon ground of affection. Then she said, "I think the trouble with all these messages, these visitors and plans and letters and schemes, is that everyone is looking at things only as Gor-don sees them." His glance was sheer genius. "Oh, not at all, my dear. If it's what you feel, why that's unfortunate, but certainly in Mrs. Herbert's—Ruth's—view and my own, you and Gordon were simply too dissimilar to manage a happy arrangement." Dissimilar! She tried desperately to keep the word from clanging in her head. Had Gordon really poisoned the dog, as she suspected? she wanted to ask, for certainly the vet had told her so, clear and round, and he had said, if you think I will stoop to so much as answer this degrading nonsense. The dog was not poisoned, they are either confused or are deliberately telling you something to cover some mistake on their own part. There was, of course, another word like dissimilar: incompatible. "I have often wondered, however, granting the fact that no one can really say what causes such desperate conditions in a marriage that divorce is the only way out—I have often wondered what I did to turn all Gordon's friends against me. Why did you hate me so much?"

"It looked that way to you, did it?" He took a small sip of French wine. "I can see how it might. We all felt, you see —protective of Gordon. He has meant, through the years, so much." "So you wanted him back to yourselves?" "There was some sort of reaction." "There certainly was," Martha agreed. "I wanted to love you," she added. "I'm sure we made it difficult for you," he admitted. "I, for one, was somewhat conscious of it at the time. I tried, in some way, do you remember, to make amends." "I remember," she said, "that you took me down to see the fish pond." "So I did." He smiled. "And wasn't that pleasant for you?" "Yes," she said, "but it was scarcely more than decent. You never said anything to let me know you saw the difficulties I was half drowning in, with everyone else." "Well, but wouldn't that have been disloyal to Gordon?"

There was the thin sound of his spoon touching down on the plate and she said, "I suppose now that this bit of land is turning out to have some value I have not heard about."

"There is no attempt afoot to give you less than every cent that could possibly be due you."

"I did not mean there was," she said. Good God! she thought, how old he makes me feel. "I only meant that I have a reasonable interest in business."

"Well, then, you may as well know that the area is being opened up as suburban property—quite in the junior executive line; maybe you aren't familiar with the term."

"Oh, yes."

"Has someone else got to you then?"

"Oh, no, it's only that I guessed that I was being treated rather well for there not to be better than average sums involved." I shouldn't have said that, she thought. Of course, I make them angry; they don't like it, of course, they don't like it, and why do I do it? "Listen," she said intensely, "I'm sorry. I never meant to—"

"You must remember, my dear, that Gordon only got interested in finance through having to manage property you were left with. He saw what a sorry mess things were in where you and your sister were concerned and he so interested himself that he could now earn fifty thousand a year as a market analyst, that is, if he cared to. Your sister Annette says she never goes to bed without thanking God for Gordon Ingram."

In Martha's view her sister Annette was a near illiterate who would have gone on comparing prices of soap powders if she had a million dollars. She felt a blind white tumult stir inside, the intellectual frustration, of always being—she could only think deliberately, but how was one to know it was—misunderstood.

"I think it's wonderful how well he manages money, but that wasn't the point of what I was saying."

"Why don't we take our coffee elsewhere, if you're agreeable." In the carrozza he hailed for them in the narrow empty street, he conversed intelligently about the city, telling her in the course of some chance recollection several things she didn't know. And in the carrozza she experienced the tug of motion as one doesn't in a car, and the easy sway of the wheels, the creak of leather. He handed her down in a comfortable way. "Well, and what a pleasant thing to do!" Moving her toward a quiet café, "Shall we just have some coffee here?"

How charming they would all be, she thought, if only one could utterly surrender the right ever to disagree with them. She wished she could have sat in the handsome bar, all white rococo and gilt, and bring him out on some old story or other: reminiscence, that was what they loved, but she had desperately to try once more, for the bar was teeming with Italians: he was all she had of America here.

"I only wish that someone would admit that a man can be as wonderful as a saint to everyone in the world, but behave like a tyrant to one person."

He gave her a quiet grey look. "I cannot see anything tyrannical about Gordon wishing you to have your share of this property settlement."

"I only want to be forgotten," she said.

"Surely a rather singular wish."

It was right there on the table that she signed it. She remembered the crash of the gun down by the stream's edge. The ink flowed easily from the pen. It was only, she thought, a question of money. His hands in receiving documents were extremely adept.

"There will of course be other papers," he said. "They will reach you through the mail."

8

AND ALL THIS time in the thick or cutting weather of that winter she had been blown adrift about the city, usually going to put in a social appearance somewhere that the Hartwells didn't have time for, and when George saw her as he did see her once, driving by in his little car—she was on the Veneto—it gave him the odd sensation that all was not well. As if to confirm it she stopped still and laughed. The sight was pleasant, but the idea worrying; she had told him something even back that far about the Boston lawyer, whom he had actually seen her having cocktails with at the Flora, but, in the days that followed the laugh, he fell to wondering what his responsibility was. He recalled the sudden break in her walking there by the high wall just past the embassy, and the giant twin baroque cupids playing with a basin into which a fountain gently spilled, and thought that if Martha was in New York she would be swelling some psychiatrist's income by now, a thing he withdrew himself from even considering. He sat meditating evenings before a Florentine fireplace covered with Della Robbia cherubs, a full-length angel or two which he called his dancing girls, and with sighs of joy sank his stone-chilled feet deeply into hot water poured into a copper pot which his wife had bought from a peasant in the Abruzzo and which was someday going to be filled to abundance with bronze chrysanthemums in some white American home among the flaming autumn hills, but right now . . . she poured another boiling kettle in. "I wish to heaven you would find out definitely once and for all that of course she does have a lover. Or even two or three. Or decide that you want her yourself. Just tell me please, so I don't have to overhear it at the opera." "It's too hot," he protested for the third time. "You don't have to scald me. And anyway, I hope she does have somebody if he's the right sort. I just don't want her jumping out of a top window of the Colosseum, or off St. Peter's balcony or even her own terrace, for Christ's sake. You know about the suicide we had in Germany." "But why should she—?" "I don't know, I can't tell. It's just a feeling I have."

An old bathrobe he had bought in Missouri to take with him to Oxford where it had been his heart's comfort and one sure joy was hugged round his shoulders, and cupids, winged but bodiless, alternating with rich purple clusters of grapes and gently prancing unicorns, looked down upon him from the low, beamed Rinascimento ceiling, justly famed. Their palazzo was listed in guidebooks and it seemed a shame that they could never remember once having been warm in it. His wife was bundled up in sweaters and an old ski jacket; she even sometimes wore gloves indoors in the damper weather, and George himself was turning into an alcoholic just from trying to get enough whiskey in himself to keep out the vicious mists. A glass of bourbon sat beside him on the marble floor.

9

WHAT GEORGE HARTWELL now recognized that in those days he must have been fighting off was no more than what Martha herself had spent so long fighting off—that around one corner he was going to run headlong into Jim Wilbourne. He told himself he was afraid she had got mixed up with an Italian, though it might not in the long run perhaps mean very much—Italians generally left the American women they made love to, or so ran the prevailing superstition. The question of her divorce would have been in it from the first, thus practically guaranteeing she would get hurt. But then he worried too that it might be the English or the Americans, whom one counted on to really mean it, or so the legends went, and hence might get lulled into trusting too implicitly for anything. That might be more damaging in the long run.

"Who is it?" he came right out at lunch once and asked her. "Who is it, Martha?" But as he had not led up to this demand in any way, she assumed, quite naturally, that he was referring to somebody who had just passed their table and told him a name they both knew of a girl from Siena who used to work at the consulate but had had to return home to live with her aunt, but what was she now doing back in Rome. He said he didn't know.

The day was misty and the light blurred, lavender and close all day, dim as the smoke from the chestnut braziers, on the branched trees of the Villa Borghese where the gravel smashed damply under the thin soles of Roman shoes. The crowds flowed out, engulfing and persistent; a passing tram blocked out whatever one might have thought one saw. Hartwell gave up worrying; suicide seemed out—she looked invariably blooming. He had enough to bother him, what with new government directives which occasioned the reorganization of the entire staff (by a miracle he stabilized himself, Martha and one or two others he wanted to keep upon the shaky scaffolding until it quieted down—these earth tremors left everybody panting). Then there was the thing of the ambassador's getting poison off the ceiling paint—*Ceiling paint?* No Roman ever believed this, just as no American ever doubted it. Solemn assurances eventually were rendered by a U.S. medical staff that the thing had actually taken place. The Romans howled. You could judge how close you came to being permanent here by how much you doubted it.

Martha forgot to come one evening and help Grace Hartwell out with the Coggins', who had to be invited somewhere occasionally; they had to be acknowledged or clamours went up from their admirers. George made a monstrous effort and kept them out of the festival plans now being talked in reference to Spoleto where no one who remotely resembled them would be included, a thing they would never have understood. Martha rang up late, excusing herself on the grounds of some trouble with her maid. Maid trouble was always a standard excuse among Americans, and though it seemed almost Italian to lie to close friends, Grace Hartwell accepted it not to risk upsetting George.

"You abandoned me, just the same," she told Martha. "And that girl now is into some trouble over her work permit."

"She never had one at all," said Martha, who knew the straight of the story. "She agreed to help at the shop or be allowed to hang around just to learn Italian. She wanted experience instead of money."

"I don't know how much experience she got," said Grace, "or for that matter had already, but the proprietor had a fight with his relatives who are all out of work and say she's taking food out of their mouths and now she's been reported somewhere. The Coggins' seem to have got her out of it just by having so many friends at the Istituto Musicale di Roma, but now she's out of work."

"Unemployment is on the rise," said Martha flippantly, making Grace cross.

"There is so little for young people in Rome," said Grace, "they don't know what to do with her. It seems all the young Italians—"

"They can always send her back," said Martha.

But seeing that she had made Grace Hartwell angry, an almost impossible feat, she invited Grace and Dorothy Coggins to tea at Babbington's on the Piazza di Spagna. They were joined by

Rita Wilbourne, who had been at Grace's. Dorothy Coggins said she used to come here often before Jean left the glove shop which was right across the street. Grace Hartwell gave full attention to Rita, who always looked tentative in Italy, rather like an ailing bird, but who, at least today, was subdued in what she wore, a navy dress and dark beret. Grace seemed to feel that given enough scones to eat she might actually be fixed in place in some way so far lacking. But Rita protested that she felt much better since some friends took her up to Switzerland, a civilized country.

Martha, who liked Grace and often used to confide in her, now felt herself so utterly bored she wondered if she could make it through to a second cup of tea, when suddenly, as if a signal had been given, they all found themselves deeply involved in talking about a new couple who had just come out from the States. They were soon examining these people in about every verbal way that exists, briskly, amiably, with enormous, almost profound curiosity, not at all unkindly, hoping for the best and not missing anything, from the two children's immediate cleverness with the language (they reminded Grace of *English* children. "Oh, yes, you're right," Martha enthusiastically agreed. "It's their *socks*!") to the woman's new U.S. clothes and probable family background, somewhat superior, they thought, to the husband's, who had worn a huge Western hat (he taught in Texas) down the Via Nazionale and was trailed around by knots of people, some of whom believed him to be a famous movie director. This was really rather funny, when one considered that he was actually an authority on Virgil, though Grace said she did not know which was funnier, to consider an authority on Virgil in a cowboy hat on the Via Nazionale, or in Texas in any sort of headgear, and Dorothy Coggins said that Texas was getting way way up, culturally speaking; that remark only proved what an ancient Roman Grace was getting to be. And Rita said that Jim loathed Italian hats and would not have one. Martha did not recall he ever had a hat at all.

"Richard doesn't mind anything Italian," said Dorothy. "He's simply gone on the place. Jean has a modelling job now," she told Martha. "I thought at first I'd have to arrange for her to go home; she was running around too much, meeting too many of these boys who just hang around places. I don't know what they do. I can never understand. Their families are well off, I suppose, but still I— You got it for her, didn't you, Martha?" "Why, no," said Martha, "I don't think so." "She mentioned you to that designer—what's her name?—Rossi. The little elegant one on the Via Boncompagni, and you were just the right one for her to know. She had to lose fifteen pounds —she ate nothing but salami for ten days. They were to call you up and she was sure—" "They didn't, but it's all right." "She thinks you got it for her." "Well, I—" Martha suddenly knew nothing to say. It looked clever of Jean to go to that one shop and mention her; but it had been perhaps merely luck. It was the sort of haphazard luck the girl had. "She admires you so," said Dorothy Coggins, with housewifely openness. "She always did. It really is amazing," she added. "I can't see anything amazing about it," said Grace, with her generous laugh. They had all paused and were looking, with more admiration than not, at Martha, and Rita said, "What a lovely pin—I must borrow it sometime to copy it." It was something she had had forever. She felt silent and alone in a certain shared secrecy with the pin—its quiet upcurving taste enclosing amethysts— and though she said she would lend it to Rita sometime she had no intention of doing so.

The women sat together, in their best suits and hats, shoes damp from the streets, handbags beside them, at a corner table while the early dusk came on and the soupy traffic thickened outside. The ceiling was low, dark and beamed in the English manner; the place a favorite haunt of the quieter English colony. The Brownings might have just gone out. Yet under the distant assurance of even that name lurked some grisly Renaissance tale. Martha found her gloves and asked for the check.

Afterwards, she drove with Grace to carry Dorothy Coggins up the Gianicolo to the American Academy to meet her husband. They left Rita to catch a cab home. "It will be a blessing," said Dorothy as Grace fended through traffic, "if she has another baby as soon as she can; she's not going to be happy until she does. I know that from my own experience."

"Well, if she could just—" Grace Hartwell broke off, fighting traffic for dear life. She and Martha were quite solidified in not wanting to hear just what Dorothy's experience had been.

When she dropped Dorothy off, she drove around for a time

among the quiet streets above the city, also above the weather, for up here it seemed clear and cold and glimpses of the city showed below them framed in a long reach of purple cloud.

"You didn't mind my bringing Rita?" she asked Martha.

"No," said Martha, and then she said, "I see a lot of Jim, you know."

"I thought something like that, this afternoon, I don't know why. I really cannot think why. I think it was when she asked you for that pin. Isn't that amazing? Well, I won't tell George."

"I know you won't," said Martha.

"I just hate seeing nice people get hurt," said Grace, somewhat shyly. She and George had fallen in love at a college dance. They had never, they did not need to tell you, loved anybody else but one another.

"I don't know who is supposed to be nice people," said Martha, with a little laugh.

Grace did not answer and Martha added, "I don't want, I honestly do not want to embarrass George in any way."

"Why, it's possible he won't ever hear about it at all. Unless everybody does. Or unless the marriage breaks up or something. Is that what you want to happen?"

Martha fell completely silent. This was the trouble with the run of women, considered as a tribe, with their husbands—George, Jim, and Richard—to talk about and other families to analyze. How they assembled all those alert, kind-tongued comparisons! How instantly they got through an enormous pot of tea and a platter of pastries! How they went right straight to the point, or what they considered to be the only point possible. To Martha it was not the point at all. The fact of her trusting Grace was the more remarkable in that she understood, even in advance, that they would from now on in some way be foreign to one another.

"I don't know that I want anything to happen," said Martha.

"Rita came over," said Grace, "to talk about—"

"Oh do stop it," said Martha, laughing, but somewhat put out as well. "You're trying to say it wasn't about me."

"You know, I honestly feel tired of it already," Grace said. She paused. "I'll think of it all as we were, as you and George and I always have been, all these years. I'm going to do that," she reiterated, and began to accelerate. Pulling her chin up sharply, a habit for preserving her chin line, and gripping the wheel with hands in worn pigskin gloves, she went swinging and swirling down the Gianicolo, past the high balustraded walls of those tall terra-cotta villas. She remained firm and skillful—a safe driver—her reddish-brown hair, streaked with grey, drawn up rather too tall from her wide freckled brow so forthrightly furrowed (like many people with warm, expressive faces, the thin skin texture of nice women, she was prematurely lined). But now, Martha noticed, her face looked strained as well.

"Confidences are a burden, I know," said Martha. "I'm sorry, Grace."

"It isn't keeping secrets I mind. You know that. No, it isn't that at all."

Martha did not ask her to define things further, for to en-counter love of the innocent, protective sort which George and Grace Hartwell offered her and which she had in the past found so necessary and comforting seemed to her now some-what like a risk, certainly an embarrassment, almost a sort of doom. Grace did not press any further observations upon her, did not kiss her when she was ready to get out of the car. She waved and smiled—there was something touching about it, a sort of gallantry, and Martha was sensitive to the exaggeration, the hint of selfishness, which this reaction contained. She did not blame Grace, but she read her accurately. She was protec-tive of her husband, the sensitive area was here, and here also was written plainly that Martha was more of a help to George Hartwell than she herself had known. Somehow she thinks now I'm in bad faith and she in good, Martha saw. Does she think I can live for George Hartwell?

She took off her damp topcoat and the hat with which she had honored the tea and saw on the telephone pad a note say-ing that Signor Wilbourne had called.

"MARTHA?"

Whether at home or in the office, at whatever time of day, the name, her own, coming at her with the curious, semi-hoarse catch in it, seemed to fall through her hearing and onward, entering deep spaces within her. She listened as though she had never heard it before, and almost at times forgot to answer. Hurried, he was generally going on anyway to what he meant to tell her, the clatter of some bar in the background, he would be shifting whatever clutch of books or briefcase he had with him to unfold a scrap of paper and read an address. Then she would write it down. There were streets she'd never heard of, areas she did not know existed, bare-swept rooms at the tops of narrow stairs, the murmur of apartment life from some other floor or some distance back of this one, the sounds of the street. The wires of small electric stoves glowed across the dim twilights of these rooms, and if she reached them first, she would sit quietly waiting for him to come, drawing the heater close to warm her damp feet, wearing one of the plain tweed suits she wore to work, her scarf and coat hung up, her face bent seriously forward. She thought of nothing, nothing at all.

She would hear his footsteps on the stair striking, as his voice on the phone did, directly against her hearing, but when the door opened she would scarcely look up, if at all, and he on his part gave her scarcely more than a passing glance, turning almost at once to put his coat up. Yet the confrontation, as brief as that, was absolute and profound. It was far more ancient than Rome.

"Is it okay here? Is it all right?" To a listener, he might have been a landlord speaking. She sat with her hands quietly placed beside her. "It's like the others. There's nothing to say about it, is there?" "Well, it's never warm enough. Someday we'll . . ." "Do what?" "I don't know. Go right into the Excelsior, I guess. Say to hell with it." "But I like it here." "You're a romana."

His cheek, the high bone that crossed in a straight, horizontal line, pressed coldly against her own; it was damp from the outside air. His hands warmed momentarily beneath her jacket. His quick remarks, murmured at her, blurred off into her hearing—stones thrown in the sea. In the long upswing of her breath she forgot to answer, and tumbled back easily with him against the bed's length. "God, there's never enough time!" "Forget it." "Yes . . . I will . . . yes. . . ."

In these beginnings, she often marvelled to know if she was being made love to or softly mauled by a panther, and that marvelling itself could dwindle, vanishing into the twin bars of the electric fire, or the flicker of a white shirt upon a chair. She could reach the point of wondering at nothing.

Yet something—some word from without them both did come to her—either then or in recollection of those little widely spaced-out little rooms hidden among the crooked roofs of Rome, where the mists curled by, and thought stood still and useless, desiccated, crumbling, and perishing; it was only a phrase: Run slowly, slowly, horses of the night. It fell through her consciousness as her own name had done, catching fire, mounting to incandescence, vanishing in a slow vast cloudy image silently among the grey skies.

Sometimes he gave her coarse Italian brandy to drink out of a bottle he might have found time to stop in a bar and buy; and she sometimes had thought of stuffing bread and cheese in her bag, but they were mainly almost without civility—there was never any glass for the brandy or any knife for the cheese, and if anyone had hung a picture or brought in a flower or two their consciousness of one another might have received, if not a killing blow, at least a heavy abrasion.

She asked him once why he did not simply come to her, but there was something about Rome he instinctively knew from the start and chose to sidestep. Ravenous for gossip, the Romans looked for it in certain chosen hunting fields—nothing would induce them to rummage around in the poorer quarters of Trastevere or wonder what went on out near San Lorenzo. And anyway—

And anyway, she understood. It was merely a question, perhaps, of furniture. The time or two he did stop by her place, ringing her up from a tobacco shop or restaurant nearby, they almost always disagreed about something. Disagreed was not quite the word; it was a surprise to her that she still found him, after everything that went on, somewhat difficult to talk to. She remembered the times in Venice and later in Rome that she had sparred with him, fighting at something intractable in his nature, and the thought of getting into that sort of thing any more made her draw back. She just didn't want to. Perhaps it was a surprise to him that she never asked him anything any more; she never tried to track him down. Did he miss that or didn't he? Did he ask himself? And if he had would he have known what to answer? He was busy—that was one thing, of course. Committees had been set up—there was a certain modest stir about economic planning on certain American lines proceeding at a level far below the top governmental rank, only in educational circles, but still— He thought of plunging off into field work, studying possibilities of industry in the south of Italy. "Then you might never come back," said Martha. "You mean to Rome?" "Oh, no, I meant—it's a separate world." She did not think he would ever do it. "You don't think I'll ever do it, do you?" She seemed even to herself to have drifted away for a time, and finally murmured or thought she had said, "I don't know." She was tired herself, with mimeograph ink on her hands and a whole new library list to set up, and her brain gone numb at so much bandying about of phrases like "the American image abroad." "What did you say?" he asked her. "I said I don't know." She rallied. "It's a worthwhile project, certainly." "Thank you, Mrs. Ingram." His tone stung her; she glanced up and tears came to her eyes. "I'm sorry," he said, with a certain stubborn slant on the words.

He had been leaning against her mantelpiece talking down to where she sat in the depths of a wing chair, sometimes toying with objects—small statuary, glass clusters and paperweights —distributed on the marble surface. When he pulled her up against him by way of breaking off a conversation that had come to nothing, his elbow struck a china image to the floor. The apartment was rented furnished, only half such things were hers and this was not. He helped her clean the fragments and must have said a dozen times how much he regretted it, asking too, "What was it?" "A little saint, or maybe goddess . . . I don't know." "If you don't know, then maybe it wasn't so good, after all." She smiled at the compliment. "I wish we were back in some starved little room," she said, "where nothing can get broken." "So do I," he agreed and left soon after.

Reflecting, she was not long in coming upon the truth the little rooms made plain: that they had struck a bargain that lay deeply below the level of ordinary speech; in fact, that in rising toward realization in the world where things were said, it only ran terrible risks of crippling and loss.

And yet one afternoon when the rain stopped and there was even a red streak of late sun in the clear simple street below, she felt gentle and happy and asked him to walk down in the street for just a little way. And then when he consented a dog trotted up and put its nose in her palm; it would have laid all of life at her feet like a bone. A cat purred near the open furnace of a pizzeria, which burned like a deep-set eye of fire in the stony non-colour of a winter day, and a child ran out with bare arms into the cold, its mother following after, shouting "Pino! Pino!" and holding up a little coat. When they left the pizzeria, he lit a cigarette leaning against a damp wall and said, All right, all right, if she wanted to they would go away for the weekend somewhere. She looked up startled and gratified, as though at an unexpected gift. It had been somewhat offhandedly thrust at her and yet its true substance was with it.

THEY DROVE to the sea in what started out to be fine weather but thickened over damply. Nevertheless, he had been full of a run of recklessly funny talk and stories ever since he got off the tram and crossed the sunlit street to meet her, way out near the Laterano, and the mood persisted. The feeling between them was, though nobody had mentioned it, that they would never be back at all. They took turns driving.

Martha admired the artichoke fields warm in the new sun and recalled a peasant who had ploughed up a whole Aphrodite in his field and didn't know what to do with her, for if he told anybody his little farm would be made an archeological area; he wouldn't get to raise any more artichokes for a decade or two. So he and his family kept hiding the statue and every now and then someone would be smuggled in to have a go at wondering how much could be got for her in devious ways and the whole thing went on for a year or so, but in the end the farmer buried her again and let her rest in peace; he could never decide whom he could trust, for everybody had a different theory, told a different story, and offered him a different sum. He then went back to raising artichokes. "So every field I see I think of Aphrodite under it," said Martha. This was not true, but she did think of it now—the small compact mindless lovely head, the blank blind exalted eyes, deep in the dark earth. "Imagine finding Aphrodite and not knowing what to do with her," he said. He began to cough.

The racking of this particular cough had gone on for weeks now. He said he would never understand Martha for never being sick. The Wilbournes were always in the thick of illnesses; there had not only been Rita's miscarriage, which had afflicted him with a tenacious sort of despair, a sense of waste and reasonlessness, the worse for being almost totally abstract. What kind of home could be had in this city, in this entire country? (Here the sun, distinctly weakening, had about faded out; he seemed to be grasping for it.) The Italians didn't even have a word for home. Casa. It was where you hung your hat, and slept, and froze, and tried to keep from dying. Oh, Lord, thought Martha, getting weary of him. To her, Rome was a magnificent city in any weather and she moved in it easily with friends in four languages at least—she had not been Gordon Ingram's student for nothing. The city's elegant, bitter surfaces were hers naturally, as a result of his taste and judgment; and there were people about who knew this, in their own way of knowing, from the instant she stepped across the threshold of a salotto. She had luck, as well. She rented from a contessa in Padova, who counted her a friend; if she told all this to Jim Wilbourne he would class her with the Coggins' who had got invited to a vendemmia in Frascati a short time after they arrived.

At the sea they sat before a rough fire in the albergo (there were no other guests) and her mind wheeled slowly round him like a gull. It was going to dawn on him some-day, she thought, how well she got along, how easily she got things, not the sort of things the Coggins' got which nobody wanted, but the sort of things one coveted. She started out of this, startling herself; this was wrong, all wrong—he was better than that. He was self-amused, even in his furies, and never lost the thread of reason (this being one reason Italians preyed on him; the reason in a reasonless quarrel delighted them, they would probably have gone on fighting with him for a generation or so, if he had remained, for when the maid stole the case of economics texts on loan from the States and was forced to admit it, she returned to him books in the same case, weighed within an etto of the original weight, the books even being in English and some, she pointed out, having been printed in the States: they were mainly mystery novels, but included a leather-bound history of World War I dedicated to the Veterans of Foreign Wars—he found this appropriate). And even he would admit that what he needed most for his nerves in a country so uncivilized was an evening at the bowling alley, a stroll through a drugstore, a ride down the turnpike, an evening at the neighborhood movie house. These things were not as much a myth to Martha as might be thought to look at her, in her classic Roman greys and black, for Woolworth's and Radio City had once stabilized her more than human voices. He believed this, and the rain sprang up off the sea, lashing in ropes against the tall windows. Her heart sank. "It's so nice here in summer," she said faintly. His face had turned silent; in Italy he had acquired a touch of despair that she felt sorry for. He could make her feel responsible for the weather.

She never knew if he heard her at all. A shift of wind off the sea had blown one of the glass doors wide, and a maid rushed through to close it, but they scarcely noticed, if at all. They had reached the shore, an extremity of sorts, and had already discovered themselves on the other side of a wall, shut, enclosed, in the garden that everyone knows is there, where even the flowers are carnivorous and stir to avid life at the first footfall. He had caught her hand, near the cup, among the silver. She sat with her face half-turned aside, until her hand and arm reddened from the fire. She did not remember leaving the table and going upstairs.

The room where they stood for a time, clinging together a step from the closed door, was unlighted, dark, though on this troubled coast it seemed a darkness prepared and waiting with something like self-knowledge, to be discovered, mapped, explored, claimed, possessed, and changed for good, no inch of it left innocent of them, nothing she had ever felt to be alive not met and dealt with. They were radical and unhurried as if under imperial orders, and it seemed no one night could contain them; yet it managed to. As she fell asleep she heard the rain stop; it had outdistanced them by a little, as though some sort of race had been going quietly on.

The next morning there was a thin light on the sea which hung leaden and waveless below their windows, its breast burnishing slightly, convexly meeting the fall of the light, like a shield. She saw a bird on the windowsill outside. Its feathers blew, ruffling in the wind, and once it shifted and looked in for a moment; she saw the tiny darting gleam of its regard.

The silver light held through the whole day. They drove far up the coast toward Pisa and she feared for a moment toward midday, voicelessly without decision as they seemed to be, they would come full circle at Genoa, where she had first seen him, in which case the sky would fall in broken masses of grey light. But the way is longer than it might be thought to be, and the slowly unwinding journey seemed perpetual, the fields and villages strict and sharply drawn with winter, the coast precipitous and wild, vanishing only to reappear; and their own speed on nearly deserted roads was deceptive—no matter what the speedometer said, they seemed adrift. They came on a fishing village and stayed there; she could never remember the name of it, but perhaps she never knew.

Where they were drifting, however, was not toward Genoa and the sky falling, nor to any mythical kingdom, but like thousands of others before and after them, it was only toward Sunday afternoon. He was sitting putting on his shoe in the pensione when the shoelace suddenly snapped in his narrow fingers, jarring him into a tension that had seemed to be gone forever; if there was anything he immediately returned himself to, after the ravishment of strange compelling voyages, it was order; he was wrenched by broken shoelaces, and it was to that slight thing she traced what he said when they were leaving: "It disturbs me to think I'm the one you aren't going to forget —yet it's true, I know it is."

His arms were around her; he was human and gentle; but she filled up instantly with panic—it was time he had let in on them, in one phrase. Had he meant to be so drastic as that? But it had always been there, she reasoned desperately, and though watching the abyss open without alarm is always something of a strain, she tried to manage it. Yet going down the stair she felt numb and scraped her wrist against a rough wall surface. Reaching the car ahead of him, she sat, looking at the surface of the harshly rubbed skin, which had shaved up in places like thinly rolled trimming of chalk, and the flecking of red beneath, the wonder of having blood at all at a moment when her ample, somewhat slow, slightly baroque body had just come to rest as finally as stone.

Miles later on the way back to Rome she asked him, "What about you? Are you going to forget it?" He glanced at her at once. "No." And repeated it: "No."

On that she would be able to stay permanently, she believed; it was her raft on the long, always outflowing tide of things, and once back in Rome could linger, not being obliged to be anywhere, in the bare strict narrow rented room, and ride the wake of his footsteps hurrying down toward the empty street, but one day she discovered on walking home alone that the rain had stopped for once, and travelling a broad street—Via

Cola di Rienzo—that rose toward a high bridge above the Tiber, the sky grew grey and broad and flashed with light into which the tramontana came bitterly streaming, drawing even the wettest and deadest leaves up into it, and the whole yawning city beneath was resonant with air like wind entering an enormous bell. This is the center of the world, she thought, this city, with a certain pride, almost like a native might, or should have.

And passing through the post office, far across the gigantic enclosed hall of a thousand rendezvous, and small disbursements for postal money orders and electric bills and letters sent pòsta aerea to catch the urgent plane and the smell of ink and blotted bureaucratic forms and contraband cigarettes, she saw Gordon Ingram leaning on a heavy mahogany cane, the sort of thing he would either bring to Europe with him or find for himself the instant he arrived. His back was toward her, that heavy-shouldered bulk, and he was leaning down to write on a sheet of paper, but even while she watched, something must have gone wrong with the pen for he shook it twice, then threw it aside and walked away. The letter fluttered to the ground and she soon went there and picked it up but by that time a heel or two had marked it in walking past.

Yet she made out clearly, in handsome script, the best Italian: "Sebbene (whereas) . . . tu m'abbia accusato di ció che ti piace chiamare inumanitá (you have accused me of what it gives you satisfaction to call inhumanity, you must realize if you have any mentality at all, that this man in spite of his youth and attractiveness is far less human than anyone of my generation could possibly be, without the least doubt. He takes an interest in you because he must live in this way to know that he is alive at all, and his behavior is certain to disappoint a woman like yourself, such as I have taught you to be, in such a manner as to make you wish that it could never be said by anyone including yourself that you were ever in any contact with him. You know that whatever else you may say or think, I have never lied to you—this you cannot deny—I have never once lied to you, whereas you have done nothing but pride yourself on your continual lying as though it were some sort of accomplishment, an art you had mastered so well you could use it carelessly [pensarci])—"

She went home holding the letter in one hand and reached the apartment with the heel of one shoe in the other, limping, because she had twisted the heel off in the irregular paving of the piazzetta below. She had spent the morning helping George Hartwell draw up a new lecture program, and there had been the interview with the priest who wanted to start a liberal newspaper in a small town near Bari. At last anyway, she had a letter, a direct word. She hung up her umbrella, coat and scarf, but dripped still, a limping trail into the big salotto, which, awaiting her in the quiet, looked utterly vacant, as disinhabited as if it were rented out afresh every three months, and she thought, He can't have written this; he is dead. Nobody is ever coming here again.

She fell face downward on the couch and slept, half-recalling and half-dreaming—which, she did not know, and why, she did not know, though the whole held no horror for her whatsoever any more than some familiar common object might—the story of a man who shot and wounded a she-wolf on his way home through the woods at twilight, and coming home, found his wife dead on the couch, a trail of blood leading inward from the door. She was awakened by a banging shutter.

She went out to the terrace and saw that the clouds had cleared before the wind and were racing in long streamers like swift ships, and that a moon, so deeply cold it would always do to think of whenever cold was mentioned, raced without motion. The city beneath it lay like a waste, mysterious, empty discovery, cold and vaulted beneath it, channelling the wind. It came to her for the first time to wonder, standing out on her empty, winter-disarrayed terrace, if a cold like that might not be life's truest definition, since there was so much of it.

And certain cold images of herself were breaking in upon her now, as though she had waked up in a thunder-ridden night and had seen an image of herself in the mirror, an image that in the jagged and sudden flash seemed to leap unnaturally close. What am I doing? Am I asleep sitting straight up? A thousand times she had said to life in the person of a bird, brilliant and wise in the cage of a friend, or a passing dog (just as she had said to Gordon Ingram), I forgive you everything, please forgive me too, but getting no answer from either, her mind went on discriminating. She had not been

Gordon Ingram's student for nothing and she longed to discuss it with him:

If life unreels from an original intuition, what if that intuition was only accident, what if it was impulse, a blind leap in the dark? An accident must be capable of being either a mistake or a stroke of luck, depending on what it is in relation to whom it happens to. So what do you think of this one, since you were the victim of it? Before you are quite gone, forever and ever, answer that for me at least.

But he was silent; Gordon Ingram was always silent.

Jim Wilbourne, however, told her many things about himself and (she had not been Gordon Ingram's student for nothing) none of them were supremely interesting things; she listened but was not utterly arrested, sometimes she half-listened. So he said, "Listen, Martha—listen," and she did stop the car (it being her turn to drive) coming back from the sea in the wet sea-heavy night, and she did try to listen, but traffic sprang up from everywhere—there was a confluence of roads and they all led to Rome, a glare and snarl and recklessness in the rain and dark, and someone shouted, "Stupida! Ma guarda! Guarda!" They poured past her like the hastening streams of the damned. She turned her face to him and he was talking, haltingly; he fell almost at once into platitudes and she wondered that the person whose face she encountered in the depths of her dreams had nothing more remarkable to say than this.

It did not escape him. He wanted to return everything to its original clear potential, to say that love, like life, is not remarkable, it is as common as bread; but every contact between the two of them was not common; it was remarkable; he was stopped before he started. "I'm listening; I'm listening," she said.

"It's the way you're listening."

"Don't let that matter to you," she said gently, kindly, for the shadow of some nature far beyond anything that had happened to her occasionally came to her. "I live in a mirror, at the bottom of a mirror somewhere."

"I think we both do; it's why we make love so well."

"There must be some way to stop it . . . to go back to where we might have been, to change. I always wanted to think of it differently. You remember I told you—"

"Yes, I remember." He urged her to drive on; the stop was dangerous, and presently said out of a long sequence of thought not told to her: "I simply can't ever believe there's any way back from anything." The force of the statement reached her, and she sensed it as distantly related to fury. He had made another jump, she realized, and now there was no turning back from that either. She had finally, like any other woman, to hold on the best way she could.

PART FOUR

12

COMING UP FROM the winter's recollections was what she and George Hartwell had to do every so often, to keep from drowning.

They were still on the terrace, and it was still Sunday morning, a healing timelessness of sun, though Hartwell went on gnawing at things he drew up out of fathomless reservoirs.

"And did you know," he was saying, "and did you fully realize, that Wilbourne got me to recommend him for an Italian government grant? He was going to study the economic picture south of Naples—the self-sacrificing servant of his times, he was harkening to duty's voice, he was going to leave the world a better place. Then what did he do but turn around and use that very grant as a lever to land his fat job back in the States."

"I'm not surprised," said Martha.

"But think what a hell of a position it put me in," Hartwell complained.

"Well, why did you let him talk you into it?"

"I thought you wanted him here. I thought you—"

"You thought *I* did it?"

"Something like that."

"It wasn't my idea," she said. "It was only that he did talk about it. I suppose, for a time, he considered staying on; he may even have believed that he meant to."

"But you said you weren't surprised."

"I wasn't . . . no . . . when he changed his mind, you mean? No, I wasn't too surprised. He only existed in relation to Gordon." There had always been the three of them, she thought; they had got stuck in the same frame forever.

"You mean destructively, of course," George Hartwell grumbled. He wondered what portion of the service they had reached in Mass, for though not a Catholic, he could hope that it was some deep and serious portion which could bite him up whole and take elaborate care to lift him back out of this pit he had blundered into on a fine Sunday morning.

"Did you see a little white-haired American lady on your way in?" Martha asked. "She was wearing a blue feather hat with a close veil over her hair and face, and a matching blue coat. She was bowlegged."

"Martha," said Hartwell, "aren't you going to spare me anything?"

He had begun to laugh. The whole thing was crazy, and probably had been all along. There wasn't any little old lady in blue. That was one certain fact. It was something to tie to. It enabled him to keep on laughing.

But there had been no laughter for him at all from any source on that February day back in the winter when the phone rang in his office and the voice said:

"This is Gordon Ingram, Mr. Hartwell; may I see you for a short time?"

"Where are you? Where are you?" was all he could think of to say; that and "Yes, Albergo Nazionale . . . of course, right away."

To his amazement a chill like a streak of ice had run down his spine; he went out in no time, breaking three appointments, grabbing a cab rather than take the car. Had the man already called his wife? Did she know? If so, she was likely driving blindly away somewhere, fodder for the next highway crash, or more deliberately, walking straight off into the Tiber would do just as well. He felt himself in the grip of fates and furies. In the dank, gusty February day, every step seemed bringing him nearer to the moment when statues speak and old loves appear.

Albergo Nazionale ran inward from a discreet doorway. The rugs were heavy and the décor firm. He searched among the sofas, the coffee tables, the écritoires, the alcoves, and bronze gods taming horses, for a shape ponderous and vast, a heavy thigh and a foot like an elephant's, and toward the last he was spinning like a top and had whirled upon the desk clerk, saying, "I'm looking for a Signor Ingram, un professore americano." But before he could get that out altogether, a hand touched his sleeve, and it was only Robert Inman, English and slight with sandy hair severely thinned, a classmate at Balliol. "I say, George, I've tried this makes three times to stop you, can't have changed so much as all that, you know." It could not have been Robert Inman who had telephoned, yet it had been. There was no Ingram on the register.

George Hartwell lived through a weak scotch in an armchair which threatened to swallow him whole, so small was he already in addition to feeling unreal, extended a dinner invitation, reviewed old histories, and afterwards, still in bleary weather, he walked up to the Campidoglio and stood looking through a heavy iron grill at something he had remembered wondering at before, back in his early days in Rome, the enormous hand from the statue of an emperor, standing among other shards in the barred recess. It was the dumbness of the detached gesture, there forever, suggesting not so much the body it was broken from as the sky it was lifted toward—one could be certain all through the centuries of similar skies. And with very little trouble he could find which step Gibbon was probably sitting on when he thought of *Decline and Fall*, but why do it unless perhaps he wanted to plant him down on the cold stone and catch pneumonia? And what indeed did he have to think of that was a match for Gibbon? He had to realize that in missing three appointments at least—two of which had to do with Italian cultural organizations interested in cooperating with American exchange programs—he had not done a good thing and that now he would have to dictate letters explaining that his son was in an accident and that he had thought for a time of flying home. Anyway, it was too late now.

He walked a bit and in passing near the post office saw the Wilbourne car, which was now fairly well known in Rome because so much had got stolen off it at one time or another, and certain quarrels had centered about it as it had once been jointly owned with another couple who complained that the Wilbournes (though the car was in their possession each time it was rifled) insisted that the expense of each misfortune be shared and shared alike. The body was a sort of dirty cream which Hartwell did not like, possibly because he did not like the Wilbournes, so why be called upon to stop and wait and why, when Jim Wilbourne appeared alone, ask him into the German beer hall nearby to share a stein and bend his ear about this odd thing—this misunderstood telephone call—as if by talking about it, it would be just odd and nothing more. And it seemed, too that only by talking could he say that from the first he had felt a concern for Martha, that she had stirred his sympathies from the first and he had learned her story a little at a time. This, too, he judged, was only a way of talking about people for once, instead of programs, programs—one built up a kind of ravenous appetite for individuals, for the old-time town life he, back in Missouri, had had once and called the past. He was winding up by saying, "Of course, don't repeat any of this to Martha," and there was a certain kind of pause hanging in the air and Jim Wilbourne carefully lit a cigarette behind his hands, worrying the match five or six times before it went out, and Hartwell thought, Oh God, Oh my God, having caught it on one side now I'm catching it on the other. I didn't know and yet I must have known.

He also thought: She is not this important to me, for all this about her to happen in one afternoon.

The trouble was she was neurotic. He had got dragged into her exile's paranoia as into a whirlpool. He foresaw the time when the only individuals would be neurotics. They were the only people who still had the nerve to demand an answer. He doubted if Jim Wilbourne was neurotic or that he would qualify as an individual, but he without a doubt had a sort of nerve balance that so obviously related him to women it seemed in the most general sense to be a sort of specific of blessing, like rain or sun, and why shouldn't she, in common with everybody else, have sun and rain? Who was to rule her out of golden shores? But with her there would always be more to it than that. Hartwell had blundered into this picture and now he wanted out.

"Did you ever know this guy?" Jim Wilbourne asked.

"Who, her husband? Well, only by reputation. He was at one time a leading American philosopher, or that was the direction he took early on. There were a couple of books . . . some theories of goodness, relating action to idealism . . . something like that. I remember one of them excited me. I read half of it standing in the college library one afternoon. . . ." One long-ago fall afternoon at Harvard. What reaches out of nowhere to touch and claim us? At a certain age, on a certain sort of afternoon, it may be any book we pick out from a shelf. "But perhaps you've read it too."

"Oh, Lord, no. I read practically nothing out of my field. I know that's not a good thing. It makes me laugh to think—I'd laid all sort of plans for doing some catching up on reading in Italy, after I learned the language, of course." He ended by coughing badly.

"You have learned it," Hartwell said, complimenting effort.

"Damned near killed me. It was a hell of a lot of work."

"You're telling me." Hartwell gulped his way into a second beer.

At the end of the encounter, catching a cab back to the office, refusing a ride, Hartwell felt outdone and silly. He envied Jim Wilbourne his cool intelligence, his quick judgments, his refusal to drink too much. I am the world's most useless citizen, he thought, an impractical cultural product, a detached hand reaching out, certainly changing nothing, not even touching anything. I am the emperor of Rome—I shall be stabbed in a corridor.

He longed for his own warm table and his wife's brown eyes, under whose regard he had so often reassembled his soul.

13

"THERE WAS always something rather depressing to me," said Hartwell with a laugh, "about all those damn ceramics. She kept on turning them out as if her life depended on it, and every one of them was in the worst possible taste."

"She knew the market back in the States," Martha said kindly. "I think that's what she had in mind."

"It's no wonder the Italians preyed on them. There was something about some chickens."

"The landlord's cousins kept some chickens out on the terrace next door, which was disturbing," Martha related, "and then when the Wilbournes got an order through the condominio to remove the chickens, they put some ducks there instead. The Wilbournes killed and ate the ducks. That was not as bad, however, as the fight over the electric bill."

"Oh, Lord," said Hartwell. "Even we had one of those. Martha, you never had a fight with Italians in your life."

"Never," said Martha, "but then I never tried setting up a business."

"I'm frankly glad as hell they're gone," said Hartwell. "If she started a business," he went on, unwisely, "it was probably out of desperation. She never seemed very well. If a vote of sympathy was taken, she'd get mine."

They had taken Rita Wilbourne for a drive one day to Tivoli —he and his wife—and had discovered near there in the low mountains a meadow full of flowers. It was as near a miracle as they could have hoped for, for it was misty when they left Rome and raining when they returned, but here she grew excited and jumped out of the car and walked out into the sun. Hartwell and his wife Grace sat in the car and spoke of her; she was unhappy, displaced in life, and alone far too much.

She had walked on away from them, here and there, in a brightly striped raincoat, always with her back to them, so that it was easy to imagine she might be crying. She talked about too many different things. Grace Hartwell worried about her. "Men like Jim Wilbourne are difficult," she said. "They're bitter, for one thing. I dislike bitter men—they are nothing but a drain." Yet when Rita came back to the car she had not been crying at all that Hartwell could see. She had found some bits of mosaic to copy in the bramble-covered remains of something—a villa, a bath, a tower—a whole acanthus leaf done in marble; her eyes were flat, bright, almost black; she was like a wound-up doll. She said it was marvellous to see the sun; she said it was wonderful to find a meadow full of flowers; she said it was quite unusual to find a whole acanthus leaf in marble. Who was she to demand George Hartwell's fealty? She was an American girl who happened to be walking across a meadow near Tivoli; she thought automatically of what she could do with what she found there. Martha Ingram hardly heard him when he spoke of sympathizing with her; she correctly judged that he was attacking Jim Wilbourne.

"What have you got against Jim? I doubt his being so bad as you think. There was nothing whatever bad about him, in an extraordinary sense."

"Yes," said Hartwell, "but who do you think is? Always excepting Gordon Ingram, of course?"

She fell silent; he wondered if he had got to her. Self-appointed and meddlesome, she could certainly call him, but he would stop her if it killed him, he thought, and it probably would. It was then she flashed at him with sudden definition, like an explosion of tinder:

"But I love them both. Haven't you understood that was the reason for it all?"

And the one to be stopped was himself.

He sat and mopped his brow as though in a period of truce, by himself, at least, much needed.

So they finally turned to business, having worn each other out.

The papers came out of her desk and he was leaning close to the shadow of the terrace wall to glance at some notes she could and did explain from memory—one thing clearly emerging from all this, like a negative from a slow developer, was how excellent she was; she seemed to have got up one morning and put her work on like a new dress. People were always calling George Hartwell up to tell him in assorted languages how lucky he was to have her, how lucky the United States of America was to have her, and in truth he himself had to marvel at how intelligently she could appear at varied distances in the conversation of salotti, terrazzi, giardini. He thought she would grow the torch of liberty out of her hand any day now, or at least show up photographed in some sleek expensive magazine, a model of the career woman abroad. She might even eclipse him: had he thought of that? He thought of it now, and decided that it did not supremely matter. In view of his long ambitious years, what a surprising thing, right now, to learn this about himself. Grace in leaving had been brimful of talk about their son, graduating at home, the solemn black mortarboard procession stretching and contracting, winding beneath green elms, every sun splotch another sort of hope and promise; the twin tears in Grace's eyes meant grandchildren beyond a doubt. Even when packing to leave, her son's future was infinitely exploding within her. She at some unknown hour had acquiesced to something: the shift in women's ambitions—true augur of the world. It was known to all, George realized, how much he drank, and Martha now was fetching him another, moving in and out among the azaleas. The truth at last emerges (he took the glass); but it had been there, relentlessly forming all this while.

"But what if the poor old bastard wants you, needs you? What if he dies?"

"I've been there already," she said, remembering how they had got the land away from her where it had all happened, she had signed the papers at Colonna's on the Piazza del Popolo and heard how the gun's roar faded along with the crash of the leaves.

"That isn't good enough!" said Hartwell, but her grey regard upon him was simply accidental, like meeting the eyes in a painting.

So there was no way around her.

I'll go myself, thought Hartwell, halfway down the scotch. In the name of humanity somebody had to, and it seemed, for one sustained, sustaining moment, that he actually would. He would go out of the apartment, reach his car, drive to the nearest telephone, call the airport for space on the first plane to New York. He could smell the seared asphalt of a New York summer, could see soot lingering on windowsills in the coarse sunlight, feel the lean of the cab turning into the hospital drive, every building in an island aspect, turning freely. An afternoon of dying. . . . A strange face in the door's dwindling square, rising above the muted murmur of a hospital at twilight: "I have come from your wife. You must understand she would come if she could, but she cannot. You must understand that she loves you, she said so: I heard her say so. She has been unavoidably detained . . . restrained? . . . stained? . . . mained?"

Then he knew it was time to go. He picked up all the documents, and put the last swallow down. The stairs were below. "Lunch with me this week." "Poor George, I think I upset you."

Poor George (he kept hearing it). Poor George, poor George, poor George. . . .

PART FIVE

14

B UT SHE had never said Poor Jim, though he too had gone down that very stairway as shaken as he had ever been in his life or ever would be. Their parting had torn at him desperately—she saw it; it was visible. And all this on the first day of sun.

"Love . . . love . . . love . . ." The word kept striking over and again like some gigantic showpiece of a clock promptly, voraciously at work to mark midnight, though actually it was noon. Returning to her was what he kept talking about. "Yes, yes, I'll always be here," she replied.

But his total motion once begun carried him rapidly down and away, cortile and fountain, stairway and hidden turning— the illusion was dropping off like a play he had been in, when, at the last flight's turning, he came to an abrupt halt and stood confronting someone who had just come through the open portone and was now looking about for mailboxes or buzzers, a fresh-faced young man whose clear candid eyes had not yet known what stamped a line between the brows.

He was wearing a tropical-weight suit which would have been too optimistic yesterday, but was exactly right today. Second year university, just arrived this morning, Jim Wilbourne thought, holding to the bannister. The young man seemed to have brought the sun. Jim Wilbourne, fresh air from the portone fanning his winter-pale cheek, thought for the first time in months of shirts that never got really white, and suits that got stained at the cleaners, of maids that stole not only books but rifled drawers for socks and handkerchiefs, of rooms that never got warm enough, and martinis that never got cold enough, and bills unfairly rendered, of the landlord's endless complaints and self-delighting rages, the doctor's prescriptions that never worked, the waste of life itself to say nothing of fine economic theory. He coughed—by now a habit—and saw, as if it belonged to someone else, his hand at rest on the stone bannister, the fingers stained from smoking, the cuff faintly grey, distinctly frayed. He felt battered, and shabby and old and here was someone to block not only the flow of his grief, but the motion of his salvaging operation, that was to say, the direction of his return; for every step now was bringing him physically closer to the land he had had to come abroad to discover, the land where things rest on solid ground and reasons may be had upon request and business is conducted in the expected manner. It all meant more than he had ever suspected it did.

"Could you possibly tell me—you are an American, aren't you—I don't speak much Italian, none at all, in fact—maybe you even know who I'm looking for—does a Mrs. Ingram live here?"

"She isn't here just now, at least I don't think so. Come to think of it, she's out of the city, at least for the time being."

He grasped at remembering how she felt about it—about these people who kept coming. She did not like it; he knew that much. But a boy like this one, anybody on earth would want to see a boy like that. He retreated from her particular complexities, the subtly ramified turnings were a sharp renewal of pain, the whats and whys he could of course if necessary deal in had always been basically outside his character, foreign to him, in the way a clear effective answer was not foreign whether it was true or not.

"Very odd. I got her address just before leaving from the States."

"When was that?"

"Oh—ten days ago."

"Well then that explains it. She's only left a couple of weeks back, or so I understand."

He ran on down the stairs. The boy fell in step with him and they went out together. The fountain at the corner played with the simple delight of a child. "You see, I have this package, rather valuable, I think. I would have telephoned, but didn't know the language well enough—the idea scared me off. Now I've gone and rented this car to go to Naples in, that scares me too, but I guess I'll make it. I just wonder what to do with the package."

"Mail it—why not? Care of the consulate. She works there. Your hotel would do it, insured, everything."

"Did you know her well then? You see, I'm her nephew, by marriage, that is. When I was a boy, younger than now at least, she used to—"

"Listen, it's too bad you and I can't have a coffee or something, but I happen to be going to catch a plane."

They shook hands and parted. He had begun to feel that another moment's delay would have mired him there forever, that he had snatched back to himself in a desperate motion his very life. Walking rapidly, he turned a corner.

He went into a bar for coffee and was standing, leaning his elbow on the smooth surface and stirring when somebody said, "Hi, Jim!" and he looked up and there was Jean Coggins. She was eating a croissant and gave him a big grin, whiskery with crumbs. He laughed in some way he had not laughed for a year. "What d'you know?" he asked her. As usual, she didn't know anything back of yesterday. "I was going down to Capri yesterday but it rained. It even hailed! And that storm last night! Now look at it. Wouldn't it kill you?" "It shouldn't be allowed." He paid for her bill and his and while doing so wondered if at any time during the entire year in Italy she had ever actually paid for anything. She skimmed along beside him for a little way, going on like a little talking dog; he soon lost track of what she was saying; she always bored him—everything named Coggins bored him, but she was at least fresh and pretty. Walking, he flung an arm around her. "I heard from Alfredo," she said, "you remember in Venice?" "I remember something about some stamps," he said. She giggled.

(Because that day they got back from the Lido, with Martha out somewhere, or so the proprietor said, and the weather getting dim, the air covered with a closing sort of brightness, she had tried to buy stamps at the desk, feeling herself all salty in all the turns of her head and creases of her arms, but the proprietor said he was out of stamps and Jim Wilbourne going up the stairway, heard her, though it was already a flight up and half across the lobby, and he said, "I've got some stamps, so just stop by number something and I'll let you have them," but when she went and scratched at the door and thought he said Come in he was asleep—she must have known they weren't talking entirely about stamps, yet when he woke up scarcely knowing in the air's heaviness, the languor the surf had brought on and the boatride back, the lingering salt smell, exactly where he was, and saw her, he could not remember who she was, but said at once, "My God you've got the whitest teeth I ever saw," and pulled her down under his arm. But she didn't want to. She liked fighting, scuffling, maybe it was what she felt like, maybe it was because he was what she told him right out, an Older Man, which made him laugh though on the street that day coming out of the bar, almost exactly a year later, it wouldn't have been funny one bit, not one little bit; and then she had bitten him too, which was what he got for mentioning her teeth. Otherwise, she might not have thought about it. He had cuffed her. "Let's stay on," she said, "I love this place. All across Italy and couldn't even swim. That old lake was slimy. Anyway I'm in love with the boy at the desk. Get them to let us stay." "You mean get rid of your parents," he said, "that's what you're driving at. Or is it her too?" "You mean Martha? Well, she makes me feel dumb, but she's okay." She came up on one elbow, a sudden inspiration. "She likes you." "Oh, stop it." "I know." "How do you know?" "I just know. I always know. I can tell." "But maybe it's you that I—" "But it's Alfredo that I—" "Alfredo? Who's that?" "You don't ever listen. The boy at the desk." She had squirmed out from under and run off, snatching up a whole block of stamps off the table—he actually had had some stamps, though this surprised him, and later in the pensione walking around restless as a big animal in the lowering weather, he had heard her talking, chattering away to the boy who kept the desk, sure enough, right halfway down on the service stairs, and the little maids stepped over and around them with a smile: "Ti voglio bene, non ti amo; dimmi, dimmi—Ti voglio bene." One way to learn the language. He thumbed an ancient German magazine, restless in an alcove, and saw Martha Ingram go by; she had come in and quietly bathed and dressed, he supposed, her hair was gleaming, damp and freshly up, her scent floated in the darkening corridor, she did not see him, rounding the stairs unconsciously in the cloud of her own particular silence. Some guy had given her one hell of a time. He thought of following her, to talk, to what? He flipped the magazine aside; his thoughts roved, constricted in dark hallways. . . .)

"I've got his picture, want to see?" "I don't have time, honey." Next she would be getting his advice. She loved getting advice about herself. He told her goodbye, taking a sharp turn away. Would he ever see her again? The thought hardly brushed him.

(Would she ever see him again? The thought did not brush her at all. What did pass through her mind—erroneously, anyone but Jean Coggins would have thought [she did not know a word like that]—was a memory of one day she was in Rossi's, the fashion shop where she worked on the Via Boncompagni, and had just taken 10,000 lire from the till [and not for the first time], to lend to a ragazzo who took pictures on the Via Veneto and was always a little bit behind though he kept a nice seicento. She would have put it back before the lunch hour was over at four, but the signora found it gone and was about to fire her, though she denied having done it except as a loan to her mother's donna di servizio, who had forgotten money for the shopping and had passed by on the way to the market. She would bring it right back from home. She faded off toward the back of the shop, for the signora was waggling her head darkly, and working away in an undertone [Figurati!]. And while she was in the back, way back where the brocade curtains and satin wallpaper faded out completely and there were only the brown-wrapped packages of stuffs [tessuti] stacked up in corners of a bare room with a gas jet and a little espresso machine, and snips and threads strewn about the floor, she heard a voice outside and it was Martha Ingram and the signora was saying with great gentilezza, "O, signora, the American girl you sent me, the Signorina Co-gins . . ." and then she heard, in the level quiet poised educated voice, almost like a murmur: "Oh, no, there was some mistake about that. I never sent her to you, signora, there was some mistake. . . . However, nondimeno. . . . I am sure she is very good . . . È una brava ragazza, sono sicura. . . ." And then there was something about some gloves. Addio, she thought, in Italian. Adesso comincia la musica . . . now the music will really begin. She thought of running out the back door. She liked working up near the Veneto, where it was fun. And then the Signora Rossi herself appeared in her trim black dress with her nails all beautifully madreperla and her gold Florentine snake bracelet with the garnet eyes and her sleek jet hair scrolled to the side and her eyes that were always asked how many mila

lire, and she twitched at the curtain and said, "Signorina Co-
gins, you are a liar—it is always la stessa cosa. . . . You have
given the money to that paparazzo, and the money was not
even yours, but mine. It would have been gentile indeed if you
had first asked me if I—io, io—had had some debt or other to
pay. Davvero. But then I do not drive you out to Frascati in a
seicento—not often, do I? No, not at all. But as for using the
name of Signora Ingram, mia cliente, to come into mia casa di
moda. . . ."

It went on and on like this, a ruffling stream of Italian, unending; as though she had stuck her head in a fountain, it went
pouring past her ears. And then she remembered, out of her
scolded-child exterior, that pensione in Venice, and Jim Wilbourne this time [rather than Alfredo]—the dim concept of
the faceless three of them—him and her and Martha Ingram
—afloat within those rain-darkening corridors and stairways.
She remembered tumbling on the damp bed and how he was
taller than she and that made her restless in some indefinable
way, so she said what was true: "She likes you." "Oh, stop it."
"I know." "How do you know?" "I just know, I always know,
I can tell." For the truth was she was not at all a liar: she was
far more honest than anybody she knew. It was the signora
who had said all along, just because she said she knew Martha
Ingram, that she had been sent there by Martha Ingram who
was close to the ambassador, and the signora could tell more
lies while selling a new gown than Jean Coggins had ever told
in her life, and another truth she knew was that Martha Ingram was bound to come in and "tell on her" someday to the
signora. It had been a certainty, a hateful certainty, because
women like Martha would always fasten to one man at a time.
She remembered her awe of Martha Ingram, her even wishing
in some minor way to be like her. And then she saw it all, in
a flash; perhaps, like that, she turned all the way into her own
grown-up self, and would never want to be like anybody else
again, for she suddenly pushed out of the corner where a tat-
ter of frayed curtain concealed a dreary little delivery entrance
from even being glimpsed by accident by anyone in the elegant
negozio, started up and flung herself full height, baring her
teeth like a fox, and spit out at the signora: "Che vuole? Non
sono una donna di servizio. I am not a servant. Faccio come

voglio . . . I will do as I like. Faccio come mi pare . . . I will do as I please. Che vuole?"

There was a sudden silence, rather like somebody had died, and the street door to the negozio could be heard to open. Signora Rossi broke into a laugh, at first an honest laugh—possibly the only one she had ever given—shading immediately into a ripple of pleasant amusement of the elegant padrona at her pretty little assistente; she turned on her narrow black stiletto heels and having touched her hair, folded her hands in that certain pleasing way, and moved toward the door.)

When Jim Wilbourne reached his own apartment, there at the head of the first flight of steps which ran down into the open courtyard, the landlord was lurking, paunchy and greasy-haired with a long straight nose and tiny whistle-sized mouth, a walking theatre of everything that had been done to him by the Wilbournes and all he could do in return because of it; here was the demon, the one soul who proved that inferno did exist, at least in Italy. Jim Wilbourne felt the back of his neck actually stiffen at the sight of Signor Micozzi in his white linen suit. The demon's energy, like the devastating continuous inexhaustible energy of Italy, was always fresh and ready for the fray; the time was always now. "Jesus, another round," Jim Wilbourne thought; "will I die before I leave this place?" Smoking, saying nothing, he climbed the stair to within two steps of the waiting figure which had bought that new white suit, it would seem, especially to quarrel in. The two of them, on perfect eye level, stared at one another. Jim Wilbourne dropped his cigarette, stepped on it, and walked deliberately past. His hand was on the bolt when the first words fell in all the smear of their mock courtesy:

"Scusi un momento, Signor Wilbourne, per cortesia."

For a moment, at the door, they ran through the paces of their usual nasty exchange. It was all he could do to keep from striking physically; in Italy that would have involved him so deeply he would never be free; Italy was the original tar baby; he knew that; getting out was the thing now; he had a sense of salvage and rescue, of swimming the ocean.

"Scusi, scusi!"

"Prego!"

They were shouting by now, their mutual contempt oozing wretchedly out of every word. He stepped inside and slammed the door.

His wife poked her head into the corridor. She was working; she was always working. Thin, in a pair of knee-length slacks of the sort nobody at all in Italy wore, which hung awkwardly, showing how much weight she'd lost in one nagging illness after another, her dark hair lank and flat, lying close to her head, framing like two heavy pencil lines her sharp face and great flat eyes: "All that bastard had to do was stand a few inches to the left when he passed the window, and I would have dropped this right on him," she said. She pointed to a ceramic umbrella stand she had made herself. It must have weighed seventy pounds at least. Her voice, slightly hoarse by nature with a ready tough fundamental coarseness in everything she observed when they were alone (she was never much "like herself" with other people), was a sort of life to him. He could not even remember life without it. "They called from the university about some survey on Neapolitan family management. It was due last week. I called your office but nobody answered." "I was there all morning but nobody rang." A world of old quarrels hung in shadowy phalanxes between every word of an exchange like this one, but both of them wearied to pour enough energy into any one of them to make it live. He stood in the doorway of her studio where she had even hung up a Van Gogh reproduction—the whole place looked American now. The Italian furniture had acquired the aspect of having been bought in a Third Avenue junk shop. "The dear old telephone system," she said, turning away, the corner of her mouth bitten in. He picked up the paper and stood reading it, leaning against a gilded chest of drawers, pushing at the dark hair above his ear with restless fingers. How would she have picked it up, he wondered, the umbrella stand? She would doubtless have managed. It was then the phone started ringing. "If that's the landlord—" he said. He knew it was. It was a favorite trick of Signor Micozzi, when the door slammed in his face, to circle down to the bar on the corner and ring upstairs, continuing the argument without the loss of a syllable. Martha Ingram would never get into this sort of mess— The thought wrote itself off the page. He crashed the paper to the floor. His wife whirled around and saw the way he looked. "Now, Jim, please—!"

"Look, you realize how much deposit he took on this place? Three hundred and fifty dollars. If he so much as hesitates about giving it back." "That's what he came for! Of course, he hesitates. He's never had the slightest intention of giving it back." "All right. Okay. He's in for a surprise or two." "But not to him, not to him! Don't you touch him!" She suddenly began to sob without crying, a grating desperate sound, biting out between the jerks of her breath, "If you touch him we'll never get out of here, we'll be here forever in this country, this horrible place, I'll die, I'll die here!" She leaped at him, latching onto his arm with both hands, and she had grown so light and he had grown so angry that when he lifted his arm she came up with it, right off the floor, as handy as a monkey. They both began to laugh—it was ludicrous, and it must have been soon after that they started figuring things out.

Her cry was over; she had even combed her hair. Then she began to bully and mock and dare him slightly; as totally disenchanted as ever, she had begun to be herself again. In some ways he listened, in others he didn't have to; most of all he was drawn back to where he was a few streets after he departed from Jean Coggins for all eternity, when, abruptly halting in a little crooked alley all alone, at some equidistance—mentally speaking, at least—between Martha and his wife, he gave over to wonder; for the first time, astringent and hard with himself, he allowed it to happen, he allowed the wonder to operate; fully, beautifully, he watched it curve and break in a clean magnificent wave.

What had he taken there, what had he conquered, so much as a city—a white, ample, ripe city, with towers, streets, parks, treasures? One bold leap of the imagination back there in Venice (the sort of thing he had always wanted to do but had never brought off quite so perfectly) had taken him soaring across the stale and turgid moat of her surrounding experience, had landed him at her very gates. It had been all blindly impulsive, perhaps cruel; but one thing had to be said for it—it had worked.

But there was something he knew and this was it: he could never have created her, and a thousand times, in turning her head, or putting on a glove, she had silently, unconsciously, praised whoever had put her together, ironically, the object of their merciless destruction—Jesus, what a trap! He rebelled at the whole godawful picture: it wasn't true. Love did not have to refer to anybody; that could all be changed in five minutes of wanting to. He had only to tell her, say so, absolutely— For an instant his mind crazed over like shattered glass, and it was some time before he hauled himself together, as though after another blind charge, this time at a wall, the first of many. Was it there or later, he allowed himself—briefly, but he did allow it—a moment's wonder at himself recognizing a young man not even thirty and what he had challenged, taken, known. He knew in what sense he was the possessor still, and in what sense no matter when he left he would always be.

(About here he came to a corner, and frowning, leaned against a wall. Grace Hartwell saw him; she was coming down from the dressmaker, hurrying home to pack.)

He was clearly aware of the many ways in which his Italian year wore the aspect of failure, of an advance halted, his professional best like chariot wheels miring in the mud, nothing, in short, to be proud of.

He walked on, at last, with a dogged, almost classical, stubbornness. This was what it had worn down to. He would live beyond himself again; he would, in future, be again gleaming and new, set right like a fine mechanism; he had to go to the States for that. But in this hour, blazed at by a sudden foreign sun, he presented to himself neither mystery nor brilliance, any more than he did to his wife or the landlord, in whose terms he did not even despise to live, if only his energy held out till the shores of Italy dropped behind him forever. But Martha too had been Italy—a city, his own, sinking forever. There was the wall again, blank and mocking. He could go crashing into it again, over and over and over, as many times as he wanted to.

15

IT WAS George Hartwell who got the full force of the Wilbourne departure after they had left Rome earlier than they had said they were going to, in the night. Now every day or so, the landlord, Signor Micozzi, called Hartwell and "Yes," he said, "Va bene," he said, and "Grazie, signor console, molto gentile, sissignore," said Signor Micozzi.

Hartwell gave Signor Micozzi appointments when no one else could get one, while the important people went across the hall to see Martha; he swivelled back in his chair and listened and listened . . . his mind wandered, sometimes he dozed, he could pick up the refrain whenever he cared to. "Gente cattiva, quei Wilbourne. Cosa potevo fare . . . cosa? Sono assolutaménte senza . . ."

"Ma Signor Micozzi, lei ha già ricevuto il deposito, non è vero?"

"Si, ma questo, signor console, non deve pensare che il deposito è abbastanza per questo . . . hanno rottoo tutto! . . . Tutto è rovinato!"

One day soon now, he was going to haul himself together. One has to wake oneself; one cannot go on forever, unravelling the waste, the inconsequential portions of a dream that was not even one's own. So one day soon now he was going to stop it. He was going to say, like any tourist in the market, Quanto allora? He might even write a check. It was his American conscience, that was it. . . .

Poor George Hartwell, there was one success he had had. Everyone assured him of it—the Coggins', of course. He could take pride in them; who would have thought that Italians would let any American tell them about opera?

He left Martha's doorway. The sun struck him a glorious blow and the little fountain pulsed from white to green in the new season.

Ah, yes, the Coggins'. Veni, vidi, vici.

He looked for his car and found it. Dorothy, Richard, and Jean.

They had gone off triumphantly to take the boat at Genoa, had been waved off at the station by contingents of Roman friends, leaving time to go by Venice and revisit that same pensione, having sent on ahead to the boat crate upon crate of tourist junk, a whole case of country wines (a gift from the landlord, by now a lifelong friend). There were also a package of citations and awards from a dozen appreciative music companies, autographed photos of half the singers in Italy, and ninety percent of all the chocolate in Perugia which had been showered upon Jean by admirers from Trastavere to the Parioli, from Milan to Palermo. Perhaps at this moment, she was talking to Alfredo again in the pensione, giggling at his soft Venetian accent, all in a palazzo set on waters crackling in the brilliant light, or strolling about the garden, hearing a motorboat churn past. Waiting for Sunday dinner in the central hallways, with one or two of the same old guests and the proprietor with his head in the books . . . waiting for Sunday dinner. It was a Western tradition, a binding point for the whole world. And why not? In his vision of Venice, for a moment, Martha Ingram and all her long mad vision stood redeemed. But not for long. Jim Wilbourne was never far enough away; his head turned slowly, his regard scorched slowly across the scene; as though the Coggins' had been in an eighteenth-century engraving deployed in each pleasant detail about their Venetian casa, the edges curled, the loosely woven paper bent backward, the images distorted, changed—one turned away.

Hartwell at last got home and opened windows in an empty flat, fetched bread and cheese from the kitchen, fought steadily against the need for whiskey, and sat down to unlock the dispatch case. His wife, so easily evoked, crossed the ocean at his nod to stand at his elbow and remark with her warm wit that along with all those dispatches, briefings, summaries, minutes, and memoranda from the embassy, he might possibly draw out a poison toad, a severed hand, some small memento of Martha Ingram.

But he did not.

The reports she had done for him were smooth and crisp, brilliant, unblemished. Their cutting edge was razor-keen, their substance unrolled like bolts of silk. There was nothing to add, nothing to take away. It was sinister, and he did not want to think about it alone. But he had to. Who has been destroyed in this as much as me? he wondered. Gordon Ingram is not alone. No, it was against George Hartwell's present and fond breast that the hurled spear struck.

Knowing this, he could not stand it any longer.

Getting up, slamming out, he got into his car and went nosing about the streets again. The Grand Hotel, a Sunday vision also, elegance and the Grand Tour, too little exercise, every wish granted, marmalade for tea, and if you're willing to pay extra, tours can be arranged through the— He had charged halfway across the lobby before he stopped to think, to enquire.

"A little signora americana in blue, sissignore. She is there, eccola là."

And there she was. He saw her. She was real. Martha was not that crazy.

She was over in a far corner before some enormous windows reaching to the ceiling, canopied with drawn satin portieres, and she was not alone. The Italian floorcleaner who had mopped and dusted the lobby there for at least ten years but had never once before this moment sat down in one of the sofas was now beside her. She had gone upstairs, and using her dictionary (as Hartwell was later to hear) had written down the message which she had to give to someone, and now she was reading it off. A piece of light blue letter paper trembled in her little crooked hand.

"Ho un amico che sta morendo . . . I have a friend who is dying. Questa mattina ho ricevuto la notizia . . . only this morning I received the news."

"O signora!" cried the floorcleaner. "Mi dispiace . . . I am so sorry!" He leaned toward her; his small-featured Latin face wrung instantly with pity; he also had lost friends.

"Mio amico era sempre buono . . . è buono . . . buono. . . ."

It was then that George Hartwell appeared. The floorcleaner sprang to his feet. "S'accomodi . . . sit down," said Hartwell. "In nome di Dio."

There was no one really around. The bright day was subdued to the décor of the great outdated windows, which made a humble group of them. And really, thought Hartwell, I've got no business here, what am I doing with these two people?

Once I had a little kingdom here. It is stolen, it is gone. Should I tell them? Would they cry?

He sat and listened.

Now the sentiment, the inaccuracy, of the usual human statement was among them; irresistibly as weeds in a great ruin, it was springing up everywhere around what was being said of Gordon Ingram. His books, his wisdom, his circle of friends, his great heart, his sad life. . . . Hartwell was translating everything to the floorcleaner, who had forgotten that he was a floorcleaner. He was, above all, a human being, and he accordingly began to weep.

George Hartwell told the lady in blue that Martha Ingram was out of town.

16

ON A day that now seemed long, long ago, had seemed long ago, in fact, almost the precipitate instant its final event occurred, she had gone out of her apartment which Jim Wilbourne had been in for an hour or so, for the last time. It was a matter of consideration to them both to give him time to get well away before she went out behind him, leaving rooms she could not for the moment bear to be alone in. She did not know that he had been delayed on the stair. She saw him, however, come out of the bar with Jean Coggins, laughing with her over something; she stepped back, almost from the curb into the street which at that point was narrow, damp, still in winter shadow; and then a car passed and she looked up in time to see Gordon Ingram's nephew driving by. She never doubted that was who it was. He had grown a lot, that was all. He did not see her; the car nosed into a turning which led away from her, away, she realized too late, icily, from her apartment. He had been there already; he had gone. From out of sight, in the chilly labyrinth where the sun would slowly seep in now and warm and dry and mellow through the long summer months, she heard Jean Coggins laugh. The boy had grown so much; she used to give him books and read to him: what college was he in, would no one tell her? She had stopped still—after her first futile steps, begun too late, of running after the car—in a small empty square. The direction of the car pulled against the direction of the laugh, in an exact mathematical pivot, herself being the central point of strain, and in this counterweight, she felt her life tear almost audibly, like ripping silk. She leaned against a wall and looked out on the little empty space, an opening in the city. The sun brought out the smell of cigarettes, but no one was about; only dumb high doorways and shadows sliced at a clear, straight angle across a field of sun.

He was driven away from me, she thought: Jim Wilbourne did it; I know that it is true. I am no more than that meeting point of shadow and sun. It is everything there is I need to know, that I am that and that is me.

It was the complex of herself that her spirit in one motion abandoned; those intricate structures, having come to their own completion, were no longer habitable. She saw them crumble, sink and go under forever. And here was what was left: a line of dark across a field of sun.

When the small package arrived for Martha—a strand of pearls which had belonged to an aunt who had left them to her in memory of—she hardly read the letter, which was not from Gordon Ingram but from the nephew who was now in Greece. The lettering on the package had been done by Gordon Ingram. There was no message inside. She went carefully, in a gentle way, downstairs and laid the strand in the crevice of the palazzo wall, like an offering to life. She felt as a spirit might, rather clever, at being able to move an object or leave a footprint. Some Italian would be telling the story for many years, waving the pearls aloft. "Dal cielo! Dal cielo! Son cadute dal cielo!"

George Hartwell's saying to the lady in blue that Martha was out of town was no lie; perhaps he was incapable of telling one. She was driving to the sea to meet Roberto there, possibly the sister and the sister's husband, possibly not, the plans were generous, promising, and vague. She more and more arranged to do things alone, a curious tendency, for loneliness once had been a torment, whereas now she regarded almost everything her eyes fell on with an equal sense of companionship; her compatibility was with the world. The equality of it all could of course be in some purely intellectual, non-nervous way disturbing. Things were not really equal, nor were people; one explanation might be that she simply did not care very deeply about anything, the emotional target she had once plainly furnished had disappeared. Was this another name for freedom? Freedom was certainly what it felt like. She bent with complete compassion, fleshless, invisible and absent, above the rapidly vanishing mortality of Gordon Ingram, at the same time she swung happily, even giddily (there went that streak again, the necessary madness), around the Colosseum, where the fresh glittering traffic, like a flight of gulls, joyous in the sunlight, seemed to float and lilt, fearless of collision. Children's bones and women's skulls had been dug up there and conjectures could be easily formed about what sort of undemocratic accidents had overtaken these fine people, but now the old ruin stood noble and ornamental to Rome, and views of it were precious to those apartments which overlooked it.

Faceless and nameless, the throng rushed on; they always had and would forever, as long as the city stood.

It was not Gordon Ingram who had died, nor was it Jim Wilbourne who was absent. It was herself, she thought. I am gone, she thought; they have taken me with them; I shall never return.

If only George Hartwell could understand that, he would know better about things, he could even bear them. But then, she saw, he might be compelled to trace a similar path in his own life; for knowing it arose merely, perhaps only, from being it. Let him be spared, she thought; let him be his poor human soul forever.

She was of those whom life had held a captive and in freeing herself she had met dissolution, and was a friend now to any landscape, a companion to cloud and sky.

SELECTED STORIES

First Dark

WHEN TOM BEAVERS started coming back to Richton, Mississippi, on weekends, after the war was over, everybody in town was surprised and pleased. They had never noticed him much before he paid them this compliment; now they could not say enough nice things. There was not much left in Richton for him to call family—just his aunt who had raised him, Miss Rita Beavers, old as God, ugly as sin, deaf as a post. So he must be fond of the town, they reasoned; certainly it was a pretty old place. Far too many young men had left it and never come back at all.

He would drive in every Friday night from Jackson, where he worked. All weekend, his Ford, dusty of flank, like a hard-ridden horse, would sit parked down the hill near Miss Rita's old wire front gate, which sagged from the top hinge and had worn a span in the ground. On Saturday morning, he would head for the drugstore, then the post office; then he would be observed walking here and there around the streets under the shade trees. It was as though he were looking for something.

He wore steel taps on his heels, and in the still the click of them on the sidewalks would sound across the big front lawns and all the way up to the porches of the houses, where two ladies might be sitting behind a row of ferns. They would identify him to one another, murmuring in their fine little voices, and say it was just too bad there was nothing here for young people. It was just a shame they didn't have one or two more old houses here, for a Pilgrimage—look how Natchez had waked up.

On Saturday morning in early October, Tom Beavers sat at the counter in the drugstore and reminded Totsie Poteet, the drugstore clerk, of a ghost story. Did he remember the strange old man who used to appear to people who were coming into Richton along the Jackson road at twilight—what they called "first dark"?

"Sure I remember," said Totsie. "Old Cud'n Jimmy Wilt-shire used to tell us about him every time we went possum hunting. I could see him plain as I can see you, the way he used to tell it. Tall, with a top hat on, yeah, and waiting in the weeds alongside the road ditch, so'n you couldn't tell if he wasn't taller than any mortal man could be, because you couldn't tell if he was standing down in the ditch or not. It would look like he just grew up out of the weeds. Then he'd signal to you."

"Them that stopped never saw anybody," said Tom Beavers, stirring his coffee. "There were lots of folks besides Mr. Jimmy that saw him."

"There was, let me see . . ." Totsie enumerated others— some men, some women, some known to drink, others who never touched a drop. There was no way to explain it. "There was that story the road gang told. Do you remember, or were you off at school? It was while they were straightening the road out to the highway—taking the curves out and building a new bridge. Anyway, they said that one night at quitting time, along in the winter and just about dark, this old guy signalled to some of 'em. They said they went over and he asked them to move a bulldozer they had left across the road, because he had a wagon back behind on a little dirt road, with a sick nigger girl in it. Had to get to the doctor and this was the only way. They claimed they knew didn't nobody live back there on that little old road, but niggers can come from anywhere. So they moved the bulldozer and cleared back a whole lot of other stuff, and waited and waited. Not only didn't no wagon ever come, but the man that had stopped them, he was gone, too. They was right shook up over it. You never heard that one?"

"No, I never did." Tom Beavers said this with his eyes looking up over his coffee cup, as though he sat behind a hand of cards. His lashes and brows were heavier than was ordinary, and worked as a veil might, to keep you away from knowing exactly what he was thinking.

"They said he was tall and had a hat on." The screen door flapped to announce a customer, but Totsie kept on talking. "But whether he was a white man or a real light-colored nigger they couldn't say. Some said one and some said another. I figured they'd been pulling on the jug a little earlier than usual. You know why? I never heard of *our* ghost *saying* nothing. Did you, Tom?"

He moved away on the last words, the way a clerk will,

talking back over his shoulder and ahead of him to his new customer at the same time, as though he had two voices and two heads. "And what'll it be today, Miss Frances?"

The young woman standing at the counter had a prescription already out of her bag. She stood with it poised between her fingers, but her attention was drawn toward Tom Beavers, his coffee cup, and the conversation she had interrupted. She was a girl whom no ordinary description would fit. One would have to know first of all who she was: Frances Harvey. After that, it was all right for her to be a little odd-looking, with her reddish hair that curled back from her brow, her light eyes, and her high, pale temples. This is not the material for being pretty, but in Frances Harvey it was what could sometimes be beauty. Her family home was laden with history that nobody but the Harveys could remember. It would have been on a Pilgrimage if Richton had had one. Frances still lived in it, looking after an invalid mother.

"What were you-all talking about?" she wanted to know.

"About that ghost they used to tell about," said Totsie, holding out his hand for the prescription. "The one people used to see just outside of town, on the Jackson road."

"But why?" she demanded. "Why were you talking about him?"

"Tom, here—" the clerk began, but Tom Beavers interrupted him.

"I was asking because I was curious," he said. He had been studying her from the corner of his eye. Her face was beginning to show the wear of her mother's long illness, but that couldn't be called change. Changing was something she didn't seem to have done, her own style being the only one natural to her.

"I was asking," he went on, "because I saw him." He turned away from her somewhat too direct gaze and said to Totsie Poteet, whose mouth had fallen open, "It was where the new road runs close to the old road, and as far as I could tell he was right on the part of the old road where people always used to see him."

"But when?" Frances Harvey demanded.

"Last night," he told her. "Just around first dark. Driving home."

A wealth of quick feeling came up in her face. "So did I! Driving home from Jackson! I saw him, too!"

For some people, a liking for the same phonograph record or for Mayan archeology is enough of an excuse to get together. Possibly, seeing the same ghost was no more than that. Anyway, a week later, on Saturday at first dark, Frances Harvey and Tom Beavers were sitting together in a car parked just off the highway, near the spot where they agreed the ghost had appeared. The season was that long, peculiar one between summer and fall, and there were so many crickets and tree frogs going full tilt in their periphery that their voices could hardly be distinguished from the background noises, though they both would have heard a single footfall in the grass. An edge of autumn was in the air at night, and Frances had put on a tweed jacket at the last minute, so the smell of mothballs was in the car, brisk and most unghostlike.

But Tom Beavers was not going to forget the value of the ghost, whether it put in an appearance or not. His questions led Frances into reminiscence.

"No, I never saw him before the other night," she admitted. "The Negroes used to talk in the kitchen, and Regina and I— you know my sister Regina—would sit there listening, scared to go and scared to stay. Then finally going to bed upstairs was no relief, either, because sometimes Aunt Henrietta was visiting us, and *she'd* seen it. Or if she wasn't visiting us, the front room next to us, where she stayed, would be empty, which was worse. There was no way to lock ourselves in, and besides, what was there to lock out? We'd lie all night like two sticks in bed, and shiver. Papa finally had to take a hand. He called us in and sat us down and said that the whole thing was easy to explain—it was all automobiles. What their headlights did with the dust and shadows out on the Jackson road. 'Oh, but Sammie and Jerry!' we said, with great big eyes, sitting side by side on the sofa, with our tennis shoes flat on the floor."

"Who were Sammie and Jerry?" asked Tom Beavers.

"Sammie was our cook. Jerry was her son, or husband, or something. Anyway, they certainly didn't have cars. Papa called them in. They were standing side by side by the bookcase, and Regina and I were on the sofa—four pairs of big eyes, and

Papa pointing his finger. Papa said, 'Now, you made up these stories about ghosts, didn't you?' 'Yes, sir,' said Sammie. 'We made them up.' 'Yes, sir,' said Jerry. 'We sho did.' 'Well, then, you can just stop it,' Papa said. 'See how peaked these children look?' Sammie and Jerry were terribly polite to us for a week, and we got in the car and rode up and down the Jackson road at first dark to see if the headlights really did it. But we never saw anything. We didn't tell Papa, but headlights had nothing whatever to do with it."

"You had your own *car* then?" He couldn't believe it.

"Oh, no!" She was emphatic. "We were too young for that. Too young to drive, really, but we did anyway."

She leaned over to let him give her cigarette a light, and saw his hand tremble. Was he afraid of the ghost or of her? She would have to stay away from talking family.

Frances remembered Tommy Beavers from her childhood —a small boy going home from school down a muddy side road alone, walking right down the middle of the road. His old aunt's house was at the bottom of a hill. It was damp there, and the yard was always muddy, with big fat chicken tracks all over it, like Egyptian writing. How did Frances know? She could not remember going there, ever. Miss Rita Beavers was said to order cold ham, mustard, bread, and condensed milk from the grocery store. "I doubt if that child ever has anything hot," Frances's mother had said once. He was always neatly dressed in the same knee pants, high socks, and checked shirt, and sat several rows ahead of Frances in study hall, right in the middle of his seat. He was three grades behind her; in those days, that much younger seemed very young indeed. What had happened to his parents? There was some story, but it was not terribly interesting, and, his people being of no importance, she had forgotten.

"I think it's past time for our ghost," she said. "He's never out so late at night."

"He gets hungry, like me," said Tom Beavers. "Are you hungry, Frances?"

They agreed on a highway restaurant where an orchestra played on weekends. Everyone went there now.

From the moment they drew up on the gravelled entrance, cheerful lights and a blare of music chased the spooks from their heads. Tom Beavers ordered well and danced well, as it turned out. Wasn't there something she had heard about his being "smart"? By "smart," Southerners mean intellectual, and they say it in an almost condescending way, smart being what you are when you can't be anything else, and it is better, at least, than being nothing. Frances Harvey had been away enough not to look at things from a completely Southern point of view, and she was encouraged to discover that she and Tom had other things in common besides a ghost, though all stemming, perhaps, from the imagination it took to see one.

They agreed about books and favorite movies and longing to see more plays. She sighed that life in Richton was so confining, but he assured her that Jackson could be just as bad; *it* was getting to be like any Middle Western city, he said, while Richton at least had a sense of the past. This was the main reason, he went on, gaining confidence in the jumble of commonplace noises—dishes, music, and a couple of drinkers chattering behind them—that he had started coming back to Richton so often. He wanted to keep a connection with the past. He lived in a modern apartment, worked in a soundproof office—he could be in any city. But Richton was where he had been born and raised, and nothing could be more old-fashioned. Too many people seemed to have their lives cut in two. He was earnest in desiring that this should not happen to him.

"You'd better be careful," Frances said lightly. Her mood did not incline her to profound conversation. "There's more than one ghost in Richton. You may turn into one yourself, like the rest of us."

"It's the last thing I'd think of you," he was quick to assure her.

Had Tommy Beavers really said such a thing, in such a natural, charming way? Was Frances Harvey really so pleased? Not only was she pleased but, feeling warmly alive amid the music and small lights, she agreed with him. She would not have agreed with him more.

"I hear that Thomas Beavers has gotten to be a very attractive man," Frances Harvey's mother said unexpectedly one afternoon.

Frances had been reading aloud—Jane Austen this time. Theirs was one house where the leather-bound sets were actually read. In Jane Austen, men and women seesawed back and forth for two or three hundred pages until they struck a point of balance; then they got married. She had just put aside the book, at the end of a chapter, and risen to lower the shade against the slant of afternoon sun. "Or so Cud'n Jennie and Mrs. Giles Antley and Miss Fannie Stapleton have been coming and telling you," she said.

"People talk, of course, but the consensus is favorable," Mrs. Harvey said. "Wonders never cease; his mother ran away with a brush salesman. But nobody can make out what he's up to, coming back to Richton."

"Does he have to be 'up to' anything?" Frances asked.

"Men are always up to something," said the old lady at once. She added, more slowly, "In Thomas's case, maybe it isn't anything it oughtn't to be. They say he reads a lot. He may just have taken up with some sort of idea."

Frances stole a long glance at her mother's face on the pillow. Age and illness had reduced the image of Mrs. Harvey to a kind of caricature, centered on a mouth that Frances could not help comparing to that of a fish. There was a tension around its rim, as though it were outlined in bone, and the underlip even stuck out a little. The mouth ate, it took medicine, it asked for things, it gasped when breath was short, it commented. But when it commented, it ceased to be just a mouth and became part of Mrs. Harvey, that witty tyrant with the infallible memory for the right detail, who was at her terrible best about men.

"And what could he be thinking of?" she was wont to inquire when some man had acted foolishly. No one could ever defend accurately the man in question, and the only conclusion was Mrs. Harvey's; namely, that he wasn't thinking, if, indeed, he could. Although she had never been a belle, never a flirt, her popularity with men was always formidable. She would be observed talking marathons with one in a corner, and could you ever be sure, when they both burst into laughter, that they had not just exchanged the most shocking stories? "Of course, *he*—" she would begin later, back with the family, and the masculinity that had just been encouraged to strut and preen a little was quickly shown up as idiotic. Perhaps Mrs. Harvey hoped by this method to train her daughters away from a lot of sentimental nonsense that was their birthright as pretty Southern girls in a house with a lawn that moonlight fell on and that was often lit also by Japanese lanterns hung for parties. "Oh, he's not like that, Mama!" the little girls would cry. They were already alert for heroes who would ride up and cart them off. "Well, then, you watch," she would say. Sure enough, if you watched, she would be right.

Mrs. Harvey's younger daughter, Regina, was a credit to her mother's long campaign; she married well. The old lady, however, never tired of pointing out behind her son-in-law's back that his fondness for money was ill-concealed, that he had the longest feet she'd ever seen, and that he sometimes made grammatical errors.

Her elder daughter, Frances, on a trip to Europe, fell in love, alas! The gentleman was of French extraction but Swiss citizenship, and Frances did not marry him, because he was already married—that much filtered back to Richton. In response to a cable, she had returned home one hot July in time to witness her father's wasted face and last weeks of life. That same September, the war began. When peace came, Richton wanted to know if Frances Harvey would go back to Europe. Certain subtly complicated European matters, little understood in Richton, seemed to be obstructing Romance; one of them was probably named Money. Meanwhile, Frances's mother took to bed, in what was generally known to be her last illness.

So no one crossed the ocean, but eventually Tom Beavers came up to Mrs. Harvey's room one afternoon, to tea.

Though almost all her other faculties were seriously impaired, in ear and tongue Mrs. Harvey was as sound as a young beagle, and she could still weave a more interesting conversation than most people who go about every day and look at the world. She was of the old school of Southern lady talkers; she vexed you with no ideas, she tried to protect you from even a moment of silence. In the old days, when a bright company filled the downstairs rooms, she could keep the ball rolling amongst a crowd. Everyone—all the men especially—got their word in, but the flow of things came back to her. If one of those twenty-minutes-to-or-after silences fell—and even with her they did occur—people would turn and look at her daughter Frances. "And what do you think?" some kind-eyed gentleman would ask. Frances did not credit that she had the sort of face people would turn to, and so did not know how to take advantage of it. What did she think? Well, to answer that honestly took a moment of reflection—a fatal moment, it always turned out. Her mother would be up instructing the maid, offering someone an ashtray or another goody, or remarking outright, "Frances is so timid. She never says a word."

Tom Beavers stayed not only past teatime that day but for a drink as well. Mrs. Harvey was induced to take a glass of sherry, and now her bed became her enormous throne. Her keenest suffering as an invalid was occasioned by the absence of men. "What is a house without a man in it?" she would often cry. From her eagerness to be charming to Frances's guest that afternoon, it seemed that she would have married Tom Beavers herself if he had asked her. The amber liquid set in her small four-sided glass glowed like a jewel, and her diamond flashed; she had put on her best ring for the company. What a pity no longer to show her ankle, that delicious bone, so remarkably slender for so ample a frame.

Since the time had flown so, they all agreed enthusiastically that Tom should wait downstairs while Frances got ready to go out to dinner with him. He was hardly past the stair landing before the old lady was seized by such a fit of coughing that she could hardly speak. "It's been— It's been too much—too *much* for me!" she gasped out.

But after Frances had found the proper sedative for her, she was calmed, and insisted on having her say.

"Thomas Beavers has a good job with an insurance company in Jackson," she informed her daughter, as though Frances were incapable of finding out anything for herself. "He makes a good appearance. He is the kind of man"—she paused —"who would value a wife of good family." She stopped, panting for breath. It was this complimenting a man behind his back that was too much for her—as much out of character, and hence as much of a strain, as if she had got out of bed and tried to tap-dance.

"Heavens, Mama," Frances said, and almost giggled.

At this, the old lady, thinking the girl had made light of her suitor, half screamed at her, "Don't be so critical, Frances! You can't be so critical of men!" and fell into an even more terrible spasm of coughing. Frances had to lift her from the pillow and hold her straight until the fit passed and her breath returned. Then Mrs. Harvey's old, dry, crooked, ineradicably feminine hand was laid on her daughter's arm, and when she spoke again she shook the arm to emphasize her words.

"When your father knew he didn't have long to live," she whispered, "we discussed whether to send for you or not. You know you were his favorite, Frances. 'Suppose our girl is happy over there,' he said. 'I wouldn't want to bring her back on my account.' I said you had to have the right to choose whether to come back or not. You'd never forgive us, I said, if you didn't have the right to choose."

Frances could visualize this very conversation taking place between her parents; she could see them, decorous and serious, talking over the fact of his approaching death as though it were a piece of property for agreeable disposition in the family. She could never remember him without thinking, with a smile, how he used to come home on Sunday from church (he being the only one of them who went) and how, immediately after hanging his hat and cane in the hall, he would say, "Let all things proceed in orderly progression to their final confusion. How long before dinner?" No, she had had to come home. Some humor had always existed between them—her father and her—and humor, of all things, cannot be betrayed.

"I meant to go back," said Frances now. "But there was the war. At first I kept waiting for it to be over. I still wake up at night sometimes thinking, I wonder how much longer before the war will be over. And then—" She stopped short. For the fact was that her lover had been married to somebody else, and her mother was the very person capable of pointing that out to her. Even in the old lady's present silence she heard the unspoken thought, and got up nervously from the bed, loosing herself from the hand on her arm, smoothing her reddish hair where it was inclined to straggle. "And then he wrote me that he had gone back to his wife. Her family and his had always been close, and the war brought them back together. This was in Switzerland—naturally, he couldn't stay on in Paris during the war. There were the children, too—all of them were Catholic. Oh, I do understand how it happened."

Mrs. Harvey turned her head impatiently on the pillow. She dabbed at her moist upper lip with a crumpled linen handkerchief; her diamond flashed once in motion. "War, religion, wife, children—yes. But men do what they want to."

Could anyone make Frances as angry as her mother could? "Believe what you like, then! You always know so much better than I do. *You* would have managed things somehow. Oh, you would have had your way!"

"Frances," said Mrs. Harvey, "I'm an old woman." The hand holding the handkerchief fell wearily, and her eyelids dropped shut. "If you should want to marry Thomas Beavers and bring him here, I will accept it. There will be no distinctions. Next, I suppose, we will be having his old deaf aunt for tea. I hope she has a hearing aid. I haven't got the strength to holler at her."

"I don't think any of these plans are necessary, Mama."

The eyelids slowly lifted. "None?"

"None."

Mrs. Harvey's breathing was as audible as a voice. She spoke, at last, without scorn, honestly. "I cannot bear the thought of leaving you alone. You, nor the house, nor your place in it—alone. I foresaw Tom Beavers here! What has he got that's better than you and this place? I knew he would come!"

Terrible as her mother's meanness was, it was not half so terrible as her love. Answering nothing, explaining nothing, Frances stood without giving in. She trembled, and tears ran down her cheeks. The two women looked at each other helplessly across the darkening room.

In the car, later that night, Tom Beavers asked, "Is your mother trying to get rid of me?" They had passed an unsatisfactory evening, and he was not going away without knowing why.

"No, it's just the other way around," said Frances, in her candid way. "She wants you so much she'd like to eat you up. She wants you in the house. Couldn't you tell?"

"She once chased me out of the yard," he recalled.

"Not really!"

They turned into Harvey Street (that was actually the name of it), and when he had drawn the car up before the dark front

steps, he related the incident. He told her that Mrs. Harvey
had been standing just there in the yard, talking to some visitor who was leaving by inches, the way ladies used to—ten
minutes' more talk for every forward step. He, a boy not more
than nine, had been crossing a corner of the lawn where a faint
path had already been worn; he had had nothing to do with
wearing the path, and had taken it quite innocently and openly.
"You, boy!" Mrs. Harvey's fan was an enormous painted thing.
She had furled it with a clack so loud he could still hear it. "You
don't cut through my yard again! Now, you stop where you are
and you go all the way back around by the walk, and don't
you ever ever do that again." He went back and all the way
around. She was fanning comfortably as he passed. "Old Miss
Rita Beavers' nephew," he heard her say, and though he did not
speak of it now to Frances, Mrs. Harvey's rich tone had been
as stuffed with wickedness as a fruitcake with goodies. In it you
could have found so many things: that, of course, he didn't
know any better, that he was poor, that she knew his first name
but would not deign to mention it, that she meant him to
understand all this and more. Her fan was probably still somewhere in the house, he reflected. If he ever opened the wrong
door, it might fall from above and brain him. It seemed impossible that nowadays he could even have the chance to open the
wrong door in the Harvey house. With its graceful rooms and
big lawn, its camellias and magnolia trees, the house had been
one of the enchanted castles of his childhood, and Frances and
Regina Harvey had been two princesses running about the
lawn one Saturday morning drying their hair with big white
towels and not noticing when he passed.

There was a strong wind that evening. On the way home,
Frances and Tom had noticed how the night was streaming,
but whether with mist or dust or the smoke from some far-off
fire in the dry winter woods they could not tell. As they stood
on the sidewalk, the clouds raced over them, and moonlight
now and again came through. A limb rubbed against a high
cornice. Inside the screened area of the porch, the swing jan-
gled its iron chains. Frances's coat blew about her, and her hair
blew. She felt herself to be no different from anything there
that the wind was blowing on, her happiness of no relevance in
the dark torrent of nature.

"I can't leave her, Tom. But I can't ask you to live with her, either. Of all the horrible ideas! She'd make demands, take all my time, laugh at you behind your back—she has to run everything. You'd hate me in a week."

He did not try to pretty up the picture, because he had a feeling that it was all too accurate. Now, obviously, was the time she should go on to say there was no good his waiting around through the years for her. But hearts are not noted for practicality, and Frances stood with her hair blowing, her hands stuck in her coat pockets, and did not go on to say anything. Tom pulled her close to him—in, as it were, out of the wind.

"I'll be coming by next weekend, just like I've been doing. And the next one, too," he said. "We'll just leave it that way, if it's O.K. with you."

"Oh, yes, it is, Tom!" Never so satisfied to be weak, she kissed him and ran inside.

He stood watching on the walk until her light flashed on. Well, he had got what he was looking for; a connection with the past, he had said. It was right upstairs, a splendid old mass of dictatorial female flesh, thinking about him. Well, they could go on, he and Frances, sitting on either side of a sickbed, drinking tea and sipping sherry, with streaks of gray broadening on their brows, while the familiar seasons came and went. So he thought. Like Frances, he believed that the old lady had a stranglehold on life.

Suddenly, in March, Mrs. Harvey died.

A heavy spring funeral, with lots of roses and other scented flowers in the house, is the worst kind of all. There is something so recklessly fecund about a South Mississippi spring that death becomes just another word in the dictionary, along with swarms of others, and even so pure and white a thing as a gardenia has too heavy a scent and may suggest decay. Mrs. Harvey, amid such odors, sank to rest with a determined pomp, surrounded by admiring eyes.

While Tom Beavers did not "sit with the family" at this time, he was often observed with the Harveys, and there was whispered speculation among those who were at the church and the cemetery that the Harvey house might soon come into new hands, "after a decent interval." No one would undertake to judge for a Harvey how long an interval was decent.

Frances suffered from insomnia in the weeks that followed, and at night she wandered about the spring-swollen air of the old house, smelling now spring and now death. "Let all things proceed in orderly progression to their final confusion." She had always thought that the final confusion referred to death, but now she began to think that it could happen any time; that final confusion, having found the door ajar, could come into a house and show no inclination to leave. The worrisome thing, the thing it all came back to, was her mother's clothes. They were numerous, expensive, and famous, and Mrs. Harvey had never discarded any of them. If you opened a closet door, hatboxes as big as crates towered above your head. The shiny black trim of a great shawl stuck out of a wardrobe door just below the lock. Beneath the lid of a cedar chest, the bright eyes of a tippet were ready to twinkle at you. And the jewels! Frances's sister had restrained her from burying them all on their mother, and had even gone off with a wad of them tangled up like fishing tackle in an envelope, on the ground of promises made now and again in the course of the years.

("Regina," said Frances, "what else were you two talking about besides jewelry?" "I don't remember," said Regina, getting mad.

"Frances makes me so mad," said Regina to her husband as they were driving home. "I guess I can love Mama and jewelry, too. Mama certainly loved *us* and jewelry, too.")

One afternoon, Frances went out to the cemetery to take two wreaths sent by somebody who had "just heard." She drove out along the winding cemetery road, stopping the car a good distance before she reached the gate, in order to walk through the woods. The dogwood was beautiful that year. She saw a field where a house used to stand but had burned down; its cedar trees remained, and two bushes of bridal wreath marked where the front gate had swung. She stopped to admire the clusters of white bloom massing up through the young, feathery leaf and stronger now than the leaf itself. In the woods, the redbud was a smoke along shadowy ridges, and the dogwood drifted in layers, like snow suspended to give you all the time you needed to wonder at it. But why, she wondered, do they call it bridal *wreath*? It's not a wreath but a little bouquet. Wreaths are for funerals, anyway. As if to prove it, she looked down at the two she held, one in each hand. She walked on, and such complete desolation came over her that it was more of a wonder than anything in the woods—more, even, than death.

As she returned to the car from the two parallel graves, she met a thin, elderly, very light-skinned Negro man in the road. He inquired if she would mind moving her car so that he could pass. He said that there was a sick colored girl in his wagon, whom he was driving in to the doctor. He pointed out politely that she had left her car right in the middle of the road. "Oh, I'm terribly sorry," said Frances, and hurried off toward the car.

That night, reading late in bed, she thought, I could have given her a ride into town. No wonder they talk about us up North. A mile into town in a wagon! She might have been having a baby. She became conscience-stricken about it—foolishly so, she realized, but if you start worrying about something in a house like the one Frances Harvey lived in, in the dead of night, alone, you will go on worrying about it until dawn. She was out of sleeping pills.

She remembered having bought a fresh box of sedatives for her mother the day before she died. She got up and went into her mother's closed room, where the bed had been dismantled for airing, its wooden parts propped along the walls. On the closet shelf she found the shoe box into which she had packed away the familiar articles of the bedside table. Inside she found the small enamelled-cardboard box, with the date and prescription inked on the cover in Totsie Poteet's somewhat prissy handwriting, but the box was empty. She was surprised, for she realized that her mother could have used only one or two of the pills. Frances was so determined to get some sleep that she searched the entire little store of things in the shoe box quite heartlessly, but there were no pills. She returned to her room and tried to read, but could not, and so smoked instead and stared out at the dawn-blackening sky. The house sighed. She could not take her mind off the Negro girl. If she died . . . When it was light, she dressed and got into the car.

In town, the postman was unlocking the post office to sort the early mail. "I declare," he said to the rural mail carrier who arrived a few minutes later, "Miss Frances Harvey is driving herself crazy. Going back out yonder to the cemetery, and it not seven o'clock in the morning."

"Aw," said the rural deliveryman skeptically, looking at the empty road.

"That's right. I was here and seen her. You wait there, you'll see her come back. She'll drive herself nuts. Them old maids like that, left in them old houses—crazy and sweet, or crazy and mean, or just plain crazy. They just ain't locked up like them that's down in the asylum. That's the only difference."

"Miss Frances Harvey ain't no more than thirty-two, -three years old."

"Then she's just got more time to get crazier in. You'll see."

That day was Friday, and Tom Beavers, back from Jackson, came up Frances Harvey's sidewalk, as usual, at exactly a quarter past seven in the evening. Frances was not "going out" yet, and Regina had telephoned her long distance to say that "in all probability" she should not be receiving gentlemen "in." "What would Mama say?" Regina asked. Frances said she didn't know, which was not true, and went right on cooking dinners for Tom every weekend.

In the dining room that night, she sat across one corner of the long table from Tom. The useless length of polished cherry stretched away from them into the shadows as sadly as a road. Her plate pushed back, her chin resting on one palm, Frances stirred her coffee and said, "I don't know what on earth to do with all of Mama's clothes. I can't give them away, I can't sell them, I can't burn them, and the attic is full already. What can I do?"

"You look better tonight," said Tom.

"I slept," said Frances. "I slept and slept. From early this morning until just 'while ago. I never slept so well."

Then she told him about the Negro near the cemetery the previous afternoon, and how she had driven back out there as soon as dawn came, and found him again. He had been walking across the open field near the remains of the house that had burned down. There was no path to him from her, and she had hurried across ground uneven from old plowing and covered with the kind of small, tender grass it takes a very skillful mule to crop. "Wait!" she had cried. "Please wait!" The Negro had stopped and waited for her to reach him. "Your daughter?" she asked, out of breath.

"Daughter?" he repeated.

"The colored girl that was in the wagon yesterday. She was sick, you said, so I wondered. I could have taken her to town in the car, but I just didn't think. I wanted to know, how is she? Is she very sick?"

He had removed his old felt nigger hat as she approached him. "She a whole lot better, Miss Frances. She going to be all right now." Then he smiled at her. He did not say thank you, or anything more. Frances turned and walked back to the road and the car. And exactly as though the recovery of the Negro girl in the wagon had been her own recovery, she felt the return of a quiet breath and a steady pulse, and sensed the blessed stirring of a morning breeze. Up in her room, she had barely time to draw an old guilt over her before she fell asleep.

"When I woke, I knew about Mama," she said now to Tom. By the deepened intensity of her voice and eyes, it was plain that this was the important part. "It isn't right to say I *knew*," she went on, "because I had known all the time—ever since last night. I just realized it, that's all. I realized she had killed herself. It had to be that."

He listened soberly through the story about the box of sedatives. "But why?" he asked her. "It maybe looks that way, but what would be her reason for doing it?"

"Well, you see—" Frances said, and stopped.

Tom Beavers talked quietly on. "She didn't suffer. With what she had, she could have lived five, ten, who knows how many years. She was well cared for. Not hard up, I wouldn't say. Why?"

The pressure of his questioning could be insistent, and her trust in him, even if he was nobody but old Miss Rita Beavers' nephew, was well-nigh complete. "Because of you and me," she said, finally. "I'm certain of it, Tom. She didn't want to stand in our way. She never knew how to express love, you see." Frances controlled herself with an effort.

He did not reply, but sat industriously balancing a match folder on the tines of an unused serving fork. Anyone who has passed a lonely childhood in the company of an old deaf aunt is not inclined to doubt things hastily, and Tom Beavers would not have said he disbelieved anything Frances had told him. In fact, it seemed only too real to him. Almost before his eyes,

that imperial, practical old hand went fumbling for the pills in
the dark. But there had been much more to it than just love, he
reflected. Bitterness, too, and pride, and control. And humor,
perhaps, and the memory of a frightened little boy chased out
of the yard by a twitch of her fan. Being invited to tea was one
thing; suicide was quite another. Times had certainly changed,
he thought.

But, of course, he could not say that he believed it, either.
There was only Frances to go by. The match folder came to
balance and rested on the tines. He glanced up at her, and a
chill walked up his spine, for she was too serene. Cheek on
palm, a lock of reddish hair fallen forward, she was staring at
nothing with the absorbed silence of a child, or of a sweet,
silver-haired old lady engaged in memory. Soon he might find
that more and more of her was vanishing beneath this placid
surface.

He himself did not know what he had seen that Friday evening so many months ago—what the figure had been that
stood forward from the roadside at the tilt of the curve and
urgently waved an arm to him. By the time he had braked and
backed, the man had disappeared. Maybe it had been somebody drunk (for Richton had plenty of those to offer), walking
it off in the cool of the woods at first dark. No such doubts had
occurred to Frances. And what if he told her now the story
Totsie had related of the road gang and the sick Negro girl
in the wagon? Another labyrinth would open before her; she
would never get out.

In Richton, the door to the past was always wide open, and
what came in through it and went out of it had made people "different." But it scarcely ever happens, even in Richton,
that one is able to see the precise moment when fact becomes
faith, when life turns into legend, and people start to bend
their finest loyalties to make themselves bemused custodians of
the grave. Tom Beavers saw that moment now, in the profile
of this dreaming girl, and he knew there was no time to lose.

He dropped the match folder into his coat pocket. "I think
we should be leaving, Frances."

"Oh, well, I don't know about going out yet," she said.
"People criticize you so. Regina even had the nerve to telephone. Word had got all the way to her that you came here to

have supper with me and we were alone in the house. When I tell the maid I want biscuits made up for two people, she looks like 'What would yo mama say?'"

"I mean," he said, "I think it's time we left for good."

"And never came back?" It was exactly like Frances to balk at going to a movie but seriously consider an elopement.

"Well, never is a long time. I like to see about Aunt Rita every once in a great while. She can't remember from one time to the next whether it's two days or two years since I last came."

She glanced about the walls and at the furniture, the pictures, and the silver. "But I thought you would want to live here, Tom. It never occurred to me. I know it never occurred to Mama . . . This house . . . It can't be just left."

"It's a fine old house," he agreed. "But what would we do with all your mother's clothes?"

Her freckled hand remained beside the porcelain cup for what seemed a long time. He waited and made no move toward her; he felt her uncertainty keenly, but he believed that some people should not be startled out of a spell.

"It's just as you said," he went on, finally. "You can't give them away, you can't sell them, you can't burn them, and you can't put them in the attic, because the attic is full already. So what are you going to do?"

Between them, the single candle flame achieved a silent altitude. Then, politely, as on any other night, though shaking back her hair in a decided way, she said, "Just let me get my coat, Tom."

She locked the door when they left, and put the key under the mat—a last obsequy to the house. Their hearts were bounding ahead faster than they could walk down the sidewalk or drive off in the car, and, mindful, perhaps, of what happened to people who did, they did not look back.

Had they done so, they would have seen that the Harvey house was more beautiful than ever. All unconscious of its rejection by so mere a person as Tom Beavers, it seemed, instead, to have got rid of what did not suit it, to be free, at last, to enter with abandon the land of mourning and shadows and memory.

A Southern Landscape

IF YOU'RE like me and sometimes turn through the paper reading anything and everything because you're too lazy to get up and do what you ought to be doing, then you already know about my home town. There's a church there that has a gilded hand on the steeple, with the finger pointing to Heaven. The hand looks normal size, but it's really as big as a Ford car. At least, that's what they used to say in those little cartoon squares in the newspaper, full of sketches and exclamation points—"Strange As It Seems," "This Curious World," or Ripley's "Believe It or Not." Along with carnivorous tropical flowers, the Rosetta stone, and the cheerful information that the entire human race could be packed into a box a mile square and dumped into Grand Canyon, there it would be every so often, that old Presbyterian hand the size of a Ford car. It made me feel right in touch with the universe to see it in the paper—something it never did accomplish all by itself. I haven't seen anything about it recently, but then, Ford cars have got bigger, and, come to think of it, maybe they don't even print those cartoons any more. The name of the town, in case you're trying your best to remember and can't, is Port Claiborne, Mississippi. Not that I'm *from* there; I'm from *near* there.

Coming down the highway from Vicksburg, you come to Port Claiborne, and then to get to our house you turn off to the right on State Highway No. 202 and follow along the prettiest road. It's just about the way it always was—worn deep down like a tunnel and thick with shade in summer. In spring, it's so full of sweet heavy odors they make you drunk, you can't think of anything—you feel you will faint or go right out of yourself. In fall, there is the rustle of leaves under your tires and the smell of them, all sad and Indian-like. Then in the winter, there are only dust and bare limbs, and mud when it rains, and everything is like an old dirt-dauber's nest up in the corner. Well, any season, you go twisting along this tunnel for a mile or so, then the road breaks down into a flat open run toward a wooden bridge that spans a swampy creek

bottom. Tall trees grow up out of the bottom—willow and cypress, gum and sycamore—and there is a jungle of brush and
vines—kudzu, Jackson vine, Spanish moss, grapevine, Virginia
creeper, and honeysuckle—looping, climbing, and festooning
the trees, and harboring every sort of snake and varmint underneath. The wooden bridge clatters when you cross, and
down far below you can see water, lying still, not a good step
wide. One bank is grassy and the other is a slant of ribbed
white sand.

Then you're going to have to stop and ask somebody. Just
say, "Can you tell me where to turn to get to the Summerall
place?" Everybody knows us. Not that we *are* anybody—I don't
mean that. It's just that we've been there forever. When you
find the right road, you go right on up through a little wood
of oaks, then across a field, across a cattle gap, and you're there.
The house is nothing special, just a one-gable affair with a bay
window and a front porch—the kind they built back around
fifty or sixty years ago. The shrubs around the porch and the
privet hedge around the bay window were all grown up too
high the last time I was there. They ought to be kept trimmed
down. The yard is a nice flat one, not much for growing grass
but wonderful for shooting marbles. There were always two
or three marble holes out near the pecan trees where I used to
play with the colored children.

Benjy Hamilton swore he twisted his ankle in one of those
same marble holes once when he came to pick me up for something my senior year in high school. For all I know, they're
still there, but Benjy was more than likely drunk and so would
hardly have needed a marble hole for an excuse to fall down.
Once, before we got the cattle gap, he couldn't open the gate,
and fell on the barbed wire trying to cross the fence. I had to
pick him out, thread at a time, he was so tangled up. Mama
said, "What were you two doing out at the gate so long last
night?" "Oh, nothing, just talking," I said. She thought for
the longest time that Benjy Hamilton was the nicest boy that
ever walked the earth. No matter how drunk he was, the presence of an innocent lady like Mama, who said "*Drinking?*" in
the same tone of voice she would have said "*Murder?*," would
bring him around faster than any number of needle showers,
massages, ice packs, prairie oysters, or quick dips in December

off the northern bank of Lake Ontario. He would straighten up and smile and say, "You made any more peach pickle lately, Miss Sadie?" (He could even say "peach pickle.") And she'd say no, but that there was always some of the old for him whenever he wanted any. And he'd say that was just the sweetest thing he'd ever heard of, but she didn't know what she was promising—anything as good as her peach pickle ought to be guarded like gold. And she'd say, well, for most anybody else she'd think twice before she offered any. And he'd say, if only everybody was as sweet to him as she was. . . . And they'd go on together like that till you'd think that all creation had ground and wound itself down through the vistas of eternity to bring the two of them face to face for exchanging compliments over peach pickle. Then I would put my arm in his so it would look like he was helping me down the porch steps out of the reflexes of his gentlemanly upbringing, and off we'd go.

It didn't happen all the time, like I've made it sound. In fact, it was only a few times when I was in school that I went anywhere with Benjy Hamilton. Benjy isn't his name, either; it's Foster. I sometimes call him "Benjy" to myself, after a big overgrown thirty-three-year-old idiot in *The Sound and the Fury*, by William Faulkner. Not that Foster was so big or overgrown, or even thirty-three years old, back then; but he certainly did behave like an idiot.

I won this prize, see, for writing a paper on the siege of Vicksburg. It was for the United Daughters of the Confederacy's annual contest, and mine was judged the best in the state. So Foster Hamilton came all the way over to the schoolhouse and got me out of class—I felt terribly important—just to "interview" me. He had just graduated from the university and had a job on the paper in Port Claiborne—that was before he started work for the *Times-Picayune*, in New Orleans. We went into an empty classroom and sat down.

He leaned over some blank sheets of coarse-grained paper and scribbled things down with a thick-leaded pencil. I was sitting in the next seat; it was a long bench divided by a number of writing arms, which was why they said that cheating was so prevalent in our school—you could just cheat without meaning to. They kept trying to raise the money for regular desks in every classroom, so as to improve morals. Anyway, I couldn't help seeing what he was writing down, so I said, "'Marilee' is all one word, and with an 'i,' not a 'y.' 'Summerall' is spelled just like it sounds." "Are you a senior?" he asked. "Just a junior," I said. He wore horn-rimmed glasses; that was back before everybody wore them. I thought they looked unusual and very distinguished. Also, I had noticed his shoulders when he went over to let the window down. I thought they were distinguished, too, if a little bit bony. "What is your ambition?" he asked me. "I hope to go to college year after next," I said. "I intend to wait until my junior year in college to choose a career."

He kept looking down at his paper while he wrote, and when he finally looked up at me I was disappointed to see why he hadn't done it before. The reason was, he couldn't keep a straight face. It had happened before that people broke out laughing just when I was being my most earnest and sincere. It must have been what I said, because I don't think I *look* funny. I guess I don't look like much of any one thing. When I see myself in the mirror, no adjective springs right to mind, unless it's "average." I am medium height, I am average weight, I buy "natural"-colored face powder and "medium"-colored lipstick. But I must say for myself, before this goes too far, that every once in a great while I look Just Right. I've never found the combination for making this happen, and no amount of reading the makeup articles in the magazines they have at the beauty parlor will do any good. But sometimes it happens anyway, with no more than soap and water, powder, lipstick, and a damp hairbrush.

My interview took place in the spring, when we were practicing for the senior play every night. Though a junior, I was in it because they always got me, after the eighth grade, to take parts in things. Those of us that lived out in the country Mrs. Arrington would take back home in her car after rehearsal. One night, we went over from the school to get a Coca-Cola before the drugstore closed, and there was Foster Hamilton. He had done a real nice article—what Mama called a "writeup." It was when he was about to walk out that he noticed me and said, "Hey." I said "Hey" back, and since he just stood there, I said, "Thank you for the writeup in the paper."

"Oh, that's all right," he said, not really listening. He wasn't laughing this time. "Are you going home?" he said.

"We are after 'while," I said. "Mrs. Arrington takes us home in her car."

"Why don't you let me take you home?" he said. "It might —it might save Mrs. Arrington an extra trip."

"Well," I said, "I guess I could ask her."

So I went to Mrs. Arrington and said, "Mrs. Arrington, Foster Hamilton said he would be glad to drive me home." She hesitated so long that I put in, "He says it might save you an extra trip." So finally she said, "Well, all right, Marilee." She told Foster to drive carefully. I could tell she was uneasy, but then, my family were known as real good people, very strict, and of course she didn't want them to feel she hadn't done the right thing.

That was the most wonderful night. I'll never forget it. It was full of spring, all restlessness and sweet smells. It was radiant, it was warm, it was serene. It was all the things you want to call it, but no word would ever be the right one, nor any ten words, either. When we got close to our turnoff, after the bridge, I said, "The next road is ours," but Foster drove right on past. I knew where he was going. He was going to Windsor.

Windsor is this big colonial mansion built back before the Civil War. It burned down during the eighteen-nineties sometime, but there were still twenty-five or more Corinthian columns, standing on a big open space of ground that is a pasture now, with cows and mules and calves grazing in it. The columns are enormously high and you can see some of the iron-grillwork railing for the second-story gallery clinging halfway up. Vines cling to the fluted white plaster surfaces, and in some places the plaster has crumbled away, showing the brick underneath. Little trees grow up out of the tops of columns, and chickens have their dust holes among the rubble. Just down the fall of the ground beyond the ruin, there are some Negro houses. A path goes down to them.

It is this ignorant way that the hand of Nature creeps back over Windsor that makes me afraid. I'd rather there'd be ghosts there, but there aren't. Just some old story about lost jewelry that every once in a while sends somebody poking around in all the trash. Still, it is magnificent, and people have compared it to the Parthenon and so on and so on, and even if it makes me feel this undertone of horror, I'm always ready to go and look at it again. When all of it was standing, back in the old days, it was higher even than the columns, and had a cupola, too. You could see the cupola from the river, they say, and the story went that Mark Twain used it to steer by. I've read that book since, *Life on the Mississippi*, and it seems he used everything else to steer by, too—crawfish mounds, old rowboats stuck in the mud, the tassels on somebody's corn patch, and every stump and stob from New Orleans to Cairo, Illinois. But it does kind of connect you up with something to know that Windsor was there, too, like seeing the Presbyterian hand in the newspaper. Some people would say at this point, "Small world," but it isn't a small world. It's an enormous world, bigger than you can imagine, but it's all connected up. What Nature does to Windsor it does to everything, including you and me—there's the horror.

But that night with Foster Hamilton, I wasn't thinking any such doleful thoughts, and though Windsor can be a pretty scary-looking sight by moonlight, it didn't scare me then. I could have got right out of the car, alone, and walked all around among the columns, and whatever I heard walking away through the weeds would not have scared me, either. We sat there, Foster and I, and never said a word. Then, after some time, he turned the car around and took the road back. Before we got to my house, though, he stopped the car by the roadside and kissed me. He held my face up to his, but outside that he didn't touch me. I had never been kissed in any deliberate and accomplished way before, and driving out to Windsor in that accidental way, the whole sweetness of the spring night, the innocence and mystery of the two of us, made me think how simple life was and how easy it was to step into happiness, like walking into your own rightful house.

This frame of mind persisted for two whole days—enough to make a nuisance of itself. I kept thinking that Foster Hamilton would come sooner or later and tell me that he loved me, and I couldn't sleep for thinking about him in various ways, and I had no appetite, and nobody could get me to answer them. I half expected him at play practice or to come to the schoolhouse, and I began to wish he would hurry up and get it over with, when, after play practice on the second night, I saw him up-town, on the corner, with this blonde.

Mrs. Arrington was driving us home, and he and the blonde were standing on the street corner, just about to get in his car. I never saw that blonde before or since, but she is printed eternally on my mind, and to this good day if I'd run into her across the counter from me in the ten-cent store, which-ever one of us is selling lipstick to the other one, I'd know her for sure because I saw her for one half of a second in the street light in Port Claiborne with Foster Hamilton. She wasn't any ordinary blonde, either—dyed hair wasn't in it. I didn't know the term "feather-bed blonde" in those days, or I guess I would have thought it. As it was, I didn't really think anything, or say anything, either, but whatever had been galloping along inside me for two solid days and nights came to a screeching halt. Somebody in the car said, being real funny, "Foster Ham-ilton's got him another girl friend." I just laughed. "Sure has," I said. "Oh, Mari-leee!" they all said, teasing me. I laughed and laughed.

I asked Foster once, a long time later, "Why didn't you come back after that night you drove me out to Windsor?"

He shook his head. "We'd have been married in two weeks," he said. "It scared me half to death."

"Then it's a mercy you didn't," I said. "It scares *me* half to death right now."

Things had changed between us, you realize, between that kiss and that conversation. What happened was—at least, the main thing that happened was—Foster asked me the next year to go to the high-school senior dance with him, so I said all right.

I knew about Foster by then, and that his reputation was not of the best—that it was, in fact, about the worst our county had to offer. I knew he had an uncommon thirst and that on weekends he went helling about the countryside with a fellow that owned the local picture show and worked at a garage in the daytime. His name was A. P. Fortenberry, and he owned a new convertible in a sickening shade of bright maroon. The convertible was always dusty—though you could see A. P. in the garage every afternoon, during the slack hour, hosing it down on the wash rack—because he and Foster were out in it almost every night, harassing the countryside. They knew every bootlegger in a radius of forty miles. They knew girls that lived on the outskirts of towns and girls that didn't. I guess "uninhibited" was the word for A. P. Fortenberry, but whatever it was, I couldn't stand him. He called me into the garage one day—to have a word with me about Foster, he said—but when I got inside he backed me into the corner and started trying it on. "Funny little old girl," he kept saying. He rattled his words out real fast. "Funny little old girl." I slapped him as hard as I could, which was pretty hard, but that only seemed to stimulate him. I thought I'd never get away from him—I can't smell the inside of a garage to this good day without thinking about A. P. Fortenberry.

When Foster drove all the way out to see me one day soon after that—we didn't have a telephone in those days—I thought he'd come to apologize for A. P., and I'm not sure yet he didn't intend for me to understand that without saying anything about it. He certainly put himself out. He sat down and swapped a lot of Port Claiborne talk with Mama—just pleased her to death—and then he went out back with Daddy and looked at the chickens and the peach trees. He even had an opinion on growing peaches, though I reckon he'd given more thought to peach brandy than he'd ever given to orchards. He said when we were walking out to his car that he'd like to take me to the senior dance, so I said O.K. I was pleased; I had to admit it.

Even knowing everything I knew by then (I didn't tell Mama and Daddy), there was something kind of glamorous about Foster Hamilton. He came of a real good family, known for being aristocratic and smart; he had uncles who were college professors and big lawyers and doctors and things. His father had died when he was a babe in arms (tragedy), and he had perfect manners. He had perfect manners, that is, when he was sober, and it was not that he departed from them in any intentional way when he was drunk. Still, you couldn't exactly blame me for being disgusted when, after ten minutes of the dance, I discovered that his face was slightly green around the temples and that whereas he could dance fairly well, he could not stand up by himself at all. He teetered like a baby that has caught on to what walking is, and knows that now is the time to do it, but hasn't had quite enough practice.

"Foster," I whispered, "have you been drinking?"

"Been *drinking*?" he repeated. He looked at me with a sort of wonder, like the national president of the W.C.T.U. might if asked the same question. "It's so close in here," he complained.

It really wasn't that close yet, but it was going to be. The gym doors were open, so that people could walk outside in the night air whenever they wanted to. "Let's go outside," I said. Well, in my many anticipations I had foreseen Foster and me strolling about on the walks outside, me in my glimmering white sheer dress with the blue underskirt (Mama and I had worked for two weeks on that dress), and Foster with his nice broad aristocratic shoulders. Then, lo and behold, he had worn a white dinner jacket! There was never anybody in creation as proud as I was when I first walked into the senior dance that night with Foster Hamilton.

Pride goeth before a fall. The fall must be the one Foster took down the gully back of the boys' privy at the schoolhouse. I still don't know quite how he did it. When we went outside, he put me carefully in his car, helped to tuck in my skirts, and closed the door in the most polite way, and then I saw him heading toward the privy in his white jacket that was swaying like a lantern through the dark, and then he just wasn't there any more. After a while, I got worried that somebody would come out, like us, for air, so I got out and went to the outside wall of the privy and said, "Foster, are you all right?" I didn't get any answer, so I knocked politely on the wall and said, "Foster?" Then I looked around behind and all around, for I was standing very close to the edge of the gully that had eroded right up to the borders of the campus (somebody was always threatening that the whole schoolhouse was going to cave in into it before another school year went by), and there at the bottom of the gully Foster Hamilton was lying face down, like the slain in battle.

What I should have done, I should have walked right off and left him there till doomsday, or till somebody came along who would use him for a model in a statue to our glorious dead in the defense of Port Claiborne against Gen. Ulysses S. Grant in 1863. That battle was over in about ten minutes, too. But I had to consider how things would look—I had my pride, after all. So I took a look around, hiked up my skirts, and went down into the gully. When I shook Foster, he grunted and rolled over, but I couldn't get him up. I wasn't strong enough. Finally, I said, "Foster, Mama's here!," and he soared up like a Roman candle. I never saw anything like it. He walked straight up the side of the gully and gave me a hand up, too. Then I guided him over toward the car and he sat in the door and lighted a cigarette.

"Where is she?" he said.

"Who?" I said.

"Your mother," he said.

"Oh, I just said that, Foster. I had to get you up someway."

At that, his shoulders slumped down and he looked terribly depressed. "I didn't mean to do this, Marilee," he said. "I didn't have any idea it would hit me this way. I'm sure I'll be all right in a minute."

I don't think he ever did fully realize that he had fallen in the gully. "Get inside," I said, and shoved him over. There were one or two couples beginning to come outside and walk around. I squeezed in beside Foster and closed the door. Inside the gym, where the hot lights were, the music was blaring and beating away. We had got a real orchestra specially for that evening, all the way down from Vicksburg, and a brass-voiced girl was singing a nineteen-thirties song. I would have given anything to be in there with it rather than out in the dark with Foster Hamilton.

I got quite a frisky reputation out of that evening. Disappearing after ten minutes of the dance, seen snuggling out in the car, and gone completely by intermission. I drove us away. Foster wouldn't be convinced that anybody would think it at all peculiar if he reappeared inside the gym with red mud smeared all over his dinner jacket. I didn't know how to drive, but I did anyway. I'm convinced you can do anything when you have to—speak French, do a double back flip off the low diving board, play Rachmaninoff on the piano, or fly an airplane. Well, maybe not fly an airplane; it's too technical. Anyway, that's how I learned to drive a car, riding us up and down the highway, holding off Foster with my elbow, marking time till midnight came and I could go home without anybody thinking anything out of the ordinary had happened.

When I got out of the car, I said, "Foster Hamilton, I never want to see you again as long as I live. And I hope you have a wreck on the way home."

Mama was awake, of course. She called out in the dark, "Did you have a good time, Marilee?"

"Oh, yes, Ma'am," I said.

Then I went back to my shed-ceilinged room in the back wing, and cried and cried. And cried.

There was a good bit of traffic coming and going out to our house after that. A. P. Fortenberry came, all pallid and sober, with a tie on and a straw hat in his hand. Then A. P. and Foster came together. Then Foster came by himself.

The story went that Foster had stopped in the garage with A. P. for a drink before the dance, and instead of water in the drink, A. P. had filled it up with grain alcohol. I was asked to believe that he did this because, seeing Foster all dressed up, he got the idea that Foster was going to some family do, and he couldn't stand Foster's family, they were all so stuckup. While Foster was draining the first glass, A. P. had got called out front to put some gas in a car, and while he was gone Foster took just a little tap more whiskey with another glassful of grain alcohol. A. P. wanted me to understand that Foster's condition that night had been all his fault, that instead of three or four ounces of whiskey, Foster had innocently put down eighteen ounces of sheer dynamite, and it was a miracle only to be surpassed by the resurrection of Jesus Christ that he had managed to drive out and get me, converse with Mama about peach pickle, and dance those famous ten minutes at all.

Well, I said I didn't know. I thought to myself I never heard of Foster Hamilton touching anything he even mistook for water.

All these conferences took place at the front gate. "I never saw a girl like you," Mama said. "Why don't you invite the boys to sit on the porch?"

"I'm not too crazy about A. P. Fortenberry," I said. "I don't think he's a very nice boy."

"Uh-*huh*," Mama said, and couldn't imagine what Foster Hamilton was doing running around with him, if he wasn't a nice boy. Mama, to this day, will not hear a word against Foster Hamilton.

I was still giving some thought to the whole matter that summer, sitting now on the front steps, now on the back steps, and now on the side steps, whichever was most in the shade, chewing on pieces of grass and thinking, when one day the mailman stopped in for a glass of Mama's cold buttermilk (it's famous) and told me that Foster and A. P. had had the most awful wreck. They had been up to Vicksburg, and coming home had collided with a whole carload of Negroes. The carnage was awful—so much blood on everybody you couldn't tell black from white. They were both going to live, though. Being so drunk, which in a way had caused the wreck, had also kept them relaxed enough to come out of it alive. I warned the mailman to leave out the drinking part when he told Mama, she thought Foster was such a nice boy.

The next time I saw Foster, he was out of the hospital and had a deep scar on his cheekbone like a sunken star. He looked handsomer and more distinguished than ever. I had gotten a scholarship to Millsaps College in Jackson, and was just about to leave. We had a couple of dates before I left, but things were not the same. We would go to the picture show and ride around afterward, having a conversation that went something like this:

"Marilee, why are you such a nice girl? You're about the only nice girl I know."

"I guess I never learned any different, so I can't help it. Will you teach me how to stop being a nice girl?"

"I certainly will not!" He looked to see how I meant it, and for a minute I thought the world was going to turn over; but it didn't.

"Why won't you, Foster?"

"You're too young. And your mama's a real sweet lady. And your daddy's too good a shot."

"Foster, why do you drink so much?"

"Marilee, I'm going to tell you the honest truth. I drink because I like to drink." He spoke with real conviction.

So I went on up to college in Jackson, where I went in for serious studies and made very good grades. Foster, in time, got a job on the paper in New Orleans, where, during off hours, or so I understood, he continued his investigation of the lower things in life and of the effects of alcohol upon the human system.

It is twenty years later now, and Foster Hamilton is down there yet.

Millions of things have happened; the war has come and gone. I live far away, and everything changes, almost every day. You can't even be sure the moon and stars are going to be the same the day after tomorrow night. So it has become more and more important to me to know that Windsor is still right where it always was, standing pure in its decay, and that the gilded hand on the Presbyterian church in Port Claiborne is still pointing to Heaven and not to Outer Space; and I earnestly feel, too, that Foster Hamilton should go right on drinking. There have got to be some things you can count on, would be an ordinary way to put it. I'd rather say that I feel the need of a land, of a sure terrain, of a sort of permanent landscape of the heart.

Sharon

UNCLE HERNAN, my mother's brother (his full name was Hernando de Soto Wirth), lived right near us—a little way down the road, if you took the road; across the pasture, if you didn't—in a house surrounded by thick privet hedge, taller than a man riding by on a mule could see over. He had live oaks around the house, and I don't remember ever going there without hearing the whisper of dry fallen leaves beneath my step on the ground. Sometimes there would be a good many Negroes about the house and yard, for Uncle Hernan worked a good deal of land, and there was always a great slamming of screen doors—people looking for something they couldn't find and hollering about where they'd looked or thought for somebody else to look, or just saying, "What'd you say?" "Huh?" "I said, 'What'd you *say*?'"—or maybe a wrangling noise of a whole clutch of colored children playing off down near the gully. But in spite of all these things, even with all of them going on at one and the same time, Uncle Hernan's place was a still place. That was how it knew itself: it kept its own stillness. When I remember that stillness, I hear again the little resistant veins of a dry oak leaf unlacing beneath my bare foot, so that the sound seems to be heard in the foot's flesh itself.

As a general rule, however, I wasn't barefoot, for Uncle Hernan was a gentleman, and I came to him when I was sent for, to eat dinner, cleaned up, in a fresh dress, and wearing shoes. "Send the child over on Thursday," he would say. Dinner was what we ate in the middle of the day—our big meal. Mama would look me over before I went—ears and nails and mosquito bites—and brush my hair, glancing at the clock. "Tell Uncle Hernan hello for me," she would say, letting me out the side door.

"Marilee?" she would say, when I got halfway to the side gate.

"Ma'am?"

"You look mighty sweet."

"Sweet" was a big word with all of them; I guess they got it from so many flowers and from the night air in South

Mississippi, almost all seasons. And maybe I did really look that way when going to Uncle Hernan's.

I would cross a shoulder of pasture, which was stubbled with bitterweed and white with glare under the high sun, go through a slit in the hedge, which towered over me, and wriggle through a gap in the fence. This gap was no haphazard thing but was arranged, the posts placed in such a way that dogs and people could go through but cows couldn't, for Uncle Hernan was a good farmer and not one to leave baggy places in his fences from people crawling over them. He built a gap instead. As I went by, the dogs that were sprawled around dozing under the trees would look up and grin at me, giving a thump or two with their tails in the dust, too lazy to get up and speak. I would go up the steps and stand outside the door and call, looking into the shadowy depths of the hall, like a reflection of itself seen in water. I had always to make my presence known just this way; this was a house that expected behavior. It was simple enough, one-story, with a square front porch, small by Southern standards, opening out from the central doorway. Two stout pillars supported the low classical triangle of white-painted wood, roofed in shingle. The house had been built back before the Civil War. Uncle Hernan and Mama and others who had died or moved away had been brought up here, but they were anxious to let you know right away that they were not pretentious people but had come to Mississippi to continue being what they'd always been—good farming people who didn't consider themselves better or worse than anybody else. Yet somebody, I realized fairly early on, had desired a façade like a Greek temple, though maybe the motive back of the desire had been missing and a prevailing style had been copied without any thought for its effect.

Uncle Hernan, however, was not one of those who protested in this vein any more, if he ever had. He lived the democratic way and had friends in every walk of life, but Sharon —that was the name of the house—had had its heyday once, and he had loved it. It had been livened with more airs and graces than anybody would have patience to listen to, if I knew them all to tell. That was when Uncle Hernan's pretty young wife was there. Mama said that Uncle Hernan used to

say that the bright and morning star had come to Sharon. It
all sounded very Biblical and right; also, he called her his Wild
Irish Rose. She was from Tennessee and brought wagonloads
of stuff with her when she came, including a small rosewood
piano. Every tasseled, brocaded, gold-leafed, or pearl-inlaid
thing in Sharon, you knew at once, had come from Tennessee with Aunt Eileen. At the long windows, for instance, she
had put draperies that fastened back with big bronze hooks,
the size of a baby's arm bent back, and ending in a lily. Even
those lilies were French—the fleur-de-lis. All this was in the
best parlor, where nobody ever went very much any more,
where the piano was, covered with the tasseled green-and-
white throw, and the stern gold-framed portraits (those belonged to our family). It was not that the parlor was closed
or that there was anything wrong with going into it. I sometimes got to play in there, and looked at everything to my
heart's content. It was just that there was no reason to use
it any more. The room opposite, across the hall, was a parlor, too, full of Uncle Hernan's books, and with his big old
plantation desk, and his round table, where he sat near the
window. The Negroes had worn a path to the window, coming there to ask him things. So life went on here now, in the
plain parlor rather than the elegant one, and had since Aunt
Eileen died.

She had not lived there very long, only about three or four
years, it seems, or anyway not more than five, when she got sick
one spring day—the result, they said at first, of having done
too much out in the yard. But she didn't get better; one thing
led to another, all during the hottest summer Mama said she
could ever remember. In September, their hopes flagged, and
in the winter she died. This was all before I could remember.
Her portrait did not hang in the best parlor with the other,
old ones, but there was a daguerreotype of her in a modest
oval gold frame hanging in the plain parlor. She had a small
face, with her hair done in the soft upswept fashion of the
times, and enormous eyes that looked a little of everything—
fearful, shy, proud, wistful, happy, adoring, amused, as though
she had just looked at Uncle Hernan. She wasn't the angel you
might think. Especially when she was sick, she'd make them

all jump like grease in a hot skillet, Uncle Hernan said, but he would say it smiling, for everything he felt about her was sheer affection. He was a strong, intelligent man; he had understood her but he had loved her, all the time.

Uncle Hernan never forgot that he'd asked me to dinner, or on which day. He would come to let me in himself. He always put on the same coat, no matter how hot it was—a rumpled white linen coat, faded yellow. He was a large, almost portly man, with a fleshy face, basically light in color but splashed with sunburn, liver spots, and freckles, and usually marked with the line of his hatband. He had untidy, graying, shaggy hair and a tobacco-stained mustache, but he kept his hands and nails scrupulously clean—a matter of pride. I was a little bit afraid of Uncle Hernan. Though I loved to come there, I was careful to do things always the same way, waiting to sit down until I was told, staying interested in whatever he told me, saying, "Yes, thank you, Uncle Hernan," and "No, thank you, Uncle Hernan," when we were at the table. He was fond of me and liked having me, but I was not his heart of hearts, so I had to be careful.

Melissa waited on us. Melissa had originally come there from Tennessee with Aunt Eileen, as her personal maid, so I had got it early through my head that she was not like the rest of the Negroes around home, any more than Aunt Eileen's tasseled, rosewood, pearl-inlaid, gold-leafed, and brocaded possessions were like the plain Wirth house had been before she got there. Melissa talked in a different style from other Negroes; for instance, she said "I'm not" instead of "I ain't" or "I isn't" (which they said when trying to be proper). She even said "He doesn't," which was more than Mama would do very often. It wasn't that she put on airs or was ambitious. But we all stood in awe of her, a little. You never know for sure when you come into a Negro house, whether you are crossing the threshold of a rightful king or queen, and I felt this way about Melissa's house. It was just Uncle Hernan's cook's cabin, but I felt awkward in it. It was so much her own domain, and there was no set of manners to go by. She had turned scraps of silk and satin into clever doilies for tables and cushion covers and had briar-stitched a spread for her bed with rich dark pieces bound with a scarlet thread; you could tell she had copied all her tastes from Aunt Eileen. The time I discovered that I really liked Melissa was when she came to our house once, the winter Mama had pneumonia. She came and stayed, to help out. She wore a white starched uniform, so then I learned that Melissa, all along, had been a nurse. It seemed that when Aunt Eileen was about to get married, Eileen's father, seeing that Uncle Hernan lived in the wilds of Mississippi, had taken Melissa and had her trained carefully in practical nursing. I guess he thought we didn't have doctors, or if we had we had no roads for them to go and come on; anyway, he wasn't taking any chances. After Mama passed the danger period, Melissa spent a lot of time reading aloud to me. I would sit in her lap by the hour and listen and listen, happy, until one day I went in to see how Mama was and she said, "I wouldn't ask Melissa to read to me too long at the time, Marilee."

"She likes to read," I said.

"I know," she said, "but I'm afraid you'll get to smell like a Negro."

Now that she mentioned it, I realized that I had liked the way Melissa smelled. I wanted to argue, but she looked weak and cross, the way sick people do, so I just said, "Yes, ma'am," and went away.

It is a mighty asset in life to be a good cook, and Melissa never spared to set the best before me when I came to Uncle Hernan's to dinner. If it was fried chicken, the crust would be golden, and as dry as popcorn, with the thinnest skim of glistening fat between the crust and the meat. If it was roast duck or turkey or hen, it would come to the table brown, gushing steam that smelled of all it was stuffed with. There were always hot biscuits—she made tiny hot biscuits, the size of a nickel three inches high—and side dishes of peach pickle, souse, chopped pepper relish, green-tomato pickle, wild-plum jelly, and blackberry jam. There were iced tea and buttermilk both, with peaches and dumplings for dessert and maybe homemade ice cream—so cold it hurt your forehead to eat it—and coconut cake.

Such food as that may have been the main excuse for having me to dinner, but Uncle Hernan also relished our conversations. After dinner, I would sit with him in the plain parlor —he with his small cup of black chicory coffee before him, and I facing him in a chair that rocked on a stand—telling him whatever he asked me to. About Mama and Daddy, first; then school—who taught me and what they said and all about their side remarks and friends and general behavior. Then we'd go into his part, which took the form of hunting stories, recollections about friends, or stories about his brother, Uncle Rex, who now lived several miles away, or about books I ought to be reading. He would enter right into those books he favored as though they were a continuation of life around us. *Les Misérables* was a great favorite of his, not so much because of the poverty and suffering it depicted but because in spite of all that Valjean was a man, he said, and one you came little at a time to see in his full stature. His stature increased, he would say, and always put his hand down low and raised it up as high as it would go. I guess he was not so widely read as he seemed to me at that time to be, but he knew what he liked and why, and thought that knowing character was the main reason for reading anything. One day, he took a small gold box from his pocket and sniffed deftly, with his hand going to each nostril in turn. When I stared at him, startled into wonder, my look in turn startled him. His hand forgot to move downward and our eyes met in a lonely, simple way, such as had not happened before.

Then he smiled. "Snuff," he said. He snapped the box to and held it out. "You want to see? Don't open it, now. You'll sneeze." I took the box in my hand and turned it—golden, with a small raised cage of worked gold above the lid. I thought at once I had come on another of Aunt Eileen's tracks, but he said, "I picked that up in New Orleans a year or so back," and here I had another facet of Uncle Hernan—a stroll past shops in that strange city I had never seen, a pause before a window, a decision to enter and buy, cane hooked over his forearm. The world was large; I was small. He let me out the front door. "You're getting to be a big girl," said Melissa, from halfway back down the hall. "I'm soon going to have to say 'Miss Marilee.'"

The one thing I could never do was to go over to Uncle Hernan's without being asked. This was laid down to me, firmly and sternly. It became, of course, the apple in the garden.

One summer afternoon when I was alone and bored, getting too big, they said, to play with Melissa's children anymore, I begged Mama to let me go over there. She denied me twice, and threatened to whip me if I asked again, and when Daddy got in from the field she got him to talk to me. They were both sterner and more serious than I ever remembered them being, and made sure I got it straight. I said to Mama, being very argumentative, "You just don't like Melissa." She looked like I had slapped her. She turned white and left the room, but not without a glance at Daddy. I knew he was commissioned to deal with me (he knew it, too), but I also knew that he was not going to treat me as badly as Mama would have if he hadn't been there. He sent me to my room and hoped for the best. There I felt very sorry for myself and told myself I didn't know why I was being treated so harshly, sent to bed in a cold room with no supper, all for making such an innocent remark. I said I would stay in my room till I died, and they'd be sorry, Mama especially. I pictured the sad words that would certainly be exchanged.

Mama relented well before I came to this tragic end. In fact, she came in the room after about an hour. She never could stand any kind of unhappiness for long, and after urging me to come and get supper (I wouldn't reply) she brought me a glass of milk and lighted a little fire to take the chill off the room. But, sweet or not, she was a feline at heart, and at a certain kind of threat her claws came out, ready for blood. She was never nice to Melissa. I overheard them once talking at the kitchen door. Uncle Hernan had sent some plums over and when Mama said, "How are you, Melissa?" in her most grudging and offhand way, Melissa told her. She stood outside the steps, not touching the railing—they had reached their hands out to the farthest limit to give and receive the bucket, and Mama had by now closed the screen door between them—and told her. She had a boil on her leg, she said; no amount of poultices seemed to draw it out and it hurt her all the way up to her hip. She had also been feeling very discouraged in her heart lately, but maybe this was due to the boil.

"I don't see why you don't go on back to Tennessee," Mama said, cold as ice. "You know you ought to, now, don't you?"

"No, ma'am," Melissa answered her politely, "I don't know that I ought to. I promised Miss Eileen I'd stay and care for Sharon."

"You aren't fooling anybody," Mama said. "If Miss Eileen—"

"Good morning, Marilee," said Melissa sweetly.

I said, "Morning, Melissa," and Mama, who hadn't noticed me, whirled around and left without another word.

The day came when I crossed over. Wrong or not, I went to Sharon when nobody had asked me. Mama was away to a church meeting, and Daddy had been called down in the pasture about some cows that had got out. It was late September, still and golden; school hadn't been started very long. I went over barefoot and looked in the window of the plain parlor, but nobody was there, so I circled round to the other side, stopping to pet and silence a dog who looked at me and half barked, then half whined. I looked through the window of the fine parlor, and there they both happened to be, Uncle Hernan and Melissa, talking together and smiling. I could see their lips move, though not hear them, for in my wrongdoing and disobedience I was frightened of being caught, and the blood was pounding in my ears. Melissa looked pretty, and her white teeth flashed with her smiling in her creamy brown face. But it was Uncle Hernan, with the lift of his arm toward her, seated as he was in a large chair with a high back that finished in carved wood above his head, whose gesture went to my heart. That motion, so much a part of him whom I loved, was for her and controlled her, as it had, I knew now, hundreds of times. She came close and they leaned together; he gathered her surely in. She gave him her strength and he drank it; they became one another.

I had forgotten even to tremble and do not remember yet how I reached home from Sharon again. I only remember finding myself in my own room, seated on the edge of my narrow bed, hands folded in my lap, hearing the wrangle of Melissa's children out in the gully playing—they were beating some iron on an old washtub—and presently how her voice shouted out at them from across the back yard at Uncle Hernan's. She had four, and though they could all look nice on Sunday, they were perfect little devils during the week, Mama complained, and Melissa often got so mad she half beat the hide off them. I felt differently about them now. Their awful racket seemed a part of me—near and powerful, realer than itself, like their living blood. That blood was ours, mingling and twining with the other. Mama could kick like a mule, fight like a wildcat in a sack, but she would never get it out. It was there for good.

Indian Summer

ONE OF my mother's three brothers, Rex Wirth, lived about ten miles from us: he had taken over his wife's family home because her parents had needed somebody on the land to look after it.

Uncle Rex had been wild in youth, had dashed around gambling, among other things, and had not settled down until years after he married. "What Martha's gone through!" was one of Mama's oft-heard remarks. I had a wild boy friend myself back then and I used to reflect that at least Uncle Rex had married Aunt Martha. Furthermore, he did, at last, settle down.

Once stabilized, it became him to be and look like a responsible country gentleman. He was clipped and spare in appearance, scarcely as tall as his horse, and just missed being frail-looking, but he had an almost military air of authority; to me, when I thought of him, I always pictured him as approaching alone. He might be in blue work pants, he might be in a suit; his smart forward step was the same, and his crinkling smile had nothing to beg about. "How you *do?*" was his greeting to everybody, family or stranger. But the place—with its rolling, piny acreage, its big two-story house, its circular drive to the gate—was not his own. He never said this, but his brother, Uncle Hernan, who lived next door to us, said that he never had to mention it because he never forgot it for a minute. "It galls him," was Uncle Hernan's judgment. He was usually right.

The family feeling toward Uncle Rex, which was complicated but filled with reality, had to do, I believe, with his having, when a boy, fallen from a tree into a tractor disk. There was still a scar on his leg and one across his back, but the momentary threat to his manhood, the pity in that, was what gave the family its special tremor about him. If he stood safe it was still a near miss, and gave to his eyes the honest, wide openness of those of our forebears in family daguerreotypes, all the more vulnerable for having died or been killed in the Civil War and yet, at the time of the picture, anyway, not knowing it, that it would happen that way, or happen at all.

To me, even stranger than the tractor disk accident and re-lating to no photograph of any family member whomsoever, was the time Uncle Rex almost burned alive. He had been sleepy from fox hunting, and out on the place in the afternoon had gone into an abandoned Negro house down in a little hollow with pine and camellia trees around it and built a fire in the empty chimney out of a busted chair and fallen sound asleep on an old pile of cotton—third picking, never ginned. He woke with the place blazing around him and what it came to was that he apparently, from those who saw it, walked out through a solid wall of flame. The house crashed in behind him. He was singed a little but unharmed. Well, he was pre-cious, Mama said, and the Lord had spared him.

Over there where he lived, however, he was a captive of the McClellands; had the Lord spared him for that? A certain way of looking at it made it a predicament. It was better to speak in ordinary terms, that he'd managed the property and taken care of his wife's parents till they died, then had stayed on.

"That farm wouldn't have been anything without you, Rex," I once heard Mama pointing out. "It would have gone to rack and ruin."

"I reckon so," he would say, and brush his hand hard across the sparse hair atop his head, the color having left hold of red for sandy gray, the permanently sun-splotched scalp showing through here and there in slats and angles. "Someday I'll pick up Martha and move in with Hernan." He had as much right, certainly, to live in the old Wirth family home as Uncle Hernan had, for it belonged to all; still, he was joking when he said a thing like that, no matter how many McClellands were always visiting him, making silently clear the place was theirs.

It wouldn't have worked anyway. He was plainer by nature than Uncle Hernan, who loved his bonded whiskey and gold-trimmed porcelain, silver, table linen, and redolent cigars. Un-cle Rex's wild days, even, had had nothing plush about them; his gambling had been done not in the carpeted *maisons* of New Orleans, but around and about with hunting compan-ions; he would hunt in the coldest weather in nothing except an old briar-scratched, dog-clawed, leather jacket, standing bareheaded on deer stands through the long drizzles of win-ter days. Sometimes he got sick, sometimes not. "Come on,

Martha," he would snort from his bed, voice muffled in cold symptoms, up to his neck in blankets, while the poor woman went off in every direction for thermometers and hot water bottles and aspirin and boiled egg and tea and the one book he wanted, which had got mislaid. "Come on! Be good for something!"

It was in the course of nature—that and pleasing the McClellands, who were strict—that Uncle Rex had given all his meanness up; he was a regular churchgoer now, first a deacon, then an elder. So all his hollering at Aunt Martha was understood as no more than prankish. Besides, Aunt Martha had been provably good for something; she'd had a son, a fine boy, so everybody said, including me; he'd gone to military academy and now he taught at one.

Once in the winter Mama and Daddy and I drove over to see Uncle Rex and found him alone. It was Sunday. Aunt Martha had gone into town to see some of her folks, who must have had some ailment, else they would have been out there.

"Come on, now," Uncle Rex said, as it was fine weather. "You want to see my filly?" He got up to get his jacket and change into some twill britches for riding in.

"How's she doing?" Daddy asked.

"She's coming on real good, a great big gal. Hope the preacher don't come. Hope Martha's not back early. Just showing a horse, Marilee," he turned to ask me, "ain't that all right on Sunday?" He fancied himself when well mounted and sat as dapper as a cavalryman. In World War I, he'd trained for that, but had never got to France.

"What's her name?" I asked him.

"Sally," he said. "How's that?" He'd put his arm across my shoulder, walking; he didn't have the mass, the complex drawing power of his brother, Uncle Hernan, but his nature was finely coiled, authentic, within him, you could tell that.

We came out to the barn all together, enwrapped (as all around us was) in the thin winter sunshine which fell without color on the smooth-worn unpainted cattle gate letting into the lot. "Mind your step," said Uncle Rex. The cows were out and grazing; two looked peacefully up; the mare was nowhere in sight. The barn stood Sunday quiet. "She must be back yonder," he said.

At the barn he reached up high to unbolt the lock on the tack room door and fling it back. The steps had rotted but a stump of wood had been upended usefully below the door jamb; if you meant business—and Uncle Rex did—about getting in, it would bear a light climbing step without toppling. Uncle Rex emerged with a bridle over his arm. The woods beyond the fenced lot were winter bare, except for some touches of oak. There were elm, pecan, and walnut, a thick stand along the bluff. Below the bluff was more pasture land, good for playing in, I remembered from childhood, handy for hunting arrowheads. It rolled pleasantly, clumped with plum bushes and one or two shade trees, down to the branch with its sandy banks.

Uncle Rex was leading the mare out now. He had found her back of the barn. He re-entered the harness room for the saddle while she stood quietly, reins flung over an iron hook set in the barn wall. Uncle Rex brushed her thick-set neck, which arched out of her shoulders in one glossy, muscular rise; he tossed on her saddle. He brought the girth under, but she spun back. "I'll hold her," Daddy said, and took the reins. "Whoa, there," he said, while Uncle Rex cinched the girth. He gathered her in then, though she wasn't sure yet that she liked it, tapped her fetlock to bring her lower for the mounting, and up he went. We stood around while he showed her off; she had a smart little singlefoot that he liked, and a long swinging walk. I still remember the straightness of his back as he rode away from us, and the jaunty swing of his elbows.

Afterward we returned to the house and there was Aunt Martha's car, back from her folks in town. She acted glad to see us: it was Uncle Rex she was cool to. The McClelland house was a country place, but it had high, white, important sides with not enough windows, like a house on a city street. The McClellands were nice people, a connection spread over two counties, yet the house was different from what we would have had. It was printed all over Aunt Martha what she was thinking; that Uncle Rex had had that horse out on Sunday. And the beast was female, too; that, I now realized, made a difference to both of them, and had all along.

Aunt Martha was pretty, with an unlined plump face, gray hair she wore curled nicely in place. She was reserved about her feelings, and if Uncle Rex had not come into her life, lighting it up for us to see it, I doubt we'd ever have thought anything about Martha McClelland. That day of the mare, she was wearing brown, but summer would see her turned out in fresh bright cotton dresses she'd made herself, trimmed in eyelet with little pleats and buttons cleverly selected. She also picked out the cars they drove; they were always green or blue. It occurred to me years after that what Aunt Martha liked was owning things. Her ownership, which was not an intrusion—she wanted nothing of anybody else's—extended to all things and persons she had any claim on. When she got to Uncle Rex, then I guess she got a little bit confused; did he belong to her or not? If so, in what way? That question, I thought, would be something like Uncle Rex's own confusion over the McClelland property: he had it, but didn't actually own it. He'd certainly improved it quite a bit. But Aunt Martha also could point to improvements; Uncle Rex was so much better than he used to be. For in former days, freshly married, with promises not to still warmly throbbing in the air, he would come in at dawn, stinking of swamp mud and corn likker, having played poker all night while listening to the fox hounds running way off in the woods—some prefer Grand Opera while playing bezique, Uncle Hernan once remarked. I wondered what bezique was. Whatever it was, it wasn't for Uncle Rex.

As we drove away, Daddy said: "She's probably raising Cain about that mare."

"I don't think so," Mama said. "I don't think Martha raises Cain. Andrew is coming home at Thanksgiving. That's keeping her happy. She's proud of that boy."

"Rex is proud of him, too," said Daddy.

"Of course he is," Mama said.

Andrew was a dark-haired square-set boy, and when we used to play, as children, looking for arrowheads in the pasture, climbing through the fence to the next property where, it was said, the high bump in the ground near the old road was really an Indian mound, I would imagine him an Indian brave

or somebody with Indian blood. My effort, I suppose, was
to make him mysterious and hence more interesting, but the
truth is there was never anything mysterious about Andrew.
He was a good boy through and through, the way Aunt Martha wanted him. She would have liked him to go in the minis-
try but he took up history and played basketball so well he was
a wonder. He wasn't so tall but he was fast and well set and had
a wondrous way of guarding the ball; he knew how to dribble
it and keep it safe. After graduating he got a job teaching and
coaching at a military academy run by the church. This was not
being a preacher but was in no way acting like his father used
to act, and Aunt Martha breathed easy once he decided on it.

He was likely to be home in the summers when not working
in some boys' camp.

That was all in the late 1940s, post-war. Andrew was younger
than me and unlike the boys my age, he had missed the con-
flict. He was old enough to play basketball but not to be
drafted. Somebody—a man of the town—on seeing him win
a whole tournament for Port Claiborne, came up afterward to
say: "Boy, it's folks like you that keeps us inter-rested here at
home. Don't think you ain't doing your part." Aunt Martha
was proud of that; she quoted it often and so did Uncle Rex.

With such a fine boy who'd turned out so well, a place
running smoothly and yielding up its harvest year by year, a
calmed-down husband with a docile wife, it seemed that Uncle
Rex and Aunt Martha could sit on their porch in the summer,
in their living room by the gas fire in the winter, smiling and
smug and more than content with themselves because of the
content they felt about Andrew. Next he would get married,
no doubt, and have children, and all would be goodness and
love and joy forever. But something happened before that and
Aunt Martha lost, I suppose, her holy vision.

It happened like this.

One of the summers when Andrew was home sort of put-
tering around farming and romancing one or two girls in town
and reading up for his schoolwork, he and Aunt Martha suddenly got thicker than thieves. They were always out in the
family car together, either uptown or driving to Jackson, or
out on the place. People leaned in the car window to tell them

how much Andrew resembled her side of the family, which was
true. The pity (at least to a Wirth) was how pleased they both
looked about it. To start really conversing with a parent for the
first time must be as strange an experience as falling in love.
Daddy and Mama and I love each other but we never say very
much about it. Maybe they talk to each other in an unknown
tongue when I'm not around. But as for Andrew and Aunt
Martha it seemed that somebody had blown up the levee of
family reticence, and water and land were mingling to their
mutual content.

Late that same summer, Uncle Rex and Uncle Hernan had
got together and taken a train trip up to visit their third and
older brother, Uncle Andrew, who had lived and worked in
Chicago for years, in the law firm of Sanders, Wirth, and Pot-
tle, but who had now retired to a farm he had bought north
of Cairo. The trip had renewed the Wirth ties of blood. There
is something wonderful about older-type gentlemen on trains.
It brings out the good living side of them and makes them
relish the table service in the diner, a highball later, and lots of
well-seasoned talk. They may even have gambled a little in the
club car. The visit with Uncle Andrew must have attained such
a joyous and measured richness they would always preserve its
privacy.

"It's the property we've looked into these last few days,"
young Andrew said to his father, on his return. "The possibilities are just great, what with that new highway coming
through."

"I think so, too," Aunt Martha said, and served them all
the new recipes she was learning. "You've just got to listen to
Andrew, Rex."

"I'm still riding the train," said Uncle Rex. "You got to wait
awhile before I can listen."

Whether they let him wait awhile or not is doubtful. They
were bursting with their plans and designs on the McClelland
property. The new highway was coming through. Forty acres
given over to real estate was something the farm would never
miss. The houses, maybe a shopping center, and even a motel
would all be too distant to be seen from the house, yet they
glimmered full formed and visible as a mirage in Andrew's talk;
and in his thoughts the large pile of money bound to result was
already mounding up in the bank.

Andrew had assembled facts and figures, and had borrowed some blueprints of suburban housing from a development firm in Vicksburg. They curled up around his ears when he talked about it all, but nobody had stopped to notice that Uncle Rex had sat the greater part of the time as stiff and straight as if his mare was under him, though the rapport he and that animal shared was not present. He listened and listened and he failed to do justice to the food, and when he couldn't stand it a minute longer he exploded like a firecracker:

"I always knew it!" he jumped up to say. "I never should have moved onto this property."

They looked up with their large brown McClelland eyes, innocent as grazing deer.

"If y'all even think," said Uncle Rex, "that you can sit here and work out all kind of plans the minute I walk out the door you can either un-think 'em or do without me. Which is it?"

"You ought to be open-minded, Father," said Andrew, exactly like he was the oldest one there. He leaned back and let the blueprints roll themselves up with a crackle. "Mother and I have gone to a lot of trouble on this."

"Just listen, Rex," Aunt Martha urged, but her new glow about life was going out like a lamp which has been switched off at the door but doesn't quite know it yet. She spoke timidly.

"I've listened enough already," said Uncle Rex.

He marched out of the room, put on his oldest, most disreputable clothes, and went off in the pickup. He eventually wound up at Uncle Hernan's. We saw him drive up, badly needing a shave. He whammed through the front door of his old home and disappeared. We didn't even dare to telephone. Something, we knew, had happened.

Aunt Martha was so stunned when Uncle Rex hit the ceiling and departed that she shook with nerves all over. She called Mama to come over there (I drove her) and sat and told Mama that everything she had belonged to Rex in her way of thinking, that the Lord had made woman subservient to man, it was put forth that way in the Bible. Did Rex think she would go against the Word of God?

"The land's all yours," Mama said, evidently aware of but not mentioning the wide gap between statements and actions. "I don't think Rex is disputing it. It just comes over him now and then. Maybe Andrew pointed it out to him."

"Andrew ought not to have mentioned it at all," said Aunt Martha. "Oh, I knew that at the time."

"I doubt his coming back to live here now, the way things are," Mama said. "They say the Wirths have got a lot of pride. Especially the men. I just don't know what to tell you. Can you move over to Hernan's with him for a while? Maybe y'all could get more chance to talk things over."

Andrew passed through, knowing everything and not stopping to talk. "He's just hardheaded," he said, in a tone of final authority, and that wasn't smart either. I recalled a saying about the McClellands, that they were so nice they didn't have to be smart. It was widely repeated.

"Hernan's got a whole empty wing," Mama said.

Aunt Martha turned red as a beet and almost cried. She kept twisting her handkerchief, knotting and unknotting it. "Do you imagine a McClelland . . ." she whispered, then she stopped. What she'd started to say was that Uncle Hernan lived with a Negro woman and everybody knew it. It was his young wife's nurse who'd come down from Tennessee with her, nursed her when she got sick and died, then stayed on to keep house. She was Melissa, a good cook—we all took her for granted. But no McClelland could be expected to be under the same roof with that! In fact, Aunt Martha may have thought of herself as sent from God to us, though Mama was also steady at the Ladies Auxiliary and of equal standing.

When we drove back home it was to learn that Uncle Rex had not only departed from Aunt Martha, he had left Uncle Hernan as well, nobody knew for where. He had gone out and loaded his mare in the horse trailer and gone off down the back road unobserved from within, while Aunt Martha was sitting there with Mama and me, crying over him. (We passed a carload of McClellands driving in as we left: at least, we, along with Uncle Rex, had escaped that.)

The next day was Sunday and a good chance for all of us over our way to get together in order to worry better.

"I'm glad I never had any children," Uncle Hernan said. Though he'd apparently had any number by Melissa, he didn't have to count them the way Uncle Rex had to count Andrew.

"I don't think for a minute Andrew and Martha calculated

the effect something like this was going to have on Rex," Daddy said.

"It's just now worked to a head," Mama said, "about being on her land and all."

"Hadn't been for Rex wouldn't be much of any land to be on," Daddy said. "The McClellands make mighty poor farmers."

"He knew that," said Uncle Hernan. "He knew that everybody knows it. But the facts speak."

"Wonder where he is right now," Mama said, and from her voice I was made to recall the slight lovable man who was her brother, threatened, in her mind, in some perpetual way.

"Down in the swamp somewhere, with that pickup and that mare, living in some hunting camp," was Uncle Hernan's judgment. "I imagine he's near the river; he'll need a road for working the mare out and some free ground not to get bit to death with mosquitoes and gnats."

"This time of year?" said Mama, because fall was coming early; we were into the first cold snap.

"All times of year down in those places."

"I worry about him, I declare I do," Mama said.

"*You* worry about him. Another week of this and Martha's going to be in the hospital," Daddy said.

"That mare," said Uncle Hernan, searching his back pocket. He drew out a gigantic linen handkerchief, blew his nose in a moderate honk, and arranged his bronze mustache. "She must be getting on for ten years old."

"She was nothing but a filly that day we were over there. You remember that, Marilee?" Daddy asked.

"When was that?" Uncle Hernan asked.

"We drove over there one Sunday," said Mama. "Martha was at one of her folks in town. Rex showed off the mare—nothing would do him but for us to see her."

"Martha came back and caught him fresh out of the lot on Sunday," Daddy said.

"Lord have mercy," said Uncle Hernan. Then he said, "How are you, Marilee?"

I was not so much involved in their discussion. I was over in the bay window reading some reports from the real estate office where I had a job now. School teaching, after two years of it, had gone sour on me. I said I was fine. I was keeping quietly in the background for the very good reason that the fault in all this crisis had been partially my own. I had once suggested to Andrew, who sometimes dropped by the office to talk to me, that the McClelland place had a gold mine in real estate if only they'd care to develop it, what with the new highway laid out to run along beside it. He'd asked me a lot of questions and had evidently got the idea well into him, like a fish appreciative of the minnow.

I knew nobody would ever reckon me responsible, simply because I was a girl in business. A girl in business, their assumptions went, was somebody that had no right to be and did not count in thinking or in conversation. I could sit in the window seat reading up on real estate not ten feet away from them, but I might as well have been reading Jane Austen for all it was going to enter their thinking about Uncle Rex.

A log broke in the fireplace while we all, for a most unusually long moment, sat pondering in silence, and a spray of sparks shot out.

"Somebody's *got* to find him," Mama said, and almost cried.

"I'd look myself," said Uncle Hernan, "but I'm down with rheumatism and hardly able to drive, much less take a jeep into a swamp. I might get snake bit into the bargain."

"What about Daddy?" I said, and added that I didn't want to go into any swamp either.

"Oh, my Lord," Daddy said, which was his own admission that the Wirth family had never given him much of a voice in their affairs, though it stirred Mama's indignation to hear about it. Daddy knew he certainly might be successful in any mission they sent him on: he was Jim Summerall—a tough little farming man and a good squirrel shot; but though you could entrust a message to him, how could anybody be sure he'd be listened to when he got there? A wild goose chase would be what he'd probably have to call it, with Mama riled up besides.

"Marilee could find him," Uncle Hernan pronounced, and everybody, including myself, looked up in amazement, but didn't get to ask him why he said it, as he picked up his walking cane and stood up to leave. Daddy walked out with him to go down and look at where the soil conservation people were at work straightening the creek in back of ours and Uncle

Hernan's properties. There was going to be a new little three-acre patch on their side to be justly divided, and a neighbor across the way to be treated with satisfaction to all. It was a nice walk.

But Uncle Hernan would have found, if not that, some other reason to leave our house. He never seemed in place there. His own house, or rather the old Wirth home where he lived, was pre–Civil War and classical in design; ours was a sturdy farming house. It was within the power of architecture to let us all know that Uncle Hernan was not in his element sitting in front of our fire in the living room, in spite of Mama's antiques and her hooked rugs and all her pretty things. Then it occurred to me that, whether totally his property by deed or inheritance or purchase or not, that house in turn had claimed Uncle Hernan; that he belonged to it and they were one, and then I knew why Uncle Rex had found no peace there either and had left after two days, as restless in search as a sparrow hawk.

When Daddy got back I walked out to speak to Uncle Hernan at the fence.

"What'd you mean, I could find him?" I asked.

"Well, you've got that fella now, that surveyor," Uncle Hernan said. "'Gully' Richard," he added, giving his nickname.

Joe Richard (pronounced in the French way, accent on the last syllable) was a man with a surveying firm over in Vicksburg whom we'd had out for a couple of jobs. He had got to calling me up lately, always at the office. For some reason, I hadn't mentioned him to anybody.

"You know how he got the name of Gully?" Uncle Hernan asked, looking at the sky.

"No, sir," I said.

"Came up to this country from down yonder in Louisiana and the first job he got to do was survey a tract was nothing but gullies. Like to never got out of there—snakes and kudzu. Says he thinks he's in there yet. Gully's not so bad, Marilee."

"No, sir," I said, and stopped. Let your family know you've seen anybody once or twice and they've already picked out the preacher and decorated the church. But Uncle Hernan wasn't like that. I thought more of him because he'd never commented on anybody I might be going with, except he did say once that the wild boy who had been my first romance could certainly put away a lot of likker. I judged if Uncle Hernan had spoken favorably of Joe Richard, it was because he esteemed him as a man, not because he was hastening to marry me off.

"What's Joe Richard got to do with Uncle Rex?" I asked, but I already knew what the connection was. He'd been surveying some bottom land over toward the river, and, furthermore, he knew people—trappers and squatters and the like. He was a tall, sunburnt, surly-looking man who kept opinions to himself. I had never liked him till I saw his humor. It was like the sun coming out. His grin showed an irregular line of teeth, attractive for some reason, and a good liveliness. He came from a distance, had the air of a divorced man, a name like a Catholic —all this, appealing to me, would be hurdles as high as a steeple to the Summeralls, the McClellands, and the Wirths (except for Uncle Hernan). But any thought that he wanted to get married at all, let alone to me, was pure speculation. Maybe what he would serve for was finding Uncle Rex.

It was a day or so before I saw him. "Will you do it?" I asked him. "Will you try?"

"Hell, he's just goofed off for a while," Joe said. "Anybody can do that. Let him come back by himself."

"He's important to us," I said, "because—" and I stopped and couldn't think of the right thing, but to Joe's credit he didn't do a thing but wait for me to finish. It came to me to put it this way, speaking with Mama's voice, I bet: "Important because he doesn't know he is."

Joe understood that, and said he'd try.

One latent truth in all this is that I was mad enough at Andrew McClelland Wirth to kill him. He'd gone about it wrong: snatching authority away from his father was what he'd obviously acted like.

During the second month of Uncle Rex's absence, with Joe Richard still reporting nothing at all, and Aunt Martha meeting with her prayer group all the time (she was sustained also by droves of McClelland relatives who were speculating on divorce), I drove up to the school where Andrew taught and got to see him between class and basketball practice. "You could have had a little more tact," I told him, when more sense was probably nearer to the point, and what I should have said. The night before I had had a dream. I had seen a little cabin in a swamp that was just catching fire, flames licking up the sides, but nobody so far, when I woke, had walked out of it. The dream was still in my head when I drove to find Andrew.

Andrew and I went to a place across the street from his little school, a conglomerate of red-brick serviceable buildings with a football field out back, a gym made out of an army-surplus aluminum airplane hangar off at the side, and a parade ground in the center, with a tall flagpole. It was a sparkling dry afternoon in the fall, chilly in shadow, hot in the sun. "If you haven't noticed anything about the Wirth pride," I continued, "you must be going through life with blinders on."

"You don't understand, Marilee," he said. "It was Mother I was trying to help. She needs something more to interest her than she's got. I thought the real estate idea you had was just about right."

"It would have been if you'd have gone through Uncle Rex."

"You may not know this, Marilee, but after a certain point I can't do a thing with Father, he just won't listen."

"You mean you tried?"

"I tried about other things. He's got an old cultivator out in back that the seat is falling off of, it's so rusty. You'd have to soak it in a swimming pool full of machine oil to get it in shape, but he won't borrow the money to buy a new one."

"He and Daddy and Uncle Hernan are going in together on one for the spring crop," I said. "It was Uncle Rex got them to do it. Didn't you know that?"

"He won't tell me anything anymore; you'd think I wasn't in the world the way he won't talk to me. I've just about quit."

I recalled that Uncle Rex had told Uncle Hernan that Aunt Martha and Andrew had got so thick he was like a stranger at his own table, but there's no use entering into family quarrels. The people themselves all tell a different tale, so how can you judge what's true?

"Promise me one thing," I said.

"What?"

"If he comes back (and you know he's bound to), glad or sad or mean or sweet or dead drunk with one ear clawed off, you go in and talk to him and tell him how it was. Don't even stop to speak to your mama. You go straight to him."

"How do you know he's bound to come back?" Andrew asked.

"I just do," I said. But I didn't; and neither did anybody else.

Andrew said: "You're bound to side with the Wirths, Marilee. You *are* one."

"Well," I said, "are you trying to break up *your* family?"

He thought it over. He was finishing his Coke because he had to go back over to the gym. He wore a coach's cap with a neat bill, a soft knit shirt, gabardine trousers, and gym shoes. He also wore white socks. All told, he looked to have stepped out of the Sears Roebuck catalogue, for he was trim as could be, but he was too regulation to be real.

"You might be right, Marilee," was his final word. "I'll try."

When I got back to Port Claiborne, Joe Richard was waiting for me. His news was that he had finally located Uncle Rex. He was living in a trapper's house down near the Mississippi River. The horse was there, and also a strange woman.

Indolent at times, in midday sun still as a turtle on a log which is stuck in the mud near some willows . . . at other times, hasty and hustling, banging away over dried-up mud roads in the pickup with a dozen or so muskrat traps in the back and the chopped bait blood-staining a sack on the floor of the seat beside him . . . at yet other times, fishing the muddy shallows of the little bayous in an old, flat-bottomed rowboat, rowing with one hand tight on a short paddle, hearing the quiet separated sounds of water dripping from paddle, pole, or line, or from the occasional bream or white perch or little mud cat he caught, lifting the string to add another: that's how it was for Rex Wirth. In spring and summer sounds run together but in the fall each is separate; I don't know why. Only insect voices mingle, choiring for a while, then dwindling into single chips of sound. The riverbanks and the bayous seem to have nothing to do with the river itself, which flows magnificently in the background, a whole horizon to itself from the banks, or glimpsed through willow fronds—the Father of Waters not minding its children.

At twilight and in the early morning hours when the dew began to sparkle, he rode the mare. He kept a smudge for her, to ward the insects off, sprayed her, too, and swabbed her with some stuff out of a bucket. The mare had nothing to worry about.

The woman was young—likely in her twenties. She came and went, sometimes with sacks of groceries. At other times she fished; sometimes a child fished with her. Another time a man came and sat talking on the porch. She had blond sunburnt hair, nothing fancy about her. Wore jeans and gingham shirts.

"A nice fanny," Joe said.

"Was it her you were studying or Uncle Rex?" I asked him.

"It's curious," he said. "I stayed longer than I meant to. I've got some good binoculars. That old guy might have found him such a paradise he ain't ever going to show up again. Ever think of that, Marilee? Some folks just looking for an excuse to leave?" I thought of it and it carried its own echo for me: Joe Richard had left Louisiana, or he wouldn't be there talking to me.

I thought that if Uncle Rex had wanted to leave forever he would have gone further than twenty miles away; he had the world to choose from, depending on which temperature and landscape he favored. There must be a reason for his choice, I thought, so I went to talk to Uncle Hernan.

"You were right," I said. "Joe Richard found him." And I told him what he'd seen.

"That would be that Bertis girl," said Uncle Hernan at once.

"Who?" I said.

"Oh, it was back before Rex was married. We all used to go down there with the Meecham brothers and Carter Bankston. It was good duck shooting in the winter and we got some deer too if you could stand the cold—cold is not too bad, but river damp goes right into your bones. Of course, we'd be pretty well fortified.

"There was a family we had, to tend camp for us, a fellow named Bertis, better than a river rat, used to work in construction in Natchez, but lost his arm in an accident, then got into a lawsuit, didn't get a cent out of it, went on relief, found him a river house, got to trapping. Well, he had a wife and a couple of kids to raise. His wife was a nice woman. Ought to have gone back to her folks. She had a college degree, if I recall correctly.

"One year, down there on the camp, Bertis came to cook and skin for us, like he'd always done, but he was worried that year over his wife, who'd come down sick. It was Rex who decided to take her to Natchez to the hospital and let the hunt go on. Some of the bunch had invited some others—a big preacher and a senator: at this late date, I don't quite know myself who all was there. It would have been hard to carry on without Bertis and Bertis needed money, too, though I reckon we might have made up a check.

"Everybody was a little surprised at what Rex offered to take on himself. He stood straight-backed and bright-eyed when he spoke up, like a man who's volunteering for a mission and ready to salute when it's granted. Somebody ought to have offered—that was true. But there's the sort of woman, Marilee, can be around ten to a thousand men all together, and every last one of them will have the same impression of her, but not a one will mention it. So we never spoke of what crossed everybody's mind.

"The funny thing was, Bertis never stirred himself to see about his wife. He was an odd sort of fellow, not mean, but what you'd call lifesick. Some people can endure life, slowly, gradually, all that comes, but with enjoyment and good spirit; but some get lightning struck and something splits off in them. In Bertis's case it was more than an arm he'd lost; it was spirit.

"Rex stayed away and stayed away. Not till the camp was breaking up did Bertis come up to me, and I offered to drive him in. We got to the hospital but his wife wasn't there, she'd gone on to Vicksburg and it was late. The next day, on a street in Vicksburg, in an old house they'd made into apartments, we found her. She was sitting in a nice room with a coal fire burning, looking quiet and at peace. She looked more than that. She looked beautiful. Her hands had turned fine, white, delicate as a lady's in a painting, don't you know. She had an afghan over her.

"When we came in, we heard footsteps out the back hall and a door slamming. 'Hello, Mr. Bertis,' was all she said. I drove them home. As far as I recall they never asked each other's news, never exchanged a word. I put them down at the front door of that house out in the wilds, not quite in the swamps but too close to the river to be healthy, not quite a cabin but too run down to call a home—it was just a house, that was all. 'You going to be all right, Mrs. Bertis?' I asked.

"'I reckon I can drive in a day or two,' was what she said. Bertis couldn't do much driving on account of his arm. Though she spoke, it seemed she wasn't really there; she was in a private haze. I remember how she went in the house, like a woman in a dream.

"And there was a little yellow-haired girl in the doorway, waiting for her. That's likely the one's down there now.

"Rex was gone completely for more than a month if I'm not mistaken. He took a trip out West and saw some places he'd always wanted to, though it was a strange time of year to do it, as some pointed out to him when he got back. Married Martha McClelland soon after.

"Marilee, does your mama mind your having a little touch of Bourbon now and then?"

"She minds," I said, "but she's given up."

"The next time you have some bright family ideas about real estate," said Joe Richard, "you better count to a hundred-and-two and keep your mouth shut."

"That's the truth," I said.

We were lying face down on a ridge thick in fallen leaves, side by side, taking turns with the binoculars. I had a blanket under me Joe had dug out of his car to keep me from catching a cold, he said, and I was studying my fill down through the trunks of tall trees—beech, oak, and flaming sycamore—way down to the low fronded willows near the old fishing camp with the weed-grown road and the brown flowing river beyond—and it was all there, just the way he'd said.

I had watched Uncle Rex come up from fishing and moor his boat, had watched a tow-headed child in faded blue overalls enter the field of vision to meet him, and then the blond woman, who'd stood talking in blue jeans and a sweater with the sleeves pushed up—exactly what I had on, truth to tell—taking the string of fish from him, while he walked away and the child ran after him. And I followed with the sights on them, the living field of their life brought as close as my own breath, though they didn't know it—do spirits feel as I did? When he came back, he was leading the mare. She looked well accustomed, and flicked her fine ears, which were furring over for winter, and stood while Uncle Rex lifted the child and set her in the saddle as her mother held the reins. The fish shone silvery on the string against the young woman's leg.

There is such a thing as father, daughter, and grandchild —such a thing as family that is not blood family but a chosen family: I was seeing that. Joe took the glasses out of my hand for his turn and while he looked I thought about Indian summer which isn't summer at all, but something else. There is the long hot summer, heavy and teeming, more real than life; and there is the other summer, pure as gold, as real as hope. Now, not needing glasses, or eyes, either, I saw the problem Rex Wirth must be solving and unsolving every day. If this was the place he belonged and the family that was—though not of blood—in a sense, his, why leave them ever? His life, like a tree drawn into the river and slipping by, must have felt the current pull and turn him every day. Wasn't this where he belonged? Come back, Uncle Rex!—should I run out of the woods and tell him that? No, the struggle was his own. We went away silent, never showing we were there.

Uncle Rex did come home.

It was when the weather broke in a big cold front out of the northwest. It must have come ruffling the water, thickening the afternoon sky, then sweeping across the river, a giant black cloak of a cloud, moaning and howling in the night, stripping the little trees and bushes bare of colored leaves and crashing against the willow thickets. It was like a seasonal motion, too, that Uncle Rex should decamp at that time, arrive back at Aunt Martha's with a pickup of frozen fish packed in ice and some muskrat pelts, even a few mink, the mare in her little cart bringing up the rear.

At least I thought he went home, as soon as somebody I knew out on that road called me at the office to say he'd gone by. If he'd gone to Uncle Hernan's that would have been a waste of all his motions, all to do again. I telephoned to Andrew.

"Get on out there," I said. "Don't even stop to coach basketball."

But Andrew couldn't do that. If he had started untying a knot in his shoelace when the last trump sounded, he would keep right on with it, before he turned his attention to anything new. So he started home after basketball practice.

There were giant upheavals of wind and hail and falling temperatures throughout the South, the breakup of Indian summer, but Andrew forged his way homeward, discovering along the road that the car heater needed fixing and that he hadn't got on a warm enough suit, or brought a coat.

He went straight in to Uncle Rex. It seemed to me later that anybody could program Andrew, but I guess on the other hand he'd worried about his father's absence and his mother's abandoned condition a great deal, and nobody except me had told him anything he could do about it. He had gone home a time or two to comfort her, but it hadn't worked miracles.

"I'm sorry for what I said about the land, Father," he said right out, even before he got through shivering. "You're the one ought to decide whatever we do."

Then he stopped. The big, white house was silent, emptied of McClellands, by what method God alone would ever know.

Uncle Rex and Aunt Martha were sitting alone by the gas heater. Aunt Martha had risen to greet him when he came in, but then she'd sat down again, looking subdued.

Uncle Rex rose up and approached Andrew with tears in his eyes. He placed his hands on each of his shoulders. "Son—" he said. "Son—" His face had got bearded during his long time away, grizzled, sun- and wind-burnt, veined, austere, like somebody who has had to deal with Indians and doesn't care to discuss it. His hands had split up in half a dozen places from hard use; his nails had blood and grime under them that no scrubbing would remove. "Son, this property . . . it's all coming to you someday. For now . . ."

If you looked deeply into Andrew's eyes, they did not have very much to tell. He said, "Yes, Father," which was about all that was required. When he told me about it, I could imagine both his parents' faces, how they stole glances at him, glowed with pride the same as ever, on account of his being so fine to look at and their own into the bargain. But I remembered that we are back in the bosom of the real family now—the blood one—and that blood is for spilling, among other things.

"Your mother wanted me on this place, Son," Uncle Rex went on, "and as long as she wants me here the only word that goes is mine. She can tell you now if that's so or not."

"But, Father, you left her worried sick. You never sent word to her! It's been awful!"

"That's not the point, Son," said Uncle Rex. "She wants me here."

"I want him here," Aunt Martha echoed. She looked at Andrew with all her love, but she was looking across a mighty wide river.

"You know how he's acted! You know what he did!"

"That's not the point," Aunt Martha murmured.

"Then what is the point?" Andrew asked, craving to know with as much passion as he'd ever have, I guess.

"That your father—that I want him here." She was studying her hands then—not even looking. They were speakers in a play.

As for Andrew, he said he felt as if he wasn't there anymore, that some force had moved through him and that life was not the same. Figuratively speaking, his voice had been taken from him. Literally, he was coming down with a cold. Aunt Martha gave him supper and poured hot chocolate down him, and he went to bed with nothing but the sounds of a shrieking wind and the ticking clock, in the old room he'd had from childhood on. He felt (he told me later) like nothing and nobody. Nothing . . . nobody: the clock was saying it too. There was an ache at the house's core and at some point he dreamed he rose and dressed and went out into the upstairs hall. There he saw his father's face, white, drawn, and small—a ghost face, floating above the stairwell.

"Why call me 'Son' when you don't mean it?"

There wasn't an answer, and he woke and heard the wind.

Uncle Rex—what dream did he have?

"We can't know that," said Uncle Hernan, when I talked to him. "Rex did what he had to. He settled it with those McClellands, once and for all. It was hard for Rex—remember that. Oh yes, Marilee! For Rex it was mighty hard."

The White Azalea

TWO LETTERS had arrived for Miss Theresa Stubblefield: she put them in her bag. She would not stop to read them in American Express, as many were doing, sitting on benches or leaning against the walls, but pushed her way out into the street. This was her first day in Rome and it was June.

An enormous sky of the most delicate blue arched overhead. In her mind's eye—her imagination responding fully, almost exhaustingly, to these shores' peculiar powers of stimulation —she saw the city as from above, telescoped on its great bare plains that the ruins marked, aqueducts and tombs, here a cypress, there a pine, and all round the low blue hills. Pictures in old Latin books returned to her: the Appian Way Today, the Colosseum, the Arch of Constantine. She would see them, looking just as they had in the books, and this would make up a part of her delight. Moreover, nursing various Stubblefields —her aunt, then her mother, then her father—through their lengthy illnesses (everybody could tell you the Stubblefields were always sick), Theresa had had a chance to read quite a lot. England, France, Germany, Switzerland, and Italy had all been rendered for her time and again, and between the prescribed hours of pills and tonics, she had conceived a dreamy passion by lamplight, to see all these places with her own eyes. The very night after her father's funeral she had thought, though never admitted to a soul: *Now I can go. There's nothing to stop me now.* So here it was, here was Italy, anyway, and terribly noisy.

In the street the traffic was really frightening. Cars, taxis, buses, and motorscooters all went plunging at once down the narrow length of it or swerving perilously around a fountain. Shoals of tourists went by her in national groups—English school girls in blue uniforms, German boys with cameras attached, smartly dressed Americans looking in shop windows. Glad to be alone, Theresa climbed the splendid outdoor staircase that opened to her left. The Spanish Steps.

Something special was going on here just now—the annual display of azalea plants. She had heard about it the night before at her hotel. It was not yet complete: workmen were unloading the potted plants from a truck and placing them in banked rows on the steps above. The azaleas were as large as shrubs, and their myriad blooms, many still tight in the bud, ranged in color from purple through fuchsia and rose to the palest pink, along with many white ones too. Marvellous, thought Theresa, climbing in her portly, well-bred way, for she was someone who had learned that if you only move slowly enough you have time to notice everything. In Rome, all over Europe, she intended to move very slowly indeed.

Halfway up the staircase she stopped and sat down. Other people were doing it, too, sitting all along the wide banisters and leaning over the parapets above, watching the azaleas mass, or just enjoying the sun. Theresa sat with her letters in her lap, breathing Mediterranean air. The sun warmed her, as it seemed to be warming everything, perhaps even the under-side of stones or the chill insides of churches. She loosened her tweed jacket and smoked a cigarette. Content . . . excited; how could you be both at once? Strange, but she was. Pres-ently, she picked up the first of the letters.

A few moments later her hands were trembling and her brow had contracted with anxiety and dismay. *Of course, one of them would have to go and do this! Poor Cousin Elec*, she thought, tears rising to sting in the sun, *but why couldn't he have ar-ranged to live through the summer? And how on earth did I ever get this letter anyway?*

She had reason indeed to wonder how the letter had man-aged to find her. Her Cousin Emma Carraway had written it, in her loose high old lady's script—t's carefully crossed, but l's inclined to wobble like an old car on the downward slope. Cousin Emma had simply put Miss Theresa Stubblefield, Rome, Italy, on the envelope, had walked up to the post office in Tuxapoka, Alabama, and mailed it with as much confidence as if it had been a birthday card to her next-door neighbor. No return address whatsoever. Somebody had scrawled Amer-ican Express, Piazza di Spagna?, across the envelope, and now Theresa had it, all as easily as if she had been the President of the Republic or the Pope. Inside were all the things they thought she ought to know concerning the last illness, death, and burial of Cousin Alexander Carraway.

Cousin Emma and Cousin Elec, brother and sister—unmarried, devoted, aging—had lived next door to the Stubblefields in Tuxapoka from time immemorial until the Stubblefields had moved to Montgomery fifteen years ago. Two days before he was taken sick, Cousin Elec was out worrying about what too much rain might do to his sweetpeas, and Cousin Elec had always preserved in the top drawer of his secretary a mother-of-pearl paper knife which Theresa had coveted as a child and which he had promised she could have when he died. *I'm supposed to care as much now as then, as much here as there,* she realized, with a sigh. *This letter would have got to me if she hadn't even put Rome, Italy, on it.*

She refolded the letter, replaced it in its envelope, and turned with relief to one from her brother George.

But alack, George, when *he* had written, had only just returned from going to Tuxapoka to Cousin Elec's funeral. He was full of heavy family reminiscence. All the fine old stock was dying out, look at the world today. His own children had suffered from the weakening of those values which he and Theresa had always taken for granted, and as for his grandchildren (he had one so far, still in diapers), he shuddered to think that the true meaning of character might never dawn on them at all. A life of gentility and principle such as Cousin Elec had lived had to be known at first hand. . . .

Poor George! The only boy, the family darling. Together with her mother, both of them tense with worry lest things should somehow go wrong, Theresa had seen him through the right college, into the right fraternity, and though pursued by various girls and various mammas of girls, safely married to the right sort, however much in the early years of that match his wife, Anne, had not seemed to understand poor George. Could it just be, Theresa wondered, that Anne had understood only too well, and that George all along was extraordinary only in the degree to which he was dull?

As for Cousin Alexander Carraway, the only thing Theresa could remember at the moment about him (except his paper knife) was that he had had exceptionally long hands and feet and one night about one o'clock in the morning the whole Stubblefield family had been aroused to go next door at Cousin Emma's call—first Papa, then Mother, then Theresa

and George. There they all did their uttermost to help Cousin
Elec get a cramp out of his foot. He had hobbled downstairs
into the parlor, in his agony, and was sitting, wrapped in his
bathrobe, on a footstool. He held his long clenched foot in
both hands, and this and his contorted face—he was trying he-
roically not to cry out—made him look like a large skinny old
monkey. They all surrounded him, the family circle, Theresa
and George as solemn as if they were watching the cat have
kittens, and Cousin Emma running back and forth with a
kettle of hot water which she poured steaming into a white
enamelled pan. "Can you think of anything to do?" she kept
repeating. "I hate to call the doctor but if this keeps up I'll just
have to! Can you think of anything to do?" "You might treat it
like the hiccups," said Papa. "Drop a cold key down his back."
"I just hope this happens to you someday," said Cousin Elec,
who was not at his best. "Poor Cousin Elec," George said. He
was younger than Theresa: she remembered looking down and
seeing his great round eyes, while at the same time she was
dimly aware that her mother and father were not unamused.
"Poor Cousin Elec."

Now, here they both were, still the same, George full of
round-eyed woe, and Cousin Emma in despair. Theresa shifted
to a new page.

"Of course (George's letter continued), there are practical
problems to be considered. Cousin Emma is alone in that big
old house and won't hear to parting from it. Robbie and Beryl
tried their best to persuade her to come and stay with them,
and Anne and I have told her she's more than welcome here,
but I think she feels that she might be an imposition, especially
as long as our Rosie is still in high school. The other possibility
is to make arrangements for her to let out one or two of the
rooms to some teacher of good family or one of those solitary
old ladies that Tuxapoka is populated with—Miss Edna Whit-
taker, for example. But there is more in this than meets the
eye. A new bathroom would certainly have to be put in. The
wallpaper in the back bedroom is literally crumbling off. . . ."
(Theresa skipped a page of details about the house.) "I hope
if you have any ideas along these lines you will write me about
them. I may settle on some makeshift arrangements for the

summer and wait until you return in the fall so we can work
out together the best. . . ."

I really shouldn't have smoked a cigarette so early in the day,
thought Theresa, it always makes me sick. I'll start sneezing in
a minute, sitting on these cold steps. She got up, standing uncertainly for a moment, then moving aside to let go past her,
talking, a group of young men. They wore shoes with pointed
toes, odd to American eyes, and narrow trousers, and their
hair looked unnaturally black and slick. Yet here they were
obviously thought to be handsome, and felt themselves to be
so. Just then a man approached her with a tray of cheap cam-
eos, Parker fountain pens, rosaries, papal portraits. "No," said
Theresa. "No, no!" she said. The man did not wish to leave.
He knew how to spread himself against the borders of the
space that had to separate them. Carrozza rides in the park,
the Colosseum by moonlight, he specialized. . . . Theresa
turned away to escape, and climbed to a higher landing where
the steps divided in two. There she walked to the far left and
leaned on a vacant section of banister, while the vendor picked
himself another well-dressed American lady, carrying a camera
and a handsome alligator bag, ascending the steps alone. Was
he ever successful, Theresa wondered. The lady with the alligator bag registered interest, doubt, then indignation; at last,
alarm. She cast about as though looking for a policeman: this
really shouldn't be allowed! Finally, she scurried away up the
steps.

Theresa Stubblefield, still holding the family letters in one
hand, realized that her whole trip to Europe was viewed in
family circles as an interlude between Cousin Elec's death and
"doing something" about Cousin Emma. They were even,
Anne and George, probably thinking themselves very considerate in not hinting that she really should cut out "one or two
countries" and come home in August to get Cousin Emma's
house ready before the teachers came to Tuxapoka in September. Of course, it wasn't Anne and George's fault that one family crisis seemed to follow another, and weren't they always
emphasizing that they really didn't know what they would do
without Theresa? *The trouble is,* Theresa thought, *that while
everything that happens there is supposed to matter supremely,*

nothing here is supposed even to exist. They would not care if all of Europe were to sink into the ocean tomorrow. It never registered with them that I had time to read all of Balzac, Dickens, and Stendhal while Papa was dying, not to mention everything in the city library after Mother's operation. It would have been exactly the same to them if I had read through all twenty-six volumes of Elsie Dinsmore.

She arranged the letters carefully, one on top of the other. Then, with a motion so suddenly violent that she amazed herself, she tore them in two.

"*Signora?*"

She became aware that two Italian workmen, carrying a large azalea pot, were standing before her and wanted her to move so that they could begin arranging a new row of the display.

"*Mi diapiace, signora, ma . . . insomma. . . .*"

"Oh . . . put it there!" She indicated a spot a little distance away. They did not understand. "*Ponere . . . la.*" A little Latin, a little French. How one got along! The workmen exchanged a glance, a shrug. Then they obeyed her. "*Va bene, signora.*" They laughed as they returned down the steps in the sun.

Theresa was still holding the torn letters, half in either hand, and the flush was fading slowly from her brow. What a strong feeling had shaken her! She observed the irregular edges of paper, so crudely wrenched apart, and began to feel guilty. The Stubblefields, it was true, were proud and prominent, but how thin, how vulnerable was that pride it was so easy to prove, and how local was that prominence there was really no need to tell even them. But none could ever deny that the Stubblefields meant well; no one had ever challenged that the Stubblefields were good. Now out of their very letters, their sorrowful eyes, full of gentility and principle, appeared to be regarding Theresa, one of their own who had turned against them, and soft voices, so ready to forgive all, seemed to be saying, "Oh, Theresa, how *could* you?"

Wasn't that exactly what they had said when, as a girl, she had fallen in love with Charlie Wharton, whose father had unfortunately been in the pen? Ever so softly, ever so distressed: "Oh, Theresa, how *could* you?" Never mind. That was long ago, over and done with, and right now something clearly had to be done about these letters.

Theresa moved forward, and leaning down she dropped the torn sheets into the azalea pot which the workmen had just left. But the matter was not so easily settled. What if the letters should blow away? One could not bear the thought of that which was personal to the Stubblefields chancing out on the steps where everyone passed, or maybe even into the piazza below to be run over by a motorscooter, walked over by the common herd, spit upon, picked up and read, or—worst of all —returned to American Express by some conscientious tourist, where tomorrow, filthy, crumpled, bedraggled, but still legibly, faithfully relating Cousin Elec's death and Cousin Emma's grief, they might be produced to confront her.

Theresa moved a little closer to the azalea pot and sat down beside it. She covered the letters deftly, smoothing the earth above them and making sure that no trace of paper showed above ground. The corner of Cousin Emma's envelope caught on a root and had to be shoved under, a painful moment, as if a letter could feel anything—how absurd! Then Theresa realized, straightening up and rubbing dirt off her hand with a piece of Kleenex from her bag, that it was not the letters but the Stubblefields that she had torn apart and consigned to the earth. This was certainly the only explanation of why the whole curious sequence, now that it was complete, had made her feel so marvellously much better.

Well, I declare! Theresa thought, astonished at herself, and in that moment it was as though she stood before the statue of some heroic classical woman whose dagger dripped with stony blood. *My goodness!* she thought, drowning in those blank exalted eyeballs: *Me!*

So thrilled she could not, for a time, move on, she stood noting that this particular azalea was one of exceptional beauty. It was white, in outline as symmetrically developed as an oak tree, and blooming in every part with a ruffled, lacy purity. The azalea was, moreover, Theresa recalled, a Southern flower, one especially cultivated in Alabama. Why, the finest in the world were said to grow in Bellingrath Gardens near Mobile, though probably they had not heard about that in Rome.

Now Miss Theresa Stubblefield descended quickly, down, down, toward the swarming square, down toward the fountain and all the racket, into the Roman crowd. There she was lost at once in the swirl, nameless, anonymous, one more nice rich American tourist lady.

But she cast one last glance back to where the white azalea stood, blooming among all the others. By now the stone of the great staircase was all but covered over. A group of young priests in scarlet cassocks went past, mounting with rapid, forward energy, weaving their way vividly aloft among the massed flowers. At the top of the steps the twin towers of a church rose, standing clearly outlined on the blue air. Some large white clouds, charged with pearly light, were passing overhead at a slow imperial pace.

Well, it certainly is beyond a doubt the most beautiful family funeral of them all! thought Theresa. *And if they should ever object to what I did to them*, she thought, recalling the stone giantess with her dagger and the gouts of blood hanging thick and gravid upon it, *they've only to read a little and learn that there have been those in my position who haven't acted in half so considerate a way.*

Ship Island

The Story of a Mermaid

THE FRENCH book was lying open on a corner of the dining-room table, between the floor lamp and the window. The floor lamp, which had come with the house, had a cover made of green glass, with a fringe. The French book must have lain just that way for two months. Nancy, coming in from the beach, tried not to look at it. It reminded her of how much she had meant to accomplish during the summer, of the strong sense of intent, something like refinement, with which she had chosen just that spot for studying. It was out of hearing of the conversations with the neighbors that went on every evening out on the side porch, it had window light in the daytime and lamplight at night, it had a small, slanting view of the beach, and it drew a breeze. The pencils were still there, still sharp, and the exercise, broken off. She sometimes stopped to read it over. "The soldiers of the emperor were crossing the bridge: *Les soldats de l'empereur traversaient le pont.* The officer has already knocked at the gate: *L'officier a déjà frappé—*" She could not have finished that sentence now if she had sat right down and tried.

Nancy could no longer find herself in relation to the girl who had sought out such a good place to study, had sharpened the pencils and opened the book and sat down to bend over it. What she did know was how—just now, when she had been down at the beach, across the boulevard—the sand scuffed beneath her step and shells lay strewn about, chipped and disorderly, near the water's edge. Some shells were empty; some, with damp drying down their backs, went for short walks. Far out, a long white shelf of cloud indicated a distance no gull could dream of gaining, though the gulls spun tirelessly up, dazzling in the white light that comes just as morning vanishes. A troop of pelicans sat like curiously carved knobs on the tops of a long series of wooden piles, which were spaced out at intervals in the water. The piles were what was left of a private pier blown away by a hurricane some years ago.

Nancy had been alone on the beach. Behind her, the boulevard glittered in the morning sun and the season's traffic rocked by the long curve of the shore in the clumps of breasting speed. She stood looking outward at the high straight distant shelf of cloud. The islands were out there, plainly visible. The walls of the old Civil War fort on the nearest one of them, the one with the lighthouse—Ship Island—were plain today as well. She had been out there once this summer with Rob Acklen, out there on the island, where the reeds grew in the wild white sand, and the water teemed so thick with seaweed that only crazy people would have tried to swim in it. The gulf had rushed white and strong through all the seaweed, frothing up the beach. On the beach, the froth turned brown, the color of softly moving crawfish claws. In the boat coming home through the sunset that day, a boy standing up in the pilothouse played "Over the Waves" on his harmonica. Rob Acklen had put his jacket around Nancy's shoulders —she had never thought to bring a sweater. The jacket swallowed her; it smelled more like Rob than he did. The boat moved, the breeze blew, the sea swelled, all to the lilt of the music. All twenty-five members of the Laurel, Mississippi, First Baptist Church Adult Bible Class, who had come out with them on the excursion boat, and to whom Rob and Nancy had yet to introduce themselves, had stopped giggling and making their silly jokes. They were tired, and stood in a huddle like sheep; they were shaped like sheep as well, with little shoulders and wide bottoms—it was somehow sad. Nancy and Rob, young and trim, stood side by side near the bow, like figureheads of the boat, hearing the music and watching the thick prow butt the swell, which the sunset had stained a deep red. Nancy felt for certain that this was the happiest she had ever been.

Alone on the sand this morning, she had spread out her beach towel and stood for a moment looking up the beach, way up, past a grove of live oaks to where Rob Acklen's house was visible. He would be standing in the kitchen, in loafers and a dirty white shirt and an old pair of shorts, drinking cold beer from the refrigerator right out of the can. He would eat lunch with his mother and sister, read the paper and write a letter, then dress and drive into town to help his father in the office, going right past Nancy's house along the boulevard. Around three, he would call her up. He did this every day. His name was Fitzrobert Conroy Acklen—one of those full-blown Confederate names. Everybody liked him, and more than a few—a general mixture of every color, size, age, sex, and religion—would say when he passed by, "I declare, I just love that boy." So he was bound to have a lot of nicknames: "Fitz" or "Bobbie" or "Cousin" or "Son"—he answered to almost anything. He was the kind of boy people have high, undefined hopes for. He had first seen Nancy Lewis one morning when he came by her house to make an insurance call for his father.

Breaking off her French—could it have been the sentence about "*l'officier*"?—she had gone out to see who it was. She was expecting Mrs. Nattier, their neighbor, who had skinny white freckled legs she never shaved and whose husband, "off" somewhere, was thought not to be doing well; or Mrs. Nattier's little boy Bernard, who thought it was fun to hide around corners after dark and jump out saying nothing more original than "Boo!" (Once, he had screamed "Raw head and bloody bones!," but Nancy was sure somebody had told him to); or one of the neighbor ladies in the back—old Mrs. Poultney, whom they rented from and who walked with a cane, or Miss Henriette Dupré, who was so devout she didn't even have to go to confession before weekday Communion and whose hands, always tucked up in the sleeves of her sack, were as cold as church candles, and to think of them touching you was like rabbits skipping over your grave on dark rainy nights in winter up in the lonely wet-leaf-covered hills. Or else it was somebody wanting to be paid something. Nancy had opened the door and looked up, and there, instead of a dozen other people, was Rob Acklen.

Not that she knew his name. She had seen boys like him down on the coast, ever since her family had moved there from Little Rock back in the spring. She had seen them playing tennis on the courts back of the hotel, where she sometimes went to jump on the trampoline. She believed that the hotel people thought she was on the staff in some sort of way, as she was about the right age for that—just a year or so beyond high school but hardly old enough to work in town. The weather was already getting hot, and the season was falling off. When she passed the courts, going and coming, she saw the boys out of the corner of her eye. Were they really so much taller than the boys up where they had moved from, up in Arkansas? They were lankier and a lot more casual. They were more assured. To Nancy, whose family was in debt and whose father, in one job after another, was always doing something wrong, the boys playing tennis had that wonderful remoteness of creatures to be admired on the screen, or those seen in whiskey ads, standing near the bar of a country club and sleekly talking about things she could not begin to imagine. But now here was one, in a heavy tan cotton suit and a light blue shirt with a buttoned-down collar and dark tie, standing on her own front porch and smiling at her.

Yet when Rob called Nancy for a date, a day or two later, she didn't have to be told that he did it partly because he liked to do nice things for people. He obviously liked to be considerate and kind, because the first time he saw her he said, "I guess you don't know many people yet?"

"No, because Daddy just got transferred," she said— "transferred" being her mother's word for it; fired was what it was. She gave him a Coke and talked to him awhile, standing around in the house, which unaccountably continued to be empty. She said she didn't know a thing about insurance.

Now, still on the beach, Nancy Lewis sat down in the middle of her beach towel and began to rub suntan lotion on her neck and shoulders. Looking down the other way, away from Rob's house and toward the yacht club, she saw a man standing alone on the sand. She had not noticed him before. He was facing out toward the gulf and staring fixedly at the horizon. He was wearing shorts and a shirt made out of red bandanna, with the tail out—a stout young man with black hair.

Just then, without warning, it began to rain. There were no clouds one could see in the overhead dazzle, but it rained anyway; the drops fell in huge discs, marking the sand, and splashing on Nancy's skin. Each drop seemed enough to fill a Dixie cup. At first, Nancy did not know what the stinging sensation was; then she knew the rain was burning her. It was scalding hot! Strange, outlandish, but also painful, was how she found it. She jumped up and began to flinch and twist away, trying to escape, and a moment later she had snatched up her beach towel and flung it around her shoulders. But the large hot drops kept falling, and there was no escape from them. She started rubbing her cheek and forehead and felt that she might blister all over; then, since it kept on and on and was all so inexplicable, she grabbed her lotion and ran up the beach and out of the sand and back across the boulevard. Once in her own front yard, under the scraggy trees, she felt the rain no longer, and looked back curiously into the dazzle beyond the boulevard.

"I thought you meant to stay for a while," her mother said. "Was it too hot? Anybody would be crazy to go out there now. There's never anybody out there at this time of day."

"It was all right," said Nancy, "but it started raining. I never felt anything like it. The rain was so hot it burned me. Look. My face—" She ran to look in the mirror. Sure enough, her face and shoulders looked splotched. It might blister. I might be scarred for life, she thought—one of those dramatic phrases left over from high school.

Nancy's mother, Mrs. Lewis, was a discouraged lady whose silky, blondish-grey hair was always slipping loose and tagging out around her face. She would not try to improve herself and talked a lot in company about her family; two of her uncles had been professors simultaneously at the University of North Carolina. One of them had written a book on phonetics. Mrs. Lewis seldom found anyone who had heard of them, or of the book, either. Some people asked what phonetics were, and others did not ask anything at all.

Mrs. Lewis now said to her daughter, "You just got too much sun."

"No, it was the rain. It was really scalding hot."

"I never heard of such a thing," her mother said. "Out of a clear sky."

"I can't help that," Nancy said. "I guess I ought to know."

Mrs. Lewis took on the kind of look she had when she would open the handkerchief drawer of a dresser and see two used, slightly bent carpet nails, some Scotch Tape melted together, an old receipt, an unanswered letter announcing a cousin's wedding, some scratched negatives saved for someone but never developed, some dusty foreign coins, a bank deposit book from a town they lived in during the summer before Nancy was born, and an old telegram whose contents, forgotten, no one would dare now to explore, for it would say something awful but absolutely true.

"I wish you wouldn't speak to me like that," Mrs. Lewis said. "All I know is, it certainly didn't rain here."

Nancy wandered away, into the dining room. She felt bad about everything—about quarrelling with her mother, about not getting a suntan, about wasting her time all summer with Rob Acklen and not learning any French. She went and took a long cool bath in the big old bathroom, where the bathtub had ball-and-claw feet painted mustard yellow and the single light bulb on the long cord dropped down one mile from the stratosphere.

What the Lewises found in a rented house was always outclassed by what they brought into it. Nancy's father, for instance, had a china donkey that bared its teeth in a great big grin. Written on one side was "If you really want to look like me" and on the other "Just keep right on talking." Her father loved the donkey and its message, and always put it on the living-room table of whatever house they were in. When he got a drink before dinner each evening, he would wander back with glass in hand and look the donkey over. "That's pretty good," he would say just before he took the first swallow. Nancy had often longed to break the donkey, by accident— that's what she would say, that it had all been an accident—but she couldn't get over the feeling that if she did, worse things than the Lewises had ever imagined would happen to them. That donkey would let in a flood of trouble, that she knew.

After Nancy got out of the tub and dried, she rubbed Jergens Lotion on all the splotches the rain had made. Then she ate a peanut-butter sandwich and more shrimp salad left over from supper the night before, and drank a cold Coke. Now and then, eating, she would go look in the mirror. By the time Rob Acklen called up, the red marks had all but disappeared.

That night, riding down to Biloxi with Rob, Nancy confided that the catalogue of people she disliked, headed by Bernard Nattier, included every single person—Miss Henriette Dupré, Mrs. Poultney, and Mrs. Nattier, and Mr. Nattier, too, when he was at home—that she had to be with these days. It even included, she was sad to say, her mother and father. If Bernard Nattier had to be mean—and it was clear he did have to—why did he have to be so corny? He put wads of wet, chewed bubble gum in her purses—that was the most original thing he ever did. Otherwise, it was just live crawfish in her bed or crabs in her shoes; anybody could think of that. And when he stole, he took things *she* wanted, nothing simple, like money—she could have forgiven him for that—but cigarettes, lipstick, and ashtrays she had stolen herself here and there. If she locked her door, he got in through the window; if she locked the window, she suffocated. Not only that, but he would crawl out from under the bed. His eyes were slightly crossed and he knew how to turn the lids back on themselves so that it looked like blood, and then he would chase her. He was browned to the color of dirt all over and he smelled like salt mud the sun had dried. He wore black tennis shoes laced too tight at the ankles and from sunup till way past dark he never thought of anything but what to do to Nancy, and she would have liked to kill him.

She made Rob Acklen laugh. She amused him. He didn't take anything Nancy Lewis could say at all to heart, but, as if she was something he had found on the beach and was teaching to talk, he, with his Phi Beta Kappa key and his good level head and his wonderful prospects, found everything she told about herself cute, funny, absurd. He did remark that he had such feelings himself from time to time—that he would occasionally get crazy mad at one of his parents or the other, and that he once planned his sister's murder down to the last razor slash. But he laughed again, and his chewing gum popped amiably in his jaws. When she told him about the hot rain, he said he didn't believe it. He said "Aw," which was what a boy like Rob Acklen said when he didn't believe something. The top of his old white Mercury convertible was down and the wind rushed past like an endless bolt of raw silk being drawn against Nancy's cheek.

In the ladies'-room mirror at the Beach View, where they stopped to eat, she saw the bright quality of her eyes, as though she had been drinking. Her skirts rustled in the narrow room; a porous white disc of deodorant hung on a hook, fuming the air. Her eyes, though blue, looked startlingly dark in her pale skin, for though she tried hard all the time, she never seemed to tan. All the sun did, as her mother was always pointing out, was bleach her hair three shades lighter; a little more and it would be almost white. Out on the island that day, out on Ship Island, she had drifted in the water like seaweed, with the tide combing her limbs and hair, tugging her through lengths of fuzzy water growth. She had lain flat on her face with her arms stretched out before her, experiencing the curious lift the water's motion gave to the tentacles of weed, wondering whether she liked it or not. Did something alive clamber the small of her back? Did something wishful grope the spiral of her ear? Rob had caught her wrist hard and waked her—waked was what he did, though to sleep in water is not possible. He said he thought she had been there too long. "Nobody can keep their face in the water that long," was what he said.

"I did," said Nancy.

Rob's brow had been blistered a little, she recalled, for that had been back early in the summer, soon after they had met—but the changes the sun made on him went without particular attention. The seasons here were old ground to him. He said that the island was new, however—or at least forgotten. He said he had never been there but once, and that many years ago, on a Boy Scout picnic. Soon they were exploring the fort, reading the dates off the metal signs whose letters glowed so smoothly in the sun, and the brief summaries of what those little boys, little military-academy boys turned into soldiers, had endured. Not old enough to fill up the name of soldier, or of prisoner, either, which is what they were—not old enough to shave, Nancy bet—still, they had died there, miserably far from home, and had been buried in the sand. There was a lot more. Rob would have been glad to read all about it, but she wasn't interested. What they knew already was plenty, just about those boys. A bright, worried lizard ran out of a hot rubble of brick. They came out of the fort and walked alone together eastward toward the dunes, now skirting near the shore that faced the sound and now wandering south, where they could hear or sometimes glimpse the gulf. They were overlooked all the way by an old white lighthouse. From far away behind, the twenty-five members of the Adult Bible Class could be overheard playing a silly, shrill Sunday-school game. It came across the ruins of the fort and the sad story of the dead soldiers like something that had happened long ago that you could not quite remember having joined in. On the beach to their right, toward the gulf, a flock of sandpipers with blinding-white breasts stepped pecking along the water's edge, and on the inner beach, toward the sound, a wrecked sailboat with a broken mast lay half buried in the sand.

Rob kept teasing her along, pulling at the soft wool strings of her bathing suit, which knotted at the nape and again under her shoulder blades, worrying loose the damp hair that she had carefully slicked back and pinned. "There isn't anybody in that house," he assured her, some minutes later, having explored most of that part of the island and almost as much of Nancy as well, having almost, but not quite—his arms around her—coaxed and caressed her down to ground level in a clump of reeds. "There hasn't been in years and years," he said, encouraging her.

"It's only those picnic people," she said, holding off, for the reeds would not have concealed a medium-sized mouse. They had been to look at the sailboat and thought about climbing inside (kissing closely, they had almost fallen right over into it), but it did have a rotten tin can in the bottom and smelled, so here they were back out in the dunes.

"They've got to drink all those Coca-Colas," Rob said, "and give out all those prizes, and anyway—"

She never learned anyway what, but it didn't matter. Maybe she began to make up all that the poor little soldiers had missed out on. The island's very spine, a warm reach of thin ground, came smoothly up into the arch of her back; and it was at least halfway the day itself, with its fair, wide-open eyes, that she went over to. She felt somewhat historical afterward, as though they had themselves added one more mark to all those that place remembered.

Having played all the games and given out the prizes, having eaten all the homemade cookies and drunk the case of soft drinks just getting warm, and gone sightseeing through the fort, the Bible Class was now coming, too, crying "Yoohoo!," to explore the island. They discovered Rob hurling shells and bits of rock into the surf, while Nancy, scavenging a little distance away, tugged up out of the sand a shell so extraordinary it was worth showing around. It was purple, pink, and violet inside—a palace of colors; the king of the oysters had no doubt lived there. When she held it shyly out to them, they cried "Look!" and "Ooo!," so there was no need for talking to them much at all, and in the meantime the evening softened, the water glowed, the glare dissolved. Far out, there were other islands one could see now, and beyond those must be many more. They had been there all along.

Going home, Nancy gave the wonderful shell to the boy who stood in the pilothouse playing "Over the Waves." She glanced back as they walked off up the pier and saw him look at the shell, try it for weight, and then throw it in the water, leaning far back on his arm and putting a good spin on the throw, the way boys like to do—the way Rob Acklen himself had been doing, too, just that afternoon.

"Why did you do that?" Rob had demanded. He was frowning; he looked angry. He had thought they should keep the shell—to remember, she supposed.

"For the music," she explained.

"But it was ours," he said. When she didn't answer, he said again, "Why did you, Nancy?"

But still she didn't answer.

When Nancy returned to their table at the Beach View, having put her lipstick back straight after eating fish, Rob was paying the check. "Why not believe me?" she asked him. "It was true. The rain was hot as fire. I thought I would be scarred for life."

It was still broad daylight, not even twilight. In the bright, air-conditioned restaurant, the light from the water glazed flatly against the broad picture windows, the chandeliers, and the glasses. It was the hour when mirrors reflect nothing and bars look tired. The restaurant was a boozy, cheap sort of place with a black-lined gambling hall in the back, but everyone went there because the food was good.

"You're just like Mama," she said. "You think I made it up."

Rob said, teasing, "I didn't say that. I just said I didn't believe it." He loved getting her caught in some sort of logic she couldn't get out of. When he opened the door for her, she got a good sidelong view of his longish, firm face and saw the way his somewhat fine brows arched up with one or two bright reddish hairs in among the dark ones; his hair was that way, too, when the sun hit it. Maybe, if nobody had told him, he wouldn't have known it; he seemed not to notice so very much about himself. Having the confidence of people who don't worry much, his grin could snare her instantly—a glance alone could make her feel how lucky she was he'd ever noticed her. But it didn't do at all to think about him now. It would be ages before they made it through the evening and back, retracing the way and then turning off to the bayou, and even then, there would be those mosquitoes.

Bayou lovemaking suited Rob just fine; he was one of those people mosquitoes didn't bite. They certainly bit Nancy. They were huge and silent, and the minute the car stopped they would even come and sit upon her eyelids, if she closed her eyes, a dozen to each tender arc of flesh. They would gather on her face, around her nose and mouth. Clothlike, like rags and tatters, like large dry ashes of burnt cloth, they came in lazy droves, in fleets, sailing on the air. They were never in any hurry, being everywhere at once and always ready to bite. Nancy had been known to jump all the way out of the car and go stamping across the grass like a calf. She grew sulky and despairing and stood on one leg at a time in the moonlight, slapping at her ankles, while Rob leaned his chin on the doorframe and watched her with his affectionate, total interest.

Nancy, riddled and stinging with beads of actual blood briar-pointed here and there upon her, longed to be almost anywhere else—she especially longed for New Orleans. She always talked about it, although, never having been there, she had to say the things that other people said—food and jazz in the French Quarter, beer and crabs out on Lake Pontchartrain. Rob said vaguely they would go sometime. But she could tell that things were wrong for him at this point. "The food's just as good around here," he said.

"Oh, Rob!" She knew it wasn't so. She could feel that city, hanging just over the horizon from them scarcely fifty miles away, like some swollen bronze moon, at once brilliant and shadowy and drenched in every sort of amplified smell. Rob was stroking her hair, and in time his repeated, gentle touch gained her attention. It seemed to tell what he liked—girls all spanking clean, with scrubbed fingernails, wearing shoes still damp with white shoe polish. Even a fresh gardenia stuck in their hair wouldn't be too much for him. There would be all sorts of differences, to him, between Ship Island and the French Quarter, but she did not have much idea just what they were. Nancy took all this in, out of his hand on her head. She decided she had better not talk anymore about New Orleans. She wriggled around, looking out over his shoulder, through the moonlight, toward where the pitch-black surface of the bayou water showed in patches through the trees. The trees were awful, hung with great spooky gray tatters of Spanish moss. Nancy was reminded of the house she and her family were living in; it had recently occurred to her that the peculiar smell it had must come from some Spanish moss that had got sealed in behind the panelling, between the walls. The moss was alive in there and growing, and that was where she was going to seal Bernard Nattier up someday, for him to see how it felt. She had tried to kill him once, by filling her purse with rocks and oyster shells—the roughest she could find. She had read somewhere that this weapon was effective for ladies in case of attack. But he had ducked when she swung the purse at him, and she had only gone spinning round and round, falling at last into a camellia tree, which had scratched her. . . .

"The Skeltons said for us to stop by there for a drink," Rob told her. They were driving again, and the car was back on the boulevard, in the still surprising daylight. "What did you say?" he asked her.

"Nothing."

"You just don't want to go?"

"No, I don't much want to go."

"Well, then, we won't stay long."

The Skelton house was right on the water, with a second-story, glassed-in, air-conditioned living room looking out over the sound. The sofas and chairs were covered with gold-and-white striped satin, and the room was full of Rob's friends. Lorna Skelton, who had been Rob's girl the summer before and who dressed so beautifully, was handing drinks round and saying, "So which is your favorite bayou, Rob?" She had a sort of fake "good sport" tone of voice and wanted to appear ready for anything. (Being so determined to be nice around Nancy, she was going to fall right over backward one day.)

"Do I have to have a favorite?" Rob asked. "They all look good to me. Full of slime and alligators."

"I should have asked Nancy."

"They're all full of mosquitos," Nancy said, hoping that was O.K. for an answer. She thought that virgins were awful people.

"Trapped, boy!" Turner Carmichael said to Rob, and banged him on the shoulder. Turner wanted to be a writer, so he thought it was all right to tell people about themselves. "Women will be your downfall, Acklen. Nancy, honey, you haven't spoken to the General."

Old General Skelton, Lorna's grandfather, sat in the corner of the living room near the mantel, drinking a Scotch highball. You had to shout at him.

"How's the election going, General?" Turner asked.

"Election? Election? What election? Oh, the election! Well—" He lowered his voice, confidentially. As with most deaf people, his tone went to extremes. "There's no question of it. The one we want is the one we know. Know Houghman's father. Knew his grandfather. His stand is the same, identical one that we are all accustomed to. On every subject—this race thing especially. Very dangerous now. Extremely touchy. But Houghman —absolute! Never experiment, never question, never turn back. These are perilous times."

"Yes, sir," said Turner, nodding in an earnestly false way, which was better than the earnestly impressed way a younger boy at the General's elbow shouted, "General Skelton, that's just what my daddy says!"

"Oh, yes," said the old man, sipping Scotch. "Oh, yes, it's true. And you, Missy?" he thundered suddenly at Nancy, making her jump. "Are you just visiting here?"

"Why, Granddaddy," Lorna explained, joining them, "Nancy lives here now. You know Nancy."

"Then why isn't she tan?" the old man continued. "Why so pale and wan, fair nymph?"

"Were you a nymph?" Turner asked. "All this time?"

"For me I'm dark," Nancy explained. But this awkward way of putting it proved more than General Skelton could hear, even after three shoutings.

Turner Carmichael said, "We used to have this crazy colored girl who went around saying, 'I'se really white, 'cause all my chillun is,'" and of course *that* was what General Skelton picked to hear. "Party's getting rough," he complained.

"Granddaddy," Lorna cried, giggling, "you don't understand!"

"Don't I?" said the old gentleman. "Well, maybe I don't."

"Here, Nancy, come help me," said Lorna, leading her guest toward the kitchen.

On the way, Nancy heard Rob ask Turner, "Just where did you have this colored girl, did you say?"

"Don't be a dope. I said she worked for us."

"Aren't they a scream?" Lorna said, dragging a quart bottle of soda out of the refrigerator. "I thank God every night Granddaddy's deaf. You know, he was in the First World War and killed I don't know how many Germans, and he still can't stand to hear what he calls loose talk before a lady."

"I thought he was in the Civil War," said Nancy, and then of course she knew that that was the wrong thing and that Lorna, who just for an instant gave her a glance less than polite, was not going to forget it. The fact was, Nancy had never thought till that minute which war General Skelton had been in. She hadn't thought because she didn't care.

It had grown dark by now, and through the kitchen windows Nancy could see that the moon had risen—a moon in the clumsy stage, swelling between three-quarters and full, yet pouring out light on the water. Its rays were bursting against a long breakwater of concrete slabs, the remains of what the hurricane had shattered.

After saying such a fool thing, Nancy felt she could not stay in that kitchen another minute with Lorna, so she asked where she could go comb her hair. Lorna showed her down a hallway, kindly switching the lights on.

The Skeltons' bathroom was all pale blue and white, with handsome jars of rose bath salts and big fat scented bars of rosy soap. The lights came on impressively and the fixtures were heavy, yet somehow it all looked dead. It came to Nancy that she had really been wondering about just what would be in this sort of bathroom ever since she had seen those boys, with maybe Rob among them, playing tennis while she jumped on the trampoline. Surely the place had the air of an inner shrine, but what was there to see? The tops of all the bottles fitted firmly tight, and the soap in the tub was dry. Somebody had picked it all out—that was the point—judging soap and bath salts just the way they judged outsiders, business, real estate, politics. Nancy's father made judgments, too. Once, he argued all evening that Hitler was a well-meaning man; another time, he said the world was ready for the Communists. You could tell he was judging wrong, because he didn't have a bathroom like this one. Nancy's face in the mirror resembled a flower in a room that was too warm.

When she went out again, they had started dancing a little— a sort of friendly shifting around before the big glass windows overlooking the sound. General Skelton's chair was empty; he was gone. Down below, Lorna's parents could be heard coming in; her mother called upstairs. Her father appeared and shook hands all around. Mrs. Skelton soon followed him. He was wearing a white jacket, and she had on a silver cocktail dress with silver shoes. They looked like people in magazines. Mrs. Skelton held a crystal platter of things to eat in one hand, with a lace handkerchief pressed between the flesh and the glass in an inevitable sort of way.

In a moment, when the faces, talking and eating, the music, the talk, and the dancing swam to a still point before Nancy's eyes, she said, "You must all come to my house next week. We'll have a party."

A silence fell. Everyone knew where Nancy lived, in that little cluster of old run-down houses the boulevard swept by. They knew that her house, especially, needed paint outside and furniture inside. Her daddy drank too much, and through her dress they could perhaps clearly discern the pin that held her slip together. Maybe, since they knew everything, they could look right through the walls of the house and see her daddy's donkey.

"Sure we will," said Rob Acklen at once. "I think that would be grand."

"Sure we will, Nancy," said Lorna Skelton, who was such a good sport and who was not seeing Rob this summer.

"A party?" said Turner Carmichael, and swallowed a whole anchovy. "Can I come, too?"

Oh, dear Lord, Nancy was wondering, what made me say it? Then she was on the stairs with her knees shaking, leaving the party, leaving with Rob to go down to Biloxi, where the two of them always went, and hearing the right things said to her and Rob, and smiling back at the right things but longing to jump off into the dark as if it were water. The dark, with the moon mixed in with it, seemed to her like good deep water to go off in.

She might have known that in the Marine Room of the Buena Vista down in Biloxi, they would run into more friends of Rob's. They always ran into somebody, and she might have known. These particular ones had already arrived and were even waiting for Rob, being somewhat bored in the process. It wasn't that Rob was so bright and witty, but he listened and liked everybody; he saw them the way they liked to be seen. So then they would go on to new heights, outdoing themselves, coming to believe how marvellous they really were. Two fraternity brothers of his were there tonight. They were sitting at a table with their dates—two tiny girls with tiny voices, like mosquitoes. They at once asked Nancy where she went to college, but before she could reply and give it away that her school so far had been only a cow college up in Arkansas and that she had gone there because her daddy couldn't afford anywhere else, Rob broke in and answered for her. "She's been in a finishing school in Little Rock," he said, "but I'm trying to talk her into going to the university."

Then the girls and their dates all four spoke together. They said, "Great!"

"Now watch," said one of the little girls, whose name was Teenie. "Cootie's getting out that little ole rush book."

Sure enough, the tiniest little notebook came out of the little cream silk bag of the other girl, who was called Cootie, and in it Nancy's name and address were written down with a sliver of a gold pencil. The whole routine was a fake, but a kind fake, as long as Rob was there. The minute those two got her into the ladies' room it would turn into another thing altogether; that she knew. Nancy knew all about mosquitoes. They'll sting me till I crumple up and die, she thought, and what will they ever care? So, when the three of them did leave the table, she stopped to straighten the strap of her shoe at the door to the ladies' room and let them go on through, talking on and on to

one another about Rush Week. Then she went down a corridor and around a corner and down a short flight of steps. She
ran down a long basement hallway where the service quarters
were, past linen closets and cases of soft drinks, and, turning
another corner and trying a door above a stairway, she came
out, as she thought she would, in a night-club place called the
Fishnet, far away in the wing. It was a good place to hide;
she and Rob had been there often. I can make up some sort
of story later, she thought, and crept up on the last barstool.
Up above the bar, New Orleans–style (or so they said), a man
was pumping tunes out of an electric organ. He wore rings on
his chubby fingers and kept a handkerchief near him to mop
his brow and to swab his triple chins with between songs. He
waved his hand at Nancy. "Where's Rob, honey?" he asked.

She smiled but didn't answer. She kept her head back in the
shadows. She wished only to be like another glass in the sparkling row of glasses lined up before the big gleam of mirrors
and under the play of lights. What made me say that about a
party, she kept wondering. To some people it would be nothing, nothing. But not to her. She fumbled in her bag for a
cigarette. Inadvertently, she drank from a glass near her hand.
The man sitting next to her smiled at her. "I didn't want it
anyway," he said.

"Oh, I didn't mean—" she began. "I'll order one." Did you
pay now? She rummaged in her bag.

But the man said "What'll it be?" and ordered for her.
"Come on now, take it easy," he said. "What's your name?"

"Nothing," she said, by accident.

She had meant to say Nancy, but the man seemed to think it
was funny. "Nothing what?" he asked. "Or is it by any chance
Miss Nothing? I used to know a large family of Nothings, over
in Mobile."

"Oh, I meant to say Nancy."

"Nancy Nothing. Is that it?"

Another teaser, she thought. She looked away from his eyes,
which glittered like metal, and what she saw across the room
made her uncertainties vanish. She felt her whole self settle and
calm itself. The man she had seen that morning on the beach
wearing a red bandanna shirt and shorts was standing near the
back of the Fishnet, looking on. Now he was wearing a white

dinner jacket and a black tie, with a red cummerbund over his large stomach, but he was unmistakably the same man. At that moment, he positively seemed to Nancy to be her own identity. She jumped up and left the teasing man at the bar and crossed the room.

"Remember me?" she said. "I saw you on the beach this morning."

"Sure I do. You ran off when it started to rain. I had to run, too."

"Why did you?" Nancy asked, growing happier every minute.

"Because the rain was so hot it burnt me. If I could roll up my sleeve, I'd show you the blisters on my arm."

"I believe you. I had some, too, but they went away." She smiled, and the man smiled back. The feeling was that they would be friends forever.

"Listen," the man said after a while. "There's a fellow here you've got to meet now. He's out on the veranda, because it's too hot in here. Anyway, he gets tired just with me. Now, you come on."

Nancy Lewis was always conscious of what she had left behind her. She knew that right now her parents and old Mrs. Poultney, with her rent collector's jaw, and Miss Henriette Dupré, with her religious calf eyes, and the Nattiers, mother and son, were all sitting on the back porch in the half-light, passing the bottle of 6-12 around, and probably right now discussing the fact that Nancy was out with Rob again. She knew that when her mother thought of Rob her heart turned beautiful and radiant as a seashell on a spring night. Her father, both at home and at his office, took his daughter's going out with Rob as a means of saying something disagreeable about Rob's father, who was a big insurance man. There was always some talk about how Mr. Acklen had trickily got out of the bulk of his hurricane-damage payments, the same as all the other insurance men had done. Nancy's mother was probably responding to such a charge at this moment. "Now, you don't know that's true," she would say. But old Mrs. Poultney would say she knew it was true with *her* insurance company (implying that she knew but wouldn't say about the Acklen company, too). Half the house she was renting to the Lewises had blown right off it—all one wing—and the upstairs bathroom was ripped in two, and you could see the wallpapered walls of all the rooms, and the bathtub, with its pipes still attached, had got blown into the telephone wires. If Mrs. Poultney had got what insurance money had been coming to her, she would have torn down this house and built a new one. And Mrs. Nattier would say that there was something terrible to her about seeing wallpapered rooms exposed that way. And Miss Henriette Dupré would say that the Dupré house had come through it all absolutely intact, meaning that the Duprés had been foresighted enough to get some sort of special heavenly insurance, and she would be just longing to embark on explaining how they came by it, and she would, too, given a tenth of a chance. And all the time this went on, Nancy could see into the Acklens' house just as clearly—see the Acklens sitting inside their sheltered game room after dinner, bathed in those soft bug-repellent lights. And what were the Acklens saying (along with their kind of talk about their kind of money) but that they certainly hoped Rob wasn't serious about that girl? Nothing had to matter if he wasn't serious. . . . Nancy could circle around all of them in her mind. She could peer into windows, overhearing; it was the only way she could look at people. No human in the whole human world seemed to her exactly made for her to stand in front of and look squarely in the eye, the way she could look Bernard Nattier in the eye (he not being a human, either) before taking careful aim to be sure not to miss him with a purseful of rocks and oyster shells, or the way she could look this big man in the red cummerbund in the eye, being convinced already that he was what her daddy called a "natural." Her daddy liked to come across people he could call that, because it made him feel superior.

As the big man steered her through the crowded room, threading among the tables, going out toward the veranda, he was telling her his life story all along the way. It seemed that his father was a terribly rich Yankee who paid him not to stay at home. He had been in love with a policeman's daughter from Pittsburgh, but his father broke it up. He was still in love with her and always would be. It was the way he was; he couldn't help being faithful, could he? His name was Alfred, but everybody called him Bub. The fellow his father paid to drive him around was right down there, he said, as they stepped through the door and out on the veranda.

Nancy looked down the length of the veranda, which ran along the side of the hotel, and there was a man sitting on a bench. He had on a white jacket and was staring straight ahead, smoking. The highway curled around the hotel grounds, following the curve of the shore, and the cars came glimmering past, one by one, sometimes with lights on inside, sometimes spilling radio music that trailed up in long waves and met the electric-organ music coming out of the bar. Nancy and Bub walked toward the man. Bub counselled her gently, "His name is Dennis." Some people in full evening dress were coming up the divided walk before the hotel, past the canna lilies blooming deeply red under the high, powerful lights, where the bugs coned in long footless whirlpools. The people were drunk and laughing.

"Hi, Dennis," Bub said. The way he said it, trying to sound confident, told her that he was scared of Dennis.

Dennis's head snapped up and around. He was an erect, strong, square-cut man, not very tall. He had put water on his light-brown hair when he combed it, so that it streaked light and dark and light again and looked like wood. He had cold eyes, which did not express anything—just the opposite of Rob Acklen's.

"What you got there?" he asked Bub.

"I met her this morning on the beach," Bub said.

"Been holding out on me?"

"Nothing like that," said Bub. "I just now saw her again."

The man called Dennis got up and thumbed his cigarette into the shrubbery. Then he carefully set his heels together and bowed. It was all a sort of joke on how he thought people here behaved. "Would you care to dance?" he inquired.

Dancing there on the veranda, Nancy noticed at once that he had a tense, strong wrist that bent back and forth like something manufactured out of steel. She also noticed that he was making her do whatever it was he called dancing; he was good at that. The music coming out of the Fishnet poured through the windows and around them. Dennis was possibly even thirty years old. He kept talking the whole time. "I guess he's told you everything, even about the policeman's daughter. He tells everybody everything, right in the first two minutes. I don't know if it's true, but how can you tell? If it wasn't true when it happened, it is now." He spun her fast as a top, then slung her out about ten feet—she thought she would certainly sail right on out over the railing and maybe never stop till she landed in the gulf, or perhaps go splat on the highway—but he got her back on the beat and finished up the thought, saying, "Know what I mean?"

"I guess so," Nancy said, and the music stopped.

The three of them sat down together on the bench.

"What do we do now?" Dennis asked.

"Let's ask her," said Bub. He was more and more delighted with Nancy. He had been tremendously encouraged when Dennis took to her.

"You ask her," Dennis said.

"Listen, Nancy," Bub said. "Now, listen. Let me just tell you. There's so much money—that's the first thing to know. You've got no idea how much money there is. Really crazy. It's something, actually, that nobody knows—"

"If anybody knew," said Dennis, "they might have to tell the government."

"Anyway, my stepmother on this yacht in Florida, her own telephone—by radio, you know—she'd be crazy to meet you. My dad is likely off somewhere, but maybe not. And there's this plane down at Palm Beach, pilot and all, with nothing to do but go to the beach every day, just to pass away the time, and if he's not there for any reason, me and Dennis can fly just as good as we can drive. There's Alaska, Beirut—would you like to go to Beirut? I've always wanted to. There's anything you say."

"See that Cad out there?" said Dennis. "The yellow one with the black leather upholstery? That's his. I drive."

"So all you got to do," Bub told her, "is wish. Now, wait—now, think. It's important!" He all but held his hand over her mouth, as if playing a child's game, until finally he said, "Now! What would you like to do most in the world?"

"Go to New Orleans," said Nancy at once, "and eat some wonderful food."

"It's a good idea," said Dennis. "This dump is getting on my nerves. I get bored most of the time anyway, but today I'm bored silly."

"So wait here!" Nancy said. "So wait right here!"

She ran off to get Rob. She had all sorts of plans in her head.

But Rob was all taken up. There were now more of his friends. The Marine Room was full of people just like him, lounging around two big tables shoved together, with about a million 7-Up bottles and soda bottles and glasses before them, and girls spangled among them, all silver, gold, and white. It was as if while Nancy was gone they had moved into mirrors to multiply themselves. They were talking to themselves about things she couldn't join in, any more than you can dance without feet. Somebody was going into politics, somebody was getting married to a girl who trained horses, somebody was just back from Europe. The two little mosquito girls weren't saying anything much anymore; they had their little chins glued to their little palms. When anybody mentioned the university, it sounded like a small country the people right there were running *in absentia* to suit themselves. Last year's Maid of Cotton was there, and so, it turned out, was the girl horse-trainer—tall, with a sheaf of upswept brown hair fastened with a glittering pin; she sat like the mast of a ship, smiling and talking about horses. Did she know personally every horse in the Southern states?

Rob scarcely looked up when he pulled Nancy in. "Where you been? What you want to drink?" He was having another good evening. He seemed to be sitting up above all the rest, as though presiding, but this was not actually so; only his fondness for every face he saw before him made him appear to be raised up a little, as if on a special chair.

And, later on, it seemed to Nancy that she herself had been, among them, like a person who wasn't a person—another order of creature passing among or even through them. Was it just that nothing, nobody, could really distract them when they got wrapped up in themselves?

"I met some people who want to meet you," she whispered to Rob. "Come on out with me."

"O.K.," he said. "In a minute. Are they from around here?"

"Come on, come on," she urged. "Come on out."

"In a minute," he said. "I will in a minute," he promised.

Then someone noticed her pulling at his sleeve, and she thought she heard Lorna Skelton laugh.

She went racing back to Bub and Dennis, who were waiting for her so docilely they seemed to be the soul of goodness, and she said, "I'll just ride around for a while, because I've never been in a Cadillac before." So they rode around and came back and sat for a while under the huge brilliant overhead lights before the hotel, where the bugs spiralled down. They did everything she said. She could make them do anything. They went to three different places, for instance, to find her some Dentyne, and when they found it they bought her a whole carton of it.

The bugs did a jagged frantic dance, trying to climb high enough to kill themselves, and occasionally a big one crashed with a harsh dry sound against the pavement. Nancy remembered dancing in the open air, and the rough salt feel of the air whipping against her skin as she spun fast against the air's drift. From behind she heard the resonant, constant whisper of the gulf. She looked toward the hotel doors and thought that if Rob came through she would hop out of the car right away, but he didn't come. A man she knew passed by, and she just all of a sudden said, "Tell Rob I'll be back in a minute," and he, without even looking up, said, "O.K., Nancy," just like it really was O.K., so she said what the motor was saying, quiet but right there, and definitely running just under the splendid skin of the car, "Let's go on for a little while."

"Nancy, I think you're the sweetest girl I ever saw," said Bub, and they drove off.

She rode between them, on the front seat of the Cadillac. The top was down and the moon spilled over them as they rode, skimming gently but powerfully along the shore and the sound, like a strong rapid cloud travelling west. Nancy watched the point where the moon actually met the water. It was moving and still at once. She thought that it was glorious, in a messy sort of way. She would have liked to poke her head up out of the water right there. She could feel the water pouring back through her white-blond hair, her face slathering over with moonlight.

"If it hadn't been for that crazy rain," Bub kept saying, "I wouldn't have met her."

"Oh, shut up about that goofy rain," said Dennis.

"It was like being spit on from above," said Nancy.

The needle crept up to eighty or more, and when they had left the sound and were driving through the swamp Nancy shivered. They wrapped her in a lap robe from the back seat and turned the radio up loud.

It was since she got back, since she got back home from New Orleans, that her mother did not put on the thin voile afternoon dress anymore and serve iced tea to the neighbors on the back porch. Just yesterday, having nothing to do in the hot silence but hear the traffic stream by on the boulevard, and not wanting a suntan and being certain the telephone would not ring, Nancy had taken some lemonade over to Bernard Nattier, who was sick in bed with the mumps. He and his mother had one room between them, over at Mrs. Poultney's house, and they had stacks of magazines—the *Ladies' Home Journal*, *McCall's*, *Life*, and *Time*—piled along the walls. Bernard lay on a bunk bed pushed up under the window, in all the close heat, with no breeze able to come in at all. His face was puffed out and his eyes feverish. "I brought you some lemonade," said Nancy, but he said he couldn't drink it because it hurt his gums. Then he smiled at her, or tried to—it must have hurt even to do that, and it certainly made him look silly, like a cartoon of himself, but it was sweet.

"I love you, Nancy," he said, most irresponsibly.

She thought she would cry. She had honestly tried to kill him with those rocks and oyster shells. He knew that very well, and he, from the moment he had seen her, had set out to make her life one long torment, so where could it come from, a smile like that, and what he said? She didn't know. From the fever, maybe. She said she loved him, too.

Then, it was last night, just the night before, that her father had got drunk and made speeches beginning "To think that a daughter of mine . . ." Nancy had sat through it all crouched in the shadows on the stair landing, in the very spot where the moss or old seaweed back of the panelling smelled the strongest and dankest, and thought of her mother upstairs, lying, clothed, straight out on the bed in the dark, with a headache and no cover on and maybe the roof above her melted away.

Nancy looked down to where her father was marching up to the donkey that said, "If you really want to look like me—Just keep right on talking," and was picking it up and throwing it down, right on the floor. She cried out, before she knew it— "Oh!"—seeing him do the very thing she had so often meant to do herself. Why had he? Why? Because the whiskey had run out on him? Or because he had got too much of it again? Or from trying to get in one good lick at everything there was? Or because the advice he loved so much seemed now being offered to him?

But the donkey did not break. It lay there, far down in the tricky shadows; Nancy could see it lying there, looking back over its shoulder with its big red grinning mouth, and teeth like piano keys, still saying the same thing, naturally. Her father was tilting uncertainly down toward it, unable, without falling flat on his face, to reach it. This made a problem for him, and he stood thinking it all over, taking every aspect of it well into account, even though the donkey gave the impression that not even with a sledgehammer would it be broken, and lay as if on some deep distant sea floor, toward which all the sediment of life was drifting, drifting, forever slowly down. . . .

Beirut! It was the first time she had remembered it. They had said they would take her there, Dennis and Bub, and then she had forgotten to ask, so why think of it right now, on the street uptown, just when she saw Rob Acklen coming along? She would have to see him sometimes, she guessed, but what did Beirut have to do with it?

"Nancy Lewis," he said pleasantly, "you ran out on me. Why did you act like that? I was always nice to you."

"I told them to tell you," she said. "I just went to ride around for a while."

"Oh, I got the word, all right. About fifty different people saw you drive off in that Cadillac. Now about a hundred claim to have. Seems like everybody saw those two characters but me. What did you do it for?"

"I didn't like those Skeltons, all those people you knew. I didn't like those sorority girls, that Teenie and Cootie. You knew I didn't, but you always took me where they were just the same."

"But the point is," said Rob Acklen, "I thought you liked me."

"Well, I did," said Nancy Lewis, as though it all had happened a hundred years ago. "Well, I did like you just fine."

They were talking on the street still. There had been the tail of a storm that morning, and the palms were blowing. There was a sense of them streaming like green flags above the low town.

Rob took Nancy to the drugstore and sat at a booth with her. He ordered her a fountain Coke and himself a cup of coffee. "What's happened to you?" he asked her.

She realized then, from what he was looking at, that something she had only half noticed was certainly there to be seen —her skin, all around the edges of her white blouse, was badly bruised and marked, and there was the purplish mark on her cheekbone she had more or less powdered over, along with the angry streak on her neck.

"You look like you fell through a cotton gin," Rob Acklen continued, in his friendly way. "You're not going to say the rain over in New Orleans is just scalding hot, are you?"

"I didn't say anything," she returned.

"Maybe the mosquitoes come pretty big over there," he suggested. "They wear boxing gloves, for one thing, and, for another—"

"Oh, stop it, Rob," she said and wished she was anywhere else.

It had all stemmed from the moment down in the French Quarter, over late drinks somewhere, when Dennis had got nasty enough with Bub to get rid of him, so that all of Dennis's attention from that point onward had gone exclusively to Nancy. This particular attention was relentless and direct, for Dennis was about as removed from any sort of affection and kindness as a human could be. Maybe it had all got boiled out of him; maybe he had never had much to get rid of. What he had to say to her was nothing she hadn't heard before, nothing she hadn't already been given more or less to understand from mosquitoes, people, life-in-general, and the rain out of the sky. It was just that he said it in a final sort of way—that was all.

"I was in a wreck," said Nancy.

"Nobody killed, I hope," said Rob.

She looked vaguely across at Rob Acklen with pretty, dark-blue eyes that seemed to be squinting to see through shifting lights down in the deep sea; for in looking at him, in spite of all he could do, she caught a glimmering impression of herself, of what he thought of her, of how soft her voice always was, her face like a warm flower.

"I was doing my best to be nice to you. Why wasn't that enough?"

"I don't know," she said.

"None of those people you didn't like were out to get you. They were all my friends."

When he spoke in this handsome, sincere, and democratic way, she had to agree; she had to say she guessed that was right.

Then he said, "I was having such a good summer. I imagined you were, too," and she thought, He's coming down deeper and deeper, but one thing is certain—if he gets down as far as I am, he'll drown.

"You better go," she told him, because he had said he was on his way up to Shreveport on business for his father. And because Bub and Dennis were back; she'd seen them drift by in the car twice, once on the boulevard and once in town, silenter than cloud, Bub in the back, with his knees propped up, reading a magazine.

"I'll be going in a minute," he said.

"You just didn't realize I'd ever go running off like that," Nancy said, winding a damp Coca-Cola straw around her finger.

"Was it the party, the one you said you wanted to give? You didn't have to feel—"

"I don't remember any party," she said quickly.

Her mother lay with the roof gone, hands folded. Nancy felt that people's mothers, like wallpapered walls after a hurricane, should not be exposed. Her father at last successfully reached the donkey, but he fell in the middle of the rug, while Nancy, on the stair landing, smelling seaweed, asked herself how a murderous child with swollen jaws happened to mention love, if love is not a fever, and the storm-driven sea struck the open reef and went roaring skyward, splashing a tattered gull that clutched at the blast—but if we will all go there immediately it is safe in the Dupré house, because they have this holy candle.

There are hidden bone-cold lairs no one knows of, in rock beneath the sea. She shook her bone-white hair.

Rob's whole sensitive face tightened harshly for saying what had to come next, and she thought for a while he wasn't going to make it, but he did. "To hell with it. To absolute hell with it then." He looked stricken, as though he had managed nothing but damaging himself.

"I guess it's just the way I am," Nancy murmured. "I just run off sometimes."

Her voice faded in a deepening glimmer where the human breath is snatched clean away and there are only bubbles, iridescent and pure. When she dove again, they rose in a curving track behind her.

The Bufords

THERE WERE the windows, high, well above the ground, large, full of sky. There were the child's eyes, settled back mid-distance in the empty room. There was the emptiness, the drowsiness of Miss Jackson's own head, tired from tackling the major problems of little people all day long, from untangling their hair ribbons, their shoelaces, their grammar, their arithmetic, their handwriting, their thoughts. Now there was the silence.

The big, clumsy building was full of silence, stoves cooling off, great boxy rooms growing cool from the floor up, cold settling around her ankles. Miss Jackson sat there two or three afternoons a week, after everybody else had gone, generally with a Buford or because of a Buford: It was agreed she had the worst grade this year, because there were Bufords in it. She read a sentence in a theme four times through. Was it really saying something about a toad-frog? Her brain was so weary —it was Thursday, late in the week—she began to think of chipmunks, instead. Suddenly her mouth began to twitch; she couldn't stand it any longer; she burst out laughing.

"Dora Mae, *what* are you doing?"

The truth was that Dora Mae was not doing anything. She was just a Buford. When she was around, you eventually laughed. Miss Jackson could never resist; but then, neither could anyone. Dora Mae, being a Buford, did not return her laugh. The Bufords never laughed unless they wanted to. She drew the book she was supposed to be studying, but wasn't, slowly downward on the desk; her chin was resting on it and came gradually down with it. She continued to stare at Miss Jackson with eyes almost as big as the windows, blue, clear, and loaded with Buford nonsense. She gave Miss Jackson the tiniest imaginable smile.

Miss Jackson continued to laugh. If someone else had been the teacher, she herself would have to be corrected, possibly kept in. It always turned out this way. Miss Jackson dried her eyes. "Sit up straight, Dora Mae," she said.

Once this very child had actually sewed through her own finger, meddling with a sewing machine the high school home-economics girls had left open upstairs. Another time, at recess, she had jumped up and down on a Sears Roebuck catalogue in the dressing room behind the stage, creating such a thunder nobody could think what was happening. She had also shot pieces of broken brick with her brother's slingshot at the walls of the gym, where they were having a 4-H Club meeting. "Head, Heart, Hands, and Health," the signs said. They were inside repeating a pledge about these four things and singing, "To the knights in the days of old, Keeping watch on the mountain height, Came a vision of Holy Grail, And a voice through the waiting night." Some of the chunks of brick, really quite large, came flying through the window.

Dora Mae, of course, had terrible brothers, the Buford boys, and a reputation to live up to—was that it? No, she was just bad, the older teachers in the higher grades would say at recess, sitting on the steps in warm weather or crossing the street for a Coke at the little cabin-size sandwich shop.

"I've got two years before I get Dora Mae," said Miss Martingale.

"Just think," said Mrs. Henry, "I've got four Bufords in my upstairs study hall. At once."

"I've had them already, all but one," said Miss Carlisle. "I've just about graduated."

"I wish they weren't so funny," said Miss Jackson, and then they all began to laugh. They couldn't finish their Cokes for laughing.

Among the exploits of Dora Mae's brothers, there always came to mind the spring day one of them brought a horse inside the school house just before closing bell, leading it with a twist of wire fastened about its lower lip and releasing it to wander right into study hall alone while the principal, Mr. Blackstone, was dozing at his desk.

The thing was, in school, everybody's mind was likely to wander, and the minute it did wander, something would be done to you by a Buford, and you would never forget it. The world you were dozing on came back with a whoosh and a bang; but it was not the same world you had dozed away from, nor was it the one you intended to wake up to or even imagined to be there. Something crazy was the matter with it: a naked horse, unattended, was walking between the rows of seats; or (another day altogether) a little girl was holding her reader up in the air between her feet, her head and shoulders having vanished below desk level, perhaps forever. Had there actually been some strange accident? Were you dreaming? Or were things meant to be this way? That was the part that just for a minute could scare you.

The Bufords lived in a large, sprawled-out, friendly house down a road nobody lived on but them. The grass was never completely cut, and in the fall the leaves never got raked. Somebody once set fire to a sagebrush pasture near their house—one of *them* had done it, doubtless—and the house was threatened, and there were Bufords up all night, stamping the earth and scraping sparks out of the charred fence posts and throwing water into chicken wallows, just in case the fire started again.

When any of the teachers went there to call, as they occasionally had to do, so that the family wouldn't get mad at the extraordinary punishment meted out to one of the children at school—Mr. Blackstone once was driven to give Billy Buford a public whipping with a buggy whip—or (another reason) to try to inform the family just how far the children were going with their devilment and to implore moral support, at least, in doing something about it—when you went there, they all came out and greeted you. They made you sit in a worn wicker rocking chair and ran to get you something—iced tea or lemonade or a Coke, cake, tea cakes, or anything they had.

Then they began to shout and holler and say how glad they were you'd come. They began to say, "Now tell the truth! Tell the truth, now! Ain't Billy Buford the worse boy you ever saw?" . . . "Did you ever see anybody as crazy as that Pete? Now tell me! Now tell the truth!" . . . "Confidentially, Miss Jackson, what on earth are we ever going to do with Dora Mae?"

And Dora Mae would sit and look at you, the whole time. She would sit on a little stool and put her chin on her hands and stare, and then you would say, "I just don't know, Mrs. Buford." And they would all look at you cautiously in their own Buford way, and then in the silence, when you couldn't, couldn't be serious, one of them would say, very quietly, "Ain't you ever going to eat your cake?"

It was like that.

There had once been something about a skunk that had upset not just the school but the whole town and that would not do to think about, just as it didn't do any good, either, to speculate on what might or could or was about to happen on this or any future Halloween.

Was it spring or fall? Dreaming, herself, in the lonely classroom with Dora Mae, Miss Jackson thought of chipmunks and skunks and toad-frogs, words written into themes on ruled paper, the lines of paper passing gradually across her brow and into her brain, until the fine ruling would eventually print itself there. Someday, if they opened her brain, they would find a child's theme inside. Even now she could often scarcely think of herself with any degree of certainty. Was she in love, was she falling in love, or getting restless and disappointed with whomever she knew, or did she want somebody new, or was she recalling somebody gone? Or: Had someone right come along, and she had said all right, she'd quit teaching and marry him, and now had it materialized or had it fallen through, or what?

Children! The Bufords existed in a haze of children and old people: old aunts, old cousins, grandfathers, friends and relatives by marriage of cousins, deceased uncles, family doctors gone alcoholic, people who never had a chance. What did they live on? Oh, enough of them knew how to make enough for everyone to feel encouraged. Enough of them were clever about money, and everybody liked them, except the unfortunate few who had to try to discipline them. A schoolteacher, for instance, was a sort of challenge. A teacher hung in their minds like the deep, softly pulsing, furry throat in the collective mind of a hound pack. They hardly thought of a teacher as human, you had to suppose. You could get your feelings hurt sadly if you left yourself open to them.

"Dora Mae, let's go," Miss Jackson suddenly said, way too early.

She had recalled that she had a date, but whether it was a spring date (with warm twilight air seeping into the car, filling the street and even entering the stale movie foyer—more excitement in the season than was left for her in this particular person) or whether it was a fall date (when the smell of her new dress brought out sharply by the gas heater she had to turn on in the late afternoon, carried with it the interest of somebody new and the lightness all beginnings have)—which it was, she had to think to say. At this moment, she had forgotten whether she was even glad or not. It was better to be going out with somebody than not; it gave a certain air, for one thing, to supper at the boardinghouse.

Even the regulars, the uptown widows and working wives and the old couples and the ancient widower who came to eat there, held themselves somewhat straighter and took some degree of pride in the matter of Miss Jackson's going out, as going out suggested a progress of sorts and put a tone of freshness and prettiness on things. It was a subject to tease and be festive about; the lady who ran the boardinghouse might even bring candles to light the table. In letting Dora Mae Buford out early, Miss Jackson was responding to that festiveness; she thought of the reprieve as a little present.

She recalled what she had told a young man last year, or maybe the year before, just as they were leaving the movies after a day similar to this one, when she had had to keep another Buford in, how she had described the Bufords to him, so that she got him to laugh about them, too, and how between them they had decided there was no reason, no reason on earth, for Bufords to go to school at all. They would be exactly the same whether they went to school or not. Nothing you told them soaked in; they were born knowing everything they knew; they never changed; the only people they really listened to were other Bufords.

"But I do sometimes wonder," Miss Jackson had said, trying hard to find a foothold that had to do with "problems," "personality," "psychology," "adjustment," all those things she had taken up in detail at teachers' college in Nashville and thought must have a small degree of truth in them—"I wonder if some people don't just feel obligated to be bad."

"There's something in that," the young man had answered. (He had said this often, come to think of it: a good answer to everything.)

Now the child trudged along beside Miss Jackson across the

campus. Miss Jackson looked down affectionately; she wanted a child of her own someday—though hardly, she thought (and almost giggled), one like this. It went along on chunky legs and was shaped like cutout paper-doll children you folded the tabs back to change dresses for. Its face was round, its brow raggedly fringed with yellow bangs. Its hands were plump—meddlesome, you'd say on sight. It wore scuffed brown shoes and navy-blue socks and a print dress and carried an old nubby red sweater slung over its books.

"Aren't you cold, Dora Mae?" said Miss Jackson, still in her mood of affection and fun.

"No, ma'am," said Dora Mae, who could and did answer directly at times. "I'm just tired of school."

Well, so am I sometimes, Miss Jackson thought, going home to bathe and dress in her best dress, and then go to the boardinghouse with the other teachers, where, waiting on the porch, if it was warm enough or in the hall if it was not, sitting or standing with hands at rest against the nice material of her frock, she would already be well over the line into her most private domain.

"I don't really like him all that much," she would have confided already—it was what she always said. "I just feel better, you know, when somebody wants to take me somewhere." All the teachers agreed that this was so; they were the same, they said.

What Miss Jackson did not say was that she enjoyed being Lelia. This was her secret, and when she went out, this was what happened: she turned into Lelia, from the time she was dressing in the afternoon until after midnight, when she got in. The next morning, she would be Miss Jackson again.

If it was a weekday.

And if it wasn't a weekday, then she might still feel like Miss Jackson, even on weekends, for they had given her a Sunday School class to teach whenever she stayed in town. If she went home, back fifty miles to the little town she was born in, she had to go to church there, too, and everybody uptown called her "Leel," a nickname. At home they called her "Sister," only it sounded more like Sustah. But Lelia was her name and what she wanted to be; it was what she said was her name to whatever man she met who asked to take her somewhere.

One day soon after she had kept Dora Mae Buford after school, she went back into the classroom from recess quite late, having been delayed at a faculty meeting, and Dora Mae was writing "LELIAJACKSONLELIAJACKSONLELIAJACKSON-LELIAJACKSON" over and over in capital letters on the blackboard. She had filled one board and had started on another, going like crazy. All the students were laughing at her.

It became clear to Miss Jackson later, when she had time to think about it, that the reason she became so angry at Dora Mae was that the child, like some diabolical spirit, had seemed to know exactly what her sensitive point was and had gone straight to it, with the purpose of ridiculing her, of exposing and summarizing her secret self in all its foolish yearning.

But at the moment she did not think anything. She experienced a flash of white-faced, passionate temper and struck the chalk from the child's hand. "Erase that board!" she ordered. A marvel she hadn't knocked her down, except that Dora Mae was as solid as a stump, and hitting her, Miss Jackson had almost sprained her wrist.

Dora Mae was shocked half to death, and the room was deadly still for the rest of the morning. Miss Jackson, so gentle and firm (though likely to get worried), had never before struck anyone.

Soon Dora Mae's mother came to see Miss Jackson, after school. She sat down in the empty classroom, a rather tall, dark woman with a narrow face full of slanted wrinkles and eyes so dark as to be almost pitch black, with no discernible white area to them. Miss Jackson looked steadfastly down at her hands.

Mrs. Buford put a large, worn, bulging black purse on the desk before her, and though she did not even remove her coat, the room seemed hers. She did not mean it that way, for she spoke in the most respectful tone, but it was true. "It's really just one thing I wanted to know, Miss Jackson. Your first name is Lelia, ain't it?"

Miss Jackson said that it was.

"So what I mean is, when Dora Mae wrote what she did on the blackboard there, it wasn't nothing like a lie or something dirty, was it?"

"No," said Miss Jackson. "Not at all."

•

"Well, I guess that's about all I wanted to make sure of."

Miss Jackson did not say anything, and Mrs. Buford finally inquired whether she had not been late coming back to the room that day, when Dora Mae was found writing on the board. Miss Jackson agreed that this was true.

"Churen are not going to sit absolutely still if you don't come back from recess," said Mrs. Buford. "You got to be there to say, 'Now y'all get out your book and turn to page so-and-so.' If you don't they're bound to get into something. You realize that? Well, good! Dora Mae's nothing but a little old scrap. That's all she is."

"Well, I know," said Miss Jackson, feeling very bad.

At this point, Mrs. Buford, alone without any of her children around her, must have got to thinking about them all in terms of Dora Mae; she began to cry.

Miss Jackson understood. She had seen them all, her entire class, heads bent at her command, pencils marching forward across their tablets, and her heart had filled with pity and love.

Mrs. Buford brushed her tears away. "You never meant it for a minute. Anybody can get aggravated, don't you know? You think I can't? I can and do!" She put her handkerchief back in her purse and, straightening her coat, stood up to go. "So, I'm just going right straight and say you're sorry about it and you never meant it."

"Oh," said Miss Jackson, all of a sudden, "but I did mean it. It's true I'm sorry. But I did mean it." Her statement, softly made, threw a barrier across Mrs. Buford's path, like bars through the slots in a fence gap.

Mrs. Buford sat back down. "Miss Jackson, just what have we been sitting here deciding?"

"I don't know," said Miss Jackson, wondering herself. "Nothing that I know of."

"Nothing! You call that nothing?"

"Call what nothing?"

"Why, everything you just got through saying."

"But what do you think I said?" Miss Jackson felt she would honestly like to know. There followed a long silence, in which Miss Jackson, whose room this after all was, felt impelled to stand up. "It's not a good thing to lose your temper. But everyone does sometimes, including me."

Mrs. Buford rose also. "Underneath all that fooling around, them kids of mine is pure gold." Drawn to full height, Mrs. Buford became about twice as tall as Miss Jackson.

"I know! I know that! But you say yourselves—" began Miss Jackson. She started to tremble. Of all the teachers in the school, she was the youngest, and she had the most over-crowding in her room. "Mrs. Buford," she begged, "do please forget about it. Go on home. Please, please go home!"

"You pore child," said Mrs. Buford, with no effort still continuing and even expanding her own authority. "I just never in my life," she added, and left the room.

She proceeded across the campus the way all her dozen or so children went, down toward their lonely road—a good, strong, sincere woman, whose right shoulder sagged lower than the left and who did not look back. From the window, Miss Jackson watched her go.

Uptown a lady gossip was soon to tell her that she was known to have struck a child in a fit of temper and also to have turned out the child's mother when she came to talk about it. Miss Jackson wearily agreed that this was true. She could feel no great surprise, though her sense of despair deepened when one of the Buford boys, Evan, older and long out of school, got to worrying her—calling up at night, running his car behind her on the sidewalk uptown. It seemed there were no lengths he wouldn't go to, no trouble he wouldn't make for her.

When the dove season started, he dropped her. He'd a little rather shoot doves than me, she thought, sitting on the edge of the bed in her room, avoiding the mirror, which said she must be five years older. It's my whole life that's being erased, she thought, mindful that Dora Mae and two of her brothers, in spite of all she could do, were inexorably failing the fourth grade. She got up her Sunday School lesson, washed her hair, went to bed, and fell asleep disconsolate. . . .

Before school was out, the Bufords invited Miss Jackson for Sunday dinner. Once the invitation had come—which pleased her about as much as if it had been extended by a tribe of Indians, but which she had to accept or be thought of as a coward—it seemed inevitable to her that they would do this. It carried out to a T their devious and deceptively simple-looking method of pleasing themselves, and of course what she might feel about it didn't matter. But here she was dressing for them, trying to look her best.

The dinner turned out to be a feast. She judged it was no different from their usual Sunday meal—three kinds of meat and a dozen spring vegetables, hot rolls, jams, pickles, peaches, and rich cakes, freshly baked and iced.

The house looked in the airiest sort of order, with hand-crocheted white doilies sprinkled about on the tables and chairs. The whole yard was shaggy with flowers and blooming shrubs; the children all were clean and neatly dressed, with shoes on as well, and the dogs were turned firmly out of doors.

She was placed near Mr. Tom Buford, the father of them all, a tall, spare man with thick white hair and a face burned brick-brown from constant exposure. He plied her ceaselessly with food, more than she could have eaten in a week, and smiled the gentle smile Miss Jackson by now knew so well.

Halfway down the opposite side of the table was Evan Buford, she at last recognized, that terrible one, wearing a spotless white shirt, shaved and spruce, with brown busy hands, looking bland and even handsome. If he remembered all those times he had got her to the phone at one and two and three in the morning, he wasn't letting on. ("Thought you'd be up grading papers, Miss Jackson! Falling down on the job?" . . . "Your family live in Tupelo? Well, the whole town got blown away in a tornado! This afternoon!") Once, in hunting clothes, his dirt-smeared, unshaven face distorted by the rush of rain on his muddy windshield, he had pursued her from the post office all the way home, almost nudging her off the sidewalk with his front fender, his wheels spewing water from the puddles all over her stockings and raincoat, while she walked resolutely on, pretending not to notice.

From way down at the foot of the table, about half a mile away, Dora Mae sat sighting at her steadily through a water glass, her eyes like the magnified eyes of insects.

"'Possum hunting!" Mr. Tom Buford was saying, carving chicken and ham with a knife a foot long, which Miss Jackson sometimes had literally to dodge. "That's where we all went last night. Way up on the ridge. You like 'possum, Miss Jackson?"

"I never had any," Miss Jackson said.

Right from dinner they all went to the back yard to see the 'possum, which had been put in a cage of chicken wire around the base of a small pecan tree. It was now hanging upside down by its tail from a limb. She felt for its helpless, unappetizing shapelessness, grizzly gray, with a long snout, its sensitive eyes shut tight, its tender black petal-like ears alone perceiving, with what terror none could know though she could guess, the presence of its captors.

"Don't smell very good, does it?" Billy Buford said. "You like it, Miss Jackson? Give it to you, you want it." He picked up a stick to punch it with.

She shook her head. "Oh, I'd just let it go back to the woods. I feel sorry for it."

The whole family turned from the creature to her and examined her as if she were crazy. Billy Buford even dropped the stick. There followed one of those long, risky silences.

As they started to go inside, Evan Buford lounged along at her elbow. He separated her out like a heifer from the herd and cornered her before a fence of climbing roses. He leaned his arm against a fence post, blocking any possible escape, and looked down at her with wide, speculative, bright brown eyes. She remembered his laughing mouth behind the car wheel that chill, rainy day, careening after her. Oh, they never got through, she desperately realized. Once they had you, they held on—if they didn't eat you up, they kept you for a pet.

"Now, Miss Jackson, how come you to fail those kids?"

Miss Jackson dug her heels in hard. "I didn't fail them. They failed themselves. Like you might fail to hit a squirrel, for instance."

"Well, now. You mean they weren't good enough. Well, I be darned." He jerked his head. "That's a real good answer."

So at last, after years of trying hard, she had got something across to a Buford, some one little thing that was true. Maybe it had never happened before. It would seem she had stopped him cold. It would seem he even admired her.

"Missed it like a squirrel!" he marveled. "The whole fourth grade. They must be mighty dumb," he reflected, walking along with her toward the house.

"No, they just don't listen," said Miss Jackson.

"Don't listen," he said after her with care, as though to prove that he, at least, did. "You get ready to go, I'll drive you to town, Miss Jackson. Your name is Lelia, ain't it?"

She looked up gratefully. "That's right," she said.

A Christian Education

IT WAS a Sunday like no other, for we were there alone for the first time. I hadn't started to school yet, and he had finished it so long ago it must have been like a dream of something that was meant to happen but had never really come about, for I can remember no story of school that he ever told me, and to think of him as sitting in a class equal with others is as beyond me now as it was then. I cannot imagine it. He read a lot and might conceivably have had a tutor—that I can imagine, in his plantation world.

But this was a town he'd finally come to, to stay with his daughter in his old age, she being also my mother. I was the only one free to be with him all the time and the same went for his being with me—we baby-sat one another.

But that word wasn't known then.

A great many things were known, however; among them, I always had to go to Sunday School.

It was an absolute that the whole world was meant to be part of the church, and if my grandfather seldom went, it was a puzzle no one tried to solve. Sermons were a fate I had only recently got big enough to be included in, but Sunday School classes had had me enrolled in them since I could be led through the door and placed on a tiny red chair, feet not even at that low height connecting to the floor. It was always cold at the church; even in summer, it was cool inside. We were given pictures to color and Bible verses to memorize, and at the end a colored card with a picture of Moses or Jesus or somebody else from the Bible, exotically bearded and robed.

Today I might not be going to Sunday School, and my regret was only for the card. I wondered what it would be like. There was no one to bring it to me. My mother and father were not even in town. They had got into the car right after breakfast and had driven away to a neighboring town. An aunt by marriage had died and they were going to the funeral. I was too little to go to funerals, my mother said.

After they left I sat on the rug near my grandfather. He was asleep in his chair before the fire, snoring. Presently his snoring woke him up. He cut himself some tobacco and put it in his mouth. "Are you going to Sunday School?" he asked me. "I can't go there by myself," I said. "Nobody said I had to take you," he remarked, more to himself than to me. It wasn't the first time I knew we were in the same boat, he and I, we had to do what they said, being outside the main scale of life where things really happened, but by the same token we didn't have to do what they didn't say. Somewhere along the line, however, my grandfather had earned rights I didn't have. Not having to attend church was one; also, he had his own money and didn't have to ask for any.

He looked out the window.

"It's going to be a pretty day," he said.

How we found ourselves on the road downtown on Sunday morning, I don't remember. It was as far to get to town as it was to get to church, though in the opposite direction, and we both must have known that, but didn't remark upon it as we went along. My grandfather walked to town every day except Sunday, when it was considered a sin to go there, for the drugstore was open and the barbershop, too, on occasions, if the weather was fair; and the filling station was open. My parents thought that the drugstore had to be open but should sell drugs only, and that filling stations and barbershops shouldn't be open at all. There should be a way to telephone the filling station in case you had to have gas for emergency use. This was all worked out between them. I had often heard them talk about it. No one should go to town on Sunday, they said, for it encouraged the error of the ones who kept their places open.

My grandfather was a very tall man; I had to reach up to hold his hand while walking. He wore dark blue and dark gray herringbone suits, and the coat flap was a long way up, the gold watch chain almost out of sight. I could see his walking cane moving opposite me, briskly swung with the rhythm of his stride: it was my companion. Along the way it occurred to me that we were terribly excited, that the familiar way looked new and different, as though a haze which had hung over everything had been whipped away all at once, like a scarf. I was also having more fun than I'd ever had before.

When he came to the barbershop, my grandfather stepped inside and spoke to the barber and to all who happened to be hanging around, brought out by the sunshine. They spoke about politics, the crops, and the weather. The barber who always cut my hair came over and looked to see if I needed another trim and my grandfather said he didn't think so, but I might need a good brushing; they'd left so soon after breakfast it was a wonder I was dressed. Somebody who'd come in after us said, "Funeral in Grenada, ain't it?" which was the first anybody had mentioned it, but I knew they hadn't needed to say anything, that everybody knew about my parents' departure and why and where. Things were aways known about, I saw, but not cared about too much either. The barber's strong arms, fleecy with reddish hair, swung me up into his big chair where I loved to be. He brushed my hair, then combed it. The great mirrors sparkled and everything was fine.

We presently moved on to the drugstore. The druggist, a small, crippled man, hobbled toward us, grinning to see us, and he and my grandfather talked for quite some time. Finally my grandfather said, "Give the child a strawberry cone," and so I had it, miraculous, and the world of which it was the center expanded about it with gracious, silent delight. It was a thing too wondrous actually to have eaten, and I do not remember eating it. It was only after we at last reached home and I entered the house, which smelled like my parents' clothes and their things, that I knew what they would think of what we had done and I became filled with anxiety and other dark feelings.

Then the car was coming up the drive and they were alighting in a post-funeral manner, full of heavy feelings and reminiscence and inclined not to speak in an ordinary way. When my mother put dinner in order, we sat around the table not saying very much.

"Did the fire hold out all right?" she asked my grandfather.

"Oh, it was warm," he said. "Didn't need much." He ate quietly and so did I.

In the afternoons on Sunday we all sat around looking at the paper. My mother had doubts about this, but we all indulged the desire anyway. After the ordeal of dressing up, of Sunday School and the long service and dinner, it seemed almost a debauchery to be able to pitch into those large crackling sheets, especially the funny papers, which were garish with color and loud with exclamation points, question marks, shouting, and all sorts of misdeeds. My grandfather had got sleepy before the fire and retired to his room while my mother and father had climbed out of their graveside feelings enough to talk a little and joke with one another.

"What did you all do?" my mother asked me. "How did you pass the time while we were gone?"

"We walked downtown," I said, for I had been laughing at something they had said to one another and wanted to share the morning's happiness with them without telling any more or letting any real trouble in. But my mother was on it, quicker than anything.

"You didn't go in the drugstore, did you?"

I looked up. Why did she have to ask? It wasn't in my scheme of thinking about things that she would ever do so. My father was looking at me now, too.

"Yes, ma'am," I slowly said. "But not for long," I added.

"You didn't get an ice cream cone, did you?"

And they both were looking. My face must have had astonishment on it as well as guilt. Not even I could have imagined them going this far. Why, on the day of a funeral, should they care if anybody bought an ice cream cone?

"Did you?" my father asked.

The thing to know is that my parents really believed everything they said they believed. They believed that awful punishments were meted out to those who did not remember the Sabbath was holy. They believed about a million other things. They were terribly honest about it.

Much later on, my mother went into my grandfather's room. I was silently behind her, and I heard her speak to him.

"She says you took her to town while we were gone and got an ice cream."

He had waked up and was reading by his lamp. At first he seemed not to hear; at last, he put his book face down in his lap and looked up. "I did," he said lightly.

A silence fell between them. Finally she turned and went away.

This, so far as I know, was all.

Because of the incident, that certain immunity of spirit my grandfather possessed was passed on to me. It came, I think, out of the precise way in which he put his book down on his lap to answer. There was a lifetime in the gesture, distilled, and I have been a good part of that long, growing up to all its meaning.

After this, though all went on as before, there was nothing much my parents could finally do about the church and me. They could lock the barn door, but the bright horse of freedom was already loose in my world. Down the hill, across the creek, in the next pasture—where? Somewhere, certainly: that much was proved; and all was different for its being so.

The Girl Who Loved Horses

SHE HAD drawn back from throwing a pan of bird scraps out the door because she heard what was coming, the two-part pounding of a full gallop, not the graceful triple notes of a canter. They were mounting the drive now, turning into the stretch along the side of the house; once before, some-one appearing at the screen door had made the horse shy, so that, barely held beneath the rider, barely restrained, he had plunged off into the flower beds. So she stepped back from the door and saw the two of them shoot past, rounding a final corner, heading for the straight run of drive into the cattle gate and the barn lot back of it.

She flung out the scraps, then walked to the other side of the kitchen and peered through the window, raised for spring, toward the barn lot. The horse had slowed, out of habit, knowing what came next. And the white shirt that had passed hugged so low as to seem some strange part of the animal's trappings, or as though he had run under a low line of drying laundry and caught something to an otherwise empty saddle and bare withers, now rose up, angling to an upright posture. A gloved hand extended to pat the lathered neck.

"Lord have mercy," the woman said. The young woman rid-ing the horse was her daughter, but she was speaking also for her son-in-law, who went in for even more reckless behavior in the jumping ring the two of them had set up. What she meant by it was that they were going to kill themselves before they ever had any children, or if they did have children safely they'd bring up the children to be just as foolish about horses and careless of life and limb as they were themselves.

The young woman's booted heel struck the back steps. The screen door banged.

"You ought not to bring him in hot like that," the mother said. "I do know that much."

"Cottrell is out there," she said.

"It's still March, even if it has got warm."

"Cottrell knows what to do."

She ran water at the sink, and cupping her hand, drank

primitive fashion out of it, bending to the tap, then wet her hands in the running water and thrust her fingers into the dusty, sweat-damp roots of her sand-colored hair. It had been a good ride.

"I hope he doesn't take up too much time," the mother said. "My beds need working."

She spoke mildly but it was always part of the same quarrel they were in like a stream that was now a trickle, now a still pool, but sometimes after a freshet could turn into a torrent. Such as: "Y'all are just crazy. Y'all are wasting everything on those things. And what are they? I know they're pretty and all that, but they're not a thing in the world but animals. Cows are animals. You can make a lot more money in cattle, than carting those things around over two states and three counties."

She could work herself up too much to eat, leaving the two of them at the table, but would see them just the same in her mind's eye, just as if she'd stayed. There were the sandy-haired young woman, already thirty—married four years and still apparently with no intention of producing a family (she was an only child and the estate, though small, was a fine piece of land)—and across from her the dark spare still young man she had married.

She knew how they would sit there alone and not even look at one another or discuss what she'd said or talk against her; they would just sit there and maybe pass each other some food or one of them would get up for the coffeepot. The fanatics of a strange cult would do the same, she often thought, loosening her long hair upstairs, brushing the gray and brown together to a colorless patina, putting on one of her long cotton gowns with the ruched neck, crawling in between white cotton sheets. She was a widow and if she didn't want to sit up and try to talk to the family after a hard day, she didn't have to. Reading was a joy, lifelong. She found her place in *Middlemarch*, one of her favorites.

But during the day not even reading (if she'd had the time) could shut out the sounds from back of the privet hedge, plainly to be heard from the house. The trudging of the trot, the pause, the low directive, the thud of hoofs, the heave and shout, and sometimes the ring of struck wood as a bar came down. And every jump a risk of life and limb. One dislocated shoulder—Clyde's, thank heaven, not Deedee's—a taping, a sling, a contraption of boards, and pain "like a hot knife," he had said. A hot knife. Wouldn't that hurt anybody enough to make him quit risking life and limb with those two blood horses, quit at least talking about getting still another one while swallowing down pain-killer he said he hated to be sissy enough to take?

"Uh-huh," the mother said. "But it'll be Deborah next. You thought about that?"

"Aw, now, Miss Emma," he'd lean back to say, charming her through his warrior's haze of pain. "Deedee and me—that's what we're hooked on. Think of us without it, Mama. You really want to kill us. We couldn't live."

He was speaking to his mother-in-law but smiling at his wife. And she, Deborah, was smiling back.

Her name was Deborah Dale, but they'd always, of course, being from LaGrange, Tennessee, right over the Mississippi border, that is to say, real South, had had a hundred nicknames for her. Deedee, her father had named her, and "Deeds" her funny cousins said—"Hey, Deeds, how ya' doin'?" Being on this property in a town of pretty properties, though theirs was a little way out, a little bit larger than most, she was always out romping, swimming in forbidden creeks, climbing forbidden fences, going barefoot too soon in the spring, the last one in at recess, the first one to turn in an exam paper. ("Are you quite sure that you have finished, Deborah?" "Yes, ma'am.")

When she graduated from ponies to that sturdy calico her uncle gave her, bringing it in from his farm because he had an eye for a good match, there was almost no finding her. "I always know she's somewhere on the place," her mother said. "We just can't see it all at once," said her father. He was ailing even back then but he undertook walks. Once when the leaves had all but gone from the trees, on a warm November afternoon, from a slight rise, he saw her down in a little-used pasture with a straight open stretch among some oaks. The ground was spongy and clotted with damp and even a child ought not to have tried to run there, on foot. But there went the calico with Deedee clinging low, going like the wind, and knowing furthermore out of what couldn't be anything but long practice, where to turn, where to veer, where to stop.

"One fine afternoon," he said to himself, suspecting even then (they hadn't told him yet) what his illness was, "and Emma's going to be left with nobody." He remarked on this privately, not without anguish and not without humor.

They stopped her riding, at least like that, by sending her off to boarding school, where a watchful ringmaster took "those girls interested in equitation" out on leafy trails, "at the walk, at the trot, and at the canter." They also, with that depth of consideration which must flourish even among those Southerners unlucky enough to wind up in the lower reaches of hell, kept her young spirit out of the worst of the dying. She just got a call from the housemother one night. Her father had "passed away."

After college she forgot it, she gave it up. It was too expensive, it took a lot of time and devotion, she was interested in boys. Some boys were interested in her. She worked in Memphis, drove home to her mother every night. In winter she had to eat breakfast in the dark. On some evenings the phone rang; on some it was silent. Her mother treated both kinds of evenings just the same.

To Emma Tyler it always seemed that Clyde Mecklin materialized out of nowhere. She ran straight into him when opening the front door one evening to get the paper off the porch, he being just about to turn the bell or knock. There he stood, dark and straight in the late light that comes after first dark and is so clear. He was clear as anything in it, clear as the first stamp of a young man ever cast.

"Is Deb'rah here?" At least no Yankee. But not Miss Tyler or Miss Deborah Tyler, or Miss Deborah. No, he was city all right.

She did not answer at first.

"What's the matter, scare you? I was just about to knock."

She still said nothing.

"Maybe this is the wrong place," he said.

"No, it's the right place," Emma Tyler finally said. She stepped back and held the door wider. "Come on in."

"Scared the life out of me," she told Deborah when she finally came down to breakfast the next day, Clyde's car having been heard to depart by Emma Tyler in her upstairs bedroom at an hour she did not care to verify. "Why didn't you tell me you were expecting him? I just opened the door and there he was."

"I liked him so much," said Deborah with grave honesty. "I guess I was scared he wouldn't come. That would have hurt."

"Do you still like him?" her mother ventured, after this confidence.

"He's all for outdoors," said Deborah, as dreamy over coffee as any mother had ever beheld. "Everybody is so indoors. He likes hunting, going fishing, farms."

"Has he got one?"

"He'd like to have. All he's got's this job. He's coming back next weekend. You can talk to him. He's interested in horses."

"But does he know we don't keep horses anymore?"

"That was just my thumbnail sketch," said Deborah. "We don't have to run out and buy any."

"No, I don't imagine so," said her mother, but Deborah hardly remarked the peculiar turn of tone, the dryness. She was letting coast through her head the scene: her mother (whom she now loved better than she ever had in her life) opening the door just before Clyde knocked, so seeing unexpectedly for the first time, that face, that head, that being. . . . When he had kissed her her ears drummed, and it came back to her once more, not thought of in years, the drumming hoofs of the calico, and the ghosting father, behind, invisible, observant, off on the bare distant November rise.

It was after she married that Deborah got beautiful. All La-Grange noticed it. "I declare," they said to her mother or sometimes right out to her face, "I always said she was nice-looking but I never thought anything like that."

Emma first saw the boy in the parking lot. He was new. In former days she'd parked in front of nearly any place she wanted to go—hardware, or drugstore, or courthouse: change for the meter was her biggest problem. But so many streets were one-way now and what with the increased numbers of cars, the growth of the town, those days were gone; she used a parking lot back of a café, near the newspaper office. The entrance to the lot was a bottleneck of a narrow drive between the two brick buildings; once in, it was hard sometimes to park.

That day the boy offered to help. He was an expert driver, she noted, whereas Emma was inclined to perspire, crane, and fret, fearful of scraping a fender or grazing a door. He spun the wheel with one hand; a glance told him all he had to know; he as good as sat the car in place, as skillful (she reluctantly thought) as her children on their horses. When she returned an hour later, the cars were denser still; he helped her again. She wondered whether to tip him. This happened twice more.

"You've been so nice to me," she said, the last time. "They're lucky to have you."

"It's not much of a job," he said. "Just all I can get for the moment. Being new and all."

"I might need some help," she said. "You can call up at the Tyler place if you want to work. It's in the book. Right now I'm in a hurry."

On the warm June day, Deborah sat the horse comfortably in the side yard and watched her mother and the young man (whose name was Willett? Williams?), who, having worked the beds and straightened a fence post, was now replacing warped fence boards with new ones.

"Who is he?" she asked her mother, not quite low enough, and meaning what a Southern woman invariably means by that question, not what is his name but where did he come from, is he anybody we know? What excuse, in other words, does he have for even being born?

"One thing, he's a good worker," her mother said, preening a little. Did they think she couldn't manage if she had to? "Now don't you make him feel bad."

"Feel bad!" But once again, if only to spite her mother, who was in a way criticizing her and Clyde by hiring anybody at all to do work that Clyde or the Negro help would have been able to do if only it weren't for those horses—once again Deborah had spoken too loudly.

If she ever had freely to admit things, even to herself, Deborah would have to say she knew she not only looked good that June day, she looked sexy as hell. Her light hair, tousled from a ride in the fields, had grown longer in the last year; it had slipped its pins on one side and lay in a sensuous lock along her cheek. A breeze stirred it, then passed by. Her soft poplin shirt was loose at the throat, the two top buttons open, the cuffs turned back to her elbows. The new horse, the third, was gentle, too much so (this worried them); she sat it easily, one leg up, crossed lazily over the flat English pommel, while the horse, head stretched down, cropped at the tender grass. In the silence between their voices, the tearing of the grass was the only sound except for a shrill jay's cry.

"Make him feel bad!" she repeated.

The boy looked up. The horse, seeking grass, had moved forward; she was closer than before, eyes looking down on him above the rise of her breasts and throat; she saw the closeness go through him, saw her presence register as strongly as if the earth's accidental shifting had slammed them physically together. For a minute there was nothing but the two of them. The jay was silent; even the horse, sensing something, had raised his head.

Stepping back, the boy stumbled over the pile of lumber, then fell in it. Deborah laughed. Nothing, that day, could have stopped her laughter. She was beautifully, languidly, atop a fine horse on the year's choice day at the peak of her life.

"You know what?" Deborah said at supper, when they were discussing her mother's helper. "I thought who he looks like. He looks like Clyde."

"The poor guy," Clyde said. "Was that the best you could do?"

Emma sat still. Now that she thought of it, he did look like Clyde. She stopped eating, to think it over. What difference did it make if he did? She returned to her plate.

Deborah ate lustily, her table manners unrestrained. She swabbed bread into the empty salad bowl, drenched it with dressing, bit it in hunks.

"The poor woman's Clyde, that's what you hired," she said. She looked up.

The screen door had just softly closed in the kitchen behind them. Emma's hired man had come in for his money.

It was the next day that the boy, whose name was Willett or Williams, broke the riding mower by running it full speed into a rock pile overgrown with weeds but clearly visible, and left without asking for pay but evidently taking with him in his car a number of selected items from barn, garage, and tack room, along with a transistor radio that Clyde kept in the kitchen for getting news with his early coffee.

Emma Tyler, vexed for a number of reasons she did not care to sort out (prime among them was the very peaceful and good time she had been having with the boy the day before in the yard when Deborah had chosen to ride over and join them), telephoned the police and reported the whole matter. But boy, car, and stolen articles vanished into the nowhere. That was all, for what they took to be forever.

Three years later, aged thirty-three, Deborah Mecklin was carrying her fine head higher than ever uptown in LaGrange. She drove herself on errands back and forth in car or station wagon, not looking to left or right, not speaking so much as before. She was trying not to hear from the outside what they were now saying about Clyde, how well he'd done with the horses, that place was as good as a stud farm now that he kept ten or a dozen, advertised and traded, as well as showed. And the money was coming in hard and fast. But, they would add, he moved with a fast set, and there was also the occasional gossip item, too often, in Clyde's case, with someone ready to report first hand; look how quick, now you thought of it, he'd taken up with Deborah, and how she'd snapped him up too soon to hear what his reputation was, even back then. It would be a cold day in August before any one woman would be enough for him. And his father before him? And his father before him. So the voices said.

Deborah, too, was trying not to hear what was still sounding from inside her head after her fall in the last big horse show:

The doctor: You barely escaped concussion, young lady.

Clyde: I just never saw your timing go off like that. I can't get over it.

Emma: You'd better let it go for a while, honey. There're other things, so many other things.

Back home, she later said to Emma: "Oh, Mama, I know you're right sometimes, and sometimes I'm sick of it all, but Clyde depends on me, he always has, and now look—"

"Yes, and 'Now look' is right, he has to be out with it to keep it all running. You got your wish, is all I can say."

Emma was frequently over at her sister-in-law Marian's farm these days. The ladies were aging, Marian especially down in the back, and those twilights in the house alone were more and more all that Deedee had to keep herself company with. Sometimes the phone rang and there'd be Clyde on it, to say he'd be late again. Or there'd be no call at all. And once she (of all people) pressed some curtains and hung them, and once hunted for old photographs, and once, standing in the middle of the little-used parlor among the walnut Victorian furniture upholstered in gold and blue and rose, she had said "Daddy?" right out loud, like he might have been there to answer, really been there. It had surprised her, the word falling out like that as though a thought took reality all by itself and made a word on its own.

And once there came a knock at the door.

All she thought, though she hadn't heard the car, was that it was Clyde and that he'd forgotten his key, or seeing her there, his arms loaded maybe, was asking her to let him in. It was past dark. Though times were a little more chancy now, LaGrange was a safe place. People nearer to town used to brag that if they went off for any length of time less than a weekend and locked the doors, the neighbors would get their feelings hurt; and if the Tylers lived further out and "locked up," the feeling for it was ritual mainly, a precaution.

She glanced through the sidelight, saw what she took for Clyde, and opened the door. There were cedars in the front yard, not too near the house, but dense enough to block out whatever gathering of light there might have been from the long slope of property beyond the front gate. There was no moon.

The man she took for Clyde, instead of stepping through the door or up to the threshold to greet her, withdrew a step and leaned down and to one side, turning outward as though to pick up something. It was she who stepped forward, to greet, help, inquire; for deep within was the idea her mother had seen to it was firmly and forever planted: that one day one of them was going to get too badly hurt by "those things" ever to be patched up.

So it was in outer dark, three paces from the safe threshold and to the left of the area where the light was falling outward, a dim single sidelight near the mantelpiece having been all she had switched on, too faint to penetrate the sheer gathered curtains of the sidelight, that the man at the door rose up, that he tried to take her. The first she knew of it, his face was in hers, not Clyde's but something like it and at Clyde's exact height, so that for the moment she thought that some joke was on, and then the strange hand caught the parting of her blouse, a new mouth fell hard on her own, one knee thrust her legs apart, the free hand diving in to clutch and press against the thin nylon between her thighs. She recoiled at the same time that she felt, touched in the quick, the painful glory of desire brought on too fast—looking back on that instant's two-edged meaning, she would never hear about rape without the lightning quiver of ambivalence within the word. However, at the time no meditation stopped her knee from coming up into the nameless groin and nothing stopped her from tearing back her mouth slathered with spit so suddenly smeared into it as to drag it into the shape of a scream she was unable yet to find a voice for. Her good right arm struck like a hard backhand against a line-smoking tennis serve. Then from the driveway came the stream of twin headlights thrusting through the cedars.

"Bitch!" The word, distorted and low, was like a groan; she had hurt him, freed herself for a moment, but the struggle would have just begun except for the lights, and the screams that were just trying to get out of her. "You fucking bitch." He saw the car lights, wavered, then turned. His leap into the shrubbery was bent, like a hunchback's. She stopped screaming suddenly. Hurt where he lived, she thought. The animal motion, wounded, drew her curiosity for a second. Saved, she saw the car sweep round the drive, but watched the bushes shake, put up her hand to touch but not to close the torn halves of the blouse, which was ripped open to her waist.

Inside, she stood looking down at herself in the dim light. There was a nail scratch near the left nipple, two teeth marks between elbow and wrist where she'd smashed into his mouth.

She wiped her own mouth on the back of her hand, gagging at the taste of cigarette smoke, bitterly staled. Animals! She'd always had a special feeling for them, a helpless tenderness. In her memory the bushes, shaking to a crippled flight, shook forever.

She went upstairs, stood trembling in her mother's room (Emma was away), combed her hair with her mother's comb. Then, hearing Clyde's voice calling her below, she stripped off her ravaged blouse and hastened across to their own rooms to hide it in a drawer, change into a fresh one, come downstairs. She had made her decision already. Who was this man? A nothing . . . an unknown. She hated women who shouted Rape! Rape! It was an incident, but once she told it everyone would know, along with the police, and would add to it: they'd say she'd been violated. It was an incident, but Clyde, once he knew, would trace him down. Clyde would kill him.

"Did you know the door was wide open?" He was standing in the living room.

"I know. I must have opened it when I heard the car. I thought you were stopping in the front."

"Well, I hardly ever do."

"Sometimes you do."

"Deedee, have you been drinking?"

"Drinking . . . ? Me?" She squinted at him, joking in her own way; it was a standing quarrel now that alone she sometimes poured one or two.

He would check her breath but not her marked body. Lust with him was mole-dark now, not desire in the soft increase of morning light, or on slowly westering afternoons, or by the night light's glow. He would kill for her because she was his wife. . . .

"Who was that man?"

Uptown one winter afternoon late, she had seen him again. He had been coming out of the hamburger place and looking back, seeing her through the street lights, he had turned quickly into an alley. She had hurried to catch up, to see. But only a form was hastening there, deeper into the unlit slit between brick walls, down toward a street and a section nobody went into without good reason.

"That man," she repeated to the owner (also the proprietor and cook) in the hamburger place. "He was in here just now."

"I don't know him. He hangs around. Wondered myself. You know him?"

"I think he used to work for us once, two or three years ago. I just wondered."

"I thought I seen him somewhere myself."

"He looks a little bit like Clyde."

"Maybe so. Now you mention it." He wiped the counter with a wet rag. "Get you anything, Miss Deb'rah?"

"I've got to get home."

"Y'all got yourselves some prizes, huh?"

"Aw, just some good luck." She was gone.

Prizes, yes. Two trophies at the Shelby County Fair, one in Brownsville where she'd almost lost control again, and Clyde not worrying about her so much as scolding her. His recent theory was that she was out to spite him. He would think it if he was guilty about the women, and she didn't doubt any more that he was. But worse than spite was what had got to her, hating as she did to admit it.

It was fear.

She'd never known it before. When it first started she hadn't even known what the name of it was.

Over two years ago, Clyde had started buying colts not broken yet from a stud farm south of Nashville, bringing them home for him and Deborah to get in shape together. It saved a pile of money to do it that way. She'd been thrown in consequence three times, trampled once, a terrifying moment as the double reins had caught up her outstretched arm so she couldn't fall free. Now when she closed her eyes at night, steel hoofs sometimes hung through the dark above them, and she felt hard ground beneath her head, smelled smeared grass on cheek and elbow. To Clyde she murmured in the dark: "I'm not good at it any more." "Why, Deeds, you were always good. It's temporary, honey. That was a bad day."

A great couple. That's what Clyde thought of them. But more than half their name had been made by her, by the sight of her, Deborah Mecklin, out in full dress, black broadcloth and white satin stock with hair drawn trimly back beneath the smooth rise of the hat, entering the show ring. She looked damned good back of the glossy neck's steep arch, the pointed ears and lacquered hoofs which hardly touched earth before springing upward, as though in the instant before actual flight. There was always the stillness, then the murmur, the rustle of the crowd. At top form she could even get applause. A fame for a time spread round them. The Mecklins. Great riders. "Ridgewood Stable. Blood horses trained. Saddle and Show." He'd had it put up in wrought iron, with a sign as well, Old English style, of a horseman spurring.

("Well, you got to make money," said Miss Emma to her son-in-law. "And don't I know it," she said. "But I just hate to think how many times I kept those historical people from putting up a marker on this place. And now all I do is worry one of y'all's going to break your neck. If it wasn't for Marian needing me and all . . . I just can't sleep a wink over here."

("You like to be over there anyway, Mama," Deborah said. "You know we want you here."

("Sure, we want you here," said Clyde. "As for the property, we talked it all out beforehand. I don't think I've damaged it any way."

("I just never saw it as a horse farm. But it's you all I worry about. It's the danger.")

Deborah drove home.

When the workingman her mother had hired three years before had stolen things and left, he had left too on the garage wall inside, a long pair of crossing diagonal lines, brown, in mud, Deborah thought, until she smelled what it was, and there were the blood-stained menstrual pads she later came across in the driveway, dug up out of the garbage, strewed out into the yard.

She told Clyde about the first but not the second discovery. "Some critters are mean," he'd shrugged it off. "Some critters are just mean."

They'd been dancing, out at the club. And so in love back then, he'd turned and turned her, far apart, then close, talking into her ear, making her laugh and answer, but finally he said: "Are you a mean critter, Deedee? Some critters are mean." And she'd remembered what she didn't tell.

But in those days Clyde was passionate and fun, both marvelously together, and the devil appearing at midnight in the bend of a country road would not have scared her. Nothing would have. It was the day of her life when they bought the first two horses.

"I thought I seen him somewhere myself."

"He looks a little bit like Clyde."

And dusk again, a third and final time.

The parking lot where she'd come after a movie was empty except for a few cars. The small office was unlighted, but a man she took for the attendant was bending to the door on the far side of a long cream-colored sedan near the back fence. "Want my ticket?" she called. The man straightened, head rising above the body frame, and she knew him. Had he been about to steal a car, or was he breaking in for whatever he could find, or was it her coming all along that he was waiting for? However it was, he knew her as instantly as she knew him. Each other was what they had, by whatever design or absence of it, found. Deborah did not cry out or stir.

Who knew how many lines life had cut away from him down through the years till the moment when an arrogant woman on a horse had ridden him down with lust and laughter? He wasn't bad-looking; his eyes were beautiful; he was the kind to whom nothing good could happen. From that bright day to this chilly dusk, it had probably just been the same old story.

Deborah waited. Someway or other, what was coming, threading through the cars like an animal lost for years catching the scent of a former owner, was her own.

("You're losing nerve, Deedee," Clyde had told her recently. "That's what's really bothering me. You're scared, aren't you?")

The bitter-stale smell of cigarette breath, though not so near as before, not forced against her mouth, was still unmistakably familiar. But the prod of a gun's muzzle just under the rise of her breast was not. It had never happened to her before. She shuddered at the touch with a chill spring-like start of something like life, which was also something like death.

"Get inside," he said.

"Are you the same one?" she asked. "Just tell me that. Three years ago, Mama hired somebody. Was that you?"

"Get in the car."

She opened the door, slid over to the driver's seat, found him beside her. The gun, thrust under his crossed arm, resumed its place against her.

"Drive."

"Was it you the other night at the door?" Her voice trembled as the motor started, the gear caught.

"He left me with the lot; ain't nobody coming."

The car eased into an empty street.

"Go out of town. The Memphis road."

She was driving past familiar, cared-for lawns and houses, trees and intersections. Someone waved from a car at a stoplight, taking them for her and Clyde. She was frightened and accepting fear, which come to think of it was all she'd been doing for months, working with those horses. ("Don't let him bluff you, Deedee. It's you or him. He'll do it if he can.")

"What do you want with me? What is it you want?"

He spoke straight outward, only his mouth moving, watching the road, never turning his head to her. "You're going out on that Memphis road and you're going up a side road with me. There's some woods I know. When I'm through with you you ain't never going to have nothing to ask nobody about me because you're going to know it all and it ain't going to make you laugh none, I guarantee."

Deborah cleared the town and swinging into the highway wondered at herself. Did she want him? She had waited when she might have run. Did she want, trembling, pleading, degraded, finally to let him have every single thing his own way?

(Do you see steel hoofs above you over and over because you want them one day to smash into your brain?

("Daddy, Daddy," she had murmured long ago when the old unshaven tramp had come up into the lawn, bleary-eyed, face bloodburst with years of drink and weather, frightening as the boogeyman, "raw head and bloody bones," like the Negro women scared her with. That day the sky streamed with end-of-the-world fire. But she hadn't called so loudly as she might have, she'd let him come closer, to look at him better, until the threatening voice of her father behind her, just on the door's slamming, had cried: "What do you want in this yard? What you think you want here? Deborah! You come in this house this minute!" But the mystery still lay dark within

her, forgotten for years, then stirring to life again: When I said
"Daddy, Daddy?" was I calling to the tramp or to the house?
Did I think the tramp was him in some sort of joke or dream
or trick? If not, why did I say it? Why?

("Why do you ride a horse so fast, Deedee? Why do you like
to do that?" *I'm going where the sky breaks open.* "I just like to."
"Why do you like to drive so fast?" "I don't know.")

Suppose he kills me, too, thought Deborah, striking the
straight stretch on the Memphis road, the beginning of the
long rolling run through farms and woods. She stole a glance
to her right. He looked like Clyde, all right. What right did
he have to look like Clyde?

("It's you or him, Deedee." All her life they'd said that to her
from the time her first pony, scared at something, didn't want
to cross a bridge. "Don't let him get away with it. It's you or
him.")

Righting the big car into the road ahead, she understood
what was demanded of her. She pressed the accelerator gradually downward toward the floor.

"And by the time he realized it," she said, sitting straight in her
chair at supper between Clyde and Emma, who by chance were
there that night together; "—by the time he knew, we were
hitting above seventy-five, and he said, 'What you speeding
for?' and I said, 'I want to get it over with.' And he said, 'Okay,
but that's too fast.' By that time we were touching eighty and
he said, 'What the fucking hell'—excuse me, Mama—'you
think you're doing? You slow this thing down.' So I said, 'I
tell you what I'm doing. This is a rolling road with high banks
and trees and lots of curves. If you try to take the wheel away
from me, I'm going to wreck us both. If you try to sit there
with that gun in my side I'm going to go faster and faster and
sooner or later something will happen, like a curve too sharp
to take or a car too many to pass with a big truck coming and
we're both going to get smashed up at the very least. It won't
do any good to shoot me when it's more than likely both of us
would die. You want that?'

"He grabbed at the wheel but I put on another spurt of
speed and when he pulled at the wheel we side-rolled, skidded
back, and another car coming almost didn't get out of the way.

I said, 'You see what you're doing, I guess.' And he said, 'Jesus God.' Then I knew I had him, had whipped him down.

"But it was another two or three miles like that before he said, 'Okay, okay, so I quit. Just slow down and let's forget it.' And I said, 'You give me that gun. The mood I'm in, I can drive with one hand or no hands at all, and don't think I won't do it.' But he wanted his gun at least, I could tell. He didn't give in till a truck was ahead and we passed but barely missed a car that was coming (it had to run off the concrete), and he put it down, in my lap."

(Like a dog, she could have said, but didn't. And I felt sorry for him, she could have added, because it was his glory's end.)

"So I said, 'Get over, way over,' and he did, and I coasted from fast to slow. I turned the gun around on him and let him out on an empty stretch of road, by a rise with a wood and a country side road rambling off, real pretty, and I thought, Maybe that's where he was talking about, where he meant to screw hell—excuse me, Mama—out of me. I held the gun till he closed the door and went down in the ditch a little way, then I put the safety catch on and threw it at him. It hit his shoulder, then fell in the weeds. I saw it fall, driving off."

"Oh, my poor baby," said Emma. "Oh, my precious child."

It was Clyde who rose, came round the table to her, drew her to her feet, held her close. "That's nerve," he said. "That's class." He let her go and she sat down again. "Why didn't you shoot him?"

"I don't know."

"He was the one we hired that time," Emma said. "I'd be willing to bet you anything."

"No, it wasn't," said Deborah quickly. "This one was blond and short, red-nosed from too much drinking, I guess. Awful like Mickey Rooney, gone and gotten old. Like the boogeyman, I guess."

"The poor woman's Mickey Rooney. You women find yourselves the damnedest men."

"She's not right about that," said Emma. "What do you want to tell that for? I know it was him. I feel like it was."

"Why'd you throw the gun away?" Clyde asked. "We could trace that."

"It's what I felt like doing," she said. She had seen it strike, how his shoulder, struck, went back a little.

Clyde Mecklin sat watching his wife. She had scarcely touched her food, and now, pale, distracted, she had risen to wander toward the windows, look out at the empty lawn, the shrubs and flowers, the stretch of white-painted fence, ghostly by moonlight.

"It's the last horse I'll ever break," she said, more to herself than not, but Clyde heard and stood up and was coming to her.

"Now, Deedee—"

"When you know you know," she said, and turned, her face set against him: her anger, her victory, held up like a blade against his stubborn willfulness. "I want my children now," she said.

At the mention of children, Emma's presence with them became multiple and vague; it trembled with thanksgiving, it spiraled on wings of joy.

Deborah turned again, back to the window. Whenever she looked away, the eyes by the road were there below her: they were worthless, nothing, but infinite, never finishing—the surface there was no touching bottom for—taking to them, into themselves, the self that was hers no longer.

The Cousins

I COULD SAY that on the train from Milan to Florence I recalled the events of thirty summers ago and the curious affair of my cousin Eric. But it wouldn't be true. I had Eric somewhere in my mind all the time, a constant. But he was never quite definable, and like a puzzle no one could ever solve, he bothered me. More recently, I had felt a restlessness I kept trying without success to lose, and I had begun to see Eric as its source.

The incident that had triggered my journey to find him had occurred while lunching with my cousin Ben in New York, his saying, "I always thought in some way I can't pin down—it was your fault we lost Eric." Surprising myself, I had felt stricken at the remark as though the point of a cold dagger had reached a vital spot. There was a story my cousins used to tell, out in the swing, under the shade trees, about a man found dead with no clues but a bloody shirt and a small pool of water on the floor beside him. Insoluble mystery. Answer. He was stabbed with a Dagger of Ice! I looked up from eating bay scallops. "*My* fault! Why?"

Ben gave some vague response, something about Eric's need for staying indifferent, no matter what. "But he could do that in spite of me," I protested. "Couldn't he?"

"Oh, forget it." He filled my glass. "I sometimes speculate out loud, Ella Mason."

Just before that he had remarked how good I was looking— good for a widow just turned fifty, I think he meant. But once he got my restlessness so stirred up, I couldn't lose it. I wanted calming, absolving. I wanted freeing and only Eric—since it was he I was in some way to blame for, or he to blame for me —could do that. So I came alone to Italy, where I had not been for thirty years.

For a while in Milan, spending a day or so to get over jet lag, I wondered if the country existed anymore in the way I remembered it. Maybe, even back then, I had invented the feelings I had, the magic I had wanted to see. But on the train to Florence, riding through the June morning, I saw a little town from the window, in the bright, slightly hazy distance. I don't know what town it was. It seemed built all of a whitish stone, with a church, part of a wall cupping around one side and a piazza with a few people moving across it. With that sight and its stillness in the distance and its sudden vanishing as the train whisked past, I caught my breath and knew it had all been real. So it still was, and would remain. I hadn't invented anything.

From the point of that glimpsed white village, spreading outward through my memory, all its veins and arteries, the whole summer woke up again, like a person coming out of a trance.

Sealed, fleet, the train was rocking on. I closed my eyes with the image of the village, lying fresh and gentle against my mind's eye. I didn't have to try, to know that everything from then would start living now.

Once at the hotel and unpacked, with my dim lamp and clean bathroom and view of a garden—Eric had reserved all this for me: we had written and talked—I placed my telephone call. "*Pronto*," said the strange voice. "Signor Mason," I said. "Ella Mason, is that you?" So there was his own Alabama voice, not a bit changed. "It's me," I said, "tired from the train." "Take a nap. I'll call for you at seven."

Whatever Southerners are, there are ways they don't change, the same manners to count on, the same tone of voice, never lost. Eric was older than I by about five years. I remember he taught me to play tennis, not so much how to play, because we all knew that, as what not to do. Tennis manners. I had wanted to keep running after balls for him when they rolled outside the court, but he stopped me from doing that. He would take them up himself, and stroke them underhand to his opponent across the net. "Once in a while's all right," he said. "Just go sit down, Ella Mason." It was his way of saying there was always a right way to do things. I was only about ten. The next year it was something else I was doing wrong, I guess, because I always had a lot to learn. My cousins had this constant fondness about them. They didn't mind telling what they knew.

Walking in Florence in the late afternoon, wondering where I was, then catching on. The air was still and warm. It had the slight haziness in the brightness that I had seen from the train, and which I had lost in the bother of the station, the hastening of the taxi through the annoyance of crowds and narrow streets, across the Arno. The little hotel, a *pensione*, really, was out near the Pitti Palace.

Even out so short a distance from the center, Florence could seem the town of thirty years ago, or even the way it must have been in the Brownings' time, narrow streets and the light that way and the same flowers and gravel walks in the gardens. Not that much changes if you build with stone. Not until I saw the stooped gray man hastening through the *pensione* door did I get slapped by change, in the face. How could Eric look like that? Not that I hadn't had photographs, letters. He at once circled me, embracing, my head right against him, sight of him temporarily lost in that. As was his of me, I realized, thinking of all those lines I must have added, along with twenty extra pounds and a high count of gray in the reddish-brown hair. So we both got bruised by the sight of each other, and hung together to blot each other out and soothe the hurt.

The shock was only momentary. We were too glad to see each other. We went some streets away, parked his car, and climbed about six flights of stone stairs. His place had a view over the river, first a great luxurious room opening past the entrance, then a terrace beyond. There were paintings, dark furniture, divans and chairs covered with good, rich fabric. A blond woman's picture in a silver frame—poised, lovely. Through an alcove, the glimpse of an impressive desk, spread with papers, a telephone. You'd be forced to say he'd done well.

"It's cooler outside on the terrace," Eric said, coming in with drinks. "You'll like it over the river." So we went out there and talked. I was getting used to him now. His profile hadn't changed. It was firm, regular, Cousin Lucy Skinner's all over. That was his mother. We were just third cousins. Kissing kin. I sat answering questions. How long would it take, I wondered, to get around to the heart of things? To whatever had carried him away, and what had brought me here?

We'd been brought up together back in Martinsville, Alabama, not far from Birmingham. There was our connection and not much else in that little town of seven thousand and something. Or so we thought. And so we would have everybody else think.

We did, though, despite a certain snobbishness—or maybe because of it—have a lot of fun. There were three leading families, in some way "connected." Eric and I had had the same great-grandfather. His mother's side were distant cousins, too. Families who had gone on living around there, through the centuries. Many were the stories and wide-ranged the knowledge, though it was mainly of local interest. As a way of living, I always told myself, it might have gone on for us, too, right through the present and into an endless future, except for that trip we took that summer.

It started with ringing phones.

Eric calling one spring morning to say, "You know the idea Jamie had last night down at Ben's about going to Europe? Well, why don't we do it?"

"This summer's impossible," I said, "I'm supposed to help Papa in the law office."

"He can get Sister to help him—" That was Eric's sister Chessie, one way of making sure she didn't decide to go with us. "You all will have to pay her a little, but she wants a job. Think it over, Ella Mason, but not for very long. Mayfred wants to, and Ben sounds serious, and there's Jamie and you makes five. Ben knows a travel agent in Birmingham. He thinks we might even get reduced rates, but we have to hurry. We should have thought this up sooner."

His light voice went racing on. He read a lot. I didn't even have to ask him where we'd go. He and Ben would plan it, both young men who had studied things, knew things, read, talked, quoted. We'd go where they wanted to go, love what they planned, admire them. Jamie was younger, my uncle Gale's son, but he was forming that year—he was becoming grown-up. Would he be like them? There was nothing else to be but like them, if at all possible. No one in his right mind would question that.

Ringing phones . . . "Oh, I'm thrilled to death! What did your folks say? It's not all that expensive what with the exchange, not as much as staying here and going somewhere like the Smokies. You can pay for the trip over with what you'd save."

We meant to go by ship. Mayfred, who read up on the latest things, wanted to fly, but nobody would hear to it. The boat was what people talked about when they mentioned their trip. It was a phrase: "On the boat going over . . . On the boat coming back . . ." The train was what we'd take to New York, or maybe we could fly. Mayfred, once redirected, began to plan everybody's clothes. She knew what things were drip-dry and crush-proof. On and on she forged through slick-paged magazines.

"It'll take the first two years of law practice to pay for it, but it might be worth it," said Eric. "*J'ai très hâte d'y aller*," said Ben. The little French he knew was a lot more than ours.

Eric was about twenty-five that summer, just finishing law school, having been delayed a year or so by his army service. I wasn't but nineteen. The real reason I had hesitated about going was a boy from Tuscaloosa I'd been dating up at the university last fall, but things were running down with him, even though I didn't want to admit it. I didn't love him so much as I wanted him to love me, and that's no good, as Eric himself told me. Ben was riding high, having gotten part of his thesis accepted for publication in the *Sewanee Review*. He had written on "The Lost Ladies of Edgar Allan Poe" and this piece was the chapter on "Ulalume." I pointed out they weren't so much lost as dead, or sealed up half-dead in tombs, but Ben didn't see the humor in that.

The syringa was blooming that year, and the spirea and bridal wreath. The flags had come and gone but not the wisteria, prettier than anybody could remember. All our mothers doted on their yards, while not a one of us ever raised so much as a petunia. No need to. We called each other from bower to bower. Our cars kept floating us through soft spring twilights. Travel folders were everywhere and Ben had scratched up enough French grammars to go around so we could practice some phrases. He thought we ought at least to know how to order in a restaurant and ask for stationery and soap in a hotel. Or buy stamps and find the bathroom. He was on to what to say to cabdrivers when somebody mentioned that we were spending all this time on French without knowing a word of Italian. What did *they* say for Hello, or How much does it cost? or Which way to the post office? Ben said we didn't have time for Italian. He thought the people you had to measure up to were the French. What Italians thought of you didn't matter all that much. We were generally over at Eric's house because his mother was away visiting his married sister Edith and the grandchildren, and Eric's father couldn't have cared less if we had drinks of real whiskey in the evening. In fact, he was often out playing poker and doing the same thing himself.

The Masons had a grand house. (Mason was Mama's maiden name and so my middle one.) I loved the house especially when nobody was in it but all of us. It was white, two-story with big high-ceilinged rooms. The tree branches laced across it by moonlight, so that you could only see patches of it. Mama was always saying they ought to thin things out, take out half the shrubs and at least three trees (she would even say which trees), but Cousin Fred, Eric's father, liked all that shaggy growth. Once inside, the house took you over—it liked us all—and we were often back in the big kitchen after supper fixing drinks or sitting out on the side porch making jokes and talking about Europe. One evening it would be peculiar things about the English, and the next, French food, how much we meant to spend on it, and so on. We had a long argument about Mont St.-Michel, which Ben had read about in a book by Henry Adams; but everybody else, though coaxed into reading at least part of the book, thought it was too far up there and we'd better stick around Paris. We hoped Ben would forget it: he was bossy when he got his head set. We just wanted to see Ver-sigh and Fontaine-blow.

"We could stop off in the southern part of France on our way to Italy" was Eric's idea. "It's where all the painting comes from."

"I'd rather see the paintings," said Mayfred. "They're mostly in Paris, aren't they?"

"That's not the point," said Ben.

Jamie was holding out for one night in Monte Carlo.

Jamie had shot up like a weed a few years back and had just never filled out. He used to regard us all as slightly opposed to him, as though none of us could possibly want to do what he most liked. He made, at times, common cause with Mayfred, who was kin to us only by a thread, so complicated I wouldn't dream of untangling it.

Mayfred was a grand-looking girl. Ben said it once: "She's got class." He said that when we were first debating whether to ask her along or not (if not her, then my roommate from Texas would be invited), and had decided that we had to ask Mayfred or smother her because we couldn't have stopped talking about our plans if our lives depended on it and she was always around. The afternoon Ben made that remark about her, we were just the three of us—Ben, Eric, and me—out to help Mama about the annual lining of the tennis court, and had stopped to sit on a bench, being sweaty and needing some shade to catch our breath in. So he said that in his meditative way, hitting the edge of a tennis racket on the ground between his feet and occasionally sighting down it to see if it had warped during a winter in the press. And Eric, after a silence in which he looked off to one side until you thought he hadn't heard (this being his way), said: "You'd think the rest of us had no class at all." "Of course we have, we just never mention it," said Ben. So we'd clicked again. I always loved that to happen.

Mayfred had a boyfriend named Donald Bailey, who came over from Georgia and took her out every Saturday night. He was fairly nice-looking was about all we knew, and Eric thought he was dumb.

"I wonder how Mayfred is going to get along without Donald," Ben said.

"I can't tell if she really likes him or not," I said. "She never talks about him."

"She just likes to have somebody," Ben said tersely, a thread of disapproval in his voice, the way he could do.

Papa was crazy about Mayfred. "You can't tell what she thinks about anything and she never misses a trick," he said. His unspoken thought was that I was always misjudging things. "Don't you *see*, Ella Mason," he would say. But are things all that easy to see?

"Do you remember," I said to Eric on the terrace, this long after, "much about Papa?"

"What about him?"

"He wanted me to be different, some way."

"Different how?"

"More like Mayfred," I said, and laughed, making it clear that I was deliberately shooting past the mark, because really I didn't know where it was.

"Well," said Eric, looking past me out to where the lights were brightening along the Arno, the towers standing out clearly in the dusky air, "I liked you the way you were."

It was good, hearing him say that. The understanding that I wanted might not come. But I had a chance, I thought, and groped for what to say, when Eric rose to suggest dinner, a really good restaurant he knew, not far away; we could even walk.

". . . Have you been to the Piazza? No, of course, you haven't had time. Well, don't go. It's covered with tourists and pigeon shit; they've moved all the real statues inside except the Cellini. Go look at that and leave quick. . . ."

"You must remember Jamie, though, how he put his head in his hands our first day in Italy and cried, 'I was just being nice to him and he took all the money!' Poor Jamie, I think something else was wrong with him, not just a couple of thousand lire."

"You think so, but what?"

"Well, Mayfred had made it plain that Donald was her choice of a man, though not present. And of course there was Ben . . ." My voice stopped just before I stepped on a crack in the sidewalk.

". . . Ben had just got into Yale that spring before we left. He was hitching to a *fu*ture, man!" It was just as well Eric said it.

"So that left poor Jamie out of everything, didn't it? He was young, another year in college to go, and nothing really outstanding about him, so he thought, and nobody he could pair with."

"There were you and me."

"You and me," I repeated. It would take a book to describe how I said that. Half-question, half-echo, a total wondering what to say next. How, after all, did *he* mean it? It wasn't like me to say nothing. "He might just have wondered what *we* had?"

"He might have," said Eric. In the corner of the white-plastered restaurant, where he was known and welcomed, he was enjoying grilled chicken and artichokes. But suddenly he put down his fork, a pause like a solstice. He looked past my shoulder: Eric's way.

"Ben said it was my fault we 'lost' you. That's how he put it. He told me that in New York, the last time I saw him, six weeks ago. He wouldn't explain. Do you understand what he meant?"

"'Lost,' am I? It's news to me."

"Well, you know, not at home. Not even in the States. Is that to do with me?"

"We'll go back and talk." He pointed to my plate. "Eat your supper, Ella Mason," he said.

My mind began wandering pleasantly. I fell to remembering the surprise Mayfred had handed us all when we got to New York. We had come up on the train, having gone up to Chattanooga to catch the Southern. Three days in New York and we would board the *Queen Mary* for Southampton. "Too romantic for anything," Mama had warbled on the phone. ("Elsa Stephens says, 'Too romantic for anything,'" she said at the table. "No, Mama, you said that, I heard you." "Well, I don't care who said it, it's true.") On the second afternoon in New York, Mayfred vanished with something vague she had to do. "Well, you know she's always tracking down dresses," Jamie told me. "I think she wants her hair restyled somewhere," I said. But not till we were having drinks in the hotel bar before dinner did Mayfred show up with Donald Bailey! She had, in addition to Donald, a new dress and a new hairstyle, and the three things looked to me about of equal value, I was thinking, when she suddenly announced with an earsplitting smile: "We're married!" There was a total silence, broken at last by Donald, who said with a shuffling around of feet and gestures, "It's just so I could come along with y'all, if y'all don't mind." "Well," said Ben, at long last, "I guess you both better sit down." Another silence followed, broken by Eric, who said he guessed it was one excuse for having champagne.

Mayfred and Donald had actually gotten married across the state line in Georgia two weeks before. Mayfred didn't want to discuss it because, she said, everybody was so taken up with talking about Europe, she wouldn't have been able to get a word in edgewise. "You better go straight and call yo' Mama," said Ben. "Either you do, or I will."

Mayfred's smile fell to ashes and she sloshed out champagne. "She can't do a thing about it till we get back home! She'll want me to explain everything. Don't y'all make me . . . please!"

I noticed that so far Mayfred never made common cause with any one of us, but always spoke to the group: Y'all. It also occurred to me both then and now that that was what had actually saved her. If one of us had gotten involved in pleading for her with Ben, he would have overruled us. But Mayfred, a lesser cousin, was keeping a distance. She could have said—and I thought she was on the verge of it—that she'd gone to a lot of trouble to satisfy us; she might have just brought him along without benefit of ceremony.

So we added Donald Bailey. Unbeknownst to us, reservations had been found for him, and though he had to share a four-berth, tourist-class cabin with three strange men, after a day out certain swaps were effected, and he wound up in second class with Mayfred. Eric overheard a conversation between Jamie and Donald which he passed on to me. Jamie: Don't you really think this is a funny way to spend a honeymoon? Donald: It was just the best I could do.

He was a polite squarish sort of boy with heavy, dark lashes. He and Mayfred used to stroll off together regularly after the noon meal on board. It was a serene crossing, for the weather cleared two days out of New York and we could spend a lot of time on deck playing shuffleboard and betting on races with wooden horses run by the purser. (I forgot to say everybody in our family but Ben's branch were inveterate gamblers and had played poker in the club car all the way up to New York on the train.) After lunch every day Mayfred got seasick and Donald in true husbandly fashion would take her to whichever side the wind was not blowing against and let her throw up neatly over the rail, like a cat. Then she'd be all right. Later, when you'd see them together they were always talking and laughing. But with us she was quiet and trim, with her fashion-blank look, and he was just quiet. He all but said "Ma'am" and "Sir." As a result of Mayfred's marriage, I was thrown a lot with Eric, Ben, and Jamie. "I think one of you ought to get married," I told them. "Just temporarily, so I wouldn't feel like the only girl." Ben promised to take a look around and Eric seemed not to have heard. It was Jamie who couldn't joke about it. He had set himself to make a pair, in some sort of way, with Mayfred, I felt. I don't know how seriously he took her. Things run deep in our family—that's what you have to know. Eric said out of the blue, "I'm wondering when they had time to see each other; Mayfred spent all her time with us." (We were prowling through the Tate Gallery.) "Those Saturday-night dates," I said, studying Turner. At times she would show up with us, without Donald, not saying much, attentive and smooth, making company. Ben told her she looked Parisian.

Eric and Ben were both well into manhood that year, and were so future conscious they seemed to be talking about it even when they weren't saying anything. Ben had decided on literature, had finished a master's at Sewanee and was going on to Yale, while Eric had just stood law school exams at Emory. He was in some considerable debate about whether he shouldn't go into literary studies, too, for unlike Ben, whose interest was scholarly, he wanted to be a writer, and he had some elaborate theory that actually studying literature reduced the possibility of your being able to write it. Ben saw his point, and though he did not entirely agree, felt that law might just be the right choice—it put you in touch with how things actually worked. "Depending, of course, on whether you tend to fiction or poetry. It would be more important in regard to fiction because the facts matter so much more." So they trod along ahead of us—through London sights, their heels coming down in tandem. They might have been two dons in an Oxford street, debating something. Next to come were Jamie and me, and behind, at times, Donald and Mayfred.

I was so fond of Jamie those days. I felt for him in a family way, almost motherly. When he said he wanted a night in Monte Carlo, I sided with him, just as I had about going at least once to the picture show in London. Why shouldn't he have his way? Jamie said one museum a day was enough. I felt the same. He was all different directions with himself: too tall, too thin, big feet, small head. Once I caught his hand: "Don't worry," I said, "everything good will happen to you." The way I remember it, we looked back just then, and there came Mayfred, alone. She caught up with us. We were standing on a street corner near Hyde Park and, for a change, it was sunny. "Donald's gone home," she said, cheerfully. "He said tell you all goodbye."

We hadn't seen her all day. We were due to leave for France the next morning. She told us, for one thing, that Donald had persistent headaches and thought he ought to see about it.

He seemed, as far as we could tell, to have limitless supplies of money, and had once taken us all for dinner at the Savoy, where only Mayfred could move into all that glitter with an air of belonging to it. He didn't like to bring up his illness and trouble us, Mayfred explained. "Maybe it was too much honeymoon for him," Eric speculated to me in private. I had to say I didn't know. I did know that Jamie had come out like the English sun—unexpected, but marvelously bright.

I held out for Jamie and Monte Carlo. He wasn't an intellectual like Ben and Eric. He would listen while they finished up a bottle of wine and then would start looking around the restaurant. "That lady didn't have anything but snails and bread," he would say, or, of a couple leaving, "He didn't even know that girl when they came in." He was just being a small-town boy. But with Mayfred he must have been different, she laughed so much. "What do they talk about?" Ben asked me, perplexed. "Ask them," I advised. "You think they'd tell me?" "I doubt it," I said. "They wouldn't know what to say," I added; "they would just tell you the last things they said." "You mean like, Why do they call it the Seine if they don't seine for fish in it? Real funny."

Jamie got worried about Mayfred in Paris because the son of the hotel owner, a young Frenchman so charming he looked like somebody had made him up whole cloth, wanted to take her out. She finally consented, with some trepidation on our part, especially from Ben, who in this case posed as her uncle, with strict orders from her father. The Frenchman, named Paul something, was not disturbed in the least: Ben fit right in with his ideas of how things ought to be. So Mayfred went out with him, looking, except for her sunny hair, more French than the natives—we all had to admit being proud of her. I also had invitations, but none so elegant. "What happened?" we all asked, the next day. "Nothing," she insisted. "We just went to this little nightclub place near some school . . . begins with an 'S.'" "The Sorbonne," said Ben, whose bemusement, at that moment, peaked. "Then what?" Eric asked. "Well, nothing. You just eat something, then talk and have some wine and get up and dance. They dance different. Like this." She locked her hands together in the air. "He thought he couldn't talk good enough for me in English, but it was O.K." Paul sent her some *marrons glacés*, which she opened on the train south, and Jamie munched one with happy jaws. Paul had not suited him. It was soon after that, he and Mayfred began their pairing off. In Jamie's mind we were moving on to Monte Carlo, and had been ever since London. The first thing he did was find out how to get to the Casino.

He got dressed for dinner better than he had since the Savoy. Mayfred seemed to know a lot about the gambling places, but her attitude was different from his. Jamie was bird-dogging toward the moment; she was just curious. "I've got to trail along," Eric said after dinner, "just to see the show." "Not only that," said Ben, "we might have to stop him in case he gets too carried away. We might have to bail him out." When we three, following up the rear (this was Jamie's night), entered the discreetly glittering rotunda, stepped on thick carpets beneath the giant, multiprismed chandeliers, heard the low chant of the croupier, the click of roulette, the rustle of money at the bank, and saw the bright, rhythmic movements of dealers and wheels and stacks of chips, it was still Jamie's face that was the sight worth watching. All was mirrored there. Straight from the bank, he visited card tables and wheels, played the blind dealing-machine—chemin de fer—and finally turned, a small sum to the good, to his real goal: roulette. Eric had by then lost a hundred francs or so, but I had about made up for it, and Ben wouldn't play at all. "It's my Presbyterian side," he told us. His mother had been one of those. "It's known as 'riotous living,'" he added.

It wasn't riotous at first, but it was before we left, because Jamie, once he advanced on the roulette, with Mayfred beside him—she was wearing some sort of gold blouse with long peasant sleeves and a low-cut neck she had picked up cheap in a shop that afternoon, and was not speaking to him but instead, with a gesture so European you'd think she'd been born there, slipping her arm through his just at the wrist and leaning her head back a little—was giving off the glow of somebody so magically aided by a presence every inch his own that he could not and would not lose. Jamie, in fact, looked suddenly aristocratic, overbred, like a Russian greyhound or a Rumanian prince. Both Eric and I suspended our own operations to watch. The little ball went clicking round as the wheel spun.

Black. Red. And red. Back to black. All wins. People stopped to look on. Two losses, then the wins again, continuing. Mayfred had a look of curious bliss around her mouth—she looked like a cat in process of a good purr. The take mounted.

Ben called Eric and me aside. "It's going on all night," he said. We all sat down at the little gold-and-white-marble bar and ordered Perriers.

"Well," said Eric, "what did he start with?"

"Couldn't have been much," said Ben, "if I didn't miss anything. He didn't change more than a couple of hundred at the desk."

"That sounds like a lot to me," said Eric.

"I mean," said Ben, "it won't ruin him to lose it all."

"You got us into this," said Eric to me.

"Oh, gosh, I know it. But look. He's having the time of his life."

Everybody in the room had stopped to watch Jamie's luck. Some people were laughing. He had a way of stopping everybody and saying: "What's *that* mean?" as if only English could or ought to be spoken in the entire world. Some man near us said, "*Le cavalier de l'Okla-hum*," and another answered, "*Du Texas, plutôt*." Then he took three more in a row and they were silent.

It was Mayfred who made him stop. It seemed like she had an adding machine in her head. All of a sudden she told him something, whispered in his ear. When he shook his head, she caught his hands. When he pulled away, she grabbed his arm. When he lifted his arm, she came up with it, right off the floor. For a minute I thought they were both going to fall over into the roulette wheel.

"You got to stop, Jamie!" Mayfred said in the loudest Alabama voice I guess they'd ever be liable to hear that side of the ocean. It was curdling, like cheering for 'Bama against Ole Miss in the Sugar Bowl. "I don't have to stop!" he yelled right back. "If you don't stop," Mayfred shouted, "I'll never speak to you again, Jamie Marshall, as long as I live!"

The croupier looked helpless, and everybody in the room was turning away like they didn't see us, while through a thin door at the end of the room, a man in black tie was approaching who could only be called the "management." Ben was already pulling Jamie toward the bank. "Cash it in now, we'll go along to another one . . . maybe tomorrow we can . . ." It was like pulling a stubborn calf across the lot, but he finally made it with some help from Mayfred, who stood over Jamie while he counted everything to the last sou. She made us all take a taxi back to the hotel because she said it was common knowledge when you won a lot they sent somebody out to rob you, first thing. Next day she couldn't rest till she got Jamie to change the francs into traveler's checks, U.S. He had won well over two thousand dollars, all told.

The next thing, as they saw it, was to keep Jamie out of the Casino. Ben haggled a long time over lunch, and Eric, who was good at scheming, figured out a way to get up to a village in the hills where there was a Matisse chapel he couldn't live longer without seeing. And Mayfred took to handholding and even gave Jamie on the sly (I caught her at it) a little nibbling kiss or two. What did they care? I wondered. I thought he should get to go back and lose it all.

It was up in the mountain village that afternoon that I blundered in where I'd rather not have gone. I had come out of the chapel where Ben and Eric were deep in discussion of whether Matisse could ever place in the front rank of French art, and had climbed part of the slope nearby where a narrow stair ran up to a small square with a dry stone fountain. Beyond that, in the French manner, was a small café with a striped awning and a few tables. From somewhere I heard Jamie's voice, saying, "I know, but what'd you do it for?" "Well, what does anybody do anything for? I wanted to." "But what would you want to *for*, Mayfred?" "Same reason you'd want to, sometime." "I wouldn't want to, except to be with you." "Well, I'm right here, aren't I? You got your wish." "What I wish is you hadn't done it." It was bound to be marrying Donald that he meant. He had a frown that would come at times between his light eyebrows. I came to associate it with Mayfred. How she was running him. When they stepped around the corner of the path, holding hands (immediately dropped), I saw that frown. Did I have to dislike Mayfred, the way she was acting? The funny thing was, I didn't even know.

We lingered around the village and ate there and the bus was late, so we never made it back to the casinos. By then all Jamie seemed to like was being with Mayfred, and the frown disappeared.

Walking back to the apartment, passing darkened doorways, picking up pieces of Eric's past like fragments in the street.

". . . And then you did or didn't marry her, and she died and left you the legacy . . ."

"Oh, we did get married, all right, the anticlimax of a number of years. I wish you could have known her. The marriage was civil. She was afraid the family would cause a row if she wanted to leave me anything. That was when she knew she hadn't long to live. Not that it was any great fortune. She had some property out near Pasquallo, a little town near here. I sold it. I had to fight them in court for a while, but it did eventually clear up."

"You've worked, too, for this other family . . . ?"

"The Rinaldi. You must have got all this from Ben, though maybe I wrote you, too. They were friends of hers. It's all connections here, like anywhere else. Right now they're all at the sea below Genoa. I'd be there too, but I'd some business in town, and you were coming. It's the export side I've helped them with. I do know English, and a little law, in spite of all."

"So it's a regular Italian life," I mused, climbing stairs, entering the *salotto*, where I saw again the woman's picture in a silver frame. Was that her, the one who had died? "Was she blond?" I asked, moving as curiously through his life as a child through a new room.

"Giana, you mean? No, part Sardinian, dark as they come. Oh, you mean her. No, that's Lisa, one of the Rinaldi, Paolo's sister . . . that's him up there."

I saw then, over a bookshelf, a man's enlarged photo: tweed jacket, pipe, all in the English style.

"So what else, Ella Mason?" His voice was amused at me.

"She's pretty," I said.

"Very pretty," he agreed.

We drifted out to the terrace once more.

It is time I talked about Ben and Eric, about how it was with me and with them and with the three of us.

When I look back on pictures of myself in those days, I see a girl in shorts, weighing a few pounds more than she thought she should, low-set, with a womanly cast to her body, chopped-off reddish hair, and a wide, freckled, almost boyish grin, happy to be posing between two tall boys, who happened to be her cousins, smiling their white, tentative smiles. Ben and Eric. They were smart. They were fun. They did everything right. And most of all, they admitted me. I was the audience they needed.

I had to run to keep up. I read Poe because of Ben's thesis; and Wallace Stevens because Eric liked his poetry. I even, finding him referred to at times, tried to read Plato. (Ben studied Greek.) But what I did was not of much interest to them. Still, they wanted me around. Sometimes Ben made a point of "conversing" with me—what courses, what books, etc.— but he made me feel like a high-school student. Eric, seldom bothering with me, was more on my level when he did. To one another, they talked at a gallop. Literature turned them on, their ideas flowed, ran back and forth like a current. I loved hearing them.

I think of little things they did. Such as Ben's coming back from Sewanee with a small Roman statue, copy of something Greek—Apollo, I think—just a fragment, a head, turned aside, shoulders and a part of a back. His professor had given it to him as a special mark of favor. He set it on his favorite pigeon-hole desk, to stay there, it would seem, for always, to be seen always by the rest of us—by me.

Such as Eric ordering his "secondhand but good condition" set of Henry James's novels with prefaces, saying, "I know this is corny but it's what I wanted," making space in his Mama's old upright secretary with glass-front bookshelves above, and my feeling that they'd always be there. I strummed my fingers across the spines lettered in gold. Someday I would draw down one or another to read them. No hurry.

Such as the three of us packing Mama's picnic basket (it seems my folks were the ones with the practical things—tennis court, croquet set: though Jamie's set up a badminton court at one time, it didn't take) to take to a place called Beulah Woods for a spring day in the sun near a creek where water ran clear over white limestone, then plunged off into a swimming hole. Ben sat on a bedspread reading Ransom's poetry aloud and we gossiped about the latest town scandal, involving a druggist, a real estate deal where some property went cheap to him, though it seemed now that his wife had been part of the bargain, being lent out on a regular basis to the man who sold him the property. The druggist was a newcomer. A man we all knew in town had been after the property and was now threatening to sue. "Do you think it was written in the deed, so many nights a week she goes off to work the property out?" Ben speculated. "Do you think they calculated the interest?" It wasn't the first time our talk had run toward sexual things; in a small town, secrets didn't often get kept for long.

More than once I'd dreamed that someday Ben or Eric would ask me somewhere alone. A few years before the picnic, romping through our big old rambling house at twilight with Jamie, who loved playing hide-and-seek, I had run into the guest room, where Ben was standing in the half-dark by the bed. He was looking at something he'd found there in the twilight, some book or ornament, and I mistook him for Jamie and threw my arms around him crying, "Caught you!" We fell over the bed together and rolled for a moment before I knew then it was Ben, but knew I'd wanted it to be; or didn't I really know all along it was Ben, but pretended I didn't? Without a doubt when his weight came down over me, I knew I wanted it to be there. I felt his body, for a moment so entirely present, draw back and up. Then he stood, turning away, leaving. "You better grow up" was what I think he said. Lingering feelings made me want to seek him out the next day or so. Sulky, I wanted to say, "I *am* growing up." But another time he said, "We're cousins, you know."

Eric for a while dated a girl from one of the next towns. She used to ask him over to parties and they would drive to Birmingham sometimes, but he never had her over to Martinsville. Ben, that summer we went to Europe, let it be known he was writing and getting letters from a girl at Sewanee. She was a pianist named Sylvia. "You want to hear music played softly in the 'drawing room,'" I clowned at him. "'Just a song at twilight.'" "Now, Ella Mason, you behave," he said.

I had boys to take me places. I could flirt and I got a rush at dances and I could go off the next-to-the-highest diving board and was good in doubles. Once I went on strike from Ben and Eric for over a week. I was going with the boy from Tuscaloosa and I had begun to think he was the right one and get ideas. Why fool around with my cousins? But I missed them. I went around one afternoon. They were talking out on the porch. The record player was going inside, something of Berlioz that Ben was on to. They waited till it finished before they'd speak to me. Then Eric, smiling from the depths of a chair, said, "Hey, Ella Mason"; and Ben, getting up to unlatch the screen, said, "Ella Mason, where on earth have you been?" I'd have to think they were glad.

Ben was dark. He had straight, dark-brown hair, dry-looking in the sun, growing thick at the brow, but flat at night when he put a damp comb through it, and darker. It fit close to his head like a monk's hood. He wore large glasses with Lucite rims. Eric had sandy hair, softly appealing and always mussed. He didn't bother much with his looks. In the day they scuffed around in open-throated shirts and loafers, crinkled seersucker pants, or shorts; tennis shoes when they played were always dirty white. At night, when they cleaned up, it was still casual but fresh laundered. But when they dressed, in shirts and ties with an inch of white cuff laid crisp against their brown hands: they were splendid!

"Ella Mason," Eric said, "if that boy doesn't like you, he's not worth worrying about." He had put his arm around me coming out of the picture show. I ought to drop it, a tired romance, but couldn't quite. Not till that moment. Then I did.

"Those boys," said Mr. Felix Gresham from across the street. "Getting time they started earning something 'stead of all time settin' around." He used to come over and tell Mama everything he thought though no kin to anybody. "I reckon there's time enough for that," Mama said. "Now going off to France," said Mr. Gresham, as though that spoke for itself. "Not just France," Mama said, "England, too, and Italy." "Ain't nothing in France," said Mr. Gresham. "I don't know if there is or not," said Mama, "I never have been." She meant that to hush him up, but the truth is, Mr. Gresham might have been to France in World War I. I never thought to ask. Now he's dead.

Eric and Ben. I guess I was in love with both of them. Wouldn't it be nice, I used to think, if one were my brother and the other my brother's best friend, and then I could just quietly and without so much as thinking about it find myself marrying the friend (now which would I choose for which?)

and so we could go on forever? At other times, frustrated, I
suppose, by their never changing toward me, I would plan on
doing something spectacular, finding a Yankee, for instance, so
impressive and brilliant and established in some important career, that they'd have to listen to him, learn what he was doing
and what he thought and what he knew, while I sat silent and
poised throughout the conversation, the cat that ate the cream,
though of course too polite to show satisfaction. Fantasies, one
by one, would sing to me for a little while.

At Christmas vacation before our summer abroad, just before Ben got accepted to Yale and just while Eric was getting
bored with law school, there was a quarrel. I didn't know the
details, but they went back to school with things still unsettled
among us. I got friendly with Jamie then, more than before.
He was down at Tuscaloosa, like me. It's when I got to know
Mayfred better, on weekends at home. Why bother with Eric
and Ben? It had been a poor season. One letter came from
Ben and I answered it, saying that I had come to like Jamie
and Mayfred so much; their parents were always giving parties
and we were having a grand time. In answer I got a long, serious letter about time passing and what it did, how we must
remember that what we had was always going to be part of
ourselves. That he thought of jonquils coming up now and
how they always looked like jonquils, just absent for a time,
and how the roots stayed the same. He was looking forward,
he said, to spring and coming home.

Just for fun I sat down and wrote him a love letter. I said he
was a fool and a dunce and didn't he know while he was writing
out all these ideas that I was a live young woman and only a
second cousin and that through the years while he was talking
about Yeats, Proust, and Edgar Allan Poe that I was longing
to have my arms around him the way they were when we fell
over in the bed that twilight romping around with Jamie and
why in the ever-loving world couldn't he see me as I was, a
live girl, instead of a cousin-spinster, listening to him and Eric
make brilliant conversation? Was he trying to turn me into an
old maid? Wasn't he supposed, at least, to be intelligent? So
why couldn't he see what I was really like? But I didn't mail
it. I didn't because, for one thing, I doubted that I meant it.
Suppose, by a miracle, Ben said, "You're right, every word."

What about Eric? I started dating somebody new at school. I tore the letter up.

Eric called soon after. He just thought it would do him good to say hello. Studying for long hours wasn't his favorite sport. He'd heard from Ben, the hard feelings were over, he was ready for spring holidays already. I said, "I hope to be in town, but I'm really not sure." A week later I forgot a date with the boy I thought I liked. The earlier one showed up again. Hadn't I liked him, after all? How to be sure? I bought a new straw hat, white-and-navy for Easter, with a ribbon down the back, and came home.

Just before Easter, Jamie's parents gave a party for us all. There had been a cold snap and we were all inside, with purplish-red punch, and a buffet laid out. Jamie's folks had this relatively new house, with new carpets and furnishings and the family dismay ran to what a big mortgage they were carrying and how it would never be paid out. Meantime his mother (no kin) looked completely unworried as she arranged tables that seemed to have been copied from magazines. I came alone, having had to help Papa with some typing, and so saw Ben and Eric for the first time, though we'd talked on the phone.

Eric looked older, a little worn. I saw something drawn in the way he laughed, a sort of restraint about him. He was standing aside and looking at a point where no one and nothing were. But he came to when I spoke and gave that laugh and then a hug. Ben was busy "conversing" with a couple in town who had somebody at Sewanee, too. He smoked a pipe now, I noticed, smelly when we hugged. He had soon come to join Eric and me, and it was at that moment, the three of us standing together for the first time since Christmas, and change having been mentioned at least once by way of Ben's letter, that I knew some tension was mounting, bringing obscure moments with it. We turned to one another but did not speak readily about anything. I had thought I was the only one, sensitive to something imagined—having "vapors," as somebody called it—but I could tell we were all at a loss for some reason none of us knew. Because if Ben and Eric knew, articulate as they were, they would have said so. In the silence so suddenly fallen, something was ticking.

Maybe, I thought, they just don't like Martinsville anymore. They always said that parties were dull and squirmed out of them when they could. I lay awake thinking, They'll move on soon; I won't see them again.

It was the next morning Eric called and we all grasped for Europe like the drowning, clinging to what we could.

After Monte Carlo, we left France by train and came down to Florence. The streets were narrow there and we joked about going single-file like Indians. "What I need is moccasins," said Jamie, who was always blundering over the uneven paving stones. At the Uffizi, the second day, Eric, in a trance before Botticelli, fell silent. Could we ever get him to speak again? Hardly a word. Five in number, we leaned over the balustrades along the Arno, all silent then from the weariness of sightseeing, and the heat; and there I heard it once more, the ticking of something hidden among us. Was it to deny it we decided to take the photograph? We had taken a lot, but this one, I think, was special. I have it still. It was in the Piazza Signoria.

"Which monument?" we kept asking. Ben wanted Donatello's lion, and Eric the steps of the Old Palace; Jamie wanted Cosimo I on his horse. I wanted the *Perseus* of Cellini, and Mayfred the *Rape of the Sabines*. So Ben made straws out of toothpicks and we drew and Mayfred won. We got lined up and Ben framed us. Then we had to find somebody, a slim Italian boy as it turned out, to snap us for a few hundred lire. It seemed we were proving something serious and good, and smiled with our straight family smiles, Jamie with his arm around Mayfred, and she with her smart new straw sun hat held to the back of her head, and me between Ben and Eric, arms entwined. A photo outlasts everybody, and this one with the frantic scene behind us, the moving torso of the warrior holding high the prey while we smiled our ordinary smiles—it was a period, the end of a phase.

Not that the photograph itself caused the end of anything. Donald Bailey caused it. He telephoned the *pensione* that night from Atlanta to say he was in the hospital, gravely ill, something they might have to operate for any day, some sort of brain tumor was what they were afraid of. Mayfred said she'd come.

We all got stunned. Ben and Eric and I straggled off together while she and Jamie went to the upstairs sitting room and sat in the corner. "Honest to God," said Eric, "I just didn't know Donald Bailey had a brain." "He had headaches," said Ben. "Oh, I knew he had a head," said Eric, "we could see that."

By night it was settled. Mayfred would fly back from Rome. Once again she got us to promise secrecy—how she did that I don't know, the youngest one and yet not even Ben could prevail on her one way or the other. By now she had spent most of her money. Donald, we knew, was rich; he came of a rich family and had, furthermore, money of his own. So if she wanted to fly back from Rome, the ticket, already purchased, would be waiting for her. Mayfred got to be privileged, in my opinion, because none of us knew her family too well. Her father was a blood cousin but not too highly regarded—he was thought to be a rather silly man who "traveled" and dealt with "all sorts of people"—and her mother was from "off," a Georgia girl, fluttery. If it had been my folks and if I had started all this wild marrying and flying off, Ben would have been on the phone to Martinsville by sundown.

One thing in the Mayfred departure that went without question: Jamie would go to Rome to see her off. We couldn't have sealed him in or held him with ropes. He had got on to something new in Italy, or so I felt, because where before then had we seen in gallery after gallery, strong men, young and old, with enraptured eyes, enthralled before a woman's painted image, wanting nothing? What he had gotten was an idea of devotion. It fit him. It suited. He would do anything for Mayfred and want nothing. If she had got pregnant and told him she was a virgin, he would have sworn to it before the Inquisition. It could positively alarm you for him to see him satisfied with the feelings he had found. Long after I went to bed, he was at the door or in the corridor with Mayfred, discussing baggage and calling a hotel in Rome to get a reservation for when he saw her off.

Mayfred had bought a lot of things. She had an eye for what she could wear with what, and she would pick up pieces of this and that for putting costumes and accessories together. She had to get some extra luggage and it was Jamie, of course, who promised to see it sent safely to her, through a shipping company in Rome. His two thousand dollars was coming in handy, was all I could think.

Hot, I couldn't sleep, so I went out in the sitting room to find a magazine. Ben was up. The three men usually took a large room together, taking turns for the extra cot. Ever since we got the news, Ben had had what Eric called his "family mood." Now he called me over. "I can't let those kids go down there alone," he said. "They seem like children to me—and Jamie . . . about all he can say is *grazie* and *quanto*." "Then let's all go," I said, "I've given up sleeping for tonight anyway." "Eric's hooked on Florence," said Ben. "Can't you tell? He counts the cypresses on every knoll. He can spot a Della Robbia a block off. If I make him leave three days early, he'll never forgive me. Besides, our reservations in that hotel can't be changed. We called for Jamie and they're full; he's staying third class somewhere till we all come. I don't mind doing that. Then we'll all meet up just the way we planned, have our week in Rome, and go catch the boat from Naples." "I think they could make it on their own," I said, "it's just that you'd worry every minute." He grinned; "our father for the duration" was what Eric called him. "I know I'm that way," he said.

Another thing was that Ben had been getting little caches of letters at various points along our trek from his girlfriend Sylvia, the one he'd been dating up at Sewanee. She was getting a job in New York that fall which would be convenient to Yale. She wrote a spidery hand on thick rippled stationery, cream-colored, and had promised in her last dispatch, received in Paris, to write to Rome. Ben could have had an itch for that. But mainly he was that way, careful and concerned. He had in mind what we all felt, that just as absolutely anything could be done by Mayfred, so could absolutely anything happen to her. He also knew what we all knew, that if the Colosseum started falling on her, Jamie would leap bodily under the rocks.

At two a.m. it was too much for me to think about. I went to bed and was so exhausted I didn't even hear Mayfred leave.

I woke up about ten with a low tapping on my door. It was Eric. "Is this the sleep of the just?" he asked me as I opened the door. The air in the corridor was fresh: it must have rained in the night. No one was about. All the guests, I supposed, were well out into the day's routine, seeing what next tour was on the list. On a trip you were always planning something. Ben planned for us. He kept a little notebook.

Standing in my doorway alone with Eric, in a loose robe with a cool morning breeze and my hair not even combed, I suddenly laughed. Eric laughed, too. "I'm glad they're gone," he said, and looked past my shoulder.

I dressed and went out with him for some breakfast, cappuccino and croissants at a café in the Signoria. We didn't talk much. It was terrible, in the sense of the Mason Skinner Marshall and Phillips sense of family, even to think you were glad they were gone, let alone say it. I took Eric's silence as one of his ironies, what he was best at. He would say, for instance, if you were discussing somebody's problem that wouldn't ever have any solution, "It's time somebody died." There wasn't much to say after that. Another time, when his daddy got into a rage with a next-door neighbor over their property line, Eric said, "You'd better marry her." Once he put things in an extreme light, nobody could talk about them anymore. Saying "I'm glad they're gone" was like that.

But it was a break. I thought of the way I'd been seeing them. How Jamie's becoming had been impressing me, every day more. How Mayfred was a kind of spirit, grown bigger than life. How Ben's dominance now seemed not worrisome but princely, his heritage. We were into a Renaissance of ourselves, I wanted to say, but was afraid they wouldn't see it the way I did. Only Eric had eluded me. What was he becoming? For once he didn't have to discuss Poe's idea of women, or the Southern code of honor, or Henry James's views of France and England.

As for me, I was, at least, sure that my style had changed. I had bought my little linen blouses and loose skirts, my sandals and braided silver bracelets. "That's great on you!" Mayfred had cried. "Now try this one!" On the streets, Italians passed me too close not to be noticed; they murmured musically in my ear, saying I didn't know just what; waiters leaned on my shoulder to describe dishes of the day.

Eric and I wandered across the river, following narrow streets lined with great stone palaces, seeing them open into small piazzas whose names were not well known. We had lunch in a friendly place with a curtain of thin twisted metal sticks in the open door, an amber-colored dog lying on the marble floor near the serving table. We ordered favorite things without looking at the menu. We drank white wine. "This is fun," I suddenly said. He turned to me. Out of his private distance, he seemed to be looking at me. "I think so, too."

He suddenly switched on to me, like somebody searching and finding with the lens of a camera. He began to ask me things. What did you think of that, Ella Mason? What about this, Ella Mason? Ella Mason, did you think Ben was right when he said . . . ? I could hardly swing on to what was being asked of me, thick and fast. But he seemed to like my answers, actually to listen. Not that all those years I'd been dumb as a stone. I had prattled quite a lot. It's just that they never treated me one to one, the way Eric was doing now. We talked for nearly an hour, then, with no one left in the restaurant but us, stopped as suddenly as we'd started. Eric said, "That's a pretty dress."

The sun was strong outside. The dog was asleep near the door. Even the one remaining waiter was drowsing on his feet. It was the shutting-up time for everything and we went out into the streets blanked out with metal shutters. We hugged the shady side and went single-file back to home base, as we'd come to call it, wherever we stayed.

A Vespa snarled by and I stepped into a cool courtyard to avoid it. I found myself in a large, yawning mouth, mysterious as a cave, shadowy, with the trickling sound of a fountain and the glimmer in the depths of water running through ferns and moss. Along the interior of the street wall, fragments of ancient sculpture, found, I guess, when they'd built the palazzo, had been set into the masonry. One was a horse, neck and shoulder, another an arm holding a shield, and a third at about my height the profile of a woman, a nymph or some such. Eric stopped to look at each, for as Ben said, Eric loved everything there, and then he said, "Come here, Ella Mason." I stood where he wanted, by the little sculptured relief, and he took my face and turned it to look at it closer; then with a strong hand (I remembered tennis), he pressed my face against the stone face and held it for a moment. The stone bit into my flesh and that was the first time that Eric, bending deliberately to do so, kissed me on the mouth. He had held one side of me against the wall, so that I couldn't raise my arm to him, and the other arm was pinned down by his elbow; the hand that pressed my face into the stone was that one, so that I couldn't move closer to him, as I wanted to do, and when he dropped away suddenly, turned on his heel and walked rapidly away, I could only hasten to follow, my voice gone, my pulses all throbbing together. I remember my anger, the old dreams about him and Ben stirred to life again, thinking, *If he thinks he can just walk away*, and knowing with anger, too, *It's got to be now*, as if in the walled land of kinship, thicker in our illustrious connection than any fortress in Europe, a door had cracked open at last. Eric, Eric, Eric. I'm always seeing your retreating heels, how they looked angry; but why? It was worth coming for, after thirty years, to ask that.

"That day you kissed me in the street, the first time," I asked him. Night on the terrace; a bottle of Chianti between our chairs. "You walked away. Were you angry? Your heels looked angry. I can see them still."

"The trip in the first place," he said, "it had to do with you, partly. Maybe you didn't understand that. We were outward bound, leaving you, a sister in a sense. We'd talked about it."

"I'd adored you so," I said. "I think I was less than a sister, more like a dog."

"For a little while you weren't either one." He found my hand in the dark. "It was a wonderful little while."

Memories: Eric in the empty corridor of the *pensione*. How Italy folds up and goes to sleep from two to four. His not looking back for me, going straight to his door. The door closing, but no key turning and me turning the door handle and stepping in. And he at the window already with his back to me and how he heard the sliding latch on the door—I slid it with my hands behind me—heard it click shut, and turned. His face and mine, what we knew. Betraying Ben.

: Walking by the Arno, watching a white-and-green scull stroking by into the twilight, the rower a boy or girl in white and green, growing dimmer to the rhythm of the long oars, vanishing into arrow shape, then pencil thickness, then movement without substance, on . . .

: A trek the next afternoon through twisted streets to a famous chapel. Sitting quiet in a cloister, drinking in the symmetry, the silence. Holding hands. "D for Donatello," said Eric. "D for Della Robbia," I said. "M for Michelangelo," he continued. "M for Medici." "L for Leonardo." "I can't think of an L," I gave up. "Lumbago. There's an old master." "Worse than Jamie." We were always going home again.

: Running into the manager of the *pensione* one morning in the corridor. He'd solemnly bowed to us and kissed my hand. "*Bella ragazza*," he remarked. "The way life ought to be," said Eric. I thought we might be free forever, but from what?

At the train station waiting the departure we were supposed to take for Rome, "Why do we have to go?" I pleaded. "Why can't we just stay here?"

"Use your common sense, Ella Mason."

"I don't have any."

He squeezed my shoulder. "We'll get by all right," he said. "That is, if you don't let on."

I promised not to. Rather languidly I watched the landscape slide past as we glided south. I would obey Eric, I thought, for always. "Once I wrote a love letter to you," I said. "I wrote it at night by candlelight at home one summer. I tore it up."

"You told me that," he recalled, "but you said you couldn't remember if it was to me or Ben."

"I just remembered," I said. "It was you . . ."

"Why did we ever leave?" I asked Eric, in the dead of night, a blackness now. "Why did we ever decide we had to go to Rome?"

"I didn't think of it as even a choice," he said. "But at that point, how could I know what was there, ahead?"

We got off the train feeling small—at least, I did. Ben was standing there, looking around him, tall, searching for us, then seeing. But no Jamie. Something to ask. I wondered if he'd gone back with Mayfred. "No, he's running around Rome." The big, smooth station, echoing, open to the warm day. "Hundreds of churches," Ben went on. "Millions. He's checking them off." He helped us in a taxi with the skill of somebody who'd lived in Rome for ten years, and gave the address. "He's got to do something now that Mayfred's gone. It's getting like something he might take seriously, is all. Finding out what Catholics believe. He's either losing all his money, or falling in love, or getting religion."

"He didn't lose any money," said Eric. "He made some."

"Well, it's the same thing," said Ben, always right and not wanting to argue with us. He seemed a lot older than the two of us, at least to me. Ben was tall.

We had mail in Rome; Ben brought it to the table that night. I read Mama's aloud to them: "When I think of you children over there, I count you all like my own chickens out in the yard, thinking I've got to go out in the dark and make sure the gate's locked because not a one ought to get out of there. To me, you're all my own, and thinking of chickens is my way of saying prayers for you to be safe at home again."

"You'd think we were off in a war," said Eric.

"It's a bold metaphor," said Ben, pouring wine for us, "but that never stopped Cousin Charlotte."

I wanted to giggle at Mama, as I usually did, but instead my eyes filled with tears, surprising me, and a minute more and I would have dared to snap at Ben. But Eric, who had got some mail, too, abruptly got up and left the table. I almost ran after him, but intent on what I'd promised about not letting on to Ben, I stayed and finished dinner. He had been pale, white. Ben thought he might be sick. He didn't return. We didn't know.

Jamie and Ben finally went to bed. "He'll come back when he wants to," said Ben.

I waited till their door had closed, and then, possessed, I crept out to the front desk. "Signor Mason," I said, "the one with the *capelli leggero*—" My Italian came from the dictionary straight to the listener. I found out later I had said that Eric's hair didn't weigh much. Still, they understood. He had taken a room, someone who spoke English explained. He wanted to be alone. I said he might be sick, and I guess they could read my face because I was guided by a porter, in a blue working jacket and cloth shoes, into a labyrinth. Italian buildings, I knew by now, are constructed like dreams. There are passages departing from central hallways, stairs that twist back upon themselves, dark silent doors. My guide stopped before one.

"*Ecco*," he said and left. I knocked softly, and the door eventually cracked open. "Oh, it's you." "Eric. Are you all right? I didn't know . . ."

He opened the door a little wider. "Ella Mason—" he began. Maybe he was sick. I caught his arm. The whole intensity of my young life in that moment shook free of everything but Eric. It was as though I'd traveled miles to find him. I came inside and we kissed and then I was sitting apart from him on the edge of the bed and he in a chair, and a letter, official-looking, the top of the envelope torn open in a jagged line, lay on a high black-marble-topped table with bowed legs, between us. He said to read it and I did, and put it back where I found it.

It said that Eric had failed his law exams. That in view of the family connection with the university (his father had gone there and some cousin was head of the board of trustees) a special meeting had been held to grant his repeating the term's work so as to graduate in the fall, but the evidences of his negligence were too numerous and the vote had gone against it. I remember saying something like "Anybody can fail exams . . ." as I knew people who had, but knew also that those people weren't "us," not one of our class or connection, not kin to the brilliant Ben, or nephew of a governor, or descended from a great Civil War general.

"All year long," he said, "I've been acting like a fool, as if I expected to get by. This last semester especially. It all seemed too easy. It is easy. It's easy and boring. I was fencing blindfold with somebody so far beneath me it wasn't worth the trouble to look at him. The only way to keep the interest up was to see how close I could come without damage. Well, I ran right into it, head on. God, does it serve me right. I'd read books Ben was reading, follow his interests, instead of boning over law. But I wanted the degree. Hot damn, I wanted it!"

"Another school," I said. "You can transfer credits and start over."

"This won't go away."

"Everybody loves you," I faltered, adding, "Especially me."

He almost laughed, at my youngness, I guess, but then said, "Ella Mason," as gently as feathers falling, and came to hold me awhile, but not like before, the way we'd been. We sat down on the bed and then fell back on it and I could hear his heart's steady thumping under his shirt. But it wasn't the beat of a lover's heart just then; it was more like the echo of a distant bell or the near march of a clock; and I fell to looking over his shoulder.

It was a curious room, one I guess they wouldn't have rented to anybody if Rome hadn't been, as they told us, so full. The shutters outside were closed on something that suggested more of a courtyard than the outside, as no streak or glimmer of light came through, and the bed was huge, with a great dark tall rectangle of a headboard and a footboard only slightly lower. There were brass sconces set ornamentally around the moldings, looking down, cupids and fauns and smiling goat faces, with bulbs concealed in them, though the only light came from the one dim lamp on the bedside table. There were heavy, dark engravings of Rome—by Piranesi or somebody like that—the avenues, the monuments, the river. And one panel of small pictures in a series showed some familiar scenes in Florence.

My thoughts, unable to reach Eric's, kept wandering off tourist-fashion among the myth faces peeking from the sconces, laughing down, among the walks of Rome—the arched bridge over the Tiber where life-size angels stood poised; the rise of the Palatine, mysterious among trees; the horseman on the Campidoglio, his hand outstretched; and Florence, beckoning still. I couldn't keep my mind at any one set with all such around me, and Eric, besides, had gone back to the table and was writing a letter on hotel stationery. When my caught breath turned to a little cry, he looked up and said, "It's my problem, Ella Mason. Just let me handle it." He came to stand by me, and pressed my head against him, then lifted my face by the chin. "Don't go talking about it. Promise." I promised.

I wandered back through the labyrinth, thinking I'd be lost in there forever like a Poe lady. Damn Ben, I thought, he's too above it all for anybody to fall in love or fail an examination. I'm better off lost, at this rate. So thinking, I turned a corner and stepped out into the hotel lobby.

It was Jamie's and Ben's assumption that Eric had picked up some girl and gone home with her. I never told them better. Let them think that.

"Your Mama wrote you a letter about some chickens once, how she counted children like counting chickens," Eric said, thirty years later. "Do you remember that?"

We fell to remembering Mama. "There's nobody like her," I said. "She has long talks with Papa. They started a year or so after he died. I wish I could talk to him."

"What would you say?"

"I'd ask him to look up Howard. See'f he's doing all right."

"Your husband?" Eric wasn't that sure of the name.

I guess joking about your husband's death isn't quite the thing. I met Howard on a trip to Texas after we got home from abroad. I was visiting my roommate. Whatever else Eric did for me, our time together had made me ready for more. I pined for him alone, but what I looked was ripe and ready for practically anybody. So Howard said. He was a widower with a Texas-size fortune. When he said I looked like a good breeder, I didn't even get mad. That's how he knew I'd do. Still, it took awhile. I kept wanting Eric, wanting my old dream: my brilliant cousins, princely, cavalier.

Howard and I had two sons, in their twenties now. Howard got killed in a jeep accident out on his cattle ranch. Don't think I didn't get married again, to a wild California boy ten years younger. It lasted six months exactly.

"What about that other one?" Eric asked me. "Number two."

I had gotten the divorce papers the same day they called to say Howard's tombstone had arrived. "Well, you know, Eric, I always was a little bit crazy."

"You thought he was cute."

"I guess so."

"You and I," said Eric, smooth as silk into the deep, silent darkness that now was ours—even the towers seemed to have folded up and gone home—"we never worked it out, did we?"

"I never knew if you really wanted to. I did, God knows. I wouldn't marry Howard for over a year because of you."

"I stayed undecided about everything. One thing that's not is a marrying frame of mind."

"Then you left for Europe."

"I felt I'd missed the boat for everywhere else. War service, then that law school thing. It was too late for me. And nothing was of interest. I could move but not with much conviction. I felt for you—maybe more than you know—but you were moving on already. You know, Ella Mason, you never are still."

"But you could have told me that!"

"I think I did, one way or another. You sat still and fidgeted." He laughed.

It's true that energy is my middle name.

The lights along the river were dim and so little was moving past by now they seemed fixed and distant, stars from some long-dead galaxy maybe. I think I slept. Then I heard Eric.

"I think back so often to the five of us—you and Ben, Jamie and Mayfred and me. There was something I could never get out of my mind. You remember when we were planning everything about Europe Europe Europe, before we left, and you'd all come over to my house and we'd sit out on the side porch, listening to Ben mainly but with Jamie asking some questions, like 'Do they have bathtubs like us?' Remember that? You would snuggle down in one of those canvas chairs like a sling, and Ben was in the big armchair—Daddy's—and Jamie sort of sprawled around on the couch among the travel folders, when we heard the front gate scrape on the sidewalk and heard the way it would clatter when it closed. A warm night and the streetlight filtering in patterns through the trees and shrubs and a smell of honeysuckle from where it was all baled up on the yard fence, and a Cape jessamine outside. I remember that, too—white flowers in among the leaves. And steps on the walk. They stopped, then they walked again, and Ben got up (I should have) and unlatched the screen. If you didn't latch the screen it wouldn't shut. Mayfred came in. Jamie said, 'Why'd you stop on the walk, Mayfred?' She said, 'There was this toad-frog. I almost stepped on him.' Then she was among us, walking in, one of us. I was sitting back in the corner, watching, and I felt, If I live to be a thousand, I'll never feel more love than I do this minute. Love of these, my blood, and this place, here. I could close my eyes for years and hear the gate scrape, the steps pause, the door latch and unlatch, hear her say, 'There was this toad-frog . . .' I would want literally to embrace that one minute, hold it forever."

"But you're not there," I said, into the dark. "You're here. Where we were. You chose it."

"There's no denying that" was all he answered.

We had sailed from Naples, a sad day under mist, with Vesuvius hardly visible and damp clinging to everything—the end of summer. We couldn't even make out the outlines of the ship, an Italian Line monster from those days called the *Independence*. It towered white over us and we tunneled in. The crossing was rainy and drab. Crossed emotions played amongst us, while Ben, noble and aware, tried to be our mast. He read aloud to us, discussed, joked, tried to get our attention.

Jamie wanted to argue about Catholicism. It didn't suit Ben for him to drift that way. Ben was headed toward Anglican belief: that's what his Sylvia was, not to mention T. S. Eliot. But in Rome Jamie had met an American Jesuit from Indiana and chummed around with him; they'd even gone to the beach. "You're wrong about that," I heard him tell Ben. "I'm going to prove it by Father Rogers when we get home."

I worried about Eric; I longed for Eric; I strolled the decks and stood by Eric at the rail. He looked with gray eyes out at a gray sea. He said: "You know, Ella Mason, I don't give a damn if Jamie joins the Catholic Church or not." "Me either," I agreed. We kissed in the dark beneath the lifeboats, and made love once in the cabin while Ben and Jamie were at the movies, but in a furtive way, as if the grown people were at church. Ben read aloud to us from a book on Hadrian's Villa, where we'd all been. There was a half day of sun.

I went to the pool to swim, and up came Jamie, out of the water. He was skinny, string beans and spaghetti. "Ella Mason," he said, in his dark croak of a voice, "I'll never be the same again." I was tired of all of them, even Jamie. "Then gain some weight," I snapped, and went pretty off the diving board.

Ben knew about the law school thing. The first day out, coming from the writing lounge, I saw Eric and Ben standing together in a corner of an enclosed deck. Ben had a letter in his hand, and just from one glance I recognized the stationery of the hotel where we'd stayed in Rome and knew it was the letter Eric had been writing. I heard Ben: "You say it's not important, but I know it is—I knew that last Christmas." And Eric, "Think what you like, it's not to me." And Ben, "What you feel about it, that's not what matters. There's a right way of looking at it. Only to make you see it." And Eric, "You'd better give up; you never will."

What kept me in my tracks was something multiple, yet single, the way a number can contain powers and elements that have gone into its making, and can be unfolded, opened up, nearly forever. Ambition and why some had it, success and failure and what the difference was, and why you had to notice it at all. These matters, back and forth across the net, were what was going on.

What had stopped me in the first place, though, and chilled me, was that they sounded angry. I knew they had quarreled last Christmas; was this why? It must have been. Ben's anger was attack, and Eric's self-defense, defiance. Hadn't they always been like brothers? Yes, and they were standing so, intent, a little apart, in hot debate, like two officers locked in different plans of attack at dawn, stubbornly held to the point of fury. Ben's position, based on rightness, classical and firm. Enforced by what he was. And Eric's wrong, except in and for himself, for holding on to himself. How to defend that? He couldn't, but he did. And equally. They were just looking up and seeing me, and nervous at my intrusion I stepped across the high shipboard sill to the deck, missed clearing it and fell sprawling. "Oh, Ella Mason!" they cried at once and picked me up, the way they always had.

One more thing I remember from that ship. It was Ben, finding me one night after dinner alone in the lounge. Everyone was below: we were docking in the morning. He sat down and lighted his pipe. "It's all passed so fast, don't you think?" he said. There was such a jumble in my mind still, I didn't answer. All I could hear was Eric saying, after we'd made love: "It's got to stop now; I've got to find some shape to things. There was promise, promises. You've got to see we're saying they're worthless, that nothing matters." What did matter to me, except Eric? "I wish I'd never come," I burst out at Ben, childish, hurting him, I guess. How much did Ben know? He never said. He came close and put his arm around me. "You're the sister I never had," he said. "I hope you change your mind about it." I said I was sorry and snuffled awhile, into his shoulder. When I looked up, I saw his love. So maybe he did know, and forgave us. He kissed my forehead.

At the New York pier, who should show up but Mayfred.

She was crisp in black and white, her long blond hair wind-shaken, her laughter a wholesome joy. "Y'all look just terrible," she told us with a friendly giggle, and as usual made us straighten up, tuck our tummies in, and look like quality. Jamie forgot religion, and Eric quit worrying over a missing bag, and Ben said, "Well, look who's here!" "How's Donald?" I asked her. I figured he was either all right or dead. The first was true. They didn't have to do a brain tumor operation; all he'd had was a pinched nerve at the base of his cortex. "What's a cortex?" Jamie asked. "It sounds too personal to inquire," said Eric, and right then they brought him his bag.

On the train home, Mayfred rode backward in our large drawing-room compartment (courtesy of Donald Bailey) and the landscape, getting more Southern every minute, went rocketing past. "You can't guess how I spent my time when Donald was in the hospital. Nothing to do but sit."

"Working crossword puzzles," said Jamie.

"Crocheting," said Eric, provoking a laugh.

"Reading *Vogue*," said Ben.

"All wrong! I read Edgar Allan Poe! What's more, I memorized that poem! That one Ben wrote on. You know? That 'Ulalume'!"

Everybody laughed but Ben, and Mayfred was laughing, too, her grand girlish sputters, innocent as sun and water, her beautiful large white teeth, even as a cover girl's. Ben, courteously at the end of the sofa, smiled faintly. It was best not to believe this was true.

> "'The skies they were ashen and sober;
>   The leaves they were crispéd and sere—
>   The leaves they were withering and sere;
>   It was the night in the lonesome October
>   Of my most immemorial year . . .'"

"By God, she's done it," said Ben.

At that point Jamie and I began to laugh, and Eric, who had at first looked quizzical, started laughing, too. Ben said, "Oh, cut it out, Mayfred," but she said, "No, sir, I'm not! I *did* all that. I know *every* word! Just wait, I'll show you." She went right on, full speed, to the "ghoul-haunted woodland of Weir."

Back as straight as a ramrod, Ben left the compartment. Mayfred stopped. An hour later, when he came back, she started again. But it wasn't till she got to Psyche "uplifting her finger" (Mayfred lifted hers), saying, "Oh, fly!—let us fly!—for we must," and all that about the "tremulous light," the "crystalline light," etc., that Ben gave up and joined in the general merriment. She actually did know it, every word. He followed along openmouthed through "Astarte" and "Sybillic," and murmured, "Oh, my God," when she got to

> ". . . 'Ulalume—Ulalume—
> 'Tis the vault of thy lost Ulalume!'"

because she let go in a wail like a hound's bugle and the conductor, who was passing, looked in to see if we were all right.

We rolled into Chattanooga in the best of humor and filed off the train into the waiting arms of my parents, Eric's parents, and selected members from Ben's and Jamie's families. There was nobody from Mayfred's but they'd sent word. They all kept checking us over, as though we might need washing, or might have gotten scarred some way. "Just promise me one thing!" Mama kept saying, just about to cry. "Don't y'all ever go away again, you hear? Not all of you! Just promise you won't do it! Promise me right now!"

I guess we must have promised, the way she was begging us to.

Ben married his Sylvia, with her pedigree and family estate in Connecticut. He's a big professor, lecturing in literature, up East. Jamie married a Catholic girl from West Virginia. He works in her father's firm and has sired a happy lot of kids. Mayfred went to New York after she left Donald and works for a big fashion house. She's been in and out of marriages, from time to time.

And Eric and I are sitting holding hands on a terrace in far-off Italy. Midnight struck long ago, and we know it. We are sitting there, talking, in the pitch black dark.

Jack of Diamonds

ONE APRIL AFTERNOON, Central Park, right across the street, turned green all at once. It was a green toned with gold and seemed less a color of leaves than a stained cloud settled down to stay. Rosalind brought her bird book out on the terrace and turned her face up to seek out something besides pigeons. She arched, to hang her long hair backward over the terrace railing, soaking in sunlight while the starlings whirled by.

The phone rang, and she went inside.

"I just knew you'd be there, Rosie," her father said. "What a gorgeous day. Going to get hotter. You know what I'm thinking about? Lake George."

"Let's go right now," Rosalind said.

The cottage was at Bolton Landing. Its balconies were built out over the water. You walked down steps and right off into the lake, or into the boat. In a lofty beamed living room, shadows of water played against the walls and ceiling. There was fine lake air, and chill pure evenings . . .

The intercom sounded. "Gristede's, Daddy. They're buzzing."

Was it being in the theater that made her father, whenever another call came, exert himself to get more into the first? "Let's think about getting up there, Rosie. Summer's too short as it is. You ask Eva when she comes in. Warm her up to it. We'll make our pitch this evening. She's never even seen it . . . can you beat that?"

"I'm not sure she'll even like it," Rosalind said.

"Won't like it? It's hardly camping out. Of course she'll love it. Get it going, Rosie baby. I'm aiming for home by seven."

The grocer's son who brought the order up wore jeans just like Rosalind's. "It's getting hot," he remarked. "It's about melted my ass off."

"Let's see if you brought everything." She had tried to give up presiding over the food after her father remarried, but when her stepmother turned out not to care much about what

happened in the kitchen, she had cautiously gone back to seeing about things.

"If I forgot, I'll get it. But if you think of something—"

"I know, I'll come myself. You think you got news?"

They were old friends. They sassed each other. His name was
Luis—Puerto Rican.

It was after the door to the service entrance closed with its
hollow echo, and was bolted, and the service elevator had risen,
opened, and closed on Luis, that Rosalind felt the changed
quality in things, a new direction, like the tilt of an airliner's
wing. She went to the terrace and found the park's greenness
surer of itself than ever. She picked up her book and went inside. A boy at school, seeing her draw birds, had given it to her.
She stored it with her special treasures.

Closing the drawer, she jerked her head straight, encounter-
ing her own wide blue gaze in her bedroom mirror. From the
entrance hall, a door was closing. She gathered up a pack of
cards spread out for solitaire and slid them into a gilded box.
She whacked at her long brown hair with a brush; then she
went out. It was Eva.

Rosalind Jennings's stepmother had short, raven-black glossy
hair, a full red mouth, jetty brows and lashes. Shortsighted, she
handled the problem in the most open way, by wearing great
round glasses trimmed in tortoiseshell. All through the winter
—a winter Rosalind would always remember as The Stepmother: Year I—Eva had gone around the apartment in gold
wedge-heeled slippers, pink slacks, and a black chiffon blouse.
Noiseless on the wall-to-wall carpets, the slippers slapped
faintly against stockings or flesh when she walked—spaced,
intimate ticks of sound. "Let's face it, Rosie," her father said,
when Eva went off to the kitchen for a fresh drink as he tossed
in his blackjack hand. "She's a sexy dame."

Sexy or not, she was kind to Rosalind. "I wouldn't have married anybody you didn't like," her father told her. "That child's
got *the* most heavenly eyes," she'd overheard Eva say.

Arriving now, having triple-locked the apartment door, Eva
set the inevitable Saks parcels down on the foyer table and
dumped her jersey jacket off her arm onto the chair with a
gasp of relief. "It's turned so hot!" Rosalind followed her to
the kitchen, where she poured orange juice and soda over ice.

Her nails were firm, hard, perfectly painted. They resembled, to Rosalind, ten small creatures who had ranked themselves on this stage of fingertips. Often they ticked off a pile of poker chips from top to bottom, red and white, as Eva pondered. "Stay . . ." or "Call . . ." or "I'm out . . ." then, "Oh, damn you, Nat . . . that's twice in a row."

"I've just been talking on the phone to Daddy," Rosalind said. "I've got to warn you. He's thinking of the cottage."

"Up there in Vermont?"

"It's in New York, on Lake George. Mother got it from her folks. You know, they lived in Albany. The thing is, Daddy's always loved it. He's hoping you will too, I think."

Eva finished her orange juice. Turning to rinse the glass in the sink, she wafted out perfume and perspiration. "It's a little far for a summer place. . . . But if it's what you and Nat like, why, then . . ." She affectionately pushed a dark strand of Rosalind's hair back behind her ear. Her fingers were chilly from the glass. "I'm yours to command." Her smile, intimate and confident, seemed to repeat its red picture on every kitchen object.

Daughter and stepmother had got a lot chummier in the six months since her father had married. At first, Rosalind was always wondering what they thought of her. For here was a new "they," like a whole new being. She had heard, for instance, right after the return from the Nassau honeymoon:

Eva: "I want to be sure and leave her room just the way it is."

Nat: "I think that's right. Change is up to her."

But Rosalind could not stop her angry thought: *You'd just better try touching my room!* Her mother had always chosen her decor, always the rose motif, roses in the wallpaper and deeper rose valances and matching draperies. This was a romantic theme with her parents, accounting for her name. Her father would warble "Sweet Rosie O'Grady" while downing his whiskey. He would waltz his little girl around the room. She'd learned to dance before she could walk, she thought.

"Daddy sets the music together with what's happening on the stage. He gets the dancers and actors to carry out the music. That's different from composing or writing lyrics." So Rosalind would explain to new friends at school, every year. Now she'd go off to some other school next fall, still ready with her lifelong lines. "You must have heard of some of his shows. Remember So-and-So, and then there was . . ." Watching their impressionable faces form their cries. "We've got the records of that!" "Was your mother an actress?" "My stepmother used to be an actress—nobody you'd know about. My mother died. She wasn't ever in the theater. She studied art history at Vassar." Yes, and married the assistant manager of his family firm: Jennings' Finest Woolen Imports; he did not do well. Back to his first love, theater. From college on they thought they'd never get him out of it, and they were right. Some purchase he had chosen in West Germany turned out to be polyester, sixty percent. "I had a will to fail," Nat Jennings would shrug, when he thought about it. "If your heart's not in something, you can't succeed" was her mother's reasoning, clinging to her own sort of knowing, which had to do with the things you picked, felt about, what went where. Now here was another woman with other thoughts about the same thing. She'd better not touch my room, thought Rosalind, or I'll . . . what? Trip her in the hallway, hide her glasses, throw the keys out the window?

"What are you giggling at, Rosie?"

Well might they ask, just back from Nassau at a time of falling leaves. "I'm wondering what to do with this leg of lamb. It's too long and skinny."

"Broil it like a great big chop." Still honeymooning, they'd be holding hands, she bet, on the living-room sofa.

"Just you leave my room alone," she sang out to this new Them. "Or I won't cook for you!"

"Atta girl, Rosie!"

Now, six months later in the balmy early evening with windows wide open, they were saying it again. Daddy had come in, hardly even an hour later than he said, and there was the big conversation, starting with cocktails, lasting through dinner, all about Lake George and how to get there, where to start, but all totally impossible until day after tomorrow at the soonest.

"One of the few unpolluted lakes left!" Daddy enthused to Eva. It was true. If you dropped anything from the boat into the water, your mother would call from the balcony, "It's right down there, darling," and you'd see it as plainly as if it lay in sunlight at your feet and you could reach down for it instead of diving. The caretaker they'd had for years, Mr. Thibodeau, reported to them from time to time. Everything was all right, said Mr. Thibodeau. He had about fifteen houses on his list, for watching over, especially during the long winters. He was good. They'd left the cottage empty for two summers, and it was still all right. She remembered the last time they were there, June three years back. She and Daddy were staying while Mother drove back to New York, planning to see Aunt Mildred from Denver before she put out for the West again. "What a nuisance she can't come here!" Mother had said. "It's going to be sticky as anything in town, and when I think of that Thruway!"

"Say you've got food poisoning," said Daddy. "Make something up."

"But Nat! Can't you understand? I really *do* want to see Mildred!" It was Mother's little cry that still sounded in Rosalind's head. "Whatever you do, please don't go to the apartment," Daddy said. He hadn't washed dishes for a week; he'd be ashamed for an in-law to have an even lower opinion of him, though he thought it wasn't possible. "It's a long drive," her mother pondered. "Take the Taconic, it's cooler." "Should I spend one night or two?"

Her mother was killed on the Taconic Parkway the next day by a man coming out of a crossover. There must have been a moment of terrible disbelief when she saw that he was actually going to cross in front of her. Wasn't he looking, didn't he see? They would never know. He died in the ambulance. She was killed at once.

Rosalind and her father, before they left, had packed all her mother's clothing and personal things, but that was all they'd had the heart for. The rest they walked off and left, just so. "Next summer," they had said, as the weeks wore on and still they'd made no move. The next summer came, and still they did not stir. One day they said, "Next summer." Mr. Thibodeau said not to worry, everything was fine. So the Navaho rugs were safe, and all the pottery, the copper and brass, the racked pewter. The books would all be lined in place on the shelves, the music in the Victorian music rack just as it had been left, Schumann's "Carnaval" (she could see it still) on top. And if everything was really fine, the canoe would be dry, though dusty and full of spiderwebs, suspended out in the boathouse, and the roof must be holding firm and dry, as Mr. Thibodeau would have reported any leak immediately. All that had happened, he said, was that the steps into the water had to have new uprights, the bottom two replaced, and that the eaves on the northeast corner had broken from a falling limb and been repaired.

Mention of the fallen limb recalled the storms. Rosalind remembered them blamming away while she and her mother huddled back of the stairway, feeling aimed at by the thunder-bolts; or if Daddy was there, they'd sing by candlelight while he played the piano. He dared the thunder by imitating it in the lower bass. . . .

"Atta girl, Rosie."

She had just said she wasn't afraid to go up there alone to-morrow, take the bus or train, and consult with Mr. Thibo-deau. The Thibodeaus had long ago taken a fancy to Rosalind; a French Canadian, Mrs. Thibodeau had taught her some French songs, and fed her on *tourtière* and beans.

"That would be wonderful," said Eva.

"I just can't let her do it," Nat said.

"I can stay at Howard Johnson's. After all, I'm seventeen."

While she begged, her father looked at her steadily from the end of the table, finishing coffee. "I'll telephone the Thi-bodeaus," he finally said. "One thing you aren't to do is stay in the house alone. Howard Johnson's is okay. We'll get you a room there." Then, because he knew what the house had meant and wanted to let her know it, he took her shoulder (Eva not being present) and squeezed it, his eyes looking deep into hers, and Irish tears rising moistly. "Life goes on, Rosie," he whispered. "It has to."

She remembered all that, riding the bus. But it was for some unspoken reason that he had wanted her to go. And she knew that it was right for her to do it, not only to see about things. It was an important journey. For both of them? Yes, for them both.

Mr. Thibodeau himself met her bus, driving up to Lake George Village.

"Not many people yet," he said. "We had a good many on the weekend, out to enjoy the sun. Starting a baseball team up here. The piers took a beating back in the winter. Not enough ice and too much wind. How's your daddy?"

"He's fine. He wants to come back here now."

"You like your new mother? Shouldn't ask. Just curious."

"She's nice," said Rosalind.

"Hard to be a match for the first one."

Rosalind did not answer. She had a quietly aware way of closing her mouth when she did not care to reply.

"Pretty?" pursued Mr. Thibodeau. Not only the caretaker, Mr. Thibodeau was also a neighbor. He lived between the property and the road. You had to be nice to the Thibodeaus; so much depended on them.

"Yes, she's awfully pretty. She was an actress. She had just a little part in the cast of the show he worked with last year."

"That's how they met, was it?"

To Rosalind, it seemed that Eva had just showed up one evening in her father's conversation at dinner. "There's somebody I want you to meet, Rosie. She's—well, she's a she. I've seen her once or twice. I think you'll like her. But if you don't, we'll scratch her, Rosie. That's a promise."

"Here's a list, Mr. Thibodeau," she said. "All the things Daddy wants done are on it. Telephone, plumbing, electricity . . . maybe Mrs. Thibodeau can come in and clean. I've got to check the linens for mildew. Then go through the canned stuff and make a grocery list."

"We got a new supermarket since you stopped coming, know that?"

"I bet."

"We'll go tomorrow. I'll take you."

The wood-lined road had been broken into over and over on the lake side, the other side, too, by new motels. Signs about pools, TV, vacancy came rudely up and at them, until, swinging left, they entered woods again and drew near the cutoff to the narrow, winding drive among the pines. "Thibodeau" the mailbox read in strong, irregular letters, and by its side a piece of weathered plywood nailed to the fence post said "Jennings," painted freshly over the ghost of old lettering beneath.

She bounced along with Mr. Thibodeau, who, his black hair grayed over, still had his same beaked nose, which in her mind gave him his Frenchness and his foreignness. Branches slapped the car window. The tires squished through ruts felted with fallout from the woods. They reached the final bend. "Stop," said Rosalind, for something white that gave out a sound like dry bones breaking had passed beneath the wheels. She jumped out. It was only birch branches, half rotted. "I'll go alone." She ran ahead of his station wagon, over pine needles and through the fallen leaves of two autumns, which slowed her motion until she felt the way she did in dreams.

The cottage was made of natural wood, no shiny lacquer covering it; boughs around it, pine and oak, pressed down like protective arms. The reach of the walls was laced over with undergrowth, so that the house at first glance looked small as a hut, not much wider than the door. Running there, Rosalind tried the knob with the confidence of a child running to her mother, only to find it locked, naturally; then with a child's abandon, she flung out her arms against the paneling, hearing her heart thump on the wood until Mr. Thibodeau gently detached her little by little as though she had got stuck there.

"Now there . . . now there . . . just let me get hold of this key." He had a huge wire ring for his keys, labels attached to each. His clientele. "*Des clients, vous en avez beaucoup,*" Rosalind had once said to him as she was starting French in school. But Mr. Thibodeau was unregretfully far from his Quebec origins. His family had come there from northern Vermont to get a milder climate. Lake George was a sun trap, a village sliding off the Adirondacks toward the lake, facing a daylong exposure.

The key ground in the lock. Mr. Thibodeau kicked the base of the door, and the hinges whined. He let her enter alone, going tactfully back to his station wagon for nothing at all. He gave her time to wander before he followed her.

She would have had to come someday, Rosalind thought, one foot following the other, moving forward: the someday was this one. It wasn't as if anything had actually "happened" there. The door frame that opened from the entrance hall into the living room did not face the front door but was about ten feet from it to the left. Thus the full scope of the high, shadowy room, which was the real heart of the cottage, opened all at once to the person entering. Suddenly, there was an interior world. The broad windows opposite, peaked in an irregular triangle at the top, like something in a modernistic church, opened onto the lake, and from the water a rippling light, muted by shade, played constantly on the high-beamed ceiling. Two large handwoven Indian rugs covered the central area of floor; on a table before the windows, a huge pot of brown-and-beige pottery was displayed, filled with money plant that had grown dusty and ragged. There were coarse-fibered curtains in off-white monk's cloth, now dragging askew, chair coverings in heavy fabric, orange-and-white cushions, and the piano, probably so out of tune now with the damp it would never sound right, which sat closed and silent in the corner. An open stairway, more like a ladder than a stair, rose to the upper-floor balcony, with bedrooms in the wing. "We're going to fall and break our silly necks someday," she could hear her mother saying. "It's pretty, though." The Indian weaving of the hawk at sunrise, all black and red, hung on the far left wall.

She thought of her mother, a small, quick woman with bronze, close-curling hair cut short, eager to have what she thought of as "just the right thing," wandering distant markets, seeking out things for the cottage. It seemed to Rosalind that when she opened the door past the stairwell into the bedroom that her parents had used, that surely she would find that choosing, active ghost in motion over a chest or moving a curtain at the window, and that surely, ascending the dangerous stair to look into the two bedrooms above, she would hear the quick voice say, "Oh, it's you, Rosalind, now you just tell me . . ." But everything was silent.

Rosalind came downstairs. She returned to the front door and saw that Mr. Thibodeau had driven away. Had he said something about going back for something? She closed the door quietly, reentered the big natural room, and let the things there speak.

For it was all self-contained, knowing and infinitely quiet. The lake gave its perpetual lapping sound, like nibbling fish in shallow water, now and then splashing up, as though a big one had flourished. Lap, lap against the wooden piles that supported the balcony. Lap against the steps, with a swishing motion on the lowest one, a passing-over instead of an against sound. The first steps were replaced, new, the color fresh blond instead of worn brown. The room heard the lapping, the occasional splash, the swish of water.

Rosalind herself was being got through to by something even less predictable than water. What she heard was memory: voices quarreling. From three years ago they woke to life. A slant of light—that had brought them back. Just at this time of day, she had been coming in from swimming. The voices had climbed the large, clear windows, clawing for exit, and finding none, had fled like people getting out of a burning theater, through the door to the far right that opened out onto the balcony. She had been coming up the steps from the water when the voices stampeded over her, frightening, intense, racing outward from the panic within. "You know you do and you know you will . . . there's no use to lie, I've been through all that. Helpless is all I can feel, all I can be. That's the awful part . . . !" "I didn't drive all this way just to get back into that. Go on, get away to New York with dear Aunt Mildred. Who's to know, for that matter, if it's Mildred at all?" "You hide your life like a card in the deck and then have the nerve—! Oh, you're a great magician, aren't you?" "Hush, she's out there . . . hush, now . . . you must realize—" "I do nothing but realize—" "Hush . . . just . . . no . . ." And their known selves returned to them as she came in, dripping, pretending nothing had happened, gradually believing her own pretense.

The way she'd learned to do, all the other times. Sitting forgotten, for the moment, in an armchair too big back in New York, listening while her heart hurt until her mother said, "Darling, go to your room, I'll be there in a minute." Even on vacation, it was sometimes the same thing. And Mother coming in later, as she half slept, half waited, to hold her hand and say, "Just forget it now, tomorrow it won't seem real. We all love each other. Tomorrow you won't even remember." Kissed and tucked in, she trusted. It didn't happen all the time. And the tomorrows were clear and bright. The only trouble was, this time there hadn't been any tomorrow, only the tomorrow of her mother's driving away. Could anybody who sounded like that, saying those things, have a wreck the very next morning and those things have nothing to do with it?

Maybe I got the times mixed up.

("She had just a little part in the cast of the show he worked with last year." "That's how they met, was it?") ("Your mother got the vapors sometimes. The theater scared her." She'd heard her father say that.)

I dreamed it all, she thought, and couldn't be sure this wasn't true, though wondered if she could dream so vividly that she could see the exact print of her wet foot just through the doorway there, beside it the drying splash from the water's runnel down her leg. But it could have been another day.

Why not just ask Daddy?

At the arrival of this simple solution, she let out a long sigh, flung her hands back of her head, and stretched out on the beautiful rug her mother had placed there. Her eyes dimmed; she felt the lashes flutter downward. . . .

A footstep and a voice awakened her from how short a sleep she did not know. Rolling over and sitting up, she saw a strange woman—short, heavyset, with faded skin, gray hair chopped off around her face, plain run-down shoes. She was wearing slacks. Then she smiled and things about her changed.

"You don't remember me, do you? I'm Marie Thibodeau. I remember you and your mom and your dad. That was all bad. *Gros dommage.* But you're back now. You'll have a good time again, eh? We thought maybe you didn't have nothing you could eat yet. You come back with me. I going make you some nice lunch. My husband said to come find you."

She rose slowly, walked through shadows toward the woman, who still had something of the quality of an apparition. Did she think that because of her mother, others must have died too? She followed. The lunch was the same as years before: the meat pie, the beans, the catsup and relish and the white bread taken sliced from its paper. And the talk, too, was nearly the same: kind things said before, repeated now; chewed, swallowed.

"You don't remember me, but I remember you. You're *the* Nat Jennings's daughter, used to come here with your folks." This was what the boy said, in Howard Johnson's.

"We're the tennis ones—Dunbar," said the girl, who was

his sister, not his date; for saying "tennis" had made Rosalind remember the big house their family owned— "the villa," her father called it—important grounds around it, and a long frontage on the lake. She remembered them as strutting around, smaller then, holding rackets that looked too large for their bodies. They had been allowed on the court only at certain hours, along with their friends, but even then they had wished to be observed. Now here they were before her, grown up and into denim, like anybody else. Paul and Elaine. They had showed up at the entrance to the motel restaurant, tan and healthy. Paul had acquired a big smile; Elaine a breathless, hesitating voice, the kind Daddy didn't like, it was so intended to tease.

"Let's all find a booth together," Paul Dunbar said.

Rosalind said, "I spent half the afternoon with the telephone man, the other half at the grocery. Getting the cottage opened."

"You can come up to our house after we eat. Not much open here yet. We're on spring holidays."

"They extended it. Outbreak of measles."

"She made that up," said the Dunbar boy, who was speaking straight and honestly to Rosalind. "We told them we had got sick and would be back next week."

"It's because we are so in-tell-i-gent. . . . Making our grades is not a prob-lem," Elaine said in her trick voice.

"We've got the whole house to ourselves. Our folks won't be coming till June. Hey, why don't you move down with us?"

"I can't," said Rosalind. "Daddy's coming up tomorrow. And my stepmother. He got married again."

"Your parents split?"

"No . . . I mean, not how you think. My mother was killed three years ago, driving in New York. She had a wreck."

"Jesus, what a break. I'm sorry, Rosalind."

"You heard about it, Paul. We both did."

"It's still a tough break."

"Mr. Thibodeau's been helping me. Mrs. Thibodeau's cleaning up. They're coming tomorrow." If this day is ever over.

She went with them after dinner. . . .

The Dunbar house could be seen from the road, a large two-story house on the lake, with white wood trim. There were two one-story wings, like smaller copies of the central house, their entrances opening at either side, the right one on a flagstone walk, winding through a sloping lawn, the left on a porte-cochere, where the Dunbars parked. Within, the large rooms were shuttered, the furniture dust-covered. The three of them went to the glassed-in room on the opposite wing and put some records on. They danced on the tiled floor amid the white wicker furniture.

Had they heard a knocking or hadn't they? A strange boy was standing in the doorway, materialized. Elaine had cried, "Oh goodness, Fenwick, you scared me!" She moved back from Paul's controlling rhythm. They were all facing the stranger. He was heavier than Paul; he was tall and grown to the measure of his big hands and feet. He looked serious and easily detachable from the surroundings; it wasn't possible to guess by looking at him where he lived or what he was doing there.

"Fenwick . . ." Paul was saying to him. What sort of name was that? He strode over to the largest chaise longue, and fitted himself into it. Paul introduced Rosalind to Fenwick.

"I have a mile-long problem to solve before Thursday," Fenwick said. "I'm getting cross-eyed. You got a beer?"

"Fenwick is a math-uh-mat-i-cul gene-i-yus," Elaine told Rosalind. The record finished and she switched off the machine.

"Fenwick wishes he was," said Fenwick.

It seemed that they were all at some school together, called Wakeley, over in Vermont. They knew people to talk about together. "I've been up about umpteen hours," Rosalind said. "I came all the way from New York this morning."

"Just let me finish this beer, and I'll take you home," said Fenwick.

"It's just Howard Johnson's," she said.

"There are those that call it home," said Fenwick, downing beer.

They walked together to the highway, where Fenwick had left his little old rickety car. The trees were bursting from the bud, you could practically smell them grow, but the branches were still dark, and cold-looking and wet, because it had rained while they were inside. The damp road seamed beneath the tires. There were not many people around. She hugged herself into her raincoat.

"The minute I saw you I remembered you," Fenwick said. "I just felt like we were friends. You used to go to that little park with all the other kids. Your daddy would put you on the seesaw. He pushed it up and down for you. But I don't guess you'd remember me."

"I guess I ought to," Rosalind said. "Maybe you grew a lot."

"You can sure say that. They thought I wasn't going to stop." The sign ahead said "Howard Johnson's." "I'd do my problem better if we had some coffee."

"Tomorrow maybe," she said. "I'm dead tired." But what she thought was, He likes me.

At the desk she found three messages, all from Daddy and Eva. "Call when you come in." "Call as soon as you can." "Call even if late." She called.

"So it'll be late tomorrow, maybe around dinner. What happened was . . ." He went on and on. With Nat Jennings, you got used to postponements, so her mother always said. "How's it going, Rosie? I've thought about you every minute."

"Everything's ready for you, or it will be when you come."

"Don't cook up a special dinner. We might be late. It's a long road."

In a dream her mother was walking with her. They were in the library at Lake George. In the past her mother had often gone there to check out books. She was waiting for a certain book she wanted, but it hadn't come back yet. "But you did promise me last week," she was saying to somebody at the desk; then she was walking up the street with Rosalind, and Rosalind saw the book in her shopping bag. "You got it after all," she said to her mother. "I just found it lying there on the walk," her mother said, and then Rosalind remembered how she had leaned down to pick up something. "That's nice," said Rosalind, satisfied that things could happen this way. "I think it's nice, too," said her mother, and they went along together.

By noon the next day her work was done, but she felt bad because she had found something—a scarf in one of the dresser drawers. It was a sumptuous French satin scarf in a jagged play of colors, mainly red, a shade her mother, with her coppery hair, had never worn. It smelled of Eva's perfume. So they had been up here before, she thought, but why—this far from New York? And why not say so? Helpless was what her mother said she felt. Can I, thought Rosalind, ask Daddy about this, too?

In the afternoon she drove up into the Adirondacks with Elaine and Paul Dunbar. They took back roads, a minor highway that crossed from the lakeshore road to the Thruway; another beyond that threaded along the bulging sides of the mountains. They passed one lake after another: some small and limpid; others half-choked with water lilies and thickly shaded where frogs by the hundreds were chorusing, invisible amid the fresh lime-green; and some larger still, marked with stumps of trees mysteriously broken off. From one of these, strange birdcalls sounded. Then the road ran upward. Paul pulled up under some tall pines and stopped.

"We're going to climb," he announced.

It suited Rosalind because Elaine had just asked her to tell her "all about the theater, every single thing you know." She wouldn't have to do that, at least. Free of the car, they stood still in deserted air. There was no feel of houses near. The brother and sister started along a path they apparently knew. It led higher, winding through trees, with occasional glimpses of a rotting lake below and promise of some triumphant view above. Rosalind followed next to Paul, with Elaine trailing behind. Under a big oak they stopped to rest.

Through the leaves a small view opened up; there was a little valley below, with a stream running through it. The three of them sat hugging their knees and talking, once their breath came back. "Very big deal," Paul was saying. "Five people sent home, weeping parents outside offices, and everybody tip-toeing past. About what? The whole school smokes pot, everybody knows it. Half the profs were on it. Remember old Borden?"

Elaine's high-pitched laugh. "He said, 'Just going for a joint,' when he pushed into the john one day. Talking back over his shoulder."

"What really rocked the boat was when everybody started cheating. Plain and fancy."

"What made them start?" Rosalind asked. Pot was passed around at her school, too, in the Upper Eighties, but you could get into trouble about it.

"You know Miss Hollander was heard to say out loud one day, 'The dean's a shit.'"

"That's the source of the whole fucking mess," said Paul. "The stoopid dean's a shit."

"Is he a fag?" asked Rosalind, not too sure of language like this.

"Not even that," said Paul, and picked up a rock to throw. He put down his hand to Rosalind. "Come on, we got a little farther to climb."

The path snaked sharply upward. She followed his long legs and brown loafers, one with the stitching breaking at the top, and stopping for breath, she looked back and discovered they were alone. "Where's Elaine?"

"She's lazy." He stopped high above to wait for her. She looked up to him and saw him turn to face her, jeans tight over his narrow thighs and flat waist. He put a large hand down to pull her up, and grinned as she came unexpectedly too fast; being thin and light, she sailed up so close they bumped together. His face skin was glossy with sweat. "Just a little farther," he encouraged her. His front teeth were not quite even. Light exploded from the tips of his ears. Grappling at roots, avoiding sheer surfaces of rock, gaining footholds on patches of earth, they burst finally out on a ledge of rough but fairly flat stone, chiseled away as though in a quarry, overlooking a dizzying sweep of New York countryside. "Oh." Rosalind caught her breath. "How gorgeous! We live high up with a terrace over Central Park," she confided excitedly. "But that's nothing like this!"

Paul put his arm around her. "Don't get too close. You know some people just love heights. They love 'em to death. Just show them one and off they go."

"Not me."

"Come here." He led her a little to the side, placing her—"Not there, here"—at a spot where two carved lines crossed, as though Indians had marked it for something. Then, his arm close around her, he pressed his mouth down on hers. Her long brown hair fell backward over his shoulder. If she struggled, she might pull them both over the edge. "Don't." She broke her mouth away. His free hand was kneading her.

"Why? Why not?" The words burrowed into her ear like objects.

"I hadn't thought of you . . . not for myself."

"Think of me now. Let's just stay here a minute."

But she slipped away and went sliding back down. Arriving in the level space with a torn jacket and a skinned elbow, she found Elaine lying back against a rock, apparently sleeping. A camera with a telescope lens was resting on the canvas shoulder bag she had carried up the hill.

Elaine sat up, opening her eyes. Rosalind stopped, and Paul's heavy stride, overtaking, halted close behind her. She did not want to look at him, and was rubbing at the blood speckled out on her scratched arm where she'd fallen against a limb.

"Paul thinks he's ir-ree-sisty-bul," Elaine said. "Now we know it isn't so."

Looking up, Rosalind could see the lofty ledge where she and Paul had been. Elaine picked up the camera, detached the lens, and fitted both into the canvas bag. "Once I took a whole home movie. That was the time he was screwing the waitress from the pizza place."

"Oh, sure, get funny," said Paul. He had turned an angry red.

In the car, Elaine leaned back to speak to Rosalind. "We're known to be a little bit crazy. Don't you worry, Ros-uh-lind."

Paul said nothing. He drove hunched forward over the wheel.

"Last summer was strictly crazy, start to finish," said Elaine. "Wasn't that true, Paul?"

"It was pretty crazy," said Paul. "Rosalind would have loved it," he added. He was getting mad at her now, she thought.

She asked to hop out at the road to the cottage, instead of going to the motel. She said she wanted to see Mr. Thibodeau.

"Sorry you didn't like the view," said Paul from the wheel. He was laughing now; his mood had changed.

Once they'd vanished, she walked down the main road to the Fenwick mailbox.

From the moment she left the road behind she had to climb again, not as strenuously as up to the mountain ledge, but a slow, winding climb up an ill-tended road. The house that finally broke into view after a sharp turn was bare of paint and run-down. There was a junk car in the wide yard, the parts just about picked off it, one side sitting on planks, and a litter of household odds and ends nearby. A front porch, sagging, was covered with a tangle of what looked to be hunting and camping things. From behind, a dog barked, a warning sound to let her know who was in charge. There was mud in the path to the door.

Through the window of a tacked-on wing to the right, there was Fenwick, sure enough, at a table with peeling paint, in a plain kitchen chair, bending over a large notebook. Textbooks and graph papers were scattered around him. She rapped on the pane and summoned his attention, as though from another planet. He came to the door.

"Oh, it's you, Rose."

"Rosalind."

"I'm working on my problem." He came out and joined her. Maybe he was a genius, Rosalind thought, to have got a fellowship to that school, making better grades than the Dunbars.

"I've been out with Paul and Elaine."

"Don't tell me Paul took you up to that lookout."

She nodded. They sat down on a bench that seemed about to fall in.

"Dunbar's got a collection of pictures—girls he's got to go up there. It's just a dumb gimmick."

"He thinks it's funny," she said, and added, "I left."

"Good. They're on probation, you know. All that about school's being suspended's not true. I'm out for another reason, studying for honors. But—"

A window ran up. A woman's voice came around the side of the house. "Henry, I told you—"

"But I need a break, Mother," he said, without turning his head.

"Is your name Henry?" Rosalind asked.

"So they tell me. Come on, I'll take you back where you're staying."

"I just wanted to see where you lived." He didn't answer. Probably it wasn't the right thing. He walked her down the hill, talking all the way, and put her into his old Volkswagen.

"The Dunbars stick too close together. You'd think they weren't kin. They're like a couple dating. They make up these jokes on people. I was there the other night to help them through some math they failed. But it didn't turn out that way.

Know why? They've got no mind for work. They think some-thing will happen, so they won't have to." He hesitated, silent, as the little car swung in and out of the wooded curves. "I think they make love," he said, very low. It was a kind of gossip. "There's talk at school. . . . Now don't go and tell about it."

"You're warning me," she said.

"That's it. There's people living back in the woods, no different from them. Mr. Thibodeau and Papa—they hunt bear together, way off from here, high up. Last winter I went, too, and there was a blizzard. We shot a bear but it looked too deep a snow to get the carcass out, but we did, after a day or so. We stayed with these folks, brother and sister. Some odd little kids running around.

"If they get thrown out of Wakeley, they can go somewhere else. Their folks have a lot of money. So no problem."

"But I guess anywhere you have to study," said Rosalind.

He had brought her to the motel, and now they got out and walked to a plot where shrubs were budding on the slant of hill above the road. Fenwick had speculative eyes that kept to themselves, and a frown from worry or too many figures, just a small thread between his light eyebrows.

"When I finish my problem, any minute now, I'll go back to school."

"My mother died three years ago, in June," said Rosalind.

"I knew that. It's too bad, Rosalind. I'm sorry."

"Did you know her?" Rosalind experienced an eagerness, expectation, as if she doubted her mother's ever having been known.

"I used to see her with you," said Fenwick. "So I guess I'd know her if I saw her." His hand had appeared on her shoulder. She was at about the right height for that.

"Nobody will ever see her again," she said. He pulled her closer.

"If I come back in the summer, I'd like to see you, Rosalind."

"Me, too," she said.

"I've got some stuff you can read." He was squinting. The sun had come through some pale clouds.

"Things you wrote?" She wondered at him.

"I do a lot of things. I'll have a car." He glanced toward it doubtfully. "It's not much of a car, though."

"It's a fine car," she said, so he could walk off to it, feeling all right, and wave to her.

Rosalind was surprised and obscurely hurt by the message she received at the motel: namely, that her father and stepmother had already arrived and had called by for her. She had some money left over from what her father had given her, and not wanting to call, she took a taxi down to the cottage.

Her hurt sprang from thwarted plans. She had meant to prepare for them, greet them, have dinner half done, develop a festive air. Now they would be greeting her.

In the taxi past Mr. Thibodeau's house, she saw a strange car coming toward them that made them draw far to one side, sink treacherously among loose fallen leaves. A Chevrolet sedan went past; the man within, a stranger, was well dressed and wore a hat. He looked up to nod at the driver and glance keenly within at his passenger.

"Who was that?" Rosalind asked.

"Griffin, I think his name is," the driver said. "Real estate," he added.

There had been a card stuck in the door when she had come, Rosalind recalled, and a printed message: "Thinking of selling? Griffin's the Guy."

Then she was alighting, crying, "Daddy! Eva! It's me!" And they were running out, crying, "There she is! You got the call?" Daddy was tossing her, forgetting she'd grown; he almost banged her head against a beam. "You nearly knocked my three brains out," she laughed. "It's beautiful!" Eva cried, about the cottage. She spread her arms wide as wings and swirled across the rugs in a solo dance. "It's simply charming!"

Daddy opened the piano with a flourish. He began thumping the old keys, some of which had gone dead from the damp. But "Sweet Rosie O'Grady" was unmistakably coming out. They were hugging and making drinks and going out to look at the boat, kneeling down to test the still stone-chill water.

"What good taste your mother had!" Eva told her, smiling. "The apartment . . . now this!" She was kind.

In the late afternoon Rosalind and her father lowered and launched the canoe, and finding that it floated without a leak and sat well in the water, they decided to test it. Daddy had changed his gray slacks and blazer for gabardine trousers and a leather jacket. He wore a denim shirt. Daddy glistened with life, and what he wore was more important than what other people wore. He thought of clothes, evidently, but he never, that she could remember, discussed them. They simply appeared on him, like various furs or fleece that he could shed suddenly and grow just as suddenly new. Above button-down collars or open-throated knit pullovers or turtlenecks or black bow ties, his face, with its slightly ruddy look, even in winter, its cleft chin and radiating crinkles, was like a law of attraction, drawing whatever interested, whatever lived. In worry or grief, he hid it, that face. Then the clothes no longer mattered. Rosalind had sometimes found him in a room alone near a window, still, his face bent down behind one shoulder covered with some old faded shirt, only the top of his head showing and that revealed as startlingly gray, the hair growing thin. But when the face came up, it would seem to resume its livingness as naturally as breath, his hair being the same as ever, barely sprinkled with gray. It was the face for her, his gift.

"Did you see the real estate man?" Rosalind asked over her shoulder, paddling with an out-of-practice wobble.

"Griffin? Oh, yes, he was here. Right on the job, those guys."

They paddled along, a stone's throw from the shore. To their right the lake stretched out wide and sunlit. One or two distant fishing boats dawdled near a small island. The lake, a creamy blue, flashed now and again in air that was still sharp.

"Daddy, did you know Eva a long time?"

There was a silence from behind her. "Not too long." Then he said what he'd said before. "She was a member of the cast. Rosie, we shouldn't have let you go off by yourself. I realized that this morning. I woke up early thinking it, and jumped straight out of bed. By six I'd packed. Who've you been seeing?"

"I ran into the Dunbars, Paul and Elaine, down in the big white house, you know. They're here from school. I have to run from Mrs. Thibodeau. She wants to catch and feed me. And then there's Fenwick."

"Some old guy up the hill who sells junk . . . is that the one?"

"No, his son. He's a mathematical genius, Daddy."

"Beware of mathematical geniuses," her father said, "especially if their fathers sell junk."

"You always told me that," said Rosalind. "I just forgot."

When they came in they were laughing. She and Eva cooked the meals. Daddy played old records, forgoing gin rummy for once. That was the first day.

"Wait! Look now! Look!"

It was Eva speaking while Daddy blindfolded Rosalind. They had built a fire. Somebody had found in a shop uptown the sort of stuff you threw on it to make it sparkle. The room on a gloomy afternoon, though shut up tight against a heavy drizzle, was full of warmth and light. Elaine and Paul Dunbar were there, sitting on the couch. Fenwick was there, choosing to crouch down on a hassock in the corner like an Indian, no matter how many times he was offered a chair. He had been followed in by one of the Fenwick dogs, a huge German shepherd with a bushy, perfectly curling tail lined with white, which he waved at times from side to side like a plume, and when seated, furled about his paws. He smelled like a wet dog owned by a junk dealer.

At the shout of "Look now!" Daddy whipped off the blindfold. The cake had been lighted—eighteen candles—a shining delight. They had cheated a little to have a party for Rosalind; her birthday wasn't till the next week. But the idea was fun. Eva had thought of it because she had found a box full of party things in the unused bedroom: tinsel, sparklers, masks, and a crepe-paper tablecloth with napkins. She had poured rum into some cherry Kool-Aid and floated orange slices across the top. She wore a printed off-the-shoulder blouse with a denim skirt and espadrilles. Her big glasses glanced back fire and candlelight. The young people watched her lighting candles for the table with a long, fancy match held in brightly tipped fingers. Daddy took the blue bandanna blindfold and wound it pirate-fashion around his forehead. He had contrived an eye patch for one eye. "Back in the fifties these things were a status symbol," he said, "but I forget what status they symbolized."

"Two-car garage but no Cadillac," Paul said.

Daddy winked at Elaine. "My daughter's friends get prettier every day."

"So does your daughter," Paul said.

Eva passed them paper plates of birthday cake.

"*She's* getting to the dangerous age, not me. Hell, I was there all the time."

Everyone laughed but Fenwick. He fed small bites of cake to the dog and large ones to himself, while Rosalind refilled his glass.

The friends had brought her presents. A teddy bear dressed in blue jeans from Elaine. A gift-shop canoe in birchbark from Paul. The figure of an old man carved in wood from Fenwick. His father had done it, he said. Rosalind held it up. She set it down. He watched her. He was redeeming his father, whom nobody thought much of. "It's grand," she said, "I love it." Fenwick sat with his hand buried in the dog's thick ruff. His nails, cleaned up for coming there, would get grimy in the dog's coat.

Rosalind's father so far had ignored Fenwick. He was sitting on a stool near Elaine and Paul, talking about theater on campuses, how most campus musicals went dead on Broadway, the rare one might survive, but usually . . . Eva approached the dog, who growled at her. "He won't bite," said Fenwick.

"Is a mathematician liable to know whether or not a dog will bite?" Eva asked.

"Why not?" asked Fenwick.

"You've got quite a reputation to live up to," Eva pursued. She was kneeling near him, close enough to touch, holding her gaze, like her voice, very steady. "I hear you called a genius more often than not."

"You can have a genius rating in something without setting the world on fire," said Fenwick. "A lot of people who've got them are just walking around doing dumb things, the same as anybody."

"I'll have to think that over," Eva said.

There came a heavy pounding at the door, and before anybody could go to it, a man with a grizzled beard, weathered skin, battered clothes, and a rambling walk entered the room. He looked all around until he found Fenwick. "There you are," he said.

Rosalind's father had risen. Nobody said anything. "I'm Nat Jennings." Daddy put out his hand. "This is my wife. What can we do for you?"

"It's my boy," said Fenwick's father, shaking hands. "His mother was looking for him, something she's wanting him for. I thought if he wasn't doing nothing . . ."

"Have a drink," said Nat.

"Just pour it straight out of the bottle," said Fenwick's father, who had taken the measure of the punch.

Fenwick got up. "That's O.K., Mr. Jennings. I'll just go on with Papa."

The dog had moved to acknowledge Mr. Fenwick, who had downed his drink already. Now the boy came to them both, the dog being no longer his. He turned to the rest of the room, which seemed suddenly to be of a different race. "We'll go," he said. He turned again at the living-room entrance. "Thanks."

Rosalind ran after them. She stood in the front door, hidden by the wall of the entrance from those in the room, and leaned out into the rain. "Oh, Mr. Fenwick, I love the carving you did!"

He glanced back. "Off on a bear hunt, deep in the snow. Had to do something."

"Goodbye, Fenwick. Thanks for coming!"

He stopped to answer, but said nothing. For a moment his look was like a voice, crying out to her from across something. For the first time in her life, Rosalind felt the force that pulls stronger than any other. Just to go with him, to be, even invisibly, near. Then the three of them—tall boy, man, and dog, stair-stepped together—were walking away on the rainy path.

When she went inside, she heard Paul Dunbar recalling how Nat Jennings used to organize a fishing derby back in one of the little lakes each summer. He would get the lake stocked, and everybody turned out with casting rods and poles to fish it out. (Rosalind remembered; she had ridden on his shoulder everywhere, till suddenly, one summer, she had got too big for that, and once it had rained.) "And then there were those funny races down in the park—you folks put them on. One year I won a prize!" (Oh, that too, she remembered, her mother running with two giant orange bows like chrysanthemums, held in either hand, orange streamers flying, her coppery hair in the sun.) "You ought to get all that started again."

"It sounds grand, but I guess you'd better learn how your-selves," Eva was saying. "We'll probably not be up here at all."

"Not be here!" Rosalind's cry as she returned from the door was like an alarm. "Not be here!" A silence was suddenly on them.

Her father glanced up, but straightened out smoothly. "Of course we'll be here. We'll have to work on it together."

It had started raining harder. Paul and Elaine, though im-plored to stay, left soon.

When the rain chilled the air, Eva had got out a fringed Spanish shawl, embroidered in bright flowers on a metallic gold background. Her glasses above this, plus one of the silly hats she'd found, made her seem a many-tiered fantasy of a woman, concocted by Picasso, or made to be carried through the streets for some Latin holiday parade.

Light of movement, wearing a knit tie, cuff links on his striped shirt ("In your honor," he said to Rosalind), impec-cable blue blazer above gray slacks, Nat Jennings played the country gentleman with pleasure to himself and everyone. His pretty daughter at her birthday party was his delight. This was what his every move had been saying. And now she had gone to her room. He was knocking on its door. "Rosie?"

"I'm drunk," said Rosalind.

He laughed. "We're going to talk at dinner, Rosie. When you sober up, come down. Did you enjoy your birthday party, baby?"

"Sure I did."

"I like your friends."

"Thank you."

"Too bad about Fenwick's father. That boy deserves better."

"I guess so."

She was holding an envelope Paul had slipped into her hand when he left. It had a photo and its negative enclosed, the one on the high point, the two of them kissing. The note said, "We're leaving tomorrow, sorry if I acted stupid. When we come back, maybe we can try some real ones. Paul."

There won't be any coming back for me, she lay thinking, dazed. But this was your place, Mother. Mother, what do I do now?

He was waiting for her at the bottom of the stairs and treated her with delightful solemnity, as though she were the visiting daughter of an old friend. He showed her to her place and held the chair for her. Eva, now changed into slacks, a silk shirt, and nubby sweater, came in with a steaming casserole. The candles were lighted again.

"I'm not a grand cook, as Rose knows." She smiled. "But you couldn't be allowed, on your birthday . . ."

"She's read a hole in the best cookbook," said Daddy.

"I'm sure it's great," Rosalind said in a little voice, and felt tension pass from one of them to the other.

"I'm in love with Fenwick," Eva announced, and dished out coq au vin.

"Won't get you anywhere," Daddy said. "I see the whole thing: he's gone on Rosie, but she's playing it cool."

"They're all going back tomorrow," Rosalind said. "Elaine and Paul were just on suspension, and Fenwick's finished his problem."

They were silent, passing dishes. Daddy and Eva exchanged glances.

"Rosie," said Daddy, filling everyone's wineglass, "we've been saving our good news till after your party. Now we want you to know. You remember the little off-Broadway musical I worked with last fall? Well, Hollywood is picking it up at quite a hefty sum. It's been in negotiation for two months. Now all's clear, and they're wanting to hire me along with the purchase. Best break I ever had."

"I'm so happy I could walk on air," said Eva.

"Are we going to *move* there!" Rosalind felt numb.

"Of course not, baby. There'll be trips, some periods out there, nothing permanent."

Before Rosalind suddenly, as she glanced from one of them to the other, they grew glossy in an extra charge of flesh and beauty. A log even broke in the fireplace, and a flame reached to some of the sparkler powder that was unignited, so that it flared up as though to hail them. They grew great as faces on a drive-in movie screen, seen floating up out of nowhere along a highway; they might mount skyward any minute and turn to constellations. He had wanted something big to happen, she knew, for a long time. "They never give me any credit" was a phrase she knew by heart. Staying her own human size, Rosalind knew that all they were saying was probably true. They had shoved her birthday up by a week to tidy her away, but they didn't look at it that way, she had to guess.

"Let's drink a toast to Daddy!" she cried, and drained her wineglass.

"Rosalind!" her father scolded happily. "What does anyone do with an alcoholic child?"

"Straight to AA," Eva filled in, "the minute we return."

"Maybe there's a branch in Lake George," Daddy worried.

"I'll cause spectacles at the Plaza," Rosalind giggled through the dizziness of wine. "I'll dance on the bar and jump in the fountain. You'll be so famous it'll make the *Daily News*."

"I've even got some dessert," said Eva, who, now the news was out, had the air of someone who intends to wait on people as seldom as possible. The cottage looked plainer and humbler all the time. How could they stand it for a single other night? Rosalind wondered. They would probably just explode out of there by some chemical process of rejection that not even Fenwick could explain.

"If things work out," Daddy was saying, "we may get to make Palm Beach winters yet. No use to plan ahead."

"Would you like that?" Rosalind asked Eva, as if she didn't know.

"Why, I just tag along with the family," Eva said. "Your rules are mine."

That night Rosalind slipped out of her upstairs room. In order to avoid the Thibodeaus, whose house had eyes and ears, she skirted through the woods and ran into part of the lake, which appeared unexpectedly before her, like a person. She bogged in spongy loam and slipped on mossy rocks, and shivered, drenched to the knees, in the chill night shade of early foliage. At last she came out of shadow onto a road, but not before some large shape, high up, had startled her, blundering among the branches. A car went past and in the glancing headlights she saw the mailbox and its lettering and turned to climb the steep road up to the Fenwicks'. What did she expect to happen there? Just whom did she expect to find? Fenwick himself, of course, but in what way? To lead her out of here, take her somewhere, take her off for good? Say she could stay on with him, and they'd get the cottage someday and share it forever? That would be her dream, even if Fenwick's daddy camped on them and smelled up the place with whiskey.

She climbed with a sense of the enveloping stillness of the woods, the breath of the lake, the distant appeal of the mountains. The road made its final turn to the right, just before the yard. But at that point she was surprised to hear, as if growing out of the wood itself, murmurous voices, not one or two, but apparently by the dozen, and the sound of a throbbing guitar string, interposing from one pause to the next. She inched a little closer and stopped in the last of the black shade. A fire was burning in a wire grating near the steps. Tatters of flame leaped up, making the shadows blacker. High overhead, the moon shone. Fenwick, too, was entitled to a last night at home, having finished some work nobody else could have understood. He would return that summer. He was sitting on the edge of the porch, near a post. Some others were on the steps, or on chairs outside, or even on the ground.

They were humming some tune she didn't know and she heard a voice rise, Mrs. Thibodeau's beyond a doubt! "Now I never said I knew that from a firsthand look, but I'd have to suppose as much." Then Mr. Thibodeau was joining in: "Seen her myself . . . more than a time or two." The Thibodeaus were everywhere, with opinions to express, but about what and whom? All went foundering in an indistinct mumble of phrases until a laugh rose and then another stroke across the strings asked them to sing together, a song she'd never heard. "Now that's enough," a woman's voice said. "I ain't pitching no more tunes." "I've sung all night, many's the time." "Just you and your jug."

From near the steps a shape rose suddenly; it was one of the dogs, barking on the instant of rising—there had been a shift of wind. He trotted toward her. She stood still. Now the snuffling muzzle ranged over her. The great tail moved its slow white fan. It was the one she knew. She patted the intelligent head. Someone whistled. It was Fenwick, who, she could see, had risen from his seat.

Something fell past him, out of the thick-bunched human shapes on the porch. It had been pushed or shoved and was yelling, a child. "Stealing cake again," some voice said, and the body hit the ground with a thump. The mother in the chair, not so much as turning, said, "Going to break ever' bone in her one o' these days." "Serve her right" came from the background—Mr. Fenwick. It was young Fenwick himself who finally went down to pick her up (by the back of her shirt, like a puppy), Mrs. Thibodeau who came to dust her off. The yelling stopped. "Hush now," said Mrs. Thibodeau. Rosalind turned and went away.

"Who's there?" Fenwick was calling toward the road. "Nobody," a man's voice, older, said. "Wants his girlfriend," said the father. "Go and git her, fella."

The mountain went on talking. Words faded to murmurs, losing outline; as she stumbled down turns of road, they lost even echoes. She was alone where she had not meant to be, but for all that, strangely detached, elated.

Back on the paved road, she padded along in sneakers. Moonlight lay bright in patterns through the trees. Finally the Dunbar house rose up, moonlight brightening one white portico, while the other stood almost eclipsed in darkness. In a lighted interior, through a downstairs window, she could see them, one standing, the other looking up, graceful hands making gestures, mouths moving—together and alone. Great white moths circling one another, planning, loving maybe. She thought they were like the photographs they took. The negative is me, she thought.

Far up the road, so far it tired her almost as much to think of it as to walk it, the old resort hotel looked out on Lake George with hundreds of empty windows, eyes with vision gone, the porticoes reaching wide their outspread arms. Water lapped with none to hear. "No Trespassing," said the sign, and other signs said "For Sale," like children calling to one another.

Rosalind looked up. Between her and the road, across the lawn, a brown bear was just standing up. He was turning his head this way and that. The head was small, wedge-shaped. The bear's pelt moved when he did, like grass in a breeze. Pointing her way, the head stopped still. She felt the gaze thrill through her with long foreverness, then drop away. On all fours, he looked small, and moved toward the lake with feet shuffling close together, rather like a rolling ball, loose and tumbling toward the water. The moon sent a shimmering golden path across the lake. She was just remembering that her mother, up here alone with her, claimed to have seen a bear late at night, looking through the window. Daddy didn't doubt she'd dreamed it. He didn't think they came so close. Rosalind knew herself as twice seen and twice known now, by dog and bear. She walked the road home.

Voices sounding in her head, Rosalind twisted and turned that night, sleepless. She got up once, and taking the red scarf she had found from the drawer, she put it down on the living-room table near the large vase of money plant. Then she went back up and slept, what night was left of it.

Daddy came in for Eva's coffee and then they both appeared, he freshly shaved and she perfect in her smooth makeup, a smartly striped caftan flowing to her ankles. Rosalind had crept down in wrinkled pajamas, her bare feet warping back from the chill floor.

"Today's for leaving," her father said. When Rosalind dropped her gaze, he observed her. They were standing in the kitchen before the stove. They were alone. He was neat, fit, in slacks, a beige shirt checked in brown and blue, and a foulard —affected for anyone but him. His amber eyes fixed on her blue ones, offered pools of sincerity for her to plunge into.

"What's this?" Eva asked. She came in with the scarf.

"I found it," said Rosalind. "Isn't it yours?"

Eva looked over her head at Nat. "It must have been your mother's."

"No," said Rosalind. "It wasn't."

After breakfast, by common consent, Rosalind and her father rose from the table and went down to the boat. Together they paddled out to the island. They had done this often in the past. The island was inviting, slanted like a turtle's back, rich with clumps of birch and bushes, trimmed with gray rock. Out

there today, their words emerged suddenly, like thoughts being printed on the air.

"We aren't coming back," said Rosalind. "This is all."

"I saw you come in last night."

A bird flew up out of the trees.

"Did you tell Eva?"

"She was asleep. Why?"

"She'll think I just sneaked off to see Fenwick. But I didn't.
I went off myself . . . by myself."

He played with rocks, seated, forearms resting on his knees,
looking at the lake. "I won't tell."

"I wanted to find Mother."

"Did you?"

"In a way . . . I know she's here, all around here. Don't
you?"

"I think she might be most everywhere."

Maybe what he was saying was something about himself.
The ground was being shifted; they were debating without saying so, and he was changing things around without saying so.

"I let you come up here alone," he went on, "because I
thought you needed it—your time alone. Maybe I was wrong."

"If you'd just say you see it too."

"See what?"

"What I was saying. That she's here. No other places. Here."

The way he didn't answer her was so much a silence she
could hear the leaves stir. "You didn't love her." The words
fell from her, by themselves, you'd have to think, because she
hadn't willed them to. They came out because they were there.

"Fool! Of course I did!"

Long after, she realized he had shouted, screamed almost.
She didn't know it at the moment, because her eyes had
blurred with what she'd accused him of, and her hearing, too,
had gone with her sight. She was barely clinging to the world.

When her vision cleared, she looked for him and saw that
he was lying down on gray rock with his eyes closed, facing
upward, exactly as though exhausted from a task. Like the reverse picture on a face card, he looked to be duplicating an
opposite image of his straight-up self; only the marked cleft
in his chin was more visible at that angle, and she recalled her

mother's holding up a card when they were playing double solitaire once while waiting for him for dinner: "Looks like Daddy. . . ." "Let me see . . . sure does. . . ." She had seen the florid printed face often enough, the smile affable, the chin cleft. "Jack of Diamonds," her mother said. For hadn't the two of them also seen the father's face turn fixed and mysterious as the painted image, unchanging from whatever it had changed to? The same twice over: she hadn't thought that till now. He reached up and took her hand. The gesture seemed to say they had blundered into the fire once, but maybe never again.

The scent of pine, the essence of oak scent, too, came warm to her senses, assertive as animals. She rubbed with her free hand at the small debris that hugged the rock. In former times she had peeled away hunks of moss for bringing back. The rock was old enough to be dead, but in school they said that rocks lived.

"You're going to sell it, aren't you? The cottage, I mean."

"I have to. I need the money."

"I thought you were getting money, lots."

"I'm getting some. But not enough."

So he had laid an ace out before her. There was nothing to say. The returned silence, known to trees, rocks, and water, went agelessly on.

Nat Jennings sat up lightly, in one motion. "What mysteries attend my Rosalind, wandering through her forest of Arden?"

"I was chased by a bear," said Rosalind, attempting to joke with him, but remembering she had almost cried just now, she blew her nose on a torn Kleenex.

"Sleeping in his bed, were you? Serves you right."

He scratched his back where something bit. "I damned near fell asleep." He got to his feet. "It's time." It's what he'd said when they left that other time, three years ago. He put out his hand.

Pulling her up, he slipped on a mossy patch of rock and nearly fell. But dancing was in his bones; if he hadn't been good at it, they both would have fallen. As it was they clung and held upright.

Rosalind and her father got into the boat and paddled toward the cottage, keeping perfect time. Eva, not visible, was busy inside. They found her in the living room.

She had the red scarf wound about her head gypsy-fashion. Above her large glasses, it looked comical, but right; sexy and friendly, the way she was always being. She had cleared up everything from breakfast and was packing.

"You two looked like a picture coming in. I should have had a camera."

"Oh, we're a photogenic pair," Nat said.

"Were you ever tempted to study theater?" Eva asked her.

"I was, but— Not now. Oh, no, not now!" She stood apart, single, separate, ready to leave.

Startled by her tone, Nat Jennings turned. "I think it was her mother," he quickly said. "She didn't like the idea."

The Business Venture

W E WERE down at the river that night. Pete Owens was there with his young wife, Hope (his name for her was Jezzie, after Jezebel in the Bible), and Charlie and me, and both the Houston boys, one with his wife and the other with the latest in a string of new girlfriends. But Nelle Townshend, his steady girl, wasn't there.

We talked and watched the water flow. It was different from those nights we used to go up to the club and dance, because we were older and hadn't bothered to dress, just wore slacks and shorts. It was a clear night but no moon.

Even five years married to him, I was in love with Charlie more than ever, and took his hand to rub the reddish hairs around his wrist. I held his hand under water and watched the flow around it, and later when the others went up to the highway for more whiskey, we kissed like two high school kids and then waded out laughing and splashed water on each other.

The next day Pete Owens looked me up at the office when my boss, Mr. McGinnis, was gone to lunch. "Charlie's never quit, you know, Eileen. He's still passing favors out."

My heart dropped. I could guess it, but wasn't letting myself know I really knew it. I put my hard mask on. "What's the matter? Isn't Hope getting enough from you?"

"Oh, I'm the one for Jezzie. You're the main one for Charlie. I just mean, don't kid yourself he's ever stopped."

"When did any of us ever stop?"

"You have. You like him that much. But don't think you're home free. The funny thing is, nobody's ever took a shotgun to Charlie. So far's I know, nobody's ever even punched him in the jaw."

"It is odd," I said, sarcastic, but he didn't notice.

"It's downright peculiar," said Pete. "But then I guess we're a special sort of bunch, Eileen."

I went back to typing and wished he'd go. He'd be asking me next. We'd dated and done a few things, but that was so long ago, it didn't count now. It never really mattered. I never thought much about it.

"What I wonder is, Eileen. Is everybody else like us, or so different from us they don't know what we're like at all?"

"The world's changing," I said. "They're all getting like us."

"You mean it?"

I nodded. "The word got out," I said. "You told somebody, and they told somebody else, and now everybody is like us."

"Or soon will be," he said.

"That's right," I said.

I kept on typing letters, reeling them on and off the platen and working on my electric machine the whole time he was talking, turning his hat over and picking at a straw or two off the synthetic weave. I had a headache that got worse after he was gone.

Also at the picnic that night was Grey Houston, one of the Houston brothers, who was always with a different girl. His former steady girlfriend, Nelle Townshend, kept a cleaning and pressing shop on her own premises. Her mother had been a stay-at-home lady for years. They had one of those beautiful old Victorian-type houses—it just missed being a photographer's and tourist attraction, being about twenty years too late and having the wooden trim too ornate for the connoisseurs to call it the real classical style. Nelle had been enterprising enough to turn one wing of the house where nobody went anymore into a cleaning shop, because she needed to make some money and felt she had to be near her mother. She had working for them off and on a Negro back from the Vietnam war who had used his veterans' educational benefits to train as a dry cleaner. She picked up the idea when her mother happened to remark one night after she had paid him for some carpenter work, "Ain't that a dumb nigger, learning dry cleaning with nothing to dry-clean."

Now, when Mrs. Townshend said "nigger," it wasn't as if one of us had said it. She went back through the centuries for her words, back to when "ain't" was good grammar. "Nigger" for her just meant "black." But it was assuming Robin had done something dumb that was the mistake. Because he wasn't dumb, and Nelle knew it. He told her he'd applied for jobs all around, but they didn't offer much and he might have to go to Biloxi or Hattiesburg or Gulfport to get one. The trouble was, he owned a house here. Nelle said, "Maybe you could work for me."

He told her about a whole dry cleaning plant up in Magee that had folded up recently due to the old man who ran it dying on his feet one day. They drove up there together and she bought it. Her mother didn't like it much when she moved the equipment in, but Nelle did it anyway. "I never get the smell out of my hair," she would say, "but if it can just make money I'll get used to it." She was dating Grey at the time, and I thought that's what gave her that much nerve.

Grey was a darling man. He was divorced from a New Orleans woman, somebody with a lot of class and money. She'd been crazy about Grey, as who wouldn't be, but he didn't "fit in," was her complaint. "Why do I have to fit in with her?" he kept asking. "Why shouldn't she fit in with us?" "She was O.K. with us," I said. "Not quite," he said. "Y'all never did relax. You never felt easy. That's why Charlie kept working at her, flirting and all. She maybe ought to have gone ahead with Charlie. Then she'd have been one of us. But she acted serious about it. I said, 'Whatever you decide about Charlie, just don't tell me.' She was too serious."

"Anybody takes it seriously ought to be me," I said.

"Oh-oh," said Grey, breaking out with fun, the way he could do—in the depths one minute, up and laughing the next. "You can't afford that, Eileen."

That time I raised a storm at Charlie. "What did you want to get married for? You're nothing but a goddamn stud!"

"What's news about it?" Charlie wanted to know. "You're just getting worked up over nothing."

"Nothing! Is what we do just nothing?"

"That's right. When it's done with, it's nothing. What I think of you—now, that's something." He had had some problem with a new car at the garage—he had the GM agency then—and he smelled of clean lubricating products and new upholstery and the rough soap where the mechanics cleaned up. He was big and gleaming, the all-over male. Oh, hell, I thought, what can I do? Then, suddenly curious, I asked: "*Did* you make out with Grey's wife?"

He laughed out loud and gave me a sidelong kiss. "Now that's more like it."

Because he'd never tell me. He'd never tell me who he made out with. "Honey," he'd say, late at night in the dark, lying straight out beside me, occasionally tangling his toes in mine or reaching for his cigarettes, "if I'd say I never had another woman outside you, would you believe it?"

I couldn't say No from sheer astonishment.

"Because it just might be true," he went on in the dark, serious as a judge. Then I would start laughing, couldn't help it. Because there are few things in the world which you know are true. You don't know (not anymore: our mamas knew) if there's a God or not, much less if He so loved the world. You don't know what your own native land is up to, or the true meaning of freedom, or the real cost of gasoline and cigarettes, or whether your insurance company will pay up. But one thing I personally know that is *not* true is that Charlie Waybridge has had only one woman. Looked at that way, it can be a comfort, one thing to be sure of.

It was soon after the picnic on the river that Grey Houston came by to see me at the office. You'd think I had nothing to do but stop and talk. What he came about was Nelle.

"She won't date me anymore," he complained. "I thought we were doing fine, but she quit me just like that. Hell, I can't tell what's the trouble with her. I want to call up and say, 'Just tell me, Nelle. What's going on?'"

"Why don't you?" I asked.

Grey is always a little worried about things to do with people, especially since his divorce. We were glad when he started dating Nelle. She was hovering around thirty and didn't have anybody, and Grey was only a year or two younger.

"If I come right out and ask her, then she might just say, 'Let's decide to be good friends,' or something like that. Hell, I got enough friends."

"It's to be thought of," I agreed.

"What would you do?" he persisted.

"I'd rather know where I stand," I said, "but in this case I think I'd wait awhile. Nelle's worrying over that business. Maybe she doesn't know herself."

"I might push her too soon. I thought that, too."

"I ought to go around and see old Mrs. Townshend," I said.

"She hardly gets out at all anymore. I mean to stop in and say hello."

"You're not going to repeat anything?"

See how he is? Skittery. "Of course not," I said. "But there's such a thing as keeping my eyes and ears open."

I went over to call on old Mrs. Townshend one Thursday afternoon when Mr. McGinnis's law office was closed anyway. The Townshend house is on a big lawn, a brick walk running up from the street to the front step and a large round plot of elephant ears in the front yard. When away and thinking of home, I see right off the Townshend yard and the elephant ears.

I wasn't even to the steps before I smelled clothes just dry-cleaned. I don't guess it's so bad, though hardly what you'd think of living with. Nor would you particularly like to see the sign outside the porte-cochere, though way to the left of the walk and not visible from the front porch. Still, it was out there clearly, saying "Townshend Dry Cleaning: Rapid Service." Better than a funeral parlor, but not much.

The Townshend house is stuffed with things. All these little Victorian tables on tall legs bowed outward, a small lower shelf, and the top covered katy-corner with a clean starched linen doily, tatting around the edge. All these chairs of various shapes, especially one that rocked squeaking on a walnut stand, and for every chair a doily at the head. Mrs. Townshend kept two birdcages, but no birds were in them. There never had been any so far as I knew. It wasn't a dark house, though. Nelle had taken out the stained glass way back when she graduated from college. That was soon after her older sister married, and her mama needed her. "If I'm going to live here," she had said, "that's got to go." So it went.

Mrs. Townshend never raised much of a fuss at Nelle. She was low to the ground because of a humpback, a rather placid old lady. The Townshends were the sort to keep everything just the way it was. Mrs. Townshend was a LeMoyne from over toward Natchez. She was an Episcopalian and had brought her daughters up in that church.

"I'm sorry about this smell," she said in her forthright way, coming in and offering me a Coke on a little tray with a folded linen napkin beside it. "Nelle told me I'd get used to it and she was right: I have. But at first I had headaches all the time. If you get one I'll get some aspirin for you."

"How's the business going?" I asked.

"Nelle will be in in a minute. She knows you're here. You can ask her." She never raised her voice. She had a soft little face and gray eyes back of her little gold-rimmed glasses. She hadn't got to the hearing-aid stage yet, but you had to speak up. We went through the whole rigmarole of mine and Charlie's families. I had a feeling she was never much interested in all that, but around home you have to do it. Then I asked her what she was reading and she woke up. We got off the ground right away, and went strong about the President and foreign affairs, the picture not being so bright but of great interest, and about her books from the library always running out, and all the things she had against book clubs—then Nelle walked in.

Nelle Townshend doesn't look like anybody else but herself. Her face is like something done on purpose to use up all the fine skin, drawing it evenly over the bones beneath, so that no matter at what age, she always would look the same. But that day she had this pinched look I'd never seen before, and her arms were splotched with what must have been a reaction to the cleaning fluids. She rolled down the sleeves of her blouse and sat in an old wicker rocker.

"I saw Grey the other day, Nelle," I said. "I think he misses you."

She didn't say anything outside of remarking she hadn't much time to go out. Then she mentioned some sort of decorating at the church she wanted to borrow some ferns for, from the florist. He's got some he rents, in washtubs. "You can't get all those ferns in our little church," Mrs. Townshend said, and Nelle said she thought two would do. She'd send Robin, she said. Then the bell rang to announce another customer. Nelle had to go because Robin was at the "plant"—actually the old cook's house in back of the property where they'd set the machinery up.

I hadn't said all I had to say to Nelle, so when I got up to go, I said to Mrs. Townshend that I'd go in the office a minute on the way out. But Mrs. Townshend got to her feet, a surprise in itself. Her usual words were, You'll excuse me if I don't get up. Of course, you would excuse her and be too polite to ask why. Like a lot of old ladies, she might have arthritis. But this time she stood.

"I wish you'd let Nelle alone. Nelle is all right now. She's the way she wants to be. She's not the way you people are. She's just not a bit that way!"

It may have been sheer surprise that kept me from telling Charlie all this till the weekend. We were hurrying to get to Pete and Hope Owens's place for a dinner they were having for some people down from the Delta, visitors.

"What did you say to that?" Charlie asked me.

"I was too surprised to open my mouth. I wouldn't have thought Mrs. Townshend would express such a low opinion as that. And why does she have it in the first place? Nelle's always been part of our crowd. She grew up with us. I thought they liked us."

"Old ladies get notions. They talk on the phone too much."

To our surprise, Nelle was at the Owenses' dinner, too. Hope told me in the kitchen that she'd asked her, and then asked Grey. But Grey had a date with the little Springer girl he'd brought to the picnic, Carole Springer. "If this keeps up," Hope said to me while I was helping her with a dip, "we're going to have a Springer in our crowd. I'm just not right ready for that." "Me either," I said. The Springers were from McComb, in lumber. They had money but they never were much fun.

"Did Nelle accept knowing you were going to ask Grey?" I asked.

"I couldn't tell that. She just said she'd love to and would come about seven."

It must have been seven, because Nelle walked in. "Can I help?"

"Your mama," I said, when Hope went out with the tray, "she sort of got upset with me the other day. I don't know why. If I said anything wrong, just tell her I'm sorry."

Nelle looked at her fresh nail polish. "Mama's a little peculiar now and then. Like everybody." So she wasn't about to open up.

"I've been feeling bad about Grey is all," I said. "You can think I'm meddling if you want to."

"Grey's all right," she said. "He's been going around with Carole Springer from McComb."

"All the more reason for feeling bad. Did you know they're coming tonight?"

She smiled a little distantly, and we went out to join the party. Charlie was already sitting up too close to the wife of the guest couple. I'd met them before. They have an antique shop. He is tall and nice, and she is short (wears spike heels) and nice. They are the sort you can't ever remember what their names are. If you get the first names right you're doing well. Shirley and Bob.

"Honey, you're just a doll," Charlie was saying (if he couldn't think of Shirley, Honey would do), and Pete said, "Watch out, Shirley, the next thing you know you'll be sitting on his lap."

"I almost went in for antiques myself," Nelle was saying to Bob, the husband. "I would have liked that better, of course, than a cleaning business, but I thought the turnover here would be too small. I do need to feel like I'm making money if I'm going to work at it. For a while, though, it was fun to go wandering around New Orleans and pick up good things cheap."

"I'd say they'd all been combed over down there," Bob objected.

"It's true about the best things," Nelle said. "I could hardly afford those anyway. But sometimes you see some pieces with really good design and you can see you might realize something on them. Real appreciation goes a long way."

"Bob has a jobber up in St. Louis," Shirley said. "We had enough of all this going around shaking the bushes. A few lucky finds was what got us started."

Nelle said, "I started thinking about it because I went in the living room a year or so back and there were some ladies I never saw before. They'd found the door open and walked in. They wanted to know the price of Mama's furniture. I said it wasn't for sale, but Mama was just coming in from the kitchen and heard them. You wouldn't believe how mad she got. 'I'm going straight and get out my pistol,' she said."

"You ought to just see her mama," said Hope. "This tiny little old lady."

"So what happened?" Shirley asked when she got through laughing.

"Nothing real bad," said Nelle. "They just got out the door as quick as they could."

"Yo' mama got a pistol?" Charlie asked, after a silence. We started to laugh again, the implication being plain that a Charlie Waybridge *needs* to know if a woman's mother has a pistol in the house.

"She does have one," said Nelle.

"So watch out, Charlie," said Pete.

Bob remarked, "Y'all certainly don't change much over here."

"Crazy as ever," Hope said proudly. It crossed my mind that Hope was always protecting herself, one way or the other.

Shirley said she thought it was just grand to be back, she wouldn't take anything for it, and after that Grey and Carole arrived. We had another drink and then went in to dinner. Everybody acted like everything was okay. After dinner, I went back in the kitchen for some water, and there was Charlie, kissing Shirley. She was so strained up on tiptoe, Charlie being over six feet, that I thought, in addition to being embarrassed, mad, and backing out before they saw me, What they need is a stepladder to do it right.

On the way home, I told Charlie about catching them. "I didn't know she was within a country mile," he said, ready with excuses. "She just plain grabbed me."

"I've been disgusted once too often," I said. "Tell it to Bob."

"If she wanted to do it right," he said, "she ought to get a stepladder." So then I had to laugh. Even if our marriage wasn't ideal, we still had the same thoughts.

It sometimes seemed to me, in considering the crowd we were always part of, from even before we went to school, straight on through, that we were all like one person, walking around different ways, but in some permanent way breathing together, feeling the same reactions, thinking each other's thoughts. What do you call that if not love? If asked, we'd all cry Yes! with one voice, but then it's not our habit to ask anything serious. We're close to religious about keeping everything light and gay. Nelle Townshend knew that, all the above, but she was drawing back. A betrayer was what she was turning into. We felt weakened because of her. What did she think she was doing?

I had to drive Mr. McGinnis way back in the woods one day to serve a subpoena on a witness. He hadn't liked to drive since his heart attack, and his usual colored man was busy with Mrs. McGinnis's garden. In the course of that little trip, coming back into town, I saw Nelle Townshend's station wagon turn off onto a side road. I couldn't see who was with her, but somebody was, definitely.

I must add that this was spring and there were drifts of dogwood all mingled in the woods at different levels. Through those same woods, along the winding roads, the redbud, simultaneous, was spreading its wonderful pink haze. Mr. McGinnis sat beside me without saying much, his old knobby hands folded over a briefcase he held upright on his lap. "A trip like this just makes me think, Eileen, that everybody owes it to himself to get out in the woods this time of year. It's just God's own garden," he said. We had just crossed a wooden bridge over a pretty little creek about a mile back. That same creek, shallower, was crossed by a ford along the road that Nelle's car had taken. I know that little road, too, maybe the prettiest one of all.

Serpents have a taste for Eden, and in a small town, if they are busy elsewhere, lots of people are glad to fill in for them. It still upsets me to think of all the gossip that went on that year, and at the same time I have to blame Nelle Townshend for it, not so much for starting it, but for being so unconscious about it. She had stepped out of line and she didn't even bother to notice.

Once the business got going, the next thing she did was enroll in a class—a "seminar," she said—over at the university at Hattiesburg. It was something to do with art theory, she said, and she was thinking of going on from there to a degree, eventually, and get hold of a subject she could teach at the junior college right up the road. So settling in to be an old maid.

I said this last rather gloomily to Pete's wife, Hope, and Pete overheard and said, "There's all kinds of those." "You stop that," said Hope. "What's supposed to be going on?" I asked. (Some say don't ask, it's better not to, but I think you have to know if only to keep on guard.)

"Just that they're saying things about Nelle and that black Robin works for her."

"Well, they're in the same business," I said.

"Whatever it is, people don't like it. They say she goes out to his house after dark. That they spend too much time over the books."

"Somebody ought to warn her," I said. "If Robin gets into trouble she won't find anybody to do that kind of work. He's the only one."

"Nelle's gotten too independent is the thing," said Pete. "She thinks she can live her own life."

"Maybe she can," said Hope.

Charlie was away that week. He had gone over to the Delta on business, and Hope and Pete had dropped in to keep me company. Hope is ten years younger than Pete. (Pete used to date her sister, Mary Ruth, one of these beauty-queen types, who had gone up to the Miss America pageant to represent Mississippi and come back first runner-up. For the talent contest part of it, she had recited passages from the Bible, and Pete always said her trouble was she was too religious but he hoped to get her over it. She used to try in a nice way to get him into church work, and that embarrassed him. It's our common habit, as Mary Ruth well knew, to go to morning service, but anything outside that is out. Anyway, around Mary Ruth's he used to keep seeing the little sister Hope, and he'd say, "Mary Ruth, you better start on that girl about church, she's growing up dynamite." Mary Ruth got involved in a promotion trip, something about getting right with America, and met a man on a plane trip to Dallas, and before the seat-belt sign went off they were in love. For Mary Ruth that meant marriage. She was strict, a woman of faith, and I don't think Pete would have been happy with her. But he had got the habit of the house by then, and Mary Ruth's parents had got fond of him and didn't want him drinking too much: they made him welcome. So one day Hope turned seventeen and came out in a new flouncy dress with heels on, and Pete saw the light.)

We had a saying by now that Pete had always been younger than Hope, that she was older than any of us. Only twenty, she worked at making their house look good and won gardening prizes. She gave grand parties, with attention to details.

"I stuck my neck out," I told Hope, "to keep Nelle dating Grey. You remember her mama took a set at me like I never dreamed possible. Nelle's been doing us all funny, but she may have to come back someday. We can't stop caring for her."

Hope thought it over. "Robin knows what it's like here, even if Nelle may have temporarily forgotten. He's not going to tempt fate. Anyway, somebody already spoke to Nelle."

"Who?"

"Grey, of course. He'll use any excuse to speak to her. She got mad as a firecracker. She said, 'Don't you know this is nineteen seventy-*six*? I've got a business to run. I've got a living to make!' But she quit going out to his house at night. And Robin quit so much as answering the phone, up at her office."

"You mean he's keeping one of those low profiles?" said Pete.

Soon after, I ran into Robin uptown in the grocery, and he said, "How do you do, Mrs. Waybridge," like a schoolteacher or a foreigner, and I figured just from that, that he was on to everything and taking no chances. Nelle must have told him. I personally knew what not many people did, that he was a real partner with Nelle, not just her hired help. They had got Mr. McGinnis to draw up the papers. And they had plans for moving the plant uptown, to an empty store building, with some investment in more equipment. So maybe they'd get by till then. I felt a mellowness in my heart about Nelle's effort and all—a Townshend (LeMoyne on her mother's side) opening a dry cleaning business. I thought of Robin's effort, too—he had a sincere, intelligent look, reserved. What I hoped for them was something like a prayer.

Busying my thoughts about all this, I had been forgetting Charlie. That will never do.

For one thing, leaving aside women, Charlie's present way of life was very nearly wild. He'd got into oil leases two years before, and when something was going on, he'd drive like a demon over to East Texas by way of Shreveport and back through Pike and Amite counties. At one time he had to sit over Mr. McGinnis for a month getting him to study up on laws governing oil rights. In the end, Charlie got to know as much or more than Mr. McGinnis. He's in and out. The in-between times are when he gets restless. Drinks too much and starts simmering up about some new woman. One thing (except for me), with Charlie it's always a new woman. Once tried, soon dropped. Or so I like to believe. Then, truth to tell, there is really part of me that not only wants to believe but at unstated times does believe that I've been the only one for Charlie Waybridge. Not that I'd begrudge him a few times of having it off down in the hollow back of the gym with some girl who came in from the country, nor would I think anything about flings in New Orleans while he was in Tulane. But as for the outlandish reputation he's acquired now, sometimes I just want to say out loud to all and sundry, "There's not a word of truth in it. He's a big, attractive, friendly guy, O.K.! But he's not the town stud. He belongs to *me*."

All this before the evening along about first dark when Charlie was seen on the Townshend property by Nelle's mother, who went and got the pistol and shot at him.

"Christ, she could have killed me," Charlie said. He was too surprised about it even to shake. He was just dazed. Fixed a stiff drink and didn't want any supper. "She's gone off her rocker," he said. "That's all I could think."

I knew I had to ask it, sooner or later. "What were you doing up there, Charlie?"

"Nothing," he said. "I'd left the car at Wharton's garage to check why I'm burning too much oil. He's getting to it in the morning. It was a nice evening and I cut through the back alley and that led to a stroll through the Townshend pasture. That's all. I saw the little lady out on the back porch. I was too far off to holler at her. She scuttled off into the house and I was going past, when here she came out again with something black weighting her hand. You know what I thought? I thought she had a kitten by the neck. Next thing I knew there was a bullet smashing through the leaves not that far off." He put his hand out.

"Wonder if Nelle was home."

I was nervous as a monkey after I heard this, and nothing would do me but to call up Nelle.

She answered right away. "Nelle," I said, "is your little mama going in for target practice these days?"

She started laughing. "Did you hear that all the way to your place? She's mad 'cause the Johnsons' old cow keeps breaking down our fence. She took a shot in the air because she's tired complaining."

"Since when was Charlie Waybridge a cow?" I asked.

"Mercy, Eileen. You don't mean Charlie was back there?"

"You better load that thing with blanks," I said, "or hide it."

"Blanks is all it's got in it," said Nelle. "Mama doesn't tell that because she feels more protected not to."

"You certainly better check it out," I said. "Charlie says it was a bullet."

There was a pause. "You're not mad or anything, are you, Eileen?"

"Oh, no," I warbled. "We've been friends too long for that."

"Come over and see us," said Nelle. "Real soon."

I don't know who told it, but knowing this town like the back of my hand, I know *how* they told it. Charlie Waybridge was up at Nelle Townshend's and old Mrs. Townshend shot at him. Enough said. At the Garden Club Auxiliary tea, I came in and heard them giggling, and how they got quiet when I passed a plate of sandwiches. I went straight to the subject, which is the way I do. "Y'all off on Mrs. Townshend?" I asked. There was a silence, and then some little cross-eyed bride, new in town, piped up that there was just always something funny going on here, and Maud Varner, an old friend, said she thought Nelle ought to watch out for Mrs. Townshend, she was showing her age. "It's not such a funny goings-on when it almost kills somebody," I said. "Charlie came straight home and told me. He was glad to be alive, but I went and called Nelle. So she does know." There was another silence during which I could tell what everybody thought. The thing is not to get too distant or above it all. If you do, your friends will pull back, too, and you won't know anything. Gradually, you'll just turn into, Poor Eileen, what does she think of all Charlie's carryings-on?

Next, the injunction. Who brought it and why? I got the answer to the first before I guessed the second.

It was against the Townshend Cleaners because the chemicals used were a hazard to health and the smell they exuded a public nuisance. But the real reason wasn't this at all.

In order to speed up the deliveries, Nelle had taken to driving the station wagon herself, so that Robin could run in with the cleaning. Some people had begun to remark on this. Would it have been different if Nelle was married or had a brother, a father, a steady boyfriend? I don't know. I used to hold my breath when they went by in the late afternoon together. Because sometimes when the back of the station wagon was full, Robin would be up on the front seat with her, and she with her head stuck in the air, driving carefully, her mind on nothing at all to do with other people. Once the cleaning load got lighter, Robin would usually sit on the back seat, as expected to do. But sometimes, busy talking to her, he wouldn't. He'd be up beside her, discussing business.

Then, suddenly, the business closed.

Nelle was beside herself. She came running to Mr. McGinnis. Her hair was every which way around her head and she was wearing an old checked shirt and no makeup.

She could hardly make herself sit still and visit with me while Mr. McGinnis got through with a client. "Now, Miss Nelle," he said, steering her through the door.

"Just when we were making a go of it!" I heard her say; then he closed the door.

I heard by way of the grapevine that very night that the person who had done it was John Houston, Grey's brother, whose wife's family lived on a property just below the Townshends. They claimed they couldn't sleep for the dry-cleaning fumes and were getting violent attacks of nausea.

"Aren't they supposed to give warnings?" I asked.

We were all at John and Rose Houston's home, a real gathering of the bunch, only Nelle being absent, though she was the most present one of all. There was a silence after every statement, in itself unusual. Finally John Houston said, "Not in cases of extreme health hazard."

"That's a lot of you-know-what," I said. "Rose, your family's not dying."

Rose said: "They never claimed to be dying." And Pete said: "Eileen, can't you sit right quiet and try to use your head?"

"In preference to running off at the mouth," said Charlie, which made me mad. I was refusing, I well knew, to see the point they all had in mind. But it seemed to me that was my privilege.

The thing to know about our crowd is that we never did go in for talking about the "Negro question." We talked about Negroes the way we always had, like people, one at a time. They were all around us, had always been, living around us, waiting on us, sharing our lives, brought up with us, nursing us, cooking for us, mourning and rejoicing with us, making us laugh, stealing from us, digging our graves. But when all the troubles started coming in on us after the Freedom Riders and the Ole Miss riots, we decided not to talk about it. I don't know but what we weren't afraid of getting nervous. We couldn't jump out of our own skins, or those of our parents, grandparents, and those before them. "Nothing you can do about it" was Charlie's view. "Whatever you decide, you're going to act the same way tomorrow as you did today. Hoping you can get Alma to cook for you, and Peabody to clean the windows, and Bayman to cut the grass." "I'm not keeping anybody from voting—yellow, blue, or pink," said Hope, who had got her "ideas" straight from the first, she said. "I don't guess any of us is," said Pete, "them days is gone forever." "But wouldn't it just be wonderful," said Rose Houston, "to have a little colored gal to pick up your handkerchief and sew on your buttons and bring you cold lemonade and fan you when you're hot, and just love you to death?"

Rose was joking, of course, the way we all liked to do. But there are always one or two of them that we seriously insist we know—really *know*—that they love us. Would do anything for us, as we would for them. Otherwise, without that feeling, I guess we couldn't rest easy. You never can really know what they think, what they feel, so there's always the one chance it might be love.

So we—the we I'm always speaking of—decided not to talk about race relations because it spoiled things too much. We didn't like to consider anyone of us really involved in some part of it. Then, in my mind's eye, I saw Nelle's car, that dogwood-laden day in the woods, headed off the road with somebody inside. Or such was my impression. I'd never mentioned it to anybody, and Mr. McGinnis hadn't, I think, seen. Was it Robin? Or maybe, I suddenly asked myself, Charlie? Mysteries multiplied.

"Nelle's got to make a living is the whole thing," said Pete, getting practical. "We can't not let her do that."

"Why doesn't somebody find her a job she'd like?" asked Grey.

"Why the hell," Charlie burst out, "don't you marry her, Grey? Women ought to get married," he announced in general. "You see what happens when they don't."

"Hell, I can't get near her," said Grey. "We dated for six months. I guess I wasn't the one," he added.

"She ought to relocate the plant uptown, then she could run the office in her house, one remove from it, acting like a lady."

"What about Robin?" said Hope.

"He could run back and forth," I said. "They do want to do that," I added, "but can't afford it yet."

"You'd think old Mrs. Townshend would have stopped it all."

"That lady's a mystery."

"If Nelle just had a brother."

"Or even an uncle."

Then the talk dwindled down to silence.

"John," said Pete, after a time, turning around to face him, "we all know it was you—not Rose's folks. Did you have to?"

John Houston was sitting quietly in his chair. He was a little older than the rest of us, turning gray, a little more settled and methodical, more like our uncle than an equal and friend. (Or was it just that he and Rose were the only ones so far to have children—what all our parents said we all ought to do, but couldn't quit having our good times.) He was sipping bourbon. He nodded slowly. "I had to." We didn't ask any more.

"Let's just go quiet," John finally added. "Wait and see."

Now, all my life I'd been hearing first one person then another (and these, it would seem, appointed by silent consensus) say that things were to be taken care of in a certain way and no other. The person in this case who had this kind of appointment was evidently John Houston, from in our midst.

But when did he get it? How did he get it? Where did it come from? There seemed to be no need to discuss it.

Rose Houston, who wore her long light hair in a sort of loose bun at the nape and who sat straight up in her chair, adjusted a fallen strand, and Grey went off to fix another drink for himself and Pete and Hope. He sang on the way out, more or less to himself, "For the times they are a-changing . . ." and that, too, found reference in all our minds. Except I couldn't help but wonder whether anything had changed at all.

The hearing on the dry cleaning injunction was due to be held in two weeks. Nelle went off to the coast. She couldn't stand the tension, she told me, having come over to Mr. McGinnis's office to see him alone. "Thinking how we've worked and all," she said, "and how just before this came up the auditor was in and told us what good shape we were in. We were just about to buy a new condenser."

"What's that?" I asked.

"Takes the smell out of the fumes," she said. "The very thing they're mad about. I could kill John Houston. Why couldn't he have come to me?"

I decided to be forthright. "Nelle, there's something you ought to evaluate . . . consider, I mean. Whatever word you want." I was shaking, surprising myself.

Nobody was around. Mr. McGinnis was in the next county.

Once when I was visiting a school friend up north, out from Philadelphia, a man at a party asked me if I would have sexual relations with a black. He wasn't black himself, so why was he curious? I said I'd never even thought about it. "It's a taboo, I think you call it," I said. "Girls like me get brainwashed early on. It's not that I'm against them," I added, feeling awkward. "Contrary to what you may think or may even believe," he told me, "you've probably thought a lot about it. You've suppressed your impulses, that's all." "Nobody can prove that," I said, "not even you," I added, thinking I was being amusing. But he only looked superior and walked away.

"It's you and Robin," I said. I could hear myself explaining to Charlie, Somebody had to, sooner or later. "You won't find anybody really believing anything, I don't guess, but it's making people speculate."

Nelle Townshend never reacted the way you'd think she would. She didn't even get annoyed, much less hit the ceiling. She just gave a little sigh. "You start a business, you'll see. I've got no time for anything but worrying about customers and money."

I was wondering whether to tell her the latest. A woman named McCorkle from out in the country, who resembled Nelle so much from the back you'd think they were the same, got pushed off the sidewalk last Saturday and fell in the concrete gutter up near the drugstore. The person who did it, somebody from outside town, must have said something nobody heard but Mrs. McCorkle, because she jumped up with her skirt muddy and stockings torn and yelled out, "I ain't no nigger lover!"

But I didn't tell her. If she was anybody but a Townshend, I might have. Odd to think that, when the only Townshends left there were Nelle and her mother. In cases such as this, the absent are present and the dead are, too. Mr. Townshend had died so long ago you had to ask your parents what he was like. The answer was always the same. "Sid Townshend was a mighty good man." Nelle had had two sisters: one died in her twenties, the victim of a rare disease, and the other got married and went to live on a place out from Helena, Arkansas. She had about six children and could be of no real help to the home branch.

"Come over to dinner," I coaxed. "You want me to ask Grey, I will. If you don't, I won't."

"Grey," she said, just blank, like that. He might have been somebody she met once a long time back. "She's a perpetual virgin," I heard Charlie say once. "Just because she won't cotton up to you," I said. But maybe he was right. Nelle and her mother lived up near the Episcopal church. Since our little town could not support a full-time rector, it was they who kept the church linens and the chalice and saw that the robes were always cleaned and hung in their proper place in the little room off the chancel. Come to think of it, keeping those robes and surplices in order may have been one thing that started Nelle into dry cleaning.

Nelle got up suddenly, her face catching the light from our old window with the wobbly glass in the panes, and I thought,

She's a grand-looking woman, sort of girlish and womanish both.

"I'm going to the coast," she said. "I'm taking some books and a sketch pad. I may look into some art courses. You have to have training to teach anything, that's the trouble."

"Look, Nelle, if it's money— Well, you do have friends, you know."

"Friends," she said, just the way she had said "Grey." I wondered just what Nelle was really like. None of us seemed to know.

"Have a good time," I said. After she left, I thought I heard the echo of that blank, soft voice saying, "Good time."

It was a week after Nelle had gone that old Mrs. Townshend rang up Mr. McGinnis at the office. Mr. McGinnis came out to tell me what it was all about.

"Mrs. Townshend says that last night somebody tore down the dry cleaning sign Nelle had put up out at the side. Some colored woman is staying with her at night, but neither one of them saw anybody. Now she can't find Robin to put it back. She's called his house but he's not there."

"Do they say he'll be back soon?"

"They say he's out of town."

"I'd get Charlie to go up and fix it, but you know what happened."

"I heard about it. Maybe in daylight the old lady won't shoot. I'll go around with our yardman after dinner." What we still mean by dinner is lunch. So they put the sign up and I sat in the empty office wondering about this and that, but mainly, Where was Robin Byers?

It's time to say that Robin Byers was not any Harry Belafonte calypso-singing sex symbol of a "black." He was strong and thoughtful-looking, not very tall, definitely chocolate, but not ebony. He wore his hair cropped short in an almost military fashion so that, being thick, it stuck straight up more often than not. From one side he could look positively frightening, as he had a long white scar running down the side of his cheek. It was said that he got it in the army, in Vietnam, but the story of just how was not known. So maybe he had not gotten it in the war, but somewhere else. His folks had been in the county

forever, his own house being not far out from town. He had
a wife, two teenaged children, a telephone, and a TV set. The
other side of Robin Byers's face was regular, smooth, and while
not especially handsome it was good-humored and likable. All
in all, he looked intelligent and conscientious, and that must
have been how Nelle Townshend saw him, as he was.

I went to the hearing. I'd have had to, to keep Mr. McGinnis's notes straight, but I would have anyway, as all our crowd
showed up, except Rose and John Houston. Rose's parents
were there, having brought the complaint, and Rose's mama's
doctor from over at Hattiesburg, to swear she'd had no end
of allergies and migraines, and attacks of nausea, all brought
on by the cleaning fumes. Sitting way in the back was Robin
Byers, in a suit (a really nice suit) with a blue-and-white-
striped "city" shirt and a knit tie. He looked like an assistant
university dean, except for the white scar. He also had the
look of a spectator, very calm, I thought, not wanting to keep
turning around and staring at him, but keeping the image in
my mind like an all-day sucker, letting it slowly melt out its
meaning. He was holding a certain surface. But he was scared.
Half across the courtroom you could see his temple throbbing, and the sweat beads. He was that tense. The whole effect
was amazing.

The complaint was read out and Mrs. Hammond, Rose's
mother, testified and the doctor testified, and Mr. Hammond
said they were both right. The way the Hammonds talk—big
Presbyterians—you would think they had the Bible on their side
every minute, so naturally everybody else had to be mistaken.
Friends and neighbors of the Townshends all these years, they
now seemed to be speaking of people they knew only slightly.
That is until Mrs. Hammond, a sort of dumpling-like woman
with a practiced way of sounding accurate about whatever she
said (she was a good gossip because she got all the details of
everything), suddenly came down to a personal level and said,
"Nelle, I just don't see why if you want to run that thing you
don't move it into town," and Nelle said back right away just
like they were in a living room instead of a courthouse, "Well,
that's because of Mama, Miss Addie. This way I'm in and out
with her." At that, everybody laughed, couldn't help it.

Then Mr. McGinnis got up and challenged that very much about Mrs. Hammond's headaches and allergies (he established her age, fifty-two, which she didn't want to tell) had to do with the cleaning plant. If they had, somebody else would have such complaints, but in case we needed to go further into it, he would ask Miss Nelle to explain what he meant.

Nelle got up front and went about as far as she could concerning the type of equipment she used and how it was guaranteed against the very thing now being complained of, that it let very few vapors escape, but then she said she would rather call on Robin Byers to come and explain because he had had special training in the chemical processes and knew all their possible negative effects.

And he came. He walked down the aisle and sat in the chair and nobody had ever seen such composure. I think he was petrified, but so might an actor be who was doing a role to high perfection. And when he started to talk you'd think that dry cleaning was a text and that his God-appointed task was to preach a sermon on it. But it wasn't quite like that, either. More modern. A professor giving a lecture to extremely ignorant students, with a good professor's accuracy, to the last degree. In the first place, he said, the cleaning fluid used was not varsol or carbon tetrachloride, which were known not only to give off harmful fumes but to damage fabrics, but something called "Perluxe" or perchlorethylene (he paused to give the chemical composition), which was approved for commercial cleaning purposes in such and such a solution by federal and state bylaws, of certain numbers and codes, which Mr. McGinnis had listed in his records and would be glad to read aloud upon request. If an operator worked closely with Perluxe for a certain number of hours a day, he might have headaches, it was true, but escaping vapor could scarcely be smelled at all more than a few feet from the exhaust pipes, and caused no harmful effects whatsoever, even to shrubs or "the leaves upon the trees." He said this last in such a lofty, rhythmic way that somebody giggled (I think it was Hope), and he stopped talking altogether.

"There might be smells down in those hollows back there," Nelle filled in from where she was sitting, "but it's not from my one little exhaust pipe."

"Then why," asked Mrs. Hammond right out, "do you keep on saying you need new equipment so you won't have any exhaust? Just answer me that."

"I'll let Robin explain," said Nelle.

"The fact is that Perluxe is an expensive product," Robin said. "At four dollars and twenty-five cents a gallon, using nearly thirty gallons each time the accumulation of the garments is put through the process, she can count on it that the overheads with two cleanings a week will run in the neighborhood of between two and three hundred dollars. So having the condenser machine would mean that the exhaust runs into it, and so converts the vapors back to the liquid, in order to use it once again."

"It's not for the neighbors," Nelle put in. "It's for us."

Everybody had spoken out of order by then, but what with the atmosphere having either declined or improved (depending on how you looked at it) to one of friendly inquiry among neighbors rather than a squabble in a court of law, the silence that finally descended was more meditative than not, having as its most impressive features, like high points in a landscape, Nelle, at some little distance down a front bench, but turned around so as to take everything in, her back straight and her Townshend head both superior and interested; and Robin Byers, who still had the chair by Judge Purvis's desk, collected and severe (he had forgotten the giggle), with testimony faultlessly delivered and nothing more he needed to say. (Would things have been any different if Charlie had been there? He was out of town.)

The judge cleared his throat and said he guessed the smells in the gullies around Tyler might be a nuisance, sure enough, but couldn't be said to be caused by dry cleaning, and he thought Miss Townshend could go on with her business. For a while, the white face and the black one seemed just the same, to be rising up quiet and superior above us all.

The judge asked, just out of curiosity, when Nelle planned to buy the condenser that was mentioned. She said whenever she could find one secondhand in good condition—they cost nearly two thousand dollars new—and Robin Byers put in that he had just been looking into one down in Biloxi, so it might not be too long. Biloxi is on the coast.

Judge Purvis said we'd adjourn now, and everybody stood up of one accord, except Mr. McGinnis, who had dozed off and was almost snoring.

Nelle, who was feeling friendly to the world, or seeming to (we all had clothes that got dirty, after all), said to all and sundry not to worry, "we plan to move the plant uptown one of these days before too long," and it was the "we" that came through again, a slip: she usually referred to the business as hers. It was just a reminder of what everybody wanted not to have to think about, and she probably hadn't intended to speak of it that way.

As if to smooth it well into the past, Judge Purvis remarked that these little towns ought to have zoning laws, but I sat there thinking there wouldn't be much support for that, not with the Gulf Oil station and garage right up on South Street between the Whitmans' and the Binghams', and the small-appliance shop on the vacant lot where the old Marshall mansion had stood, and the Tackett house, still elegant as you please, doing steady business as a funeral home. You can separate black from white but not business from nonbusiness. Not in our town.

Nelle came down and shook hands with Mr. McGinnis. "I don't know when I can afford to pay you." "Court costs go to them," he said. "Don't worry about the rest."

Back at the office, Mr. McGinnis closed the street door and said to me, "The fumes in this case have got nothing to do with dry cleaning. Has anybody talked to Miss Nelle?"

"They have," I said, "but she doesn't seem to pay any attention."

He said I could go home for the day and much obliged for my help at the courthouse. I powdered my nose and went out into the street. It wasn't but eleven-thirty.

Everything was still, and nobody around. The blue jays were having a good time on the courthouse yard, squalling and swooping from the lowest oak limbs, close to the ground, then mounting back up. There were some sparrows out near the old horse trough, which still ran water. They were splashing around. But except for somebody driving up for the mail at the post office, then driving off, there wasn't a soul around. I started walking, and just automatically I went by for the mail because as a rule Charlie didn't stop in for it till noon, even when in town. On the way I was mulling over the hearing and how Mrs. Hammond had said at the door of the courtroom to Nelle, "Aw right, Miss Nellie, you just wait." It wasn't said in any unpleasant way; in fact, it sounded right friendly. Except that she wasn't looking at Nelle, but past her, and except that being older, it wasn't the ordinary thing to call her "Miss," and except that Nelle is a pretty name but Nellie isn't. But Nelle in reply had suddenly laughed in that unexpected but delightful way she has, because something has struck her as really funny. "What am I supposed to wait *for*, Miss Addie?" Whatever else, Nelle wasn't scared. I looked for Robin Byers, but he had got sensible and gone off in that old little blue German car he drives. I saw Nelle drive home alone.

Then, because the lay of my home direction was a short-cut from the post office, and because the spring had been dry and the back lanes nice to walk in, I went through the same way Charlie had that time Mrs. Townshend had about killed him, and enjoyed, the way I had from childhood on, the soft fragrances of springtime, the brown wisps of spent jonquils withered on their stalks, the forsythia turned from yellow to green fronds, but the spirea still white as a bride's veil worked in blossoms, and the climbing roses, mainly wild, just opening a delicate, simple pink bloom all along the back fences. I was crossing down that way when what I saw was a blue car.

It was stopped way back down the Townshend property on a little connecting road that made an entrance through to a lower town road, one that nobody used anymore. I stopped in the clump of bowdarc trees on the next property from the Townshends'. Then I saw Nelle, running down the hill. She still had that same laugh, honest and joyous, that she had shown the first of to Mrs. Hammond. And there coming to meet her was Robin, his teeth white as his scar. They grabbed each other's hands, black on white and white on black. They started whirling each other around, like two schoolchildren in a game, and I saw Nelle's mouth forming the words I could scarcely hear: "We won! We won!" And his, the same, a bari-tone underneath. It was pure joy. Washing the color out, say-ing that the dye didn't, this time, hold, they could have been brother and sister, happy at some good family news, or old lov-ers (Charlie and I sometimes meet like that, too happy at some piece of luck to really stop to talk about it, just dancing out our joy). But, my God, I thought, don't they know they're black and white and this is Tyler, Mississippi? Well, of course they do, I thought next—that's more than half the joy—getting away with it! Dare and double-dare! Dumbfounded, I just stood, hidden, never seen by them at all, and let the image of black on white and white on black—those pale, aristocratic Townshend hands and his strong, square-cut black ones—linked perpetually now in my mind's eye—soak in.

It's going to stay with me forever, I thought, but what does it mean? I never told. I didn't think they were lovers. But they were into a triumph of the sort that lovers feel. They had acted as they pleased. They were above everything. They lived in another world because of a dry cleaning business. They had proved it when they had to. They knew it.

But nobody could be counted on to see it the way I did. It was too complicated for any two people to know about it.

Soon after this we got a call from Hope, Pete's wife. "I've got tired of all this foolishness," she said. "How did we ever get hung up on dry cleaning, of all things? Can you feature it? I'm going to give a party. Mary Foote Williams is coming home to see her folks and bringing Keith, so that's good enough for me. And don't kid yourself. I'm personally going to get Nelle Townshend to come, and Grey Houston is going to bring her. I'm getting good and ready for everybody to start acting normal again. I don't know what's been the matter with everybody, and furthermore I don't want to know."

Well, this is a kettle of fish, I thought: Hope, the youngest, taking us over. Of course, she did have the perspective to see everything whole.

I no sooner put down the phone than Pete called up from his office. "Jezzie's on the warpath," he said. (He calls her Jezzie because she used to tell all kinds of lies to some little high school boy she had crazy about her—her own age—just so she could go out with Pete and the older crowd. It was easy to see through that. She thought she might just be getting a short run with us and would have to fall back on her own bunch when we shoved her out, so she was keeping a foothold. Pete caught her at it, but all it did was make him like her better.

Hope was pert. She had a sharp little chin she liked to stick up
in the air, and a turned-up nose. "Both signs of meanness," said
Mr. Owens, Pete's father, "especially the nose," and buried his
own in the newspaper.)

"Well," I said doubtfully, "if you think it's a good idea . . ."

"No stopping her," said Pete, with the voice of a spectator at
the game. "If anybody can swing it, she can."

So we finally said yes.

The morning of Hope's party there was some ugly weather,
one nasty little black cloud after another and a lot of restless
crosswinds. There was a tornado watch out for our county and
two others, making you know it was a widespread weather system. I had promised to bring a platter of shrimp for the buffet
table, and that meant a whole morning shucking them after
driving out to pick up the order at the Fish Shack. At times the
lightning was popping so close I had to get out of the kitchen.
I would go sit in the living room with the thunder blamming
so hard I couldn't even read the paper. Looking out at my
backyard through the picture window, the colors of the marigolds and pansies seemed to be electric bright, blazing, then
shuddering in the wind.

I was bound to connect all this with the anxiety that had got
into things about that party. Charlie's being over in Louisiana
didn't help. Maybe all was calm and bright over there, but I
doubted it.

However, along about two the sky did clear, and the sun
came out. When I drove out to Hope and Pete's place with the
shrimp—it's a little way north of town, reached by its own side
road, on a hill—everything was wonderful. There was a warm
buoyancy in the air that made you feel young and remember
what it was like to skip home from school.

"It's cleared off," said Hope, as though in personal triumph
over Nature.

Pete was behind her at the door, enveloped in a huge apron.
"I feel like playing softball," he said.

"Me, too," I agreed. "If I could just hear from Charlie."

"Oh, he'll be back," said Pete. "Charlie miss a party? Never!"

Well, it was quite an affair. The effort was to get us all launched
in a new and happy period and the method was the tried and

true one of drinking and feasting, dancing, pranking, laughing, flirting, and having fun. I had a new knife-pleated silk skirt, ankle length, dark blue shot with green and cyclamen, and a new off-the-shoulder blouse, and Mary Foote Williams, the visitor, wore a slit skirt, but Hope took the cake in her hoop skirts from her senior-high-school days, and her hair in a coarse gold net.

"The shrimp are gorgeous," she said. "Come look. I called Mama and requested prayer for good weather. It never fails."

"Charlie called," I said. "He said he'd be maybe thirty minutes late and would come on his own."

A car pulled up in the drive and there was Grey circling around and holding the door for Nelle herself. She had on a simple silk dress with her fine hair brushed loose and a pair of sexy new high-heeled sandals. It looked natural to see them together and I breathed easier without knowing I hadn't been doing it for quite a while. Hope was right, we'd had enough of all this foolishness.

"That just leaves John and Rose," said Hope, "and I have my own ideas about them."

"What?" I asked.

"Well, I shouldn't say. It's y'all's crowd." She was quick in her kitchen, clicking around with her skirts swaying. She had got a nice little colored girl, Perline, dressed up in black with a white ruffled apron. "I just think John's halfway to a stuffed shirt and Rose is going to get him all the way there."

So, our crowd or not, she was going right ahead.

"I think this has to do with you-know-what," I said.

"We aren't going to mention you-know-what," said Hope. "From now on, honey, my only four-letter words are 'dry' and 'cleaning.'"

John and Rose didn't show up, but two new couples did, a pair from Hattiesburg and the Kellmans, new in town but promising. Hope had let them in. Pete exercised himself at the bar and there was a strong punch as well. We strolled out to the pool and sat on white-painted iron chairs with cushions in green flowered plastic. Nelle sat with her pretty legs crossed, talking to Mary Foote. Grey was at her elbow. The little maid passed out canapés and shrimp. Light was still lingering in a clear sky barely pink at the edges. Pete skimmed leaves from the pool surface with a long-handled net. Lightning bugs winked and drifted, and the new little wife from Hattiesburg caught one or two in her palm and watched them crawl away, then take wing. "I used to do that," said Nelle. Then she shivered and Grey went for a shawl. It grew suddenly darker and one or two pale stars could be seen, then dozens. Pete, vanished inside, had started some records. Some people began to trail back in. And with another drink (the third, maybe?), it wasn't clear how much time had passed, when there came the harsh roar of a motor from the private road, growing stronger the nearer it got, a slashing of gravel in the drive out front, and a door slamming. And the first thing you knew there was Charlie Waybridge, filling the whole doorframe before Pete or Hope could even go to open it. He put his arms out to everybody. "Well, whaddaya know!" he said.

His tie was loose two buttons down and his light seersucker dress coat was crumpled and open but at least had it on. I went right to him. He'd been drinking, of course, I'd known it from the first sound of the car—but who wasn't drinking? "Hi ya, baby!" he said, and grabbed me.

Then Pete and Hope were getting their greetings and were leading him up to meet the new people, till he got to the bar, where he dropped off to help himself.

It was that minute that Perline, the little maid, came in with a plate in her hand. Charlie swaggered up to her and said, "Well, if it ain't Mayola's daughter." He caught her chin in his hand. "Ain't that so?" "Yes, sir," said Perline. "I am." "Used to know yo' mama," said Charlie. Perline looked confused for a minute; then she lowered her eyes and giggled like she knew she was supposed to. "Gosh sake, Charlie," I said, "quit horsing around and let's dance." It was hard to get him out of these moods. But I'd managed it more than once, dancing.

Charlie was a good strong leader and the way he danced, one hand firm to my waist, he would take my free hand in his and knuckle it tight against his chest. I could follow him better than I could anybody. Sometimes everybody would stop just to watch us, but the prize that night was going to Pete and Hope, they were shining around with some new steps that made the hoop skirts jounce. Charlie was half drunk, too, and bad on the turns.

"Try to remember what's important about this evening," I said. "You know what Hope and Pete are trying for, don't you?"

"I know I'm always coming home to a lecture," said Charlie and swung me out, spinning. "What a woman for sounding like a wife." He got me back and I couldn't tell if he was mad or not, I guess it was half and half; but right then he almost knocked over one of Hope's floral arrangements, so I said, "Why don't you go upstairs and catch your forty winks? Then you can come down fresh and start over." The music stopped. He blinked, looked tired all of a sudden, and, for a miracle, like a dog that never once chose to hear you, he minded.

I breathed a sigh when I saw him going up the stairs. But now I know I never once mentioned Nelle to him or reminded him right out, him with his head full of oil leases, bourbon, and the road, that she was the real cause of the party. Nelle was somewhere else, off in the back sitting room on a couch, to be exact, swapping family news with Mary Foote, who was her cousin.

Dancing with Charlie like that had put me in a romantic mood, and I fell to remembering the time we had first got serious, down on the coast where one summer we had all rented a fishing schooner. We had come into port at Mobile for more provisions and I had showered and dressed and was standing on deck in some leather sandals that tied around the ankle, a fresh white T-shirt, and some clean navy shorts. I had washed my hair, which was short then, and clustered in dark damp curls at the forehead. I say this about myself because when Charlie was coming on board with a six-pack in either hand, he stopped dead still. It was like it was the first time he'd ever seen me. He actually said that very thing later on after we'd finished with the boat and stayed on an extra day or so with all the crowd, to eat shrimp and gumbo and dance every night. We'd had our flare-ups before, but nothing had ever caught like that one. "I can't forget seeing you on the boat that day," he would say. "Don't be crazy, you'd seen me on that boat every day for a week." "Not like that," he'd rave, "like something fresh from the sea." "A catfish," I said. "Stop it, Eileen," he'd say, and dance me off the floor to the dark outside, and kiss me. "I can't get enough of you," he'd say, and take me in so close I'd get dizzy.

I kept thinking through all this in a warm frame of mind while making the rounds and talking to everybody, and maybe an hour, more or less, passed that way, when I heard a voice from the stairwell (Charlie) say: "God Almighty, if it isn't Nelle," and I turned around and saw all there was to see.

Charlie was fresh from his nap, the red faded from his face and his tie in place (he'd even buzzed off his five-o'clock shadow with Pete's electric razor). He was about five steps up from the bottom of the stairs. And Nelle, just coming back into the living room to join everybody, had on a Chinese-red silk shawl with a fringe. Her hair, so simple and shining, wasn't dark or blond either, just the color of hair, and she had on the plain dove-gray silk dress and the elegant sandals. She was framed in the door. Then I saw Charlie's face, how he was drinking her in, and I remembered the day on the boat.

"God damn, Nelle," said Charlie. He came down the steps and straight to her. "Where you been?"

"Oh, hello, Charlie," said Nelle in her friendly way. "Where have *you* been?"

"Honey, that's not even a question," said Charlie. "The point is, I'm *here*."

Then he fixed them both a drink and led her over to a couch in the far corner of the room. There was a side porch at the Owenses', spacious, with a tile floor—that's where we'd all been dancing. The living room was a little off center to the party. I kept on with my partying, but I had eyes in the back of my head where Charlie was concerned. I knew they were there on the couch and that he was crowding her toward one end. I hoped he was talking to her about Grey. I danced with Grey.

"Why don't you go and break that up?" I said.

"Why don't you?" said Grey.

"Marriage is different," I said.

"She can break it up herself if she wants to," he said.

I'd made a blunder and knew it was too late. Charlie was holding both Nelle's hands, talking over something. I fixed myself a stiff drink. It had begun to rain, quietly, with no advance warning. The couple from Hattiesburg had started doing some kind of talking blues number on the piano. Then we were singing. The couch was empty. Nelle and Charlie weren't there. . . .

It was Grey who came to see me the next afternoon. I was hung over but working anyway. Mr. McGinnis didn't recognize hangovers.

"I'm not asking her anywhere again," said Grey. "I'm through and she's through. I've had it. She kept saying in the car, 'Sure, I did like Charlie Waybridge, we all liked Charlie Waybridge. Maybe I was in love with Charlie Waybridge. But why start it up all over again? Why?' 'Why did you?' I said. 'That's more the question.' 'I never meant to, just there he was, making me feel that way.' 'You won't let me make you feel any way,' I said. 'My foot hurts,' she said, like a little girl. She looked a mess. Mud all over her dress and her hair gone to pieces. She had sprained her ankle. It had swelled up. That big."

"Oh, Lord," I said. "All Pete and Hope wanted was for you all— Look, can't you see Nelle was just drunk? Maybe somebody slugged her drink."

"She didn't have to drink it."

I was hearing Charlie: "All she did was get too much. Hadn't partied anywhere in months. Said she wanted some fresh air. First thing I knew she goes tearing out in the rain and whoops! in those high-heeled shoes—sprawling."

"Charlie and her," Grey went on. Okay, so he was hurt. Was that any reason to hurt me? But on he went. "Her and Charlie, that summer you went away up north, they were dating every night. Then her sister got sick, the one that died? She couldn't go on the coast trip with us."

"You think I don't know all that?" Then I said: "Oh, Grey!" and he left.

Yes, I sat thinking, unable to type anything: it was the summer her sister died and she'd had to stay home. I was facing up to Charlie Waybridge. I didn't want to, but there it was. If Nelle had been standing that day where I had stood, if Nelle had been wearing those sandals, that shirt, those shorts— Why pretend not to know Charlie Waybridge, through and through? What was he really doing on the Townshend property that night?

Pete, led by Hope, refused to believe anything but that the party had been a big success. "Like old times," said Pete. "What's wrong with new times?" said Hope. In our weakness and disarray, she was moving on in. (Damn Nelle Townshend.) Hope loved the new people; she was working everybody in together. "The thing for you to do about *that* . . ." she was now fond of saying on the phone, taking on problems of every sort.

When Hope heard that Nelle had sprained her ankle and hadn't been seen out in a day or so, she even got Pete one afternoon and went to call. She had telephoned but nobody answered. They walked up the long front walk between the elephant ears and up the front porch steps and rang the old turning bell half a dozen times. Hope had a plate of cake and Pete was carrying a bunch of flowers.

Finally Mrs. Townshend came shuffling to the door. Humpbacked, she had to look way up to see them, at a mole's angle. "Oh, it's you," she said.

"We just came to see Nelle," Hope chirped. "I understand she hurt her ankle at our party. We'd just like to commiserate."

"She's in bed," said Mrs. Townshend; and made no further move, either to open the door or take the flowers. Then she said, "I just wish you all would leave Nelle alone. You're no good for her. You're no good I know of for anybody. She went through all those years with you. She doesn't want you anymore. I'm of the same opinion." Then she leaned over and from an old-fashioned umbrella stand she drew up and out what could only be called a shotgun. "I keep myself prepared," she said. She cautiously lowered the gun into the umbrella stand. Then she looked up once again at them, touching the rims of her little oval glasses. "When I say you all, I mean all of you. You're drinking and you're doing all sorts of things that waste time, and you call that having fun. It's not my business unless you come here and make me say so, but Nelle's too nice to say so. Nelle never would—" She paused a long time, considering in the mildest sort of way. "Nelle can't shoot," she concluded, like this fact had for the first time occurred to her. She closed the door, softly and firmly.

I heard all this from Hope a few days later. Charlie was off again and I was feeling lower than low. This time we hadn't even quarreled. It seemed more serious than that. A total re-evaluation. All I could come to was a question: Why doesn't he reassure me? All I could answer was that he must be in love with Nelle. He tried to call her when I wasn't near. He sneaked off to do it, time and again.

Alone, I tried getting drunk to drown out my thoughts, but couldn't, and alone for a day too long, I called up Grey. Grey and I used to date, pretty heavy. "Hell," said Grey, "I'm fed up to here and so are you. Let's blow it." I was tight enough to say yes and we met out at the intersection. I left my car at the shopping-center parking lot. I remember the sway of his Buick Century, turning onto the Interstate. We went up to Jackson.

The world is spinning now and I am spinning along with it. It doesn't stand still anymore to the stillness inside that murmurs to me, I know my love and I belong to my love when all is said and done, down through foreverness and into eternity. No, when I got back I was just part of it all, ordinary, a twenty-eight-year-old attractive married woman with family and friends and a nice house in Tyler, Mississippi. But with nothing absolute.

When I had a drink too many now, I would drive out to the woods and stop the car and walk around among places always known. One day, not even thinking about them, I saw Nelle drive by and this time there was no doubt who was with her— Robin Byers. They were talking. Well, Robin's wife mended the clothes when they were ripped or torn, and she sewed buttons on. Maybe they were going there. I went home.

At some point the phone rang. I had seen to it that it was "out of order" when I went up to Jackson with Grey, but now it was "repaired," so I answered it. It was Nelle.

"Eileen, I guess you heard Mama turned Pete and Hope out the other day. She was just in the mood for telling everybody off." Nelle laughed her clear, pure laugh. You can't have a laugh like that unless you've got a right to it, I thought.

"How's your ankle?" I asked.

"I'm still hobbling around. What I called for, Mama wanted me to tell you something. She said, 'I didn't mean quite everybody. Eileen can still come. You tell her that.'"

Singled out. If she only knew, I thought. I shook when I put down the phone.

But I did go. I climbed up to Nelle's bedroom with Mrs. Townshend toiling behind me, and sat in one of those old rocking chairs near a bay window with oak paneling and cane plant, green and purple, in a window box. I stayed quite a while. Nelle kept her ankle propped up and Mrs. Townshend sat in a tiny chair about the size of a twelve-year-old's, which was about the size she was. They told stories and laughed with that innocence that seemed like all clear things—a spring in the woods, a dogwood bloom, a carpet of pine needles along a sun-dappled road. Like Nelle's ankle, I felt myself getting well. It was a new kind of wellness, hard to describe. It didn't have much to do with Charlie and me.

"Niggers used to come to our church," Mrs. Townshend recalled. "They had benches in the back. I don't know why they quit. Maybe they all died out—the ones we had, I mean."

"Maybe they didn't like the back," said Nelle.

"It was better than nothing at all. The other churches didn't even have that. There was one girl going to have a baby. I was scared she would have it right in the church. Your father said, 'What's wrong with that? Dr. Erskine could deliver it, and we could baptize it on the spot.'"

I saw a picture on one of those little tables they had by the dozen, with the starched linen doilies and the bowed-out legs. It was of two gentlemen, one taller than the other, standing side by side in shirtsleeves and bow ties and each with elastic bands around their upper arms, the kind that used to hold the sleeves to a correct length of cuff. They were smiling in a fine natural way, out of friendship. One must have been Nelle's father, dead so long ago. I asked about the other. "Child," said Mrs. Townshend, "don't you know your own grandfather? He and Sid thought the world of one another." I had a better feeling when I left. Would it last? Could I get it past the elephant ears?

I didn't tell Charlie about going there. Charlie got it from some horse's mouth that Grey and I were up in Jackson that time, and he pushed me off the back steps. An accident, he said; he didn't see me when he came whamming out the door. For a minute I thought I, too, had sprained or broken something, but a skinned knee was all it was. He watched me clean the knee, watched the bandage go on. He wouldn't go out—not to Pete and Hope's, not to Rose and John's, not to anywhere —and the whiskey went down in the bottle.

I dreamed one night of Robin Byers, that I ran into him uptown but didn't see a scar on his face. I followed him, asking, Where is it? What happened? Where's it gone? But he walked straight on, not seeming to hear. But it was no dream that his house caught fire, soon after the cleaning shop opened again. Both Robin and Nelle said it was only lightning struck the back wing and burned out a shed room before Robin could stop the blaze. Robin's daughter got jumped on at school by some other black children who yelled about her daddy being a "Tom." They kept her at home for a while to do her school-work there. What's next?

Next for me was going to an old lady's apartment for Mr. McGinnis, so she could sign her will, and on the long steps to her door, running into Robin Byers, fresh from one of his deliveries.

"Robin," I said, at once, out of nowhere, surprising myself, "you got to leave here, Robin. You're tempting fate, every day."

And he, just as quick, replied: "I got to stay here. I got to help Miss Nelle."

Where had it come from, what we said? Mine wasn't a bit like me; I might have been my mother or grandmother talking. Certainly not the fun girl who danced on piers in whirling miniskirts and dove off a fishing boat to reach a beach, swimming, they said, between the fishhooks and the sharks. And Robin's? From a thousand years back, maybe, superior and firm, speaking out of sworn duty, his honored trust. He was standing above me on the steps. It was just at dark, and in the first streetlight I could see the white scar, running riverlike down the flesh, like the mark lightning leaves on a smooth tree. When we passed each other, it was like erasing what we'd said and that we'd ever met.

But one day I am walking in the house and picking up the telephone, only to find Charlie talking on the extension. "Nelle . . ." I hear. "Listen, Nelle. If you really are foolin' around with that black bastard, he's answering to *me*." And *blam!* goes the phone from her end, loud as any gun of her mother's.

I think we are all hanging on a golden thread, but who has got the other end? Dreaming or awake, I'm praying it will hold us all suspended.

Yes, praying—for the first time in years.

The Legacy

IN THE STILLNESS, from three blocks over, Dottie Almond could hear a big diesel truck out on the highway, climbing the grade up to the stoplight, stopping, shifting gears, and passing on.

She went and brushed her hair that was whiter than pull candy and rubbed a little dime-store lipstick on her mouth. In the bathroom window, her cousin Tandy's big white buckskin shoes all but covered the sill. They were outlined with swirling perforated leather strips, toe and heel and nest for laces, and had been placed there to dry. When he got back from Memphis, he would probably be going out on a date or out on the highway someplace or "just out," which was what he said when you never knew. He never asked Dottie anywhere, never told her anything, never talked to her once. She kept notes on him from such things as cleaned-up shoes.

She had heard them—Aunt Hazel and Tandy—out in the living room the night she came. They had thought she was asleep, she had been so dead tired when she'd gone to bed.

"One more mouth to feed, huh?" Tandy said. Whatever he said, it was always as if he were telling jokes, the subject of this present joke being what his mother had got into about Dottie.

"You don't have to look at it that way," Aunt Hazel said. "She had to be somewhere."

"Just keep her out of my things. She gets in my things, she's going to know it."

"Try and be nice to her."

"Not paying us a cent."

"Well, I know, but try your best. Be nice to her."

"Oh, I'll be nice to her." The tone went up; it was an unpromising voice, off center. If it made a promise, the promise might be its opposite because a word had got twisted around. "I'll be nice to her, all right."

Dottie's father worked in Birmingham and did not make much money. She'd had to go somewhere, which was why Aunt Hazel had taken her in. There was also a Great-aunt Maggie Lee Asquith, who (she had said) would have done the same and that she ought to, but she was too old, all alone in a big house in the middle of a Delta "place." A young girl like that—gull, she called it—a young gull like that ought to have young people around. Aunt Hazel and Tandy lived in a town with young people in it. They were the ones to take her in.

"How long you been with Miss Hazel?" The speaker was a Mr. Avery Donelson, to whose law office Dottie had just been summoned.

"About a year."

Hanging down from the straight chair one foot couldn't quite touch the floor. She crossed her legs, in order to resemble any other girl, though the man at the desk gave no sign of noticing. She had heard her father once say that Mr. Avery Donelson was a high-class fellow.

"Your family has a high mortality rate," he remarked, and seemed almost prepared to be amused about it.

Dottie didn't laugh. Death to her had nothing to do with anybody except her mother (who had held her hand when she hurt from polio and who was right there, everything they did to her. "When you hurt, I hurt, baby. Just think about that. Only I hurt twice as bad." Nobody else who had died—or lived either—had ever said that). However, Aunt Hazel's husband, Uncle Jack, had died of a stroke uptown one hot day three years ago, and Aunt Maggie Lee had gone quick, from cancer, just last spring. Dottie hadn't attended the funeral. Her daddy wouldn't let her. He had come over from Birmingham to stay with her while Aunt Hazel went. Aunt Maggie Lee was on her mother's side of the family. "You go on, Hazel," Daddy said. "My little ole sugar's not going to any more ole funerals." He had taken her out to eat in a restaurant and then, as they couldn't find anything to talk about, he took her to the picture show. The show was sad, so she got to cry in it. What she was thinking about was her mother's funeral. Maybe he had known that because he held her hand. When they got home Aunt Hazel and Tandy had got back from the Delta, where Aunt Maggie Lee's funeral was held that afternoon, and Daddy gave Dottie a lot of wet, smacking kisses and called her his little old honey bun, and went off back to Birmingham, late as it was.

She thought that Aunt Hazel made him nervous. "He's always got business somewhere," was what Aunt Hazel said . . .

"I knew your aunt Miss Maggie Lee pretty well," Mr. Avery Donelson said. "She was quite a stepper." He seemed to be enjoying himself.

"What's a stepper?" Dottie asked. So far she hadn't smiled; feeling herself observed, she kept her blue eyes steady, thought of her skin, which was darker than her taffy-white hair.

"She was a fine lady," he said. "Knew how to dress, how to talk. Kept a good house, set a good table. Lived in good circumstances. Husband was a planter. Left her well-fixed."

Dottie had herself known Aunt Maggie Lee. She and her mother had gone once or twice to visit her and stayed overnight, in the Delta, a long way from Birmingham. Mother was a little nervous and hoped Dottie and she were behaving all right, especially at the table. Aunt Maggie Lee sat up straight in graceful antique chairs; yet on the second day she lay down on the sofa for a while. ("Maggie Lee's tired," Mother said to someone when they returned. "I think something's wrong.") She had a kind of cosmetics Dottie had never seen in stores, and her bathrooms were rosy, her house soft with rugs and dim lights because the Delta in the summer was full of glare; air-conditioning was essential and curtains had to stay drawn. With her mother out of the room, Aunt Maggie Lee questioned Dottie extensively on a number of subjects. "Do you have a hobby?" she asked. "I collect things," Dottie said. "What, for instance?" "Bird cards from Arm and Hammer soda boxes, for one thing." "What else?" "Pencils, all different colors." When she was sick, for some reason, everybody had started giving her boxes of pencils. She had all colors now. If she got one the same color as another she would go out and exchange it for a color she didn't have. "Birds are of some interest," said Aunt Maggie Lee. "But pencils . . ."

"She kept up with you," Mr. Avery Donelson went on. "She knew about your making good grades in school. She thought you must have a little bit of what it took. I wanted to see you alone because of what she did for you. She made a special bequest for you before she died."

"Bequest?"

"A settlement . . . money . . . all yours. But—a secret."

Dottie was quaking again now; another one had known of her, thought and spoken of her, made her a secret and formal gift. It sounded like something God might do.

"You're not interested in how much?" Mr. Avery Donelson finally said.

"Five hundred dollars?" Then she blushed. Greedy was what she knew she'd sounded like.

"How about ten thousand?"

"Ten thousand? What? Pennies?" A wisecrack was not the right thing. She had just reached the conclusion that it was all a big joke.

"Dollars, young lady. And if you don't want 'em, there's plenty that will."

"I didn't mean that. It seemed like—. It was a surprise, that's all."

"Don't you like surprises?"

"It was a big surprise."

"You sing in school, I hear."

So he knew that, too. Her contralto voice had a rich thrill in it when she let go with a song. She and everybody else had found out about this by accident, trying out songs. They all liked to hear her, even the teachers, and they got her to sing at school programs sometimes. There would be dances, too, to sing at, but she wouldn't go to them. If you were crippled, it was better not to go. But on rainy days she could hold the student body in the auditorium at recess, singing almost anything anybody wanted to play for her. Her mother had never known she could sing, not like that.

"What do you want to be?" Mr. Avery Donelson pressed her. "That's a good sum of money, you know. Set up in trust until you turned eighteen, it could see you some of the way through college. Your Aunt Hazel wouldn't be able to afford to send you to college."

"Tandy doesn't like it because I live there free of charge," said Dottie. "He thinks I ought to pay. Maybe Aunt Hazel would think it, too, if she knew I could."

"Then don't mention it," he said at once. "You don't have to. We can say it's in trust for you, just for college."

"But it's not, is it?"

"She wanted you to decide, that's all. Me to administrate, advise. You to decide."

Through slats in the venetian blinds Dottie could see the town water tank, painted silver, the tops of the trees, see the still, hot, morning sky. The window air conditioner purred. Mr. Avery Donelson had brown-and-white horizontally striped curtains, a rug, a desk, some black leather chairs. His secretary was outside and the door was closed. He would never call a daughter "little old honey bun," and if he took her to dinner he would know what to talk about. He had known Aunt Maggie Lee, who was a stepper like himself and who had picked Dottie out for possible entry into a world different from Aunt Hazel's.

But did she *have* to be what they had decided, whatever it was? They had taken her consent for granted. She was dazed.

"I get to think it over, don't I?"

The carpet took her halting walk. The man at the desk—gray, unmoving, nicely suited but casually rumpled—had stopped smiling, sat watching instead, his attention all finally upon her. He rose to open the door. She was a small girl, came hardly to his top vest button.

"It's in the bank for you. I'm supposed to do anything you say, young lady." He pressed her hand.

Then she was through the office, down the stairs, and on the hot sidewalk that led back to Aunt Hazel's, hot and chill together in the scald of sun, a jerky progress through the dazzle.

All that money poured out on me, *me*, ME! She almost struck herself on the forehead. Transparent as a locust's wing, the frail self within tried to stir, to take up whatever was meant by it; since it was recognized, it ought to emerge and fly. But all it was was Dorothy Almond, plodding back toward her few small treasures and necessities, toward pencils and bird cards no two the same, her four or five cotton dresses, her slacks and blouses, her new white sandals.

When she came in the front door the phone was ringing. "I called you twice," said Aunt Hazel, on the other end.

"I was in the bathtub."

"You must have stayed till you shriveled. I have to work through dinner. Just fix yourself something."

"Yessum."

"Did the paper ever come?"

"Yessum."

"Did Tandy call?"

"No'm. I don't guess he did."

"I don't reckon so. I'll see you this evening, honey."

Dottie went and looked to see if the big white male shoes were still on the bathroom windowsill. They were. There was nowhere else they could have gone. Men's shoes, white, heavy, secretive, knowledgeable—they derided her as much after as before Mr. Avery Donelson's call had smashed into her silence. All else had changed and diminished; *they* were the same. What did she expect? She had heard of a distant cousin who had stuck his finger up an empty socket to see whether, since the bulb would not work, the lamp was broken. It wasn't. Was it a shock she had expected when she put her hand out and put her fingers over those shoes, heel to vamp to toe? Shoes like these, only brown, were now treading pavement in Memphis, Tennessee, with Tandy in them. He was going to know the minute he looked that something had happened to her, and he would find out what it was, right away. Now she was scared. A call to life was one thing, but getting the first breath kicked straight out of you—. It would happen if she wasn't careful. She called up Avery Donelson.

"You said I could have anything, any time."

"That's right."

"Can I have five hundred dollars, then?"

"Certainly."

"Can I get it at two o'clock?"

"That's possible."

"Will you put all the rest where nobody can get it, just tell them if they ask you that five hundred dollars was all there was, that was all?"

A hesitance. "If you say so."

She had climbed his answers like stair steps, one by one; they had taken her higher and higher, to the very top, and at that top—like saying "Walk!" the way they had in the hospital and she had held her breath and walked, the leg feeling liquid at first and numb, then thin as a toothpick but holding—so at this final moment in what was happening now, she had to jump, which was more than walk; and the jump was trust.

"Do you promise?" She clutched the receiver. Her eyes were squinched up tight.

"I promise." She was held, so far, unfalling.

The bus to Birmingham had left, as Dottie had known it would from visiting her father, at two-thirty. She was on it. Near a window, bolt upright with five hundred dollars—less the price of the ticket—in her purse, she was drawn forward above the landscape like a pulled-out string. In the Birmingham bus station, she dialed Daddy on the pay telephone, holding her finger on his number in the book. A woman's voice answered "Hell-o?" too loud. Dottie asked for Mr. Almond, then added for some reason, "I'm his daughter," but the woman said she had the wrong number. She tried again, but though she let the phone ring six times, nobody answered it. Maybe he was still at work. She tried Southern Railway, where he had his office, but only got the ticket counter, and when she tried to explain, they couldn't hear her, there was such a lot of noise at the other end, and then she was out of dimes. She walked out of the station, which smelled of frying hamburgers, still remembering the woman's voice on the phone. She attained to an enormous lack of conviction about things involved in finding Daddy, and seeing a bus with MIAMI on the front, she bought a ticket and climbed into it. On the bus, at intervals, she slept. Miami was not till the next day. When she got there, she didn't know what to do, so took another bus that said KEY WEST. In Key West there was nothing to do either, but it was the end. Dottie went to a motel of separate cabins in a shady park full of plants, rented one, and fell asleep.

It was the end of running; that she knew. Like a small planet, she had set.

Another day, freshly risen, she sat in a newly bought bathing suit on a sandy beach with one leg tucked under her, looking out at the sea. There were large clouds above her, all the same color as her hair, which made them seem more personal than they might have been to brunettes or redheads.

There was a boy circling round, a man, really, though younger than Tandy and certainly better to look at. He was all bronze and gold, like a large, well-formed wasp, she thought, and he had the same copper hair on his head, chest, arms, and

legs. And his drift—the way he spoke to her, looked at her—
was something like that of a wasp, which might or might not
be thinking favorably of you. He asked her if she wanted to
swim, and she told him no.

"You're getting sunburned," he said.

"I'm all right," she said.

"Where are you staying?"

"The Hibiscus."

"Walk you home?"

She shook her head, gazing up at the clouds. But he was
right. She *was* getting sunburned. She wished he'd go. She
wished he'd leave her alone. Then he did.

Dottie had told him the truth about the Hibiscus because
she had done nothing lately but tell lies. The first night away,
for instance, at a bus stop, she had phoned Aunt Hazel so Aunt
Hazel wouldn't call out the FBI, or the highway patrol, or
whatever you called out, to look for her. She had said:

"Aunt Hazel, I hope you found the letter I left."

What followed was such a volley of words that Dottie felt
sorry for Aunt Hazel, who when she got to worrying about
things there was no stopping her. "Let me tell you something,
honey. It's just ridiculous for you to go off like that. If Maggie
Lee had known you'd be spending all her money at the beach,
she never would have left you a dime, let alone five hundred
dollars. But there you are throwing it away, *five hundred dollars*, and with any number of things you really need, and I can't
think of why anybody would be that inconsiderate, as good as
Tandy and I have been to you. Why didn't you at least go to
see your daddy in Birmingham?"

"I tried to call him, but he wasn't there."

"You ain't *with* anybody?"

"No'm."

"Well, you'd just better mind out," Aunt Hazel said. And
when Dottie didn't answer she said, "You'll phone me every
night until you get home? I'm going to worry about you every
single night."

Dottie stayed in the shady little cabin she had rented at Hibiscus Cottages All Conveniences Pool TV. You reached the
cabins through winding paved paths bordered by plants and

flowering shrubs, shaded by palms. It was a pretty place, and not many people were there. Not that many people came to Key West in the summer, so they said. If you swam in the pool, the water felt like you could just as well take a bath in it. She read some movie magazines, then a paperback mystery book, then made a ham sandwich and ate it, ate a tomato whole with salt, ate some coconut marshmallow cookies, some pink, some white, and drank a glass of milk. Then she lay down and looked at TV and fell asleep with the air conditioner purring. At four o'clock she went walking. It was still hot all over town, hot as an oven, but the clouds had got bigger, and from somewhere off she heard a rumble of thunder.

At the end of a street, she could look at the gulf, and way out there she saw the big clouds piled higher than ever before, the silver color darkening from the top downward. She turned her back on them and walked into town, past houses with plants round them, oleanders, a stubby sort of grass, pale faded green or artificial funeral-parlor green, not like the grass up home, and always palms, some bent and low as plants, some the size of real trees. The trees she liked the best were—she'd been told by an old lady on the bus coming down—royal palms. The trunks of the palms were round, swelled out at mid-height but narrow at top and bottom, and looked to be made of stone, with a bunch of thick palm fronds coming out of the top, as though stuck in a too-tall vase. They were pretty trees, Dottie decided, and when the afternoon rain hit Key West and she had no idea which way to go to get back, she went and sat under one of them, at the corner of somebody's property. It was probably the most dangerous place to be, as the tree was high and would attract a lightning bolt possibly, but its top was waving in such an impressive way she thought she'd rather be there than elsewhere. She crouched there as the rain fell in ropes. Soon she was soaked to the skin.

When the sun burst out again she started returning by trial and error and so came into the Hibiscus from the back, before she knew it. Standing in the garden, also wet, wearing beige cotton trousers, a T-shirt, and a dripping slicker was the copper-haired boy she had met at the beach. She ran right into him and then, seeing it wasn't just a coincidence, that he was coming toward her, she turned around and started off through the paths. He had to run to catch her arm. She stopped, head down and shuddering, like she'd seen wild animals do in the country the minute some boy would get his hands on them. She drooped like that and didn't look.

"What'd you come for?" she said.

"You're not from around here, are you?"

She shook her head.

"What are you limping about?"

"Something fell on me."

The boy looked around at the maze of paths, the village of cottages spotted out among the dripping foliage. "Where's yours?"

"Number ten."

He was half holding her up, but before he got to the door he thought it simpler to carry her, and so did. "Give me your key." She took out the key, but being let down, stood holding herself upright by the door, downcast still, and tremulous. "Nothing really fell on me," she said.

"But you're hurt, obviously."

"I'm crippled."

"Is that why you wouldn't go swimming?"

"Please."

She felt his large warm hand drop from her arm. "Okay." He drew back, looking at her with a different air altogether. Was she glad or not? She didn't know. She thought she must have looked terrible after the rain. Like a drowned white rat, she thought, closing the door on him, leaning against it.

She was still hearing his voice and not answering it. New feelings—fresh, sharp, hurting—had sprung up as though branches of her blood had turned into vines that were determined all by themselves to flourish in her. It was what she thought it would never do any good to look for. She fell face down across the bed. She might have known, but hadn't. She could have said that in addition to being lame, her mother had died, and that the lawyer Mr. Avery Donelson had sent for her, and that her aunt Miss Maggie Lee Asquith, well known in the Delta, had left her a legacy of ten thousand dollars, a part of which, in the opinion of Aunt Hazel, she was now throwing away in Florida. She was somebody picked out. Being lame in *itself* was being picked out. But he wouldn't see any of that.

He wasn't from where she was. All that traveled with her was a short leg.

And her white hair, whiter than taffy, born white, said the streak of sun coming through the one slat of blinds that had got twisted.

Late in the afternoon, her hair brushed and combed, face washed, she walked down the main street of Key West, past the big square hotel. She was looking for somewhere to eat and went past a big open bar where a sign said Ernest Hemingway used to sit and drink. Among palms, and near a large spreading tree with red flowers, she saw a barnlike building painted brick red whose sign, also outside, said it was a playhouse. Another sign, of hastily lettered green on white cardboard, said that tryouts for a play were being held. Dottie hobbled to the door and found it open. She went through an empty foyer plastered with posters, and through a second large heavy door into an auditorium with a stage before it and rows of folding chairs, some disarranged, some open and placed in regular lines, others closed and propped against the walls.

A tall dark woman like the statue of a goddess, wearing a crumpled linen dress and leather sandals, was standing near the center of the stage, which was lighted artificially, with a large bound sheaf of pages in her hand, open half the way through, back folded on itself. Her hands were long, and tanned, and aware of themselves; her whole self was aware and nurtured; her black hair tumbled the way she wanted it to around her face. She was pointing out to three or four others on the stage with her, younger than she, what they ought to do, what she thought they ought to do, how this, how that. She turned, walked away, leaned back against a table, and picked up a half-smoked cigarette from an ashtray, inhaling, pluming smoke; her body gave life to the clinging linen. At the lift of her fingers, the young actors, all about Dottie's age, holding smaller books, began to read aloud. Dottie hated the large woman of authority in linen and sandals . . . she was afraid of her by instinct. She turned to go away, but was called to.

"Hey, blondie!"

Obedient, not showing what she felt, she turned back and limped forward, down between the raggedly arranged chairs.

The woman had come to the footlights, and as Dottie approached, the former went down on one knee, as though kneeling by the edge of a pool to retrieve something. She did it like poetry. Dottie's face was a mask, looking up at her.

"You want to try out? What can you do?"

"Sing," said Dottie.

"Sing what?"

The boys were talking now, over the footlights, the words falling toward her lifted face: "Rock? . . . Revival? . . . Country-western?"

"Just sing," Dottie said. "Popular mostly."

"There's all kinds of popular," one of the boys said. "But, hey—stick around. We expected more people. . . . Take a script."

"Take mine," another boy said.

"You know this play? It's *Picnic*. There's a song in it somewhere, at least I think there is."

"Or we'll put one in," somebody said, and another: "She looks like Kim Novak."

"I'm crippled," Dottie said, right out. "I can sing, that's all."

There was a quick silence, like a whole orchestra gone dead. Then they reached their arms down and pulled her up over the footlights, out of the dark and onto the bright stage. She hobbled over to the piano and a girl about her age came and sat down to play for her. She sang one of the songs she liked, and they clapped, saying with astonished voices how wonderful she was, and she knew it, too.

She had bought herself a little cap, like a sailor's cap, at an open-air shop along the way where things were all displayed, and when she sang her song she held this in her small hands and knew it made a good effect. When they shot a spotlight on her face she didn't mind a bit. A sissy boy at school used to turn his spotlight on her: she was used to it. Her face and voice went floating away from her legs, off from the part they could forget while she sang. She heard them applaud again and she heard what they said and then she sang again and told them that was all.

The light switched off. The large woman seemed to her to have gone completely, but this was not so; she had gone out of the circle of light to sit on the edge of a table.

Then they were leaving. Dottie was moving with them, or they with her, as she was not going with them in spirit, but only moving alone though among them, through the disarray of chairs in the big dusky barnlike room, and feeling not so far from home, for it resembled the high school auditorium where she had held many more people for an even longer time. She heard them speaking to her but was not answering; and then the daylight struck through the second door they opened, not glaring as when she had entered, but softened by evening. There was a car freshly pulled up beside a yellow Pontiac that had been parked there when Dottie went in, and the boy was in it, the one from the beach and the storm, just getting out when he saw them come through the door. She saw him get out, turning as he closed the door the way she had seen good basketball players turn without seeming to move at all, the way dancers follow each other. He was there for them, she knew at once: his approach said so. And she knew too why she had been afraid of the dark woman.

Dottie left the crowd and walked across the street.

"Hi." The boy was following her.

"Hi." She didn't stop walking.

"You're in the play?"

"Ask them," she said and kept limping on.

The pool was a quiet rectangle with no one swimming in it, and the people who circled, stood, wound, and twined and drank and talked with one another moved like columns, slowly revolving and changing place, one to another, in long dresses, in white jackets, reflecting in the water. The house was built around this open area, with a balustrade above in white painted wood such as Dottie thought she'd seen in pictures or paintings. There were brick-colored urns of geraniums and a long twining plant with purplish blue blooms as if a head of hair had decked itself that way, and there were others, yellow and pink and white. No one walked on the balustrades, or climbed the stairs. They turned, columnar and decorous, with muted voices, around the still pool. They sipped from glasses that sparkled with amber whiskey or white gin or crystal ice.

"No, thank you," said Dottie. "Just some water," she said.

She refused not from righteousness or inexperience but simply because she was drunk already, having earlier ordered three martinis in a restaurant somewhere near the Hibiscus. Later, she'd been found wandering around the old Spanish fort, jumping off and onto the parapet, pretending nothing was the matter with her while all sorts of wild ideas somersaulted through her head—been found by the copper-haired boy and another, his friend.

In the friend's car, all of Key West had looped and dived around her like a dolphin. If you got drunk, how long did you have to stay drunk? She was wondering this when the friend stopped before a Spanish-type house and, once inside, began pulling evening skirts out of a closet.

"Try any one you want."

"You got a sister?" Dottie said.

"She's not here. Besides, she wouldn't mind. She swaps clothes all the time," he said with a laugh to the boy Dottie knew, the copper-haired boy. Johnny was his name.

The phone rang and Johnny's friend went to answer it. Johnny threw his arms around Dottie and tumbled her back on the bed. She lay there a little while with his arms around her. Then they heard the other boy coming back and she got up to try the skirts on. In the long skirt she felt uncrippled. She moved her built-up sandal in a different way, just like her hips were swaying. Pretty, pretty, she thought, looking in the mirror. I can be like magic.

Then they drove to another house, the big one with the drive. There Dottie saw the dark woman whom in linen she had hated, only she was columnar now, standing by the still pool in a bold drop of yellow with great white wings or fronds and a white binding against the tan of her bare arms and her hair in rich careless coils.

"They tell me you sing, young lady."

The speaker was a man, the host here, with dark thinning hair combed straight back. He smiled at Dottie and showed teeth that looked false.

"Yes, sir," she said.

He asked her where she'd come from, where she went to school, where she wanted to go to college. She must have been saying things back.

"Can you sing for us?" he said. "Sometime this evening, I mean."

"I'm sorry."

"Oh, you must," he said.

"I got drunk," Dottie said.

The beautiful dark head above the bare brown back showed it had heard her and was turning. The carefully painted mask hung perfectly. Dottie wanted to be with people who wouldn't notice her too much. Nobody would have cared what she said except the dark woman, who was, of course, her enemy, and said nothing.

Dottie started climbing the flight of stairs. A Cuban-looking man in a white jacket had said she would find the bathroom up there. In passing she saw that a pottery urn filled with blooms was just above the head of the hostess, the dark woman, Pam, the enemy who did not want her to live. Dottie placed her hands, one on either side of the urn, and gazed, calculating, as one might along the barrel of a cousin's BB gun. She drank up the possibility of the action as she might another martini. This was what she needed to do, but couldn't. A door opened off in the shadowy passageway behind her, and she turned, surprised, unable to see anyone.

Later, coming out of the bathroom, she thought about the urn again but in a distant way. Johnny met her at the foot of the stairs with a banana daiquiri and somebody from above screamed, "Watch out!" They all looked up. An old woman with too bright blond hair, too scarlet a mouth was clutching at that same terra-cotta urn, and everyone leaped aside as it swung, tottered, slipped past her painted nails and long pink chiffon handkerchief, smashing on the marble paving near the pool.

"Grandmother!"

The old woman, like a mad witch entered on a balcony during a play, leaned far out into the velvet air, calling, "I hit it by mistake! It just fell!"

To Dottie, who could not stop gazing above, it was like seeing herself sixty years from now, a grotesque double. Was it the old lady's door she had heard a while ago?

The Cuban, a servant it seemed, was picking up pieces of broken pottery that had scattered near Pam's skirt. Pam's husband, whom someone had jerked from the falling urn's path, mounted the stairs toward the old woman.

Conversation resumed. There was a drift toward a table of food. Someone remarked that half of Key West was there. Many of them were young, the age of Johnny, more or less.

I'll just sneak out, Dottie thought. I'll go home alone.

But she didn't go home alone, because Johnny reappeared to drive her, and not with the boy whose sister's skirt she wore, but Johnny alone and driving like the wind, racing out from Key West up the long highway that arrowed toward Marathon, then swirling off along back shell roads because he was high on something maybe liquor maybe not and talking a blue streak, and she was piecing it out the best she could, she Dottie Almond, to whom all of life was gradually reducing itself to one single problem: How to Stay Awake Another Minute. The day must have already been sixty-four hours long. She could hear him the way she might hear the sea rustling when asleep by it, or the way you'd hear prayers in church.

"Morrissey knew about it from the first and that I wasn't any killer, not a thief, and certainly that if I went too far that time, it was out of my own principles . . . how they got out of bounds. He had some good inside stuff about them, but when they put on the pressure, he was even able to swing a position elsewhere, it's how he got the big appointment . . . oh, Pam's money . . . you saw that house . . . where'd he be without it, nobody can say, only it's not so much money . . . just that he saw a way of getting me out, out of the country till it blew over . . . that was when Pam came looking. It was her idea . . . I'd swear to it anytime . . ."

"Out of the country where?" she mumbled, her mouth sticky inside from being sleepy.

"Think of anywhere. Mexico. Think of Canada."

She thought of Canada, but only saw polar bears. They had got back. He turned at the Hibiscus sign and, drifting in, stopped the car. Hundred-pound weights sat on her eyelids. "Look." He held his hands forward and turned up the dash light, then showed her his fingers, palms up. She could discern by the dim light what she'd seen before, the healed skin over fingertips that had been cut or burnt. She was still hearing the soft crush of shells beneath the tires, and then she felt the broken fingertips like pieces of screen printing her cheek and neck, then her mouth pressed and opened with his own. She remembered earlier how he'd pushed her down, knew her body had taken a note of it, like a secretary might write down a call to be made at a later moment, which had now arrived. She was dead for sleep, opened the door herself to stumble out and find her cabin but instead was being carried, floating, skimming silently down along a smooth and swollen stream, face rising up above the surface, eyes closed, branches of oleander, vines of bougainvillea, hibiscus like trumpets, crisp and red.

She woke with the sun coming in through the blinds, the long borrowed skirt crumpled on a chair, herself a trampled field with a game over, the score standing.

She lay there till she got hungry. No one came in the door and no message was to be found. She dressed, folded up the skirt, and put it in a grocery sack. Outside, it was clear and hot, without a cloud. The breathless immensity of the Florida day entered her breathing self and made it light and pure. She could find him. The skirt was her excuse.

He wasn't at play practice, nor was anyone. A tolling bell reminded her: This was Sunday. She turned strange corners until she saw—far down a street in the ever-heating sunlight—a couple of shore patrols in white uniforms struggling with a man they were dragging out of a front walk between red flowers. All down the street she could hear their heaving breath but no words . . . nothing to say.

She grew faint and around eleven-thirty went into a drugstore, sat down at the lunch counter, and ate a sandwich. A fan was turning overhead. In a jar of pickling brine, some large eggs were floating. The man at the counter was darkly thinking of things not before him. The whiteness of the eggs in the huge jar frightened Dottie vaguely. From the mirror a smooth little face, her own, watched and noted that she looked about the same.

Move closer, or go far, she thought and folded up her paper napkin. She knew which already. She paid her check and gathered up her bundle as responsibly as if it bore a child inside. She had wandered in; now, committed and compelled, she went a chosen way. She was lame, yes, and motherless, yes, and she'd been left with a legacy greater than she needed, but the one thing she knew she bore was a right to be seen, to be answered.

Everything, she guessed, was in the precise look of that big luxurious white stucco house when she finally found it by the blaze of the afternoon sun. She trudged in through the gate, her footsteps making unequal crushes into the gravel, her height not reaching halfway up the square sentinel posts of the entrance drive. The house looked blank, green-shuttered, sheltered and curtained and cool within. She remembered the patio, the pond, the trailing vines, thick as a head of hair, a house with a woman inside whom she didn't like, an intricate mystery. In one sense she drove herself forward; in another, it was all she could possibly do. Her vital thread, whose touch was her life, was leading her.

From the upper-floor windows, she supposed, you could see the water. The entrance was recessed into the shadow of an arch, and a grillwork gate of iron stood ajar before a closed front door of dark-stained wood. A fanlike spread of steps led down to the gravel drive, and above them and below, a paving of square yellow tiles gave off a flat gloss to the sun. At either end of the tiled area below, large cement urns of verbena stood on square pedestals.

Clambering upward, step by halting step, she gained the entrance, but before approaching the door, she turned and looked around her. Out at the side where the pool was situated, she could see the coconut head of the Cuban, motionless, out of hearing. She walked three steps backward, and looked up to where, on a balcony above, the dark woman stood. She shielded her face from the sun.

"I thought you'd be at play practice," Dottie said.

"Not on Sunday. Wait there. I'm coming down."

Sandals on the long white walkways, the white-railed stairs, the marble floors, approaching expensively.

Then Dottie heard the sound of a car turning into the drive. She dropped the sack and ran.

Hidden behind a large stone urn full of verbena, Dottie watched as her enemy greeted Johnny at the door. Where did she go? Pam was probably asking him. Where did *who* go? You know, that girl you brought. The lame one. The *singer*, dopey.

Dottie looked up to where, gazing down from an upper window, the drunk blond grandmother was regarding her silently. When Pam and Johnny went inside, Dottie remained behind the verbena pot, alone and miserable, for even the old lady had closed the window, and the Cuban was out there asleep. He had to be asleep. Nobody could sit that still.

I want! I want! thought Dottie Almond; and alone, not just in that place but in the world, in the grand presence of her wishes, she turned and put her arms around the verbena urn and wet the harsh cement surface with streaming tears. Not only for Johnny but for herself, outside like that, and for her grand aplomb in seeing herself the possessor of the cool lovely house alone with him there in it, sometimes hidden from each other, wandering shadowy passages, sometimes discovering by chance or by search the other that each sought constantly, bedding for whole afternoons, and at night gathering moonlight in through windows, joining like twin divers in the pool, tangling like vines from sunny breakfasts onward, lords to the last fence corner and rock of gravel at the drive's head of all. All. *All.*

A drapery slid across a distant window, and Dottie limped out and away. Home. Nothing was merited; that, she knew. Nothing was ever deserved.

When, two days later, she saw him on the beach, he asked her where she'd been. "I thought about you," he said. "About the other night."

"What were you thinking?"

"How sweet you were." He touched her cheek, then caught her hand, and sat, holding it. "Why don't you come up to the university?" he said. "School's not far off. Morrissey can get you in."

"Pam's husband."

"Sure, Pam's husband. You met him. Morrissey."

"Pam—" she started, then gave out.

"What about Pam?" he asked.

"You're something—to her."

"I know I did a lot of talking the other night. Maybe I said things—things you didn't understand."

"Or maybe I did." Some force she didn't know the name of was pushing her on to the next thing to say. "Ron Morrissey—"

"What about him?"

"He got you out of something bad."

The boy did not answer.

"Is Johnny even your real name?"

He dropped his arm away, and whereas before they had been blending warm with each other while one breath did for both, he was now sitting separate from her, stonily silent. Dottie felt exhausted, like a sea creature who had struggled up on the beach, then to a rock, attaining, while the damp dried from its panting sides, a visible, singular identity. There wasn't any need to go further.

"Come to practice," he said, and bent to kiss her.

"Be glad you're just crippled," they used to say, "you might be dead." "But why be either one?" she had asked.

From the beach she watched jet streams like scars fade into the sky. There was nothing left to do but pack her clothes, say good-bye to the room, get ready to take the bus all the way up Florida, across Alabama, all the way to north Mississippi in unbroken silence. And once on the road, she would drift in and out of sleep, thinking, Aunt Maggie Lee Asquith, it's you I'm riding with; Mr. Avery Donelson, I am traveling with you.

The Runaways

EVERY DAY Edward walked down to the village. Joclyn saw him go, usually with a list from her in his pocket. It was a long walk. If she was going to walk, she said, staying near the ridge was preferable. She could stop and talk to some of the children in the native houses, out of sight but not so far away. She could practice her Spanish. She had learned it wasn't wise to hand out favors. Even when she did go to town, she did not go with Edward, as a rule. He always asked her, "Anything from below?" It would be hot there. Up here on the ridge, cool nights, temperate afternoons.

The Hacienda Sol y Agua was not really a hacienda, but rather a cluster of cottages, recently built, spaced out along a ridge above a long green valley. Perhaps there would be a hacienda some day, the guests speculated. Or perhaps there had been one in the past. The ruins of a mining project far down the eastern drop of the hill made them think that. Crumbling walls down that way were grown up in vines, a jungle of bloom. Some said copper was mined here once, some said silver. No one knew for sure. As for *agua*, there was nothing to swim in either; they were far inland from the ocean, with no lake in sight. The theory ran that the new swimming pool, now only a red gash down the western slope, looking abandoned, was what was meant. The feeling was that its not being finished was what made the rents so reasonable. Others gave credit to the recent struggles of the peso. But the level ridge top where the little houses stood was beautifully laid out with winding walks and rock-bordered beds. And the sun, at least, was certainly there. The nights were velvety, starlit, clear, and calm. Days, the path to the village beckoned downward.

But Joclyn seldom felt like the climb back. She did her graphics, a series of them, promised for book illustrations. The mail was important to her. Edward had her written permission to pick it up. The packets with the San Francisco postmark, he knew those were the ones she waited for. She had told him.

When she had gone, a time or two, she had discovered a long winding path, in addition to the sharp climb he preferred.

She could dawdle and rest, coming up by stages. She had not been well. She was thin, and as with many very thin people, it was hard to tell her age. She didn't volunteer to reveal it. Mystery in Mexico, a mysterious country. She felt it part of being here not to come right out with everything. And unlike the other renters, he didn't inquire.

"You can come if you want to." He always said that, but on the climb the one time she came along, he seldom spoke. One evening, though, he waited till after sunset to see that she did indeed return up the longer path. He met her. "What took you so long? I was worried." "I ran into a woman and talked to her. She's got three children and another one coming. She's hardly older than twenty, if that. Her husband needs a job. I guess it's a common story." "You see where practicing Spanish can get you? Into sympathizing." It seemed a harsh comment, but she let it pass. It was the slurred way he spoke, Southern obviously, that made irony seem like sarcasm or even contempt. Leaning back slightly, talking down. Maybe just joking. "Come sit," he offered. He'd placed a chair before his entrance door. "Take the weight off yo' feet." She had so little weight, she thought that might be a joke, too. She shook her head. "Another time." She walked back to her own cottage, at the far end.

It was an unspoken code among the renters that they either met for drinks separately, in households or alone, or all together, gathering. "Our time next." It was said easily, two or three times weekly. There were seven of the units, five occupied at present. The month was about to terminate, meaning a turnover for a number of them. The hilltop had been laid out amply; the beds held jacarandas, pepper trees, lemon trees, oleanders, hibiscuses, geraniums. Footsteps crunched on the gravel walks that branched off to individual cottages. "Efficiencies," somebody had said early on, during drinks. "I hate that word," Edward had said under his breath, and Joclyn had heard him, being accidentally nearby.

Later on the day of the long climb, her supper finished, she was about to shower and go to bed, legs aching from the effort of the afternoon, when she heard a knock at the windowpane toward the back. It was Edward, the only name for him that she knew. "I forgot to give you the mail." She let him in. "But

I went down today. I was at the post office." "I got there first. They passed it over without asking. I just forgot." He handed her two letters. Family mail, a bill. She put them aside. He was standing there rather awkwardly, not like his usual way. "Well, come in." She was irritated. The feeling was that he had gotten her mail, then kept it from her. Was he finally losing his distance? Why should she mind? Certainly, he was attractive, sensitive looking, his intelligence communicated without any particular proof needed, and he too was mysterious. Unasked and unanswered questions about him doubtless had occurred to everyone there, and had actually been put to him by the less reticent ones, like that Hartley couple, for instance. "Now, just what brought you down all this way?" they wanted to know. "I saw an ad." (Period.) Mussed brown hair, well-set, fairly tall. Late thirties? Hard to tell. Tan trousers usually, T-shirt and dirty tennis shoes, not very good for walking. But as he stood there with her mail in hand, she noticed that he had bathed and smelled like good soap. His shirt was clean.

"I get tired very easily," she said, by way of getting him out of there after the one drink she was now going to fetch for him. "I was recently sick."

"That's too bad. Are you better?" Memory stirred for her, out of the soap smell: tub baths in the slow, soft California twilight, clean pajamas, the murmur of a family talking on the side porch.

"It's slow."

He sat down and was a leisurely while taking the first swallow from his glass. "It was breaking up my marriage is the trouble with me," he said. "Ten years of it and all over. Gone. I had to get off and think."

"Is that what you do here?" she asked him. "Think?"

"I call it that. Really it's just going over it again. Like hitting yourself where it hurts the most. The first time you can't stand it, the second time you think you'll die, the third time is worst of all, but then by the tenth or twelfth or twentieth time, being still alive, you get surprised at yourself. By the hundredth time, you're numb."

"And finally you don't care?"

"I must be getting there. But lately I've wondered if I want to."

"Ever?"

"I believe I never really want not to care."

With that, to her surprise, he got up and left. Then why had he dressed? she wondered. Maybe just for himself.

At week's end the company changed. The inquisitive Hartleys left, as did the retired minister Mr. Telfair and his wife, with talk of their "kiddies," meaning grandchildren, and the Maynards, who wondered the whole time if their Labrador was all right at the vet's, and if the lawn was being watered, what with a drought all over the Midwest.

Edward and Joclyn were the only ones still there. The new list had gone up in the guardhouse, as they called the caretaker's unit, but the names—though one seemed Russian and another distinctly Jewish—meant little or nothing, Edward and Joclyn agreed, as long as the people who owned them were okay.

"I'm fairly antisocial," he told her, having wandered into the office while she was studying over the notice. "Some good nasty characters might be interesting." He then knocked on the caretaker's door to say in Spanish that his stove needed repair.

Those who had cars or had rented jeeps, which were more common, took the road down the back side of the mountain to sightsee, explore, shop, or dine. There was a small convenience store connected with the cottages, but it was often locked up, the old senora and her daughter who ran it gone somewhere best known to themselves. They always said any absence was for washing clothes down below at the river, and maybe it was. "It's where they meet and talk to everybody," Edward explained. "They gossip." Still, it got to be a saying among the renters: "Gone to wash clothes."

"I think you'd better go and wash clothes," was what Edward had the misfortune to say to the blond wife of one of the new arrivals. She had made a dead set for him right away the first evening. The next day, having found a window open, she was into his quarters when he came back up the hill from town. The newcomers' arrival party, held regularly for a get-together drink, had been her first appearance. After a couple of drinks, she had draped her arm around Edward and had pushed her head up under his chin. Her name was Gail Loftis. Her husband, Bill, said he was in investments. Edward told him that he had no money to invest, and then he had to reveal to the wife that he had no wish to invest in her either. The clothes-washing remark offended her, however, so she went around the next morning telling everyone how insulting he was.

"It's a saying we have," Joclyn explained. "An 'in' joke. About the little shop that's never open."

"God, does he think everything on two legs is after him?" Evidently, Gail Loftis wanted to start dropping in for coffee or beer or just anything anybody had. It was Joclyn's turn for her visit. "Most of us have some little work to develop here," Joclyn explained. "Mr. Rotovsky is a writer, isn't he? So he must work, too, for one." "It's what he said," Gail sulked, and finished the cup of instant coffee. She was not offered more. "You can take some nice trips," Joclyn counseled. "I'd like to myself, but I have a commission for some graphics to finish. I have a deadline." Her voice had gotten firmer, and finally even Gail Loftis understood that she was supposed to leave. "Bill's such a bore," she said. "He's keeping us on this awful budget. We ought to see more of the country." She got up. "He's not gay, is he?" It was Edward she meant. Joclyn sensed the trap. "I wouldn't think so," she was quick enough to reply.

After lunch, Edward talked with Mr. Rotovsky. They sat on lawn chairs, looking out over the back slope toward a low mountain range behind. A blue fringe of light hung evenly over the summit.

"But if you go existential," Edward said, "you plunge toward something new, and then how're you to know you'll wind up any better than at first?"

"Well, then you must feel so strongly that you plunge anyway. There is no time for the questions of this nature."

Joclyn heard all this while passing behind them. She was off to pick some wildflowers for her rooms, as the beds near the walkways were off-limits. Knee-deep in weeds—something like sedge—she picked blue flowers whose name she didn't know. She saw an iguana stretched on a rock in the sun. She straightened and looked toward the blue mountains.

After dark that evening, Edward came to see her for the second time. "It's that damn woman," he said when she let him in. "She waits around after dinner. If she gets in again, I'm going to throw her out bodily. Then there'll be a big row. At least I speak enough Spanish so they'll let me explain, possibly even believe me."

"Her husband's gone all around explaining already," Joclyn said. "You didn't hear him? 'It's just when she's drinking,' was what he said. He thinks she undergoes a female Jekyll-Hyde personality shift."

"It doesn't do me much good," Edward said. "She's not apt to stop."

The knock at the door was her, of course. Joclyn went and cracked it open. The hectic face, hair streaming half across it, peered out of the dark. "I knew it! He's here! Well, you two little bugs in a rug! . . . Have fun!" The door slammed in her face. Joclyn had got mad enough for that.

She turned to Edward. "I don't care if you don't."

He didn't answer. His glass was empty. She got him another drink.

Presently, she went over to the large folding table she kept set up in one corner and switched on her work light, the one she had brought with her. A white sheet, held down with steel rulers on either side, was half covered with the black outlines of what might be just a design but was really a half-formed picture. He did not come closer or inquire.

"I killed my wife," he said into the semidark of his side of the room. She did not look up. "She was a crazy wild one, too, a nuisance every way you'd care to imagine. I had loved her too long. It all ran dry. She wasn't living in the family home with us anymore. She'd rented an apartment for herself. I had to go there for something she wanted to talk about. The argument —well, who'd want to hear about it? I hit her. She fell and died. The weapon was a heavy piece of green Venetian glass my sister got on a summer trip. She'd liked it, so took it. She had taking ways."

"Weren't you arrested?"

"It looked like an accident. Everybody knew she was on whatever it took to have one. Nobody knew I was even in town. I spent a lot of time off fishing last summer. I think, though, that maybe everybody knows but doesn't blame me. We—my family is well known, prominent—. What can I say? In a Southern small town—. No way to explain just how it is. If you didn't do it, you didn't do it, no matter if you and everybody else knows that you did, including your mother."

"Most of all your mother," was what came to her to say. She leaned forward to smudge a line. Her hand was shaking. It wouldn't stop. She turned out the light.

In the newly dark room she crossed the floor and came to him. Groping, she pulled a hassock forward and sat near him.

"I'm going to die," she said.

He put his hand on her head. "I know. I thought so." She leaned forward and laid her head on his knee. Close and warm, his hand moved on her hair.

He said: "Today, down in the village, I saw this Mexican, an older guy, riding a bicycle in a muddy street, holding this kid, a little girl, before him on the seat. She had grabbed onto the handlebars, close to the middle. They were both laughing. I never saw two people so happy. I guess it was his granddaughter —it would have to be. I think I'll remember it forever. There in a muddy street of a dirt-poor town on a half-broke old bicycle —pure happiness. You don't see it often."

"You didn't kill your wife," she said.

"I was walking the steep way back and sat down to rest at that turn, you remember, from the first time you tried it."

"The only time. It's too taxing."

"There's a path I hadn't noticed before, it slopes off down to the left if you're coming up, to the right otherwise. Down there, I heard something move and a girl came up, a Mexican girl, Indian I would think, old skirt, black hair, broad face with no expression on it. When she left I walked down a piece and saw where this spring was welling up, just a thread of water trickling down, and some kind of little statue there, I couldn't tell of what. A face, half worn off, but whose? Surrounded by flowers, bunches tied together. About ten or a dozen bunches, some dead, some fresh, some wilted. I wondered if she'd left some flowers, and if that's their way of saying prayers. Do you know?"

"You didn't kill your wife," said Joclyn.

"No, I didn't kill her. I wanted to, but I didn't. I was lying."

"I wasn't."

"I know."

She stayed where she was, cheek laid on his knee, head silently beneath his hand. This was the happiest she had felt, in such a long time.

The Master of Shongalo

W<small>E HAVE</small> it now before us and know at least that it isn't any dream. The name is plain enough, written down in the old guidebook of the state I just yesterday found by accident on the shelves. The book was done by a WPA commission back in the Depression. But where did that name come from? Out of the Bible, like Sharon (rose of), Mizpah, Gennesaret, Galilee, or Gilead (balm in)? No, probably an Indian name—what tribe? Read further. We find that it was an old Mississippi town, long since absorbed into another one. I know no one who remembers it. But the name, though I dream about it, is a real name. In the dream I know its reality without doubt, though when waking I doubt and am glad to have it proved. Once I see it proved, I can return to the dream. I can see it all.

There is a large house of mellow old red brick trimmed in white, still in the baking afternoon sun, and an entrance at the side with a small portico. Seldom used, it matches in a minor modest way the imposing front portico. Here wasps may have built in the overhang, or large bright colored flies, trapped, may have died and fallen in the space between the outer door and the screen. The door is hard to pull inward, the wood having swollen after many rains, and the screen sticks at the bottom, so that a sharp kick is needed to help it along.

Now go into the garden. It is like this. A sunken garden laid out in a rectangle, slightly shorter and narrower than a tennis court. A low slope of grass, trimly mowed, frames it on every side. There are four sets of three steps each, with low balustrades. Each terminates in a square flagstone plateau, a place for setting out pairs of clay pots for flowering plants, or ornamental urns in a classical design. On one side there is a small statue of a goat figure, dancing, about two feet high, a copy of something Roman. He has no mate; the space for one is bare. There is a fountain in the center, composed only of four equal spray heads, slanting upward, not often turned on. But there is water in the shallow rectangular pool, and lily pads at one end, at the other a few lazy goldfish, with one ordinary lake fish, gray among their brilliance, dropped there from the sky or by someone who caught it and judged it too small to eat. Life spared, it swims with a strange race. Such is its destiny.

At the far end of the sunken garden there is a stone bench with scrolled arms. It looks to be for ornament only, as if no one had ever actually sat on it. But I go and sit on it anyway. This visit must be complete.

Let me say who I am. I said "we" at first because I wanted to include you, whoever you are. And because, though not everyone should go to Shongalo, you may be among those who should. It is mysterious. It is beautiful. Even in the full glare of Mississippi July afternoon sun, it raises questions no one will remember to ask, and if they do, and if someone begins to answer, an interruption will occur and no one will recall afterward what was being said.

There, I have done it too. Started to say who I am, then got interrupted by another train of thought. Well, I'll start again.

I'm nobody really. A teacher from the town. One of the children here, a girl in my class during the school year, which concluded two months ago, admired me, favored me, liked being my student. Nothing would do but an invitation here, where before I had been invited only once, for Sunday dinner, nothing so exciting as a dinner party. She persisted. Miss Weldon must have a chance to visit during the summer. We would read some more, we could go swim at the country club pool, we could talk some more, and I could get to know her brother, home from school, her parents, and maybe even a cousin or two, some well known, even from as far away as Washington. They came in the summer, at intervals.

My thoughts were wary. I wondered how I would be treated. A student's enthusiasm in no way makes a haughty family democratic. Wouldn't the favored-teacher role set me in a category: poor relation? The decision to chunk me whole into that box would be so immediate they would never stop to think about it. Not saying it, but making me feel it. Yet my clothes were in good taste, and my manners beyond criticism. Money? Was that what gave me pause? It was obviously not plentiful or I wouldn't be teaching in a Mississippi high school. And what about my single status? Matter of choice—mine or others'?

Who does she "go with"? These were the questions that no one would bring up, but everyone would think them anyway. Better they would be asked openly, like some impossibly bad visiting boy cousin who belched at the table, or jumped out of stairwell closets in the dark.

Nevertheless, the following was true: I had gone back for the summer to my hometown, a hundred miles to the south. I was completing work on a thesis for a graduate degree. The town was named Stubbins, Mississippi. It was dull and hot and tiresome. So I accepted Maida's invitation. Her mother had written as well—swirling initials engraved on ivory notepaper, confidently scrawling script. Using plain but decent drugstore notepaper, I replied. I could drive there as suggested on a Thursday, planning to stay for the weekend. I tried not to pack my misgivings with my clothes. I came.

So why was I all alone on a hot Friday afternoon, out in the sunken garden, sitting on the stone bench, observing the pool? Everyone was taking a nap—that was one reason. I had gone to my room (air conditioner in the window, cool high ceilings, four-poster bed, ruffled snow-white pillow shams), agreeing to nap also, but wanting a book, any book, I drifted downstairs. If there were bookshelves, a library somewhere, it was hard to find. The house was silent, as though they'd all gone off and died. Far out on a corner of the front porch, under the shade of the portico, beyond the line of ferns, a large dog was sleeping. A stranger, I hesitated to go that way. He might rouse up, bark, disturb them all. My books were in my car, parked somewhere out back on a large sweep of gravel near the yawning mouth of a garage. I had come out the side door, seen the garden, been tempted to wander and explore.

What lingers in some of us, in me, of the child exploring the mysterious castle, the château we took refuge in from a twilight storm, the sudden looming structure at the end of a winding road that a mistaken turn has led us on to follow? Once it is seen there, the feeling comes: "I am no stranger here." I mean to say that houses like this were part of my heritage, and since I had never lived in one, they were to be possessed only in this way of wandering, a native not to be told she wasn't to explore. For what was I exploring in this case but my own spiritual property?

But, hindering, there was the heat. Just like Stubbins. Something stung my ankle, sweat glazed my eyes. The nap here was a required ritual I should be observing. I would try it tomorrow. From the sunken garden I went toward the back, where the cars were parked, crunching through gravel as softly as possible, for one or two windows, high up above, were open. I sorted out a couple of books from the back seat of my own modest Ford and returned, entering on tiptoe through the side door.

Something seen out of the corner of my eye as I passed now was developing. Could it have been the tail end of a strange car? I thought so. I thought I had seen the sleekly tapered rear of something decidedly foreign. I didn't go back to check on it. The sight gave me, for no good reason, a start, a qualm, as if someone had come on purpose to unsettle things. To threaten?

Maybe I was wrong. Even if right, why feel it as disturbing? I tiptoed through the dining room, its windows shuttered against the heat, the long cherry table polished and quiet, not yet set for dinner. The chairs were arranged symmetrically back against the walls. The doors throughout the house towered high above my head. I pushed open the door between the dining room and the hall. There was the stair, ready to lead me up to my room. But still wondering where they kept their books, thinking that I remembered Maida, my student, mentioning "the library," I wandered across into the formal living room. Last night before dinner we had sat in the less formal room, adjacent to the dining room. Chairs and sofas there were slip-covered in cool faded fabric; furniture in the formal room wore satin, draperies were in lustrous brocade.

Perhaps my real reason was just to see the room once more, meditatively, alone. Its proportions had struck me as beautiful. There was ornamental scrollwork around the moldings; and a medallion of similar design on the ceiling surrounded the hanging point of the chandelier. A round table of inlaid polished wood stood central to the room beneath the chandelier, and a man was bending over it, his back to me. He was pulling out one of the drawers, or closing it. He turned: a stranger. We looked at each other. He was tall and rather messily dressed in a long-sleeved shirt but no tie, rumpled tan trousers, loafers. His hair was light, fading to gray. His expression, however, was dark, annoyed.

"Who are you?"

It seemed he had every right to ask that.

"Just a visitor," I said. "I'm sorry. I didn't mean . . ." Just what didn't I mean? "I mean, I didn't know you were here."

He laughed in an odd way, somewhere between amused and scornful. "You still don't, do you? *I* mean, you don't know who I am."

"That's true," I said. I supposed he wanted me to go, but when I reached for the door he said, "Wait." I turned back and he said, "Come here . . . closer."

"What is it?" I said, moving halfway toward him.

"No one . . . nobody knows I'm here. I'd rather they didn't." Then he smiled. Charming. He wanted something. "I'd rather you didn't mention it." That was it.

"Then just tell me who you are. I ought to know; that is, if I'm not supposed to mention you."

"I'm just a cousin," he said. "That will have to do."

"Wouldn't they want to see you?"

"Well, sometimes they might. It depends." He glanced up and around, as though regarding the whole large structure: Shongalo. Its vast shoulders sturdily asleep in the full afternoon light. "Nap time," he remarked, returning his gaze to me. "It never fails. Come at nap time, you won't see anybody. You, too—you're supposed to be napping."

"I just wanted something to read. Do you know where they keep the books?"

The smile again. "You've got some in your hand."

"I mean theirs. These are mine."

"The books—oh, yes." He swung away, quickly, on his heel. "Come here. I've just a minute." He opened a door I hadn't noticed; it adjoined the small fireplace, with its cold grate protected by curved bars. "Here." He beckoned. I came and looked inside. The room was oblong, running along the right flank of the house, with two shuttered windows set equidistant from the center of the outer wall. The shelves were all around, between the windows, covering the walls, on either side of the door. A table with a reading lamp was central and two straight chairs were drawn up to it, facing. Two others stood in the corners. I stepped across the threshold, following, and looked admiringly up at the shelves, which were pressed to overflowing with row after row of books.

I went farther inside. He pulled at a shutter, letting in a tilt of light. I could see the side yard, the drive, and a few shrubs just beyond. I was turning to stare all around, upward at the sets of Dickens and Scott, medium height to biographies and novels, then downward to an encyclopedia in rows and piled-up *National Geographics*, when I noticed he had moved away from the window. Leaving? Well, he had mentioned haste.

But then I sensed him right behind me and turned directly into him, astonished, but with a sense of rightness in being exactly there. His smile up close had a quality I was wanting without knowing it to find—that of letting himself be just himself. The scorn was out of it.

"A pretty woman here." Marveling, he almost laughed, the way he might at sudden luck—that being how he meant it, I had to conclude.

The room needed airing. The book smell was dense. I stood still as he raked a careful finger around my hairline, damp from the heat, just as my lip would be beaded.

"What are you, besides a visitor? Did you fall out of a plane? Wander off the road?"

"Teacher," I said; one word was all I had breath for. The pull of kissing had come to both of us at once. It was what we did. "Maida's," I murmured, my hand resting naturally on his shoulder. "You must know her."

"Lord, that little brat. Well . . . it's all for the best." I didn't ask what he meant. Later, I pondered it through the years. It may be that it was just a phrase. It didn't have to mean anything. What was for the best? Something to do with Maida or with himself? "Please tell me . . ." I began, about to ask him any number of things. But all he did was kiss me again. The only time I moved was to set the books down on the table, so as to free my arms. I still have no idea how much time passed before he made that slight movement that could only mean looking at his watch. "What a cryin' shame."

He moved away, going toward the door, but turned to me again, looking as intent as anyone ever had since time began. "Remember, you're not to mention me, please, ma'am." Then he smiled in a different way. "Can you possibly help it?" He had brought his distance back, gathered it all in. Then he left.

I stood stock-still for long moments in the sought-for room full of books, but after hearing the muted rustle of gravel as his car backed cautiously and turned, the roll of tires past the windows and their dwindling sound, I still could not break with the room itself where this unexpected magic had occurred, but circled about it like a trapped bee. I might well have buzzed but didn't know how. I heard the afternoon house waking, the creak of beds, the shuffle of footsteps. Leave? Yes, I must.

"I found the library," I told Maida in the hallway, seeing her come pattering down the stairs.

"Oh, there you are. I was calling you."

"I hope you don't mind if I explored."

"Course not. Want to get your suit? We'll drive in and swim."

"Where?" I was dazed and languid, as if more had happened.

"At the club. You know. It's not all that far. I told you."

Maida Stratton was blond and plump, a bouncy girl, always looking about ready to laugh. When I'd first seen her last September at the start of school, I had put her down in my mental notes as possibly dumb, or one of those students with native intelligence but who, try as I might, would not be induced to proper study. Later, when the students were discussing stories and poems that we read together, assigned or introduced in class, her perceptions astonished me. They were quick and sure. "Wouldn't that mean she was just uncertain what to do?" . . . "Didn't he feel he was lots better than the girl he was with?" . . . "Aren't they really trying to hide something?" She would get the point, quick as a blink. And make it sound easy. Her hair was long and untidy; she wore it bound back in a little scarf. Pieces kept slipping through and getting in the way as she bent to write something. But her homework was neat, brief, intelligent. High school English was her favorite class, she told me with a blush, turning a paper in. "Hasn't it always been your favorite?" I asked. A gulp. Then, "Mainly just since you came." That touched me. The Sunday dinner invitation came not long after. Mrs. Stratton, her mother, sent a note to me at school. "Mother sent you this," Maida said. She turned and almost ran away. It is painful to be young.

We drove to the club in one of the family cars. The minute we left the entrance gates, Maida, silent till then, began to talk rapidly. She was reading the Ibsen play I had given her. She loved reading plays. She could visualize how the scene might look before her on the stage. "Or a movie screen," I said.

"No! I'd rather imagine the stage . . . me in the audience." That refreshing giggle. "You could be there, too, long as I'm imagining."

"Why not on the stage . . . you, I mean?"

"Maybe later I'll think about it. But in Norway they have a lot of old dark furniture. They have stuffy old parlors, I bet."

"Why stuffy?"

"It's cold there. They'd have to keep the windows closed, wouldn't they? I bet they all have colds."

At the pool, she dove and splashed, greeted her friends, laughed a lot. But her delight, I had to recognize, was in having me there, her teacher now becoming her friend. A breathless change. "Yes, I'm from Stubbins," I kept saying, to some I hadn't met, home for the summer. Then I had to explain where it was. These south Mississippi towns might have been out West as far as the Delta mentality went. "Isn't that near Wimbly?" one boy asked, and everyone laughed. I said that it was. He had only said that because the names were funny. What did they recognize except each other? Maida confided on the way home that her father had wanted to have a swimming pool put in at Shongalo, but gave up the idea. "He didn't know how he would keep the poor children out. He'd hate not to be democratic. We're all democratic," she added. I wondered if she thought the Glenwood country club was democratic. We went riding happily home. Home was Shongalo.

"Somebody was here this afternoon," Bobby said at dinner. Bobby was Maida's brother, a husky boy, freckled and friendly, home from his first year in college. A bath before dinner, strenuously urged upon him by his mother, had reddened the mosquito bites along his arms. The water had darkened and subdued his light hair.

Mrs. Stratton laughed. "Lots of people were here." Her gaze on him was almost doting. Her children were her idols. Missing him through the school year had made her twice as fond. "The four of us, at least."

"Don't leave Miss Weldon out," Mr. Stratton said kindly.

"Milly, please," I said.

"All right. Milly. Is that for Mildred?"

"Yes, but I like it better. I never liked Mildred."

"I'm telling you there was this car here." Bobby was getting cross at them, but I could imagine it happened quite a lot—they had a strange habit of talking past or around a point somebody was trying to make.

"Lots of cars," his father teased.

"Aw 'ight, y'all don't wanna listen." Now he was mocking country speech, another trick. "What if I said it was a Jaguar?"

That stopped them. Now they paid attention. "I was coming back from the creek. Down there fishing with R.C. I came up the bank by the tennis court and saw it drive off. I swear I did."

"Well," his mother said after a pause, "who was it?"

"Don't know. Just told you what I saw." He shut up, sealed up tight, getting them back. He finished his plate.

Nothing was quite the same since he'd mentioned a Jaguar. "How did you know that's what it was?" Mr. Stratton pursued.

"Saw it."

"I guess it's all right to have a Jaguar," Mrs. Stratton meditated. "I just don't know anyone who owns one."

"Came for Milly," Mr. Stratton bantered. "Down in Stubbins they all drive around in 'em. Yes, sir."

"In Stubbins they raise pickles," I laughed.

"Lots of money in pickles," Mr. Stratton said. "Maida, you must have seen it. You never go to sleep."

"I was trying on bathing suits," Maida said. "It wasn't at the club," she added. It would naturally be there.

"I bet it was Edward," Mrs. Stratton suddenly said.

Mr. Stratton looked sharply up. Bobby and Maida stopped eating. Everyone but me knew who Edward was.

"Well," Mrs. Stratton explained, "the time before it was a Mercedes, wasn't it?"

"He'd borrowed that one from some friend," Mr. Stratton said drily. "With friends like that, anything is possible."

"You always think the worst," Mrs. Stratton said. She was not wanting to quarrel.

"Edward got some money out of that old place of theirs. Finally sold it, I understand. Maybe he just came to visit in his brand-new car."

"But nobody really saw him," Maida complained. "You don't know it was him." She sounded like what she was, a bright student arguing a firm point.

Mrs. Stratton smiled at her. "It just seems like it would have to be Edward."

Mr. Stratton turned to me. "Edward, Miss Weldon—Milly, I mean—is a cousin of ours. He—well, how *do* we explain Edward?"

"He does unexpected things," Mrs. Stratton said. "Going off to Mexico, for instance. I was always fond of Edward," she added, and looked a little wistfully, I thought, down at her wedge of icebox pie.

"He *wants* unexpected things," Mr. Stratton continued. "All sorts of records on this house, for instance."

"That you won't give him," Mrs. Stratton almost flared. "No reason on earth not to."

"None of his business. The Glenns sold it. George Glenn preferred not to hold on. So it's finished."

"You like refusing," his wife returned. "Jeannie never meant the slightest harm." Strange names were flying, tempers close behind.

"I like minding my own business."

"It's a simple request. You like defeating him. You won't admit it."

"I want some more tea," said Bobby. Mrs. Stratton rang the bell.

As for me, I said nothing. No more than Bobby did I know for sure that the man I'd seen was Edward. I wanted to know and yet didn't want to speak of it. Yet didn't they have a right to find out that a stranger was in the house, looking for something? I guessed they did, but still I never said. I went floating through the encounter once again, moment by moment.

"It's the funniest thing! I can't help laughing out loud. It's just most awfully funny." Maida was reading Noël Coward, *Hay Fever*.

"You're sounding British already," I said.

"We could go there someday."

"Go where?"

"To England."

"Maybe." I had to be vague. I had gotten into her plans; her future delights included me.

"I used to love reading," Mrs. Stratton volunteered from across the room, putting aside the paper. "But, you know, when I met Robert and married . . . well, it's foolish to say so, but all the things I was reading *for* were all around me, right near instead of somewhere else. I mean I read about these girls who admired some man and then found he liked them too, and so finally they had some sort of romance or got married after a lot of hitches and all that. But wasn't there always a big estate in it somewhere? A wonderful house and all that? Well, all of a sudden I had Shongalo. Why read about some place I might not even like? This one was good enough." Her little laugh was young, a lot like Maida's. "I saw lots of splendid old houses on a trip to England. You know, I wouldn't take any of them for this place right here. Did you know Maida started there?"

"Oh, Mama, don't tell that."

"We rode somewhere I forget, a little bit out from the center of London, Robert and I. We were trying out the 'tube,' as they call it there. I looked up and saw this station that said 'Maida Vale.' It sounded so pretty, I just couldn't get over how pretty that did sound. So I said to Robert, 'If we ever have our little girl, I'm going to name her that. Maida Vale.' We just don't use all of it, though I think double names are nice. They're often very melodic, don't you think so, Milly?"

"Well, I don't think much of Mildred Carrothers Weldon."

"A family name. That's different. They're often awkward. Mine is double, too. Linda May. I always liked both, but to Robert I'm just Linda—or Lin. Only then you'd spell it different."

"Differently," Maida corrected.

"I'm going to spank you," Mrs. Stratton said without meaning it.

It was late on Saturday morning, nearly lunchtime. Among the rooms at Shongalo trivial conversations could spin on forever. They were like iced tea, cold in tall glasses packed with ice cubes, pale with a moon-shaped slice of lemon. Outside the heat almost audibly prickled on the lawn, baked hot the flagstone path to the sunken garden; within, a breeze stirred through the tall windows, the blade fan turned slowly above, taking it up, passing it on. Maida ran out of the room—seeking bathroom or dictionary or following some whim about what to read next.

Mrs. Stratton put down the paper with a definite gesture.

"You can't know how pleased I am with this interest you've stirred in Maida Vale. She's always been so active. I get worried sometimes when she gets active in the wrong direction. You can imagine. We joined the club for her. Bobby too, of course. Robert and I couldn't care less about all those meetings and club doings. He never golfs. But the children . . . socially, I suppose . . ." She trailed off. She was about to say, I think, that social affairs didn't interest her much. The lack of interest went with her inward air, her absence of any detailed care for clothes or looks. It made sense that she would be content in her place as Robert Stratton's wife at Shongalo, not needing to seek anything to fill her time. There were relatives they spoke of, not only the mysterious Edward but others, some in the North, and others in Alabama who had "needed them" for a time but now were "straightening up again." I never inquired. I listened.

"Maida," I began, but did not know how to follow up.

"Yes?" said Mrs. Stratton.

"Maida may be getting too fond of me." I felt awkward and blushed.

"Oh yes, I know what you mean." Mrs. Stratton should have been sewing. Her speech went like that. She could have stopped from time to time to smooth out fabric, straighten thread, inspect her work, then continue. She smiled. "Things of that sort pass. Maybe it's a phase. Can you stay?"

"Stay?" I was surprised. I had meant to leave the next morning.

"Robert will speak to you. We have to be away on Monday. It's some business over near Leland. I want to go along with him to see about Maggie Lee . . . I don't suppose you know her . . . Maggie Lee Asquith?" Linda Stratton lived in a world where everybody knew Maggie Lee Asquith. I said that I didn't. "Well, she's just this wonderful person, an aunt of ours by marriage. She doesn't have long, they tell us." Here, I thought she should have been drawing a thread through an intricate turn. By "have long" she meant, I guessed, that the

aunt was dying. "Leaving Maida Vale here just with Bobby.
Just boy like, he won't pay her a bit of attention except when
he feels like it. And besides, she's just wild for you to stay."

"Well, I—"

"Robert will speak to you." At that she did their strange
trick of turning into someone else. Laid aside the imaginary
sewing, rising, efficient. "Excuse me a minute. I've just got
to see about—" The chatelaine. I had learned that word,
somewhere along the way. It suited her. Her reading now—
romances from the sound of them, but maybe not the cheap
kind. Magazines were her choice at present, probably. Or mysteries. TV had not caught such a firm hold here, scarcely into
the fifties. Bobby was showing signs of interest. There was a
set with rabbit ears such as people had back then, in the upstairs hall. He would sit there in an old wicker armchair covered in faded cretonne, looking at the images. In those days
before color they often looked grayish, and the frames would
jump around depending on the weather. "You're going to
ruin your eyes," Mrs. Stratton would say, passing him on the
way to her own room. I could glimpse its spaciousness when
she opened her door. Sparsely furnished with a large oval rug
on the dark-stained, wide-boarded floor, the huge hexagonal
mahogany posts of the bed. On two sides, tall windows let in
light, which seemed to bring in the color blue, like the sky.

Robert did speak to me, as she had said.

"We want you to stay on a day or two, Milly," he earnestly
told me.

He had asked me out for a stroll just before dinner to see
his new plan for a terrace with chairs and tables near the tennis court. "The children are always eating out here. No place
to put things." Was he asking my advice? I thought it only
a pretense, a preface to something important. But was it so
important to stay with Maida? He raised a hand, like someone
warding off an interruption. "I've no right to ask for your time.
Only if you could."

"I never dreamed it was so crucial." I wanted to ask why.

"Oh, I wouldn't undertake to say crucial. Maida is at a
time when things are shaping up for her future. We're looking at colleges. We feel the presence of someone she respects

—and loves"—he said it right out: loves—"would be the best thing for her. Besides, she's got her heart set on your staying. Maida. . . . There can't be a better gift to the world, Milly, than a woman who just goes into life with all that wonderful wildness about her. Right now, she's just a sight to behold, all her reading this, and thinking that. I confess none of it gets me worked up, not at my age. But she's just plain head over heels about it. Your going off . . . it would seem like leaving her high and dry. We'd have a regular crybaby. No telling how we'd manage."

We were walking side by side in a vague semicircle around the empty tennis court. It was after the ritual nap, also after the trip to the pool, cut short because there was such a crowd. Saturday afternoon. There had also been the ritual bath.

Mr. Stratton was not an imposing man. He might have been attractive, in a boyish way, when younger. He had discerning gray eyes, fair skin, and an open way of talking, his regard traveling all about you as he spoke. Evaluating, noting, though never staring exactly . . . kindly, I supposed. He always seemed to know much more than he chose to say. His business in town, for instance. I knew he ran an insurance company and went in daily on its affairs. He kept "some few head of cattle," as he once remarked, at Shongalo, though where they were escaped me, never having heard them so much as moo. He was glad to be through with row-farming, he had also once remarked.

He had asked me questions before, but always in company, had never spoken to me alone. Yet now we strolled together amiably, like old friends, possibly relatives. The feeling was of having known him since childhood. My thoughts drifted around him.

He was rapidly becoming more bald than any man would have liked. A pale, high forehead crowned him, made his eyes prominent. He was scarcely taller than I; though not frail exactly, he was not rugged either. His regard was for his property. Wherever those cows were, they were being cared for. Careful, he picked up a fallen pecan branch and looked at it before he hurled it aside into some weeds in an untended part of the yard beyond us. His property included Maida; he was looking after her. But she was more than that, of course, and he next let me know it.

"There was all that trouble last year."

I turned in surprise. "What trouble?"

"Some boy she got crazy about here. I say 'some boy.' Let's just say he wasn't anybody who would do for her. We'll leave it there."

"Is he in school?" I thought I might as well know who.

"No . . . gone. Well, not exactly gone. He has some sort of local job." It had a dark ring to it, the way he said it, and I knew I wasn't to learn any more from him.

As we walked back to the house, he talked about what kind of chairs and tables we might like best for the terrace. His saying "we" that way made me feel a little alarmed. He asked again if I would stay. Looking up at the house, mysterious in the westering light that slanted before us, I marveled at how weightless its presence before us seemed. I could suddenly not imagine being anywhere else. "I kissed a strange man in the library," I almost said, almost adding, "I live here." I had found in the thought a different meaning for that simple phrase, *I live here*. I turned it in my mind, just as in an exercise I had often had my students do. *Here, I live.*

I told Robert Stratton I would stay for a day or so longer.

"Good," he answered, and having gained the front steps, he ran up them to the porch. In that motion I saw him become imposing. He had the air of the owner of Shongalo. He held the door for me.

Monday morning.

"They've gone!" Maida said, gloating, full of jumps and twirls, running to fetch me coffee, make me toast, find the special jar of peach preserves.

Sunday had passed in a jumble of decisions about church. I went to the service with Mrs. Stratton, and Maida, dressing in a topsy-turvy rush, trying to find some good shoes and a piece of something she called a hat, went with us at the last minute. She sat close beside me in the pew; we read the responses in unison. In the afternoon, a clutch of chattering people came and went—relatives, friends. Names went up around them like a flock of birds. Who knew anything about me? That day, I did decide on napping. I dreamed.

Then Sunday was gone, like a day misplaced.

"They've gone!" said Maida.

Bobby, sleeping late, was soon to be seen plodding downstairs, a firm hand on the bannister. He passed squint-eyed into the kitchen. The cook was off also, let go for the day. Bobby soon came to the table with a plate of cold fried potatoes and some leftover apple pie. He poured coffee and picked his fork up with his fist. Boys were often like that, pretending to be workmen or cowboys out of a movie. Maida ignored him. Whenever someone else was with us, she was waiting for them to leave. Since the evening before, we had been reading Tennyson aloud.

When I asked Bobby's plans for the day, he said he meant to go off fishing with R.C. and Clayton, whoever they were, but that it looked like rain. "I'll just go over there anyway," he concluded. He gave a look that plainly said any place was better than here in the house with us. I asked him, teacher fashion, if he'd seen any more Jaguars.

"Naw. I know it was Edward though."

"How'd you know that?" Maida was a great one for probing. She always had her curiosity working, one thing that made her such a good student. "I mean," she added, "nobody saw him."

"I just think it was," said Bobby, shoveling pie into his mouth.

"But who," I asked, "is Edward?"

There was a small silence, and Bobby said, "A cousin."

I laughed. "You said that before. Isn't everybody your cousin?"

Bobby was already heading out the door. Maida began to clear the table. She was thinking already of *Idylls of the King*. "He just comes and goes so funny," she said.

"Why 'funny'?" I asked. How to get to know without seeming to want to know?

She came back from the kitchen for more of the breakfast things, but stopped to look out the window of the smaller dining room, where we sat. The family hardly ever breakfasted together. They, too, came and went. "It's so pretty out there," she remarked, seeing the morning yard with its rose garden, its birdbath, its shrubs. She all but clapped her hands. Bobby was gone. We had the place to ourselves. "I want to always live at Shongalo!"

"I can't say I blame you."

"Don't you love it?"

"I love it," I said, sincere as ever I could be. "Can I come and go," I ventured, "like this Edward person?"

Maida whirled on me, jumping forward in a little rabbitlike spring, throwing slightly sticky arms around my neck. "You can come and *never* go! We'll read and read! Everything there is! I'll know as much as you!"

"Lots more, I hope."

"Promise?"

"Promise what?"

"You'll never leave."

"I promise we'll find our book wherever we left it yesterday."

"You won't promise?"

"Now, Maida. I'll come and go, whenever you let me. Soon you'll be saying I come and go 'funny,' like Edward."

She sat down; her bouncing fit was passing. "But Edward just comes without telling anybody. He just shows up. Daddy says Edward thinks he belongs here."

"What do you think of that?"

"Just that you wouldn't. I don't guess you would. Mother likes to see him, though. He makes Daddy mad."

"Why?"

"Oh . . . he thinks she likes him."

"Do you like to see him?"

"I would . . . but he calls me a brat. And I'm not. Am I?" The question was a tease, but before I could answer she was off at a run, leaving the breakfast things to me.

A brat. . . . Yes, he had said that.

Gently, the rain had started.

All that long day while the rain plunged us both into our separate dreams, we read in the library, in the family room, in the formal living room at the round inlaid table beneath the chandelier. Curious as Maida, but for different reasons, I pulled a drawer a little way out. "Look," I noted. "The table's like a pie." Indeed it was: The five drawers with bronze pulls were triangular, ending in a point at the center. Maida hardly noticed. In one brief glimpse I had seen that the drawer was empty. Bad manners were something I could not afford to let her notice my having. Were the other drawers empty, too? We had reached the magical story of Sir Gawain's vision. The rain continued.

It hadn't started in the usual rush of wind and flash-bang of thunder, but only as a rustle, muted as a whisper, then growing louder. It seemed to have put out gray arms and enveloped the day. The interiors of Shongalo were shadowy, dim. At night we might have found strong light in corners, not the cloudy mist that permeated every room, drank up the lamplight, and left us sometimes unable to make out the words on the page. In the corner of a sofa, Maida leaned against my shoulder as I read. We were about to go on to Mordred's betrayal of Lancelot and Guinevere to Arthur. I finished a long descriptive passage.

"You know," Maida remarked, "it's pretty, but it makes me sleepy."

"Later on," I promised, "it will make you cry."

"Let's skip to that," she said. Maida and I had talked of it one day: Why do people like to read what makes them cry? "Emotions get to show themselves," I explained. "You can sympathize and cry over people you never met, so it does your own feelings good." She puzzled over it, and really it wasn't a very good answer. Why do teachers think they have to answer things that students ask?

One thing I was glad about: the rain made it impossible to go in and swim. Maida was always taking chances, diving, chasing somebody underwater. She had some of the boys there daring her. One of them called her at times. He asked her to go with him to a picnic or the movies. She would tell him that Miss Weldon was still here, though to her I'd long since become just Milly. "Go on if you want to see him." "Maybe I don't," was all she'd say. She'd let it out that a boy she'd liked last year was always around wherever she went with somebody else. "You don't want to see him?" She was vague in replying. So that must have been the one her father spoke of. One day, leaving the pool, I had seen him too. He was lingering out near the entrance, a tall, rather swart boy, with thick hair of a color that habitually looked dirty, a serious face half turned away. Maida had given a little wave and he had nodded. "That's Garth," she'd told me. "Who?" "You know . . . the one they didn't like."

The rain was shifting around, blowing softly in through an open window. Maida jumped up to close it. "I know. Let's go upstairs. There's a good lamp in the little room. You haven't seen the little room, I bet." She was running already, up the stairs. I followed.

The door to the "little room" was between the one opening on her parents' bedroom and another, farther up the hall, that was Bobby's. No telling what was behind that one, though I could imagine pennants and posters, a jumble of everything and nothing. In the little room there was a jumble, too.

Sewing! Not for nothing had I connected Mrs. Stratton with that. She had obviously put everything pertaining to it here. There stood her dress form, armless, chastely plastered over with brown paper, though her own lines were visible, low-set and full-fleshed, a friendly shape. An old quilt was folded, lying on top of a large oval basket, woven from broad withes. Mending must be inside. Both a hanging lamp and a standing one were fitted with strong bulbs. Maida had switched them on already. The one window looked down to the lawn far below and the path that led to the sunken garden. "Now . . ." A sofa bed against the wall was waiting for us to sit and read more. But though she sat down as though waiting for me, she did not open the book or offer it to me. She just sat holding it, frowning and thinking of something very hard. The rain stood at the window, a gray presence, but here it was full of secluded light. An armchair too big for the small space was opposite. When I sat in it, our knees were almost touching. "Are you tired of reading?" I asked. She didn't answer.

Maida Vale had a charming face, mainly, I had often thought, because it was so changeable. Serious, she might almost seem to sulk; her thoughts were inward, running over something that puzzled, maybe even offended her. She had chubby cheeks when she smiled, lighting up at something from the outside world, small teeth, bursts of crinkles, upturning lips when she laughed, her eyes half-shut with all-out fun. A boy might want to kiss her a lot, I thought. I felt she wanted to confide something in me, so was waiting; but then the telephone rang. It rang persistently, five times or more. Maida, not especially wanting to go, finally went out to the extension near the TV in the upper hall. She came back distractedly.

"It's for you."

"For me?"

My mother, of course, knew where I was. I had called to tell her that I would stay longer, but why would she call me now? Sickness, maybe, or an accident.

Of course, there was Willie.

I had kept Willie under wraps because there was nothing much to say about him, the necessary escort in the small town, the one you went to the movies with, asked to parties, gave routine good-night kisses to. There'd been others before him, one at college I'd rather not think about, but others, too, here and there, no more than average. Willie would hardly call.

"Hello," the voice said in answer to mine. Then I knew. "Still there?"

"A little longer," I stumbled.

"I've thought of you. But . . . what's your name—?"

"My name?"

"Yes, your name. I didn't get it."

"Mildred . . . I mean, Milly. . . . What's yours?"

"Can't hear." There was a sputtering on the line, then a crackle. "Can't hear you," he said again.

"Who are you?" I all but shouted. Some word began to form, but the sound mangled and the line went dead.

I returned slowly.

"Who was it?" Maida asked me.

"I don't know. The wrong number, I suppose."

"But you said your name."

"It's how he knew it was wrong, I guess."

She gave me the kind of look that comes out of knowing a friend has told a lie. Her mouth was slightly open; a thinking went on. "He said 'that pretty woman staying there.' It's what he said."

"I guess women stay everywhere," I said lightly. I picked up *Idylls of the King*. "I lost the place," I said, searching.

But Maida was not listening. She was staring at me, her mood so altered that mentioning the book seemed totally irrelevant. "Did you ever fall in love?" she suddenly inquired.

"Everybody does," I said, "sooner or later."

"I was in love last year. It was Garth. They said it wouldn't do."

"Who said so?"

"Mother did and Daddy. Daddy was the worst."

"They think of you," I said firmly. I couldn't be ganging up against them. Nor did I want to deny her confidence. It was dangerous ground.

"It was when his mother came. She came here and wanted to talk to Mother." She suddenly picked up a cushion and held it on her lap, lifting and shaking it. "Mother said it was awful."

"You mean, his mother was awful? Then you saw what they meant—your parents, I mean."

"I don't know if I saw what they meant. I just don't know. It was all such a big lot of talking all of a sudden." She hit the cushion. "I just hated everything."

I smiled. "It's all behind you, isn't it? Back there last year somewhere?" At her age a year was a long time.

"I don't know," she said, still thinking. "I guess."

I had found the place in *Idylls of the King.*

"Do you think sex is bad? Making love, I mean. Is that so bad?"

"Well, no, but I think you ought to get older before you decide about it."

"Do you know about it?"

I began to read on from where we had stopped. Not a doubt that she wasn't listening, but like someone walking ahead on a path I hoped she'd follow.

"Somebody wanted you," Maida insisted. "They wanted to talk to you."

"Why don't you read for a change?" I held out the book.

She stared a moment, then got up and ran from the room, stumbling over the large basket, which tilted open, spilling its contents. Between friends, what lie will ever do? The answer is: none.

I knew that I didn't care quite enough what Maida thought. I knew that. I sat with my heart beating like a drum. He had remembered me. He had called. "What's your name?" It kept chanting. I could even hear again the snarled static on the phone. Rumbling thunder shook the house softly, like a dog worrying a worn-out toy. Then there was the rumble of the cattle gap, from far off at the entrance. The Strattons had returned.

As the car drew up, stopping near the front, I wondered where Maida had gone. I searched, intending, I suppose, to take her hands, to say I was sorry for whatever had upset her. But I didn't find her. She would reappear. Open and frank always, she would tell me what was wrong. We would find another book, a different sort, snappy satire or hard-surfaced mystery. Things would resume as before.

From an upstairs window I saw the sky clearing, long broken clouds turning to pink scarves, light gleaming on the wet trees. There was evening still left, and part of the late afternoon. Shoes were crunching the gravel, tapping up the wooden steps. "Maida! Bobby? Milly! We're home!"

I dressed for dinner with more care than usual. I brushed my hair till it shone, a mix of blond and brown, sun-streaked in summer. I dampened it and fastened it with a brown clasp like tortoiseshell. I put on a full flowered skirt I had not worn before, and a blouse in ivory cotton latticed with embroidery, cut low. In my Stubbins vision of what might happen at Shongalo, I had prepared for a possible party, a dance at the country club, who knew what? But these were not to be, and so far I had not dared to appear in such a getup. But now I didn't care.

Where was Maida? The heavy steps I heard battering up and down the stairs were Bobby's. First he was explaining something, then his father called him back, he was quarreling with his mother, from the sound of water pouring out he was taking a shower, he was hollering from the door that he couldn't hear what they were saying. He was much too big for the house, for any house. Something fell and crashed in his room. He was mad. He was furious. A few minutes later, the smell of ham and biscuits drifting up from below, he was dressed in slacks and a fresh shirt and smiled with calm beatitude when we encountered each other at the top of the stairs.

At dinner no one even mentioned the trip to Leland, or the aunt Maggie Lee. Robert Stratton, responding to my dressed-up state, drew my chair out for me. He waited a moment to start serving the plates, as Maida was not present but could be heard descending the stairs. She came in quietly and sat with her head tucked, her face quiet and pale, not looking my way. "Are you all right, honey?" asked her mother. She said that she was.

"We drove through some awful weather," Robert Stratton said. "Coming back between here and Leland. The worst was over when we arrived."

"A whole roof blown off and some trees down. The house was dark when we came. Didn't you all have sense enough to turn the lights on?" She was asking Bobby.

"I thought it was like that other time we lost power," Mr. Stratton recalled. "Candlelight and lamps, I thought."

"It was pretty," said Mrs. Stratton. "But everything got cold."

"We've got no old range anymore to build a fire with stove wood. I well remember that other time. I went out back and found that son of Annie's. Or was it Delia's?"

"No, sir, it was Annie's," Delia said from the kitchen.

"I said, 'Can you bring us in some stove wood.' He had just got home from Chicago for a visit. He didn't know what stove wood was. What happened to that old range, Lin?"

"Gave it away. One of Annie's daughters wanted it."

"Now she's got electricity too. Time marches on."

"Speaking of time," I said, "I think it's time for me to be going home tomorrow."

Maida looked up, startled. They were all silent.

"Oh? Make it the day after." Robert Stratton put it that way, for reasons he knew best. He didn't say, Stay on and on. He didn't say, What could we do without you? I found out why the next evening, when we talked in the sunken garden, out near the lily pool.

We sat on the stone bench. It had grown warm again that day, though the freshness from the rain had lingered.

"Maida isn't so taken up," he remarked. I had got to know his train of thought. His conversation up to then had seemed to absorb him, changes in the Delta, more to come, things his little trip had brought to mind. But this was his real subject, now appearing.

"'Taken up'?" I repeated. I could already guess what he meant.

"All this reading . . . you, the marvelous teacher. It's slacked off."

"So you thought it was a bad thing?" I saw that, unconsciously, I had used the past tense. Maida and I had talked, but had not mentioned a book all day long. We had talked about movies, one we had missed in town. Some friends of Bobby's had showed up and she had wanted to go out to play tennis with them. I had to join, she insisted, so as to have another girl.

"I think," said Robert Stratton, and crossed his ankle over his knee, "that anything done to exclusion is not such a good thing." He glanced at me through the late lingering light. "Don't you agree?"

"I never thought it was forever," I said. "It's been such fun—her enthusiasm, I mean. To think I stirred it up. I love books, too, you know." I thought I should point that out.

"Oh, I'm sure she won't forget. Nor will we." He leaned against me, pressed my knee, took my hand. He was a great one for patting. "We'll always thank you, Milly." And time, as he had so lightly mentioned it at table, had not marched; it had jumped right out at us.

I saw how neatly he had taken everything away from me. I wanted to protest. But I knew whatever I said to him would leave me biting my lip, feeling it was wrong at that moment, as in the future I would feel it, looking back.

I said something anyhow. "Thank me for what? What is it you think I did?"

"Oh, I expect you see that, or will if you don't now. She had to live through it, you see. So one day . . . why, you'll see."

Angry! But how, if I didn't have words to say why, could I flash out at him? I murmured something about having to pack and walked away, inside. My planned speech—how wonderful it had been at Shongalo, getting to know them, make friends, plan a return visit. . . . What was the use of going through a useless exchange? I left Robert Stratton sitting meditatively, smoking a pipe, which he would presently knock out against the stone bench before he went inside. It was another ritual, a habit he had.

Mrs. Stratton heard me come in and called from the living room. Would I have coffee? I pleaded a headache. I went trembling up the stairs. Wasn't it part of my perception of them that they were different from the ordinary run of people? Not to be easily, if ever, completely seen into? But I'd been used! It was that that hurt, more than if they'd coarsely scorned me at the beginning, or given me a caretaker's shed room at the back.

I looked around the room, at the muted luster of its polished walnut and mahogany, its wide dark-stained floorboards, its rugs a little worn, a little sun-stained. My things were all around, more confident than I. I drew my suitcase from the big closet and set it open on the bed. That headache was no lie. I took two aspirin and lay down beside the open case. I fell asleep.

When I woke I wondered what time it was. Everything was quiet. I found my watch: two o'clock. Tiptoeing to the broad hall outside, I knew I had gained control again. I would have this place, in memory at least, from now on. I moved to the front of the central upper hall, where the broad curved windows looked down on the lawns below. I could see the path to the sunken garden and part of the garden itself, not the pool but an urn and the one small statue, clearly visible in the moonlight.

Someone was out there. A shadow moved, going toward the line of shrubs between the house and the garden, returning with the deliberate rhythm of a tall man walking slowly, hands thrust in pockets. It was not Robert Stratton.

I knew who it was.

I floated downward, drawn through the silence of thinking about it. I found no obstacle, not a creaking floorboard or a resistant door. The path to the garden was plain; I turned the corner by the hedge. There lay the pool, smooth as carbon paper. The grass had been mowed that day and the fresh smell lingered. I had noticed it earlier, mingling with the scent of Robert Stratton's whiskey. No one was about. I circled outward, moving toward the heavy line of trees, dense in their dew-wet mystery. I went to them and peered into the wood. The insects had stopped chanting, but I heard no footstep, no breach or rustle. I saw no one. Nothing. I returned to the house. On the path, the old dog snuffled up beside me. He put a damp nose in my palm, and we walked up the front steps together. On the porch he went to his accustomed corner and lay down. He was not allowed inside.

All that was forty years ago.

For years I received a Christmas message from the Strattons, a card with a letter enclosed, telling me about Bobby and

Maida, also about themselves and what had gone on during the year at Shongalo. The children went off to school, had various mishaps and triumphs. Bobby barely missed having to go to Vietnam. After finishing school and college at Duke, Maida almost moved to New York to work. Instead, she married a Charleston boy, a young doctor. Maida wrote me, too, for a time, but the correspondence faded into postcards and finally vanished. I sent a wedding present.

Before I left, I took something. I went into the little room to find the book we had been reading. It was lying face down where we'd left it. The woven basket had turned over with Maida's rush from the room. Scraps of fabric had spilled out, and a packet of letters. They had been held together with a rubber band, but it had broken. I saw at once, among all the others, a long envelope, faded yellow, with "Edward Glenn" written across it in black ink in an old-fashioned flowing hand. There was no address, just the name, so it was meant to be given by hand. It was by instinct that I picked it up, without thought. Perhaps what I had in mind was a sort of revenge.

Once away, I opened it, but found nothing surprising. A wish from an elderly man, some aging relative, that "my boy," the young Edward, would have a profitable time at school, and would make the family proud, as they had always been of him heretofore. It was handsomely stated, with feeling as real as heartbeats. It was such as this he felt worth returning to search for in the crevices of Shongalo. And Linda Stratton thought worth saving for him? Yes, and so did I; and I would tell him, "This is yours," if the chance came my way.

Return Trip

IT WAS during a summer season Patricia and Boyd were spending together in the North Carolina mountains that Edward reappeared. He left a message on the answerphone predicting arrival the next afternoon, saying not to give a thought to driving into Asheville for him, that he would rent a car and come out, if at all welcome.

"At all welcome" sounded more than slightly aware that he might not be. Yet, of course, Patricia thought at once, they were going to say, "Come ahead, we'd love to see you," whether it was true or not. And for me, she thought, it really is true, though she doubted it was for Boyd. Edward had a charming way of annoying Boyd, she thought, though Boyd wouldn't say charming.

Patricia stood out on the porch of the cottage (theirs for the summer) and looked out at the nearest mountain, thinking about Edward. Boyd soon joined her. "Wonder what he's got in mind."

"Oh, he won't be a bother. He'll probably be going on someplace else."

She could have asked, but didn't, just what it was Boyd thought Edward had in mind. Money used to be a problem for him, but family business might also be involved. Boyd never cared for him; she knew Edward was acknowledging that.

"Maybe he just wants to see us," she offered.

"Why not a dozen other people?"

"Those, too. He has affections. And God knows after what's happened he needs to find some."

"Nobody on the West Coast has any?"

"Well, but his wife died. Outside of that—"

"You'll ask."

"Certainly I'll ask. He'll tell me."

"But then you won't know either."

She whirled around, annoyed. "Don't brand him as a liar before he even gets here." Boyd apologized. "He's your cousin," he allowed.

Patricia said what she always said, "But we're not close kin. In fact, hardly at all." Boyd had learned that just as there were complicated ways Mississippians took of proving kin, so there were also similar ways of disproving it. "God knows," he once remarked, "all of you down there seem to be kin." They dropped the subject of Edward.

Boyd spent the afternoon picking up fallen tree limbs from the slope back of the house. There were pinecones too. He built a fire every night, pleased to be in the mountains in midsummer and need one. Boyd was from Raleigh, in flatter country, but he loved the Smokies. "My native land," he crooned to Patricia, "from the mountains to the sea." Patricia said she liked to look at them, but never ask her to climb one. She wasn't all that keen on driving in them either, though the next afternoon would find her whirling down the curves to Asheville. "I've got to go in anyway, to pick up groceries, oh, and mail off Mama's birthday present, else she won't get it in time."

"And pick up Edward," Boyd said.

"You won't mind," she said. "He'll be nice. I'll cook something good, you'll see."

But she had hardly made it out to the car when she heard the hornet buzz of a motorcycle coming up the Asheville road. It banked to pull in their drive and under the helmet and goggles she recognized her son. Oh Lord, thought Patricia. Why now? Then she was running forward to embrace him and hear about why now and calling to Boyd and finally getting into the car, leaving father and son to their backslapping and Whatderyaknows. A long weekend away from school. He might have told them. Boyd's shout of "Wonderful surprise!" followed her down the swirl of the mountain.

And all the way she wondered if the mystery could possibly come up again. They had been over it before and decided it was just a joke of nature, unfortunate, but only extended family to blame for their son looking so much like Edward.

Airport.

The heat in Asheville had about wilted her. She entered airconditioning with a sigh and headed for the ladies' room to repair her makeup and make sure she looked her pretty best.

But before she could get there, a voice said "Hey wait up,

Tricia," and there he was when she turned, Edward himself, standing still and grinning at her.

He came forward and planted a sidewise kiss. But even those few feet of distance had let her notice that he didn't look so great. Older, and not very well kept up. Scruffy shoes, wilted jacket, tee shirt open. The blond hair was mingled with gray, but the smile, certainly, was just as she remembered.

He was carrying only a light satchel. "I checked the big one." He caught her arm. "We're heading somewhere right away and we're going to eat something edible. I nearly choked on dry pretzels."

She managed to find an ancient restaurant, still there from former days, dim and uncrowded, a rathskeller. She sat across from him, her questions still unasked.

Boyd was fine, she told him. Mark had just appeared. For a minute, she could plainly see, he didn't recall just who Mark was. Then he remembered. "Oh great!" he said. A silence. Food ordered. Time for confidence.

Yes, his wife had died. Yes, she said; she had heard and was sorry. He had taken up with Joclyn in Mexico, followed her out to Pasadena, knew all along she didn't have long to live. Why do it at all? Patricia had wondered then, now wondered again. Love, was what he said. It was reason enough. That was Edward.

"Oh, yes, Joclyn's gone," he said. "I tried but I simply couldn't stay on out there after losing her. I began to think Where else is there? I mapped out a plan. Friends in Texas, a covey of cousins in Chicago. Brother Marvin in Washington. You here. I picked you first. And then, possibly, back to Mississippi. It's always there. Maybe not the happiest of choices. But there is where Mama used to be. But she's gone, too, and so is the house."

"And Aline?" She had to be mentioned sometime.

"Oh, Lord," said Edward. "The eternal Aline. Don't ex-wives ever go away?"

"What do you mean? Die?"

"Or something."

"I always liked her," Patricia murmured.

"Spare me," said Edward.

Suddenly, Patricia felt terribly much older.

Boyd was showing Mark around the cottage.

"Isn't it a good place?" he enthused. "It is owned by Jim Sloan at the office. They couldn't take it this summer. You can bunk in here. Pat will make up the bed and so forth. And the bathroom's here. But now come on out and look at the view. We can see the New River. And the nights . . . ! Breathe in the cool. How's the new course?"

"I need to talk to you. I may be changing majors."

Boyd groaned. "Not again. Well, we'll discuss it. Meantime, do you remember Edward Glenn?"

Mark, thin but sturdy, often called handsome, given to pleasing smiles, looked puzzled. "Cousin of Mother's?" he finally said. "Didn't she—?"

"Didn't she what?"

"I don't know, Dad. I just thought I remembered something."

"You better disremember it," Boyd grumbled. He was not given to subtlety but he felt he was in a situation where such was required. "He just called up and said he was coming. Uninvited. She went down to meet the plane."

Mark's young brow wrinkled. "I thought of what I remembered—or what I couldn't remember. Didn't Mama date him or something?"

Boyd whirled on him so sharply he startled him. "Do me a favor? When he comes, act like you never heard anything about him."

"If that's how you feel." He concentrated, then said: "But why?"

Boyd was irritable. "I'll tell you later. After he leaves. Promise. Okay?"

Outside in a flat side yard, Boyd explained he was trying to set up a fish pond. "Sort of kidney-shaped," he said. "Something to leave for the Sloans—they insisted on lending us the place. Just the utilities to pay, though I guess if the roof blew off . . ."

"But do they really want a fish pond?"

"No trouble in summer. Just stock it. Feed 'em. Winter comes, scoop out the fish, drain it, leave it. We can start it while you're here." Mark had a look he got when something sounded like work. But then he got on better with his father when they worked together. Quarrels came when they pulled in opposite ways. He knows that, too, thought Mark. That's why he'd brought this up. Mark knew he had to ease his father into his new plans. Boyd went to a toolshed and produced two shovels. With a plastic measuring cup, he dribbled lime to mark the outline. He stood looking for a moment before he took up a shovel. A sudden thought. "Have you eaten?"

"I'm okay," said Mark, and drove his shovel in the turf.

In Asheville, Edward and Patricia sat in front of a large house that was half burned down, surrounded by guard ropes, now well into reconstruction, which was not at the moment proceeding. It was the remains of My Old Kentucky Home, the house Thomas Wolfe had lived in and wrote about. Though why Edward had to see it, she wasn't quite clear.

"It's for my soul," he explained. "Tricia! I've got to live again. Every little bit helps."

She was wondering what little bit Thomas Wolfe had to offer.

"Didn't Wolfe have to put up with an awful family?" Edward recalled. "I wonder how he stood it. We were luckier than that."

"Are we getting into family?" She was tentative.

"It's what we share," said Edward.

"Boyd's family . . ." she began again.

"What about them?"

"I've managed somehow. I even get on with his mother." She switched subjects. "You met Joclyn in Mexico."

"Yes, and I knew even then she was dying by degrees. After that she went back to Pasadena. I followed. Then there was chemo, all sorts of cures. But through it all she was happy. We were happy."

"Was that your reward?"

"Um. The trouble now is, she was terribly rich. I didn't know how rich. It was some family legacy. Who's ever going to believe I didn't do it for that? Didn't even know a lot about it. Who'd believe it?"

"Nobody in Mississippi," she was quick to say.

Edward laughed. "Right on." A pause, then, "How did this house burn?"

"If I knew I've forgotten."

"I read Wolfe long ago. You learn something from other people's bad times."

"Like what?"

"How to get through your own."

"Edward?"

"Um."

"It's Mark. My son Mark."

"Of course. What about him?"

"Well . . . I better tell you." She laughed a little nervously. "He looks a lot like you."

"Poor kid . . . only . . . Well, now you've said it." He sat quietly, slowly digesting the implications. "I thought that was a dead issue . . . Want me to leave?" He was half-joking.

She was silent.

"Tricia . . . what if he does? Nothing happened . . . We both know that. We've been all over it. I don't even think about it, haven't for ages." He stopped again, realizing he was getting off on the wrong tack. "Let the past go."

"Boyd might not be the friendliest in the world."

"Maybe we can charm him with a drink or so."

"Just play it straight and we'll be okay. He's such a nice guy. At this moment you need us . . . need me. You said so. Besides, nothing happened."

"Tricia, *nothing did happen*."

"Right."

"Think of all Wolfe's talent in that one house. Busting to get out. And it did."

She started the car and backed away. Old-fashioned and rambling, the house had still managed to assert itself. The long-ago meetings, quarrels, seductions and heartaches of that big, lumbering man's life, the family's torments, had all smoked up right out of the windows and porches to sit on the backseat of the car, leaning awkwardly over, speaking in their ears. So time to let it out and then move on. Patricia thought she would read his book again. *Look Homeward, Angel*. Wasn't that it?

Later than it should have been, they pulled up to the cottage. Boyd and Mark were out on the terrace, drinking beer and admiring the view. But the stunning moment soon arrived, as Patricia and Edward appeared. All they did, naturally, was shake hands, then stood there, boy and newcomer, look-alikes, though not quite carbon copies. Patricia removed herself hastily to the kitchen to stash away groceries, while Boyd turned and looked out down the mountain. The talk was perfunctory —weather, national news. Edward to Mark: "So what are you into at the university?" Mark to Edward: "It was history, but I'm trying to switch. I came home to talk about it." Boyd, disgruntled: "He's switched once already. Not good to keep on switching." Mark: "Computer science is a must these days." Boyd: "History is a great base. You can always take up the computer stuff when you finish that." Mark: "That's postponing." Edward: "I shouldn't have asked." Silence.

Patricia appeared with drinks. Bourbon for Edward with a little splash of water. Scotch straight for Boyd. Another beer for Mark. She had changed and smelled fresh. She settled into a lounge chair with gin and tonic.

"We started the fish pond," said Boyd.

"You can see the New River," said Patricia.

"It wasn't so much that I didn't like history. Old Douglas was interesting about the Greeks."

"The Greeks are important," said Boyd. "Ask Edward."

"So I'm told," said Edward.

"You all always knew each other," said Mark. "Funny, but I don't even remember kids I knew growing up."

"Well, being kin . . ." Edward began. "It makes a difference."

"Always at Aunt Sadie's," Boyd said with a shading of contempt, but maybe he was only recognizing their nostalgia for those youthful days. Patricia doubted it. She was bound to remember that one last evening. And so was Boyd. And so was Edward. And so soon after getting married too. Which made it worse.

She had often replayed it. Scene by scene, like a rented movie, its sequence never varied.

Edward was drunk and turning in. Boyd was drunk and staying up. Patricia was drunk and had gone to bed.

A house party given at Aunt Sadie's for Patricia and Boyd, bride and groom. What a glorious afternoon it had been! They had spent it walking to familiar places on the big property: the garden swing out near the lily pond, the winding path down to the stables, now empty, the old tennis court. Aunt Sadie, widowed but content these past years, with two gardeners to help, kept it all up. She had Lolly, too, a wonderful cook. Late as usual, Edward had appeared. "Well, it's about time," Aunt Sadie scolded. "We'd about given you out. Where's Aline?" "Home with a headache." Edward's code response, everyone knew. He and Aline were famous for pitched battles. Aunt Sadie gave him a drink. The guests were trooping in. It had turned black and was about to rain. Thunder grumbled. They all crowded inside.

"We'll play games," somebody suggested, trying to ignore the weather threat, though the sky had turned purple and looked low enough to touch. They were setting up a table for bridge when the lightning flash crashed right into the room and the lights went out. "Too dark to see aces," Patricia said. Edward declared it was too dark to do anything but drink.

"We could all go to bed," said Boyd, provoking laughter to acknowledge his honeymoon state of mind. Aunt Sadie said no, they could eat, as everything was done. She began looking for candles.

By the time they sat down everybody had taken a drink too many. They alternated between silly remarks, some known only in the family, and gossip about absent relatives. Both subjects made Boyd cross. Patricia could sense this, but didn't see it was so important or why they should stop having fun. The family didn't get together that often. He could stand them this once.

Somebody (must have been Aunt Sadie's big son Harry) also sensed the unease. He said to Boyd, "You can see what a crazy family you've got into."

"Well," Patricia chimed in, just being funny, "you ought to see Boyd's family."

That remark didn't work the agreeable way Patricia had hoped, but by then it was pouring rain. She was never sure why Boyd was so angry. He put down his napkin and got up from the table. Everybody tried to look like maybe he was just going to the bathroom. They ate steadily on, as though nothing was wrong but the weather. Edward tried to get Aunt Sadie to make a fourth for bridge. Everybody had another drink, which they didn't need. No lights came on. Patricia finally groped up to bed with a flashlight thinking she would find Boyd, but nobody was there. He couldn't be out in the rain, she thought, undressing, but as soon as her head hit the pillow, she went out like a light. So when the body landed in bed, it hardly registered, if at all.

It seemed scarcely a minute later but must have been an hour or so that she started straight up wide awake with the lights blazing and Boyd in the middle of the room, yelling, "What the hell you think you're doing!" And ohmigod, it was Edward saying "Huhuhuh," rubbing at his head and straightening up from where he was sprawled out next to her. Patricia had always maintained he was fully clothed, though why she had to maintain it was the real question.

"You'd have to see he hadn't even undressed," she kept saying to Boyd, as they drove away that very morning, hardly saying goodbye.

"Yes, all right," said Boyd, "but what was the bastard doing in my bed in the first place?"

"It was always his room when he came to Aunt Sadie." Patricia had said it so often she was about to shriek.

"We won't discuss it," said Boyd. And wouldn't. Period.

But slowly it dawned on her that the reason he shut her up was that he didn't care for any of them, especially Edward. *He wants to get rid of all of us!* Such was the thought that kept hanging around like a bad child or a smelly stray dog, no matter how many times she told it to go away.

Now the thought had followed them all the way into the mountains. Patricia was so annoyed she actually considered leaving them before dinner, with nothing to eat. But staying, she had to face it that the only really difficult person was Boyd. Edward was grieving over his loss. Mark was worrying about changing majors. But Boyd was sinking into a mood of long ago. Yet when she came in with a smoking casserole, everyone seemed amiable, even smiling. Talking college days.

"What's Pasadena like?" Boyd wanted to know.

"I thought it was pretty nice. People out west aren't made like us. You had to make efforts to know them. Then it might not even register. They don't get into the politeness routines. Of course, Joclyn had friends, family too."

"I wish I had known her," Patricia said.

"It's what I mean," Edward said, half to himself. "Out there, nobody would say a nice thing like that." He smiled at her. Their kinship came back.

"We stopped by the Wolfe house," Patricia said, leaping to a subject.

Boyd looked blank. "The what house?"

"Oh, you know, Boyd. The Old Kentucky Home. Thomas Wolfe's mamma kept a boardinghouse. It's in Asheville."

"Of course, I know that. Insured with the firm. When it caught fire, we had a struggle over payments."

"Did somebody set it?"

"The facts kept dodging us. It could have been some sort of family jealousy coming out that way."

Mark said brightly, "If you get mad in a family, it just goes on and on. There's this boy at school can't see his daddy because—" He stopped.

"So what will you do next?" Patricia asked Edward.

"When my round of visits are over, you mean? I'll have to sit down and think about it."

Boyd regarded him as though he might be half-wit. For a grown man just not to know what to do next seemed hard to believe.

Edward said, "I'd move back home if it weren't for Aline."

"That's his first wife," Patricia told Mark. "He doesn't like her."

"She wouldn't be all over the state," Boyd said.

"Yes, she would," said Edward. "She's got a talent for it."

"Word gets around," Patricia laughed. "We never knew what to make of Aline. But we tried."

"I tried too," said Edward.

"Do you remember that evening when you had gone fishing and came in to Aline's dinner party with a string of catfish, when she had made up this important meeting you had to attend?" Starting that story made Patricia choke on laughter.

But Boyd was getting stiff. "All that family stuff . . ."

Patricia retreated. "I won't start it," she vowed. "I promise, cross my heart, hope to die."

Boyd laughed. He suddenly decided to be a good host. He went to work at it, asking if they had passed a highway project on the way from the airport. "Funny thing," he started out, and went into the funding, the business deal, the election that interrupted it, knocking out a campaign promise. He got them interested. His facts were certain to be correct. Boyd always said that to be funny you didn't have to exaggerate, just tell the truth. He said it was one thing Mississippi people knew very well. He said that now.

"Going to Mississippi is what I'd like to do," said Mark.

"It's not like it used to be," said Patricia. "All changed."

"Changed how?"

Boyd explained: "They don't have these big properties kept up by old ladies with lots of black help kowtowing and yes-ma'aming."

"Aunt Sadie was wonderful at it," Edward recalled, half to himself.

"She was getting dotty," said Boyd. "That's all I remember."

"She did her best," said Patricia fondly. "Right to the last."

"Was she my aunt, too?" Mark wondered.

"Great-aunt, I guess," Patricia allowed, then asked about football.

Mark was their only child. In spite of efforts, she had never conceived again.

In the dark evening on the terrace they sat listening to a faint whispering of nighttime creatures, an occasional splash from the river.

"We could get the canoe out tomorrow," Mark said. "Is it still down there?"

"I haven't checked," said Boyd. "I'm sure they wouldn't have taken it to Europe."

"Maybe I'll go abroad," Edward mused.

"Ever been?" Patricia asked.

"Once with Joclyn. It was interesting, but we moved around too much. It might be nice just to find some place and sit in it."

"Wondering what to do next?" Boyd asked.

"Right," Edward agreed.

"Well," said Boyd, who was commencing to feel control, "you could go some place like Sweden. I always wanted to go there, but I never found the time."

"What would I do?"

"You said you would just like to sit," Boyd pointed out.

"The summers are too short."

"Try Mexico. That's summer all year round."

"I did try Mexico. It's where I met Joclyn."

"Oh."

Edward was silent. He seemed to have faded into the night shadows. He had declined dessert and coffee, wanted no more to drink. He came up out of his silence to say: "It was a pretty place."

Patricia knew he meant Aunt Sadie's place and she saw, as if it was actually there, the slope of the yard in the twilight and down beyond the drive the myrtle hedge and the fireflies.

"Lightning bugs," said Edward, echoing her own thought exactly. "Remember the time that—"

"I'm going to bed," said Boyd.

But when he left Mark wanted to know what time he meant.

"I bet he means the time about the pig," said Patricia, guessing. She was right.

"She made a pet of it and wanted it in the house," said Edward.

On they went, laughing and remembering, until Mark left for bed. Edward, finally rising, crossed to Patricia and kissed her on the forehead. She threw her arms up to him, and he was gone.

While still at morning coffee, Boyd and Patricia saw Mark outside with Edward, bending intently over Mark's motorcycle. Straightened upright and started, it gave a nasty cough and snarled. Mark shut off the motor while Edward speculated. He seemed to know what was wrong. Mark came in with a grease smear down one cheek. "We need to go down to the store. Can we take the car?"

"What do you want?" Boyd asked.

"It's something to clean the gas line. They'll know at the filling station. Edward says he can tell them."

"I had one in Pasadena," Edward explained.

Boyd gave his consent. The two got in the car and went away.

Patricia finished in the kitchen and came out to the terrace. Boyd joined her.

"They're gone," she said.

Nobody had ever doubted that Boyd was right for Patricia. She had had a definite wild streak which she explained by saying nobody understood her. There had been escapades in the sorority at Ole Miss, sneaking out with that Osmond boy who wasn't the right kind, and then that wild night in the cemetery. Several had got expelled. It was said she escaped because of her good family. But then her own mother had run her out of church for showing up at Easter service in a low-cut silver dress with spangles. Yes, Boyd Stewart was the right one. For one thing he had a no-nonsense approach. He corrected her right before the whole family. "That won't do, Pat," and once he just said "Hush up!" The remarkable thing was she minded him. And after a year or so, remarked on in stages by home visits, she "settled down."

As for all the running around during those years that she and Edward had done—if nobody exactly minded, it was because they were kin, or near kin, thought of that way.

Boyd made money. He took life seriously. Insurance was a complicated business. He was still learning, he said. "But he must be fun, too," Aunt Sadie remarked. "How come?" her daughter Gladys asked. "Patricia wouldn't have had him if he wasn't fun."

They pondered over what the fun might be. They accepted Boyd. When he visited, he unpacked and hung his clothes up carefully. Driving away with Patricia after that first visit, he had remarked, "They're going to lose that place." "How come?" she asked. He laughed and said in his brushing-off way, "They drink too much." That wasn't what he meant, and a few years later, they had to sell. By then Patricia was raising her baby and had settled down even more.

Patricia and Boyd had lunch alone. Boyd wondered if he should call the filling station. Patricia giggled. "Maybe they went back to My Old Kentucky Home."

"Why do that?" Boyd asked.

"To look for Thomas Wolfe's ghost."

Boyd went out to work on the fish pond. At three o'clock he came in. The sky had thickened darkly. He was sweaty; his shirt and trousers smeared with dirt. Patricia was checking the weather station on t.v. He stood in the door and announced: "I do love you, Pat." He sounded angry. "Why, honey," she said, "of course you do."

Something was happening, but where it was happening, they didn't know. The first thunder rumbled.

Patricia came to Boyd. "And we both love Mark." Impulsively, they hugged. There was a rush of rain and closer lightning. They ran around closing windows and troubling about Mark and Edward, who did not come.

At twilight with the rain over and Boyd tired of ringing up with queries, they heard the car enter the drive and leaped up to see.

It was Mark.

"Gosh we were worried," Boyd reproved.

"It was just raining. We thought you'd know. We had a couple of beers."

"Where is Edward?"

"Oh, he's gone. He said you'd understand."

Patricia felt the breath go out of her, permanently, it seemed. "Why?"

"He said just throw away the stuff in that little bag. He had a big one checked at the airport. He got a ride into Asheville. I offered to drive him but he said no."

"Well," said Boyd, "I guess that's that." Relief, unmistakably, was what he meant. "He gave me a great big hug," Mark said. "He said, 'Carry on!' Then he jumped in the car."

Patricia went inside.

At dinner nobody talked but Mark and he talked his head off. He had been to drink beer with Edward! Edward was great to talk to! Mark could tell him things! He listened!

"About what?" Boyd asked.

"Everything. Girls and school and all. I could really talk to him. I'm sorry he went away."

Patricia got up to clear but Boyd said, "Don't worry, honey. I'll do all this. You go on out on the porch. It's cool out there. Look for the lightning bugs."

She sat in the dark and heard them quarreling. "If you think like that, son, just go on back to school and don't ever listen to me." They could say it was about school, but it was really about Edward.

There was no way possible she and Edward could have done anything at all that long-ago night, both drunk as coots. No, it wasn't possible.

Patricia got up from the porch and walked in the dark down to the New River. She kicked off her shoes, sat on the boat pier and put her feet in the cool, silky water. It was then she heard the Mississippi voices for the first time. She knew each one for who it was, though they had died years ago or hadn't been seen for ages. Sometimes they mentioned Edward and sometimes herself. They talked on and on about unimportant things and she knew them all, each one. She sat and listened, and let the water curl around her feet. She knew she would hear them always, from now on.

First Child

T HE STATION WAGON had eased into the cottage drive a little past three. The man and woman got out, each turning
to reach back for the child. The storekeeper across the highway noted them and wondered if he could recall them from
the summer before. He concluded that they were new, and
when after an hour they came across the road in the sun glare
to shop, he proved to be right.

"We've rented from the Stimsons. Just for this weekend,"
the man said. "Do you know them?"

"Sure thing," the storekeeper said.

"How's fishing?"

"Catching some, but mainly far out."

"I'll stick to shore. You got minnows?"

"Some. Take a look."

A barrel stood in the cool back of the store. It was past the end
of the glass-front counters and the shelves loaded with canned
goods and specialty items. A net hung on a hook near the barrel.

"You got dinosaurs?" the child asked.

"Haven't noticed any today," the storekeeper said. "In the
hot weather, they mainly stay out in the swamp."

The woman laughed. "He means rubber ones, I think. The
kind you can blow up and float in the water."

"You'll have to go up the road for those. K-mart maybe."

"So you'll have to wait," the woman said to the boy, who
looked uncertain about it.

The boy's name was Cooper. He was not her son. His
mother was her brother's wife, only her brother had left for
other parts, somewhere out West, and remarried. Had anyone
told him his ex-wife was in the hospital, gravely ill? Had anyone told him the mother of his son was ill?

Questions like these might float around in the atmosphere,
might come in on the repetitive waves of thought. But no one
asked, so no one answered.

Packard, who was neither the boy's father nor the woman's
husband, sat out on the porch and watched the sea. He had

already brought poles up from the basement and strung the lines, but still he made no move toward going out. He let the sea sound, the salt air invade him, like water permeating dry fabric. He had brought work with him, but he did not think about it. He wondered if they had done the right thing. The Stimsons' unexpected offer was hard to refuse. A vacant weekend for their cottage at Ocean Isle. But there was this illness. The tide was out and the waves reached the long sand beach in a slow measure, unfurling, retreating, but not breaking open. The water seemed like satin, glossy, swelling and shrinking.

Inside, Elsa was taking the few staples from the store out of sacks, stocking the cabinets and the refrigerator. "I'm sorry," she had told Packard back in Eltonville, "but we'll have to take Cooper. There's nobody else to keep him."

"Aren't you going to fish?" her voice floated through the open window.

"Later. Where's Cooper?"

"Watching TV."

Packard snorted. "If I had a kid . . ."

"You'd what?"

"I'd take that damn box five miles out and dump it."

"There'd just be more, more, more. You'd never stop them. Nothing will."

"But don't you watch it, too?" He hadn't learned a lot about her.

"Some things. Don't you?"

"Mighty few."

"But some."

He dropped the argument. Reading was always Packard's preference. Only there was too much to read.

"TV and dinosaurs," he muttered, half to himself. "Just proves he's a normal kid." He was learning about Cooper, too.

The refrigerator door closed with a definitive sound. "I have to drive up for more groceries. Are you coming?"

"I'm staying. See if they're biting."

"Cooper! Come and shop." She had to call twice.

There was a burst from the spare bedroom. Packard turned to look. Cooper was a nice brown little boy, about seven. He went to grammar school, not the high school where Packard worked as assistant administrator. "TV is a tool," he often lectured students. "An educational crutch. It's not for you to devote your life to. If you're not learning anything, switch it off. Go play basketball."

"You're not making a dent, I bet," Elsa told him.

"Maybe not. Maybe some of them listen."

Cooper was barefoot. "Better put your sneakers on," Packard advised. Elsa agreed. "You'll have dinosaurs stepping on your toes."

Cooper giggled. He believed in them and he didn't at the same time.

Packard dropped his magazine and went inside. He helped Cooper tie his sneakers. They were red with a white rubber rim around the soles. Cooper ran back in the room to get something. Before he came back, Packard kissed the back of Elsa's neck. "We're going to get through it somehow," he assured her.

She made a face. "Just like Margery to get sick."

Elsa and Cooper drove the highway to the shopping mall. They stopped at the fish market for shrimp, in case Packard didn't catch anything. Elsa had a feeling that he wouldn't. She kept her eyes on the road with almost too much concentration, a frown between her eyes. Margery was no kin to her was what she was thinking. Whatever Cooper said she answered yes and no. He rode beside her, his feet in red sneakers stuck straight out.

"Wish you taught at the school," Packard had told her. She worked at the county tax office, collating answers to particular surveys, sending out notices.

"I wouldn't try to control those brats for anything," had been her answer. Cooper, fallen silent, kept pulling at a rip in the vinyl upholstery. "Don't," Elsa told him, twice. Then she slapped his hand. He tried not to cry. "I'm sorry, Cooper," she said. "Where's Mommy?" he asked, though he knew very well. She told him again. "She's in the hospital. She'll be all right." He said nothing, his round little face shut up tight.

Cooper trailed Elsa through the supermarket without saying anything, but when they had hauled the sacks out to the car, he said "K-mart."

Oh Lord, Elsa thought, and supposed that she had to. Women her age, twenty-eight, were supposed to have kids already. She sometimes wondered why she hadn't. It was that early marriage maybe. It was that liquid regard and ripe no-nonsense mouth that showed her cool to motherhood. But now she had to buy a dinosaur.

They came in large plastic envelopes, each with a colored picture of the one waiting within. Cooper chose a brontosaurus. As he knew already, the next step was the filling station to have it blown up. Elsa knew she had to do that too and pulled in under a Texaco sign.

The attendant, who came out to help, spread the large expanse of rubber on the pavement. He then found the entry valve and plugged in the air nozzle. A hissing sound continued for several minutes, and when he turned around he said, "My God!"

Elsa was astounded and Cooper was delighted. The creature, in all its painted glory, soared up in the air above them. Cooper jumped up to circle its lofty neck, but couldn't reach it. It smiled down with a stupid lizard grin. All lizards grin, thought Elsa, and looking at the massive feet, the long, tapering tail, wondered how to get it in the station wagon.

But there was no parting Cooper from it now. He was jumping with delight and looking ready to wet his pants, though he said he didn't need to go.

The attendant helped Elsa squeeze the creature through the back: a tight fit. Not much more than a boy himself, he was obviously having fun. They laid it on its side. They had to bend and fold the tail across its back. When they sat in the front seat, the tiny head reached over and stuck itself between them. Elsa shoved at it. A glance showed her not only that lizard grin but eyelashes painted on. One eye was staring into hers. "It has funny ears," said Cooper.

"What you got there, sport?" Packard wanted to know. But this was just when they started unloading. "Jesus," he next remarked.

"You're mighty right," said Elsa. They set the dinosaur upright on the lawn and stood staring at it.

Like all the houses so near the sea, the cottage had living quarters on the second floor, utility and storage space below. There was no way to get the dinosaur up the outside stairs.

They circled the house to the beach side and managed to get him into the porch. He filled most of the floor space, where they placed him, huge feet planted, tail hanging out the door, foolish head nudging the ceiling. "His name is Billy," said Cooper.

It was getting late. "We'll have to hurry if you want to swim," said Packard.

Cooper said that Billy didn't want to swim.

"I thought that's why you bought him," Packard said to Elsa.

"Don't ask me why I bought him," said Elsa. "Forty damn dollars' worth of rubber monster."

"Come on, Coop," said Packard. "Let's take him in the water for a ride. Let's see if Billy can swim."

Elsa went inside. She heard Cooper say again that Billy didn't want to.

By the next afternoon, however, they had all gone swimming with Billy and they had walked with Billy on the beach. They had tied a rope around the rise of the neck, painted like the rest of him all gray, green, and orange. They had pulled and nudged him along. His lengthy tail wagged across the sand. He was light with all the air inside, but also awkward. He towered over them, grinning at people, grinning at the sea. People pointed and laughed. Some had taken pictures.

The three had had lunch in the cottage. Packard had even caught a fish. And though they had made love in the night, it hadn't been the best ever. Elsa kept dreaming about dinosaurs. "I'm fucking with the damned things," she confided. "Better stop it," Packard advised. But now it was afternoon. One thing they had always agreed on: Love in the afternoon was the best. Since they didn't live together, it was why they liked to go away. Now it was afternoon.

"All parents have the problem," Elsa said to Packard. "We can't send him out to swim. He might drown."

"Just leave him with the TV," said Packard.

She laughed. "It's what you're against."

"Maybe this is all it's good for."

"He'll see more sex on that than if he sat and watched."

"Don't be so graphic," Packard said. He was squeamish. He didn't like talking about sexy behavior. When he got going he would let out little cries and whispers. Elsa liked to talk dirty, once she got into it.

Out on the porch, Cooper was sitting in the swing with the dinosaur beside him on the floor. He had to hold it by one arm to keep it from sliding away from him. Sometimes he put his arm all the way around it. He was swinging and singing something tuneless.

"Let's give it up," Elsa said.

They then stared at each other as though someone else, invisible, had spoken. For desire was with them now, knocking about in the blood.

For the first time, since they came, the phone rang.

It took them both a while to quit looking at it and answer it. They both knew why.

Elsa finally went to it. All she said was Yes and No and Of course. She straightened up and bit her lip.

Packard went out on the porch. He sat in a rocker very near Cooper and the dinosaur. "Did Billy like his swim?" he asked.

"He'd rather walk with us," said Cooper.

Packard forbade himself even to look at the creature. He thought maybe he hated all this dinosaur craze as much as he hated TV. It's off the same bolt of cloth, he thought.

He had an inspiration. "If I give you ten dollars, will you go across the street and buy something?"

"Like what?"

"Something I might want and something you might want —two things or one thing for us both. Will you?"

"What about Billy?"

"Something for Billy too. I'll look after him. I promise." He held out the money.

Cooper put Billy in the living room. He left for the store. "Look both ways when you cross the road," Packard advised. Then he turned to Elsa. "When he comes back in, we'll hear the door."

"You hope," said Elsa, but she was already ahead of him, hurrying to the bedroom, shedding her jeans, getting out of her blouse.

"A quickie," she said, head flung back against the pillows, eagerly and happily, laughing. She was stripped to her bikini briefs and bra, leaving them for Packard, who liked taking them off.

He turned her and smoothed her, he murmured to her. He really was good at it. Now he was over her once again, and she could draw her fingers down the V of black chest hair. ("You've got brown hair," she had told him the first time she saw it. "Do you dye all this?") Her firm fingers explored the black thicket below. She watched his sex emerge to stand all white and sturdy, ready to lean right in. "Ooh!" said Elsa. "Oh-ohhh!" she said.

Better than nothing at all, Packard said, when the short time passed. They lay a little apart and listened. "He should be back by now," said Elsa. "The door squeaks," Packard had assured her. "We'll be certain to hear him."

But the whole house was silent.

From the first time they met, they had known what they wanted. Packard, still in his twenties, felt he had plenty of time to think about marriage, for the truth was he was hesitant about it. He took responsibility too seriously. At the high school, he was always fretting the details. Marriage meant smaller kids than those, with their interminable demands. But he liked sex.

He had run into Elsa, literally run into her at the door of the gym one night before a basketball game. She was hurrying not to miss the start. She had Cooper with her, and her sister-in-law was trailing behind. She had bumped straight into him, though it wouldn't have happened if he hadn't been looking back over his shoulder and talking with someone. "Oh, sorry." "My fault." Packard had stepped on Cooper's foot. Cooper was saying, "You hurt my foot."

Later on, Packard went and found them. "Is your little boy all right?" "He's not mine," said Elsa, "but he's all right. I've got no kids," she continued amiably. "I know how to keep out of that," she found herself going on to say, and not exactly without knowing what she was saying, for he had attracted her from the bumping point. Just the right height for her, and lean in the bargain. *Umm*, she was already thinking.

Elsa had run off and got married at sixteen, but had got her fill of it in less than a year. She'd discovered the unconscious selfishness of men, and furthermore that she had no intention of getting used to it. She left as abruptly as she had come. He had to claim desertion. So that was over with. But she liked sex.

Wasn't there just enough time for a little more? She leaned her thigh into Packard's, touching again, starting him up. There was a persistent whisper in her mind, like a little night wind.

"What was that phone call about?" asked Packard.

She had to tell him. "Margy."

"Better?" he asked, turning his head to her on the pillow, frowning when she didn't answer, then finally said,

"No."

He came up suddenly on his elbow. "Very serious then?" Again she didn't answer. "Why didn't you say?"

But he knew why she hadn't and that it was the same reason that he, when the call came, had gone out on the porch.

"Jesus," she flared up, "I can't do miracles."

But what miracle did she mean? She didn't know, she only felt accused.

He flung back the fold of sheet he had drawn partway over his legs and, rising off the bed, began grabbing for his clothes.

"Don't you realize . . . ?"

A fight was in the air. They had been careful, all these past months, never to get quarreling, as, they both assured each other, all they wanted was the same thing, nothing to quarrel over. Now he was going to accuse her. She knew it.

But he didn't, unless his sudden cutoff of feeling, his urgency, was an accusation.

"I'll go get him from the store," he said.

"If he's there," she flung after him, making him turn back.

"What on earth do you mean?"

"I mean that he hasn't come back, so he must have gone somewhere else."

"God in heaven," Packard said, and plunged through the living room. He ran to the top of the steps that ran to ground level.

Cooper, she thought, *I'm doing something to you. But then Margy wanted us to take you. What could she do with him, was what she said. And now I'm supposed to be. . . .* What? What was she supposed to be? She remembered the exact words of the call, though she hadn't told them to Packard. "We'd urge you to come as soon as possible. She's not improving." But Packard hadn't wanted to hear. It's why he'd gone on the porch. Like a signal that had told her. And they both knew it. Yes, both of them.

Packard was still on the steps when a man in blue jeans and a faded T-shirt walked into the yard.

"Oh, hello," said Packard.

"Hi yer doin'. Say, is one of you over here named Billy?"

"No . . . well, yes and no. He's a . . . well, he's our . . . relative."

"A kid was over to the store. He was talking about Billy."

"Where's he now?"

"He just struck out."

"Struck out?"

"Preston over there, he come to the conclusion the kid was with you. But he just wasn't sure."

"You mean he left? For where?" He was gazing hard into a country face, sun-reddened, with sun-scaled skin and eyebrows speckled gray under a cap bill.

"Beats me, if he ain't here."

Packard was stricken. He stood fixed on the stair, feeling his feet grow numb as if set in cement. Elsa, all dressed, came out beside him. "Don't tell me he's lost." He turned on her in something like the start of an outburst, but then said hurriedly, "We're going to the store."

They crossed the road together.

Preston had no more to offer than what they'd heard already. "Just struck out. Kept talking about Billy. Are you Billy?"

"No," said Packard.

A woman came from the back of the store. She was well-informed. "How come you letting him out like that? How old is he?"

"Seven," said Elsa.

"You ought not to let him out like that."

"He was supposed to come right back," said Packard.

"He said something about his mother, too," said the store-keeper, Preston. "You his mother? He was talking about her and Billy."

Elsa and Packard got in the station wagon and rode up and down the highway. They stopped at every place of business to inquire about Cooper. They described him so much they knew him by heart. The last phrase was always red tennis shoes.

They went back to the beach house and called the police. Then they sat and tried not to look at each other. It seemed like the first bad afternoon in Eden.

It was after dark that a car pulled up in the yard below. Packard and Elsa rushed to the stair. An elderly couple were alighting from their car, and here came Cooper.

"We should have stopped and called," they said. "But we decided to hurry back instead."

The story was simple enough. They had filled up with gas at Preston's store and Cooper had heard them say they were heading to Eltonville. He wanted to see his mother and tell her about Billy. She was sick and he thought it would be good for her to know. He had crawled into the back seat. What happened next was never quite clear because everybody started talking at once. Did they notice him there before they heard the announcement on the radio, or afterward? The man had judged he had got in at the store, only place they'd stopped for gas. He'd turned right around to come back. And then the radio. . . . But there—after all was said, and never to be understood—there was Cooper, standing so small and so separate from Packard and herself. Separate from the others too. So separate he was almost nameless, like a kid without a name, Elsa thought. She cried out "Cooper!" and suddenly closed the distance. She threw her arms around him and burst into tears. Cooper hugged her back.

"Golly, sport," said Packard. "You sure scared us silly."

"How's Billy?" Cooper asked.

The elderly couple said they were glad to have been a help. It was their little adventure, they said. They gave their name and address and telephone number and Packard, giving his, said "we"—"we live at," etc. Letting out they weren't married seemed not quite the thing. Probably he would never see them again, except maybe in the grocery.

In the dew-damp early night, the three of them stood in the dark, waving good-bye to the nice people as they backed away and moved into the highway.

Then Packard and Elsa turned and followed Cooper up the stairs to where the brontosaurus waited in the living room.

"We're leaving now," Packard said firmly. "We've got to get to Margery."

Packard and Elsa never went away together again. Elsa kept remembering what she had felt about Cooper, how she had seen and seen and seen again, in her mind's vivid memory, the hurt face when she'd slapped him, the firm little shoulders trudging ahead of her, eagerly leading her down the aisles at K-mart, the two smudges of blood on his legs from mosquito bites, the march of the red tennis shoes. And her inward cry in the awful afternoon of "Come back, my darling, please." It had all surprised her. She had never thought of Cooper as her darling. She never cried. She didn't know she could. Once, long ago, she had cried. It was not long after her mother died and had to do with something about some roller skates, but what she couldn't remember. She thought it didn't matter anymore.

Margery didn't die, she just almost did.

Elsa got married and moved away to Oklahoma. She had children one after another. She even had twins. Packard got a better job up in Maryland, and he got married too. Soon he had a son. He would stare at him in loving amazement.

But wherever they were, Packard and Elsa always thought of Cooper as their first child. They didn't know that they each thought this. One day Packard drove down to Raleigh on some school business. Being near Eltonville, he went over and looked Cooper up.

He had grown into a great boy, rather brusk, but friendly. He didn't remember much about Ocean Isle, only going off somewhere in a car. But when Packard mentioned Billy, he grinned. "He stayed blown up for a long time," said Cooper. "But the air finally faded right out of him." He turned to his mother, Margery. "It was that dinosaur I had once," he explained. "Oh, yes," she said. "It went down a little at a time. There was nothing left but his little old head." Cooper was laughing. "That silly grin just wouldn't go away."

Packard wanted to tell that to Elsa.

On the Hill

REGARDING BARRY and Jan Daugherty you first had to know that they lived out about two miles from town. Lots of people do live out in wooded areas here; the whole town is filled with trees so that the extent of it is not easily determined. Even so the Daughertys were to be thought of as distant. The little maps which accompanied their frequent invitations were faithfully followed, for they gave wonderful parties.

They had not been very long in Eltonville, only since last winter, it would seem. Exact dates of their arrival and acquisition of the property were not known. The fact was nobody could pin down any exact information about the Daughertys. Jan, in fact, sometimes went by another name—Fisher. But it was easy to think she was in the modern habit of retaining her maiden name, or was it the name of a former husband? The Daughertys, if asked, gave rather roundabout answers. Jan said, in regard to the name, "Oh, I keep it for Riley." Riley was her son. Then was there a Mr. Fisher, somewhere off in her past? It was hard not to sound too inquisitive. Riley was a blond little boy of about ten. When guests arrived, he ran about taking everybody's coats and then vanished with them, upstairs. He reappeared at departure time, looking sleepy but holding wraps by the armload.

As for the girl, younger, probably six, she clearly was Barry's daughter. But was she Jan's? Were there two divorces in the background? Not unusual: who cared? It wasn't really that anyone would care, one way or the other; it was just that nobody knew.

Going to the Daugherty house was like a progress to an estate. The road off the state highway wound through trees, but broke into the open on a final climb. The house itself sat free of all but a couple of flanking oaks. Its galleries suggested an outlook over vistas.

It was a joy to come there. How had they managed so soon to find such nice people? For a dinner invitation, you arrived just before dark and parked in an ample space. Barry himself would be just inside the door. He had a broad smile, skin that always looked lightly tanned. Sometimes a tie, sometimes not. He had picked up easily on local habits. His hair was dark brown, sprinkled with gray. He never slicked it down. And Jan? Well, she knew how to dress and how to greet. The feeling imparted was that everything was under control, and that the arriving guests were the choice people of the earth.

It would soon be dark. Looking out toward the terrace from where she sat at the end of her table, pouring coffee while Barry refilled wineglasses, Jan would say, "Last winter during the snow, what a lot of creatures wandered in." "It happens in town, too," one guest would offer. "I admired them, as much as you can admire a 'possum—is that it? Those things with the long snouts and skinny tails. I'd hate to dream of one. I wonder if they bite."

"We'll ask Riley to find out at school," Barry said.

"They certainly bite," one of the men volunteered, speaking from country knowledge. "But just if you corner them. They're sort of timid."

Where on earth were they from, not to know about 'possums?

"Then there was the raccoon," Jan continued. "What a precious little guy. All black circles under his eyes."

"You must have put food out."

"Oh, just a few scraps."

"They'll love you to death. They'll certainly bite you."

Somebody had a story about a raccoon his aunt had let in the house, because he looked so cute. He had rifled the cupboards and climbed on the shelves. He had tried to get in the refrigerator. How to get rid of him?

"They carry rabies," the same informing man said.

"Don't disillusion me," pled Jan.

Evenings there sped by, but when the guests spoke of them later, there was not much more to remember later than talk of possums and raccoons.

Do we really like them? Eva Rooke asked herself that, all the while observing with fascination, as they were leaving the table for the living room, how Jan Daugherty wielded a silver candle snuffer, tapering in her slender hand, elongating her white arm where two bracelets circled.

Suppose I used a candle snuffer? Eva wondered. What would Dick say to that?

The Rookes lived nearby. It was easy to come there. Dick was with her sometimes. He could seldom be led out to parties. Eva gave excuses for him—as one of the county commissioners he often came in late and tired or had to go to some night meeting. But the true reason was his passion for music. He liked nothing better than turning up the stereo full force, four speakers blaring *Le Mariage de Figaro*, *The Barber of Seville*. Now and then something by Wagner or Massenet. He even listened to CDs of Broadway musicals—*Oklahoma!*, *South Pacific*. He wasn't choosy. Eva bought earplugs and swore she didn't mind. Once in the middle of gossip about local sexual affairs, how everybody wondered whose marriage would be next—she brought out that she was safe until Aida showed up. Someone who heard her caught on slow, trying to place the name.

Another truth was that people around Dick Rooke were a little timid. He was brusque with a habit of looking as if he had got himself bathed and dressed reluctantly. Everybody liked him, but found him hard to talk to. He said abrupt things. Something you had asked him five minutes before he would suddenly answer, having thought it over.

Eva, loving, knew she wouldn't be with anybody else but Dick. They had lost one child from a miscarriage but were hoping for another.

Three times a week, Eva drove to her part-time job in a law office, about ten miles. There was a back road she took which led through some few unexpected places—a Chinese restaurant sat out on a graveled parking lot. A shabby old abandoned house with children's toys scattered on the porch. And a church with an odd name—Holy Brotherhood of Jesus. Eva always looked at the building, which was plain and small with a sort of square pedestal on the roof; it seemed to have been put there in expectation of a steeple. Soon they'll raise money for the steeple, Eva thought. But then one day, in the tail of her eyes, she saw the door of the church open and Barry Daugherty came out.

A man in a black suit followed and stood talking. She swerved, almost ran off the road, considered going back, decided not to, and went on her way. Perhaps she was mistaken. He had looked accustomed there, and she was sure the more she thought of it that it had been Barry. He had a certain unique quality, not easily confused with another. But Barry in a Holy Brotherhood?

That evening Eva told Dick about it. "Well, maybe he belongs to it," Dick said. The church was in his section of the county and he knew about it.

"What are they like?" Eva wanted to know.

"A bunch of kooks," said Dick, though he thought this same thing about most religions.

"How do you know?"

"Well . . ." he was slow to confess, "I stopped there to listen once. I sat in the back. They stand up and talk about it all."

"What all?"

"Oh, salvation . . . Jesus . . . stuff like that. They stomp on the floor."

"I cannot believe that Barry Dougherty is into that sort of thing. I expected they would join in with us, but they didn't."

"Us" was Episcopalian, the sort of religion that went with the wines and the candlelight.

Dick Rooke professed himself tired of all these dinner parties. Eva thought you had to pay people back. He helped out reluctantly when they did and Eva bit her nails, hoping things would go well. "You don't have to do all this," he would say, stacking wood to start a fire. She worked hard at it and was so exhausted afterwards she had to rest up for three days. But she loved those parties; everybody was so interesting. They were getting friendly with prominent people—the head of a university department, a member of the town council, a bank president. "You knew them all already," Dick objected. But it was the setting, the way the Daughertys did things. And the sense of mystery, the sense of belonging. Eva always thought they should have more of a social life. They had simply lucked up on the Daughertys. Dick had run into Barry in a line at the post office. They had got talking and the result was an invitation, the first.

Barry Daugherty answered clearly enough when asked about his vocation. He was involved in a scientific project which might lead to breakthroughs in selected fields of cancer research. The basic work he had done at Hopkins had interested the leading research team here so they had enticed him to relocate. But where did you come from before that? Up around Philadelphia. What did you ask him next? Certainly he would answer, but what did anyone know about corrective laser surgery leading to alteration of enzyme deficiency? You switched to personal questions: Where did he meet Jan? Easy. "Skiing at Aspen. She fell and thought something was broken. Only a sprain." He laughed. "I picked her up."

So now, you knew everything you had asked. Could you possibly say, "What church do you go to?" Certainly, Eva's mother, active in the altar guild, could do that. But nowadays it seemed something you didn't ask, especially considering the Holy Brotherhood of Jesus.

She stood near a wall, looking at a three-panel picture, a natural wooded scene, each part a trifle different from the others. Barry noticed her. "It looks like Cézanne," she remarked, fishing up art knowledge from university days. "Exactly what I thought when I bought it," he praised her. In warming days, the guests spilled out on the back terrace. Once Eva was standing there, looking out toward a line of trees. She heard a distant thrashing sound. "What's that?" Barry asked. She shook her head. "You're from here," he teased her. "You should know. Have you got bears too?" It could be, she told him, recounting a story about a bear in somebody's backyard. Jan came out with another couple. "Don't scare me," she said, and remarked that Eva's dress was lovely. "You must tell me where you shop." If she hadn't come out, would Eva have asked Barry what church he went to? Not more about bears.

The time of year was leaning toward Christmas holidays. One day Eva went to the door and found little Riley Daugherty standing there in the cold.

"Riley!" she exclaimed. "What are you doing here?" She at once looked out to the drive expecting to see Jan in her gray Buick, having sent the boy with a message. But there wasn't any car or any Jan.

"Mamma's gone away," said Riley.

"Gone where?"

"I don't know. I'm scared." He was shaking, not altogether from cold.

"Come in," said Eva. "It's warm in here. Come on in," she repeated when he didn't move.

Eva gave him some hot cocoa and let him warm up.

"Why did you come to visit me?"

He looked at her steadily with large gray eyes. "Just 'cause I wanted to."

Eva had a feeling that was not wholly true. She told him she was about to call his mother. He only stared at her.

No one answered the call. *I'd better drive there*, thought Eva. "Come on," she said to Riley. "We'll go out to your house." He followed.

They were up the driveway and on the flat summit within shouting distance of the house, when Eva sensed that something was wrong. "I'm going to find your mamma," she said to Riley. "Now you just wait and we'll come back for you."

Riley said nothing. He continued to stare out the window.

She went toward the house with what she hoped looked like confidence, but the truth was, she was a little afraid. But why? She didn't really know.

She reached the door. The big bronze knocker with its lion head seemed to be meeting her eye. It crashed twice. She heard nothing from within. She circled to the right and looked in on the living room where the curtains were partially drawn. There sat Jan in a large armchair, facing a younger blond woman, who lolled in another chair. It was obvious, even without noting the glasses and half-empty whisky bottle on the low table between them, that they were both "out," as Dick called it. Stoned.

Eva went back to the car. "Your mother's not here," she told Riley. "Nobody's home. She must have sent you some message you didn't get. Now let's go have some ice cream, and I'll drive you back later."

"The car's here," said Riley. Had he trudged home from the school bus, then come to her? She didn't ask.

"I expect your dad came and now they're off in the other car. They'll both be back." I'm getting good at this, she thought. But dismay was growing within.

She did take him for ice cream; then, thinking Dick would be home and tell her what to do next, she rang her house. But what could she say? Talking on her cell in the ice cream shop she was in hearing distance of Riley. She clicked off before there could be an answer. "I need to stop by my house," she said to the boy. "Then we'll go to yours." So on they went.

"Isn't it fun to ride around like this?" Eva said. Riley said nothing.

"If it was me, I'd stay out of mysteries," Dick advised her, having listened to all of it. He had gone with her to take Riley home once again. They had found Barry Daugherty out on the lawn. He thanked them profusely, saying that all that time he had just been upstairs taking a nap. Returning, Eva puzzled on.

"But you went in the church," she said. "You were curious too."

"That was before we met these folks. I wonder about weird religions. I had heard some complaints."

"But when they ring up again."

"For dinner, you mean? Just say no."

She sighed. She thought it was fun to go there. But she also wondered about Riley. Dick said she wondered too much. Wanting children herself, it was easy to let her mind drift toward the boy. What situation was he in? Who knew?

Then Riley showed up again.

It was an afternoon in late February, barely tinged with spring. Riley, having rung the bell to good effect, stood before the door and looked up at her. "Now, Riley, what's the matter this time?"

"I thought maybe we could ride around," said Riley.

It was just as far to the Daughertys' house from the bus stop as it was to the Rookes'. She pointed that out to him. He said he knew that. "I like to ride," said Riley.

She took a long way around. A tribe of crows sped by them, turned and circled. They looked as if they were going somewhere on purpose. "What if you could fly?" Eva asked. "I wouldn't be a crow," said Riley. "Let's go away."

Eva was astounded. "Go away where?"

"Anywhere. Up in the mountains."

"That's a long way."

"Maybe the beach."

"Don't you want to go home?"

He thought it over. "Okay." So she took him there.

In the Daughertys' yard everything was quiet. The car stood there.

"Come on," said Eva. "We'll go in together."

She glanced at him. He sat very still and looked ahead.

"Don't you want to?"

Riley turned his head and pressed his face into the seat back.

Eva put out her hand to him, touched him to get his attention, saw he was crying.

"Why, Riley. What's the matter, honey?"

"He'll drown me."

"Who will? Your daddy?"

Riley suddenly jumped forward, opened the door, sprang out and ran to the house. He rushed in through the front door not looking back.

That evening Dick was downright firm. "You leave those folks alone."

"I'm not sure if he even said that. I thought he did."

"There's trouble in that house. It's not our business."

But now she had office work to do and thought he was right and went about her daily life. But at times she wondered if Riley might appear again and there was a catch in her heart from that very wondering. Uptown she ran into Amy Waldron who said, "Those people quit inviting us, how about you?" Eva agreed. "I think her sister's been here," said Amy, "but even so—" Anyway, no more invitations. It seemed all that glow and elegance had just been phenomena of seasons past.

Despite herself, she would detour and drive past the Daughertys' just to glance at it as it stood on the rise among trees with the front drive opening and disappearing. All was silent, and nobody seemed at home, though sometimes a car could be seen, high up.

Next, the truant officer. The son of some people she knew had been reported as not in school, they said, but the school couldn't find out why. They had visited but no one was at home and so had reported the absence. "I understood you all were friends. I couldn't find anybody."

"If I go there and ring, they might let me in. They have a girl too, I think."

The officer thought it over. "Try, then. But let us know."

Dick was out. She dressed carefully and then drove there. Why did her heart beat so fast when she rang the bell?

Footsteps, then the door and there stood Jan Daugherty in an old dressing gown that could only be called a wrapper. She looked drained, tired, maybe hungover. "Oh, it's you."

"Why, Jan, I just stopped by to say hello. I was wondering about Riley. Someone told me he hadn't been in school."

"He's sick. I'm keeping him in for a while." Behind her the little girl was lingering palely at the foot of the stair.

"Nothing serious, I hope?"

She stepped back, half closing the door between them. "Same thing his father had. Sorry, but I need to see about . . ."

See about what, she never said. Only "Thanks for coming," and the closed door.

"Well then a mystery," was all Dick would say. She had called the truant officer. He had thanked her.

"His real father must have died of something or other," she speculated.

"Will you stop all this? I never liked them anyway. Too slick and smooth. Something's bound to be wrong."

"It's that church," she pondered.

"Not our problem," Dick said, and put on Wagner.

Seeing no more of them then, she agreed, was the only right way. Still she thought of Riley. There was something about a needful child, but what did he need? She remembered the large gray eyes, asking for something. One day, well and hearty, he appeared again. She drove him home once more. He told her he wanted to go see his grandmother. He said that she lived in Hollowell, a town some miles away.

"I can't take you," said Eva. "Ask your mom and dad."

"They don't like her."

This time, she dropped him in his driveway and left.

Long after the Daughertys had moved away, Eva found a list of Hollowell citizens but none of their name, nor Fisher either.

It was only a year they had been there. The house sat empty for a good while. It looked lonely. Eva was happily pregnant again. Hoping this time to succeed, she quit her job. Dick had persuaded her. In the afternoons she walked, sometimes by the Daugherty house. One afternoon in the woods across from the entrance, she saw a small boy who beckoned to her. She followed but he disappeared into the woods. She stood a few steps into the trees and called out, "Riley?" *He's looking for me.*

Oh but that was absurd, she realized. The family had long gone and now the For Sale sign was down, someone else would move in.

It was inevitable she would go to that church. She found out the time—it was the normal Sunday eleven o'clock hour. To Dick, at home with a pile of Sunday papers, she had only said she was going to church.

She parked near some other cars and sat quietly, listening. The church windows were open to the warm day. The people who entered did not look her way. They mostly wore dark clothes, even black. She saw no one she knew. She heard murmuring that died away and a piano began to play a tune she'd never heard. Singing too, then silence. The speaking voice— a minister?—was too low to make out the words, but before long it began to rise, even to shouting, and she heard "Water? Fire? Blood?" There began a sort of chanting and a shuffling like feet moving and then a positive shout: "We consume or we will be consumed!"

Good Lord, Eva thought. She slid from the car and moved nearer to the open door. She wanted to peer inside. A man in black stood in front of the audience, waving something like a pitcher full of liquid. A line of children kneeled before him. On the table beside him, a large torch-like candle was alight. The feet began to move again, the rhythm mounting, almost stamping the floor.

The door closed in her face. A man was standing beside her.

"What are you doing?" he demanded.

"I was passing by," she stammered. "I wanted to hear."

"Come in if you wish," he said sternly. "We celebrate God's power. You can join us. But do not spy."

"Those children," she said. "What is happening?"

"They are souls before God," he all but intoned. From within she heard a child's frightened cry. She turned and hastened back to her car.

It was telling Dick about it when she got home that relieved her.

"Jesus," he said. "I told you to stay away."

"But you went there yourself."

"I didn't see them trying to kill anybody."

"But you had heard things. You investigated."

"Yes, I had heard things. People complained. But what are you going to do about it? The Baptists keep a lake for dunking people. Some people wash feet. Up in the mountains, they play around with snakes."

"It ought to be stopped," she insisted. "What did they mean by fire or by blood?"

"People just like to go crazy. Religion's the best way. 'Do it my way, you'll be saved.'"

"Barry Daugherty had a scar on his face."

"Maybe they branded him."

They both began to laugh. She felt it had been a bad dream.

After lunch he lay down beside her. "What cold little hands." He fondled one. "Let me warm them for you." One of those operas, she forgot which. He sang it in the foreign words. *"Se la lasci riscaldar."* She felt a thrill. His hands were warm. For the first time, the baby stirred in her womb.

"You ought to go to your own church," her mother advised. She was a model in attending. "We could get all that out of you. Anyway, what do you care what they do?"

"It was the boy. He was frightened. And then the crying I heard . . ."

The next Sunday she did go to church. She sat by her mother and listened though did not remember later what was said, but came out feeling calm.

So now the past had dissolved everything about the Daughertys. They had vanished like a road.

Still, when she passed by, she looked up at the house. Then that habit too faded. She kept her appointments, doing everything as she was told, making ready for the child.

But one day, driving past on an errand, she saw at the top of the hill above the trees the high yellow lift of a crane. What on earth? She parked by the roadside and began to walk slowly up the drive. The crane was in the backyard of the house, which seemed to be vacant. There were two men in the back around the crane. They looked up at her. Another man was sitting on the small back terrace where Jan Daugherty, in warm weather, had liked to serve cocktails. She could almost hear the laughter. The man rose and came to her.

"You want something?"

"Why no . . . I was just curious, that's all."

He looked puzzled. She felt awkward, so obviously pregnant, so intrusive on the scene.

"I—I used to know the people who lived here."

"Well, they moved away. I bought the house." She still stood there. "It's mine," he added, as if she hadn't heard.

"Not the last ones," she said. "The ones before that. The Daughertys. They had children, I remember."

He laughed. "Don't ask me." He nodded at the crane. "Drainage problems. We've got to uproot the pipes. Hey, you walked here? I can drive you home."

"No, I'm okay." Coming closer to the house, she peered through a window, seeing the shadowy, empty space inside, as if she hadn't believed it could be. She could glimpse the living room, even see the entrance hall if she craned. Inside, she thought something moved.

"You look here—" The voice had turned harsh. He meant business. She hastened away past the house, down the drive. At a turn a deer came out from the trees and stood still, regarding her for a long moment. *I'm an intruder*, she thought. The deer turned and leaped back into the wood.

Before anybody lived here, before there was even a house, the deer were here. The place was theirs. She recalled the talk about 'possums and coons. The bear they might have heard. Didn't someone mention snakes? Animal life started spinning through her mind, all but clouding her vision. She sat in the car, waiting for it to clear. Inside her, the baby was stirring.

At dinner that night she told Dick, "I saw a deer."

"They're everywhere, especially at night."

On the way to the hospital where he had to rush her that night, they saw no deer at all. By dawn there was another child in the world, a boy. Her mother came to stay with them. She sat and rocked and changed the diapers and Dick was nice to her.

"I prayed she would be all right," she told him. "I asked for prayers at church." She was a comfortable woman, wearing old-fashioned shoes that laced.

Dick had arranged for a nurse who now sat there too. There was a changing table, a bassinet. "I always pray," the nurse said, and added, "I'm a Methodist."

At the hospital Dick had run into one of the doctors he knew from an illness in his family. Oncology. "There was a guy here doing computer research in cancer. Daugherty. He left last year." "They come and go," said the doctor. "Can't say I remember him." He bent to a computer and found a few leads. "Seems it fell through," was all he could report. "But I do remember now. Something about a child that died."

Eva dozed and woke. She put out her arms and the nurse lifted the baby to lie in them. Bliss was crowding into her confusion and remembered pain. "What's all this about Riley?" the nurse asked.

Her mother said, "She wants to name him that."

Dick thought, looking in on the scene, *three women and a baby son.* He heard what they were saying. "His name's Richard," he clearly pronounced. "We'll call him Rick." *I'll teach him music,* he comfortably thought. He sat down on the bed and stroked his child's head. He took his wife's hand.

"What's gone is gone," he said. "What's real remains."

So they built the wall. From back of it, came the faint echo of stamping feet, and on the hill a bear explored, a deer was watchful, and a little boy wandered, searching forever.

The Wedding Visitor

IT SEEMED a good thing to do and because he hadn't come there in so long, he went slowly. Approaching the house from the road before it spiraled up the drive, he sat for a while and gave it a long look.

Like many Southern houses, the original structure was almost lost among the many extensions. There was the added side porch where everyone lived out each day, enjoying sun through the enveloping series of windows. He recalled another, earlier porch out back, screened in, added to escape the hot summer nights. They had slept under mosquito nets and hoped not to hear a wicked buzz. To one side of that, there was the kitchen with doors opening on one of two dining rooms. And up front, jutting out, a sturdy new entrance porch with a handsome hanging lamp. Inside all these tack-ons, the original house nested peacefully. It was nothing splendid, dating from the 1890s, he supposed, but sturdy, white, comfortable.

In the yard, recently mowed, the familiar trees had grown taller. He remembered climbing them.

Shifting gear, he wound up the driveway.

But where was everybody?

He went to the side porch, the family entrance, and getting no answer to his knock, he walked in.

Far in the back, a cousin named Emily saw him and jumped up.

"It must be Rob Ellis!"

"It's me," he said, exchanging hugs. "I came for Norma's wedding."

"So did everybody," said Emily. "They're up at the church."

Then calmly, as they both sat down, she picked up *Time* magazine and continued reading. He felt a stir of his old childhood resentment about the odd way they treated him, but then laughed at himself. Emily had always been that way, doing what she wanted and not noticing anybody.

"Where's the groom?" he asked, not quite sure he could recall the name engraved on the handsome invitation.

"Sandy? He comes around after work."

"Do you like him?"

She had yet to look up. "He's okay." One of her sandals slipped off. She scratched her ankle with her toe. "Are you going to vote for Reagan?"

"Isn't everybody?" He had hoped to get away from politics.

"Normie's in the living room."

He began to feel peaceful, unwilling to do anything. It must be about one o'clock, time they all used to fold up after lunch at noon. They called it dinner. Nap time. He yawned. It was quiet—end-of-the-road quiet. When he stayed there in the summers, twenty years ago, Emily had not been born. He had seen her whenever he visited from law school at Ole Miss. Twenty years ago he had been twelve. Maybe then he had been a different person.

Whichever person he was, eventually walked through the hallway to the living room. Sure enough, his cousin Norma was there, sitting in a beautifully upholstered chair, her feet on a matching stool, reading a book. The room was shadowy, the blinds half-drawn. A tall lamp gave light on her page.

"Cousin Rob!" she exclaimed. She jumped up, hugged him close, and sat back down.

"I came to your wedding. Where is everybody?"

She laughed. "Off talking about me, I guess."

"Saying what?"

"Oh, I'm in the doghouse."

He looked around. The rich draperies, the beautiful chairs, the fireplace with logs ready for lighting, the flanking bookshelves. A room seldom used.

"It doesn't look much like a doghouse to me."

"The dog is me," she smiled, and filled him in. "It's because of my dress." She was wearing blue jeans and a checkered shirt. "I want to wear what I want to wear. It's *my* wedding. A beige dress, just with pleats and a slit up the side. You'd think I wanted to wear a bikini. And Aunt Alicia is coming all this way from Chicago, she and Uncle Harry. Everybody is mad at me. They're choosing up sides, but nobody much is on mine. Even Muzzy."

Muzzy was what they called her mother, his Aunt Molly. He looked at what she was reading. *Middlemarch*. Old classic. She was like that. Liked to keep ahead of them all. Along with the rest, he had mocked her. But later he admired her for it.

"Where's . . . your fiancé?" The name again escaped him.

"Sandy? Oh, he'll be along. He works with the road crew."

"He's not from here?"

"No, practically a Yankee."

All those porch nights. Before they had shortened the front porch and no longer used it (the change was blamed on the weather, TV, air-conditioning). Norma in her teens had sat in the swing every evening after supper. And regularly through the night air, the boys would come down the road, and up the drive, by ones and twos. She would sit and swing a little, while each one who came sat on the steps, or up in one of the rockers, talking and laughing. Sometimes one was allowed to sit beside her. Rob Ellis guessed that Sandy must have made it to the swing.

"How'd you meet him?"

"Daddy was helping out the road crew with town people. They didn't know where to find rooms, or where to eat. They wanted to stay over in the Delta. He got to asking them here for dinner once or twice, making suggestions, lining up their business. Sandy keeps their accounts. He started talking to me."

"Out in the swing?"

"The swing's out of date. He asked me to the picture show. He's fun. He doesn't care a bit what I wear to get married in. In fact, he'd just as soon not have a wedding in church. He's a Catholic. We'll have to do it all over again anyway. I haven't told them, so don't you tell them either."

"I always liked you," Rob Ellis said. When his own marriage broke up, he thought of coming back and finding Norma, but he never did it. Courting cousins didn't work. He lived on in Memphis. He worked for a congressman, wrote his press releases, tried (often unsuccessfully) to keep him away from booze and women. Helped him talk up Reagan for a second term, along with himself.

Norma shook back her rich dark hair. "We all liked you, too."

"I was wished on you every summer."

His father, divorced, had him in charge in the summers and plopped him down with relatives. A busy father, often on the road.

Norma said: "They're building this new highway just outside town. It's going to miss us completely. I guess you knew that."

He nodded. Once again, in the continued quiet of that place, he felt absorbed into it, his own spirit drowsing.

Norma dropped her book on the floor. "Let's have a drink."

A *drink*? Well, he had heard some passing talk about her, that way. Family disapproval. But she did smile in a lovely, conspiratorial way, as if to say, We can have fun, just you and me.

"It's too early," he said.

"Hell," said Norma. "You're just like all the rest. Don't tell them I asked you."

He promised.

She picked up her book. Then she thought to ask about Memphis and didn't hear what he said. Even with the fun gone from her face, she was still so pretty, such a candidate for happiness. The tilt of her head, her soft Mississippi drawl. Once when they were kids and fighting, he had caught a wad of her thick hair and pushed her aside and such a charge went prancing through him as he had never felt before. He wondered if she remembered.

Rob wandered toward the back of the house. There was bound to be somebody in the kitchen. He wondered if they had the same old black cook, whose name also he had forgotten.

But then to his surprise, he ran into another extension, a tack-on he didn't know about. The door was open and there in a chair, an old lady was sitting, reading the paper. There was also a Bible, resting in her lap. Did everybody in the house do nothing but read?

"Hello? Can I come in?"

She removed some small slivers of eyeglasses which had slid down her nose and examined him.

"I'm trying to think who it is. No, don't tell me . . . Larry Eilis's boy . . . Now wait . . . Bob . . . no . . ."

"Rob," he finally said.

"Of course!" She stretched out a hand.

She sat enclosed in a long comfortable skirt, with roomy shoes peeping out below. He recalled her only vaguely. She had worked somewhere as a teacher and visited at intervals.

"I'm your cousin Marty," she supplied, helping him. "You're here about Norma."

"Her wedding, yes."

"I hope it works this time. She been lined up for it twice before, you know."

"No, I didn't know."

"Well, it never got as far as sending invitations. Always fizzled out. Something wrong, I reckon. That child is in her thirties. Don't watch out, she'll wind up an old maid like me. Nobody would want that."

Time to say something Southern-nice, but he didn't. "This is a nice room," he said.

"Mack built it for me." It was his uncle she meant, her sister's husband, owner and provider, taking care of everybody the best he could. "He wanted to keep me shut off from the rest of them, I guess." Now she was at it again, suspicious. Nobody wished her well. Nobody liked her. A theme song. "I'd no place else to go. I had to accept."

I'm sure they are glad to have you . . . he knew what he ought to say but didn't. You were supposed to compliment everybody.

"At least I don't have to see them all the time. And they're rid of me. Except for meals."

Considering everything told, she replaced her glasses. Her dress was loose over her frail shoulders. He wondered at her. She had worked all her life, but had wound up here, dependent on her sister's husband for a place to live out the rest of her years. She could have lived frugally alone. She needed family, he imagined. Company. Her intelligent eyes and trim face, bare of makeup, made him wonder why she'd never married.

"I remember your mamma. An energetic soul. Why your father left her, I never knew. Did you?"

"They couldn't get along." At times he hadn't blamed him. Fierce in her advertising work, she had hired various caretakers for her son. What if he didn't like them? Too bad. There was always school.

"This wedding . . ." said Marty. "I'll have to dress and go."

"Don't you want to?"

"I have to be with the family." She gave an instructive, schoolteacherish smile. "Family is all we have, like them or not. Oh, not that I criticize. Don't tell them that."

He promised not to. The voice pursued him.

He wandered out to where the old screened porch still stood in place. Some kitchen things leaned around, broom and mop and bucket, a chair or two. He heard a humming, a hymn, out in the kitchen. He found the steps and went down into the yard, walking toward some pecan trees, now grown into a shady grove.

Somebody was out there, sitting in an old wicker chair, maybe another cousin. A dog detached from the scene, and came toward him, a bronze Lab who gave a low woof, tail wagging, curious but friendly. Sniffing, then following.

"How you doin'?" the possible cousin said.

He saw a pleasant face, amiable, smiling under thick blond hair, unfamiliar in memory. There was a second wicker chair. Rob sat in it.

"Hi there." They shook hands. "I'm Rob. What cousin are you?"

"Not a cousin yet. About to be. I'm Sandy."

The bridegroom! "They said you were at work."

"Supposed to be. But I had to get the right suit. Dark. Rules all over the place."

"Normie's inside."

"Yeah, I know. They're worrying her to death."

"The dress?"

"Yeah, the dress. I don't give a happy damn. I just want Normie away from here."

"To where?"

"Anywhere."

Rob thought it wasn't a good answer. If there was an *away* there had to be a *where*. The dog lay down with a grunt. Rob leaned to stroke the low head.

"Say," said Sandy, "you like him? His name's Remus."

"Sure I do."

"You might want to keep Remus, while we're gone. We'll be taking a little trip. Maybe Florida. Why don't you?"

Rob said he didn't think so.

"Well how do I take a dog along? Maybe Normie wouldn't mind." He thought it over.

There was a rustle of gravel from the drive, a car arriving.

Now the onslaught, Rob thought. But he was wrong. The door slammed and only one arrival made his concerned way to the side door. His Uncle Mack himself. Worried. Head down. Walking inside.

Rob left Sandy, who said he thought he was better off outside. "Tell Normie I'm out here."

On to Uncle Mack. He kept a small office, tucked away, one of the bedrooms organized to harbor his files, his typewriter, his big fat checkbook.

"Why," he exclaimed, "if it isn't Rob. How's the boy?"

The pleasure seemed genuine. In the past, it always seemed Uncle Mack was cordial to him because he had to be. He was obliged to fulfill his duty toward his brother, who had this boy nobody knew what to do with. Especially in the summers. They stood awkwardly in the hall.

"Old Stockton working you hard?"

So he had kept up enough to know about the congressman.

"Keeping schedules. Writing speeches." Rob could have continued, but something about his uncle's presence stopped him. MacKenzie Ellis was an imposing man, a strong face above a thickened body, its heavy waistline always buttoned up in a cream-colored vest which might be satin or heavy cotton or wool.

"Supports Reagan, I guess. Up in Tennessee I'd probably vote for him. Come in."

In the office Uncle Mack sat down at his desk, then leaned his head forward on his hand, frowning.

"Where is everybody?" Rob asked again.

Uncle Mack started. "Oh, they all went up to decorate the church. Then they went over to Gert Henderson's, I imagine to talk about it all and drink coffee. Then the rehearsal and after that we go to the club for dinner." He let out a sigh.

It was two o'clock, and the sense of things to come was in the air. Uncle Mack swiveled. He had a struggle going on behind his eyes. He needed to confide. But with Rob Ellis? He scarcely ever saw the boy, clearly not a boy any longer. A man with a political job, or something like it. But not so deeply in the family he was apt to run around telling secrets. So not too big a risk. Decision.

"I'm telling you, Rob. I'm upset."

"Yes, sir."

"You may know this guy here with the road people. Milton Ward?"

"No, sir."

"I thought you might. I think he knows Stockton. He's from Memphis. Well, he runs the bunch making the new highway. I helped them all quite a bit. Just this morning he told me."

"Told you what?"

"That boy's about to be my son-in-law. And do you know what? He's been helping himself to the road crew's expense money!"

"He's right out in the backyard," Rob said.

"Where's Norma?"

"In the living room. Reading a book."

Uncle Mack let out a groan. "And now we're supposed to have this wedding. He's going to marry her!"

"I know. It's what I came for."

"Do I stop it? What do I do?" Then he added in a voice that broke, "I want her to be happy."

"So do I," Rob said. He had never imagined his uncle crying. "Maybe it's not true," he ventured.

"Oh, it's true all right. But how'd he expect to get by with it? And how much was it? Ward didn't tell me. Just said forget it. But how can I let her do it? Marry a thief?"

He suddenly rose. "Now you listen here . . ." Rob stood as well, and confronting that heavyset tower of a man, he felt like a dwarf. He had never grown tall. He was a little guy and he got even smaller when his uncle caught his lapels and all but lifted him off the floor.

"Don't you tell any of this! You hear me? I have to face it alone. It's up to me!"

Rob promised, reflecting that everybody so far, excepting Emily, had asked him not to tell something. It was as bad as politics.

From the front came a grinding crunch of gravel followed by a car door slam, steps on the walk, at the door, a welcoming call from Emily. Norma must be gone from the living room.

Stamp of feet and the usual passage toward the big side porch. Emily would have to part with Ronald Reagan and *Time* magazine. Cries of greeting.

"May the Lord help me," said Uncle Mack. "I've got to greet them."

The bunch of cousins were talking loud. They were staying at the Homestead Inn . . . my, it was nice as could be . . . and where on earth was Molly (some said Muzzy), and where was Norma (some said Normie).

Rob listened and decided not to appear, be identified, screamed over, kissed and pounded. He crept through the house, tending toward the back, but did not escape running into the cook, big black Louise (he remembered the name), who knew him at once. "Lawd, Mister Rob, you ain't grown a inch."

He must have said something, escaping, looking toward the back where he had left Sandy. But Sandy now had Norma with him, standing, his arm around her, her hand resting on him, and the way they tilted Rob knew this was real to them and right. Remus seemed to know it too. He lay contentedly at their feet, as though already in a house they lived in. It seemed to grow up around them. Rob walked forward until they looked up.

"The cousins," he said to Norma. "I think it's Maud Oakley and that gang. They come by four and sixes," he explained to Sandy.

"Oh God, it's my bridesmaids!" Norma ran toward the house.

"Listen," he said to Sandy. His tone was not to be mistaken. Sandy listened. "How much did you take?"

In no more than a half a minute Sandy guessed what he meant.

"God," he said, "they never look at that account."

"Well they have now."

"Just for my dark suit. And the trip to Florida. I thought they wouldn't look."

"They've told Uncle Mack." He paused to let this be digested, then asked, "Where can we find them?"

Sandy said he didn't know but could guess. He had driven down with Norma, so Rob piled him in his car. Remus jumped into the backseat and lay down. The house was buzzing with the cousins' voices, sounding like a swarm of bees just deciding to hive.

Sandy protested all the way to town.

"They stretch that account to the limit. I cover up for them. Buying liquor. Paying off debts. I don't think they'd tell all that to Norma's dad."

Rob felt he'd never left Memphis, cleaning up behind Congressman Stockton. Not at all what he came for.

The town unfolded in its ancient way, up past the filling station, the drugstore, the courthouse, and on to dusty old Homestead Inn with its white columns needing paint and cracked brick walk, but inside nice and homey. The boy at reception looked up with a ready smile, but Rob waved him silent, while Sandy made a cautious circuit around the lobby and ducked into a passage back of the desk.

It opened into an office, with files ranked along one wall and two ample sofas cornered near a back window. On one of them a heavyset man sprawled at leisure. He sat his tall glass down beside the half-empty bourbon bottle and snorted with delight.

"If it ain't the bridegroom! Who's your friend?"

Rob got presented to Milton Ward, head of the road crew. There was a second man, sitting on the rug under the window, likewise nursing a tall glass of amber-colored drink. Jamie Hackett. Friday had come for them both.

"This is serious," Rob announced. His tone left no doubt. He refused a drink. "We've got to talk."

He sat on the vacant couch and bent forward. Jamie Hackett got up to listen. Milton Ward leaned closer. Sandy kept nodding agreement, but also stuck in his own comments. He hadn't thought it was serious to borrow a little. It had seemed like an emergency.

"Why in hell did I tell him?" Ward marveled at himself. "Just to watch out for this shyster here. It's all I said." He slapped Sandy on the shoulder. "It was a joke."

"You don't know Uncle Mack," Rob said. "He's got these Presbyterian ideas. He knows what sin is. He's always thinking about money. Also, he's a teetotaler. He might stop the whole show. They're already mad at Normie."

"That pretty girl? Why?"

"Her dress," Sandy explained. "She doesn't want to dress pretty."

"Well, that's easy," said Milton Ward. He had raised two daughters. "Just tell her she's got to."

"You don't know Norma," said Rob.

"Seems like I don't know anybody. So what you want from me?"

"Sober up," Rob advised. "Then get hold of Uncle Mack. Say it was all a mistake. Sandy's paid it back."

"I can't," said Sandy. "I got to have it. I paid for that suit. And Florida is coming up fast."

"We'll figure it out," Rob said, and wondered how much was in his bank account. Oh, those summers when he stayed with these kinfolks, paying nothing. Just freeloading, as they sometimes even told him, the mean ones, playing tennis or cards, shoving him aside. He was such a little squirt, one of them said. *You gonna ever grow up?* That was one of the bunch from Jackson, not close kin.

"We've got to get to the bank," Rob said, pushing Sandy toward the door.

"I'm due at the church pretty soon," Milton Ward said. "I'm the best man. What time is it?"

"Don't come drunk," Rob said. "Butter him up about Sandy. Lie if you have to."

"Not exactly lying. I owe this boy here a favor, don't I?"

"Lots of 'em," said Sandy, in a whisper.

A clutter of voices came from the lobby. *Oh Lord, the cousins,* thought Rob. "Is there some way out the back?"

There was.

He and Sandy found a door and sneaked out the back of the old hotel to the car. Nobody saw them.

Then the bank.

It was nearly four. Rob had read somewhere that four o'clock was the dead hour. If you could live through four o'clock you would get to another day. Rob reckoned he would make it, as after concluding the bank business, he dropped off Sandy and Remus. ("Can't you keep Remus?" Sandy asked. "No, I can't," said Rob. Remus licked his face.) He drove to the house to catch his breath and get ready for dinner at the club.

The house was quiet. He welcomed its peace and the chance to feel what he had come for, reflection and memories. There was a narrow stair, he recalled, leading up to a single large room, made from what was once the attic. In that room, his aunt had often sat with her sewing machine. She would bend forward to guide the cloth beneath the needle, turning it, stopping to release it, pushing it forward again. Again the clicking.

Sometimes alone with her he had sat on the floor near enough to lean against her and at times she would stop stitching and bend over to muss his hair. He might be discouraged at some way they had acted down below and she might know that without his saying anything because when she touched him, she would press him encouragingly and say "How's Rob? Bless your heart." He liked having his heart blessed.

The sewing machine was shoved back in a corner and looked sidetracked. He sat down on a couch and felt a breeze through the open window. Like a scent in the air, he thought of her as a mother.

But then he heard footsteps on the stair. Emily.

"Not at the church?" he asked.

"I didn't want to go. I'm not in it."

"Why not?"

"I had a fuss with Normie. I wanted to borrow her eye makeup but she wouldn't let me. I called her a bitch. Then she said I couldn't be in it. I said I didn't care."

She sat down on a stool.

"Aunt Alicia showed up, with Uncle Harry. They rented the big suite at the inn. They drove a Jaguar. It's long and shiny."

Rob said he imagined so. They sat silently. So much he could ask her . . . school . . . friends . . . parents . . . But she seemed content. A moth floated through the air and landed on the blind.

"I guess you've seen it," said Emily.

"Seen what?"

She got up, a slight girl, sturdy, getting grown-up looks. She moved to open a cupboard door, wanting him to look.

The dress, which was clothing a headless manikin, was white, ruffled and so sculpted to fit it appeared to have grown in place. Rob caught his breath at the sight, for it seemed all the weddings that had ever been were stated by it, and he felt Norma's presence glowing in its lines. He remembered his own modest wedding and his heart ached for all the hopes wrapped up in all weddings, everywhere in the world.

"Now she won't wear it," Emily said, and stood beside him. She stood on a level with him. On impulse from the dress, they turned and kissed.

The swirl of getting to the dinner at the club drew them in, like the suction pipe at the gin. Dressing, racing, driving, then on through the doors at the country club. A rush of voices.

"Why Rob Ellis, come all this way!" He was hustled up to Aunt Alicia and Uncle Harry, who exclaimed over his job in politics and wanted to know . . . to know . . . know . . . Drink in hand, he tried to answer, to keep a light tone, say something funny. The very look of them said Important People. Aunt Alicia was not so much plump as stout, not so much stout as filling space. Her satiny outfit was handsome. Uncle Harry, thin beside her, wore the look of doing everything right. They had favored everyone by coming.

Uncle Mack was pulling him aside. "Say, you know? When I finally got to Milton Ward he said that was all a mistake about Sandy. If he borrowed it at all, it's been paid back. Maybe it was somebody else."

"It could be."

"Stockton called for you from Memphis. Wanted to talk to you . . . had to, he said."

"Said what about?"

"A speech. One of the clubs in Memphis. Rotary, I think he said."

"I better call back. He just needs a start-up, then he's off full speed."

"Important job you've got, old boy." Odd to be called that.

Across the room, Norma in discreet silk, smiled and chatted to the right, her arm hooked in Sandy's, while he talked to the left. But where was her mother? *Muzzy*, he thought.

"Why, Rob," he heard at his shoulder, almost in his ear. "If it isn't Rob. Bless your heart." And so she remembered. Or did she just bless everybody's heart? He gave his hug and took his kiss and looked into her eyes. They were a pale gray, not melting brown or declaring blue. What filled them was love, the kind of love just previous to tears. He all but wept himself.

In a last meeting his wife Doris had stood before him and said "I love you and I don't really want to go." It was only that they bored each other. They never had much to say. Her family never liked him. Did they like anybody? And then the quarrels set in. And the flirting. And the lies. But she stood there saying she loved him and not going anywhere. Until she did. His heart was not so much broken. He did not know what that was. What afflicted his heart, like a virus maybe, was yearning. *Please*, he would whisper to no one sometimes when he was alone, not quite knowing what he meant. He thought it now, then he drank enough to forget it.

But where should he sleep? They forgot to tell him. Back at the house, he gravitated upstairs to the same old sewing room where he felt at home. He passed one of them below the stair and said, "Is this all right?" "Sure it is," was the answer. He climbed, laid down his small suitcase, and closed the door. He sat down and sighed. It had been a long day.

Minutes later, a tap at the door and he knew it wasn't over yet. He opened and found Norma standing there, holding a bottle and two glasses.

She sat down on the step, handed him a glass, and poured out whiskey.

"I was good at the dinner," she whispered. "I didn't have but one drink. I brought your old glass."

She had indeed. It was a heavy carved crystal glass, unlike any other, that Muzzy put aside for him long ago. Chocolate milk. Iced tea. Now whiskey.

"Won't they find us?"

"No. Everybody's too tired."

"So you conformed about likker," he teased her. "But not about the dress."

"The dress." She was suddenly quiet and serious.

"Nobody understands anything. How could I parade around in white? They all know I'm no shy little virgin. Except Muzzy. She never believes I do anything bad."

"She loves you. She made it for you."

"No she didn't. She had to get Miss Amy Johnson to do the

ruffles. Miss Amy is expert. Twice before I almost got married. But we never made it to a dress with Pete and Horace."

He did not inquire about Pete and Horace. She rushed on.

"You remember the time when we were growing up and you were here for the summer? We put you in that trolley we had strung up between two trees. Halfway down it fell. If you hadn't tucked up your legs, they would have broken, half in two."

"I'd be even shorter. A midget."

"I was thinking the other day . . ." Off on the past. The games—tennis, cards—the picnics, the swims, the quarrels. How happy they had been. Protected, playing, arguing, safe. They hadn't known how lucky they were. As she spoke of it, he thought so too. Else what had he come back to discover? Another tilt from the bottle . . . He interrupted. "This glass. It used to be mine."

"I know," she said. "I brought it for you. We kept it. But why couldn't we keep those happy days?"

"They still want you to be happy. Your father told me. He cried."

"Daddy cried? Feature that."

"I saw the dress," he said.

She started. "How?"

"Emily showed me."

"Oh Lord, Emily . . . I want to wear what I want! I want it to state something. I want to say I'm my own person. I'm going to be happy again with Sandy, even if he's not from around here. Everybody will see it. I want to be myself! I want to say who *I am*!!" But in her excitement what she said came out like *jam*.

"Strawberry jam?" Rob inquired. They both fell to laughing. They laughed until they cried, they couldn't stop laughing.

"Are youall still up?" A voice from below. And there in the shadows Aunt Molly appeared in her long pale housecoat, a faintly glowing outline, like a spirit.

Norma leaned toward him, not to hug as he thought, but to hide the bottle. She left it and the glasses with him and tee-tered off down the stair.

What a day! Rob's mind was fairly clear, and what pressed into it as Norma's tirade melted, was how Sandy had sought him out at the club, ambushed him in an alcove near the men's room. His face was strained with appeal, under the topping of thick blond hair, the eyes pleading.

"Do you know how much I thank you? This wouldn't have happened at all except for you. You saved me. I want you to know—"

"It's okay."

"No, you have to realize. And of course I'll pay back, every cent. Soon's I can."

"I know. It's okay."

"You know why they looked at that account? It was Jamie Hackett. That guy you met at the hotel. He wanted to borrow some money. He got the boss to check the account. They saw where it had gone. Maybe I could have straightened it out somehow. But if it hadn't been for you—"

"It's okay."

He slept, and suddenly it was morning. He remembered that he had to call Stockton, then go to the wedding.

On the way out he was waylaid by his cousin Marty. The old lady had the sleeve of her dress caught in her fine hair. He had to help untangle her, threads and hairs, one by one.

He went to the inn to call Stockton. The call was a long one. He barely made it to the church before Mendelssohn. And with the music there came Norma and Uncle Mack. She was wearing the white dress. Was it their laughter on the stair that had changed her? Or her mother's calling? Or her father's tears? Something had. Emily spread flowers in the aisle. She must have got the eye shadow. The little cousins who were bridesmaids looked solemn and exalted. Sandy, tame in his dark suit, discovered dignity.

Why had anyone worried?

The reception was held at the inn where once again Uncle Mack drew him aside.

"Rob, I think you must have helped that boy out."

He pretended puzzlement.

"I mean the one she just married. The Clemons boy at the bank gave me a clue."

Did nobody ever keep a promise not to tell? Rob wondered. They had all but pinned Al Clemons to the floor to swear him to silence.

"If you gave him anything, I want to pay you everything back. Every cent."

"Oh, no. Better talk to Sandy. He would know."

"I'm in the dark."

They were standing apart in an alcove room, meant for small dinners. Rob watched Uncle Mack as he stood reflecting over all he knew and what he didn't know. Uncle Mack liked control. Decision.

"Son," he said, "I know your father died not long ago and you got nobody left. But you got us. You got me for your father, and Molly for your mother, and Normie too and all the rest of us. But mainly me. I want you to call this home. It's a sacred word, son. It's yours."

So now at last, a father. The words struck through Rob's breast. Words from an honest man who meant what he said. There were none who ever doubted him, none he ever failed. *Did I come for this?*

Leaving time. He had promised Stockton he would drive back that very night. Storing his bag in the car, he checked to see if by any chance Remus was in the backseat.

He drove out in the late afternoon. He passed the orange-colored monsters of the road construction, towering over the old hills now crumbled, shaping into a highway that would sweep thoughtlessly past the little town of his youth.

He fell to wondering what he had come here and done. His bank account was considerably diminished. Had he secured the marriage of a possible alcoholic to a possible crook? But he remembered the scene beneath the pecan trees and refused a dark scenario. He held to the warmth of his uncle's words. They grew like a firm standing place beneath his feet.

At the reception, Emily had crept closer. She had squeezed his hand. He felt he could come back to her. But courting cousins wouldn't work.

The miles fled beneath him. "You're going with me to Washington, son," Stockton had said. "It will be a whole new world."

CHRONOLOGY

NOTE ON THE TEXTS

NOTES

Chronology

Catherine Elizabeth Spencer born July 19, 1921, in Carrollton, Mississippi, the seat of Carroll County, an agricultural
community of five hundred people in the range of hills that
rises to the east of the Mississippi Delta; the nearest town
of consequence is Greenwood, seventeen miles to the
west. She is the second child and only daughter of James
Luther, a shopkeeper, and Mary James McCain Spencer, a
former music teacher; her older brother, James (b. 1914),
will eventually become a physician but plays little role in
her life. Known as Luther, Spencer's father, the son of a
Confederate veteran, is originally from the nearby settlement of McCarley, where his family has a farm and runs a
store. Her mother grew up on the two thousand-acre Teoc
plantation to the north of town, the daughter of John and
Elizabeth McCain; the plantation's name comes from a
Choctaw word meaning "Tall Pines."

1922–33 Brought up in a strict Presbyterian household, Spencer herself will remain a churchgoer throughout her life, though
becoming an Episcopalian as an adult. Observes as a child
that though there are some black Episcopalians in Car-
rolton, sitting on benches at the rear of the church, there
are no black Presbyterians; and is told to hush when she
asks why. Attends Carrollton's local schools, and passes her
childhood between the town and Teoc, acutely aware of
the differences between the two sides of her family. Father
is competitive and quarrelsome, known as a "go-getter,"
and recognizes no one's authority but his own and God's;
he believes that the arts are both foolish and womanish
if not actively sinful. The better-educated McCains, in
contrast, value books and storytelling and the pleasures of
conversation. Often sick and kept in bed as a child, Spencer
learns to read early and finds a resource in exploring the
McCains' library of classic novels, Scott and Dickens, Austen and Hawthorne.

1933–37 At twelve begins to ride the thirteen miles between Carrollton and Teoc alone, traveling cross-country on horse-
back. Reads Victor Hugo's *Les Misérables*, at the insistence

of her mother's youngest brother, Joe, and discusses it and other novels with him at length. At school realizes how sheltered she has been, and finds that the reading her mother has encouraged makes her unpopular; will later describe herself as having been a skinny child with grown-up manners and no hope at all of fitting in. Largely accepts the social and racial hierarchy of Mississippi's Jim Crow world. But is shocked by the condition of the house in which her parents expect the family's African American servants to live, and retains an indelible memory of her parents' cook, Laura Henley, appearing at their back door one night, in fear for her life, badly beaten and bloodied for having allegedly "sassed" a white woman; Spencer's father helps Henley leave town. Luther Spencer's business interests and prosperity grow, eventually including a cattle ranch in the Delta, a hunting lodge, a cotton gin, cropland and other real estate, a Chevrolet dealership as well as the local Standard Oil Franchise, and many other ventures besides.

1938   Graduates in spring as valedictorian of Carrollton's local J.Z. George High School. Although her own preference is to attend the University of Mississippi in the fall, Spencer's parents enroll her at Belhaven College in the state capital of Jackson, a Presbyterian women's college with some three hundred students.

1939–42   At Belhaven majors in English and studies Latin as well, while beginning to write fiction; as a sophomore, receives second prize for one of her stories at the Southern Literary Festival, a regional conference for undergraduates. Possesses a growing awareness of William Faulkner, whose work is shunned in her parents' milieu but praised by others, though she will not seriously engage with his writing until graduate school or later. As a junior reads T. S. Eliot's *The Waste Land* and feels she has stepped into the modern world. During her senior year she telephones local writer Eudora Welty, who lives across the street from Belhaven, and asks her to come speak to the college's literary society. Welty accepts the invitation; this encounter marks the beginning of a lifelong friendship. Spencer graduates from Belhaven in spring 1942. In the fall enters the masters's program in English at Vanderbilt University in Nashville. Her department is the founding home of both the New Criticism, which sees literature as a privileged realm of ideal forms, and the Nashville Agrarians, who looks to an imagined agricultural past as an alternative to modern capitalist society. Names associated with both movements include the poets Robert Penn Warren and Allen Tate; each has moved elsewhere by the time Spencer arrives, but Warren in particular will support and encourage her early work. Studies with the charismatic yet intimidating Donald Davidson, the most conservative of Vanderbilt's remaining Agrarians, reading Faulkner and Henry James, and writing a thesis on "Irish Mythology in the Early Poetry of William Butler Yeats." World War II has made the future seem on hold, but after Belhaven nevertheless enjoys the social opportunities of Nashville: men in uniform, dances, learning to smoke cigarettes and drink beer. Spends one wartime summer taking care of her young cousin and future U.S. senator, John McCain, each of them on an extended visit to Teoc.

1943 After completing requirements for the MA in English at Vanderbilt, takes a job as an instructor in English at Northwest Junior College in Senatobia, Mississippi, the first of three jobs in three successive years.

1944 Takes a position as a teacher at Ward-Belmont, a private school for girls in Nashville.

1945 Works as a reporter on the city desk of the *Tennessean*, Nashville's leading newspaper, where she is assigned minor stories, obituaries, and rewrites. While living in Nashville, enrolls in a creative writing class taught by mystery writer Raymond Goldman at the Watkins Institute, a night school. Submits a story, "The Little Brown Girl," to *The New Yorker*, which is rejected; the same story, unrevised, will be accepted and published by the magazine in 1957.

1946–47 Resigns from the *Tennessean* in summer 1946 to work full-time on her first novel. Her father vehemently objects, believing she has destroyed her chances for future employment. Later that summer Donald Davidson introduces her to David Clay, an editor at Dodd, Mead, who accepts the book, offering a $500 advance and inviting her to New York to discuss its completion. (Clay will become an important figure in her publishing career and a close friend until they have a falling-out after she leaves his failing literary agency.) On that first trip north Spencer realizes that her accent is so thick that she has trouble making people understand her. Returns to Nashville from New York to finish manuscript. Takes a brief substitute teaching job in winter 1946–47 at Belhaven. While waiting for her novel to appear, renews her friendship with Eudora Welty.

1948   Takes a position as an instructor in the English Department at the University of Mississippi in Oxford. *Fire in the Morning*, a story of enduring small-town feuds and rivalries, published by Dodd, Mead in October. Reviews are positive, but the book shocks Spencer's parents with its occasional profanity and awareness of sex. Spencer takes a position as an instructor in the English Department at the University of Mississippi in Oxford.

1949   In April, at an Ole Miss cocktail party in honor of writer Stark Young, sees but does not speak to Faulkner, who stands silently in the corner, an untouched glass in his hand. Still feels at home in Mississippi but is increasingly drawn to the world outside, and in June 1949 takes a freighter from New Orleans for her first trip abroad. In Paris meets Saul Bellow, then moves on to stay with a friend from home in Germany, and afterward travels down to Italy: a determinative visit, where she goes from Milan to Rome, with many stops in between, losing herself in art and opera, romance, and the life of the streets. Returns to Oxford that fall, where she will teach for the next two years.

1950   In summer attends the Bread Loaf Writers' Conference in Vermont.

1951   Takes a leave from the university during the academic year to work on her second novel, living briefly in Pass Christian, Mississippi, on the Gulf Coast. Eudora Welty visits twice during Spencer's time on the Gulf; on the first visit she brings Katherine Anne Porter with her, on the second Elizabeth Bowen. This remains a mysterious period in Spencer's life, marked by the end of a long affair with an unnamed man that dates back to her postwar years in Nashville, when after military service he entered the PhD program in Vanderbilt's English Department. Spencer writes that their relationship represented a desired continuance of the southern life she had always known, but that over time it became increasingly frayed, marked by his mood swings and drinking. Repeatedly tries to break things off but remains drawn by his wit and intelligence, and the relationship starts up again, briefly, destructively, during her time on the Gulf, where he teaches at a nearby college. Later recognizes that he has suffered for years from schizophrenia, a condition that neither of them understood or was even aware of.

1952   *This Crooked Way*, a tale of religious obsession, published by Dodd, Mead in March. Spencer receives an award of $1,000 from the National Institute of Arts and Letters and uses it to spend the summer in New York City. Returns to teach at the University of Mississippi in fall, this time renting a room in the house of Maud Falkner, the famous novelist's mother.

1953–55   In spring 1953 mother's brother Joe dies from a self-inflicted gunshot—whether suicide or accident is never determined. Spencer suffers a debilitating nervous collapse, losing weight and energy, and spends several months in hospital. Learns that she has been awarded a Guggenheim Fellowship. In October 1953, against her parents' wishes, travels to New York, where she boards an Italian liner for Italy and settles in Rome, living in a *pensione* near the via Vittorio Veneto. Spencer will spend the next two years in Italy. Rome is full of American expatriates and visitors, and she enjoys an active social life, seeing, among others, the Agrarian poet Allen Tate and his wife, the fiction writer Caroline Gordon, the Renaissance historian Garrett Mattingly, and the Italian novelist Alberto Moravia. Meets Faulkner, then traveling for the State Department, at a series of receptions. Works on her third novel, *The Voice at the Back Door*, its title growing from her childhood memory of Laura Henley. Spends part of summer 1954 in Florence, with a side trip to London to meet Victor Gollancz, her English publisher. After dating what she describes as "enough men of different nationalities to form a sizable committee for the United Nations," in Rome meets an Englishman, John Rusher (b. 1920), a former teacher at Berlitz now working with private pupils, who hails from a family of Cornish gentry. But cannot yet decide to marry and accept the uncertainties of life abroad, and in September 1955 returns instead to Mississippi. Back in Carrollton, Spencer's parents show no interest in her work or experiences abroad, and they fall immediately into a political argument. Her attitudes toward race have changed during her time in Europe. Things she had accepted all her life now seem "outrageous," and argues with her father about the lynching of Emmett Till, the Chicago fourteen-year-old who, while visiting Mississippi relatives, had recently been murdered in a nearby town, for allegedly whistling at a white woman. She had always seen Luther Spencer as "fair-thinking" though rigid, but now recognizes him as a reactionary and within two days leaves home for Oxford. Her former colleagues at the university are ready to renew her teaching position but decides instead to move to New York. Luther Spencer offers her $2,000 to go away, and signals that she can expect no more money from him. (After her parents' death Spencer will, however, receive a small continuing income from family land.) But it takes her some time to accept, as she later writes, that she no longer belongs in the South. In fall 1955 travels by train north to New York, where she rents an apartment on East 22nd Street. Revises *The Voice at the Back Door*. Enjoys growing friendship with Robert Penn Warren and his wife Eleanor Clark, and with John and Mary Cheever, to whose daughter Susan she becomes godmother; but remains lonely.

1956–57   Learning of Rusher's matching loneliness in Europe, decides to visit him in England in summer. After she meets his family in Cornwall, they marry in the village of St. Columb Minor on September 29, and then return to Rome. *The Voice at the Back Door* published by McGraw-Hill in October. The novel is quickly a commercial success, with three printings by end of year. Reviews are uniformly strong, though Spencer will later note that during her "absence from the state a precipitate moment had come and gone": The novel describes a world that had already vanished at time of publication, the ever violent but still apparently stable Mississippi of the time before Emmett Till's murder. Nevertheless, the novel causes great consternation in her home state, with some white readers branding her a traitor. In 1957 the judges for the Pulitzer Prize recommend it for the award in fiction, while noting that they consider the year as a whole undistinguished (other novels published in 1956 include James Baldwin's *Giovanni's Room* and Saul Bellow's *Seize the Day*). But the Pulitzer board decides to make no award, a decision that has never been adequately explained.

1958–59   With money running low and few economic prospects for a life abroad, Spencer and Rusher return to the Americas in 1958, settling in Montreal where he has relatives.

On their first visit back to Mississippi Spencer's father asks Rusher to make her stop writing. He refuses. Spencer and Rusher settle in the Montreal suburb of Lachine; he takes a job in business but soon uses an inheritance to establish a language school, the Cambridge Language Centre, teaching English and French to the city's growing immigrant population.

1960   *The Light in the Piazza* published in *The New Yorker* in June, and in book form by McGraw-Hill in the fall. A short, quickly written, and deceptively idyllic novel about an Italian-American courtship, it hits the *New York Times* best seller list and will remain Spencer's most popular book, selling more than a million copies over the years. Nevertheless, she comes to see it as an "albatross" that occludes an awareness of her other work. It is a finalist for the National Book Award. Film rights are sold to MGM. "First Dark" (1959) chosen for the annual O. Henry Prize volume. Spencer receives the McGraw-Hill Fiction Award.

1962   Spends 1962–63 as Donnelly Fellow at Bryn Mawr College, the first of many visiting positions at colleges and universities. Directed by Guy Green, shot largely on location in Florence and Rome, and starring Olivia de Havilland, Rossano Brazzi, and Yvette Mimieux, the film adaptation of *The Light in the Piazza* opens to mixed reviews and a disappointing box office.

1964   Makes the first of several donations of her manuscripts, letters, and other materials to the rare books library at the University of Kentucky, using their valuation of the material as a tax deduction.

1965   Written during a period of prolonged depression, *Knights and Dragons* published by *Rebook* (July) in an abridged form. About the same time, McGraw-Hill publishes it in book form. Set in Rome, it is a "dark companion" piece to *The Light in the Piazza*. Reviews are mostly negative. Spencer expresses regret at having published it as a stand-alone book.

1966   "Ship Island" appears in the annual O. Henry Prize volume.

1967   *No Place for an Angel* published by McGraw-Hill in fall; a novel about art, power, and money in the age of America's Cold War might, it is set in Italy, New York, and Texas.

1968   Spencer first story collection, *Ship Island and Other Stories*, published by McGraw-Hill in August. Later tells an interviewer that in its brevity the short story suited the increasingly fragmented nature of her experience after leaving the South. It is the form for which she will become best known.

1969   Is a creative writing fellow at the University of North Carolina, Chapel Hill.

1970   Spencer and Rusher move into an apartment in Westmount, an affluent Anglophone enclave within Montreal proper, and she takes a studio in which to work near McGill University. Begins friendships with Canadian writers, including Alice Munro and especially Mavis Gallant. In March teaches as a visiting writer at Gulf Park College for Women in Mississippi.

1972   *The Snare* published by McGraw-Hill in November 1972. Spencer comes to feel her longest novel, a dark psychological thriller set in New Orleans, is underappreciated.

1973   Is a writer-in-residence at Hollins College, Virginia.

1974   Mother dies at eighty-five on May 20.

1976   Father dies at eighty-eight on August 20. Spencer begins teaching in a continuing position at Concordia University in Montreal.

1981   *The Stories of Elizabeth Spencer* published by Doubleday in February, with a preface by Eudora Welty; the volume comprises all the author's short fiction and *Knights and Dragons*. *Marilee*, a limited edition bringing together three stories narrated by the endearing Marilee Summerall, published by University of Mississippi Press in summer. In August Spencer lectures at the annual Faulkner and Yoknapatawpha Conference at the University of Mississippi.

1982   In spring is a resident at Yaddo in Saratoga Springs, New York, where she works on a new novel.

1983   Receives the Award of Merit Medal for the Short Story from the American Academy and Institute of Arts and Letters, the first of many such recognitions of her career.

1984   Set on the Gulf Coast in the aftermath of 1969's destructive Hurricane Camille, *The Salt Line* published by Doubleday in February. It is her first novel in more than ten years. In

April Spencer reads at a celebration of her friend Eudora Welty's seventy-fifth birthday. In May, during a residency at the Rockefeller Foundation Center at Bellagio, on Lake Como, writes "The Cousins," the last of her Italian stories. "By accident" learns of the death of her former editor, agent, and friend David Clay. Makes a donation of manuscripts and other literary materials to the National Library of Canada in exchange for a tax deduction.

1985   Elected to the American Academy and Institute of Arts and Letters.

1986   "The Cousins" published in annual O. Henry Prize volume. Suffering from chronic bronchitis, Spencer has begun to feel the effects of Montreal's long winters, and she and Rusher are both troubled as well by the bitterness of Quebec's linguistic politics. The southern literary historian Louis D. Rubin persuades her to accept a five-year appointment as a visiting professor of creative writing at the University of North Carolina, and the couple leave Montreal in June 1986 for Chapel Hill, settling at 402 Longleaf Drive, a few miles from the city center, where they will live for the rest of their lives. The university's library will become the final repository of her papers. Spencer later says that though she was happy in Canada it took her away from the material she knew best, and that they had remained a decade too long. Continues to travel, with repeated visits to France and Italy as well as throughout the American South in the next dozen years.

1987   Travels to Russia with the Mississippi novelist Ellen Douglass and other friends. Helps found the Fellowship of Southern Writers, a self-selecting literary society for the promotion of the literatures of the American South.

1988   Awarded an honorary doctorate by Concordia University. "The Business Venture" published in annual O. Henry Prize volume. *Jack of Diamonds and Other Stories* published by Doubleday in August.

1989   *For Lease or Sale*, Spencer's only play, in which she introduces the character of Edward Glenn, opens at Playmakers Repertory in Chapel Hill on January 28 and runs through February 12.

1991   *The Night Travellers*, Spencer's final novel, published by Doubleday in August to strong reviews; it examines the life of Americans living underground in Canada during the Vietnam era. *On the Gulf*, an illustrated edition of previously published stories, and *Conversations with Elizabeth Spencer*, a book of interviews, published by University Press of Mississippi. Spencer receives the John Dos Passos Prize for Literature, a career award given to a currently underrecognized American writer.

1995   Brother, James, dies on October 8.

1996   Serves as a judge for the National Book Award in Fiction, with the prize going to Andrea Barrett's *Ship Fever and Other Stories*. *The Light in the Piazza and Other Italian Tales* published by University Press of Mississippi, helping to introduce her work to a new generation of readers.

1998   *Landscapes of the Heart*, a memoir concentrating on her early life, published by Random House in January. On December 17 John Rusher suffers a fatal heart attack, just managing to pull his car off the road while driving to a doctor's appointment. After Rusher's death, Spencer maintains a steady correspondence with her English in-laws—cousins, nieces, nephews. But it is years before she feels the strength she needs to write again, and tells friends that she still hears her husband coming through the door and putting his keys down—an explanation she offers whenever asked why she continues to live in a large house alone.

1999   Receives honorary doctorate from what is now Belhaven University. As early as 1995 the composer Adam Guettel had suggested writing a musical based on *The Light in the Piazza*, and Spencer now options the work to him, with the book to be written by playwright Alfred Uhry.

2000   Speaks in October at a centenary celebration of Thomas Wolfe in the novelist's hometown of Asheville, North Carolina.

2001   *The Southern Woman: New and Selected Fiction* published by The Modern Library in August. Comprising a selection from earlier collections along with *The Light in the Piazza* and six new stories from the 1990s, it earns some of the best reviews of her career.

2002–19 Playwright Craig Lucas replaces Alfred Uhry in 2002 as writer for *The Light in the Piazza*, which goes into development at the Intiman Playhouse in Seattle in 2003 and the Goodman Theatre in Chicago in 2004. The musical opens on Broadway on April 18, 2005; the initial cast includes Victoria Clark as Margaret Johnson and Kelli O'Hara as her daughter Clara. *The Light in the Piazza* runs for 504 performances at Lincoln Center's Vivian Beaumont Theater. Nominated for eleven Tony Awards, it wins six, including Guettel's score and Clark for Best Actress in a Musical. A national tour runs for a year, with subsequent productions throughout the United States and Canada, as well as in Japan and the United Kingdom. In 2019 an opera house version opens in London with Renee Fleming as Margaret Johnson, and then moves to Los Angeles and Chicago. Spencer's share of the royalties allows her to afford the round-the-clock medical care she needs to remain in her house during her final years. Spencer has always voted Democratic but during the 2008 presidential campaign cannot bring herself to vote against her cousin John McCain, and does not cast a ballot for president. Votes for Barack Obama in 2012. Among the honors with which her career is recognized in her last years are the PEN/Malamud Award for the Short Story in 2007 and the Rea Award for the Short Story in 2013. *Starting Over*, a collection of nine recent stories, published by W. W. Norton in January 2014. Spencer is increasingly frail, and by 2015 has stopped writing, while telling a friend that "I miss it, like the death of a person that you know." Early in 2016 falls and breaks her hip; moves to a downstairs room and will thereafter remain housebound, though alert and talkative.

2019   Elizabeth Spencer dies at her home in Chapel Hill on December 22, at ninety-eight.

Note on the Texts

This volume contains three novels by Elizabeth Spencer—*The Voice at the Back Door* (1956), *The Light in the Piazza* (1961), and *Knights and Dragons* (1965)—as well as a selection of nineteen stories published from 1959 to 2013.

In 1953 Spencer traveled to Rome on a Guggenheim Fellowship and lived in Italy for the next two years. It was during this time abroad that she completed a draft of *The Voice at the Back Door*, her candid novel about race relations in Mississippi during the Jim Crow era. Spencer returned briefly in September 1955 to her parents' home in Carrollton, Mississippi, where she quarreled with her father about the recent lynching of Emmett Till. That disagreement precipitated a move to New York City. In an apartment on East 22nd Street, Spencer worked strenuously to revise her novel. *Fire in the Morning* (1948) and *This Crooked Way* (1952) had been published by Dodd, Mead, but Spencer found a new publisher for her third novel. Published in October 1956 by McGraw-Hill, *The Voice at the Back Door* quickly became a commercial success, with three printings before the end of the year, and it was reviewed widely and favorably by critics. Despite or perhaps because of its success, the novel caused outrage back home in Mississippi, with some white readers branding Spencer a traitor and threatening retribution should she ever return to the state. Spencer's former Vanderbilt teacher Donald Davidson, a fierce segregationist, never spoke to her again after the novel's publication. In 1957 the Pulitzer jurors recommended it for the fiction prize, but the governing board elected to make no award that year. That decision has caused much speculation about the board's motives. (See also the Chronology in this volume, page 838.) In 1957 Victor Gollancz published *The Voice at the Back Door* in England, using the McGraw-Hill settings. *The Voice at the Back Door* was reissued in Spencer's lifetime by several American publishers, including Louisiana State University Press in 1994 as a part of its Voices of the South series. Spencer did not revise the novel after its initial publication. The text presented here is that of the 1956 McGraw-Hill edition.

Reflecting later in life on *The Light in the Piazza*, Spencer said in her memoir (*Landscapes of the Heart*, 1998) that it "came close to writing itself." The typescript was completed quickly, in three or four weeks in 1959, while Spencer and her husband were living in the Montreal suburb of Lachine: "I would write through some hours at the library, then come back to the apartment and type up the day's scribblings." Submitted to *The New Yorker* by her agent and former editor at Dodd, Mead, David Clay, it was first rejected and then accepted after Spencer completed a small number of revisions urged by Clay. *The Light in the Piazza* appeared in *The New Yorker* on June 18, 1960. Spencer revised the novel for the book version, published in November 1960 by McGraw-Hill. Heinemann published an English edition of the novel in London in 1961, apparently without the author's involvement. *The Light in the Piazza* was a critical and commercial success, climbing onto *The New York Times* best seller list and getting recognition from the National Book Committee in 1961 as a finalist for the fiction award. An MGM adaptation directed by Guy Green and starring Olivia de Havilland, Rossano Brazzi, and Yvette Mimieux was released in theaters on February 7, 1962. Four decades later, *The Light in the Piazza* was developed as a musical by the Intiman Playhouse in Seattle in 2003 and the Goodman Theatre in Chicago in 2004. It opened on Broadway on April 18, 2005, and ran for 504 performances, winning six Tony Awards and five Drama Desk Awards. Spencer came to have mixed feelings about the "slight" novel that seemed to define her career, complaining in interviews that it had eclipsed other, more significant work. *The Light in the Piazza* was reprinted numerous times in her lifetime and appeared in two retrospective anthologies of her work: *The Southern Woman: New and Selected Fiction* (Modern Library, 2001) and *The Light in the Piazza and Other Italian Tales* (University Press of Mississippi, 1996). The 1960 McGraw-Hill edition of *The Light in the Piazza* provides the text printed here.

Knights and Dragons, Spencer's "other" Italian novel, gave its author trouble from the start. Composed during the mid-1960s during a period of prolonged depression, it was difficult to write, she later recalled, "because I got involved with something in my own psyche in maybe an unpleasant way. . . . I had to back up and rewrite over and over and over." *Knights and Dragons* was published in *Redbook* (July 1965) in an abridged form its author found "hardly recognizable." Book publication by McGraw-Hill followed soon after in summer 1965. Heinemann published *Knights and Dragons* in England in 1966, using the McGraw-Hill settings. Reviews were mostly negative and Spencer came to feel her "dark companion" to *The Light in the Piazza* should not have been published as an independent book. When *The Stories of Elizabeth Spencer* was published (Doubleday, 1981), Spencer included it among the thirty-three stories selected for that volume; she also later included it in *The Light in the Piazza and Other Italian Tales*. The text presented here is that of the 1965 McGraw-Hill edition.

Although Spencer thought of herself primarily as a novelist, the short story was the form for which she was best known in the latter half of her career. Her first collection of stories, *Ship Island and Other Stories* (1968), appeared two decades after the publication of *Fire in the Morning*. Many of the early short stories first appeared in *The New Yorker*, but by the mid-1970s the primary venue for the first publication of her short fiction was literary journals. She gathered her stories into eight collections published during her lifetime, including *The Stories of Elizabeth Spencer* and *The Southern Woman: New and Selected Fiction*.

The stories selected for this volume are arranged chronologically by date of their first publication with these two exceptions: the stories featuring Marilee Summerall are grouped together, as are those about Edward Glenn. These groupings are suggested by Spencer's decision to publish *Marilee* (University Press of Mississippi, 1981), a limited edition bringing together the author's stories about her protagonist of the same name. Spencer sometimes revised her stories for their first book publication, but she is not known to have subsequently revisited them. The texts of the stories printed here are taken from their first American book publications. In the list that follows, the story's first magazine or chapbook publication is given.

From *Ship Island and Other Stories* (New York: McGraw Hill, 1968): "First Dark," *The New Yorker*, June 20, 1959; "A Southern Landscape," *The New Yorker*, March 26, 1960; "The White Azalea," *Texas Quarterly*, 4 (Winter 1961); "Ship Island," *The New Yorker*, September 12, 1964.

From *The Stories of Elizabeth Spencer* (New York: Doubleday, 1981): "The Bufords," first published as "Those Bufords," *McCall's*, January 1967; "Sharon," *The New Yorker*, May 9, 1970; "A Christian Education," *The Atlantic Monthly*, March 1974; "The Girl Who Loved Horses," *Ontario Review*, 10 (Spring–Summer 1979).

From *Jack of Diamonds and Other Stories* (New York: Viking, 1988): "The Cousins," *The Southern Review*, 21 (Spring 1985); "Jack of Diamonds," *The Kenyon Review*, n.s. 8 (Summer 1986); "The Business Venture," *The Southern Review*, 23 (Spring 1987).

From *On the Gulf* (Jackson: University Press of Mississippi, 1991): "The Legacy," first published as a chapbook (Chapel Hill, NC: The Mud Puppy Press, 1988).

From *The Southern Woman: New and Selected Fiction* (New York: Modern Library, 2001): "The Runaways," *Antaeus*, 73/74 (Spring 1994); "The Master of Shongalo," *The Southern Review*, 31 (Winter 1995); "First Child," *The Southern Review*, 36 (Spring 2000).

From *Starting Over: Stories* (New York: Liveright, 2014): "Return Trip," *Five Points*, 13 (Spring 2009); "On the Hill," *Five Points*, 15 (Spring 2013); "The Wedding Visitor," *ZYZZYVA*, 98 (July 2013).

This volume presents the texts of the original printings chosen for inclusion here, but it does not attempt to reproduce nontextual features of their typographic design. The texts are presented without change, except for the correction of typographical errors. Spelling, punctuation, and capitalization are often expressive features and are not altered, even when inconsistent or irregular. The following is a list of typographical errors corrected, cited by page and line number: 24.24, fifthy,; 83.28 and .30, Philip; 84.3 (and *passim*), Clark; 109.22, threshhold; 135.18, Jimmy,; 137.27, white, without; 158.24, touch it,"; 182.7, I'll; 198.38, daguerrotype; 199.2, daguerrotype; 242.22, that; 258.36, steps."; 286.5, that; 314.40, manuevering; 340.7, Squardo; 349.38, Guiseppe's; 381.23, langourously,; 383.23, musicans,; 465.18, in a; 541.9, than; 543.34, alone.; 626.16–17, beneth; 690.5, She'd; 780.13, half-joking; 781.4, perfunctory; 783.7, of room,; 783.33, cassarole,; 802.16, tailes.; 802.19, of men; 813.31, forever; 819.15, waging,; 824.8, me?'; 829.6, know—.

Notes

In the notes below, the reference numbers denote page and line of this volume (the line count includes headings). Biblical quotations are keyed to the King James Version. Quotations from Shakespeare are keyed to *The Riverside Shakespeare*, ed. G. Blakemore Evans (Boston: Houghton Mifflin, 1974). For further biographical background than is provided in the Chronology, see Elizabeth Spencer, *Landscapes of the Heart: A Memoir* (New York: Random House, 1998) and Peggy Whitman Prenshaw, *Elizabeth Spencer* (Boston: Twayne Publishers, 1985).

THE VOICE AT THE BACK DOOR

2.1 *To David and Justine Clay*] Spencer's literary agent and former editor, David Clay, and his wife, Justine Clay; friends of Spencer.

5.25 feist] A type of small, scrappy mixed-breed hunting dog popular in the American South; largely descended from English terriers and known for their fearlessness.

6.4 tie plant] Factory or mill manufacturing railroad ties: rough-cut pieces of wood, laid perpendicular to the steel tracks that rest upon them; often made of pine and smeared with creosote as a preservative.

8.8 Beat Two] For much of the twentieth century Mississippi counties were divided into five districts, with an elected supervisor as the administrator of each district or "beat." Supervisors were responsible for maintaining roads and bridges, and for allocating the tax monies meant for that purpose. This decentralized and often corrupt system was reformed in the 1980s, but some counties have voted to preserve it.

10.23 the university] The University of Mississippi at Oxford, the seat of Lafayette County, in the state's north.

11.10 Camp Shelby] Army National Guard and Reserves training site in the De Soto National Forest in southern Mississippi.

11.24 OCS] Officer Candidate School.

24.7 *illegal whisky.*"] A movement of Protestant ministers and temperance organizations such as the Anti-Saloon League and the Woman's Christian Temperance Union (WCTU) led to Mississippi's passage of a law prohibiting the sale of alcohol in 1907; in 1918 the state became the first to ratify the Eighteenth Amendment to the Constitution, which prohibited that sale nationwide. In 1933 the Twenty-first Amendment ended Prohibition nationally, but

Mississippi kept its state ban in force until 1966. New legislation then allowed each county to establish its own ordinances; some chose to continue that ban. In practice the state was both legally dry and everywhere wet, with bootlegged liquor or locally distilled moonshine available in virtually every town.

24.28–29   Stromberg-Carlsons] Founded in 1894, Stromberg-Carlson at first manufactured telephones and then moved into other forms of consumer electronics; here, a large wood-encased radio.

29.39   Dixiecrat movement] A breakaway faction of the Democratic Party: fiercely segregationist southern politicians who bolted over President Harry Truman's 1948 integration of the armed forces. Known formally as the States' Rights Democratic Party, it fielded a presidential candidate in the 1948 election; South Carolina governor Strom Thurmond won four states, Mississippi included.

33.29   Rabbit Foot Minstrels] A white-owned touring company of African American musicians and variety performers, who played throughout the Deep South until 1959, often setting up a tent for one-night stands in small towns. Singers such as Ma Rainey and Bessie Smith spent part of their early careers with the troupe.

49.18   the Delta."] A fertile wedge-shaped floodplain formed by the meeting of the Mississippi and Yazoo Rivers at the town of Vicksburg, Mississippi, and stretching two hundred miles north to the Tennessee border; bounded on the east by the range of low hills in which Spencer's hometown of Carrollton sits. In the years after the Civil War and for much of the twentieth century its large landholdings were usually worked by sharecroppers. The Delta cotton fields generated much of the state's white-owned wealth, and for white Mississippians the term was shorthand for both prosperity and an open-handed hospitality. For black Mississippians, the vast majority of the Delta's population, the term connoted grinding poverty and unending labor; but it was also the home of the blues.

58.38   twelve niggers . . . courthouse upstairs.] This incident is based on the Carroll County Courthouse Massacre of 1886, in Spencer's hometown of Carrollton. A minor and quickly resolved dispute between Robert Moore, a white man, and Ed and Charley Brown, two brothers of mixed African American and Native American heritage, led to the involvement of a second white man, James Liddell. A month later the Browns and Liddell exchanged gunfire, and the brothers then tried to prosecute him for attempted murder. On the day of the trial a group of between fifty and one hundred armed white men stormed the courthouse and opened fire. Over twenty people (the exact figure has never been determined), all of them black, were either killed immediately or later died from their wounds. Some victims tried to escape by jumping from second-floor windows but were shot as they hit the ground. No one was ever prosecuted, and the bullet holes remained visible in the courthouse walls until the 1990s. In the minds of the county's white citizens the massacre stood as a buried memory, one discussed only in the most veiled and elliptical of terms. Spencer herself writes of it in her 1998 memoir, *Landscapes of the Heart*, as "the crime, the old crime, the one nobody ever talked about . . . overheard, half-heard, not clearly understood" and one that continued to haunt her for decades after this novel was published.

62.31   buzz-bomb] V-1 Rocket, an early missile used by Germany for attacks on Great Britain in 1944–45; so called because of the sound it made in flying.

67.13   FHA] Federal Housing Administration; houses built in accordance with its safety regulations and standards.

67.15–16   "Gone-with-the-Wind" lamp] Hurricane lamps characterized by a globelike shape and hand-painted floral decorations; popularized and renamed after their use in *Gone with the Wind*, the 1939 film adapted from Margaret Mitchell's 1936 novel.

70.14   Epworth League?] Founded in 1889, a national association of young Methodists, a forerunner of modern church youth groups.

86.17   *True Detective.*] Pulp magazine concentrating on true crime stories, many of them involving sex crimes; it popularized the genre and at its peak in the 1930s and '40s the magazine sold over two million copies a month. Typical cover stories bore titles like "The Nylon Strangler" or "Cathy's Blackjack Killer."

101.30–31   twelve Negroes . . . cold blood."] See note 58.38.

134.7   Palm Beach suit] Palm Beach cloth was a blend of cotton and mohair, a lightweight fabric suitable for hot weather. First introduced in 1911, it was especially popular in the 1930s and was often though not always white or cream-colored.

135.3   Tippah County] Rural and hilly county, on Mississippi's northern border, with its seat in the town of Ripley. One of the few actual places in the state that Spencer mentions, in contrast to the imaginary Winfield County and Lacey of the novel's setting.

152.1   Tarawa] Tarawa Atoll, in the Gilbert Islands in the Central Pacific. The site of a major World War II battle, November 20–23, 1943.

153.1   LCI] Landing Craft Infantry, used in amphibious military operations such as Tarawa.

189.14   the Delta,'] See note 49.18.

200.17   *Shiloh*] The battle of Shiloh, a Civil War battle that took place on April 6–7, 1862, near Pittsburg, Tennessee, resulting in a Union victory. The United States forces were led by Ulysses S. Grant; the Confederates by Albert Sidney Johnston, who was fatally wounded at Shiloh. The battle led to the federal seizure of the important rail junction at Corinth, Mississippi; more importantly, the combined Union and Confederate casualities were nearly twenty-four thousand men killed, wounded, or missing provided the first demonstration of how long, bitter, and bloody the war would become.

205.39 Vardaman] James K. Vardaman (1861–1930), a Democrat, served in the Mississippi house of representatives, 1890–96; as governor, 1904–8; and the U.S. Senate, 1913–19, where he warned that the conscription of African Americans during World War I would threaten white supremacy. His ascendancy marked a shift in political power away from the state's old planter aristocracy, with yeoman farmers and poorer whites taking their place.

213.12–13 have you churched] Disciplined, cleansed. Here used colloquially, the term derives from the ritual blessing with which women were once welcomed back into church after recovering from childbirth.

214.26–30 "Shall we gather . . . the river . . ."] Popular Baptist hymn, based on Revelation 22:1–2. Words and music written in 1864 by the Brooklyn minister Robert Lowry (1826–1899).

255.13–14 red tie . . . Bilbo.] Theodore G. Bilbo (1877–1947), a Mississippi Democrat and white supremacist successor to James K. Vardaman, who twice served as governor of Mississippi, 1916–20, 1928–32; and later was elected a U.S. senator, 1935–1947. He and his supporters were often accused of being "rednecks," an accusation they embraced by wearing red neckties in response.

266.20–21 "Let Me Call You Sweetheart,"] 1910 popular song, music by Leo Friedman, lyrics by Beth Slater Whitson. It featured in the 1940 movie *Waterloo Bridge*; the most noted of its many recorded versions include those by Bing Crosby in both 1934 and 1944, and by Patti Page in 1958. It was an almost inescapable standard of the novel's period, heard at dances, proms, campus homecoming festivities, and beauty pageants.

274.3–5 "The *Tribune*! . . . the *Commercial*] The Memphis *Daily Tribune* was published from 1866 to 1899, but the city had no newspaper of that name in the twentieth century. The *Commercial Appeal* was Memphis's most important newspaper throughout the twentieth century.

296.27–28 Gustave Doré] French artist (1832–1883) who worked in all visual media but known especially for the often nightmarish wood engravings with which he illustrated literary works, including an 1866 edition of the Bible and a posthumously published edition of John Milton's *Paradise Lost* (1885).

THE LIGHT IN THE PIAZZA

306.1 *To John*] John Rusher (1920–1998), Spencer's husband. Spencer and Rusher married on September 29, 1956, four years before the publication of *The Light in the Piazza*.

307.4–14 Piazza della Signoria. . . . Palazzo Vecchio . . . Perseus] The Piazza della Signoria is the historic site of Florence's municipal government, with the crenellated Palazzo Vecchio—the Old Palace—as its city hall. *Perseus with the Head of Medusa* (1545–54), a bronze by the goldsmith, sculptor, and autobiographer Benvenuto Cellini (1500–1571), stands with other Renaissance and classical sculptures in the Loggia dei Lanza along one side of the piazza.

307.29–32 The tall white boy . . . a monk."] Michelangelo Buonarroti's (1475–1564) marble statue of David (1501–4), stood next to the Palazzo Vecchio until 1873, when it was moved to the Galleria d'Accademia, Florence's sculpture museum. "The tall white boy" is the replica that stands in the piazza itself. The charismatic Dominican friar Girolamo Savonarola (1452–1498), whose apocalyptic and puritanical sermons had made him the city's de facto ruler, was burned to death in the piazza after falling from public favor.

308.9 Fiesole] A town in the hills above Florence, three miles from the city center. Now a wealthy suburb, it is prized for its view onto the city below.

308.22 Piazza della Repubblica—] The city's commercial center.

308.23–24 si fanno la musica.] Italian: that's where they make music.

309.11 Van Johnson!"] American movie and television star (1916–2008).

309.13 cugino] Italian: cousin.

310.6 the Medici] Florence's dominant family, in their various branches, from circa 1400 until the middle of the eighteenth century, their fortune derived from banking and made respectable by their patronage of the arts. The one-time commoners eventually became Dukes of Florence and then Grand Dukes of Tuscany, producing along the way four popes and two queens of France.

310.7 stranieri] Italian: foreigners.

310.32 Piazzale Michelangelo] Hilltop square (actually an oval) to the south of Florence's center, on the left bank of the Arno River, providing splendid views of the city's Duomo or cathedral.

313.12 carrozza] Italian: horse-drawn carriages.

315.13 Ma sono belli.] Italian: But it's beautiful.

316.16 non credo] Italian: I don't think so.

316.23–24 "Fortuna! Signora, signorina, permette.] Italian: What luck! Ma'am, miss, allow me.

317.4 The Grand.] Now the St. Regis Florence, an old-fashioned luxury hotel on Piazza Ognissanti, facing its rival, the Excelsior, across the square.

317.6 saint's day, San Giovanni.] The feast of San Giovanni is celebrated on June 24.

317.19 Che figura!] Italian: How embarrassing!

317.37 the Palio] A horse race run twice each summer around the Piazza del Campo in Siena, with the horses and their jockeys representing the city's different wards. The winning horse is indeed brought into the cathedral and presented before the altar.

322.2   paese] Italian: village.

322.23   Ti ricordi come ti ho detto. . . ."] Italian: You remember what I told you.

323.4–5   "Mio figlio . . . è buono. Capisce?"] Italian: My son is good. Do you understand?

323.7–10   "Non lui . . . Ma lui. Si, è buono. Va in chiesa, capisce?"] Italian: Not him. . . . But him. Yes, he is good. Goes to church, do you understand?

323.12   Che roba!"] Italian: Wow!

323.13   "Si, è vero,"] Italian: Yes, it's true.

327.15–16   Due mila!"] Italian: Two thousand lire.

330.20   Ponte Vecchio] Literally, the "Old Bridge," and along with the city's cathedral and Palazzo Vecchio one of Florence's enduring images. A bridge has crossed the Arno at its site for over a thousand years; the current structure dates from 1345. It is for pedestrians only and lined with small shops, most of them selling jewelry. During World War II, it was the only one of the city's bridges not to be blown up in 1944 by German occupiers.

334.18   Tivoli] A resort town outside of Rome, famous for its villas, classical ruins, springs, and waterfalls.

334.23   Spanish Steps] Magnificent stairway, constructed 1723–25, that climbs the Pincian hill from the Piazza di Spagna to the church of Trinita dei Monti; a favorite place for tourists to sit and gather.

340.7   Bello Sguardo] A hill on the south side of the Arno, offering fine views of the city and its surrounding countryside; a place of villas and gardens, and long a favorite of Florence's Anglo-American expatriate community.

340.28   contadina] Italian: a peasant or countrywoman.

340.34   figlio di mamma] Italian: a mama's boy.

342.13   "Ma che generoso!"] Italian: But that's generous!

343.6   "come stai?"] Italian: How are you?

346.21   Un-American Activities Committee.] An investigative committee of the U.S. House of Representatives, established in 1938 and formally dissolved in 1975, by which time its power had long waned. It was much feared at its height in the late 1940s and early 1950s, when it investigated Communist influence in Hollywood, the academy, and the federal government, along with other so-called un-American practices such as homosexuality.

355.16–17   Via Tornabuoni—] Florence's most fashionable shopping street.

356.27 "Capisce, signora? In chiesa! Capisce?"] Italian: Do you understand, madame? In church! Do you understand?

356.31 parrocco] Italian: parish.

358.13 "Ma Papà! Non possiamo fare nulla—!"] Italian: But Father! There is nothing we can do—!

364.7 Boboli Gardens] Large formal gardens, with fountains, grottoes, and tree-lined walkways, attached to the Pitti Palace, on the south or left bank of the Arno.

365.6 Vallambrosa] Forested summer resort town and monastery fifteen miles to the east of Florence.

365.12–13 just as a Florentine had said] Galileo Galilei (1564–1642), Pisan-born astronomer and physicist, the first to use the telescope systematically in the observation of the skies; tried, convicted, and sentenced to house arrest for heresy (1633) by the Roman Catholic Inquisition after holding that Earth moved around the sun and not the other way around.

366.7–8 *Botticelli*] Allesandro di Mariano di Vanni Filipepi, known as Sandro Botticelli (1445–1510), Florentine painter especially celebrated for his pictures of women, often the Virgin Mary but also the Roman goddess Venus, whom he depicted as a blonde.

KNIGHTS AND DRAGONS

377.20 *Lucia* for fifty lire] *Lucia di Lammermoor* (1835), opera by Gaetano Donizetti (1797–1848), based on *The Bride of Lammermoor* (1819), a novel by Sir Walter Scott (1771–1832). Fifty *lire* in Italian currency was worth rather less than ten cents at the time *Knights and Dragons* was published.

377.40 cortili] Italian: courtyards.

379.27 "Scusatemi, per favore. . . ."] Italian: Excuse me, please.

380.23 campo] In Venetian parlance, a square or piazza. Only the Piazza San Marco in that city is called a "piazza"; all others, no matter how large, are called "campo," e.g., Campo Santa Margherita.

380.34 Lido] The Italian word for beach; as a proper name it designates the barrier island that encloses the Venetian lagoon, with swimming beaches found on its outer, Adriatic edge.

380.37 Tintoretto's Scuola] The Scuola Grande di San Rocco, the headquarters of a Venetian confraternity, a charitable organization and club; decorated throughout with paintings of biblical and mythological scenes by Jacopo Robusti (1518–1594), known as Tintoretto.

381.8 Che vuol fa', che vuol fa'?"] Italian: What does he do, what does he do?

381.16 sciròcco] A hot wind, often dusty or rainy, that blows from North Africa across the Mediterranean to Europe.

382.37 la dolce vita] Italian: the sweet life, a phrase popularized by Federico Fellini's 1960 movie of that title.

383.24 fiasco] Italian: flask or bottle.

385.2 Piazza San Marco] An oblong, arcaded plaza that attracts numerous tourists, bounded at one end by the cathedral of San Marco, and on its other sides lined with cafés and shops. Napoleon is said to have called it "the drawing room of Europe." It extends at a right angle to the Grand Canal through the Piazzetta, or little piazza, where the Doge's Palace is located, the historic center of Venice's city-state republic.

385.31 ragazzo . . . 'O soave fanciulla,'] *Ragazzo* is Italian for "boy"; "O Soave Fanciulla"—"Oh, Lovely Girl"—is an aria from *La Bohème* (1895) by Giacomo Puccini.

390.8 St. George slew the dragon] St. George is one of Venice's several patron saints, and the legend of his exploit, in which he rescued a young woman about to be eaten by a monster, is commemorated throughout the city, often in sculpted panels carved in relief and set into the facades of houses.

390.33–34 Perchè in questo mondo è stato veramente un errore terribile.] Italian: Because in this world there truly has been a terrible mistake.

391.12–13 la spesa—] Italian: shopping (noun).

398.25 Tramontana] Italian: The north wind; literally, "from beyond or across the mountains."

398.26 campagna] Italian: countryside; but around Rome it functions as a proper name for the low-lying plain around the city.

399.15–16 Piazza di Spagna.] Fashionable area associated for centuries with foreign visitors, and more recently with luxury shopping.

399.25 Bis, bis!] Italian: encore; literally, "More, more!"

404.26 Lambretta] Classic but now defunct brand of motor scooters, made in Milan from 1947 to 1972.

406.9 topolinos] Italian: the original Fiat 500 automobile (manufactured 1936–1955), here given as an English plural. The word literally means "little mouse," and "Topolino" is also the Italian name of Mickey Mouse.

410.1 portone] Italian: front door, main entrance.

410.22 Via de' Portoghesi.] A short narrow street in the Campo Marzio district of Rome. Near Piazza Navona, it serves as a setting in Nathaniel Hawthorne's *The Marble Faun* (1860), one of the first American novels of expatriate life.

414.40–415.1 "La Signora Ingram . . . Roma."] Italian: Mrs. Ingram isn't here, Mrs. Ingram has left Rome.

415.3 'Si, si . . . vista."] Italian: Yes, yes, there, the lady there? I just saw her.

415.4–5 "O, scusi . . . uno sbaglio. . . ."] Italian: Oh, excuse me. A mistake.

415.8–9 "Non parlo inglese, signora. Mi dispaice. . . ."] Italian: I don't speak English, ma'am. I'm sorry.

415.31 "Voglio parlare . . . per cortesia."] Italian: I would like to speak with Mrs. Ingram, please. *Per cortesia* is formal and rather old-fashioned.

415.35–36 "No, signora. . . . è vuoto."] Italian: No, ma'am, Mrs. Ingram isn't there. The apartment is empty.

423.1 Ciampino] Rome's principal international airport at the time, now largely superseded by the new terminal at Fiumicino.

423.5 Flora lobby near the Porta Pinciana.] The Grand Hotel Flora is a luxury hotel on the via Vittorio Veneto, then the center of Roman nightlife, next to the gardens of the Villa Borghese; the Porta Pinciana is a gate in a surviving fragment of the city's Aurelian wall, where the via Vittorio Veneto meets the Villa Borghese.

427.19–20 Della Robbia] Family of Florentine sculptors and ceramic artists, known especially for the glistening white and deep blues and greens with which they glazed terra-cotta medallions, plaques, and altarpieces. Luca (1399/1400–1482) and his nephew Andrea (1435–1525) are the most famous.

428.6 Rinascimento] Italian: Renaissance.

429.26 Villa Borghese] A large park, once the gardens surrounding the villa of the Borghese family, in the center of Rome, usually reached from the top of the Spanish Steps or through the Porta Pinciana. The villa itself, in the park's center, now houses the Galleria Borghese, one of Rome's best art museums.

430.11 Spoleto] Hill town in Umbria with an ancient Roman theater, the site since 1958 of a summer arts festival drawing an international audience.

432.5 Via Boncompagni] A street of hotels and elegant shops, off the via Vittorio Veneto.

432.32 American Academy] A research and arts institute, founded in 1897, hosting American scholars, artists, and writers, in a modern villa (1914; designed by McKim, Mead & White) on the Gianicolo, high above the city on the west side of the Tiber.

439.6 Laterano] The term includes both the Basilica di San Giovanni in Laterano and the complex of ecclesiastical buildings and palaces around it. Located on the eastern side of the historic city, beyond the Colosseum, the basilica is the cathedral church of Rome, and the seat of the pope in his function as bishop of Rome.

440.11 vendemmia] Italian: grape harvest or vintage.

440.27 etto] 100 grams; a distinctly Italian unit of measurement, often used in weighing out cheese and charcuterie.

445.20 Ma guarda! Guarda!"] Italian: Look out, look what you've done!

451.7 Campidoglio] The Piazza del Campidoglio, atop a hill on the site of Rome's ancient capitol, was designed by Michelangelo (1475–1564); the equestrian statue of the emperor Marcus, at the center of the piazza, is a replica, and the original sits in the adjacent Capitoline Museum.

451.15–16 Gibbon . . . *Decline and Fall*] The church of Santa Maria in Aracoeli is adjacent to the Campidoglio, though reached by a separate flight of stairs, each beginning to climb from the same piazza. The English historian Edward Gibbon (1737–1794) said that he got the idea for his *Decline and Fall of the Roman Empire* (6 vols, 1776–88) while sitting on the steps leading up to the church.

454.24 Tivoli] See note 334.18.

456.2 salotti, terrazzi, giardini.] Italian: rooms (salons), terraces, gardens.

456.26 Piazza del Popolo] People's Square, though the name derives from the poplar trees that once stood on the site. With an ancient Egyptian obelisk erected in its center, it is a large and bustling space, and the historic entrance to the city from the north.

463.13–14 Capri] Fashionable resort island in the bay of Naples, marked by both lively nightlife and rugged hills.

464.26–27 "Ti voglio bene . . . Ti voglio bene."] Italian: I care for you, but I don't love you. Tell me, tell me—I care for you.

465.11 seicento] Italian: Fiat 600 automobile, manufactured from 1955 to 1969.

465.14 donna di servizio] Italian: maid.

465.19 Figurati!] Italian: an idiomatic expression, covering many situations, its meaning dependent entirely on context: Don't mention it, imagine that, that figures, no way.

465.21 tessuti] Italian: textiles, cloth.

465.30 nondimeno] Italian: nevertheless.

465.32 Addio] Italian: Goodbye.

466.2 la stessa cosa. . . .] Italian: the same thing.

466.6 Davvero] Italian: Really.

466.39   "Che vuole?] Italian: literally, Who wants, but here with the force of an expletive.

467.39   "Prego!"] Italian: Please!

471.12–19   "Gente cattiva . . . Tutto è rovinato!"] Italian: "Nasty people, those Wilbournes. What could I do, what? I am absolutely without . . ." "But Mr. Micozzi, you have already received the deposit, haven't you?" "Yes, Signor Consul, but you cannot think that this deposit is enough . . . They broke everything! . . . Everything is ruined!"

471.24–25   Quanto allora?] Italian: How much?

471.34   Veni, vidi, vici.] Latin: I came, I saw, I conquered. Attributed to Julius Caesar after he defeated Pharnaces II.

473.32   "Mio amico era sempre buono . . . buono. . . ."] Italian: My friend was always good . . . he was good . . . good.

476.16–17   "Dal cielo! . . . dal cielo!"] Italian: From the sky! From the sky! A gift from the sky!

SELECTED STORIES

481.27   Pilgrimage] A celebration of the slaveholding Old South, usually held in March and April, in which historic homes are elaborately decorated and open for tours, and townspeople dress in the clothes of the antebellum period. Several cities in Mississippi hold such festivals; the most famous is in Natchez, where it has provided a major part of the city's tourism income since the 1930s.

500.10–11   "Strange As It Seems," . . . or Not."] Popular syndicated newspaper columns of the mid-twentieth century that relied on presenting odd and marvelous facts. They were illustrated and usually appeared on the comics page.

501.25   "Benjy"] Benjy Compson, one of the three brothers who narrate William Faulkner's 1929 novel, *The Sound and the Fury*. Benjy is both entirely reliable and entirely uncomprehending, a mentally disabled man who can neither speak nor distinguish past from present, but who has a total sensory recall of particular moments in his earlier life.

502.25–26   siege of Vicksburg.] A strategically important port city on the Mississippi River, the Confederate citadel of Vicksburg surrendered on July 4, 1863, after a forty-day siege, to United States forces under Ulysses S. Grant (1822–1885), thereby giving the Union control of the river.

502.26–27   United Daughters of the Confederacy's] United Daughters of the Confederacy, an organization for southern white women, founded in 1894 and dedicated to the commemoration of the Confederacy. Among other things, the UDC worked to ensure that the textbooks used in southern schools presented a pro-Confederate version of history, in which slavery was benign and the Civil War was fought over the issue of states' rights.

502.32 *Times-Picayune*] New Orleans's leading newspaper throughout the twentieth century.

504.22 Windsor] Greek Revival plantation house, built 1859–61 in Claiborne County, Mississippi, along the Mississippi River between Vicksburg and Natchez, which was destroyed by fire in 1890. Often photographed, e.g., by Eudora Welty (1942) and Sally Mann (1998), it survives as twenty-three blackened and freestanding Corinthian columns.

505.7 *Life on the Mississippi*] 1883 travel book and memoir by Mark Twain (1835–1910).

508.5 W.C.T.U.] See note 24.7.

508.39 defense of Port Claiborne] Civil War battle of Port Gibson in Claiborne County, Mississippi, fought on May 1, 1863; an early Union victory in Grant's Vicksburg campaign.

511.24 Millsaps College] Private liberal arts college in Jackson, Mississippi, founded in 1890 and affiliated with the Methodist Church.

513.1 *Sharon*] In the Hebrew Bible, a fertile plain lying between the Samarian hills and the coast; in the United States frequently used as a placename, and also as that of a variety of hibiscus, the flowering plant known as rose-of-Sharon.

518.10 *Les Misérables*] 1862 novel by the French writer Victor Hugo (1802–1885).

526.25 bezique] Two-handed, trick-taking card game, most popular in nineteenth-century France.

536.35 Father of Waters] The Mississippi River; a literal translation of the Algonkian word "Mississippi."

543.4 American Express] The American Express office in Rome is located in Piazza di Spagna, a fashionable area associated for centuries with foreign visitors, and more recently with luxury shopping. The office provided travel services, hotel bookings and traveler's checks among them, and also functioned as a *poste restante* for letters.

543.35 Spanish Steps.] A favorite place for tourists to sit and gather, the Spanish Steps (designed by Francesco de Sanctis, constructed 1723–25) climb the Pincian hill from the Piazza di Spagna to the church of Trinita dei Monti.

547.15 Carrozza] See note 313.12.

548.7 *Elsie Dinsmore*.] The heroine of a popular series of children's books by Martha Finley (1828–1909), set largely in the American South and with a marked emphasis on Christian virtues; published from 1867 to 1905.

548.15 *"Mi dispiace, signora, ma . . . insomma. . . ."*] Italian: I'm sorry ma'am, but . . . well . . .

548.19–20 *"Va bene, signora."*] Italian: Okay, ma'am.

551.1 *Ship Island*] A barrier island in the Gulf of Mexico, twelve miles off Gulfport, Mississippi.

552.16 "Over the Waves"] Translation of "Sobre Las Olas," a popular, lilting, 1888 waltz by Mexican composer Juventino Rosas (1868–1894).

553.19–20 "Raw head and bloody bones!,"] Bogeyman figures from English folktales, used to frighten children. John Locke records the phrase in 1693, and such tales migrated to and were popular in the American South, where Rawhead is often figured as a skull stripped of its skin that bites its victims, and Bloody Bones as a dancing headless skeleton. In the twentieth century, it is sometimes used as a shorthand formula for the horrors and pleasures of southern Gothic fiction.

597.33 *Middlemarch*] Victorian multiplotted novel (1871–72), subtitled *A Study of Provincial Life*, by George Eliot (1819–1880).

610.33 "raw head and bloody bones,"] See note 553.19–20.

612.32 Mickey Rooney] Stage name of Ninnian Joseph Yule, Jr. (1920–2014), redheaded American actor, famous in the 1930s and '40s for the MGM "Andy Hardy" films, which presented an idealized version of small-town life, as well as several musicals costarring Judy Garland. He was later known for his string of eight marriages and six divorces.

615.19 *"Pronto,"*] Italian: literally, "Ready"; in practice, the first word one says on answering the telephone.

616.7 the Brownings' time] The English poets Robert (1812–1889) and Elizabeth Barrett Browning (1806–1861) lived in Florence from the time of their 1846 marriage until her death. Each used the city as a setting for their poetry, and Casa Guidi, their house on the south side of the Arno River, opposite the Pitti Palace, became the center of Florence's Anglo-American expatriate community.

618.9 *"J'ai très hâte d'y aller,"*] French: I can't wait to go.

618.19 *Sewanee Review.*] The oldest American literary quarterly, founded in 1892, and published by the University of the South in Sewanee, Tennessee.

618.21 "Ulalume."] 1847 poem by Edgar Allan Poe (1809–1949), a mournful work on Poe's favorite topic, the celebration of a beautiful dead mistress.

619.19–21 Mont St.-Michel . . . Henry Adams] Mont St. Michel is a monastery on the coast of Normandy in France; it sits in a tidal plain and at high tide was historically cut off from the mainland, though it is now connected by a causeway. *Mont Saint Michel and Chartres* (1904), by the American historian

Henry Adams (1838–1918), used its study of medieval faith and architecture to mount a critique of the modern world.

621.10   the Cellini] See note 307.4–14.

626.2   *marrons glacés*] French: candied chestnuts.

627.21–22   "*Le cavalier de l'Okla-hum . . . Du Texas plutôt.*"] French: The cowboy from Oklahoma . . . From Texas, rather.

630.37   Ransom's poetry] John Crowe Ransom (1888–1974), American poet, critic, and apologist for white southern tradition, who was born in Tennessee. Ransom taught first at Vanderbilt University in Nashville and then at Kenyon College in Gambier, Ohio, where he was founder and editor of the quarterly *Kenyon Review* (1939). His students included Robert Penn Warren, Robert Lowell, and Allen Tate.

635.11–12   Uffizi . . . Botticelli] The Uffizzi is Florence's most important museum, housed in a set of former municipal offices by Giorgio Vasari (1511–1574). Its treasures include many paintings by the Florentine master Sandro Botticelli (1445–1510).

635.19–22   Donatello's lion . . . Cosimo I on his horse . . . *Rape of the Sabines.*] Monuments in the Piazza della Signoria. The lion is a heraldic symbol of Florence, here by Donata di Niccolo di Betto Bardi, called Donatello (1386–1466). The bronze equestrian statue (1594) of Cosimo I, Grand Duke of Tuscany (1519–1574), is by Giambologna (1529–1608), who also made *The Rape of the Sabines* (1574–82), a marble statue located with Cellini's "Perseus" in the Loggia dei Lanzi.

637.9   *grazie* and *quanto.*"] Italian: Thank you and How much?

637.12   Della Robbia] See note 427.19–20.

641.10   "*Bella ragazza,*"] Italian: Beautiful girl.

642.30   *capelli leggero—*"] Italian: light hair.

643.1   "*Ecco,*"] Italian: Here.

644.16   Piranesi] Giambattista Piranesi (1720–1778), Italian artist known for his etchings of Roman scenes and buildings, as well as for the *Carceri* (1745–61), frightening depictions of a series of imaginary prisons.

644.24–25   the horseman on the Campidoglio] Equestrian statue of the emperor Marcus Aurelius (121–180 C.E.), erected in his lifetime. The Piazza del Campidoglio, atop a hill on the site of Rome's ancient capitol, was designed by Michelangelo (1475–1564); the statue now on public display is a replica, and the original sits in the adjacent Capitoline Museum.

647.23   Hadrian's Villa] An enormous complex, including temples, reflecting pools, and colonnades, constructed for the emperor Hadrian (76–138 C.E.) at Tivoli outside of Rome in the second and third decades of the second century

C.E. The de facto capitol of the empire in the last years of his reign, it is now a set of splendid ruins.

651.15   Bolton Landing.] Resort village on Lake George in upstate New York, seventy miles north of Albany.

651.20   Gristede's] Chain of New York City supermarkets.

653.33   "Sweet Rosie O'Grady"] Popular 1896 song by Maude Nugent (1873/74–1958); its title was picked up for a 1943 Technicolor musical starring Betty Grable and Robert Young.

656.3   Schumann's "Carnaval"] Op. 9 by the German composer Robert Schumann (1810–1856). It is a suite of twenty-one brief pieces for solo piano, dating from 1834–35, with each meant to depict a masked reveler at Carnival time.

656.23   *tourtière*] A double-crusted meat pie, one of the classic dishes of French-Canadian cuisine. There are many local variations, but the filling is usually based on ground meat and potatoes.

658.26   *"Des clients, vous en avez beaucoup,"*] French: You have a lot of clients.

661.25   *Gros dommage.*] French: Great pity.

684.4   Jezebel in the Bible] The wife of Ahab, king of Israel; Phoenician by birth and a worshipper of Baal and Astarte rather than the Hebrew Yahweh. Her name is associated with the pursuit of false prophets and idolatry; in the twentieth century it became a term for fallen, shameless, or abandoned women, and linked with promiscuity. Often used ironically. See 1 Kings 16:31.

721.6–7   pull candy] Taffy.

722.2   Delta] See note 49.18.

749.1   *Shongalo*] The first town incorporated (1840) in Carroll County, Mississippi, where Spencer was born; built on the site of a Choctaw settlement of that name. The town was abandoned c. 1859 when its population moved a mile away to the new settlement of Vaiden along the railroad.

749.5   WPA] Works Progress Administration, founded 1935, and renamed Work Projects Administration in 1939. A New Deal–era jobs program, it involved everything from building streets and dams to writing travel guides and painting murals.

756.1   Ibsen] Henrik Ibsen (1828–1906), Norwegian playwright, best known for his realistic and often tragic depictions of middle-class domestic life in such works as *A Doll's House* (1879) and *Hedda Gabler* (1890).

759.21   'Maida Vale.'] Affluent London residential neighborhood, to the west of Regent's Park; developed in the late nineteenth century and also known as Little Venice because of the Regent's Park Canal.

764.29   *Idylls of the King*] A set of twelve blank-verse narrative poems (1859–85) by English poet Alfred, Lord Tennyson (1809–1892), that retell the legends of King Arthur and the Round Table. The cycle's account of Arthur's attempt and failure to establish a perfect kingdom is usually read as an allegory of Victorian Britain.

779.13   Thomas Wolfe] American writer (1900–1938), born Asheville, North Carolina and known for his torrential prose. His heavily autobiographical novels include *Look Homeward, Angel* (1929) and *Of Time and the River* (1935).

803.11–17   *Le Mariage de Figaro . . .* Aida] *The Marriage of Figaro* (1786), opera by Salzburg-born composer Wolfgang Amadeus Mozart; *The Barber of Seville* (1816), opera by Italian composer Gioachino Rossini; Wagner, German composer Richard Wagner (1813–1883); Massenet, French composer Jules Massenet (1842–1912); *Oklahoma!* (1943) and *South Pacific* (1949), musicals by American songwriters Richard Rodgers and Oscar Hammerstein II; Aida, the title character of Italian composer Guiseppe Verdi's 1871 opera.

811.23–24   *"Se la lasci riscaldar."*] Italian: From the aria "Che gelida manina," in the first act of Giacomo Puccini's opera *La Boheme* (1895). It begins "*Che gelida manina, se la lasci riscaldar*"—"What a cold little hand, let me warm it for you"—and is sung by the tenor Rodolfo to the doomed consumptive soprano Mimi.

815.40   *Middlemarch*] See note 597.33.

829.23   Mendelssohn] The "Wedding March," also known as "Here Comes the Bride," composed in 1843, from Felix Mendelssohn's incidental music for Shakespeare's *Midsummer Night's Dream* (Op. 61).

*This book is set in 10 point ITC Galliard, a face designed
for digital composition by Matthew Carter and based
on the sixteenth-century face Granjon. The paper is acid-free
lightweight opaque that will not turn yellow or brittle with age.
The binding is sewn, which allows the book to open easily and lie flat.
The binding board is covered in Brillianta, a woven rayon cloth
made by Van Heek–Scholco Textielfabrieken, Holland.
Composition by Dianna Logan, Clearmont, MO.
Printing by Sheridan Grand Rapids, Grand Rapids, MI.
Binding by Dekker Bookbinding, Wyoming, MI.
Designed by Bruce Campbell.*

THE LIBRARY OF AMERICA SERIES

Library of America fosters appreciation of America's literary heritage by publishing, and keeping permanently in print, authoritative editions of America's best and most significant writing. An independent nonprofit organization, it was founded in 1979 with seed funding from the National Endowment for the Humanities and the Ford Foundation.

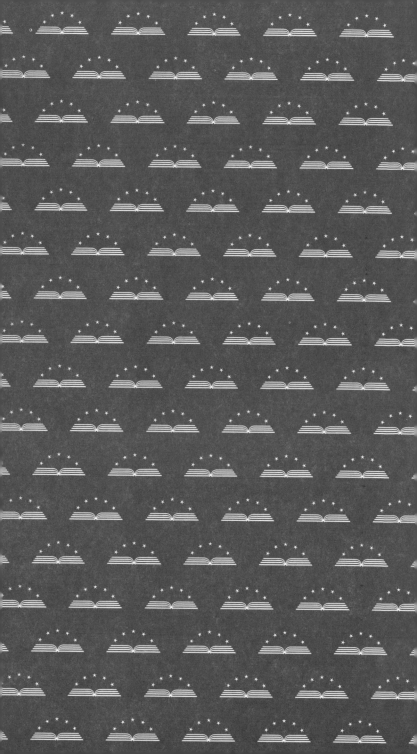